BOOK I: THE BIRTH

BY

BRIAN MCLAUGHLIN

FIRST EDITION
0830
https://www.worldofthran.com

Cover Art By: Natalie Marten

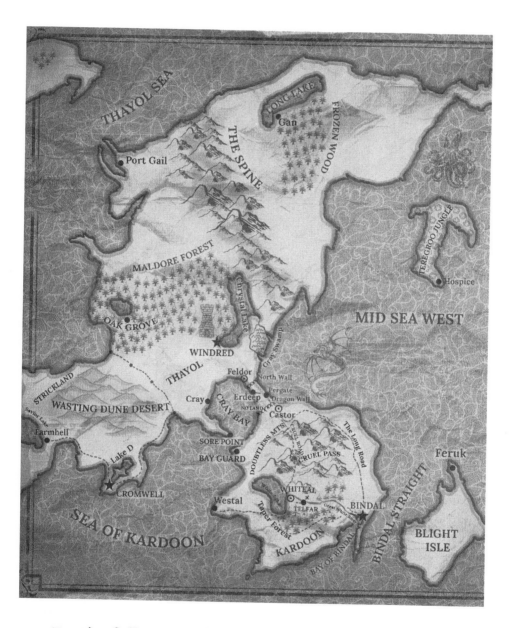

For the full map and more information about Thran
visit: worldofthran.com

For the full map and more information about Thran
visit: worldofthran.com

DEDICATION

To those who inspired me:

I played my last game of Dungeons and Dragons® in 1994, twenty-four years ago, but prior to that, from 1984 to 1994, I played that wonderful role-playing game with a passion and dedication that only a teenager and young adult, with no other responsibilities, could afford to carve out of their day (and nights!), and I was very fortunate to have a great group of friends that shared my love of the game. During those years, in the vast majority of cases, I played the role of dungeon master, which meant it was up to me to throw together one adventure after another and keep it interesting. I had to draw the maps, create a plot, and fill the adventure with obstacles, challenges, and, oh yes, of course, monsters and treasure. I never thought of it back then as storytelling, but that's what I was doing: creating a framework for the players, who, with their own characters and personalities, fleshed out the tale. What emerged out of all those hours, days, and years of gaming, was an ability (at least the desire!) to tell stories. To the gang: Toby, Mike, Brad, Jim, Ian, and Romesh. Thank you for being such great friends, and for sharing your creativity, personalities, and characters that fueled our adventures. I hope you see glimpses of the characters you played, and that the story brings back some fond memories of too many guys in one room, consuming too much soda and too much pizza, but creating everlasting friendships and memories. Thank you!

To those who gave me the time and support:

In 1994, my life changed. I graduated college and I married Lynda, the love of my life, and soon followed that up with Garrett and Rachel, the best children a father could ask for. I was a lucky man, with the golden, happy family and a fast track career that was professionally rewarding. In 2012, I found my career wasn't as fulfilling as it once was, and I began to think about what else I could do to fill that void, and even all those years later, I could sense the pull of Dungeons and Dragons® in my mind, but rather than play the game, I decided to try my hand at writing a book. At first, it was a toy I tinkered with on the weekends, but, over time, it actually began to flesh itself out and turn into a real novel, and soon I was spending hours on Saturdays and Sundays, hoping to write two thousand words a weekend. To Lynda, Garrett, and Rachel: thank you for all your love, support, and understanding, while never once complaining, always encouraging, about the thousands of hours I spent staring into the screen, typing away.

To those who read this book:

Finally, I want to dedicate this novel to all the gamers out there, old and new, that love to game and roll the dice. I hope this story hits home for you, tugging on your heartstrings and taking you, at least temporarily, into the World of Thran, where anything is truly possible, and you can be anyone or anything you desire. For those of you who have never tried a role-playing game: put down the joystick, the keyboard, and the mouse, and get your two, three, or four best friends together, or even your brothers and sisters, and make your own adventures. It's not what you think it will be; it will be deeper, more fun, and a much more memorable experience than you imagine.

Thank you to everyone! Let the dice roll!
Brian McLaughlin

PROLOGUE

Heavy with moisture from their days of travel over the Sea of Kardoon, the clouds continued their lazy westward drift until finally encountering the western edge of the Doubtless Mountains. Ushered unceasingly by the wind, and confronted with a mountainous wall, the clouds, as they had done since the beginning of time, began to rise, releasing as they did so their treasured stores of life-giving water. As the pristine water fell, the clouds ascended the peaks, floating over and around the summits of the imposing chain. Portions of the falling rain found rest in the multitude of caves and other crags found in the heights, but the majority of the water flowed down the steep mountain faces in thousands of small streams that, over time and distance, eventually converged and pooled to form one of the greatest lakes known in Thran. This lake, growing in size and depth, finally surged, uninhibited, beyond its banks to the east with such powerful force that its water clawed through soil and rock, felling trees as it moved, creating the fastest, deepest, widest, and longest river in all of Thran. Flowing east and eventually turning southeast, nothing could stop the might of the river but the end of land itself, where it emptied back into the ocean, from whence it came. This abundant source of fresh water for drinking and irrigation combined with the fertile soil along the banks of the river created a perfect spot for civilization to begin, and so it did.

Bindal Kardoon, an adventurer from the port city of Plinth on the far western edge of the Kingdom of Nemisa, set sail with a crew of thirty men and thirty women, having convinced the farming community he lived in that they could build a new life on their own terms in a distant, unsettled land. They set out on a due westward course, and after a long, hard, trying voyage, they landed on the eastern shore of Blight Isle. At first, the crew was overjoyed to have discovered land, but after exploring inland, they soon found the conditions to be synonymous with its name. Downhearted, they set sail again, this time heading north and then southwest, following the coastline of Blight Isle. It was during their voyage southward that Bindal had a vision of lush, fertile soil, clean mountain water, and a majestic city rising up from the land, but watching the gray, arid, cold coastline slipping by as their ship cruised along, Bindal knew it wasn't to be found here. Despite the pleas of the other crew members, he took control of the helm and wouldn't let go, steering the ship westward, out into the open ocean once again. After six days of heading west, without having left the helm for any reason or necessity, and barely able to stand on his own, he spotted land again, but this time it was full of trees and life, clearly visible from the ship. The crew rejoiced, but Bindal still would not let anyone land, claiming this was not the bay he had foreseen. Changing course once again, Bindal began following the new coastline southward, still refusing to give up the helm. After four more days, they came to the end of what turned out to be a long peninsula, and Bindal, rounding the tip, turned the ship 180 degrees and began heading north up the other side. Finally, having run out of food, the rest of the crew were about to forcibly take control of the ship -- it would not have been difficult, as Bindal had lost all his strength, leaning on the steering wheel of the helm for balance. As fortune would have it, Bindal finally saw the land he had envisioned, landing in the lush location where a mighty river emptied into the ocean. Bindal, guiding his crew, created a fortified settlement along the northern bank of the river, which due to its purity, unusually cold temperature, and occasional small icebergs that flowed by, he named the White River. Leading excursions back to Plinth, Bindal was able to attract more settlers, enamored with the lushness and opportunity presented by the now famous explorer. As time ticked by, the village grew into a town, and the town into the city of Bindal. Always an adventurer at heart, Bindal led multiple excursions, following the banks of the White River north to find its source, where he soon discovered, and named, the Great White Lake. Bindal was so taken with the utopia of the setting where the White River began that he christened the site as the future city of Whiteal, and, wanting construction to begin immediately, left his nephew, Gaol Cragstaff, behind with an armed contingent to oversee its progress.

Trees, fed for centuries by the abundant water of the White River, flourished along the southern bank, creating a forest of unusual trees that slowly sprawled southward over time. The water, carrying a hint of iron from the mountains from whence it came, created the Taper tree, or

Iron tree, as Gaol and the small contingent soon were apt to call it. The wood of the Taper tree was exceptionally hard, but that in and of itself was not what made Taper wood so coveted. The wood, containing minuscule air pockets, also made it very light and buoyant; this in conjunction with its hardness was what made Taper wood unique. Such qualities made it perfect for building materials, weapons, and, even more particularly, for shipbuilding. People used it for all three purposes, but shipbuilding became the primary use, and as the Kingdom of Kardoon grew, the need for ocean-going vessels grew with it.

As supplies and people continuously moved upriver from Bindal to Whiteal, a road began to take form along the southern bank, worn into the ground by thousands of feet, hooves, and wheels. One hundred miles east of Whiteal, where the Taper wood forest began, accompanied by a sharp bend in the river, the settlement of Telfar was born. Initially a logging camp, sourcing Taper wood for both Whiteal and Bindal, it began as an outpost of woodsmen. But after only a few years, the first shipyard was built, with a dry dock facility and a lone pier jutting out into the river. Soon, carpenters, shipbuilders, a blacksmith, a sail makers loft, a tavern, an inn, and other general stores began opening in, and around, the growing town to support the burgeoning population and businesses. But as the town grew in both size and population, law and order receded, making the village rife with nefarious characters all vying for control of the flow of money and taking their rightful cut, as they saw it. As the conflicts escalated, it finally caught the attention of Gaol Cragstaff in Whiteal, who dispatched his older brother Fuhr Cragstaff and one hundred soldiers to the settlement, with instructions to re-institute law and order as Reeve of Telfar.

Fuhr, wanting to make a name for himself, took to the task with vehemence. First, discreetly sending in several waves of scouts, under the guise of travelers on their way to Whiteal, to learn how many factions there were in the village and the names of their leaders and high-level henchmen. Once informed, he marched his soldiers into the village, seeking out and killing, some say murdering, over forty suspected gang leaders and members. Erecting a dozen posts in the middle of the village, he hung leaders of the gangs, some dead and some briefly alive, upside down by their feet, nailed to the post with a long nail, soon to be called a Fuhr nail, through the abdomen. After the initial day of skirmishes and hangings, Fuhr would walk around the village with a ring full of long "Fuhr" nails, the clanking of the nails giving away his location wherever he went. If he found someone undesirable, or for any reason decided that the person needed to go, he would take a nail off the ring and hand it to the person, saying coldly, "This nail has your name on it. Tomorrow it gets nailed." This tactic had the desired effect. Many people fled the village, mostly unidentified gang members, or other persons envisioning easier profit elsewhere, but most assuredly nobody waited for the next day when their nail would be hammered home as they hung upside down from a large pole. This went on for seven more days, with fewer and fewer nails being handed out, and eventually none on the seventh and last day. On the eighth day, he ordered all poles and bodies to be taken down and, casting them into the river, declared the village purged, purified, and open for business to the honest citizens of Telfar. As an ominous reminder to anyone coming to Telfar in the future, Fuhr commissioned one large pole to be erected in the center of the village, with two large chains that dangled and clanked in whatever breeze so moved them, with a plaque that read, "The reward for criminals in Telfar: A final view of the world, turned upside down." Newcomers to Telfar, of course, wouldn't know exactly what that meant, but it usually was one of the first questions they asked.

With order restored, Fuhr began the second phase of his plan: the construction of fortified walls around the town, an act which seemed odd to the citizens, since Telfar never seemed in danger, never having been attacked, but nevertheless the Taper wood walls went up and have remained stout, though untested, in their defense of the village ever since.

Protected by the river itself to the north, fortified on all other sides by the strong Taper wood walls, and accompanied by harsh governance within the walls, Telfar became a safe haven for travelers heading upstream to Whiteal. For folks traveling south to Bindal, they usually opted for a fast ride down the river from one of the many river pilots from Whiteal, although an experienced river pilot could be costly both to purse and patience. Of course, purchasing passage with less experienced pilots may reduce idle time and coin spent, but it is a dangerous trip to the uninitiated, and once on the water, the lives of everyone, and everything, are in the hands of the pilot. As such, some people prefer the longer but possibly safer trip south down the White Road and that too would take them through Telfar. As the travelers passed through, they brought with them a trove of information, rumors, and, of course, gold coins, making it an ideal place for mercenaries to hire themselves out as guards for caravans, merchants, or anyone moving over land in either direction.

Time passed and Fuhr Cragstaff passed away, allowing for his eldest son, Strix Cragstaff, to became Reeve of Telfar. His first act was to create a monument and tomb for his father near the center of the village. He has carried on his father's tradition of strict, but fair order, and supported the business owners and citizens of the town.

The current year is now AG1175, in the month of Sepu, with the seasonal warmth of Heatal finally giving way to the shorter days and colder nights of Ebbal, and the eightieth anniversary of Bindal landing on the mainland and creating the first vestige of the Kingdom of Kardoon.

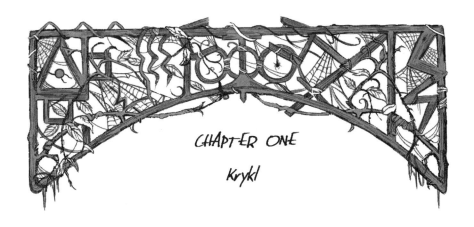

CHAPTER ONE
Krykl

YEAR: AG 1172, The Month of Sepu, Three Years Prior to Current Day

THE BUGBEAR, WITH ITS BULLDOG-LIKE HEAD, stood over seven feet tall. Its arms and legs, bulging with muscles, were thick and pulsing with visible veins. Armed with a huge spiked club, the beast was intimidating as all hell. 'It looks more like a bear than a bug,' thought Anthall Mixnor to himself. The beast began slowly sidestepping, keeping its distance, as it looked for an opening to strike with its large club that was dripping a disturbing amount of blood from recent victims. The bugbear held the weapon high, waggling the spiked end of the club behind its head, as if drawing imaginary circles in the air. Not seeing an opening develop, it bellowed a challenging and deafening roar as it towered above Anthall. This, however, was not a solitary conflict. The two combatants were in the midst of a great battle and, as the battle raged around them, one of Anthall's men appeared out of the surrounding fray, charging the bugbear. The beast saw the new threat out of the corner of its eye and, spinning, swung its club with deadly effect. The man didn't have a chance. The spike first punctured completely through and then, as the bugbear followed through, ripped out of the man's side leaving a gaping hole. The stricken warrior was spun around and thrown off his feet, landing in a groaning heap. The bugbear had little time to celebrate its victory, and before it knew what had happened, Anthall closed the gap and, with practiced fluidity, he struck. He first swung Slice, his bastard sword, in a downward motion, severing the bugbear's thick leg just above the knee. Continuing the attack, he spun on his heel and sunk Slice deep into the beast's right arm. The bugbear howled as it toppled to the ground, writhing for the final moment of its life next to its last, and now motionless, victim.

The battle had been raging for some time now, and both sides were beginning to tire but, from what Anthall could see, the battle was not going well. Spying a large boulder twenty yards away, he gathered a dozen men and ordered them to follow him. Anthall moved quickly but limped slightly on his right leg as he made his way to the boulder where he rested for a moment by propping himself up against the side of the large rock. He was wearing his full battle armor, which over time had become a dull and darkened shade of gray with each dent, scratch, stain, and imperfection belying a past conflict and though it offered him excellent protection, it was also extremely heavy.

As the soldiers formed up around him, a ragged footman stepped forward and asked, "Sir, are you okay? Is your leg hurt?"

Anthall turned to face the soldier, causing the young man to back up at the sight of his commander, whom he had never seen before in his battle armor. The helmet Anthall was wearing only covered the top half of his face, leaving his mouth and square, whiskered, jaw visible. The helm covering the rest of his head and face gave the deathly appearance of a skull and, as an added measure of dread, it also bore an enchantment that made the wearer's eyes glow red from within its eye sockets. Anthall knew it struck fear into weaker opponents, an effect that he often used to his advantage. Leaning Slice against the boulder, Anthall reached up and removed his helmet and tucked it into the crook of his arm, revealing his brown hair and green eyes. Looking human once again, Anthall replied, "I am fine, soldier. My limp is from a battle long before this one, and today we have far greater things to worry about. You three," he said, pointing to a small cluster of soldiers, "help lift me up onto this damn boulder, I want to get a better look at what is going on."

The soldiers jumped into action and after Anthall set his helmet down on the ground they heaved their commander up onto the boulder. Anthall climbed to his feet and surveyed the battlefield. He could see General Krugar two hundred yards back behind the main battle. 'The fool,' he thought to himself; the general had led them right into a trap, where they were surrounded on three sides by the hordes of this bugbear army. The men were fighting bravely and, thankfully, had enough discipline not to run, but Anthall had seen many battles, and this one was well on its way to being lost. From his new vantage point, he could see the corpses of the mages that marshal Krugar had placed so much faith in -- they were the first casualties in the battle, being killed by a pack of hellhounds that seemed to come out of nowhere when the battle began. 'That was a clever move... Too clever for a bugbear,' he thought to himself. "Where are you?" Anthall whispered into the wind, looking for the man or beast that was holding this wild band of bugbears together. Anthall waited patiently, scanning the battlefield for signs of...something. The field was relatively flat, though there were several rock outcroppings, like the one he was now standing on, with the grass that had covered the field just a few hours ago having been trampled out of existence by thousands of feet. The flattened ground was littered with what looked like logs from a distance -- some stacked on top of each other, while others lay off on their own, alone -- but they weren't logs, and Anthall knew the wake of sorrow that each fallen soldier left behind. Anthall chided himself for letting his thoughts drift and refocused his mind on his search for the leader of the bugbears. "Where are you, you son of a bitch," Anthall whispered again, using his hand to shield his eyes from the sun, which was getting perilously low in the sky, and then he saw it. A huge ogre blinked into view, surrounded by a pocket of bugbears. It wasn't obvious before, but now, with the ogre appearing, he could see the protective ring of bugbears around it. The ogre was wielding a gigantic longbow, shooting huge javelin-like arrows. Each time the ogre unleashed an arrow, it broke the invisibility spell and became visible for just a moment, and then it would vanish again. An ogre with the power of invisibility could mean only one thing. "Ogre mage..." Anthall groaned to himself. During his travels, he had been in enough taverns to hear folks bragging about this or that, and so he had heard of them, but the blunt fact was that most people did not survive an encounter with an ogre, much less an ogre mage. The end result meant there were only a handful of people on Thran who would know how to fight one and, looking down at the tired soldiers gathering around his boulder, he knew he was going to have to go into this battle ignorant of his opponent; an opponent, unfortunately, that was fearsome enough to inspire myths.

Turning back to address his handful of soldiers, Anthall was surprised to see that many more soldiers were gathering around his boulder. Calculating that there were perhaps fifty men, his spirits rose a bit, as that would give their mission an added chance for success. Anthall, looking at the sergeant standing six feet below him, commanded, "Sergeant, hand me my helmet and sword."

The sergeant nodded, replying, "Yes, sir," as he first grabbed the helmet and handed it up to Anthall. Next, he fixed his eyes on the sword, reaching out to pick up the enormous weapon. Most men used two hands to wield such a heavy blade, but the sergeant's hand jerked up into the air with unexpected ease, his eyes widening in surprise to find that the sword was almost weightless.

"You...are...not...worthy," hissed a venomous, snake-like, voice that seemed so close it could have been a whisper in his ear. The startled sergeant, now holding the sword, whipped his head around, looking for the source of the voice, but saw no one close enough to have made the comment. The hair on the back of his neck stood on end, as he quickly handed the sword up to Anthall, who immediately took it.

Anthall could see the perplexed and anxious look on the sergeant's face. "Not what you were expecting, soldier?", Anthall asked with a mischievous tone.

The Sergeant shook his head, "N-No, sir. I ain't never held a sword like that one before. It be darn near light as the air."

Anthall studied the soldier's face and could see that Slice had shaken the man's will, wondering what sordid message the blade had delivered. Time was short, so Anthall gave the soldier a quick wink before putting his helmet back on and standing back up as tall as he could make himself, he addressed the assembled soldiers. "Men, we are facing defeat here today, and we will likely lose this battle." Anthall paused to let the statement settle in, and he could see it had an impact as the soldiers fidgeted nervously. "But," continued Anthall, "we have not lost it yet. The truth is, as much as you do not want to be here, right now, those damn bugbears," he pointed out into the battlefield, "want to be here less! But they are here because of one reason: they fear their master, and I have seen who that is." Pointing in the ogre mage's direction, Anthall continued, "There is an ogre, two hundred yards to our east. We have no way to win this battle other than killing that ogre, which will cause the remaining bugbears to scatter." Or so he hoped, Anthall thought to himself. "Who will go into the teeth of the enemy with me and bring this battle to an end...and a victory!" he shouted with all his might, his eyes glowing ferociously red behind his helmet. The soldiers cheered in unison, raising their swords high in salute.

It was difficult in his heavy battle armor, but Anthall managed to leap down from the boulder, landing on the hard ground with a loud thud and sinking to one knee to absorb the impact. Rising back up to his feet, he motioned with his sword to move forward, and the company of soldiers that had rallied around him charged into the bugbear lines like a human wedge, using their leverage to open a narrow path for Anthall to make his way to the ogre. The fighting was fierce and fanatical, with both bugbears and humans falling in the melee. Soon after penetrating the front line, the group of soldiers found themselves surrounded, but they fought on, forcing their way deeper into the bugbear ranks until at last they could see the protective pocket around the ogre.

Anthall reached the last layer of bugbears guarding the ogre with about twenty of his men still left standing, and as they neared the pocket, Anthall heard a deep growly laugh from behind the bugbears, which he knew would be the ogre, but due to its invisibility, it was nowhere to be seen. As he continued to fight his way closer, the ogre blinked back into sight, just fifteen feet in front of him with its huge arm outstretched in his direction. The ogre was bigger than he had thought it would be, the distance from which he had viewed the ogre, back on the boulder, having deceived his judgment. It towered over twelve feet tall, and while its arms and legs were not as thick as the bugbears, they were ripped with sinewy muscles that denoted a better mix of agility and strength. Its skin, light green, had a mottled look and bore a myriad of arcane tattoos. The ogre wore a fine suit of leather armor that was covered with intricate runes and carried a bow, now slung over its shoulder, freeing up its hands. Its two large, intelligent eyes, one being milky white, focused in on Anthall and his small band of remaining men.

"Ah, well met, little clever ones. You got close to Krykl," growled the ogre mage, tapping his chest gently with two of his huge fingers, "but that is as far as you fucking little maggots will get!" And then, with a savage grin, the ogre drew upon the depths of his arcane knowledge and, with no more effort than a simple extension of his index finger in Anthall's direction, uttered the vocal trigger. "Invoco un cono di morte gelata." The hurricane blast of cold air summoned by the ogre mage was nothing like Anthall had ever experienced; it was as if he had jumped into an icy lake from one hundred feet. First, the crushing blow, the force of it knocking him backwards and the air out of his lungs, followed in the next instant by the hurricane sensation of extreme cold, like being stabbed by a thousand knives of ice that mingled with the sound of shattering ice echoing in his mind, and then finally, with his senses being overwhelmed...nothing.

CHAPTER TWO
Home

YEAR: AG 1175, The 17th Day of Sepu, Three Years After the Bugbear Battle

THE NIGHT, WITH ITS COOL BREEZE rustling the leaves of the great oak tree just outside his window, should have beckoned sleep, but for Brutal Mixnor, the quiet of the night was unwelcome, offering no distraction to the fact that his father was gone and almost certainly dead. Particularly, it was during the quiet, lonely, moments that Brutal most often thought of his father. Time after time, he found himself praying to Soulmite, the good goddess of combat, to bring peace to his soul and some acceptance of the loss, but in this, of all things, Soulmite had so far forsaken him. Shifting from his back to lie on his side, tucking his arm under the pillow, he fidgeted until it felt right under his head, as if the new position would somehow guard him from further thoughts of his father. "Honored Lady," Brutal whispered into the darkness, "why will you not hear my prayer, my plea, for peace? I am so very weary...three years it has been, is that punishment not long enough? Why am I cursed with such lingering discontent?" As thoughts and questions boomeranged around inside his head, he took a deep breath to calm his mind, focusing on his family: his mother, Fey, and his siblings, Lila, Percival, Trinity, and Nicholas. He knew he was blessed to have such a family, and he suddenly felt the tug of war inside his soul: the selfishness of missing his father and wanting to know more about where and what had happened, versus being thankful for the family Soulmite had blessed him with. He asked himself, 'Was it so wrong to want it all?' To have his family and answers about what happened to his father in the hills of the Cruel Pass?

Emerging from the storm of his circular thoughts, he noticed his hands, unconsciously, had balled up into fists, his mind urging him to hit something. With a deep sigh, as if to exhale the tension, he relaxed, letting his hands unclench, but he couldn't shake the collage of sadness, loss, uneasiness, and mystery that he felt, all stemming from his missing father. Admitting that lying on his side did not offer the distraction he was seeking, he shifted again to his back, tucking both arms behind his head. He stared up at the ceiling of his cottage, the half-moon shining enough light through the window so that he could still make out the familiar knot in the beam above his bed: the outer rings curving, making the outline of a wooden, unblinking eye, with the dark, hardened center forming a dark pupil, staring down at him, always watching, always silent, mocking him. Brutal found strength in this adversarial relationship, giving his pent-up ire a focal point. "You son of a bitch," Brutal said, but his words were cut off by something unexpected: sleep.

Cresting the horizon, the sun was making its bid to begin another day. The morning rays made their way into his small room, but did little to provide any warmth. The dwindling days of Ebbal would soon give way to the frozen season of Darkal and its short days and even colder nights. Brutal awoke to the sound of his mother, Fey, making breakfast. Opening his eyes, he saw the knot, his old nemesis, clearer now in the morning light, still staring down at him. Sitting up and turning to sit on the edge of the bed, he whispered, as if the knot could hear him, "What spell did you cast on me last night, you old bastard?" With his bare feet resting on the floor, the wood felt cold, sending a chill up his legs, but its familiar grooves and ridges still offered a comforting feeling. Yawning, he slipped his light brown shirt over his head, then, standing up, stepped into his brown leather leggings. Sitting back down on his bed, he slipped his leather boots onto his feet, feeling a bit more formidable now that he was clothed.

Glancing outside, past the great oak, he could see dark clouds off in the distance to the west. 'Great, rain,' he thought to himself, already feeling a dark mood descending. Eyeing a small wooden bowl sitting on his window ledge, he stood up and, leaning down and cupping his hands, splashed his face with the cool water, simultaneously sending a shiver down his spine and a rude jolt through his consciousness, removing any shred of the sleepy feeling that had been lingering. Brutal ran a wet hand through his brown hair which, like his father's, was of medium length on top but with the sides shaved close to his head. With one more splash on his face, he finally felt fully awake, and, leaning against the window frame, watching the distant storm clouds, he enjoyed a few more moments of rest before taking a deep sigh and walking into the living area of the cottage.

All the rooms in the house were small by design, with just enough space to sleep the family. There was no reason to build a large home that would require more repairs, cleaning, and most importantly, more wood to heat. The main living area was no different, with just enough room for a table and six chairs that dominated the northern half of the room. Four openings along the west side led to the bedrooms: a small space used to store wood was converted into Brutal's own bedroom, one for the younger boys, one for his sisters, and, of course, his mother's...and father's. The fireplace and chimney were tucked into the northeastern corner, where a fire was already crackling, casting shadows along the wooden walls. It wasn't a large fire, but enough to heat up some porridge and some small portions of ham. Brutal watched as his mother went about setting the table with simple bowls and wooden spoons for everyone, and as she leaned over to do her work, he noticed the holy symbol of Soulmite that was carved into a Taper wood disc, three simple dots arranged as if on the corners of a triangle, that dangled on her leather necklace. He couldn't remember a time when she didn't have it, and they prayed every night to the good warrior goddess. 'Had we not been faithful servants?' He thought to himself, as a sense of abandonment, perhaps even a hint of betrayal began welling up inside of him, but those dark feelings were fleeting, replaced by a wave of guilt for allowing himself to think such blasphemous thoughts. That was the struggle he felt each day. With a deep sigh, he tried to put the feelings aside as it only took Brutal three good strides to reach Fey, who had just finished setting the table. Giving her a quick kiss on the cheek, he said, "Good morning, Mother."

Fey's black hair, fashioned into a long braid, went to the middle of her back, highlighting her slender stature, but she was never mistaken as dainty - her strength and stamina were legendary in the household. She wore a plain brown working tunic that went down to her plain brown leather boots, almost covering them up, but not quite. "Good morning," she said, a little more abruptly than she intended, but continued, "Were you planning to begin harvesting today?"

Yawning, betraying his lack of sleep, Brutal gestured to the west. "Aye, but rain is coming, and keeping the sheaves dry is hard enough without --"

"When then?" Fey interrupted in frustration. "I tasted the grain two weeks ago, it was firm then, it was ready then, Brutal. But here we are, the wheat still in the field." She sighed and took a deep breath. "You keep finding reasons to put it off. It is not like you to delay, what is the matter?"

As if in reply, Brutal squeezed Fey's shoulder gently and moved toward the door. Opening it, he leaned on the frame, squinting. Looking out to the east, he could see the barn, the well, and, beyond that, the wheat fields, creating a sea of gold as the sun, rising, lit upon it. "It has been three years, Mother, do you not still miss him and wonder what happened?" he asked, but before Fey could answer, he added, "I do."

Fey bristled, initially, but seeing Brutal's slumped shoulders as he gazed out over the fields, she felt compassion for her son's pain, saying, "Aye, of course, I miss Anthall." Walking over to him, she put her hand on his shoulder. "But I do not want to know more, nor should you seek more of his death. The truth is, he was a fighter, Brutal, he died on the battlefield like any warrior would want. Even now, as we speak, he is in Soulmite's company and a member of her Righteous Guard, where he continues the fight against evil. It was his choice to go, and now that he is gone, he would want... Nay," she continued more firmly, poking him on the shoulder, "he would expect us to go on with our lives and find happiness."

Brutal listened to his mother, hoping and wishing she was right, but the cold pit in his stomach, and the weight he felt on his soul, only served to fuel his doubts. Just then, Brutal heard the sounds of Percival and Nicholas getting ready in their room and, glad for the distraction, he gave Fey a kiss on her tanned forehead. "Send them out then," he said, nodding in the direction of the boys. Brutal stepped out, saying as he did so, "We will do what we can today."

Fey watched Brutal as he made his way to the small barn, hating the feeling of helplessness oppressing her. Her right hand, unconsciously reaching up, touched the wooden holy symbol that was always close to her heart. As her thoughts turned to Soulmite, she felt the closeness of the good deity's presence, as she always had throughout her life. Filling her soul with the positive energy, she felt the comfort and relief fueling her iron will as she closed the wooden door, its hinges creaking in protest.

∗ ∗ ∗ ∗

As Brutal trudged his way across the open thirty feet to the barn, he looked out over his fields, the wheat was top-heavy -- a sure sign that it needed to be harvested soon, the stalks bending slightly toward the ground in submission to gravity, as if accepting their inevitable destruction. His mother was right, he knew he had been delaying, but for what reason he, himself, did not know. He was not ready, he thought to himself, but not ready for what? Shifting his gaze back to the barn, he noticed as he approached that the hand bolt on the double doors to the small twenty-five by fifty foot barn was unbolted, the doors slightly ajar, lightly banging together in the morning breeze. Getting closer, he could hear the grinding of metal coming from inside. "Who goes there?" demanded Brutal, bracing himself, wishing suddenly that he had a dagger or something to defend himself.

The grinding sound stopped, heavy footsteps moved toward the large barn doors, then paused, and finally the doors swung outward. Brutal had to jump backwards to avoid being hit. "Tyberius! What in the eight hells are you doing in there?"

Like a bear on two feet, Tyberius, grinning, as he was known to do, from behind his scraggly red goatee, barged out of the barn carrying a large scythe. Looking down at Brutal, he said, "Saving your arse, I suppose!

I seen your wheat has been ready to harvest for weeks now. What the hell have ya been doing? Do ya want to lose the crop, I mean, what will ya trade in Telfar to survive the winter on? Not your damn looks, that much is for certain." Not giving his friend time to answer, Tyberius shoved the scythe toward Brutal. "No wonder ya have not begun, this blade is duller than...than...well, it be damn dull, I tell ya." Tyberius chuckled again. "Ya could have been out there hacking away into the damn winter and gotten nowhere with this thing...ya might as well..."

Brutal cut him off, dramatically taking the offered scythe. "Yes, yes! I get it! I planned to sharpen the damn thing before I used it."

Tyberius put his hand on Brutal's shoulder as if to quiet him. He raised an eyebrow and, like a dog catching a scent, raised his nose for more clarity -- the westerly breeze carrying a familiar smell with it. "Ah, if that ain't ham or bacon, I be a halfling." Glancing past Brutal at the house, he licked his lips.

Shaking his head, Brutal said, "I will go sharpen this damnable thing while you go get a bite to eat..." But just as Tyberius's grin expanded, he concluded, "And then you can help me in the field until mid-day."

"Seems like a fair trade to me, but I was plan'in to help anyway," Tyberius said with a wink and a grin.

* * * *

Back in the house, Fey peered through the front window, watching Tyberius coming out of the barn. Her brow furrowed a bit, deepening wrinkles on her forehead that were not there just a year ago.

Percival was seventeen now, his boyish body from just two or three years ago making its transformation into a man. His weight, lagging behind his height, resulted in a tall, thin frame, but his face was already sprouting stubbles of whiskers on his square jaw that brooked seriousness. Noticing the change in his mother's disposition, he swallowed a mouthful of porridge and asked, "What is it, Ma?"

"Oh, nothing," Fey paused for a moment, but could not help herself, "Oh, Tyberius is out there with your brother," she added, absently drumming her fingers on the sill of the window. "I know Brutal thinks the world of him, and 'tis true that he has been a great help to us since, well, you know..." Chiding herself for bringing up the subject of their father, she paused to recover before continuing, "but that boy cannot be trusted, mark my words."

Sitting taller in his chair, a growth spurt and a straight back helping him gain some height on his sister, Trinity, just two years his elder and sitting next to him, Nicholas blurted out, "Ah, Ma, Tyberius is a good guy, why would you say that?"

Fey, turning her back to the window, looked at Nicholas and Percival, noticing that Lila and Trinity were now making their way to the table. "Tyberius has a good heart, I know that, but he has a crazy streak in him, and may the gods help anyone on the wrong side of his crazy." It was then that Fey noticed all four children looking over her shoulder. Turning to look, she saw Tyberius had made his way to the window where she was standing.

"'Ello, Momma," Tyberius stated affectionately, like a fourth son, "is Percy there actin' crazy again?" he asked with another grin.

"You best not sneak up on me, Tyberius," Fey scolded with a dagger-like finger. "That window is for looking out, not looking in. Did they not teach you any manners over yonder?" She gestured in the direction of Tyberius's home, which was the field to the north of their own.

"Oh, they taught me good, Momma. But I smelt the good cookin' in here. Ya'know," Tyberius added with a little cunning, "I am aiming to help Brutal today do a little harvestin'. A quick bite sure would make the day more..." Tyberius's voice trailed off as he looked up to the heavens, as if the word he was searching for would fall from the gods themselves.

"I think the word you be looking for is: productive," quipped Fey. "And," she added, "save that grin for Ariana or whatever girl you have your eye on these days -- you know you are always welcome at our table, working or not."

Victorious in his endless search for food, Tyberius happily said, "Thank ya, Momma!" As he walked to the front door, he yelled back to Brutal, announcing that he was going to get something to eat, as if Brutal didn't already know. Opening the door, Tyberius entered the house, ducking his head slightly to keep from bumping into the top of the door frame. Closing the door, taking off his worn leather hat and hanging it on the rack by the door, he took a seat at the end of the table where Brutal usually sat.

Fey served Tyberius a hot piece of bread and a piece of ham on it. "Do they not feed you back home?" she asked rhetorically.

Grinning, he readily accepted the plate, picked up the piece of ham, and gulped down a bite. "You see, it takes two families to feed me, Momma." Tyberius took another bite before turning his attention to Lila, who happened to be sitting next to him. One year younger than Tyberius, she wore her black hair pulled away from her face into a pony tail which was was held in place by a purple piece of cloth. Pointing a piece of ham at her, he stated, "I swear, girl, you look pert-ier every day."

Lila, flushing a bit self-consciously, averted her eyes and, using her spoon, toyed with the porridge in front of her. "Tyberius, Ariana would flay you if she heard you saying such nonsense."

Tyberius snorted in disagreement. "She would not. Why, in fact, she would agree with me, I am sure of it. Am I blind, am I not able to speak the truth no more? Should I be...well, one of them damn people that cannot speak?" he sarcastically fussed.

"No!" Both Nicholas and Trinity chimed in, making their opinion known.

"Youse two," Tyberius said, pointing the diminishing piece of ham at them, "are wise beyond yer young years. Momma, ya have two budding sages here, mark my words." Gulping down the last piece of ham, taking a swig of well water from Lila's cup, despite her futile gasp as he did so, he wiped his hands on his leather leggings as a finishing touch. "Thank you, Momma. I feel so much more...productive," he said with a wink and, of course, a grin. "Come along now, boys, the wheat is callin' yer names." With that, Tyberius, Percival, and Nicholas rose from the table, picking their hats from the rack by the door, and headed outside, the storm clouds getting closer.

* * * *

It was backbreaking work, made worse by the built-up humidity preceding the oncoming storm. Tyberius paired up with Percival, while Nicholas worked with Brutal. Brutal stopped swinging the scythe to let Nicholas catch up, and he smiled as he watched his little brother stacking the fallen stalks of wheat. Brutal chuckled, catching a glimpse of Nicholas's small leather hat, which was an ordinary in all respects, except for two jagged teeth that adorned the front. Brutal remembered finding them in the field during the harvest two years ago and, after convincing Nicholas that they were from a dire wolf, asked Fey to sew them into place on the hat. Once complete, Brutal handed the hat to his little brother and told him the teeth would help ward off evil.

Brutal's thoughts were interrupted by Nicholas, who had finally caught up. "C'mon," he whined, "let us call it a day already." Pointing to the clouds that were nearly upon them, he said, "It will rain soon..."

"Afraid of a little rain?" said Brutal playfully.

Ignoring the prod, Nicholas replied, "The wheat ain't going anywhere. We can do some more tomorrow."

Brutal turned away and resumed swinging the big scythe back and forth, ignoring the pleas of his little brother, the cradle catching the wheat and dropping it at the end of each swing into a neat pile as he walked. Nicholas, exasperated, followed behind and built the sheaves, standing four or five together to make a standing stack. After a few minutes, Brutal looked over his shoulder and said, "Just a little longer, lad, then we will head in."

Lila was working in the garden along the north side of the barn, picking some peas and carrots to help Fey make the midday meal. Shaking her head, she picked a few more than normal, knowing Tyberius would stay for the extra meal. A flash of lightning caught the corner of her eye, then after a short moment, the low echoing rumble of thunder washed over her like a slow wave, disappearing into the hills, like her father, she thought. She looked out into the field where the boys were working, all of them having taken their shirts off to help stay cool. She could not help but notice how strong Tyberius and Brutal looked as they swung their scythes back and forth. Tyberius, being taller, a little thinner, was more sinewy. Amazing, she thought, considering he ate like a pig. Brutal, though a few inches shorter, looked more muscular, making each swing of the scythe look easy, though she was sure it was not. Well, she thought analytically, the hard work that had to be done on a farm, day in and day out, built strong foundations. Interrupting her thoughts, a drop of rain landed on her cheek. Standing up, with the basket tucked in the crook of her arm, she headed back to the house to help start preparing the meal.

Brutal felt the drops of rain hit his bare back. It felt cool and refreshing, and the humidity was beginning to break with the first few drops. He could see Tyberius and Percival, already heading in, having stacked the last of their sheaves. Brutal laid the scythe down and helped Nicholas tie and stack the last of the fallen wheat. Once done, he picked up the scythe and the two brothers ran to catch up with Tyberius and Percival.

Stashing their tools in the barn, they could hear the rain start to increase its intensity. Tyberius, pushing Brutal and Percival out of the way, whooped, "Last one to the house is a wet pig!" and he bounded out of the barn in a full sprint, grin and all, Nicholas trying desperately to follow.

* * * *

Watching from the corner of the barn was a small black and white ferret. For others, humanoids mostly, the first glance was disconcerting as the immediate thought was a small, skinny, skunk -- but upon closer inspection, they saw a white body with a black patch on its head and two black stripes that ran along its sides and into its tail. However, it had a thin body and agile gait, not the thick bulk and waddle of a skunk. His name was Foetore, though only one person knew that -- and that was just fine, he thought to himself. As the boys ran across the now muddy space from the barn to the house, he groaned in displeasure; he did not like getting wet, nor the idea of crossing the open ground to the house. There were too many owls and other critters to worry about, but with no choice, he scurried as fast as he could over to the house. Making it safely there, with a quiet squeak of relief, he scouted around the outside of the house where he found a window partially open on the west side. Fortunately, a branch from the large oak tree reached out far enough to touch the wall of the house. The ferret hurriedly made its way to the trunk of the tree then, using his sharp claws, climbed up the trunk to the branch. With great dexterity, he easily scampered down the length of the branch and leapt onto the small windowsill, and with just enough space, slipped through the shutters and into the house. Once inside, he did a quick violent shake to shed some of the water, then, looking around for any dangers like a cat or dog but not seeing any, stealthily made his way onto a bed and then onto the floor. The room was extraordinarily plain and small, he thought, nothing adorning the walls and no room for anything but the bed. The only other things in the room that he could see, or smell, as it worked his nose hard, was a sword leaning in the southeastern corner where a small pile of neatly stacked books lay. 'Interesting, could Brutal read?' he wondered. Finding nothing else worthy of note, he hugged the eastern wall until it came close to the opening that led into the main living area. There, Foetore curled up into a small ball -- for warmth and comfort but not to sleep. Things were going well, he thought, pleased and proud with himself.

* * * *

They all just made it in, the rain starting to pour as Brutal, the last one to the house, shut the door of the house behind them. Fey raised her voice over the din of the activity in the small overcrowded room. "Well, what an unexpected surprise! Tyberius, you made it just in time for the mid-day meal."

Grinning, with his hat still in his hand, he looked down at her. "Darn the weather, it looks that way, Momma." Reaching down, he gave her a big bear hug, picking her up off the ground.

"Ugh, you are all wet, put me down, Tyberius, right now!" she hollered at him, everyone getting a good laugh, including Brutal. "You see, you see! There is that crazy streak I was warning you kids about!" As he put her gently back down, all she could think of saying was, "Honestly," as she smoothed out her dress and apron, now covered with splotches of wet spots.

A stool was pushed up to the table for Tyberius, and once everyone settled into their usual spots, Brutal, sitting at his end of the table, surveyed his family, feeling the love that held them all together through the last three hard years. It was in the midst of this happy setting, the sound of rain pattering on the roof, the eager hand of Tyberius being slapped by a scolding Fey, the giggling of Nicholas and Trinity, that the reason for his delaying the harvest came to him, like a ship coming out of the fog, a ghostly shape finally taking form, a blessing from Soulmite herself, he was sure. A peace washing over him, the shackles on his spirit undone, sweeping away three years of anguish, Brutal smiled.

"Tyberius," Fey admonished, slapping his hand reaching for a piece of bread on the table, "not until we say the blessing."

"Oh, sorry, Momma," Tyberius, recoiling his hand, said somewhat sheepishly.

Brutal began, "Dear Lady, thank you for all your blessings, for this family, our friends, and for the food you have provided. No lover of war, but war against evil a righteous duty. Soulmite, we offer our services to you as we offer our lives."

The meal was a simple stew of rabbit and fresh vegetables from the garden, accompanied by the bread that Fey had made that morning, but to Brutal, it was the most satisfying meal he had eaten in years, its smells, flavors, and the company elevating by his rising spirit, only made possible by his recent epiphany: This would be his last harvest and his last fall at the farm, he was leaving to find out what happened to his father.

* * * *

As the sounds of the mid-day meal wound down and the chair legs screeched on the floor announcing that the people were getting up, Foetore, the ferret, looked up and cocked his head to better hear exactly what was happening. The smells were wonderful, and he thought with regret that he could not investigate the floor underneath the table for scraps that were sure to be there; humans were so messy. He heard Brutal say, "I will walk you home, then I am going into Telfar to see Mikell. But, first, I must grab my sword." Foetore quickly glanced at the sword in the corner, then with the sound of footsteps coming closer, he jumped to his feet and in an instant bounded up onto the bed and back through the small gap between the shutters. With no time to spare, he saw Brutal walk in and pick up the sheathed longsword, which he attached to the brown belt he was wearing. As he was about to leave the small room, he stopped and turned back to the window. "Damn it," he heard Brutal whisper, reaching over the bed to close the shutters completely and latching them tight. "Great, the bed got wet..."

Foetore didn't waste any time, he jumped the four feet to the ground and scurried around the north end of the house, rounded the corner, and waited in a woodpile at the northeast corner of the house for Brutal and Tyberius.

* * * *

"It is still raining, why not wait a little while before heading out?" Fey asked.

"The rain has almost passed, and I want to get back before dark. Besides," added Brutal, pushing his friend toward the door, "Tyberius would not want to miss the mid-day meal back at his house."

"Can I go with you to the village?" asked Nicholas, hopeful, racing up to Brutal's side.

Ruffling Nicholas's hair, he replied, "Not this time, lad -- I have to be quick, and besides, there is nothing exciting about the village."

"Says you -- I never get to go to the village. It sounds exciting to me," replied Nicholas.

"Maybe next time, lad." Brutal gave Nicholas a quick hug, and then he and Tyberius grabbed their hats from the rack on the wall by the door and headed out.

"Thank ya for the grub, Momma!" Tyberius managed to say as Brutal was closing the door. Outside, he turned to his friend. "What the hell was that all about? Though ya do have a good point of getting back for another mid-day meal."

"Come on," Brutal said, heading toward the barn, "I need to get Sally saddled up, it will just take a minute." Together, the two men walked across the small courtyard.

* * * *

The ferret could not risk the open ground to the barn, there were too many people moving around, but no matter -- 'I have what I need,' he thought to himself -- and after watching Brutal and Tyberius walk into the barn together, the white and black ferret took a moment to scan the still overcast sky. 'Damn birds,' he thought. Seeing nothing, he dashed out of the woodpile and disappeared into the safety of the tall grass, leaving no trace he was ever there.

* * * *

Opening the barn doors, Tyberius and Brutal went inside, each grabbing a brush that hung on the barn wall as they approached Sally's stall. Sally was Brutal's draft horse, she was brown with white markings on her right side and was more at home behind a plow than under a saddle, but capable either way. As Brutal brushed the loose hair and dirt from Sally's back, Tyberius watched his face. "Ya have that far off look in your eye, my friend. And ya did not answer my question, so what is the big rush to see Mikell?"

"I learned something today.... Soulmite finally answered my prayers," responded Brutal.

"What do ya mean? She told you what happened to your pa?"

"No, she did not directly speak to me, of course...she gave me --" Brutal paused, looking for the right word, "direction."

"So she told you to ride to Telfar?" asked a confused Tyberius.

Brutal chuckled a bit. "No, you are taking what I am saying too literally."

"I did not," huffed Tyberius, "I am hearing what ya are saying, and it makes no sense. I mean, listen to yourself," raising the pitch of his voice in mockery, "'she gave me direction but did not tell me where to go.' Who can make sense of that?"

Putting his brush down, Brutal grabbed the saddle blanket and placed it onto Sally's back. "I guess you are right, it was more like...a feeling...which is why I need to talk to Mikell. He knows more about that kind of stuff than us."

"Now, that I understand," said Tyberius. "It has been a while since I seen Mikell. Hey - since we is going into town, we should stop and see if Bealty is around. He always has good stories and info."

Brutal sat the saddle gently down on the blanket covering Sally's back and passed the cinch straps underneath to Tyberius, Sally snorting as they did so. "Good, you track down Bealty while I talk to Mikell, and we will meet you two later at the Drip. Sound like a plan?"

"That will work," agreed Tyberius. "I will run back home to get me a horse."

"Alright, I will see you on the path then," said Brutal as he slipped the bit into Sally's mouth and positioned the bridle on her head. But Tyberius was already out of the barn and was disappearing to the north as he sped homeward. Tyberius had always been extraordinarily fleet of foot, and Brutal knew from personal experience that there was no way to keep up with him when walking or running. Brutal did the math in his mind: it was a two mile run back to Tyberius's house. Once there, he would eat his second mid-day meal, as Brutal knew there was no way he was going to pass that up, then he would have to get saddled and on his way. If it were anyone else, they would never catch up, but, chuckling to himself, he knew Tyberius could.

CHAPTER THREE
The Road To Telfar

THE VILLAGE OF TELFAR WAS OVER TEN MILES, and Brutal knew he could make the trip in just about two hours if he let Sally walk the distance, a little less if he had her trot occasionally, which is normally what he would do, but because Tyberius was still behind him, he decided to slow Sally down, knowing that once his tall friend caught up, they could make up the time. Although the area was quite safe, Telfar did have armed patrols that came out as far as Brutal's farm, but being on the north side of the White River, it was still a wild region and they were close enough to the hills of the Cruel Pass that it wasn't unheard of to find tracks and other signs of kobolds, orcs, goblins, hobgoblins, and other nefarious creatures passing through. With such thoughts rolling around his head, Brutal kept Sally on the beaten path to Telfar, scanning the sides of the road for any danger, but all he saw were the rolling plains of green and brown grass, and off in the distance to the north, he could see the foothills of the Cruel Pass. Farther off, beyond the foothills, somewhere over the horizon, he knew the Doubtless Mountains loomed, refuge to all sorts of denizens, some good and some bad… 'Mostly bad,' he thought to himself. 'Whatever happened to Father,' his mind continued, 'happened in those hills or those mountains.' Brutal patted the side of Sally's muscular neck, it was warm to the touch and felt like sculpted granite on his palm. "It is about damn time we find out what happened to him, ain't it, Sally?" he asked rhetorically, a little surprised when Sally let out a loud snort in what, to him, seemed like agreement.

The rain stopped shortly after he started on his way, and the sun, a hazy orb overhead, was trying to burn its way through the overcast skies, with little success -- but it did succeed in ramping up the heat and humidity in the wake of the storm. Always someone who broke into a sweat easily, Brutal already found himself wiping his forehead occasionally, and, reaching down, he grabbed his water-skin, taking a refreshing swig of the still cool well water. Plugging the cork back in, he tucked the waterskin back into his saddlebag, hiding it from the direct rays of the sun as he glanced backwards down the path behind him. "Where the hell are you?" he mumbled out loud, already expecting to see Tyberius -- but there was still no sign of him. With only six good hours of daylight left, Brutal was beginning to worry that his slow pace would force him, and Tyberius, to ride home from Telfar in the dark -- and safe or not, patrols or not, he did not relish that idea.

While Brutal was looking backwards, the wind, blowing from the west, brought with it a faint stench. Wrinkling his nose, he swiveled in his saddle to face forward, looking around to see if he could find the source, one hand on the reins and the other moving unconsciously to rest on the hilt of the longsword. He knew he wasn't a skilled fighter -- hell, he thought to himself, he was just a farmer with a sword, but it was better to be a farmer with a sword than a farmer without a sword. Continuing to scan the area in front of him, he urged Sally slowly down the path heading west. The smell grew worse with each step Sally took, but when the wind shifted, blowing out of the north, the awful smell vanished. Something was dead and rotting, he thought to himself, probably a carcass of a small animal, he tried to reassure himself, but one thing was for certain: he was heading right for it.

"Alright, Sally, whoa," he said as he pulled up on the reins, and, obeying, Sally came to a halt. Brutal tried to swing his right leg over her back and hop down, but his foot caught on Sally's hind quarter, and he started to fall. Falling upside down in an awkward position, he held out his left hand to try and break his fall but was only partially successful, still landing hard on his back. Grunting, the air being forced out of his lungs, he lay there for just a moment, shaken from the unexpected fall. Regaining his senses, Brutal rolled over and quickly pushed himself back up to a standing position. His face flushed in a mixture of anger and embarrassment, looking around quickly to see who might be out there who could have seen his absurd display. But still nothing.

"Son of a bitch," he said through gritted teeth, admonishing himself, and leaned against Sally with one arm over her neck, pausing for a moment to regain his composure. The adrenaline slowly leaving his system, he stood back up and whispered to Sally, "Let us keep that little, incident, to ourselves. There is a carrot with your name on it back at the farmhouse." Wincing just a bit, he noticed for the first time the pain in his left hand, which was beginning to throb and bleed. Examining it closer, he found a half inch triangular-shaped rock embedded into the flesh of his left palm, near his thumb. "Damn it..." he fumed. Digging into his saddlebag, he pulled out a crumpled-up piece of cloth, tearing off a half-inch wide strip. Putting the bundle back into the saddlebag, he wrapped the cloth around his left hand and, using his teeth and right hand, pulled it tight and knotted it. Not perfect, he thought, but it would work for now, and grabbing Sally's reins with his right hand, he started walking down the path toward Telfar.

It wasn't much further until Brutal reached "the turn," as they called it, where their trail met the main road to Telfar. The road ran southwest and northeast, beginning at the Telfar ferry crossing and stretched all the way into the hills of the Cruel Pass. 'Halfway there,' Brutal thought to himself. Another path, seldom traveled, veiled by untrammeled grass, continued on the other side of the main road, heading northwest, making Brutal think about Julius, a friend with a small house, several miles in that direction. Not being one for cities, or villages, Julius kept to the wilds and so the path was seldom used. It had been many tendays since he had seen Julius, and Brutal made a mental note that he should see how he was doing, maybe when the harvesting was done.

Turning left, Brutal headed southwest down the road, walking Sally toward Telfar. Less than a quarter mile down the road, scanning the grassy plains to the northwest, Brutal noticed a faint trail where some of the grass had been recently trodden. "Huh, that's interesting, why would someone just go off the road there?" he quietly asked himself. Looking behind him again, hoping, expecting, to see Tyberius any minute, he hesitated, debating about seeing where the mysterious trail went. "I do not have time for this," he said, shaking his head, admonishing himself. He was about to continue down the road, when the wind shifted again, blowing from the north, bringing with it an intense foul smell. Raising his left arm up, covering his nose and mouth with the crook of his arm, he gave the path another look. "What is that smell?" he said from behind his elbow. Looking one more time for his friend, then to the west, down the main road, Brutal decided he would follow the trail for a small distance and see where or what it led to. The heat and humidity continued to grow, and sweat was already running down his face. Brutal wiped the sweat away using the crook of his arm. With the mysterious stench palpable, Brutal led Sally off the main road.

Entering the path, Brutal, for the first time, noticed how quiet it was. Normally there were crickets, birds, or small animals making sounds as they flew, scurried, crawled, or otherwise went about their daily tasks, but now there was nothing to be heard. Pausing, moving to Sally's right side, Brutal took the reins in his bandaged, still bleeding, left hand, allowing him to draw the longsword from the scabbard clipped to his left side. Its weight and balance comforting him, he continued down the faded trail. With each step, the smell grew stronger, causing his heart to beat quicker, filling his head with the rhythmic thump; he had never smelled anything like it. It was difficult to keep track of the faint trail since the grass was blowing in the wind, which would occasionally erase all the evidence. Being several hundred yards into the tall grass, Brutal paused to look back toward the main road, which was getting more difficult to make out. If something happened to him out here, nobody would find him or be able to help, and that made him start to think twice about what he was doing. With still no sign of Tyberius, Brutal fought back the instinct to wait for his friend and started moving along the mysterious path. 'Just a little further,' he thought to himself. He could make out a small rise another seventy-five yards farther and figured he would at least go that far.

Reaching the small hill and walking up the low incline, he came upon a swale in the grassy plain, a small bowl about one hundred feet in diameter and twenty feet deep in the middle -- a feature that disguised it from view, at least from the road -- the tall grass surrounding it giving the illusion of a continuous plain. Standing on the small rim, looking down, the hairs on the back of his neck snapping on end, his fingers flexing as he tightened his grip on the hilt of his sword, he could hardly believe what he was seeing. "What in the eight hells?" Whispered Brutal out loud.

CHAPTER FOUR
Bealty

CLIMBING OUT OF BED LATE TODAY, the sun already high in the late morning sky, the two foot ten inch halfling, Bealty Bexter, pulled on his black leather leggings, a brown cloth shirt, and his brown leather walking boots. Grabbing a belt with several pouches sewn into it for concealment, he buckled it on and headed out. Pushing his dark black hair back, he put on his brown leather day cap, revealing the boyish features of his face. At first glance, he might pass as a five-year-old human boy, but on second glance, the face had an older, wiser look to it, not quite fitting the small body, and if that didn't give away his halfling race, the short stubble growing on his chin and jawline, along with the pointed ears that his hat neatly tucked behind, surely did. Opening his front door, he headed out into the bright sunlight. It must have rained, he thought to himself, noticing puddles already disappearing into the soil and evaporating in the uncommonly warm Sepu air. Telfar, being a pass-through town, changed on a daily and weekly basis -- sure, people lived here, and he knew almost everyone, even if they didn't know him, but there was a transient nature to the city, which is why he liked it; anything could happen on any given day and the best spot to find out what was going on in town was the Drip, making it an almost irresistible destination for the small rogue. The Drip was the only real tavern and inn in the village of Telfar, although the Gustav was an inn, too, but it was comparatively boring, people only going there, mostly, to sleep. Making his way from his home in the southwest corner of the town, dodging between small cramped houses, avoiding being trampled by the much larger humans, it was but a few moments before he found himself in front of the entrance to the Drip. Looking around with his keen eyes, it was unusually quiet for being close to mid-day, he thought to himself. The door was open, as it always was during the day, so Bealty, with practiced quiet, stepped into the tavern and quickly found his best friend, a shadow, and melded into the darkness. The tavern, like many buildings, was illuminated by candlelight and lanterns during the night, but relied on the sun and open windows and doors during the day. Either way, shadows abounded in the fifty foot by forty foot room of the tavern's first floor. Oddly, there wasn't anyone else around, except for Syd behind the old wooden bar in the southeast corner. With only one good eye, wearing a grotesque patch to cover the other one, Syd wasn't the keenest observer, but what he lacked in sight he made up for with bat-like hearing, so Bealty, carefully watching his footing, made his way from shadow to shadow. Barely having to duck to walk under the tables, he made his way to the bar and gracefully hopped up, like a cat, onto one of the empty bar stools.

"Hey there, Syd," he said with a half grin as he slapped two copper pieces down on the bar with a dull thud. "Give me a brew."

Startled by the sudden appearance of the halfling, Syd's weathered face twisted into a grimace. "I should charge ya double, ya drink like a damn bird, and for being as small as ye are, you still take up a blasted chair or stool," Syd said in his gravelly voice, worn by years of pipe smoking, and pointed a grizzled finger at the halfling. "I changed me mind, make it four times over for ye, cause it feels like I be serving a toddler ev'ry time ya come in here," and punctuating his point, added, "I like it not." Despite the protests, Syd poured some ale from one of the many barrels behind the bar into a mug, and placing it in front of Bealty, quickly took the two copper pieces and stuffed them into his pocket.

Bealty had heard it all before. Every joke, every insult about his diminutive stature. Being a halfling, a race where giants broke the four foot mark and fifty pounds, it came with the territory. "Do we have to go through this every time I come in here, Syd?" asked Bealty, hoping to avoid the conversation.

Syd started again, "And you..."

"Make the customers nervous." Bealty finished Syd's sentence.

Waving his arm around the room that had eleven wooden tables, each with four sturdy, functional chairs, all of which were presently empty, he said, "But there are no other customers, so relax."

"Do not be telling me to relax in me own joint. Durn, halfling." Syd said gruffly as he wiped the bar down.

Taking a sip from the relatively huge mug in front of him, pulling out a copper piece from some hidden source, and deftly flipping it through his fingers as if putting on a show, Bealty asked, "Is not my coin as good as the next, though? Especially since I seem to be your sole customer."

"Aye, ye coin is just as good," Syd admitted. "But look at what ya's doin' with that there coin," Syd complained. "I bet ya could lift a gold coin out of a dwarf's puckered arse, and he would have just thought he passed wind. Watchin' ya do that stuff makes me feel like checking me own pockets," which he then did.

With a subtle flick of his wrist, the coin disappeared back into its hidden pouch. "Syd," Bealty said plainly, "that is an unfair comment. I locksmith for my money, I do not steal."

Rubbing his stubbly chin, Syd looked at the halfling with his one good eye. "Aye, and ye be a good locksmith at that." He paused and leaned a little closer. "Likely, a little too good -- and not enough locks to be picked 'round here, I imagine." Leaning back and picking up a mug to wipe it out with a dirty towel, he said, "But it be true, I have not known ye to steal from me. I only said such a thing cause the guests do not know ye like I do. They see a halfling showing off, and they tighten their purses. That be all I is saying, lad."

Bealty considered that as he sipped from the gigantic mug. "Yeah, I can see how that might be."

Just then, the door creaked open as two humans entered the tavern, both were medium height, though one was a little hunched over, their faces were bearded but otherwise plain and they both wore basic clothing of brown cloth shirts and brown leggings, with leather boots. Bealty didn't recognize them, so they weren't from the village, but that wasn't unusual. As they walked over to the bar, he couldn't see any visible weapons; just merchants traveling, he guessed. As they neared the bar, the hunched-over man, who was closest to Bealty, looked at the halfling and put his hand on a pouch tied to his belt and frowned.

This too was nothing new to Bealty and he did not take such receptions as an insult, but rather as a compliment. As a diminutive race with renown natural dexterity, and some would say luck, add to that the ability to fit into the smallest of places, meant that thievery was practically a given trade for all halflings. Of course, not all were thieves, but when encountering an unknown halfling, it was always wise to assume so. As such, with no outward reaction, Bealty took a sip of ale from the big mug, ignoring the frown, but like a moth to a flame, his gaze lingered briefly to peek at the pouch the man clasped, noticing the light bulge of coins, their edges pressing against the leather bag, wondering how much money was in there. 'So easy,' he thought, his nimble fingers flexing around the handle of his mug, imagining it was the leather strap holding the man's bag on his belt, his finger knife effortlessly cutting through it. But, suppressing his instincts, Bealty took one final sip from the mug, and, setting it back down on the bar, sprang off the stool. "See ya around, Syd, thanks for the drink." The two new guests watched warily as the spry halfling breezed out of the tavern.

Picking up the mug and finding it practically full, Syd mumbled under his raspy breath, "Like a damn bird..." Syd, ever the pragmatist and not wanting to waste good ale, took a long pull. Turning to his new guests, now appearing a little more at ease with the departure of the halfling, he asked, "How may I help ye boys?"

* * * *

Finding himself back outside the northern door of the Drip, Bealty scanned the buildings around him. The guild hall, where all the craftsmen went to find work and handle grievances, was directly across the street to the north. It was one of the finest buildings in Telfar, proudly built by the most skilled carpenters and adorned with fine metalwork and glassware, all the trades wanting to out-perform the others in its construction. The large engraved double doors were the centerpiece and showed a collage of different crafts constructing a ship. The Farley stables, kitty-corner to the northwest, was a place where there was usually steady traffic, since most folks traveling needed a place for their horses and other livestock to rest while they conducted their business in Telfar. It was a large building, but very plain and functional looking, Bealty thought to himself. Across the main street, directly west of the Drip, was the sheriff's office. The building was over fifty years old, but though its Taper wood had a slightly more golden look after years of being bleached in the sun, it was as solid and forbidding as ever. A tall spire that went up fifty feet to a lookout, dominated the village and was always manned. Looking up, Bealty could see two figures in the parapet, one of them, his hands on the railing as he was looking out, seemed to be looking down right at him, but that was probably just his imagination, Bealty assured himself. Right at the intersection, next to the stables, Bealty could see the massive Fuhr pole, jutting straight up into the sky, like the gods themselves had hurled a huge dart into the ground. The two chains dangling, could, when the wind was strong enough, make an eerie sound as the air whistled through the large links, but today they just gently clanked in the light breeze.

Looking the other direction, to the east, Bealty could see the temple to Zuel, the good god of healing, where his friend Mikell was a priest. He could also see, across the street from the temple, his own small building, just bigger than a shack, really, that had a sign above it that read: "Bexter Locksmith." Originally from Whiteal, Bealty came to Telfar in AG1170, five years ago, and purchased two small plots, one for his home and the other for his shop. Though it was small by human standards, it was plenty large enough for Bealty, and suited all his needs, which consisted mostly of being a safe secure place to practice his "skills," but occasionally an actual customer would, surprisingly, show up.

With one more glance at the Fuhr Pole, Bealty turned and headed down the street toward the Zuel Temple. The church was relatively new to the village, having been built in AG1165, five years before Bealty had even come to Telfar. The Taper wood was dark and still had a fresh, almost minty smell. It was a modest size, just two stories, with the lower level for worship, and the upper level serving as the living quarters for Mikell and his father. Standing at the small wooden steps, looking up, Bealty paused for just a second, admiring the only extraordinary feature of the church: the entrance, with its stained glass double doors. The glass depicted the cross and double dot symbol of Zuel, a welcoming sight, Bealty thought, and as grand entrances weren't his style, he opened the doors a crack and slipped into the chapel, gently closing the door behind him.

CHAPTER FIVE
Mikell

EYES CLOSED, HIS HANDS CLASPED IN HIS LAP, a broom leaning against the side of his pew, Mikell sat in silent prayer. Hearing a small creak from behind him, opening his eyes, and turning, Mikell looked back at the double door entrance to the church, expecting someone to be there. Instead, all he saw was the empty main floor of the temple, with its ten rows of pews, split down the middle by the narrow walkway that led from the double doors straight to the altar, and beyond that, a large brass symbol of Zuel hanging on the wall. Unlit candles lined the walls and unlit torches in their sconces leaned inward from the walls where they were positioned. Two large torches, held up by poles, stood on either side of the altar and two more on either side of the holy symbol at the back of the church. A doorway in the northwestern corner of the room was the only other visible feature.

Mikell was dressed in his work clothes, a white over-shirt, leather leggings, and, of course, his silver necklace with the holy symbol of Zuel hanging around his neck; its cool metal, a cross with two small circles diagonally across from each other in opposite quadrants, resting comfortably against his chest. Not quite five feet eight inches tall, he was stout in stature with a powerful build, and although his head was bald -- only the shadowy outline of his receding hairline visible -- it was contrasted by bushy eyebrows and a thick black mustache that went from ear to ear, lending emphasis to the two solid loop gold earrings in each ear, making him look more like an exotic pirate than a holy priest of Zuel. His physical appearance, deep voice, and bright brown eyes that could look through to your soul, presented a powerful figure that, all told, gave Mikell a commanding presence and a charisma that drew people into him, like a moth to a flame. Mikell, his forehead dampened by sweat from the humidity and heat that was building up in the mid-day air, stood up, and, grabbing the broom, he continued sweeping the endless amount of dirt that always seemed to find its way into the chapel, corralling it toward the double doors.

With a few more sweeps toward the doors, and without pausing, Mikell spoke, his voice deep, into the supposed emptiness. "Bealty, I have no idea where you are, but if you jump out at me, I promise you: you will feel the end of this broom going where it should not." Mikell, now pausing to look around again, this time with more scrutiny, raised the broom, turning it into a club. "I mean it," said Mikell.

Popping up five feet away, with a pew between him and Mikell, Bealty revealed himself, holding his hands up in the air in mock surrender. "Merciful gods, no need to get violent, cannot I come to say a prayer without getting assaulted?"

Mikell, still armed with the broom, spun around to see the small halfling. "A prayer, my arse. Prayers to Graff will be in vain in this house, Bealty, and you know that much." Graff, the good god of luck, Mikell knew, was the deity that Bealty, and almost all halflings, paid homage to. "We have known each other for what, five years now, and I have yet to ever hear or see you pray."

"That is because Graff knows I am faithful and does not require such nonsense," Bealty retorted, with a wave of his small hand.

Mikell pondered that for a second. "Well, well, is that not convenient for you? Someday, Bealty, you may need Graff's aid, and you will not know where to begin." After a moment's thought, Mikell, lowering his voice in seriousness, continued, "But, because Graff does not require it, would it not make it more meaningful if you were to do it?"

"Huh, that is an interesting point, I have never thought of that." Pausing to consider Mikell's statement further, hopping up onto the pew, and sitting on the backrest, resting his stubbled chin in his hand, he looked up and, seeing Mikell standing there, a sly smirk forming on the cleric's face, he groaned. "Aw, shit. You miserable priest, why do I even

44

listen to you? I am not falling for that guilt trip. I suppose you use that on all your sheepish followers? Yeah, I bet that gets the donations flowing."

Mikell did not answer, as they both had a good hearty laugh, their voices echoing in the otherwise empty temple. Mikell, feeling weak from the gut-rolls, sat down on the pew to let the last few chuckles pass. "Your presence here can mean only one thing: there must be nothing happening at the Drip today."

Wiping away a tear of laughter and suppressing a chuckle, Bealty mused, "Yeah, it was just me and Syd for a little while. Telfar seems unusually quiet today. Maybe the passing storm has something to do with it. Being Ex-day, maybe folks decided to stay home."

"Aye, maybe," agreed Mikell. "Hey, why not help me sweep up in here? Then walk over to Dory's with me?"

Bealty groaned. "What? Help you sweep? You know how I hate manual labor, and for what? So we can walk a short way to a smelly candle-maker's shop?" he asked rhetorically. Then without hesitating, he punctuated his feelings with a wave of his hand. "I will pass on that offer, thank you very much."

Mikell, sensing an error in his approach, said, "Just to help a friend out, will you?" Seeing the lack of motivation in the halfling's green eyes, he added, "Alright, I will buy you a drink at the Drip on our way back."

Bealty's face brightened. "Well, what are friends for?"

Mikell handed Bealty his broom and headed toward the door in the northeast corner. "I will go get a second broom and be right back. You start over there," he said, pointing toward the western corner. "And get under the pews," he said with a grin, "that should be no problem for you."

Holding the broom, what looked like a giant oar in his small hands, Bealty walked over to his assigned corner, grumbling, "Oh, ha-ha, like I never have heard that before..."

CHAPTER SIX
Discovery

LOOKING DOWN INTO THE BOWL OF THE SWALE, Brutal found the source of the ghastly smell. In the center of the bowl lay a large and mixed pile of bones and carcasses, of what Brutal could not discern from the distance of his vantage point. Looking around, he could not see what, or who, might have caused the horrid scene, but the myriad of tracks leading in and out showed this area was well traveled. So much so that a wide area at the bottom of the swale had the grass worn away, exposing the dark black fertile soil. It wasn't obvious at first, but looking with renewed awareness, he could definitely make out traces of paths leading out into the grassy plains surrounding the swale, one of which he was now standing on.

Sally neighed nervously and began to back away from the rim. "Whoa, girl," Brutal whispered to her comfortingly. Then Brutal felt it, a vibration in the ground that sent tingles up his legs, accompanied by the grinding sound of metal on stone. Looking around frantically, he finally saw it. An opening started to appear in the side of the slope ahead of and below him. He let go of Sally's reins, and she trotted a distance away while Brutal dropped to the ground, trying to hide in the tall grass around the rim. He could hear some sort of guttural language coming from below, and taking a chance, he crawled forward just a bit so he could see through the grass.

It was two humanoids, standing nearly seven feet tall, Brutal guessed, wearing crude leather armor, and each had a large hand ax strapped to their belts. Their heads and bodies were dog-like, including

46

their pawed feet -- but they had hands like a human. One of them was carrying the carcass of what looked like a deer, the flesh having been stripped off, leaving a pile of gristle and bones. The beast heaved the carcass onto the pile and turned around, saying something to his companion. It pointed to the southwest and made some comment he couldn't understand. Now that the beast was facing in Brutal's direction, he could see the muzzle, loaded with discolored but sharp, teeth, and the eyes were large, alert, and had a crazed look about them.

Brutal felt like a coward hiding in the tall grass, but he didn't know how many -- things -- could be down there, and he wasn't going to take them on alone; after all, he was just a farmer, he thought to himself. Lying motionless, he watched as the two beasts slowly started walking back toward the entrance from whence they came, both scanning their surroundings as they did so. Raising their dog-like snouts into the air, they started sniffing for scents -- or had they already caught a whiff of something? As beads of sweat fell from Brutal's forehead and landed on his forearm, he wondered about the possibility that they could smell him from that far away. As if finishing his thought for him, the taller of the two beasts abruptly halted, extending his pole-like arm to stop his companion, and, with his eyes looking in his direction, growled something. The slightly shorter humanoid, barely pausing, aggressively shoved the outstretched arm out of his way with his left hand and punched his taller companion hard in the shoulder. Yelping and cowering at the blow, the taller beast rubbed his wounded shoulder and watched as his shorter companion stomped back through the hillside door. The remaining beast, reaching back with his right hand, drew his large war ax from his belt. Still sniffing the air, he cautiously moved away from the doorway, looking for a less steep place to ascend the hill.

Brutal's mind began to spin through his options, the adrenaline kicking in full force, and his heart pounded like a drum in his head. Hiding wasn't an option anymore, once that beast got to the crest of the swale, it would certainly see Sally, then it would know someone was around, if it didn't already. So it was down to the basics: fight or flight? Sizing up his adversary who was a seven foot, dog-like humanoid, there was no way he could outrun it back to Sally, so he was going to have to fight this

47

thing. If he was going to fight, he was determined to keep the advantage of the high ground. Moving slightly to get his arms underneath his body, he readied himself, but just as he was about to spring up, a loud bark and guttural growl broke the intense silence. Brutal froze, watching how the tall humanoid reacted to the new sound. Pausing halfway up the hill, Brutal could see it snarl, revealing yellowed fangs, and it let out a loud low growl that made the hair on Brutal's neck stand on end. It hacked in frustration at the grass in front of it with its ax, but, after a short pause, turned around and walked back down toward the entrance, disappearing inside. As the door began to close, he distinctly heard one word come from the inside before the door shut. It was heavily accented, but it was distinct, the word he heard the beast utter was: "Human..."

Not wasting any time, Brutal sprang up, sheathed his sword, and started running back down the trail. He could see Sally looking in his direction, waiting for him about halfway back to the main road. Brutal was out of breath as he finally reached Sally. "Smart girl," he said as he grabbed the reins, and getting one foot in the stirrup, he leaped onto her back with a grunt. He gave Sally a quick kick with his heels, and needing no further encouragement, the horse galloped back to the main road. Pausing for a moment, he looked back in the direction of home. "Where the hell are you, Tyberius?" With that, Brutal urged Sally southwest at a fast trot toward Telfar.

CHAPTER SEVEN
Crossing

BRUTAL MADE GOOD TIME and was almost to the ferry crossing. He knew he was close to where the road would begin its descent into the Great White River valley and sure enough, with each step Sally took, a small portion of the panoramic view unveiled itself. Once at the crest, Brutal had Sally stop so that he could admire the grand view. The frothy water of the Great White River could be seen stretching from the horizon to the northwest, past the town of Telfar, and disappearing over the horizon to the southeast. The difference between the north and south banks could not be starker. Aside from the sturdy and fortified structure of the ferry building, the north bank looked pristine, its sea of grass undulating with the wind, with no sign of civilization and only the occasional grove of Taper wood trees dotting the view. The south bank, however, was a beehive of activity. The town of Telfar hugged the river, its four piers jutting out like a huge claw. Usually there was at least one ship docked, but today there were none, though he could make out two ships under construction in the dry docks next to the piers. Trails of smoke drifted up into the sky from numerous sources within the city, some from homes and others from the work being done by all the different craftsmen.

Outside the town walls, the guards maintained a fifty-foot perimeter to prevent anyone, or anything, from scaling the walls, going under the walls, or otherwise trying to damage the walls -- though their Taper wood construction would make that task very difficult. Outside the fifty-foot perimeter, tents speckled the area around Telfar's walls like dandelions in a field, and the people, looking like ants, could be seen scurrying from one place to another. The south bank ferry landing, located just outside the walls of the town, wasn't fortified; its sole pier jabbing out into the river provided a sturdy platform for travelers to embark and disembark. The large ferry barge was currently tied up alongside its pier, with the long ropes used to haul it back and forth spanning the river, like a giant spiderweb, from bank to bank. The current of the deep, cold, river being so strong, it required multiple ropes to safely guide the ferry across the treacherous one hundred and fifty yard crossing.

Even more impressive than the man-made features, Brutal thought, was the dominating feature beyond the town, on the south bank: the Taper wood forest. The steely greenish-gray canopy of the trees stretched over the horizon to the southeast. One of the taller features in the town of Telfar, was the spire on the Temple of Notria, the good goddess of nature, whose holy symbol, a tree, Brutal could see towering above the town. The wind shifting direction, blowing out of the southeast, Brutal could detect just a hint of the robust, minty smell of freshly worked Taper wood coming from town. Taking a deep breath of the fresh air, he allowed himself one more glance backwards. His brow furrowed, a growing sense of worry for his missing friend crowding his thoughts, and for what seemed like the hundredth time today, he muttered to himself, "Where are you, Tyberius?" But Brutal could see no sign of his friend and the only sounds were that of rushing water from the Great White River in the distance, and the wind swishing through the tall grass. Sally interrupted his thoughts with a snort and pawed a nervous front hoof into the dirt road. Brutal turned back forward in the saddle and patted her neck. "Alright, girl, let us get moving; Tyberius has always been able to take care of himself." With that, he urged Sally onward, down the sloping and curving road that led to the north bank ferry landing.

* * * *

As Brutal approached the fortified walls of the north bank ferry crossing, he could see two Telfar soldiers walking the parapet, armed with crossbows. As he neared, the soldiers quit their patrol of the wall and took up a position over the closed portcullis. Finally at the gate, Brutal raised his right hand in greeting and said, "Well met!"

The guard with corporal chevrons on his chest returned the greeting. "Well met, traveler. What brings you to Telfar this day?"

Brutal was used to the questioning, they always recorded the coming and going of travelers, and replied, "I am here to see a friend at the temple of Zuel. My stay will be brief, and I will return this way yet later today."

Noticing the bloodied bandage on his left hand, which Brutal was resting carefully on his thigh. "What happened to ye hand?"

Feeling embarrassed about his fall, Brutal's mind raced to conjure up a more fitting reason for his injury, but his mind was not cooperating, so he stuck to the truth -- almost. "My horse got spooked on the way here, and I was thrown," He shook his head and, raising the injured hand, added, "Thankfully, she did not run too far, and I was able to catch up with her." After a moment's thought, he said, with a chuckle, "She is a workhorse first but leaves some to be desired as a mount, as she is not as used to that."

"I see," replied the corporal somewhat indifferently and humorlessly. "Do you have the toll to cross?"

Thankful that the questioning was done, Brutal patted the saddlebag. "Yes, I do, sir."

"Very well then," said the corporal. Looking down behind him, he said in a booming voice, "Raise the gate!"

From behind the wall, came a return shout, "Aye, raising the gate!" With that, he could hear a team of oxen grunting, and the portcullis, creaking in protest, started to rise. When it was up far enough, Brutal trotted Sally through the opening, ducking out of instinct as he rode under the heavy iron gate. Once inside, he could see two more soldiers with crossbows slung on their back working the team of oxen. "Lowering the gate!" one of them shouted, and the oxen began to back up until finally with a thud, the pointed ends of the gate once again slammed into the road below with a loud thud.

Carefully, this time, Brutal dismounted. It felt good to get off his horse and, with his feet back on the ground, took a moment to stretch out his legs and back. Eyeing the bloodied bandage on his hand, Brutal shook his head in quiet disgust, and deciding to change the bandage, he reached into his saddlebag and pulled out the piece of cloth and tore another long strip. Unwrapping the soiled bandage, he assessed the wound. It looked worse to him now than it had when it first happened. Brutal had been able to remove the rock that had caused the injury, but the jagged puncture was clotted with a mixture of dirt and congealed blood. The only good thing, Brutal thought, was that, at least, the bleeding had stopped.

From down by the edge of the river, a shout rang out. "Brutal?!"

Brutal was surprised to hear his name, and even more so to hear the familiar voice. Looking up from his hand, he saw Tyberius waving at him from the western dock. Brutal, watching as Tyberius tied his horse to the dock railing, marveled at the swiftness of his friend, whose long strides carried him off the dock and up the path to the gate, and before he could answer, Tyberius was at his side.

"What happened to yer hand?" Tyberius asked, reaching out to grab the wounded extremity.

Pulling his hand back reflexively to save it from being mauled further by his well-intentioned friend, Brutal replied, "Sally got spooked and threw me at the turn," referencing where the road that led to their farms met the Telfar road.

"Did she now?" he asked, his big smile, a raised eyebrow, and a chuckle betraying some doubt.

"I do not know why that should amuse you, as it is halfway your fault," Brutal said, pointing with an accusing finger from his good hand.

"My fault, you say?" Another laugh. "You think I spooked her? I was never even near the turn."

"No," Brutal said defensively, "but I was waiting for you at the turn when it happened."

Standing up a bit straighter and stroking Sally's nose gently, Tyberius argued back, "We agreed to meet at the Drip, did we not?" After a short pause and a puzzled look, he added, "There was no talk of meeting at the turn."

Brutal could see the honesty written on Tyberius's face. "Well, let us not worry about this," he said, holding up his hand. "It is just a trivial wound," he said, looking around the small compound, "I would like to clean it out, though." There was a single square one-story building, about thirty feet by thirty feet, located in the middle that functioned as a shelter, a place to sleep, and as a small armory for the few soldiers on duty. Three long tables, each with a canopy, were lined up in parallel in the courtyard and provided a resting spot for guests to wait. An outhouse building was tucked into the southeast corner where the outer wall went into the river. The only other construction were the two symmetrical ferry docks extending fifty feet into the Great White River, with a forty foot gap of open water between them. They were mirror images of each other, with railings protecting the three outer sides of each dock. Between the docks, built at the water's edge, was the huge rope system that moved the ferry boat from bank to bank, consisting of three grooved wheels, each with a four-inch rope running around it. These wheels were set on a single-geared shaft that was spun by a massive outer gear that was turned by a team of oxen on each side of the river. As the oxen turned the large outer gear, the center shaft spun the ropes in whichever direction they wanted the ferry to move. Currently the ferry was being pulled closer to their side of the river, and as it drew closer, a soldier down on the dock blew his horn two times, and the animal handlers on both sides of the river reduced their oxen's pace, which slowed the ferry as it neared the gap between the two docks.

The Great White River, like all rivers, would rise and fall with the seasons; during the season of Annewal with the snow melts, the river would surge and had been known to rise as much as five feet for short periods of time, but then would recede through the seasons of Heatal, Ebbal, and Darkal. Being that it was already in the season of Ebbal, the river was relatively low, making the banks of the river dangerous due to their precipitous nature, which also made it difficult for travelers waiting for the ferry to reach the water for a drink. To solve that problem, there were several buckets along each dock that could be safely lowered with a rope to the water below.

Pulling on Sally's reins, Brutal started walking her down the path to the docks. "C'mon, let us get down to the docks, the ferry will be here soon, and I want to get a couple buckets of water; Sally needs a drink and I want to wash my hand."

"Sure, I will run ahead and get some water." Tyberius bounded down the path ahead of Brutal and Sally, heading toward the western dock. Once on the dock, he picked up one of the buckets and heaved it over the railing. It filled quickly, and Tyberius hoisted it back up.

Brutal, noticing that there was one other traveler waiting for the ferry, groaned to himself. The other traveler had a wagon with supplies that were covered up by a canvas sheet tied over the wagon bed -- it would take extra time for the wagon and team of horses to get loaded onto the ferry, and Brutal was impatient to get across. Once on the dock, Sally's hooves clopped loudly as the thirsty workhorse zeroed in on the bucket of fresh water that Tyberius had just fetched from the river, immediately lapping up the fresh cold water with fervor.

Once Sally had her fill, Tyberius launched the bucket back over the railing into the river and retrieved a fresh bucket of cool water, handing it to Brutal. There were a few extra buckets on the dock, and both Brutal and Tyberius each turned one over to use as an improvised chair.

Brutal placed the bucket in front of him and plunged his left hand into the water and began to gently scrub the wound. A small flap of skin made touching the wound sensitive, causing him to grimace. Looking up, he saw Tyberius watching. "Do you have a knife handy?" Brutal asked.

"Aye," replied Tyberius and, standing up, walked over to his mount and dug out a large hunting knife from a saddlebag.

As Tyberius walked back, Brutal chuckled and said with a sarcastic tone, "Do you not have a bigger knife?"

Tyberius, smiling and returning the sarcasm, responded, "Well, I did not plan on do'in no barberin', so I left my wee little boo-boo knife at home."

Holding up the flap of skin, Brutal said, "Real funny," with a half grin, then asked more seriously, "are you good enough with that cleaver to just cut this damnable flap of useless skin off? It keeps getting in the way."

"I could cut the pecker off a mosquito with this knife," Tyberius answered confidently. Tyberius scooted his bucket a little closer to Brutal and had his friend set his arm on his thigh. Bringing the knife closer to make the cut, he paused, adding, "If it were a really gigantic mosquito." Brutal started to laugh, but as Tyberius's blade trimmed off the flap of skin, all he could do was grit his teeth.

"Thanks, I think," Brutal said as he again dipped his hand into the water and started cleaning out the gash. His face winced in pain as he did so, the water turning a light shade of red as his wound began to bleed again. Pulling his hand out, he quickly dried it off with a scrap of cloth, then wrapped a dry strip of it around the wound. Holding his hand out, he asked, "Here, can you tie the ends for me?" Nodding, Tyberius tied the two ends of the cloth snugly around Brutal's hand. "Thank you, that should do the trick for now," Brutal said.

"Yeah, no problem," said Tyberius. As he watched Brutal make a minor adjustment to the bandage, Tyberius asked, "So, what spooked Sally at the turn?"

Brutal, hoping that embarrassing question had been left behind, snapped, his tone a bit harsher than he had intended, "I have no idea, probably some damn snake or such thing."

Tyberius held up his hands as if in surrender. "Okay, okay, no more questions about the 'spooking.'" After a short pause, he changed the subject. "So...did Soulmite offer you any more advice on your way?" But before Brutal had a chance to answer, he added, "She never speaks to me, I wonder why?"

"Well, first of all, she does speak to you, but you do not listen." Letting that sink in, Brutal continued, "And no she did not drop from the heavens to speak with me -- but I believe she did point me to something significant."

Baited and unable to resist, Tyberius asked, "What was that?" leaning in a little closer.

"How long were you here before me?" asked Brutal.

"Not long, why?" Asked Tyberius.

"Well, I did not see you pass me on the road. How did you get here so quickly?" Brutal asked.

"Once home, I headed straight for the ferry crossing rather than take the road." Then quickly, he added, "After a quick bite to eat, that is."

"Did you stop at Ariana's?" Brutal asked. Ariana Pulgari lived on the farm to the west of Brutal and would have been right in Tyberius's path. Ariana and Tyberius were given to each other and planned to be married, though Tyberius had not picked a date, or rather, knowing her dominating personality, thought Brutal, perhaps Ariana had not agreed to a date.

Tyberius shook his head and said with a mixture of determination and apprehension, "Heck no. I would have been stuck there for a half-day and there be no way I could have left without tellin' her we was planning to go to Telfar."

As Tyberius was talking, they could hear the guard at the gate shout out the familiar order, "Raise the gate!" and the sound of the grunting oxen and the creaking ropes signaled the arrival of a new passenger. Both men looked up toward the gate, but from the docks, they could not see over the lip of the bank.

"If you had followed the road," Brutal gave his friend a look, then continued, "you would have seen the markings of a trail leading west from the main road -- just after the turn."

Brushing off Brutal's admonishing glance, he said, "Now I wish I had taken the road. Go on then, what did you find?"

The thought of his close encounter brought back some of the adrenaline he had felt. "It led to a swale in the plain..."

"A what?" interrupted Tyberius.

Brutal explained, "Like a big depression in the plains, a bowl of sorts. It cannot be seen from the road, but you can smell the place from a ways away -- it smells awful."

"It smells?" asked Tyberius.

"On account of all the animal carcasses that are piled in there." Then with a wry smile and dramatic pause Brutal added, "But that is not the most interesting thing I saw."

"What in the eight hells would pile up carcasses there?" Tyberius asked, his excitement growing as well.

"I do not know what they were, but I saw them," Brutal answered. He could see the astonishment on Tyberius's face and continued, "They came out of some secret door made into the side of the hill and they looked like half-dogs and half men. And they were huge -- like seven feet tall," Brutal raised his good hand over his head, indicating their height.

Tyberius chuckled and slowly sat up straight, a look of

disappointment washing over his face. "Oh, I get it now...very funny, B," he said, waving his hand as if brushing the tale away.

Brutal sat up, too, somewhat indignant. "What, you do not believe me?"

"Yeah, and I saw a half-pig, half-man, fishing in the pond on my way here, too." With more sarcasm, he added, "I said 'Hello,' but he just snorted at me."

Brutal raised his right hand and, putting it over his heart, said, "Soulmite can strike me down, if what I am telling you is a lie."

Leaning back in, his elbows on his thighs, Tyberius now looked serious. "Okay, so what did you do, did they see you?"

Brutal continued his story. "I only saw two of them and they never did see me, but one of them smelled me. I swear on my father's life -- he smelled me. I know because he was sniffing the air and started to come up the hill toward me -- with a large war ax in his hand."

"Holy shit..." commented Tyberius, stretching the words out for emphasis, then asked in awe, "it carried an ax?"

"Yes, they have human-like hands. But for whatever reason his pal called from inside the, um," Brutal paused for a second to think, "a lair, I guess it would be called... Anyway, one of his pals called from inside and -- though he looked pissed about it -- he ended up turning around. Once it was back inside and the door closed, I high-tailed it out of there."

Taking off his hat, Tyberius wiped his brow with his forearm and exclaimed, "That is fucking amazing." Then, with a little more thought, he added, "We ought to tell the sheriff of Telfar about it so they can root those things out of there before they start piling human carcasses in there."

Brutal raised his hand in a halting gesture. "Hell no. Like I said, Soulmite led me there -- obviously she wants me to go in there."

Tyberius let out a hearty laugh, his big smile leaping back onto his face. "You know me, B. I admit I am the first to come up with hair-brained ideas and to do whatever crazy thing comes across my mind," his face grew serious, "but you have to be joking, right? You want to go and attack some seven-foot dog beasts that wield axes? That sounds like more than we can handle."

Brutal was not dissuaded. "Why? I have my sword, and I was two shakes of a lamb's tail from taking one of them down myself -- alone."

"If you had attacked that beast out there by yourself, ya would not be here speaking to me right now -- sword or no," snapped Tyberius, his voice rising a bit. He drew in a breath to continue his rant, but just as he was about to go on, something caught his attention behind Brutal, and all that came out was, "Oh shit... What the hell?"

Brutal, bracing himself for the argument, saw the look on his friend's face and quickly turned his head around to see what Tyberius was looking at. Up on the path, at the crest of the river bank, was Ariana sitting on her pony, distinctive due to its black coat. He could see she was looking right at them, a sly smile forming on her lips as she started the pony down the path to their dock. Brutal whipped his head back around. "You lied, you said you passed her farm."

Tyberius met his friend's eyes as he rose to greet his fiancée and said, "I did not stop, I swear..." Then standing up, a perplexed look washed across his face. "I am as surprised as you to see her." Mumbling to himself, he added, "A day full of surprises..."

The "clop-clop" of the pony's hoofs on the Taper wood dock announced Ariana's arrival, and Brutal turned around to greet her. Tyberius, moving past him, extended an outstretched hand in an offer to help Ariana down. More than declining the help, she ignored the offer, sliding her leg over the pony and letting herself down the small drop. Brutal had always thought she was beautiful. She had long brown hair that she almost always wore in some sort of braid with her leather headdress, as she did today. Her brown eyes could be seductive or intimidating -- or both he thought to himself. A smaller nose and mouth rounded out the slightly almond shape of her head. She had a svelte frame but not fragile. Today, for the ride, she had on her leather riding leggings and a short-sleeved brown leather shirt that was tight to her torso. On her right arm, slightly above the bicep, she wore a silver-looking armband that had some intricate graving. She had several pouches attached to her belt and a dagger was visible, held snug to her right thigh. Brutal raised an eyebrow, he had never seen Ariana carry a weapon before, but neither would he have figured her to ride from the farm to Telfar alone.

"Well, boys, fancy meeting you here," Ariana stated with a hint of sarcasm, folding her arms across her chest.

Tyberius was quick to reply. "Wh-what are you doin' here?"

Ariana, looking up at Tyberius with mild disdain and with a slight shake of her head, replied, "Always asking the obvious question." Then leaning to look around Tyberius and to the river behind him, Ariana stated, "Ah, good, it looks like I am just in time to catch the ferry."

Tyberius moved his body in front of her gaze. "You know what I mean. You just happened to be going to Telfar today...and you did not ask me to accompany you?"

Ariana, her eyes sparkling with defiance, said, "I do not need your permission or protection," her eyes narrowed, "nor should you ever think to try and require it," she said, finishing with her finger poking into Tyberius's chest.

Tyberius, laughing despite his rising temper, retorted, "Oh -- do not worry yourself about that." Pushing her finger to the side, he bent down and wrapped his long arms around her and picked her up in an affectionate bear hug.

With her arms trapped against her sides in Tyberius's hug, Ariana squirmed to free herself. "Put me down, you oaf!" Though her arms were trapped, Brutal could see Ariana's hand wrap itself for a brief moment around the hilt of the dagger on her thigh. Her hand was just able to reach it -- but as quickly as she had it gripped, she let it go, though he could still see true anger in her eyes as Tyberius set her back down.

Ariana's face flushed red, and she smoothed out her leather shirt, regaining her composure. "I do not like to be handled like that -- I mean it."

"Alright...fine," Tyberius said with some finality, but then his grin returned. "You win, as usual, my queen," he added with a figurative bow.

Stepping forward, seeing an opening in the discussion, Brutal approached the couple. "Well met, Ariana," Brutal said greeting his long-time friend. "What is so urgent that you dare the ride by yourself?" Brutal inquired.

Ariana replied coolly, "What brings yourself to Telfar so urgently?" But then, holding up her hand before Brutal could answer, she said, "Nay, I do not care -- though I do wonder why you have dragged Tyberius with you and, more importantly, why was I excluded?"

Perplexed, he furrowed his brow causing a bead of sweat to trickle down onto his nose, which he wiped away with his forearm. "Wait, so you knew I was coming to Telfar today? How could that be," he asked, looking back to Tyberius.

Tyberius shrugged and shook his head, raising his arms palms up in ignorance. "Do not look at me, I am in hot water over this..." Then grinning back at Brutal, he said, "Just as much as you."

Brutal, looking back at Ariana, asked again, "How did you know?"

Walking past Brutal, guiding her pony to stand next to Sally and Tyberius's horse near the railing, she grabbed the rod connected to the overturned bucket that Brutal had been sitting on and pitched the bucket over the side. Carefully leaning over the railing, she watched the bucket fill with water and answered, "I did not know you were coming to Telfar." As she hefted the bucket back onto the dock, she looked up at Brutal and added, "That I did know is your own presumption -- a foolish one at that," she added with some reprove.

It didn't make sense to Brutal. Some piece of the puzzle was missing, but he decided to just let it go -- she was here now, 'and that was that,' he thought to himself.

As Ariana's pony drank from the bucket, she asked Brutal, "So what does bring you to Telfar today? Is something wrong?" she quickly tacked on with concern in her voice.

Brutal paused, fidgeting with the bandage on his hand. "We have been friends for a long time, heck, I cannot remember a time without either of you." He could see true concern on Ariana's face, but Tyberius's expression was more one of interest than concern as he continued, "But Soulmite blessed me this morning with the realization that I will never find peace if I do not try and find out more about what happened to my father in those hills," he said, pointing northward, toward the Cruel Pass.

Like a duet, both Ariana and Tyberius exhaled and said in unison, "Holy shit."

Tyberius quickly followed up. "I thought you were just going to ask Mikell a few questions about Soulmite talking to you."

Ariana's eyes went wide. "Soulmite visited you?"

Brutal, shaking his head and waving a hand, answered, "No, nothing direct like that... But you know how I am haunted by my father's disappearance -- when awake I think about him, when asleep, I dream about him. The last few tendays have been worse, something changed in me. I can hardly think of anything else -- so much that I have been putting off harvesting the wheat."

Tyberius, listening intently, chimed in. "Aye, that is a fact."

Ariana, irritated at the interruption, nudged Tyberius's shoulder with her forearm. "We do not need you to verify the state of his fields -- let him finish," she said, gesturing to Brutal.

Looking his friends in the eyes, Brutal said, "The wheat was calling to me -- I knew it was time to bring it in -- but I did not." Shaking his head, he continued, "Something was holding me back...like an invisible force. But then..."

Brutal was interrupted by the loud thud of the boarding ramp slamming down onto their side of the dock with a loud thud. Brutal could see the travelers that had just disembarked the ferry, working their way up the embankment path to the gate. A short crewman with a noticeably crooked nose and weathered face, standing by the boarding plank, waved the three of them aboard, shouting, "Load 'em up!"

Flashing a scornful look at the crewman, Ariana then quickly turned her attention back to Brutal, and with an eager look, asked, "Then what? Go on."

Brutal paused for a second. "We had better get on board, these guys do not wait. I will have to tell Mikell anyway, then I do not have to tell it more than once." Ariana huffed, and then mumbling something that Brutal could not hear, started walking her pony toward the ferry.

Tyberius patted Brutal on the shoulder. "Do not worry, she is just used to getting her way." Grabbing the reins of his horse, he joined Ariana, standing by the boarding plank, where they watched the wagon of goods being loaded onto the Ferry.

Brutal lingered behind, preferring to keep the quiet moment for himself. As the wagon of goods was loaded, Tyberius put his arm around Ariana and pulled her tighter to his side. It took a few moments, but the wagon was finally loaded onto the ferry with its team of horses. Then

61

the short crewman turned his attention back to Ariana and Tyberius. Remembering the look Ariana had given him, the crewman asked, with dripping sarcasm, "Mind getting on board now, your queeny?" Some words were exchanged, Brutal could tell, but Tyberius and Ariana boarded the ferry. Brutal, holding Sally's reins, quickly led her up the plank, pausing for just a brief second to look down over the edge of the ramp to see the Great White River swiftly flowing beneath him, forever racing to its destination. But, before drawing the ire of the ferry crew, he finished the short climb and boarded the ferry which rocked slightly in the river current.

Boarding the ferry, Brutal and his companions tied up their horses to hitching posts located in the center of the ferry. Around the stable were two spacious open areas where wagons or goods could be stored safely for the trip across. There were benches built into the deck that ringed the outer edge of the ferry just inside the gunwale. The ferry was relatively empty, as there was only one other traveler crossing with them, so there were many benches open. Tyberius and Ariana found a bench on the port side and sitting down motioned for Brutal to join them, but Brutal held up his hand as if saying thanks but no, and pointed to the starboard side. Brutal, walking around the horses, selecting a bench, sat down with a sigh of relief -- it felt good to be off his feet and in the safety of the ferry. Closing his eyes, letting the cool breeze brush against his stubbled face, he finally allowed himself to relax. For a moment the only sound was that of the rushing water underneath the ferry, and he felt the peace of Soulmite comforting him. But the siesta was quickly broken by a horn blast from the ferry crew on the north side of the river signaling they were ready to start moving the ferry across. It was quickly answered by a horn blast from the other side of the river and the ropes, creaking under the strain, pulled taught. The ferry lurched and the ropes strained as the wide, large, vessel began to traverse the rushing waters of the Great White River.

CHAPTER EIGHT
The Decision

THE FERRY JERKED TO A STOP, coming to rest between the pair of south bank docks that jutted out into the river. The ferrymen scurried around the deck securing the mooring lines and as each rope hugged a cleat, the deck of the ferry stopped moving. Brutal, Tyberius, and Ariana waited impatiently until finally the off-ramp was unceremoniously lowered with a loud thud. The three companions quickly walked their mounts off the Ferry and were promptly greeted by the town toll master. Waddling with surprising speed, on short stubby legs, and waving his arms, he intercepted the small band of friends.

"Hold up! Hold up!" croaked the toll keeper, looking up with his dirty face at Brutal. Looking over each of them with an uncomfortable level of scrutiny, his gaze lingered especially long on Ariana, before reminding them, "That will be a silver piece each, since ye have steeds with ya."

"A silver piece?!" Brutal exclaimed in surprise. "That is ridiculous."

The toll keeper's face was inscrutable. "If you cannot pay, you will be put to work. Two days of work for each crossing," he added holding up two nubby fingers, several adorned with rings. "Of course, we could come to some other agreement, if necessary," he offered, his eyes returning to Ariana, betraying his lewd quid pro quo thoughts.

Tyberius and Ariana each dug out a silver coin and handed it to the toll keeper, the disappointment on the keeper's face being quite visible. Dropping the coins into a bag on his belt, the keeper turned to face Brutal again. "Well, what is going to be?"

Indignantly, Brutal reached into an inside pocket of the shirt and pulled out a silver piece and handed it over. "Highway robbery is what this is. When did the cost of the ferry go up to a silver piece?"

The keeper looked at him with disinterest and pushed Brutal aside as he made his way past, waddling over to the wagon of goods just coming off the ferry.

Seeing Brutal's face begin to twist in outrage, Tyberius quickly stepped in. "C'mon, let us go find Mikell -- we are losing daylight." Brutal kept staring at the backside of the toll keeper as his friend pulled on his arm to turn him. Applying a little more force to his pull, Tyberius got Brutal to turn his head and look at him. "We cannot talk to Mikell hanging from a Fuhr pole."

Ariana climbed up onto her pony. "We cannot assault public officials for enforcing every tax we do not like, can we?" With that, she made two quick clicks and her pony started heading toward Telfar.

Brutal, feeling his anger ebb, gave the keeper, now engaged with the merchant owner of the wagon, one last glance. "He ought to be careful who he is shoving around." With that, using his good hand, he swung up onto Sally's back and urged her down the road.

The only way into Telfar was on its south side, through its massive Taper wood gates; thus, the road from the ferry had to curve around the western side of Telfar before it finally merged with the main road leading into the town. It was a half mile from the ferry to the town gates, and the road was lined with wagons and tents of travelers, merchants, gypsies, mercenaries, thieves, or anyone who couldn't or didn't want to go inside the town. The cacophony of noises and the bustle of activity was distracting, but for the most part, people stayed out of the way of the horses, making the short half mile go by quickly and they were soon at the gates of Telfar, which were currently open, with several guards visible standing along catwalks, above the gate, and along the walls.

As the party approached, a sergeant, clad in chain mail armor and a metal helmet with a "T" emblazoned on it, and a longsword sheathed in its leather scabbard that hung from a belt around his waist, moved from the gate opening with his hand raised in a halting gesture. "Well met, travelers, state your name and your business in Telfar."

Brutal had Sally take a step forward. "My name is Brutal Mixnor, and we are here to see Mikell Corvas at the temple of Zuel." Brutal could see another soldier sitting at a desk inside the gate, scribbling something into a book.

The sergeant looked at the other two companions. "And your names?"

"Ariana Pulgari," Ariana said with a little arrogance in her voice.

"Tyberius Elgar," Tyberius added.

The sergeant, still looking that Tyberius and Ariana, said, "And what is your purpose coming here?"

"We come from the north side," Tyberius said, referring to the north side of the White River. "Travel there is not as safe on the south side, so we came together." Brutal could see the scribe scratching notes into the book.

"How long are you planning to stay in Telfar?" asked the sergeant.

"Not long, we need to be headed back yet today," answered Brutal.

The sergeant's eyebrows raised slightly in surprise. "What is so important at the temple that you would ride so far for such a short visit?"

Tyberius and Brutal hesitated and looked at each other, there was nothing nefarious about coming to Telfar to talk to Mikell, but somehow now that they had to explain it to a stranger, it seemed like an unbelievable reason for such a long day's ride.

"He needs to have his hand attended to," interjected Ariana. All three men shifted their gaze to her.

Brutal, grateful for her quick thinking, played along, displaying his injured hand to the sergeant, he added, "Uh, yes...I injured my hand while working the fields, and it has gotten worse...I cannot afford to lose my hand...I could not do my farm work."

Although they had just put some fresh wraps on his hand, blood was already beginning to soak its way through again. The sergeant, after a quick look seemed satisfied. "I see...okay, move along then," and resting one hand on the hilt of his sword, he waved them into Telfar using the other. The soldier sitting at the desk was in uniform but was not wearing his helmet, thus revealing the features of his face. Passing the clerk, Brutal thought the man had an odd, unfriendly look about him and watched as he scribbled some more notes into the large book, dabbing his pen into his little bottle of ink frequently.

* * * *

The companions rode their mounts through the main gate and past its two large guard towers, where they could see several guards in each, some of whom had their attention on the activities outside the wall, but also some who were watching what was happening inside the town. They were on the main street leading through the town, which went all the way to the docks and building yard along the river. They couldn't see all the way down to the docks, but they knew there were six roads that crossed the main avenue.

The streets were relatively quiet today, though they were far from empty as folks went about their way on whatever errand they were on. Sometimes navigating the roads could be difficult, but today they were able to ride pretty much down the middle of the main avenue. They made their way past Harn's General store on their right and Boral's Blacksmith on their left, then at the next block was the sheriff's office on their right and the Drip on their left. Standing at the intersection, the towering, bloodstained Fuhr pole cast a shadow across the main avenue, its chains hanging motionless, despite the light breeze coming off the river. Turning west off the main avenue, the three companions made their way down the side street, passing the Drip on their left, and the guildhall on their right. The guildhall had numerous people going in and out of the building, as was typical, being a hub of activity as tradesmen offered their services and waited for work. Today was no different, the hustle and bustle carried into the streets, and the three friends had to guide their mounts toward the left side of the street to get around the throng of people. Once around the crowd, they continued down the side street to the next intersection. On their left was Bealty's locksmith shop, and on the right was the Temple of Zuel. A large sign hung on the door handle of Bealty's shop that read "Not Here."

Tyberius could not read, but he knew Bealty was almost never there, and he knew what was written on the sign. "Right," Tyberius said. "We," motioning to Ariana, "will go find Bealty while you go talk to Mikell."

"We will not," countered Ariana. "I thought we were all going to see Mikell?" she asked.

"No, Brutal will go talk to Mikell... We will find Bealty and meet them at the Drip in a little bit," informed Tyberius.

"What do we need Bealty for?" asked Ariana, stressing his name with some disdain. "Are we robbing someone today?" she added sarcastically. "No, we should all go talk to Mikell, and later we can find Bealty if we need to, though I still do not understand why we would."

"I know he is not your favorite person..." Tyberius began to say.

"Halfling, you mean," Ariana interrupted.

Sighing out of frustration, Tyberius said, "He is still a person. I do not know what you have against him -- he has been nothing but a friend to all of us."

"Even so, you cannot trust a halfling," Ariana stated with conviction in her voice.

Brutal, growing a bit impatient with the argument, said, "Look, I will go talk to Mikell alone, that is what I came here to do. Like Tyberius says, Mikell and I will meet up with you at the Drip as soon as we are done."

Ariana huffed, motioning at Bealty's, "So what is your plan? He is never at home, or his...his shop...if you can call it that."

"It ain't that big of a town, Ariana, we will find him," assured Tyberius.

"I will see you two a little later," Brutal said, guiding Sally over to a hitching post on the north side of the street where he hopped down, being careful not to use his bad hand. Tying her up, he started walking across the street to the Temple of Zuel. As he was nearing the door to the temple, it began to open. A slight figure burst through the small opening and then as the door opened wider, much wider, a larger figure emerged into the afternoon light.

The small figure, dressed in familiar black leggings and brown shirt, stopped at the top of the stairs leading to the temple door. "Brutal! What are you doing here?" asked the surprised halfling.

From the middle of the intersection, Tyberius patted Ariana on the back. "See, this town ain't big enough to hide even the likes of Bealty

Bexter for very long." With that, he and Ariana hopped down from their mounts and walked them over to the hitch by Sally.

Mikell, nudging the small halfling from blocking the doorway, made his way out as well. "Well met, good friends! It is so good to see you all. Come on in, let us talk," he said, motioning for the group to come into the temple -- but nobody moved. Confused, he was about to ask a question but noticed everyone was looking at something else. Tracking their gaze to its target, he discovered Brutal was their focus. It took a second, but then his face lit up in recognition. Eyeing the bloody hand, Mikell headed down the steps of the temple toward his friend. "What happened to your hand? Is it bad?"

Brutal continued walking and met Mikell halfway across the street. Holding up his hand, feeling a bit ashamed at the truth behind it, said, "Oh, no, this is not serious."

Putting his hand on Brutal's shoulder, Mikell insisted, "Well, let me see it anyway."

"Actually," Brutal said while lowering his hand, "I would like to talk to you alone for a bit first, I mean, that is why I came here today."

The puzzlement showed on Mikell's face. "Really? What about?" Mikell asked with some concern in his voice.

"Yeah, what about Brutal?" asked Bealty, who seemingly appeared out of nowhere behind Brutal.

"Do you have to sneak everywhere you go?" asked Brutal, a little irritated.

"What? Did I sneak?" asked Bealty, looking at Tyberius and Ariana for their objective point of view. With no sympathy forthcoming, he raised his small arms up in exasperation. "Well, I cannot help that I am small and inconspicuous. All I did was follow Mikell over here."

"Sorry, Bealty, I am just tired from the ride. I should not have said that," Brutal said apologetically.

"How about I buy you a thimble full of ale at the Drip, my little friend?" Tyberius asked Bealty, walking over to the small halfling.

"Yes," said Mikell, "you all should go enjoy yourselves. I will talk with Brutal and then we will join you."

"A thimble full?" asked Bealty, wrenching his neck to look upward at his tall friend. "Really?"

"Well, you drink like a damn bird -- you think I would buy you a full mug?" asked Tyberius, giving the halfling a wink and a grin.

Bealty stopped in his tracks, thinking back to Syd's comment earlier. "It is so funny you should say that..."

* * * *

Back inside the Temple of Zuel, Mikell and Brutal sat in the front pew together. "Let me guess," Mikell began, "this has to do with your father? You have to learn to let him go, he would not want you to be miserable for the rest of your life because he died on the battlefield -- a place he chose to go."

Brutal, fidgeting with his hand, looked Mikell in the eyes. "Aye, he chose, or so he said. But if he died on the battlefield like you say, Soulmite would have brought me peace a long time ago. I really believe that."

"Has something changed?" asked Mikell.

With his elbows on his knees, leaning forward, Brutal began carefully unwrapping the bandage. "Today," Brutal said, "I had an epiphany: that I need to go find out what happened out there. Maybe he did just die on the battlefield, but I do not think so. In the last three years, I have never felt such peace as washed over me when I finally came to that conclusion. For the first time, I feel blessed again by Soulmite." Pausing for a second and making eye contact with Mikell, Brutal asked, "I want your opinion: Do you believe that Soulmite is guiding me to this decision?"

Mikell sat up a bit straighter in the pew, and holding out a hand, said, "Let me see the wound."

"Are you going to answer my question?" asked Brutal.

"First, let me see your hand," insisted Mikell. Brutal presented his hand to Mikell who examined the wound. It was a deep, jagged puncture that was still bleeding and weeping pus. Dirt and small rock fragments were mixed into the congealed blood that partially filled the void in his palm, and Brutal grimaced as Mikell touched the flesh around it. "This needs to be healed, it is deeper than you think."

Pulling his hand back from Mikell, Brutal said, "I cannot afford a healing spell. It will be fine, I just need to wash it out better."

"It needs to be healed, I have seen many wounds, and that is a deep puncture. How did you get it?" asked Mikell.

"Oh, for the love of the gods," exclaimed Brutal, fed up with the injury and the embarrassment of how it happened. "I fell off Sally on my way here." Calming down a bit, Brutal continued, "As I fell, I was able to get my hand down to break my fall. Unfortunately, a sharp rock stuck in my hand, and it got pretty dirty, too."

"Let me heal it for you," Mikell said.

Brutal raised an eyebrow. "You? When did you learn to do that? And how much does that cost?"

"I would not charge you -- you are my friend," Mikell said, his gruff voice reassuring but tinged with a hint of scolding.

"Your father would not heal me without paying," stated Brutal. He knew Mikell's father, Pardor Corvas, was a good man, but he was also a bit of a miser.

"Well, Father has good reasons not to hand out free healing. Can you imagine the line out the door if word got out that there was free healing at the Temple of Zuel?" defended Mikell.

"Oh, I suppose. I never thought of it that way," admitted Brutal. "Sorry."

"That is okay. I understand why you would think that way. Now let us fix that hand," said Mikell. "You are not a disciple of Zuel, so this may not feel pleasant, but Zuel will heal your wounds, trusting in my free will to request it, and my belief to enact it."

"Okay, go ahead then," said Brutal, with a touch of nervousness, as he had never had a spell cast on him before -- at least that he knew. Holding out his hand again, Brutal braced for the unknown.

Taking a deep breath, Mikell turned slightly to better face Brutal. Touching his right hand to his holy symbol, Mikell uttered, "Zuel, Benedici il mio tocco con il potere di guarire le ferite lievi." Completing the verbal component, Mikell touched Brutal's injured hand, transforming the prayer into energy. Brutal felt the energy surge into his body as an uncomfortable freezing sensation in his hand -- but the feeling was brief and before he knew it, it was gone.

"The pain is gone," Brutal said in amazement, flexing his fingers, testing his hand. "I have never seen or felt anything like that before." Looking at his hand, the flesh had knitted completely, the only remaining sign of the injury was a small faint scar outlining where the rock had punctured his skin.

"Zuel is great," Mikell said with a gentle smile, contrasted by his otherwise rough features.

"How long have you been able to heal?" asked Brutal.

"Over a year now. Father helped teach me the verbal component of the prayer. It looks easy, but believe me, it is not," assured Mikell.

"You never mentioned it to me before, why not?" asked Brutal.

"I never needed to. I was not hiding it, nor is it something to boast about, so it just never came up," said Mikell.

"I guess I owe you one. How can I repay you?" asked Brutal.

Mikell shook his head. "There is no need for that. Like I said, you are a good friend -- for you, anytime." Looking toward the door in the northeastern corner that led upstairs to Mikell and his father's living quarters, he whispered, "But no need to tell father about it, if you know what I mean."

Smiling, Brutal nodded. "No problem there." Pausing a moment in reflection, Brutal continued, "You know, that is the second amazing thing that has happened to me today," then correcting himself,"-- no make that the third thing."

"Oh, what else happened?" asked Mikell with sincere interest.

Brutal explained his discovery of the swale and his encounter with the 'dog-men.' "Tyberius thinks I should just tell the sheriff and let them take care of it," Brutal paused briefly, "but I feel Soulmite very specifically led me to that site. I mean, I stink at tracking, yet somehow I made out the faint old trail, and then something urged me to follow it. I do not know what is in their lair, but I feel I need to find out." Brutal locked onto Mikell's eyes. "Whatever it is, it is going to lead me to my father."

Mikell, now leaning on his knees, let out a soft whistle. "That sounds pretty damn dangerous, and foolish. I am not sure what kind of beast they are, but this is life and death, Brutal -- I mean, if you go back there, what are you gonna do? Knock on the door and start hacking away?" asked Mikell.

Brutal stiffened a bit. "Well, no, obviously I have to have a plan. I am just trying to piece all of what has happened to me today together."

"Sorry," said Mikell, "of course, you have had quite the day." Quickly changing the subject, Mikell asked, "What was the third amazing thing?"

"Ariana," stated Brutal.

"What did she do?" asked Mikell.

"She just showed up at the ferry today while Tyberius and I were sitting on the dock," answered Brutal, still trying to figure that event out.

"Tyberius probably told her," added Mikell.

Shaking his head, Brutal replied, "No, I do not think he did, that is the strange part. At least he said he did not, and I believe him. So that means, she just showed up for some...some reason."

"Well, indeed, you definitely have had an interesting day," Mikell said, then after a second added, "a lot of coincidences."

Brutal nodded in agreement. "Yeah, that is it exactly -- a lot of coincidences."

"Yes," stated Mikell.

"Yes what?" asked Brutal.

"I think, yes," stated Mikell again, "Soulmite could be playing a hand in your drive to seek out your father."

Brightening at hearing Mikell's opinion, Brutal looked at his friend. "I am so glad to hear you say that, but..." Brutal did not finish his sentence and looked back down at the floor.

"But what?" asked Mikell.

Looking back up at his friend, he said, "I have to admit, I am a little scared...you know, to just venture forth," Brutal said, gesturing with his arms. "I mean, I have almost no money, and just this sword. I cannot take Sally -- they will need her on the farm. I do not even know where to start."

Mikell placed a powerful hand on Brutal's shoulder and gave it a hard squeeze. "Do not look at the whole journey -- just take the first step, then the next. Soulmite will guide you." Standing up, Mikell said, "C'mon, I am thirsty. We should go to the Drip and see what our friends are up to."

* * * *

The Drip was just one block east of the Temple. Brutal and Mikell entering the tavern via the north entrance, they surveyed the scene as the stepped into the darkened, slightly smoky room. Only three out of the eleven tables were now occupied, including the table where Bealty, Tyberius, and Ariana sat. The other two tables were occupied by what looked to be merchants taking a mid-day break. A lone waitress, tall with shoulder-length blond hair, skittered around the room making sure mugs were full. Mikell knew her name was Gaylee. She was still very young and modestly attractive but, more importantly, she was Syd's, the owner and bartender, granddaughter and he was very protective of her. Mikell nodded at Syd as he and Brutal weaved through the tables to the back of the room where their friends were sitting.

"Can I getch'a anything, boys?" Gaylee asked as she passed by Mikell and Brutal on their way in.

Brutal shook his head and waved a hand. "Nothing for me ma'am, thank you."

"Make that two mugs of ale," interjected Mikell with a smile. "This round is on me."

"I do not like to owe coin to anyone, Mikell," reminded Brutal.

"Then it is a gift...a going-away gift," answered Mikell. As they neared their friends' table, he added, "Besides, you will need every coin you have."

Reaching the table, Mikell sat in the remaining open chair while Brutal picked up a chair from the empty table next to theirs and squeezed between Bealty and Tyberius just as Gaylee was bringing the two new mugs of ale, carrying them deftly in one hand. Arriving at the table she set the mugs down in front of Mikell and Brutal. Holding out her hand, she said, "Four copper, Mikell." Looking over the others at the table with a critical eye, she added, "Quite the bunch tonight."

Handing the copper pieces over, Mikell said with a polite smile, "Just a couple friends from the north side of the river."

"They grow their men big on the north side, eh?" said Gaylee, looking at Brutal and Tyberius, at which both men blushed a bit at the comment, not knowing quite how to respond.

"Aye, they have to be big," added Ariana, "it helps compensate for their puny minds."

Gaylee laughed at the slight, and pocketing the coins, said, "Let me know if any of ya's need a refill," then she turned and left to tend to the other customers.

"Alright, Brutal, daylight is slipping by, time to start talking," Ariana said with some authority in her voice. "What is going on?"

Brutal could feel the weight of everyone's eyes on him. He felt like he was standing at the crossroads of his life; if he said nothing, he could stay on the current path and live out his life on his farm, albeit with the knowledge that he did not have the courage to take the unknown road that could lead him to his father. All he had to do was speak to take his first step down the unknown path -- seemingly so simple, just a few words. He watched as his friends took a sip of ale, waiting for him to tell them why he had come to Telfar. Saying a silent prayer to Soulmite, Brutal felt a surge of courage, and he took his first step, just like Mikell had told him. "I am leaving the farm and going to look for my father."

"But what about Soulmite? Tell us how she talked to you." asked Ariana.

"Soulmite talked to you?" asked Bealty, intrigued already.

Answering quickly, Brutal said, "No, no, she never said a word to me, but I have been praying for three years to be at peace with my father's death, and that prayer has never been answered. The feelings have grown more intense over the last couple months and today I realized what I must do: I must find my father, dead or alive. Once I made that decision in my mind, I felt the hand of Soulmite and a peace wash over me like I have not felt for years." With his mouth feeling a bit dry, he took a sip of the luke-warm ale, then continued, "I came to Telfar because I knew Mikell could help me figure out if I am just going crazy, or if Soulmite could really be giving me direction through my feelings."

"That is incredible," said Bealty, then looking at Mikell, "so what do you think? Is he just crazy?"

Mikell shook his head. "No, he is not crazy; I think there are enough coincidences that it is possible that Soulmite could be reaching out to him."

"Like what?" asked Bealty.

Using his fingers as he listed off the reasons, Mikell said, "One, he felt at peace with his decision, he was led to the swale with the dog-men, he hurt his hand, requiring my aid, Ariana showed up at the ferry crossing." At mention of her arrival, Ariana began to twirl the end of her long brown hair. "And Bealty and I walked out of my temple together just as you all arrived. It is like we all were drawn here, to be together tonight."

"What was that about dog-men?" asked Bealty.

"Yeah, you never mentioned anything about that," added Ariana, still twirling her hair.

Brutal watched Ariana. He had seen her do it all his life, and her habit of twirling her hair was mesmerizing to him, but he managed to keep his focus and finally diverting his eyes to Bealty, said, "Very near the turn, I followed a faint trail off the main road and it led to a large swale in the plains. There I found a lair, I guess you would call it. Two beasts that stood probably seven feet tall and looked like half-men, half-dogs came out to look around."

"Did they walk on two feet or four?" asked Bealty.

Brutal answered, "They walked upright, but had human-like hands." Pausing to think for a moment, he added, "And they wore some primitive-looking armor and wielded large axes."

"I bet they were gnolls," Bealty said with a casual look of pride.

Now everyone's eyes shifted to the small halfling. Tyberius asked what everyone was thinking, "You know of these creatures?"

"Well, I have never seen one, but I have heard stories of them -- all halflings have," said Bealty, taking a small sip from his mug.

"Can you tell us anything about them?" asked Mikell.

Swallowing his sip and wiping his mouth, Bealty looked up at his friends around the table and said, "They are strong and fast, but not too smart -- and," Bealty paused for effect, "they prefer to eat the meat of intelligent creatures rather than animals."

"Bah! What nonsense!" Tyberius said, slapping the table and added with a snort of skepticism, "That is just a tale to frighten little halfling children."

"No, it is not," said Bealty. "It is true."

"You just said you never seen one, how would you know if it was true?" asked Tyberius.

"Look, it does not matter if it is true or not," said Brutal. "All that matters is I was led there by Soulmite, and I know have to do something about it."

"We should tell Sheriff Afgar," Mikell said.

"That is what I told him," said Tyberius.

"No," said Brutal and Ariana simultaneously. Brutal and Ariana looked at each other in surprise.

Everyone seemed stunned, and looking at Ariana, Tyberius asked, "What did you say?"

Ariana sat up straighter, holding her ground, and said, "He should not tell the sheriff. We can take care of these gnolls, if that is what they are, by ourselves."

Mikell said, "This is not a game, Ariana. If we go up there, people could get killed."

"Wait," Brutal said, "I do not want any of you to go up there with me. Mikell is right, it will be dangerous, and I cannot ask that of you."

Turning to face Brutal, Mikell said, "Well, that is craziness, Brutal. You cannot just walk up there alone and fight your way through -- whatever it is that is up there. You would be killed for sure."

"I am not afraid of those things," said Brutal. "Soulmite guided me up there, so I will prevail...somehow. I will figure it out."

"You do not know what is five feet behind that door. How can you plan for that?" asked Tyberius.

"I do not know, Tyberius, I have not thought about it yet...it all just happened!" Brutal said, his temper rising a bit.

"Let us all just calm down," said Mikell. "We are all friends here. Brutal, we are just worried that you are going to do something rash and get yourself hurt -- or worse, even killed."

"He will not get hurt if we help him," said Ariana.

Tyberius turned again to look at his fiancée. "What are you doing? Urging him on?" He asked.

"We can do it," said Ariana.

"Are you serious?" asked Tyberius. "Even if all of us went up there, we do not know how many there are or what else we would find. We could all end up dead. And besides, what the hell are you going to do -- stab them with your dagger?" he said, pointing at the blade on her thigh.

"Damn right I would, if I have to," said Ariana, "but I can do much more than that, but you would not know or understand."

Mikell asked, "What do you mean: 'much more than that'?" His eyes glancing quickly, almost imperceptibly, at the tattoo on Ariana's shoulder.

Ariana, catching Mikell's glance, stopped twirling her hair, and said, "I have been blessed too -- just like Brutal."

Tyberius grabbed his head with both his hands in disbelief, saying, "By the gods...what is happening here?! You have been blessed? By Soulmite?" Ariana gave Tyberius a cold, silent look, clearly indicating it was not Soulmite.

"It is a fair question," said Mikell.

"We can do it," Ariana said, crossing her arms defiantly, ignoring Mikell.

"I agree with Ariana -- I think we can do it, too," said Bealty.

"Oh, well now I know it is a bad idea if the damn halfling is for it," said Tyberius giving the halfling a hard look.

"What is that supposed to mean?" asked Bealty, putting his mug down on the table.

"I like you, Bealty, but we all know halflings make foolish decisions," said Tyberius.

Bealty started to say something, but Mikell slapped the table with his hand, making a loud thud. Everyone looked at him, including some of the other patrons in the tavern. Mikell said, "Enough, Tyberius! You need to settle down. Insulting your friends will not make this any easier or solve any problem."

"This is not what I wanted to happen," Brutal said.

"But it has happened, Brutal," said Ariana, "and like Mikell said, we were all brought here for a reason -- and I believe that reason was to help you find your father. The first step being to take out that lair." Looking around at the now quiet table, Ariana concluded, "I say we do it."

Tyberius picked up his mug and tilting it back, gulped it all down. Putting the mug down, he said, "Then I am in. If this is what we were meant to do, then I will not stand in the way." After a short pause he added, "Besides, you fools will need me."

Mikell said, "I must confess, I want to do it, too." Fidgeting with his mug, he continued, "My father spent several years exploring when he was my age, and I cannot think of a better reason to see the world than to help you find your father...or at least what happened to your father."

"We are going to need some equipment," said Bealty. "We cannot just walk up there with a couple swords. We do not know what is in that lair, so we need to be prepared."

Brutal said, "I do not have any money to buy supplies. I was planning on getting the harvest done first, then using some of that money to help me get on my way. Besides, I need to get the harvest done before I leave."

"I can help you with that," said Tyberius.

"How much time do you need?" asked Mikell.

Thinking it over, Brutal said, "Two tendays."

Tyberius shook his head and said, "No, we can get it done in one tenday."

Mikell said, "Good. Then it is settled. We will meet back here in a tenday. We will gear up, and we will start our journey, beginning with the gnolls up over the hill by the turn."

Brutal said, "I did not intend for any of this to involve any of you, but I am glad to have friends like you, and I will not let you down -- nor forget what you are doing for me." Looking at Tyberius, Brutal continued, "We had better be getting back. We have some work to do."

"Aye," agreed Tyberius, "that we do."

Brutal, Tyberius, and Ariana all scooched their chairs backwards and stood up. Saying their farewells to Mikell and Bealty, they wove their way through the growing crowd inside the tavern and exited through the north door.

Bealty, taking another sip from his still almost full mug of ale, gazed around the bar. He could see several purses that bulged with coins. Mikell snapped his fingers in front of Bealty's eyes and said, "No stealing, Bealty...now is not the time to start any of that foolishness."

A smile played across Bealty's small face and with his green eyes focusing upon an unknown purse in the crowd, said, "Not here, Mikell, I would not do that to Syd." After a brief pause, he added, "But I think I might head to Whiteal for a couple days."

Shaking his head, Mikell said, "I do not want to know."

CHAPTER NINE
Harvesting

BRUTAL, TYBERIUS, AND ARIANA CROSSED THE STREET and headed toward their mounts. Unhitching the reins, they each climbed up into their saddles and began heading back down the street to the east and at the Fuhr pole turned south to head out of town. Arriving at the gate, the familiar sergeant greeted them, raising his mailed hand for them to stop.

"You," the sergeant said, pointing to Brutal, "with the wounded hand -- let me see it."

Brutal raised his healed left hand, opening and closing it to show that it had been healed, and said, "It feels much better now. I am glad I made the trip."

"Let me see your other hand," said the sergeant, who was watching Brutal carefully. Complying, Brutal showed his other hand to the guard. "Alright then," said the sergeant, "state your name for the clerk on your way out and safe travels to all of you."

The clerking soldier made some notes as Tyberius and Ariana passed by. When Brutal approached and stated his name, the clerk looked up. His hair was clean cut, but he had a small thin mustache that looked incomplete, and his eyes were small and close together. The clerk said, "You are a liar, mister. I ain't never heard such a bullshit story as you be tell'in." Waving his hand in the direction of Brutal's hand, he continued, "You may have healed your hand, but that ain't why you came here."

"What did you say?" asked Brutal, at first surprised, then angered, giving the clerk a glaring look.

"I says you is a liar -- and your little buddies, too," said the clerk, motioning toward Tyberius and Ariana, who were turning around to see what was happening. The tension in the air was quickly escalating, but before Brutal could say anything, the clerk said, "But I suppose there ain't no way to prove your lies, so git! Be on your way! But just so you knows, I made a note by your name, and I will be watching for you next time."

"What do you mean?" asked Brutal. But the clerk said nothing, instead closing his eyes and leaning back in his wooden chair. Clasping his ink-stained hands behind his head, he closed his eyes as if to go to sleep.

"C'mon, Brutal, let us be going," said Tyberius.

Brutal gave the clerk one last look, but the soldier's eyes were still closed. Looking around, Brutal could see guards with crossbows up on the wall, watching him with lazy but curious looks as if daring -- maybe hoping -- for him to do something. Gritting his teeth, Brutal urged Sally to move forward, and he headed out of Telfar. Catching up with his friends, Brutal said, "What an asshole."

They hurried the short distance back to the crossing, making it just in time to catch the ferry before it departed for the north side. The short ferry trip was uneventful and soon they found themselves back on north bank. Heading out the gate of the north bank outpost, they once again found themselves in the open plains of their homeland. Taking a deep breath, Brutal said, "It feels good to be back on the north side, it feels like home already."

"Aye," Tyberius said, "I do not think I am much of a city dweller. Give me the open space any day."

Ariana said, "I like the city...there is more going on. It is more interesting."

"I knew you were going to say that," said Tyberius, shaking his head slightly.

"Oh, what else am I going to say?" asked Ariana coldly.

A confused look came across Tyberius's face as he asked, "What do you mean?" Giving her fiancé a scolding glare, Ariana urged her pony ahead of the two men.

Seizing the moment, alone with his friend, Brutal asked, "What do you think she meant when she said she was 'blessed,' too?"

"I have no idea -- that is the first I have heard of it," said Tyberius.

"Do you mind if I ask her about it?" asked Brutal.

"No," Tyberius said, motioning Brutal forward. "Please do...the gods know, she will not tell me." Then with his grin making an appearance, he said, "I will go on ahead a bit and scout the way. You never know, those things could be out there waiting for us to return."

Tyberius trotted his horse out ahead, vigilantly scanning the surrounding area as he did so. Soon he was well beyond earshot. Brutal kept Sally behind Ariana for a few minutes more, watching her. She was a very graceful rider, the leather outfit, which he had never seen her wear, made him see her in a new light -- in some ways even more beautiful than before, but also a certain... 'What was it?' he thought to himself. With that question still lingering on his mind, Brutal trotted his horse up to Ariana.

Hardly acknowledging Brutal except for a look out of the corner of her eye, she said, "I was wondering if you were going to just stay back there looking at me."

"W-what?" asked Brutal, his face blushing a bit at being called out. "No, I was just thinking about the events of the day and how amazing it has been."

Ariana turned her head to look at him, her brown almond eyes locked on his. "That is not what you were thinking. We have known each other for too long, Brutal."

"I do not know what you are talking about," said Brutal, lying.

Ariana rode for a moment, letting the silence weigh uncomfortably on Brutal, but before it became unbearable she said, "So, now that Tyberius is far ahead, go ahead and ask your questions."

"How do you always know so much about things?" asked Brutal.

Ariana snorted slightly but a smile played across her lips. "Look, Brutal, I love Tyberius and you, but the day you two lug-heads come up with something beyond the most obvious tactic, that is the day I will be surprised." Without missing a beat, Ariana switched the subject. "So, when did you start reading?"

Brutal's eyes widened, and he asked, "How in the gods do you know about that?"

Ariana smiled fully now and let out a laugh. Wagging a finger in the air, she said, "Never give out your secrets, my mother taught me that early on. So, answer my question and I will answer yours. Of course, I know what your question is...unless today is the day you are going to surprise me?"

Brutal asked, "Have you been talking to Fey? I did not even think she knew."

Ariana said, "How I know is irrelevant, just answer my question."

Brutal knew he was cornered, so with no way out, he confessed the truth. "Mikell has been helping me. I went to Telfar about a year ago and asked him if he could help me. He agreed to do it, and so he would come out to the farm for a few days at a time. Each day I would tell Fey he was helping me with some odd job or another but, really, he was helping me learn to read. I did not like lying to Fey, but I thought she would think it was a waste of time...heck, it probably would have been, but now do you not see?" Brutal looked at Ariana intensely and continued, "Now it seems clear: being able to read will be invaluable to me as I search for my father."

"We," stated Ariana. "You mean: 'we' will search for your father."

"Well, that brings us back to my question. Since you already know what it is, answer it," said Brutal. Seeing Ariana halt her pony, he had Sally stop as well. With the horses resting, Brutal noticed how quiet it was. The only noise was the sound of the grass shush-ing in the wind, as millions of blades of grass waved back and forth in seemingly random directions.

"You and Tyberius think I would be more of a burden than a help, but you are wrong," said Ariana, breaking the silence.

"How would you help? You cannot fight," said Brutal.

Pointing to the tattoo on her right shoulder, which depicted two vertical arrows, one pointing up and the other down, she asked, "Do you know what this symbol is?"

Brutal looked more closely at the symbol, its lines and edges were so crisp and perfect, the snake-like "S" curving, connecting the tips of the two arrows...it was like no tattoo he had ever seen before. Furrowing his brow, he shook his head, and said, "No, I do not recognize it. Should I?"

"Being a farmer, probably not," then pausing for a moment in thought, placing a finger on her lips, she continued, "though honestly, I thought Mikell, or even the halfling, might have recognized it. But they probably would not have said so if they did."

"Mikell asked who had blessed you -- he must not have known...or maybe he did not see the tattoo," said Brutal.

Giving Brutal a look of reproach, she said, "Oh please, everyone saw it, I am sure. No...he wanted me to say it, not him," said Ariana, "-- but I respect that about him. I suppose as a priest you have to learn to be discreet."

"So what is the symbol? What does it mean?" asked Brutal.

Ariana reached out and gently touched Brutal's arm. Her touch was warm and comforting, and sent a wave of emotion through his body. While gently holding his forearm, she said, "I have a power now that I never dreamed of having. I can certainly help you on your quest." Her gaze was intense, her eyes serious. "I need to see how far I can push myself, and our search for your father is the perfect opportunity."

Brutal, enjoying her warm and most welcomed touch, could see a new drive smoldering in her brown eyes. All he could think to ask was, "What is this power?"

Pulling her hand back, Ariana could see the disappointment in his face, saying, "You will not be impressed by this, but I assure you I can do much more." Pausing for a moment, then pointing at Brutal's sword, she said, "Draw your sword and point it at me."

Brutal moved his hand to the hilt of his longsword, but did not draw the blade. Hesitating, he asked, "Why? What are you going to do?" Ariana gave him her commanding look, one he had seen her give Tyberius many times. There was something very uncomfortable about being the recipient, so he acquiesced. Drawing his sword, he leveled the blade with its tip pointing at her.

Without looking down, Ariana reached into one of the small pouches that hung on her belt. Brutal could not see what she pulled out, but it looked as if she had something pinched between her right forefinger and thumb. She rubbed her finger and thumb together and, speaking not much above a whisper, said, "Invoco la luce." The tip of her finger glowed slightly and she reached out to touch the tip of his sword. Upon her touch, the tip of his blade burst into a bright light.

"Holy shit," said Brutal. "What in the eight hells did you just do?"

Smiling at her work, Ariana could not contain a look of pride, and said, "It is a simple light spell."

Brutal swung the sword, gently waving it around in the air, and said, "I have never seen such magic, but I have read about it a little." Looking back at Ariana, he asked, "How long will my sword glow like this?"

Ariana said, "A short while. And then," gesturing with her hand as if it were a small puff, "poof -- it will just blink out."

"Wow -- that is impressive," said Brutal with true fascination. Resting his sword across his lap to give himself a moment to think, Brutal thought about his next choice of words, which, like steps across a thin sheet of ice, needed to be delicate. With a little uncertainty in his voice, Brutal asked, "But, you know we would bring torches with us, I do not think we would need a light spell," then raising his free hand in a gesture of awe, "-- as awesome as that spell was."

Ariana's eyes squinted slightly at the comment, and she said, "That is one of the simplest spells I can cast." Without hesitating, and determination in her voice, she said, "Abbaglia e stordisci il mio nemico," and instantly, a burst of intensely bright light flashed in front of Brutal.

"Argh!" he screamed, reflexively his hands flying up to his face, covering his eyes, and in doing so dropped his sword, the heavy blade landing on the dirt road. In the same instant, startled by the combination of the flash, Brutal's reaction, and the sword landing by her feet, Sally bolted a few yards ahead, sending Brutal tumbling off her back. This time he was fortunate, being able to break his fall and roll safely to the side of the road. From his prone position on the ground, Brutal regained his senses and looked up at Ariana, who was still sitting on her pony.

Looking down on him now, a triumphant look on her face, Ariana said, "That too was just a simple spell. I have more powerful spells, but I will not cast them on you," then with her beguiling smile again returning, she continued. "you will just have to trust me -- as you always should."

"Are you mad? You could have killed me with that trick!" said Brutal, his face flush with both embarrassment and anger. Pushing himself up onto his knees, he shook his head to clear the now fading bright spots still dancing in his vision. Still on his hands and knees, he looked up again and said, "What can you do with your more powerful spells?"

Ariana, still smiling at Brutal, gave him a wink, and giving her pony a gentle kick, started off down the road. Brutal watched as she rode away, her sleek silhouette highlighted by the setting sun, glowing orange, behind them. Outwardly she was the same, he thought, but she had surely changed. "What happened to you?" whispered Brutal to himself as he got back up on his feet and dusted himself off. Collecting his longsword from the road, its tip still shining brilliantly, he sheathed it, snuffing out the light. Remounting Sally, he urged her into a trot. Catching up to Ariana, Brutal slowed Sally down to keep pace. They rode in silence, taking in the view of the plains in the waning of the day, the sun sinking slowly toward the horizon to the west, casting increasingly long shadows, as if the darkness was taking over the landscape, from the ground up. About three miles from the turn, they caught up to Tyberius, who was waiting for them.

"We should cut off the path and head northeast from here," said Tyberius, pointing out the direction.

"Just like old times," said Brutal with a smile, thinking about the countless times they had taken the short cut through the plains while growing up; more often than not, with Ariana. The three friends shared the quiet moment together, watching the sun slowly disappear, like a fiery ship, over the western horizon. For a fleeting moment, the plains looked like they were aflame as the red dying rays of sunlight strained to burn, perpendicularly, through the endless blades of grass. In contrast, the brightest stars began to peek from behind their blue veil, as the sky slowly began to darken.

"Alright, the show is over, let us get on our way," said Tyberius, breaking the silence. Without another word being said, the three companions headed off the path to the northeast.

Drawing his sword out of its sheath, Brutal checked to see if the tip was still shining, but the blade was dark. "How about another light spell?" Brutal asked.

"In your dreams, Brutal," Ariana replied.

"A light what?" asked Tyberius. Ariana and Brutal looked at each other and began to laugh. "What? What did I miss?" pleaded Tyberius.

"I will fill you in later, my dear," said Ariana, trying to regain her composure. "Let us get home, it has been a long day."

* * * *

The next day, Tyberius showed up at the Mixnor farm early enough that the sun had yet to fully rise, but just in time to catch Fey serving breakfast. After a quick bite to eat, the boys split up again into their two-man teams, as they had on the day before, Brutal with Nicholas and Percival with Tyberius. The men and boys once again set out to harvest Brutal's field. The work was back-breaking, with the constant swinging of the scythe back and forth, accompanied by an unusual heat wave for Sepu making the task even more difficult. The silver lining, regarding the heat, Brutal knew, was that the heat would also help dry out the myriad of stacks they were producing. Pausing for a moment in the hot sun, taking off his hat to wipe his brow with his forearm, Brutal surveyed his fields, the stacks of wheat looked like an army of tents dotting the hills around his small farmhouse. Normally it would take Brutal a facet, two tendays, of time to stack the wheat with his brothers -- but with Tyberius's help, over the last seven days they had three quarters of the field stacked. As amazing as their progress was, thought Brutal, it was still not quick enough as they only had two more days to get the field stacked before they were supposed to meet their friends back at the Drip.

Because of the heat, Brutal, like the other three men, worked shirtless, wearing only his wool leggings and leather boots. Each of them also had a waterskin on a leather strap that slung around their shoulder. Brutal reached for his waterskin, and upon grabbing it, noted that it was almost empty. Looking back at Nicholas, he could see his younger brother was dragging a bit, the gusto he had in the morning was gone, and his stacking had become more methodical; he was falling farther behind. Noting that the sun was directly overhead, Brutal called to his brother, "Hey, Nicholas, I am beat! What do you say we take a break and grab the mid-day meal?" Nicholas's face brightened immediately into a wide grin and he nodded his head. The twelve-year-old boy hustled to finish the stack he was setting up and with a renewed bounce in his step began jogging toward the house. Still smiling at seeing the youthfulness of his young brother, Brutal whistled loudly in the direction of Tyberius and Percival. Gaining their attention, Brutal gestured toward the house and then laying his scythe down, he began walking back to the house.

* * * *

It was easy to keep a safe distance from the humans. They were loud under normal circumstances and, today, out in the fields, hacking away at the wheat, they were grunting and groaning even more. For the small black and white ferret, the uncut wheat offered not only shade, but easy concealment as well. Every so often, Foetore would have to get up and move over a few feet deeper into the uncut wheat, but for the most part this was an easy assignment. At hearing Brutal's whistle, and the sound of footsteps walking away, he rose to his feet and did a couple stretches. With a yawn, he moved to the edge of the remaining wheat and peeked out to see all four men heading to the little house. With a final stretch, he took off at a brisk pace, zig-zagging through the wheat, as he did not want to miss any of the conversation at the house.

It took a couple extra minutes since he had to make his way a little farther around the barn in order to approach the table using the well to block their sight. Fortunately, the wheat still had not been cut by the well, or it would have been more difficult -- but luck was on his side today, and as soon as the humans settled around the table, the ferret was able to scurry quietly up to the opposite side of the well, hidden from view. Proud of himself, the ferret lay down with its long body hugging the stones along the base of the well, and with his ears perked, was in a perfect spot to eavesdrop.

* * * *

The men converged on the table outside the farmhouse where Fey, Lila, and Trinity had set the table with some fresh well water, some bread, and some apples cut into slices. Of course, Tyberius, with his uncanny speed, was the first to make it to the table and sit down -- but he could see Fey watching him and giving him that look which meant: do not start eating yet. When Brutal and his brothers arrived, he said with a grin, "Damn, you boys are slow," then looking over at Fey, added with all the charm he could muster, "This looks awful good, Mother, thank you."

Immune to the sweet talk, Fey gave Tyberius a look. "If I put bark on the table you would say the same thing, Tyberius."

"If you put bark on the table, I would eat it, 'cause I know it would be good!" said Tyberius.

Walking to the table, Fey chuckled a bit and sat down next to Brutal. "I have not asked, because I am glad to see it get done -- but what is the big hurry to get the wheat stacked? It seems like you are in a race or something to finish," Fey said, looking at her eldest son. Brutal was chewing a piece of apple, but stopped at hearing her question. He looked at Tyberius for a moment and then looked out at the field behind him.

Tyberius stopped chewing as well and asked, "You mean she does not know yet?"

Fey's face flushed red a bit, fear creeping into her mind for the first time. "What is he talking about?" she asked Brutal. Then quickly, her brown eyes darkened and she gave Tyberius a menacing look. "What have you gotten Brutal into?"

Tyberius's grin vanished, replaced by a look of indecision. "I, um, I did not, um..." he said, fumbling his words uncomfortably as he looked to Brutal to say something.

"It is my doing, Ma, not Tyberius," said Brutal, once again looking at his mother.

"Did you get into trouble at Telfar the other day?" asked Fey.

"No, no, nothing like that, Ma," assured Brutal, "but you will not like it."

Fey's once flushed face went pale, and Brutal could see the dread in her eyes, but also the recognition. "You are leaving to go look for Anthall," Fey stated as if in a trance, referring to Brutal's father.

Brutal nodded and said, "Yes, Ma, I have to -- if I do not, I will never be at peace with myself."

"Then I am going with you," said Percival, who stood up as if to punctuate his determination.

"No," said Brutal, "you will be needed more than ever here at the farm -- you will need to step up and lead the household," then Brutal paused for a second, "at least until I get back."

"If you get back. Do not fool yourself, Brutal, it is dangerous out there," Fey said, pointing to the north, the color slowly returning to her face, "those hills took Anthall's life and they will take yours, too, if you go looking for his body."

"If he were dead, Soulmite, bless her name, would have comforted me long ago -- so he must be alive...and what if he is a prisoner out there and needs help -- my help?" Brutal said, pointing at himself.

"Do not be such a fool...you miss him and that is normal," said Fey, touching Brutal's forearm comfortingly.

Brutal pulled his arm away, saying, "No! It is more than that! He is alive, and I am going to find out where he is!" said Brutal, standing up and tossing his piece of apple into the dirt. "Come on, boys, let us get back to work, we have to get this field stacked, and we only have two days left," said Brutal, who began walking back out into the field.

Fey's arm hung in the air as if it were still resting on Brutal's arm, then slowly it sank down onto her thigh. With her focused gaze still following Brutal, she said, "Kids, go to your chores. Leave me and Tyberius alone for a moment." The girls walked back to the house with some of the food and Nicholas and Percival hurried to catch up to Brutal.

"Well, Mama, I should get out into the field myself..." said Tyberius in a vain attempt to get away.

Fey turned her attention to Tyberius, her usually soft brown eyes now hardened, and she said, pointing a finger at him and then at the ground indicating he dare not move. "Not yet -- you are staying here. Brutal would not do this alone -- I want you to tell him you are NOT going... No matter what he says -- you tell him 'no!'"

Tyberius, fidgeting with a piece of apple, his eyes trying to avoid Fey's glare, said with an uncomfortable chuckle, "Well, Mama..."

Fey interrupted, "Forget that crap, Tyberius -- stop the 'mother' crap and do what is right for this family. Do not let him walk away to his death...and if you go with him, it will be your death too - and for what? Anthall is DEAD...it has been three years, Tyberius, not even you can be so stupid to think he is still alive!"

Tyberius stiffened at the word 'stupid,' his expression changing from polite uncertainty to a harder, fiercer determination. "Fey, it is not just me who is going with him..."

Fey, her eyes beginning to moisten, shaking her head in disbelief, interrupted again. "I suppose Ariana is tagging along, too, that makes sense..." she said, throwing up a hand.

Tyberius quickly stood up, bumping the table as he did so. Several of the mugs of water to tipped over, spilling their contents, which ran down the slight angle of the table until finally they dripped through the small cracks between the boards, hitting the ground. Tyberius raising his voice, said, "Fey, let me finish. It is not just me. Yes, Ariana is going to come along, and so is Mikell and Bealty. I is going to ask Julius as well. As you said, this is going to be dangerous, and the more of us that go, the better our chances are of getting back here alive."

A tear slowly made its way down Fey's face, leaving behind a moist trail. Wiping it away, she said, "A priest and a halfling? What good will either of those two do you out there? You are wrong, Tyberius. You are not equipped and you do not know what is out there. There are terrible beasts -- monsters, literally -- waiting for groups like you," she said, pointing to Tyberius, "filled with over-confidence, to go stumbling into those hills."

"Brutal is going, with or without us, he said as much, and I believe him," said Tyberius. "And I ain't going to let my best friend just walk out to his death -- and I think if enough of us go, we at least have a chance to do some good."

Fey standing up, straightened her brown gown, and said, "Come with me, Tyberius." Without waiting for Tyberius to answer, she began walking toward the barn.

Tyberius looked around uncomfortably. "Okay, Momma," he said, following her into the barn, worried he had said too much.

* * * *

It was dark inside the barn, so Fey opened a window on the eastern end, allowing a flood of sunlight to brighten the interior. In the corner of the last stall, at the far eastern end of the barn, Tyberius watched as Fey bent down and rummaged around. He could hear her moving the hay around, and then he heard the sound of creaking wood as she opened something on the floor of the barn. He quickly moved to get a better angle to see what she was doing, and as he neared, he could see her reaching into a built-in space beneath the barn floor. "What are you doing there?" he asked.

Fey quickly closed the compartment door and stood up, holding a small wooden box with its top missing. Walking toward Tyberius, she said, "Hold out your hand."

Tyberius did so, holding out his left hand, into which Fey placed a small scroll case, just a little wider than the width of his palm, "What is this?" he asked.

"Do not open it, if the seal is broken, it will not help you," Fey said, in a serious tone, adding weight to her command.

"I do not know how a small little thing like this is gonna be helpful no matter what I do with it...what the heck is it?" he asked, flashing his big grin.

"This is not a joke, Tyberius, so wipe the grin away, and pay attention," Fey said, waggling her finger. Tyberius did as he was told. "This scroll case contains a document that could help you if you get into trouble in Whiteal, Bindal, Westal, or Castor -- or if you get into a bind with..."

"Fey," Tyberius said, followed by a small chuckle, interrupting her, "I ain't never heard of those places, except Whiteal, of course."

"Then you better buy a fucking map!" Fey snapped. Tyberius's face couldn't hide his shock at hearing Fey's vulgar language. He swore all the time, but Fey was like an angel to him, stern, yes, but always kind and helpful. This was not the Fey he knew, and he took a step back. "Oh, now I have your attention?" she asked rhetorically. "It is time to wake up, Tyberius. You, my son, and all your little friends are about to embark on something you are not ready for -- so listen up!" Tyberius nodded. "Keep the scroll in a safe place -- and heed what I said before -- it can help you if you find yourself in trouble in one of the larger cities in Kardoon."

Tyberius nodded again. "Yes, ma'am," he added as he tucked the small scroll into a pocket on the inside of his cloth shirt

"One more thing, Tyberius," Fey said. "Hold out your hand again."

Tyberius extended his left hand again, and Fey, reaching into the small box, pulled out a platinum ring, which she placed onto his palm. The pale gray ring was etched with a roping, interweaving, pattern around its circumference, but otherwise it seemed ordinary. "You really should give

92

this stuff to Brutal, not me," said Tyberius.

Fey shook her head. "No, it is your burden to carry these items -- you need to do this for Brutal and me. I want you to have them. Take great care of the scroll and do not let the halfling sell the ring for coin or some other foolishness," said Fey, pointing her finger again at Tyberius and jabbing it into his chest as punctuation. Tyberius had a puzzled look on his face, so Fey continued, "The ring is just a trifle, but it is magical."

Tyberius's face twisted in disgust and he recoiled, extending his left hand out, as if to get the ring as far away from his body as possible. "Magical? I...I do not like magical things -- it...it cannot be trusted. Fey, take it back...Please. Please, give it to Brutal," he begged.

"No," she said sternly, folding Tyberius's fingers backwards around the ring in his palm and pushing his hand back into his chest. "Tyberius, this is a fool's errand. Going out to find Anthall will likely get all, or some of you killed, and Anthall is already dead, so there is nothing to find, except maybe a grave," Fay looked away and down, "but I doubt even that exists."

"How do you know he is dead?" asked Tyberius.

Fey looked up into Tyberius's eyes, for a moment, then looked away, crossing her arms. "It does not matter."

Tyberius thought for a second. "Well, shit, then just tell Brutal he be dead and how you know, and we can end all this...this...madness," he said, raising his arms in desperation, then realizing he still had the ring in his hand, he continued to hold his left hand away from his body.

"I wish it were that simple, but, like so many things, it is not," Fey said, shaking her head. "He is convinced that Soulmite, bless her being, wants him to do this."

Tyberius let out a long breath. "Okay, okay, but I still do not understand how the ring will help us, an' I do not know why you cannot just give it to your SON," he said, emphasizing the last word.

Fey sat down on a bale of hay. "When Anthall and I were in Feldor, we decided to get married and settle down. After the ceremony, the priest, for a small donation, offered to cast a spell on the rings. It was a mere cantrip. Oh, we were so young and so foolish. We paid an extra fifty gold pieces to enchant the rings so that when they were near to each other, they would faintly pulse, like a slow heartbeat." Standing back up, she walked over to the open window, and leaning on the sill, she laid her head down on her forearms as she picked at a few stray straws of hay. Looking up into the sky and a long way into the past, she chuckled a little, but it was a sad chuckle -- as if it was her only option other than crying -- then said, "We were just children back then, years younger than you are now, Tyberius." A slight smile danced on her lips for a brief moment as good memories of Anthall, so long suppressed, once again returned to her thoughts...but it was fleeting.

"Fifty gold pieces?!" said Tyberius. "That be a small fortune, why would you waste that much gold on magic?"

Fey moved away from the window as her memories faded back into the darkness. She looked at Tyberius again, and said, "Tyberius, even if Anthall is buried in the ground, if the ring he wore is with his body, you will know when you get close. Since that is most likely where he is, I am entrusting you with this ring, and that is the ONLY reason I am giving it to you now." Passing Tyberius, she moved toward the open barn doors, then turned back again. "If you do find his body, please bring both rings back. I would very much like to have them."

Tyberius, walking with his arm extended, asked, "Wait, wait -- why cannot Brutal take this? You said it yourself, it...it will help us find him." Fey stopped by the large double doors, the sun glinting off her dark brown hair, and tanned skin, she looked back at him. He had never really noticed, or thought about it, but in that moment, he could see how beautiful she was.

"I cannot stop him from going out into the world, to look for a father he will never find," Fey said, her voice filled with sadness, "but even Brutal will eventually see the fruitlessness of the search, at some point." Fey looked up and into Tyberius's blue eyes. "But if he knows the ring can help him locate the body, he will never stop -- he will search all of Kardoon, and that will get him killed for certain. You see, our only hope is that he gives up on this crazy search before he, and the rest of you, die." Fey grabbed Tyberius's left hand, which was still holding the ring. "I am holding you to your word that you will not reveal any of this to anyone -- not even Ariana."

Tyberius hesitated, swallowing hard, he was not good at keeping secrets, especially from Ariana, but eventually he nodded. "Aye, you have my word."

* * * *

Fey and Tyberius, walking out of the barn, passed right by Foetore, who was nestled underneath some hay, and closed and latched the doors as they left. Fortunately, they had left the window open at the eastern end. Foetore waited a few more minutes, his nose wrinkling at the foul-smelling hay that he used for concealment. Cursing silently at himself for hesitating and being tardy to the scene, 'What had Fey given Tyberius and why could he not give it to Brutal? Or even tell Ariana' he thought to himself, using his paws to smooth out his whiskers. Well, one thing was for certain, he would learn nothing staying here -- so, cautiously, he made his way to the open window. There were several bales of hay stacked by the window, so it was easy to make the climb. Peeking out the window, he surveyed the area: Brutal and Nicholas were already at work, and Percival had begun cutting the wheat on his own. 'There,' he thought, spotting the lanky Tyberius who was heading back into the field. Foetore scanned his surroundings for the usual predators, but seeing nothing concerning, he leapt down to the ground and dashed back into the safety of the uncut wheat, heading in the direction of the tall redheaded man.

* * * *

Later that night, Brutal lay awake in his bed. He was running out of time, there was no way to finish stacking the wheat with just two days left. He would have to send Tyberius to Telfar and let their friends know he would need a few more days. It was getting colder every day, and it would feel even colder out in those hills with no roof over their head, so the delay nagged at him. Closing his eyes, he said a little prayer to Soulmite, "Most beloved Soulmite, I know my plight is trivial, but I feel you have set me on this path, so I humbly ask for your guidance and help. I am anxious to begin my search, please help me find a way to get the harvest done in the two remaining days." The night was quiet, not even the wind was blowing, and opening his eyes he could see the eye-like knot in the beam overhead staring down at him, its dull gaze full of mockery

95

and laughter at his prayer. But Brutal stared back, determined to break the will of the wooden incarnation.

Brutal awoke. It was very early, the sun not quite cracking the horizon, but the rays of sunshine bent over the terrain as they filled the farmhouse with their light. Rolling onto his back, he rubbed his face and cleared his eyes. The knot was still there, still staring, but it never looked the same in the sunlight as it did in the moonlight. Interesting how that works, Brutal thought to himself. Remembering his prayer from the other night, he again felt the weight of disappointing his friends -- who were all risking their lives to help him -- resting on his shoulders. Looking at the longsword, leaning against the corner of his room, he felt inspired to get up and get on with the day. The morning was cool, but he pulled on his dirt-caked wool leggings and boots, leaving his shirt hanging on the wall. He walked into his brother's room and woke them up. "C'mon, boys, let us get going. We have a lot of work to do, and not much time to do it. I will be in the field," he said.

Opening the door, Brutal walked out into the courtyard and headed to the well to get a drink of water. While pulling the rope to raise the bucket, Brutal looked out into the field. Amazed at what he saw, he stopped pulling on the rope, the bucket now suspended in the air, and stared in disbelief. Four people were in his field, cutting and stacking the wheat. He could tell that two of them were Tyberius and Mikell, and the third was Julius Hallow, a friend of Tyberius, but he could not make out the fourth man. The four men apparently saw him, too, as they put their tools down and started walking toward him and the well. Brutal knew they would be thirsty, so he hurried inside and grabbed five mugs, which he brought back to the well and, filling each to the brim with water, set them on the outdoor table and waited.

"Just like a Mixnor to be sleeping in when there be work to be done," said Tyberius loudly as they got closer, smiling his big grin.

Brutal couldn't help cracking a smile at the comment as he rose from the bench at the table. "Well met, my friends! I am surprised to see you all here, especially so early."

Mikell was wearing what was obviously new clothing -- as the wool leggings were practically spotless. "Praise Zuel," Mikell said as he approached, with extra enthusiasm, "if it ain't the great Brutal Mixnor." Sticking out a thick arm, which Brutal took in a warrior's handshake, the priest added with a wry grin of his own. "We thought you might need some help finishing up."

Brutal couldn't help but chuckle a bit at his friend, who was obviously out of his element on the farm, and gesturing to his friend's pants, said, "I appreciate the help, but I would hate to see your new pants get dirty on my account."

"Oh, nice...pick on the priest, eh?" said Mikell, still grinning, as he joined in his friend's laughter, which he suddenly stopped, in dramatic fashion. "I will remember that when you all are lying on the ground, bleeding out," he continued, pointing his priestly finger at each of them, "and when I do not have enough power to heal all of you, it will help make my decision easier." The laughter quickly died down as they each looked at the ground as if to cover up their participation in the joke.

Crossing his arms over his chest, Tyberius said, "Well, Brutal made the comment...I guess it sucks to be you," at which they all had a good laugh again, including Mikell, who gave Brutal a wink.

"Julius!" Brutal exclaimed, extending his hand. "It has been too long. How have you been?"

Julius was moderate in height, and unless you knew him, he just looked like a slender human, but if you looked closer, you could make out his true heritage. He had soft green eyes, dark black eyebrows, highlighting a narrow face with distinguished cheekbones, almost as if his skin were being pulled back tightly across his face. His nose was narrow, but also a little large, contrasting with the sharpness of his other features, but what really made it stand out was the noticeable bend in it from several breaks. His face was clean shaven, but only from meticulous effort, and it was impossible to completely hide the fact that his dark beard was being held in check. Julius had straight jet black hair reaching just below his shoulders, with his bangs cleanly cut, keeping it away from his face. It was, of course, his ears that that ultimately gave his mixed race away -- his thick straight hair flowing in front and behind his muted, but still pointed, and most noticeable elven feature. "Well met, Brutal," Julius said, grasping and shaking his friend's hand. "Tyberius found me last night and said you needed an extra hand for a couple days."

"Certainly, your help is greatly appreciated," replied Brutal, a little more formal than he might have intended, but he had only met Julius a few times, so was surprised to see him here and a little embarrassed at needing the help.

Julius let Brutal's hand go, saying, "I would also like to accompany you on your search. I would like to see more of the world, and if I can do that helping the friend of a friend, then I am in."

"Thank you, Julius, your woodland skills will be invaluable to all of us, I am sure," said Brutal.

"Brutal," said Mikell, stepping forward and placing his hand on the shoulder of the man standing next to him, who Brutal did not know. "I would like to introduce you to a friend of mine."

Brutal examined the man. He was dressed like all of them, in brown leggings, but he was wearing a white wool shirt. He was a little shorter than himself, not quite as muscular, but he had a confident look about him. He had short brown hair, kind of a military look about him. His face was dominated by two features: his blue eyes were set just a little farther apart than seemed normal, and he had a red acorn-sized birthmark on his forehead. If he had been wearing a different type of hat, it might not have been visible, but in the growing daylight, it was noticeable under the brim of his leather working hat that sat on his head, tilting up slightly. Extending out his hand, Brutal said, "Well met, my name is Brutal. Thank you for your help today."

The man eagerly shook Brutal's hand and said, "Well met, Brutal, my name is, well, just call me Hammer...and you are very welcome." Looking in Mikell's direction, he continued, "Mikell has told me a lot about you and explained your situation regarding your father...I would like to help."

Brutal let Hammer's hand go and, sizing him up further, said, "Oh, what is it that you do?"

"I may not look it," said Hammer, "but I am pretty good with my war hammer. My father has spent some time training me over the years -- you see, he was a soldier in the Kardoon army for many years before he came up to Telfar." The men started walking toward the table and they each took a spot on the benches. Hammer continued, "My father now works as a caravan guard for a group that sells their services between here and Whiteal. I went on a few runs with him, we never saw any real action -- but," he added with some conviction, "I did get some good training."

Brutal nodded. "Well, that is more experience than we can boast. How did you meet Mikell?"

Mikell spoke up before Hammer had a chance. "He is a follower of Zuel and comes into the temple to pray when he is in town. It just so happened that he showed up the day after you were in Telfar. We started talking and I told him I might not be around for a while..."

Hammer jumped into the conversation. "And that is when he told me about you. I think what you are doing is great -- I would do the same if my father went missing."

"Well, Soulmite knows we need all the help we can get, so you are more than welcome to join us," said Brutal. "I hope you realize," Brutal said, "that this could be very dangerous. I do not know where my search will take us or what we will find out there."

"We all know that, Brutal," Mikell said. "I cannot speak for everyone, but I am going, not only because you are my friend, but I feel I need to go -- it is like there is something pulling me, and if I do not go... well, strangely, I feel I almost have no choice."

"Fuck all that," said Tyberius. "I wanna just crush some damn skulls, besides, you would not last a day out there without me," he said, looking at Brutal, exposing his wide grin.

"I will be just fine, you can stay here and eat both my family and yours out of house and home, if that suits you better," said Brutal.

The door to the house cracked open and Nicholas and Percival walked out, joining the men at the table. "Hey there, boys," said Tyberius, "you ready to finish off this field today?"

Nicholas was always eager in the morning, but being the youngest, had a hard time keeping up all day. "I will be glad to get it done, are you all here to help?" Nicholas asked. All the men nodded.

"Great, that way you can get going sooner," Percival said, a sour look on his face, directing his comment at Brutal, before turning away and heading out into the field.

"Not too happy about you going?" asked Mikell.

"Shit, no. He is pissed because he wants to go with, and I told him 'no,' that he needs to stay back and run the farm," said Brutal.

"He will see the truth and appreciate your advice when we are gone," said Julius.

"I am sure I would feel the same way if our roles were reversed, but I hope you are right," said Brutal.

"Well, the fields will not work themselves," said Mikell, standing up. "Let us get to work!" he concluded with some gusto, sealing it with a clap of his hands.

Brutal, noticing a new stain on the rear of Mikell's otherwise pristine pants, no doubt from sitting on a small berry that was on the bench, chuckled. "Well, Mikell, it looks like you had a little accident there," at which they all had a good laugh.

"Laugh now, boys...laugh now," said Mikell, wagging his finger at each of them.

* * * *

The heat remained oppressive, making the chore of harvesting the wheat more difficult and uncomfortable, but with the all the extra help the men were able to finish stacking the wheat by the end of the second day -- just in time so they all could get to Telfar as planned. The sun still had a few hours left in the sky when Brutal and Nicholas finished up the last stack. Brutal, looking around at the work they all had accomplished, took an extra few minutes to enjoy the moment with Nicholas, and putting his arm around his little brother gave him a quick, heartfelt squeeze, and said, "Well, we did it. I am glad we were able to do it together."

"Yeah," said Nicholas, "so am I." Then looking up at his big brother, with concern in his eyes, he asked, "Are you going to die out there when you leave? I mean," Nicholas fidgeted with a stray stalk of wheat that he had picked up, "am I ever going to see you again after tomorrow?"

Brutal's focus was jolted from the serenity of the stacks of wheat back to his little brother, then bending down to get face to face said, "Of course, you will, I am just going to see if I can find out what happened to Pa." Brutal searched for the right words. "I believe he needs help."

"Ma thinks you are gonna die out there," Nicholas said.

"All Ma's worry too much, besides, she does not know what is out there, and I am going to be traveling with a lot of good, strong friends."

With a nervous look on his face, Nicholas said, "Do not tell Ma, but I hope she is wrong."

Brutal smiled and gave Nicholas another quick squeeze. "C'mon, we are done here, let us go join the others at the house." The two brothers turned and started heading back to the house, and as they did so, Nicholas let the now broken stalk of wheat fall from his hands, landing in the fertile dirt.

Brutal and Nicholas were the last ones back to the outside table where all the others were sitting, enjoying a drink of the fresh cold water as Fey, Lila, and Trinity had prepared a supper of bread, apples, and some smoked ham. "Well," said Brutal, as he clapped, knocking some of the dirt off his hands, forming a small cloud, "that is it. Thank you all for helping get the field harvested so quickly. We can get a good night's rest and head to Telfar where we can get equipped for our journey."

Fey, who was filling up the pitcher of water at the well, looked over her shoulder and said, "You boys have no idea what you are getting yourself into. If you did, you would not be so anxious to begin this foolishness."

Brutal's shoulders slumped slightly at the rebuff, feeling the weight of her disappointment. "Ma, we all know you do not approve, but we are going to go -- so, please, let us just enjoy the rest of the night together."

Fey, having filled the pitcher full of water, walked back to set it on the table near Tyberius. "I cannot enjoy the night," said Fey, giving the men at the table a cutting glare, "knowing that it will likely be the last time I will see you. If you can enjoy the night, do not let me stop you, but I will be in the house." Brutal stepped forward to grab onto his mother's arm as she moved past, but she quickly broke his grasp and continued, disappearing into the house.

"Let her be," said Tyberius, "she does not understand right now, but when we return, she will see that we -- that you," he jabbed a finger at Brutal, "did the right thing."

"Why is she so certain of our failure? What does she know of the hills?" asked Mikell. "We all hear the rumors, but she acts like she knows something."

Brutal, turning back to face his friends at the table, said, "She knows nothing, she has never been anywhere."

Tyberius shifted uncomfortably in his seat, wanting to say something, but remembering his promise to Fey, he kept his mouth shut. Thinking of his conversation with her, when she had given him the ring and scroll just a couple days ago, he felt Brutal didn't know his mother as well as he thought. "She might have been around more than ye think," he added reluctantly.

Brutal shook his head. "Nah, she grew up in Whiteal but moved here with Pa when King Bindal offered free land to folks who wanted to farm. She ain't been in those hills." Tyberius raised a skeptical eyebrow but said nothing.

Mikell thought for a moment, then said, "Your ma is a smart woman. I do not know what she does or does not know, but she is right in one respect: we need to be careful. Everyone knows the Cruel Pass is a dangerous place."

"Shit yeah, it is," added Hammer. "My pa says the caravans are stacked with guards, and even some wizards, when they go up to Castor."

"Castor?" asked Brutal.

"Oh man, you boys really ain't got a clue, do you? You ain't heard of Castor?" asked Hammer incredulously.

"I heard of that city," said Tyberius, again recalling his conversation with Fey.

Brutal looked at Tyberius. "Where have you heard of that city?"

The redheaded warrior's face flushed. "Um... Shit, I heard Ariana talkin' about it one time."

"It is the northern city in Kardoon. The Cruel Road goes between there and Whiteal," added Hammer, "and the shit can get messy on the road." Nobody knew what to say to that. The comment, sparking their inner fears, silenced them as their minds each conjured up different, horrible, monsters that could be lurking in the Cruel hills, and the dire consequences of coming face to face with such evils.

* * * *

Their dark-colored fur and light leather armor helped them blend into the field of stacked wheat and the dry dirt. Skulking along on their bellies, the two gnolls, Vilnesk and Huppkif, still a hundred yards away from the table of men, moved a little closer to get a better look. "Is that the man?" asked Huppkif in their low, growly dialect.

"Normally it is hard to tell, human scum all look alike to me," answered Vilnesk, "but I am sure that it was the last one that left the field. He had short brown hair and looked very strong for a human."

"What? That little one?" asked Huppkif.

"No, you idiot, not the little human, the fucking big one that was with the little one," snipped Vilnesk.

"Do not piss me off, Vilnesk, it is your fault we are out here right now," growled Huppkif.

"Fuck you, I was about to kill him...but Fellpon insisted I go back inside," Vilnesk said.

"Okay, okay, at least we finally found the bastard. Let us get back and report this location to Fellpon" said Huppkif.

Staring at the table in the distance where the humans had gathered, drool began running down the side of Vilnesk's mouth. He licked his lips, exposing his large canine teeth, and with a smile on his dog-like muzzle, he growled, "Agreed. Tomorrow. Though, I get the first taste." The two gnolls, still on their bellies, carefully made their way back to cover before disappearing into the fading light of the day.

CHAPTER TEN
Return

BRUTAL AWOKE THE NEXT DAY to find fey sitting on the end of his bed. She was bent over, using his longsword to prop herself up, as she rested her forehead on her hands that cupped the hilt. She rocked back and forth slightly, causing the sharp point of the sword to dig lightly into the floorboard of his room.

She raised her head, a tired look on her face, the impression of her knuckles, like small red coins, visible on her forehead. "We did not want this," said Fey, glancing at the sword in her hands, "for you...or any of the kids."

Brutal sat up and rubbed his face to help wake himself up, "What-what are you talking about?" he asked.

"I told him not to go," she said, shaking her head, "but I could tell he was getting that 'itch' again. I felt it, too, but for me it was manageable, I was happy here on the farm -- but for him it was much more tangible and irresistible." Fey could see the confused look on Brutal's face. Of course, he was confused, he could not possibly understand, she thought to herself. "Did Anthall ever tell you how we met?" she asked.

"Not really, only vaguely..." Brutal tried to remember. "You met in Whiteal, but I cannot remember how. But what..."

Fey laughed a little. The laugh was hollow though, as if one realized a terrible irony, and interrupting Brutal, she asked, "He told you Whiteal?"

"Yeah, you both grew up there," said Brutal.

Shaking her head slowly. "No, we did not grow up in Whiteal, nor did we meet there. We met in the city of Cray."

Rubbing his forehead, Brutal asked, "Cray? Is that not far to the north in Thayol? What in the name of Soulmite were you doing up there?"

"Ah, that is good, you know some geography then. I have seen the books," Fey said, looking into the corner of his room where they lay under his brown leggings, "I did not expect you to learn to read. That is not a skill I thought you would need on a farm. But then, I see you have been thinking far beyond the farm. Books..." Fey thought for a moment. "Books most likely come from a temple, so that makes Mikell your likely tutor. I like him, he is someone you can always trust and rely on. If you must go, I am glad he is going with you."

"Ma, why were you in Cray?" asked Brutal again.

Fey shifted, crossing one leg on the bed in front of her, placing the longsword on the bed between them. "There is probably nothing I can say at this point, but you should know that your father was a very skilled fighter -- so much so that he was sought out by Dertah and Strix Cragstaff to help lead the Kardoon forces against the bugbears in the hills. It is difficult to see how Anthall could have fallen against such a disorganized lot, but obviously he did -- or he would have returned."

Brutal, pushing himself up, sat a little straighter. "I cannot believe you never told me this before..." said Brutal.

"You are missing my point," said Fey with some impatience. "Whatever killed Anthall in those hills will surely kill you, and," Fey paused to emphasize her next statement, "-- and anyone you bring with you. Are you ready for that kind of weight on your conscience?"

"They are choosing to go, I am not forcing anyone..." said Brutal.

"Bah! Do you really believe that?" Fey said, waving her hand through the air as if physically brushing his comment aside. "These boys think this is going to be some grand camping trip into the Cruel Pass, I am sure. Today, you can save your life and all of theirs. All you have to do is get up and tell them you have decided to wait until the spring of next year -- that the weather will be getting too cold in the hills to leave now."

"What does it matter if we go now or next spring if we are going to die anyway?" asked Brutal with sarcasm in his voice.

"Brutal," she said, gripping both of his shoulders in her strong hands, "if you delay it to the spring, it will never happen, and it will be easier for you, and them, to let it go. You can all get a drink at the Drip and talk about what a crazy thing you almost did 'last year.'"

"I cannot do that. I have not slept well for three years, until the day I decided to go looking for Father. Soulmite is urging me to go, I feel it," said Brutal. He could see the fierce resistance fade within Fey and tears began to well up in her eyes. He could not remember seeing her cry before, and it struck at his heart to think it was from his doing. "Ma, we will be back, I promise," he said.

Leaving the sword on the bed, Fey stood up and turned around, so her back was to Brutal. Without turning around, after straightening her blouse and quickly wiping her face, she said, "I put a pouch by your books that has two hundred gold pieces in it. That will be enough to get you equipped in Telfar, plus a little left over to help with your travels."

"What?" asked Brutal with outright shock. "How did you get a huge sum of coin like that?"

Still not facing her son, she sighed a deep sigh and gripped her holy symbol of Soulmite, taking the moment to pray for the strength to face the morning. "Well," she said, "I will get breakfast going, you will need to be off soon," and she walked out of his room and went to wake the girls.

＊ ＊ ＊ ＊

The breakfast was good, but there was not much in the way of conversation. The mood was very melancholy as everyone's thoughts were on Brutal's imminent departure, possibly to never be seen again. After finishing, they all went outside to see him off. Standing outside the house, Brutal had his brown leggings and white wool work shirt on, and of course, had his longsword sheathed at his side, with one hand resting on the hilt. Everyone was there except Percival, who seemed to be taking it the hardest, as he had ventured off into the field.

"Well, I know this feels like goodbye, but I will be back -- I promise," said Brutal, at which point Nicholas ran up and giving him a big hug.

"Do not go! Pa will come back on his own someday," said Nicholas.

"I wish I believed that, then I would wait, too... But he is in trouble and needs my help," said Brutal. Lila and Trinity now stepped forward and gave him a hug as well.

"We expect you to keep that promise," said Lila, "make sure you come back."

"I will," said Brutal with a smile.

"Do not make promises you cannot keep," warned Fey, who also stepped forward, giving him a hug and light kiss on his cheek. "May Soulmite bless you and keep you safe, so you can fulfill that promise. I do know the kinds of beasts that are out there, but, thank the gods, I do not know what will happen to you -- so I will carry the hope of your return until we meet again. I do have one hard-earned piece of advice to give you: do not trust anyone you meet until they have proven themselves to you. Remember that." Fighting back her tears like a hardened soldier who had just lost a long-time comrade, Fey stepped back and said, "Good luck, Brutal."

"I will, Ma, I will remember that advice," said Brutal. With that, he started down the trail in the direction of the main road where he would meet Tyberius, Julius, Hammer, and Mikell. He soaked in the view of the fields and looked back one more time to see his family standing there, watching him go. He waved one more time and then lowered his head and told himself no more looking back until he returned either with his father or at least with the knowledge of what happened.

* * * *

As his farm disappeared from view, a feeling of freedom overtook him, and he wondered where Soulmite's will would take him. His own mother had been all the way to Cray, he thought. It was hard to imagine going that far, but there was really no way to know; the possibilities were almost endless, and it awoke a feeling of adventure within him that he had never experienced before. It was just a little over a mile to where several paths met at a junction, and as he neared, he could see his friends waiting. Tyberius was sitting on the ground with his back up against a rock, and Mikell and Hammer were half leaning and half sitting on the large rock.

"It is about blasted time!" Tyberius said as Brutal neared the junction. While getting to his feet, he continued, "I thought Fey might have finally convinced you to give it up."

Brutal could see the large grin on his friend's face, which was always a comfort, and said, "No way, nothing could change my mind now."

Mikell picked up a small backpack and slung it onto his shoulder and said, "Good morning, Brutal, it sounds like you are ready to go." Then looking at the other three men, said, "Do you all feel it, too?"

"What are you talk'n about you goofy priest," said Tyberius, "I do not feel anything except ready to get moving -- I hate sit'n around."

"I feel it," said Brutal.

"So do I," said Hammer. "It is the same feeling I get at the start of a new caravan run...you never know what is going to happen that day -- it could be your last day, or your best day ever."

"Yeah, it is an exhilarating feeling," said Brutal. Then it occurred to Brutal that Julius was not there. "Where is Julius?"

Mikell said, "He decided to head home. He said he had a couple things to take care of and that he would meet us at the turn."

"This ain't gonna be our last day. Hell, we have hardly started," said Tyberius who started down the path. "Go on then, let us each have a big 'girl' hug and let us get going! Heck, Ariana is probably already waiting too, and she ain't gonna like waiting for us."

The four men hustled to keep up with Tyberius and it wasn't long before Hammer asked, "Can he keep up this pace?"

Brutal and Mikell laughed, both having experienced the pain of traveling on foot with Tyberius. "Yeah," said Brutal, "he cannot help himself. I do not know how he does it, but I have never seen anyone even close to as fast as he is on foot..."

"Nor the endurance," said Mikell, "he just keeps on going."

As if on cue, Tyberius turned around and saw how far ahead he was getting. Putting his hands on his hips in disgust, he shouted back to the three men, "I am going to go on ahead...Ariana and me will wait for you at the end of her trail!" Then he bounded off, the gap quickly expanding between himself and the others. Once out of view, and well enough ahead, he paused in the path, the tall grass on either side of him rhythmically blowing in the wind. He breathed a sigh of relief, and reached into a pouch on his belt and pulled out the platinum ring Fey had given him. He looked at the ring lying in the palm of his hand, handling it as though it were contaminated with a contagious disease, and with a mixed look of disgust and horror on his face, said out loud to himself, "A god-damned magic ring, and she had to give it to me." Mocking Fey's voice, he added, "Do not tell anyone..." He looked around, comforted by the tall grass, building up the courage for what he was about to do. He said a short prayer, "Soulmite, forgive me, but I cannot carry this...this thing." Cringing as he closed his hand around the ring, he took off running, moving even faster than before, hoping Ariana would be at the path waiting for him so he could unload his burden...at least for now.

It was close to three miles to where the trail to Ariana's farm met the main trail he, and the others were moving down. It was another two miles beyond Ariana's, to get to the turn. Tyberius made good time, even for him, and to his relief, Ariana was already waiting for him at the intersection, sitting atop her black pony. At the sight of her, he grinned, and couldn't help but admire her beauty, and he thought how lucky he was. As he neared, she slipped off the pony and they embraced in a hug.

"The others could not keep up?" asked Ariana, almost rhetorically.

A little out of breath, from pushing his pace over the last mile or so, Tyberius, motioning back down the trail, said, "Yeah, they all move like old ladies, but they should be here pretty soon."

"Great, more waiting," said Ariana, crossing her arms. "Let us go down to the turn and meet them there."

"I told them we would meet them here, besides, I have something for you," said Tyberius.

"Oh really, what is it?" asked Ariana, with a bored expression on her face. "It better not be some stupid flower you picked on the way here."

"Well, no, but I will remember that comment. Well, if you do not care, never mind," said Tyberius as he began to fidget with the pouch on his belt.

"Tyberius, do not do that...what is it?" she asked with curiosity creeping into her voice.

Tyberius grinned again and pulled his hand back from the pouch. "We have been promised to each other for a long time now," said Tyberius.

"I figure it is time I give you a promise ring." He opened his hand for Ariana to see. The platinum ring sparkled in the early light of the day, it's beauty enhanced by its simplicity.

Ariana's eyes widened at the sight of the ring, and she looked from his hand to his eyes, and said, "It is beautiful. But when did you get this, and how could you afford something like this?"

Tyberius paused, he hadn't thought she would ask such questions and didn't know what to say, "Well, uh, it has been in a safe place for a while, and I just felt the time was right -- us going off with Brutal and all."

"Not a very elegant answer," said Ariana, taking the ring from his palm, "but then elegance is not why I love you." The metal felt warm in her hand, having been in Tyberius's palm during his run. She slipped the ring over her left index finger and, admiring it, said, "Thank you, Tyberius," as she gave him another hug and then a long kiss. Then in a playful voice, she said, "I suppose we can wait here for the others..."

Ariana and Tyberius enjoyed the little time they had to be alone. Finding a comfortable spot in the tall green grass and lying down together, Ariana rested her head on Tyberius's shoulder. "Are you scared, Tyberius?" Ariana asked as she played with a stray thread of wool on Tyberius's shirt.

"Nah," Tyberius snorted, "my guess is we are back in our homes within a month, maybe even quicker."

"What about the gnoll lair -- there will be a fight for sure there," said Ariana.

"That is true, but how many could there be? And besides, there are a lot of us," said Tyberius, "and Mikell can heal wounds -- I saw what he did for Brutal's hand." After a short silence, Tyberius changed the subject. "Ya know, there is no need to be making a big fuss to the others about the ring."

Ariana raised her head up a bit. "You do not want me to tell anyone about it?" Ariana asked with some suspicion in her voice.

"Uh, no, it is not a secret...just, ya do not have to go bragging about it and such," said Tyberius.

Resting her head back down on his shoulder, she said, "Well, they would not care anyway, they all know we are promised." But Tyberius's statement had awakened her curiosity about the ring's origin and how he came about it. "C'mon, tell me: Where did you get it?" asked Ariana.

The voices of Brutal, Mikell, and Hammer could now be heard not too far off, as well as their loud footsteps, crunching the dried-up trail beneath their boots. Tyberius gave Ariana a kiss on her forehead and said, "Well, damn, the boys are comin', let us get ready to start movin'."

Ariana stood up, dusting off her leather leggings, and straightened her headdress. "You did not answer my question," she said with some annoyance.

Tyberius, grunting as he pushed himself up and onto his feet, looked at his fiancée, his grin was wide. "Oh, c'mon, it is a gift, I thought you would be happy...not...well, suspicious."

"'Suspicious,' well that is an interesting choice of words," said Ariana, her hands drifting to her hips, her eyes narrowing slightly.

"Hello, Ariana!" shouted Mikell, waving as he, Brutal, and Hammer approached.

"Hello, boys," said Ariana. Then flashing Tyberius a knowing glance, she stepped forward to greet them, holding out her hand for them all to see, the ring glinting in the morning sun, and said, "Look what Tyberius gave me today, is it not beautiful?"

Tyberius's grin faded from his face, and he looked at Brutal to see his reaction. All he could hope for now was that Brutal would not somehow recognize the ring. It felt like slow-motion to Tyberius, as he watched Brutal approach Ariana. Upon reaching Ariana, Brutal gave the ring a quick look and said, "Very nice, I did not know Tyberius could be such a romantic."

"Neither did I," said Ariana. Shifting her attention to the third man, whom she did not recognize. "Who might you be?"

Mikell stepped forward. "Ariana, this is Hammer. He is a friend of mine from the temple, he is a follower of Zuel and handy in a fight."

Hammer took Ariana's already outstretched hand and gave it a gentle shake. "Well met, Ariana, I look forward to traveling with you."

"Hammer. That is an unusual name, what is your real name?" asked Ariana as she pulled her hand back from out of his grasp.

A smile crept across his face, and Hammer said, "My parents gave me a shitty name, and I do not care for it." As he spoke he unslung the war hammer that was on his back, displaying it to her. "When I started my caravan duties, I learned to fight with my war hammer, and the other guys started calling me Hammer, and it stuck."

"Mikell is a good judge of character, so if he trusts you then you must be Alright, and we can always use another fighter," said Ariana.

"I am so glad you approve," said Hammer with a hint of sarcasm.

Mikell, seeing Ariana's face darken a bit at the comment, quickly changed the subject. "Yes, we can always use another fighter," and then stepping between Ariana and Hammer, continued, "we should probably get going, Julius is waiting for us at the turn." Mikell put his arm around Ariana and guided her back to her black pony that was grazing in the grass nearby, as the rest of the group began walking down the trail toward the turn.

The trail made the walking easy going, and the small band of companions was already talking easily. Before they knew it, they had reached the turn, where they saw that Julius was waiting for them. Tyberius, naturally, had walked ahead of the others and was already talking to the half-elf ranger, who was holding the reins of his light warhorse while it grazed on the fresh green grass of the plains. As Brutal approached, he could see that Julius looked like he was already equipped. He wore brown leather leggings like himself, but he had on a chain mail shirt, a light backpack that looked full, and he had two swords strapped to his hip by a belt: one was a longsword, like his, and the other was a short sword. Most notable, though, was the powerful and well-crafted longbow attached to the side of his horse, and the full quiver of arrows. The half-elf waved hello as the group closed in around him and Tyberius.

"Where did you get all that equipment?" asked Brutal.

"I asked him the same question!" said Tyberius, who was obviously impressed as well.

"As I told Tyberius, I have been around a bit longer than you, and I have been as far as Westal." Gathering up the reins, Julius swung himself up onto the gray mare, and said, "I have not always been a farmer, and for the last few years, the life of peace that it affords has suited me."

"A life of peace?" asked Brutal.

"Like I said, Brutal, I have not always been a farmer." Then turning his horse in the direction of the main road just a hundred yards off, he said, "I scouted ahead and found the trail you spoke of, and indeed it did lead to a swale in the grass, just like Tyberius described. I could see humanoid tracks all around, going in and out, but I did not see any door."

"You should not have gone up there alone," said Mikell. "If they think people are snooping around, they could either leave or reinforce it, either way it is not good..." then after a pause added, "or worse, you could have gotten killed."

"Nah," said Julius, "I was careful, and they would not be able to find me if they tried, unless it was night out, then maybe."

"Why at night? It would be harder eatin' Taper wood bark than to see you at night," asked Tyberius.

"Infravision," said Ariana, causing everyone to look at her.

"Or perhaps, dark-vision," said Julius, causing everyone's attention to shift back to the half-elf.

"How the hell do you know about inter-vision? Have you been talk'n to Bealty?" Tyberius asked Ariana.

"Some people can actually read, Tyberius," said Ariana, who then gave Brutal a look as she added, "a useful skill for those who take the time to learn. Would you not agree, Brutal?" She could tell, and was pleased to see, the wheels were spinning inside Brutal's head, wondering why she singled him out, and still mystified at how she had known about his books. Caught off guard by her comment, he looked at Mikell, who innocently shrugged his shoulders.

After an awkward moment, with nobody saying anything, Tyberius raised his hands up in the air as his patience wore out, saying, "So, will one of you care to explain what, in the name of the gods, life-vision, and dark-vision are?"

Julius smiled, answering, "Some beings are gifted to be able to see heat, so at night I would stick out like a sore thumb. And dark vision is the ability to see in complete darkness."

"Well that is great then," said Tyberius, "they will be able to see me bashing their friends under any light conditions." The group had a good laugh, easing the tension that had built up.

"Let us keep moving," said Mikell, who, taking advantage of the distraction, began walking down the main road leading to Telfar. "We need to get to Telfar, get equipped, and then figure out how we are going to root out those gnolls." The rest of the small group dutifully fell in behind the priest, except for Tyberius who announced he would scout ahead and quickly moved out in front, soon disappearing over the gentle rolling hills of the Kardoon plains. The excitement in the air was palpable, yet the conversations seemed hushed and sparse as each individual tried to wrap their mind around what the next couple days would entail. Lost in their thoughts, the miles passed by quickly, and a little after mid-day, the companions arrived at the hill crest leading down into the valley through which the Great White River flowed.

Tyberius was waiting for them there, apparently enjoying the grand view, and munching on some dried meat. Swallowing, he said, "Sure is quiet today, I did not see any animals at all, all the way here. That seems odd."

"You are just being paranoid, knowing the gnolls are out there," said Brutal, "obviously there are animals around."

"I am just saying," said Tyberius, "I usually see little animals here and there on the way to Telfar, and I saw none today. Somethin' feels off."

"Let us not get all wrapped up in superstitious-ness," said Mikell, "-- we are being overly sensitive, because we can all sense the danger ahead of us. And that is a new feeling."

"Aye," said Hammer, "I do not feel anything is wrong. It is just that feeling you get when you know you are about to get in a fight."

"Alright," Mikell said forcefully, gaining everyone's attention and pointing toward the distant town, and said, "Telfar is right down there, so let us keep moving. Our nerves can only be calmed by action." Nobody said anything, but everyone seemed to agree, and they all began to move down the winding road that would lead them to the north side fort of the ferry crossing. As the new group of adventurers made their descent down to the bank of the Great White River, the air of excitement, with which the day had begun, waned just a bit -- being replaced by a sliver of uncertainty and fear.

The group descended quietly in a single file down the hillside, each lost in their own thoughts about the upcoming days. Soon they were at the gate of the fort. The tower guard was wary at first, eyeing the six armed figures with some caution, but after a short discussion, gave the order to open the gate. As it began to creak open, Tyberius said, "Ariana and me are gonna wait outside on the bank. We will come in when we sees the ferry gett'in close."

Brutal, a concerned look on his face, said, "Are you okay?"

Tyberius gave him a grin. "Of course, we just feels like waiting outside is all." With that, they headed off on a small trail that led to the south side of the fort.

The rest of the group trudged inside. Once in, Julius stabled his horse and paid to have it looked after for one day, knowing he would be back tomorrow to pick it up on their way back to the turn, and the gnolls. While Julius did that, the three others walked over to one of three long tables located in the courtyard, each with a canopy to protect its guests from the elements.

Mikell let out a pained groan as he sat down on one of the long benches, then lifted his leg over it so he could sit facing the table. "Oh, it feels good to sit, and my hands," said Mikell, holding his palms up so Brutal and Hammer could see the blisters, "look what that damned scythe did to my hands; they are killing me."

Hammer laughed and, nudging Mikell with his elbow as he sat down, said, "Your pa ain't working you hard enough that temple. Does he tuck you in at night, too?"

Mikell gave Hammer, who was sitting next to him, a sideways glance. "Okay, okay, I know my work at the temple is not as physical as what you guys do," then gesturing with his marred hand, as if pinching the air, continued, "but how about a smidgen of sympathy for the only person here who is gonna be healing you tomorrow?" Then looking at his hands again and grimacing while he flexing his fingers, he said, "That is, of course, unless my hands are too swollen for me to cast the spells properly."

"Why do you not just heal yourself? I mean your hands..." asked Hammer.

"Are you kidding?" said Mikell with a rhetorical air.

"What? Why not? I would..." said Hammer.

"You want me to call down the blessed power of Zuel to heal a few blisters?" asked Mikell, snorting in disgust.

Hammer looked at Brutal, who was still standing on the other side of the table listening to their conversation. Then looking back at Mikell, said, "Well, when you put it like that...I guess not."

Brutal, fidgeting with the hilt of his sword, said, "I am going down to the river."

"What for?" asked Hammer.

Brutal didn't respond and just turned and walked away, making his way down the road that led to the docks.

"What was that all about?" asked Hammer.

"Just let him be. He just needs some time to think; I am sure he feels a lot of pressure right now," said Mikell.

"Pressure?" asked Hammer.

Mikell gave Hammer a scholarly look. "He just left everything he knows, to begin a journey of which he knows nothing. And if that is not enough, he feels we are all putting our lives on the line for him."

Hammer, raising his eyebrows in understanding, said, "I guess that makes sense," then, as the question just popped into his mind, he asked, "How did you get so smart?"

"I work with my mind," said Mikell, pointing to his head and then again holding up his hands to show the blisters, "not my hands. I listen to people all day long."

Hammer chuckled, then, looking a bit more seriously, said, "You know, I am not doing this because of his father...It just sounds like, well, fun."

Mikell looked toward the river where Brutal was leaning against the railing, and said, "I do not think we share the same definition of 'fun.'"

"I am just saying," said Hammer, "maybe it would help Brutal to know that he is not responsible for me...heck I am my own man-- ain't nobody responsible for me but me."

Julius, just arriving from the stable, overheard the last comment and sat down at the table across from Mikell and Hammer. "What is with Brutal? Did I miss something?"

Mikell, shook his head, saying, "No, let us just give him some time

116

alone."

* * * *

It took an hour for the ferry to make its way across the great White River, finally slowing as it approached the docks on the north-side bank. Seeing the ferry draw near, Tyberius and Ariana made their way inside the fort. Once inside, Ariana also stabled her pony and paid the groom the overnight fee to avoid the much larger cost of carrying the animal back and forth across the river. Before letting the groom take the pony, she removed a small backpack tied to her pony's saddle, and after carefully slinging it over her shoulders, the couple walked down the cobbled path that led to the docks and they rejoined their companions who were already aboard and sitting on several wooden benches located in the midsection of the ferry. The benches were nailed down onto the deck to keep them from moving during the sometimes bumpy ride across the river, and being in the middle of the vessel, offered the most comfortable ride.

Mikell smiled as Ariana and Tyberius joined them. Once they were seated he said, "Alright, let us talk about what we are doing today." Everyone leaned in a little closer, as if he were about to share a secret. "We will all stay at my temple tonight, so first we go there and drop off the gear we are carrying. Bealty will most assuredly find us on his own," at the mention of the halfling, Ariana sat up a bit, as if in silent disapproval, "so there is no need to wait for him or to find him. From the temple we will go to Boral's Blacksmith." Mikell paused and, avoiding any eye contact, focused his gaze on the Taper wood deck at his feet, "I guess the first questions is, should we pool our money together and decide together what is most important to buy? Or is it everyone for themselves?"

There was an awkward silence until Brutal broke it, saying, "I say we pool it. One party, one sum."

Hammer now sat up a little straighter as well, his eyes narrowing a bit. "Well, maybe for just this one time, but I expect to walk away from this thing at some point with a lot more coin than I have right now. I mean, I am here to help and all, but I have stuff I want to do after all this."

"Not a problem," said Brutal, "If someone decides to leave, they take their share of coin, but," Brutal said, raising his index finger to make

117

a visible point, "until someone leaves, the money is spent as a group."

Ariana now spoke up. "No. I do not like it. If we get more coin along the way, then I want a share to do with as I see fit, without asking anyone for, 'permission,'" she said with emphasis." Then, relaxing her tone, she added, "However, I do agree that we should pool our resources for today. We cannot start out with the fighters ill-equipped."

Brutal sat up a little straighter, his fingers were interlaced, his elbows resting on his thighs, and said, "We need to trust each other, and fighting over shares of money will not help."

Before anyone else could speak, Mikell said, "At least for now, I think we can all agree that we need to pool our money so that we can best equip everyone." Looking around at everyone's face, he asked, "Does everyone agree with that?" Seeing several nods, he said, "After we get our equipment we can go to the Drip for a drink and a meal, and then I say we go back to the temple and get a good night's rest."

Tyberius started laughing and, seeing everyone look at him, he said, trying to control himself, "Okay, Grandpa -- an early bedtime, eh? This could be the last night of our lives, I am going to enjoy it!"

"Yeah, I second that!" added Hammer.

"Well," said Mikell, looking over his nose at the two young fighters. "Do as you please, but remember, we need you at your best tomorrow. Do not let your enjoyment of today cost us tomorrow."

"Do not worry, Mikell," said Tyberius, "I will be ready -- I always am," and his large grin confirmed it.

* * * *

The ride across the river was uneventful as was the short walk to the entrance to Telfar. Once at the gate, the familiar sergeant approached the group, raising his hand, though it was unclear if it was a greeting or a demand to halt. "Quite the group today. I recognize some of you from a few days ago, and, of course, you," he said, pointing to Mikell. "Out on some missionary work, eh?" he asked the cleric, who had taken a position at the front of the six companions.

Mikell let out a short laugh and said, "No, not at all. We all helped my friend Brutal, here," at which point Brutal stepped forward, "with his harvest. Now that we are done, we all came back to enjoy a night in Telfar together."

The sergeant looked at Brutal. "Yes, I remember you. How is the hand?"

Brutal raised his hand for the guard to see, saying, "It is all good now."

The sergeant moved closer and grabbed Brutal's hand to look closer at it. "You did this?" he asked looking at Mikell.

Mikell said, "The easiest answer is: yes. But in truth, Zuel performed the healing, I am just the instrument."

Letting Brutal's hand go, the sergeant moved further into the midst of the small group. Eyeing Ariana, he moved closer to her, leaving an uncomfortably small gap between the two of them, saying, "I suppose you helped with the harvesting, too?"

Ariana locked her eyes onto the sergeant's, but in her peripheral vision she could see Tyberius starting to move. Without taking her eyes off the sergeant, she put her hand on Tyberius's forearm, and said, "Of course not, I am not particularly good with a scythe." Then taking her hand off Tyberius, she gently put her index finger on the chest of the sergeant. "I am here just to enjoy the night with my friends." Then, applying some more pressure, she pushed on the sergeant's chest, his chain mail shirt felt cold and hard on the tip of her finger, one of the small interlaced rings leaving a small, oval impression. The little extra push caused the sergeant to take a half step backwards. "Be a darling and give a lady some space," said Ariana.

The sergeant's face flushed, and after regaining a solid footing, he motioned to the clerk by the entrance, saying, "Fine. State your name for the clerk before going in and give the reason for your visit."

Everyone In the group filed by the soldier who wrote down their names and their reason for requesting entrance. Brutal was relieved to see that the clerk was not the same one that had given them so much grief a few days ago -- that's all they needed right now, he thought to himself. Fortunately, there were no more delays or new incidents, and once through the gate, the group made their way to the Temple of Zuel. Compared to their last visit, Telfar seemed abuzz with activity today, the streets being crowded with town folk and travelers going to and fro on their respective errands. The first two buildings they encountered, entering the town, was Boral's Blacksmith on the east side of the street and Harn's General Supply on the west side. Everyone gave the buildings a long look as they walked past, thinking about the weapons, armor, and supplies they would need for their journey, and wondering how they would pay for it all. The next two buildings along the street were the Drip, next to Boral's Blacksmith, on the east, and the Sheriff's office to the west. It was a little early in the day for the Drip to be so crowded, but after all it was Ex-day and perhaps some of the residents were getting an early start for the coming two days of rest. Despite the noonday hour, whatever the reason was, patrons were already spilling out into the streets with mugs in hand, drinking ale. A lot of commotion could be heard from the inside of the Tavern, and then they heard a roar of shouts in unison; some of the shouts were loud angry curses and some of the shouts were those of joy and glee, like those of spectators watching a jousting match as one knight falls to the ground.

"Oh, I cannot take it anymore I have to go see what is going on inside there," said Tyberius.

"If you go in there, we will not see you until dark," said Brutal.

Tyberius shook his head. "No, I just want to go inside and see what is happening."

"They play games inside there all the time, it is probably just a big card game or maybe dice," said Mikell.

Tyberius grinned and pointing a long finger toward the tavern said, "That is no card game, I can tell ya that."

Brutal step toward Tyberius and said, "Just come with us to the temple and let us get organized first. We cannot let ourselves get distracted before we have even begun."

"I want to see was going on inside there, too, Tyberius," said Hammer, "but I agree with Mikell and Brutal. All those drunks will still be there after we stop at the Temple."

Brutal could see the curiosity burning in Tyberius's eyes and he knew his friend sometimes struggled to control his urges. Fey had often warned him to be wary of Tyberius for that reason -- that people who could not control their own urges could not be trusted, especially in critical situations. That was easy for Fey to say, but Tyberius was his best friend and Brutal knew he could be trusted, even more so on the big things, than the little things. Unfortunately, this was a little thing and he wondered what Tyberius would do.

Tyberius's eyes darted back and forth between the group and the Tavern and then he let out a long breath. "Okay, okay, I will go to the temple first, then we will go see what's happening at the Drip." And with that the tall warrior began striding forward on the short trip to the temple of Zuel.

It only took a few minutes to walk the short distance through the town and soon they were all standing in front of the Zuel Temple. Leading the way, Mikell walked up the three short steps to the main entrance, and as he opened the familiar Taper wood door, with its beautiful stained glass windows, he could feel the comforting wash of Zuel, cleansing his soul, as he stepped through the doorway and into the sanctuary itself. As if returning to the surface from a long, deep, dive, he breathed in the reviving air and thanked his God for his blessings.

"Mikell! It is good to see you back," said his father, Pardor Corvas, who was purifying some water by the altar when his son walked through the door. After drying off his hands on a small towel, he shuffled down the main aisle toward Mikell. The long white robe he was wearing had intricate gold stitching and was held together with a red sash that was tied and hung down his left side to about his knee. The white robe made a slight brushing sound as it lightly touched the wooden floor of the temple with each of his short strides. Reaching his son, he gave him a brief, but strong embrace, slapping Mikell's back a couple times as if in punctuation.

The rest of the group filed in, standing just inside the entrance. Tyberius, seeing Pardor walking down the aisle toward Mikell chuckled and said, "Well, it is not hard to see that they are related," commenting on their near identical physical stature of Mikell and Pardor. Ariana jabbed Tyberius in the side. "What?" the tall redheaded warrior asked, truly bewildered.

"It is okay, missy," said Pardor, smiling and slapping his belly. "Zuel has been good to me, and fortunately he has managed to keep my table full over the years. And," he added, "besides, Tyberius has been given the blessings of a good heart and straight-forwardness -- those are admirable qualities, you know."

"I will grant you the good heart," said a smiling Brutal, "but what you call straight-forwardness, some might call just being an asshole." The group had a good laugh.

Tyberius, with his familiar grin acknowledging the clever slight, gave Brutal a quick shove, hard enough to knock him off balance just a bit, and said, "Asshole, is it? I will remember that, B!" Shifting his attention back to the rest of the group, he said, "Hey, all this talk about blessings and food is making me hungry. Can we go to the Drip now?"

"You have the attention span of an ant," said Ariana. "Now that we have Tyberius distracted from the tavern for a moment, why do we not see how much coin we have so we can put a plan together for when we go to Boral's?"

"That is an excellent idea," said Mikell, and everyone in the group except Tyberius nodded approval.

Seeing that he stood alone, Tyberius raised his hands and mock surrender and said, "Alright...Alright, let us go count the money. How long could it take to count a few copper pieces?"

Brutal padded Tyberius on the back, saying, "Thank you, Tyberius."

"Great. We can use the table in my kitchen area upstairs to sort the coins and add up how much we have," said Mikell, as he led them through the door in the northwest corner of the Temple which opened up to a flight of stairs leading up.

Brutal climbed the Taper wood stairs, their fragile minty scent belying their strength which supported him and his friends without even one creak. As he topped the stairs, he found himself on the second level of the temple. It seemed like an odd space, there were no walls, as it was a completely open; more fit for storage than living. There were two straw mattresses along the east wall, with a holy symbol of Zuel nailed into the wall between them. Bookshelves, completely full, lined the north wall, like a small library, and overflowed into a large pile of books neatly stacked on the floor. There was a small round table, and two chairs, near the bookshelves, and the table were also cluttered with books, with barely enough room for the two large candles in the center. Because it was still light outside, they weren't lit now, but the large drips of wax, now solidified, told that someone had spent many hours reading by their light. The rectangular kitchen table was by the south wall, and had four chairs neatly tucked in on each side. The only indication that it was even a kitchen was a small cabinet along the wall next to it which held several plates and mugs, and a large bucket of water. The whole area was uncomfortable, thought Brutal; it was missing a woman's touch. Brutal knew that Mikell's mother had died when he was very young, and looking around, he felt sad for his priestly friend. It made him think back to the home that he had just left, which although it was by any definition simple -- it still felt like a home, filled with positive energy and love. Not like this space, which felt empty. But Mikell didn't seem to think anything of it, or if he did, it certainly did not show. There were two windows, Brutal saw. One on the east wall that overlooked a small courtyard past which the guildhall and the Drip could easily be seen. Brutal walked over to it, careful not to step on the mattresses and peered out. The courtyard was empty at the moment, but he could still see plenty of activity around the Drip as the muffled shouts and applause indicated. The second window was on the south wall, just above the small table. The light coming through the south window, made it the brightest area in the room.

"Alright," said Mikell as he led his friends over to the table, "you can leave your backpacks or anything you would like, up here, it is all very safe." Julius, Hammer, and Brutal each took off their backpacks and placed them in the southeast corner near the sole cabinet in the room. Tyberius began to help Ariana remove her backpack, but she quickly turned away, forcing the backpack to be ripped from Tyberius's grasp.

"No!" Ariana shouted, feeling a little embarrassed at the unintended volume of her voice. Everyone stopped what they were doing, looking to see if it was something they'd done. Flushing a bit, she continued, "I mean, thank you, but I will keep my backpack for now."

"Why lug it around town?" asked Tyberius.

Regaining her composure, her eyes became icy as she gave Tyberius a look. "Because it has things I need."

"Okay, fine," said Tyberius, adding grumpily, "but do not ask me to carry it for you later." With that, he also took off his backpack and set it in the corner and then dug out a small pouch of coins.

Mikell, Hammer, and Julius were already sitting at the table, each with a pouch of coins in front of them. Tyberius and Brutal remained standing as Ariana took off the backpack and fished out her own small bag of coins and then took her seat at the table, setting the backpack right at her feet. Brutal took out his bag of gold, that Fey had given him, and set it down on the table in front of him; it was conspicuously larger than all the others.

Tyberius, of course, was the first to comment. "What is that? A bag of copper pieces? I thought I was going to be the low man here!" he added with a chuckle." Picking up his tiny bag, he pulled on the string and dumped out five small gold pieces. "It ain't much, but it is all I got. It is not like I planned on going anywhere or something."

Ariana looked down at her left hand that was resting on the small brown leather pouch that had her coins. The slender platinum ring glinted in the sunlight coming through the window. Every slight move of her finger made the sunlight dance in her eye. The ring must have cost him nearly everything he had, she thought to herself with a mixture of selfishness and appreciation.

Hammer let out a deep chuckle and said, "Five gold pieces? What the hell do you spend your money on to have so little?"

"Hey, we live off the land on the north side," said Tyberius and then, gesturing with his large arms, added, "we are not traveling across the land getting paid." Eyeing the bag Hammer was holding in his lap, which bulged substantially, said tentatively, "So, let us see it, how much do you have?"

Hammer looked down and hesitated, as if he did not want to show his sum, but after a few seconds, he slowly lifted the bag up, like a gambler about to bet his life's savings, and poured the contents onto the table. He licked his lips, his mouth was dry and it seemed to be an effort for him to speak, "It...It is about 150 gold pieces," said Hammer. Then looking around the table at the group, upon which he now depended, he absentmindedly picked up a single gold piece and let it fall back into the pile and he said, "It is all I have in the world, but hopefully it will help us kill them damn gnolls and we will find much more gold."

Tyberius shifted uncomfortably on his feet, "Wow, that is a lot of gold -- did they pay you that well for being a caravan guard?" asked Tyberius.

Hammer was staring at his pile of gold pieces, but his eyes looked up at Tyberius. "Yeah, it paid okay, and I saved up for a couple years. But we got a lot of it from an abandoned wagon on the trail to Whiteal. Someone got waylaid, a man and a woman, but for some reason whoever killed them left the wagon alone." Hammer shrugged his shoulders. "I do not know why it was not taken, but there was a lot of gold in a chest stashed in the wagon and we all split it up. I felt a little guilty, but there was no way to know who they were and they obviously did not need it anymore." Hammer, as if finally letting the money go in his mind, pushed his gold into the center of the table and said, "We need it now, so I am glad to contribute, but I expect to be rewarded too when this is done."

"We all do," said Brutal. "My reward will be information, yours can be in gold."

Hammer looked at Brutal. "That works for me."

Mikell placed a small leather pouch of his own on the table and emptied the contents onto the table. "Father and I prayed to Zuel and we felt that these fifty-five gold pieces should be used for this righteous cause. Not only will we find out what happened to Brutal's father but we will wipe out evil along the way." Mikell's eyes narrowed a bit as he pushed his coins into the center pile with Hammer's, and continued, "Starting with these godforsaken gnolls on the north bank."

Julius pushed his leather hat up a bit to uncover his face, the light from the window illuminating his blue eyes, and he squinted. Lightly tossing his bag into the middle of the table, it landed with a thud into the growing pile of gold. "Eighty-five gold is what I have. I have been alive for a long time, but acquiring coin has not been what I seek. I still do not know what that is, but I feel that I will find it on this journey."

Ariana, her eyes looking down at the table, feeling a little embarrassed, pushed her small bag of coins into the middle as well. "Twenty-two gold. I used to think it was a lot, but now it feels like a paltry amount."

"It is a fortune compared to Tyberius," said Hammer, which drew a quick round of laughter from the others.

Tyberius leaned over and put both his hands on the table, and said, "Oh, laugh it up. Let us count the copper pieces Brutal has squirreled away and then we will see who is laughing." A smile crept across Brutal's face while Tyberius's grin faded away, as if melted away by the sunlight on his face, and he asked his friend, "what are you smiling about?"

Brutal hefted the bulging bag and placed it in the middle with all the other coins. Untying the top string, he reached in and pulled out a few gold coins. "Two hundred gold pieces, boys," then, noticing Ariana, quickly added, "and girls."

Tyberius slowly reached up and took off his hat. Hat in hand, he looked at his friend and said, "Where in the eight hells did you get that much gold?"

Ariana's eyes widened in surprise too. Nobody had that kind of money on the north side bank, it was a farming community, and Tyberius was right when he said they lived off the land. "Yes, please tell us, Brutal," she asked, letting her curiosity get the better of her.

"I wish I could say I did some heroic deed to earn it, but the truth is: Fey had it."

Brutal had not even finished his answer when Ariana asked, "Where would Fey have gotten that much gold?"

Brutal looked at Ariana. "She did not say exactly. But it would seem that Fey and Anthall have not always been farmers. And this," Brutal said, pointing at the bag of gold, "was something from that time in their lives."

"I will have to talk to Fey about that," said Ariana, "I would like to know more about what they did."

"Well, there is no time for that now," said Tyberius, we will not be back to the farms for a while now." Then looking back at the table, he asked, "How much do we have?"

Mikell quickly answered, "I calculate 517 gold pieces."

"I never dreamed I would see such a fortune," said Tyberius, "it is amazing." A loud cheer erupted from outside and Tyberius walked over to the window and leaned out, trying to see what was happening. A man came out of the Drip holding and rubbing his right arm. Tyberius could not hear exactly what he was saying, but it sounded like a torrent of obscenities. Pulling his head back inside and standing up, he turned back to the group and asked excitedly, "Okay, now can we go to the Drip and see what is going on!?"

"Aye," said Hammer, "I am hungry and thirsty, too, and I must admit, a little curious myself." Sliding the chair back, with a screech, along the floor, Hammer stood up, then looking at the table, pointed at the small pile of gold and said, "What are we going to do with all that? It might be safe up here, but I am not leaving my gold sitting here, unguarded, temple or no."

Mikell took the largest leather pouch and placed all the coins in it. He took out two of the small gold pieces and said, "This will be more than enough to get us all something to eat and drink at the Drip." Then he placed the two coins in a small pouch and attached it to his belt. Taking the large pouch of coins, he walked over to the bookcase on the north wall where he moved a few of the books and placed the bag in a compartment behind them. After putting the books back in place, the bag was perfectly concealed. "There, that ought to be safe enough. Everyone agreed?" asked Mikell. Everyone nodded, impressed with the secret compartment. "Zuel has many secrets," said Mikell with a wry smile. Everyone filed down the stairs and back out through the front doors of the temple.

At the bottom of the stairs, Ariana paused. "On second thought, I will leave my backpack here. Go ahead, I will catch up!" And with that Ariana bounded up the stairs. Back upstairs, she carefully took off the backpack and placed it on the outer edge of the pile of everyone else's stuff. Bending down, she untied the loops that held the bag closed, paused as if considering something, then quickly patted the bag and hurried back down the stairs.

Back out on the street, Ariana hustled to catch up as the group began the short walk down the block to the Drip. As they neared the tavern the sounds grew louder. Tyberius thought he recognized the man he saw coming out of the drip sitting on the wooden porch running along the outside of the tavern. There was another man sitting with him and they were obviously talking. The one man was still rubbing his right arm and he was hunched over slightly as if in some pain. Curious, he walked over to the two men and introduced himself, "Well met, friends," he said with a slight wave of his hand.

The two men looked up. The one holding his arm grimaced. "Well met," he said with a guarded tone, "what do you want?" Just then another cheer went up from inside the tavern. "Another poor sod just got his arm ripped off in there," said the injured man.

"What is going on in there?" asked Tyberius, then added, "I have never seen the Drip so busy or noisy before."

The hurt man let out a quick growl. "There is a monk in there, or so his friend says -- but I do not believe it. No monk is stronger than me." The man's face contorted in pain as he tried to move his arm. By this time the rest of the group had caught up and were standing behind Tyberius.

"What happened to your arm?" asked Mikell with concern in his voice.

"That monk inside nearly ripped it off my body," the man said through gritted teeth.

Tyberius stepped forward and asked again. "What the hell is going on in there?"

This time the other man spoke. He was shorter and thinner than his injured friend, wore a plain leather travelers cap, and his face was covered by a scruffy looking beard. When he spoke, it was in a quiet voice, which was unexpected from his gruff appearance, "There are two people inside. I do not even think they are even traveling together, but anyway, one is a monk who is just sitting at a table."

Tyberius interrupted, "sitting at a table? Doing what?" he asked.

Pausing as if to scold, the scruffy man continued, "Well, if you would let me finish. As I was saying, the monk just sits there at his," then the man paused as if contemplating some complex problem. Looking at his injured friend and raising his hand to his face, he gave his face a scratch and said, "Humph, well, I do not know if it was a man or a woman, now that you ask."

The injured man quickly turned and then groaned in pain as his arm shifted. Through his gritted teeth he said to his friend, "No woman did this to me. You better not go telling people it was a woman neither."

"Well, it does not matter anyway. The monk does not say anything,

128

but sits there mute as the Fuhr pole outside," the scruffy man said, jabbing his thumb in the direction of the pole down the street.

Tyberius groaned in impatience, asking both men, "So what the hell does the monk have to do with his arm?"

The scruffy man spoke first. "The monk has a sign on its table that says for two gold pieces he will arm wrestle any challenger. If the monk wins, he keeps your gold, and if the challenger wins, he will be a slave for thirty days to the victor....whatever that means." After a second he scruffy man continued, "Well, at least that is what we assume. The sign just says: '2gp. I win I keep. You win I slave 30 day.'"

Mikell exhaled in distaste. "Who would want a slave? That is an awful thing to win."

The scruffy man looked at Mikell. "Maybe to you. I could use a slave, especially one that strong."

Tyberius's eyes sparkled in the afternoon sun, and Brutal could see the obsession beginning to take hold of his friend. As if on cue, Tyberius said, "I am going in, I gotta see this."

As Tyberius started to leave, Hammer asked, "how many people have tried?"

Tyberius stopped, interested in hearing the answer. The injured man spoke this time. "I seen at least six or seven guys had a go at him, but they were already in there when we showed up, so who knows."

Hammer quickly asked again, "Anyone come close to beating him?" Both men shook their heads, and Hammer said, "Damn, I hate to say it, but I gotta see this too."

Mikell asked, "What about the other guy? You said there were two people."

The scruffy man answered, "There is a bard, or I guess that is what he is, and he is like announcing all the matches, and writing them in some book of his. Says he is gonna write a story about it all and tell it to others in his travels. Who would not want a story being written about them? But I know I am not that strong, so I did not even try."

Mikell stepped closer to the injured man. "What do you do for a living, and where are you from?"

The man looked up, the pain evident on his face, which was worn from years of work in the sun. "Why do you ask?"

Mikell said, "I can help you with your arm, but I want to know why you would deserve the blessing of Zuel."

The man's face seemed to soften at the mention of Zuel, the good god of health. "I am a merchant from Whiteal and I come to Telfar every few tendays to sell my wares."

Mikell studied the man's face, looking for tells that would indicate deceit or maliciousness. Mikell had always been a good judge of character, which was an important skill when dealing with the public, as he often had to do with the temple services. This man seemed genuine and good to him, making his decision easy. "Will you allow me to help you?" Mikell asked. The man nodded, and even that caused him to grimace in pain. Mikell placed one hand on the holy symbol of Zuel, which hung around his neck, and the other hand began to trace invisible symbols into the air in front of him as he chanted a soft prayer to Zuel, "Benedici il mio tocco con il potere di guarire le ferite lievi..." The others stood, astounded, watching in awe what Mikell was doing. Mikell's free hand, tracing the somatic portion of the spell, began to lightly glow. It took only a moment, and then Mikell, finishing his prayer, touched the man's arm. The energy crackled for an instant as it leapt from Mikell into the injured man. The man's body spasmed slightly and then an instant later the pain disappeared from the man's face and a restful appearance replaced his haggard look.

The man could feel the energy working its way through his body, and could feel the bone and tendons reforming underneath his skin. It was a peculiar feeling, not painful but not pleasant either. It all happened in just a few seconds and before he knew it the odd sensation was gone, and his arm felt...normal. "Oh...my...god," was all the man could say. He gingerly began to move his arm around testing the range of motion, his eyes wide with amazement. "I-I thought you were going to give me a sling or something for my arm...I-I did not know you could heal me like this."

"It feels better now?" asked a smiling Mikell, proud of his Zuel's handiwork. "And remember, I did not do this," he said, pausing for effect and tapping his holy symbol. "Zuel did it. Praise be to Zuel," he said, his arms partially upraised.

"That is fucking awesome," said Hammer. "I know priests could heal and stuff, but I have never seen it done before."

Tyberius, impressed, but more impatient, blurted out, "Yeah, that was fucking great, now I am going inside." And with that, both he and Hammer worked their way through the throng of people standing around the outside of the Drip and soon disappeared inside.

The man stood up, cautiously rubbing his arm as if it the pain might suddenly return. He extended his hand to Mikell. "I am Rucknor Delbith, and you are well met." Mikell took the man's hand and they both shook. "What can I offer you in return for this kindness?"

Ariana started to speak, but Mikell raised his hand silencing her and said, "I do not heal for profit. You owe me nothing, as I said," Mikell gave Ariana a quick glance, "it is Zuel's work."

"Well, thank you then for your aid, and good luck in your travels," than man said. The scruffy man stood up, too, shook Mikell's hand, and then both men walked down the street, blending into the mass of people, and soon gone from sight.

"Do not silence me, Mikell," said Ariana, her arms crossed.

Mikell turned to look at her. "And you, do not try to profit from Zuel's healing...I know you were going to ask for money."

Ariana stiffened and said, "We need the coin, Mikell." Her eyes narrowed a bit as she continued, "Some of us could be dead tomorrow. I hope for yours and Zuel's sake it's not because we lacked the coin for proper weapons or armor."

Brutal stepped between the Ariana and Mikell, putting a hand on each of their shoulders. "We have plenty of coin for what we will need," said Brutal. "Julius is already equipped," he said, gesturing toward the ranger, "and so is Hammer. So that means Mikell, Tyberius, and myself are the only ones in need of anything, and I already have a good sword," he said, his left hand drifting down to the hilt as if in punctuation.

Ariana, arms still crossed, replied, "Do not be so naive, Brutal. That coin has to do more than just buy armor and weapons. Are we going to walk everywhere? No, so we each need a horse...each horse needs a saddle, saddlebags, and we need provisions...or were you planning to carry everything we find in your arms and hunt for all our food? There are a lot of things that will require coin, especially if we end up in any cities."

Brutal could see he had not thought their needs all the way through. "So far Soulmite has provided everything we need, I believe she will continue to do that. Perhaps we will find more money with the gnolls."

"You call that a plan?" she asked, and then added, "I hope you are right, Brutal. I really do." With that, she pushed her way between Brutal and Mikell, heading toward the door to the Drip.

"An independent-minded person," commented Julius, "and she is always watching out for herself."

"Nobody likes being shushed," said Brutal in her defense. "Besides," he said, "she was looking out for the group, not herself."

Julius considered that. "Perhaps," he said, patting Brutal on the back. "Let us go inside and see this monk, Tyberius is probably already trying to figure out how to get 2gp from someone."

Brutal nodded. "You are right, it will not take him long to get into trouble in there. Although, I must admit, I am just as curious as Tyberius to see this monk."

Mikell smiled and clasped his friend on the shoulder and gave him a knowing smile, "Aye, you are not the only one." With that, the three men followed close behind Ariana. With so many people piling into the tavern, the doorway and windows were effectively blocked, making the Drip unusually dark inside for being mid-day and difficult for the three friends to make their way inside.

CHAPTER ELEVEN
York

PUSHING HIS WAY THROUGH THE CROWD, brutal finally made it to the entrance of the drip, and he could feel the heat from inside rushing past him, warming his skin, as it escaped into the open air. Ariana, Julius, and Mikell followed behind Brutal, who was finally able to push his way through the doorway and make his way inside. Along with the heat, inside the room, came a powerful odor, a mixture of sweat, ale, dirt, and cooked meat; an unpleasant smell to say the least. Pushing onward, once inside, he spotted Tyberius, the tall warrior's head, his short red hair, sticking out like a sore thumb in the crowd. The crowd of people, impossibly, grew denser as they moved toward the corner, but Brutal was able to twist and shove his way, with his three friends following his lead, to Tyberius and Hammer.

Seated at the corner table was someone wearing a monk's robe, a large hood was pulled over their head, hiding their face in its shadows. With the robe covering so much, it was difficult to gauge but, sizing up the monk, Brutal did not think it was taller than himself, and certainly not as tall as Tyberius. However, the build was obviously powerful, as even the loose-fitting robe could not hide the massively broad shoulders. The monk was sitting quietly and statue still, with his hands resting in his lap and hidden by the long sleeves on the robe. On the table was a poorly scrawled note, that read just as Rucknor, the man outside, had explained: '2gp. I win I keep. You win I slave 30 day.'" A brown clay bowl containing the gold from previous challengers rested on the table to the monk's right.

"Will no one pay the paltry sum of two gold pieces to challenge this kind and fair monk? It is a small price to pay for your chance at instant fame!" shouted a man over the noise of the room, which suddenly quieted down. He was standing behind the monk, and placed a hand on the monk's shoulder as he spoke. The difference between the two men could not have been starker. The man sitting at the table, had immensely, almost absurdly, broad shoulders, and although the plain and soiled robe hid much, it was obvious that he was very deep chested and powerfully built. The man standing, and shouting, was thin and graceful, clothed in fine studded leather armor, that looked impeccably maintained, and a sheathed longsword dangled at his side. His long, flowing, blond hair was combed back, just long enough to touch his shoulders, and plainly revealing his pointed ears, betrayed the elven blood that ran in his veins, and far from trying to hide his heritage, he wore two diamond stud earrings in each ear, which drew attention to them. His sharp facial features, classic by elven standards: a skinny nose, oval eyes, and a smaller mouth. "Surely there is a man in this room that is in search of glory!?" he challenged the crowd.

" 'Ave him take off that dang hood -- we want to see 'is face!" shouted someone from the crowd. Then another man shouted, "Aw, it be all trick -- do not waste yer coin on 'im!" The crowd grumbled in agreement.

The man behind the monk stepped forward in the direction of the voices and pointed at the monk. "This is an honorable monk and a fair competition, I stake my reputation on it!"

"Bah -- who the hell are you?! And what is your name to any of us?" asked an angry and drunken voice from the crowd.

The elf gracefully bowed, as if just completing a performance, saying, "So kind of you to ask. My name is York O'Lurn, and I am the most famous bard in Kardoon and Thayol. I retell only the most amazing -- and TRUE -- stories you have ever heard. And this monk here," he continued, patting the monk's shoulders again, "and the legends born this night, will be among the stories I tell across the lands!" York gave the crowd a steely look and pointed in an arc that spanned the entire crowd. "And what name will I be telling in the cities of Bindal, Castor, Westal, Whiteal, and even as far as Cray? Yours?!," he shouted, as a question, pointing at a man in the front of the crowd.

The man shook his head and stepped back. "Not mine, good bard, I have seen this monk beat men that I know are far stronger than me."

York was not deterred and stepped forward, grabbing the man by both shoulders. "Ohhh, it is often the person you least expect who rises to glory -- and people love that kind of story the best! Give it a go!" The crowd, feeding off York's energy, roared in approval, urging the man to try.

Then a large round man stepped out of the crowd. "I will take the challenge!" he shouted. The crowd roared in a frenzied delight as people began placing bets on who they think would win. While they were doing that, the large man made his way to the table and sat in the chair opposite the monk.

Quickly abandoning the apprehensive man, York approached the round man and bent down to talk in his ear. "Excellent, Excellent! And what is your name, good sir? And what do you do?" asked York.

"Verlo Woodlife. I am a Taper wood logger, if it is of any matter to the likes of you," the man answered gruffly.

York stood up, rubbing his hand on his chin for a moment as he thought. "No, no, no...Verlo will not do...How about Venom? Ah yes, that sounds much better!" Before the man could object, York turned around and shouted above the crowd, "Ladies and Gentlemen, I give you...Venom Woodlife!! He is a prodigal lumberjack taking down Taper wood trees with one fell blow! Such work has made him very strong -- be careful should you bet against him!" This information ignited a new round of betting amongst the crowd. York returned to the table, standing between the monk and 'Venom,' smiling for a few more minutes to allow the betting to finalize. As the hum of betting died down, York raised his hands in the air, the noisy crowd slowly began to hush, to the point where all that could be heard were a few metallic clinks of mugs, and a burp or two. Turning back to the table, the bard leaned down, placing both hands on the table, and said, "Okay, Venom, first, place your two gold pieces into the bowl," York said, gesturing to the clay bowl on the table. Verlo already had the two gold pieces in his hand and he dropped the coins into the bowl, making the familiar and tantalizing clinking sound coins make as they collide.

York smiled again. "Wonderful! This is a fair match -- no spells, no tricks. Just one on one. Man versus monk. Which arm do you prefer, Venom?"

Verlo looked a little uncomfortable at the continued incorrect use of his name, but answered in his gruff voice, "Right hand."

York nearly leapt from the ground. "The right hand!" he shouted, his right hand raised, and the crowd bellowed and clapped in applause. "Let me see your arm," York instructed Verlo, who held out his arm. It was a very thick arm, but how much muscle was hard to tell. York felt up and down the Verlo's extended arm as if looking for any possible cheats. Finding nothing, York shouted, "Venom is true and ready!" Then turning to the monk, he said, "Now you must show us your arm, good monk."

The monk, who had not moved at all, finally raised his right arm. Leaving the hood on, the monk rolled up the large right sleeve of his robe, allowing York to inspect his arm again. There were several scars, the skin had an ashen appearance, but most noticeably, the monk's arm bulged with muscles. Brutal's eyebrows raised in astonishment; he had rarely seen someone he thought could be as strong as himself, aside from Tyberius, but this monk might be just that. Brutal looked at Tyberius, knowing his friend would be thinking similar thoughts, but what really worried him was that his friend was going get sucked into it all excitement. Fortunately, he thought to himself, he knew Tyberius did not have the necessary two gold pieces, but it was obvious looking at the intent and focused gaze of his tall friend, that Tyberius was indeed enraptured by the spectacle unfolding in front of him.

"Look at the size of his fucking arms," Tyberius said as he flexed his right arm, feeling his bicep with his left hand.

"Do you see the color of his skin? What kind of humanoid do you think he is?" asked Ariana.

"I have no idea," said Brutal.

"Could be a half-orc," stated Julius, "I knew one when I lived in Whiteal for a couple seasons. They are broad in the shoulders, just like this guy, and have that gray-ish look to their skin. But we could not know for sure without seeing his face."

"I am impressed, Julius," said Ariana.

Julius smiled and shrugged his shoulders at the compliment. "As I said, I have been around a little."

"The rules are simple: one," said York, holding up the index finger of his right hand, "keep your elbow on the table. Two," York held up two fingers, "force your opponent's hand to the table, and you win! Three," he held up a third finger, "if your elbow comes off the table, you lose!" The crowd cheered again, some yelling encouragement to 'Venom" and some to the 'monk,' depending on where their money was bet. "Are each of you ready?" York asked.

The monk nodded from behind his hood. Verlo nodded his chinless head, saying, "Aye, I am ready." With that Verlo put his right elbow on the table, holding out an open hand. The monk put his elbow on the table and grasped Verlo's hand. The monk's hand was slightly larger, and the two combatants fiddled with their grips, each vying for a slightly better position. York placed both his hands over the top of their interlocked grips, and squeezing down, he did his best to hold them in place. A nervous hush settled over the room, the anticipation of the contest grew with everyone staring at the clasped hands. York let the moment hang in the excitement of the unknown for just a few seconds longer, then, releasing their hands, he shouted, "Pull! Pull!!" as he dramatically jumped backwards.

The room exploded in a thunderous mixture of encouragements and heckles for each combatant. At York's word, Verlo pulled with all his might, his face began to flush as he struggled against the monk's counter effort. With the hood still covering the monk's face, Brutal could not see the monk's expression, but he could tell Verlo was giving everything he had as sweat began to bead up on his forehead, and his face began to jiggle, turning red, as he put more and more effort into the fight. But the monk's hand did not move. Then, slowly, the monk began pushing Verlo's hand down toward the table. Verlo gasped for air and shifted his weight to his left foot and used his weight to help pull his hand back to the center. It started to work, Verlo was able to get his hand back over center and a smile began to form at the corner of Verlo's mouth as he got a whiff of hope. But his hope was quickly extinguished, like that of a candle being blown out with a single breath.

In a raspy voice the monk shouted, "Ki-a!" and in a flash Verlo's arm slammed down onto the table, hard enough to make the bowl of gold coins, on the opposite side of the table to jump up, almost spilling its contents on the floor, but it wobbled for a second before stabilizing back down on its base. Verlo howled in pain, but it was muted by the cacophony of exclamations from the crowd at the outcome. Verlo, holding his arm gingerly, gave the bard and the monk a dirty look, then stood up and quickly disappeared into the crowd.

Tyberius turned to his friends. "Hell, I can take that monk; someone give me two gold pieces?"

Ariana spoke first. "We are not wasting two gold pieces so you can arm wrestle that beast."

"Why not? We could use an extra hand with the gnolls," stated Tyberius.

"You are assuming you would win," Ariana shot back. "Besides," she added, "we cannot rely on a monk we do not know -- even if you did win."

"She is right Tyberius," said Brutal, "we need every coin we have, and even if you did win, we could not depend on him in a fight."

"Fine, I will free him right away, we do not need him." Then, turning to Mikell, he said, "I know you have the coin...our coin," he added with emphasis. "C'mon, give me the two gold pieces," he asked again, but seeing the look on Mikell's face, he could see the priest was not convinced, "Aw, c'mon, we have a pile back in the temple...just give me two."

Mikell looked around. "Keep your voice down and be careful what you are saying, many people here are looking for easy coin tonight. We are not giving you two gold pieces to do this insane and honestly, pointless, challenge."

"I will," said a small but familiar voice from behind Mikell. Bealty, from out of nowhere, gracefully appeared in front of Mikell with two gold pieces in the palm of his hand, which he extended up to Tyberius. "I want to see if Ty can do it," he added, as he handed the coins to Tyberius.

"Oh, shit yeah! Yes!" exclaimed Tyberius with the excitement of a child. "Thanks a bunch, Bealty! I did not know you were back - Great god-damned timing!"

"Yeah, great timing," said Mikell, "How long have you been there?"

"Long enough," Bealty said with a sly grin.

"You ought to keep to your own business, Bealty," said Ariana. "This will cause nothing but trouble. Tyberius," she said, her voice clear and commanding, "give him the coins back and let us get out of here." Tyberius looked nervously between Ariana and the table where the monk now sat, again, motionless. He jingled the coins in his large hand, trying to decide what he was going to do.

As if on cue, York again addressed the gathering. "Alas, poor Venom did not prevail -- but it was a great match and he almost had the victory! What a story that would have made -- one kings and queens no doubt would pay to hear! Who is the next challenger?! I can sense a victor in the room, all we need is for him to reveal himself!"

Ariana glared at Tyberius. "I think he means victim -- not victor."

"Aye, I am the one you seek!" said Tyberius, raising his hand with the two gold pieces and stepping out of the crowd toward the table.

Ariana gave Bealty a cold look and shook her finger at him. "You wait and see what trouble you just caused."

Halflings were used to being blamed for many things, so Bealty took the rebuke in stride, and looking up at Ariana as she spoke to him, shrugged. "Something good will come of it, you will see," he said, shifting his focus back to Tyberius. Ariana crossed her arms, glaring down at the top of the halfling's head, covered by his brown day cap, looking up, finally, at the sound of York's voice ringing out.

York turned to face the new challenger. "Wonderful! My, oh my, what a beastly human you are -- has anyone ever seen such a tall man before?! Certainly, the odds favor this man!" The crowd cheered in unison as he hurried over to Tyberius and asked in a quiet voice, "What is your name?"

"Tyberius," answered Tyberius, "but some people just call me Ty."

"Tyberius...Hmm, that is not bad," said York. "It kind of has a regal sound to it." Patting him on the chest, York turned to face the crowd again. "Everyone, let me introduce our largest and newest challenger: Tyberius!" The crowd yelled and clapped in response, filling the room with raw energy once again.

Mikell flicked Bealty's ear with his finger. "Ow," yelped the halfling, rubbing his ear, "why did you do that?"

Mikell gave the halfling a scolding look. "You know why," he said, gesturing toward Tyberius, who was now seating himself at the table. "Ariana is right, you know -- the best we can hope for is that this is just a waste of two gold...but it could end up a lot worse. I do not know how, but it could."

"Nah," said Bealty, waving his hand dismissively. "If he loses, which he probably will, at least he got to try. The worst that can happen is his ego takes a beating. If he wins, then he has a monk to pick up after him instead of Ariana, for a few days. By the way, I bet ten gold against him. I am afraid he is not favored to win; the best I could get was one to two odds. If you want in on that, I know who to talk to."

Mikell snorted in disgust. "I do not want any part of this, and you are wasting gold that we could really use right now."

"Saving coin was never my strong suit," Bealty admitted. Mikell shook his head in disapproval but turned his attention, like everyone else in the tavern, to the table where Tyberius and the monk were now sitting.

Tyberius sat down and tried to see into the darkness of the monk's hooded head, pointing a long finger at the monk, he said, "I am going to kick your ass...monk or not."

The monk turned his head slightly, then in a raspy voice, halting voice, said, "No...you, will, lose."

Tyberius grinned. "I am already inside your head little monk." And with that Tyberius dropped the two gold pieces into the clay bowl and began rolling up his shirt sleeve.

York turned his attention back to the table. "Hold on there partner, we have to give folks time to get their bets in -- and do not forget we have to put on a good show."

Tyberius continued to stare at the monk. "This ain't no show, I am gonna rip his arm off."

York laughed. "That may be, and I hope you do – that would make a wonderful story...but we cannot disappoint the folks by going too quickly...we need to build up the anticipation!"

"Fuck that, let us get this thing done," and with that Tyberius put his right arm on the table and motioned the monk to take his hand.

The monk leaned onto the table with his immense weight, causing the boards to creak, while he placed his right elbow on the table and clasping Tyberius's hand.

York gave Tyberius an irritated look and then his face suddenly transformed into a smile as he turned back to the crowd. "Well, folks, better finish up your bets -- these two are anxious to get on with it!"

Tyberius and the monk wrestled with their grip for a moment, and then they got into a position that each liked. York quickly got his hands on theirs and said, "Hold...hold....Go!"

Tyberius quickly pulled the monk's arm down halfway, but then the monk's resistance stiffened.

Ariana watched, her eyes wide with excitement and widening more as Tyberius pulled the monk's arm down, with an easy victory, almost in hand. "Go Tyberius!" she shouted with all her might, although it was lost within the explosive roar of the tavern. Just as victory seemed inevitable, the monk halted Tyberius's progress and began pulling Tyberius's arm back up. "Oh shit," she said as the monk was almost back to the starting position. "Oh shit, pull Tyberius, pull!!" she screamed. Mikell, Julius, and Hammer couldn't resist the primal urge, seeing their friend locked in the struggle, they began yelling support to Tyberius as well. Everyone except Bealty, who was yelling for the monk to pull harder, at which Ariana shoved the little rogue. "Are you rooting for the monk?" she asked in a mixture of disbelief and anger.

"Well, heck yeah...look at how big the monk is," he answered, shrugging his shoulders and gesturing toward the table. "I bet ten gold on him to win!"

Ariana's face flushed, and she was about to say something when her attention was riveted back to the table, as the monk yelled, "Ki-a!" and with a great heave pushed Tyberius's arm down to within a needle's width of touching the table. York moved quickly, placing one cheek on the table so he could judge the final touch.

"No touch, no touch!" yelled York, and the crowd thundered again. Tyberius's face was flushing red as he held his breath and put all he had into bringing his arm up, but the monk's arm felt like a rock, unmoving, and his own arm was getting so tired. Tyberius let out a terrible roar as he heaved. His arm made some progress back upwards and the crowd gasped.

"He is doing it, he is doing it!" shouted Ariana. "Keep fighting Tyberius!"

Tyberius continued to fight on and as his arm slowly made its way back up, little by little. As their hands approached the top again, the monk shifted his weight to put more force into his pull. In one great motion, the monk slammed Tyberius's hand down onto the table. The force of the blow again, nearly tipping the bowl of coins over, but as before, the bowl finally stabilized itself.

York jumped up, waving his hands. "Victory for the monk!!! Victory for the monk!!"

Tyberius's face was still flushing red as he stood up, giving York a hard shove in the chest. "I want another go!"

York, surprised by the shove, nearly lost his balance, but regained it after a couple steps backwards. Holding up a hand to keep Tyberius at bay, he said, "Be a good chap now -- do not be a sorry loser, it was a fair fight."

Tyberius knocked York's hand away and bent down until his face was inches from York's. With their eyes locked together, Tyberius growled in a low, strained voice. "Give me another go..."

York did not flinch at the closeness and held his ground. "No, no, you have already lost! No second tries! But thank you for your brave and valiant effort! I will not forget to mention you in my retelling as it was a magnificent bout!"

"Fuck your stories, I want another go!" said Tyberius again.

Brutal and Mikell ran out and grabbed Tyberius by the shoulders. "Come on, Tyberius," said Brutal. "Let us get out of here! You had your shot! We do not want any trouble here."

Tyberius, turning to face Mikell and holding out his hand, shouted, "Give me two more gold, damn you! Give it to me!"

"No! We need to get out of here," said Mikell.

Tyberius, shoving Mikell to the ground and breaking free from Brutal's grasp, plunged into the crowd, who quickly parted for him. In a flash, Tyberius was gone, his path marked only by the curses of the people he had pushed aside.

As Mikell lay on the floor, he said, "We better go after him." Hammer and Julius ran to help Mikell up.

Brutal, looking in the direction that Tyberius took off, said, "Wherever he is going, we will not catch him. He needs to cool down."

"So, what now?" asked Hammer.

"I say we go over to the Gustav Inn to get something to eat... this place is too crazy right now," said Brutal.

"I agree, I would like to sit down and collect myself," said Mikell, dusting himself off.

"Are you happy now?" snapped Ariana at Bealty.

"Yeah," said Bealty. "I just won five gold pieces...although I lost the two that I gave Ty. But hey, I am up three gold!"

"You little son of a bitch," Ariana growled at the halfling.

Mikell stepped between Ariana and Bealty. "Come on now, Ariana. He should not have given Tyberius the gold, but Tyberius wanted to do it."

"I told you nothing good would come of this, Bealty!" said Ariana, scolding the halfling, and leaning down, jammed her index finger into his chest.

"He is a big boy, Ariana, I do not see what the big deal is," said Bealty, who stepping backwards, easily brushed away her finger.

Ariana opened her mouth to say her next piece, but stopped, her expression suddenly changing from that of anger to shock, as if she had just seen something of great concern. Brutal put his hand on Ariana's shoulder and asked, "What is it, Ariana?"

Ariana continued to stare off into the distance for several long seconds, until finally her eyes refocused and locked on Brutal. "Oh shit, the gold!" said Ariana. "The gold!"

"Oh, do not worry about it, Ariana -- I gave it to him, so I do not expect it paid back," said Bealty.

"No, you little shit," said Ariana, "not your stupid two gold pieces -- OUR gold," she said, gesturing to the group.

"Do you think he went back to get two more gold pieces, from our stash?" asked Hammer.

Ariana shook her head, and her face paled. "No...he took it all," her voice trailed off.

"Why would he do that?" asked Brutal, concern now creeping into his voice.

"Are you fucking kidding?" asked Hammer, in a sharp tone, the situation suddenly becoming more personal for him.

Just then a loud commotion at the door on the northern side of Drip erupted and everyone turned to see what was going on. Standing there, a head taller than all the others in the crowd stood Tyberius holding, high above his head, the bag of gold which they had stashed away in the temple. "Five hundred gold pieces says I can beat the monk!" yelled Tyberius in a fierce challenge. "If I win, I keep the bag, and the monk serves me for the thirty days." A hush took over the tavern, and all the eyes shifted from Tyberius to York and the monk at the small table in the corner.

York hesitated, looking at the monk. The monk, still sitting statuesque, nodded his robed head. "Five hundred gold pieces!" yelled York with great excitement. "Well, bring the bag here and let us all see what you have there. If indeed it is such a sum, then we accept your challenge!"

The crowd parted, again, for the big warrior, and the only sounds were his footsteps falling on the Taper wood floorboards and, with each step, the slight jingle of coins in the bag. Before he made it to the corner, Brutal stepped out in front of Tyberius, blocking his path to the monk.

"This is not your coin to risk, Tyberius," said Brutal, staring into his friend's eyes. But all Brutal could see was a blind rage in Tyberius's eyes, it was as if his friend was gone.

Ariana appeared behind Brutal, her arms crossed. "Do not do it, Tyberius," she said, giving him her icy stare. "You cannot!"

Tyberius stopped for a second in front of Brutal but said nothing as he strode with purpose past his friend and fiancée. Ariana gasped as he passed her, giving her no acknowledgment, as if she were a ghost. He placed the heavy bag onto the table where the monk was sitting, and said, giving the bard a malevolent stare, "Go ahead and count it, if you need to, you fucker -- but do it quickly."

York smiled pleasantly, but kept a wary, green, eye on the tall human as he pulled on the leather string holding the bag closed, and to his amazement, as the bag opened, some gold tumbled out. York quickly snatched up the few pieces that had fallen out and put them back into the bag, and then he resealed it. York turned to the crowd, raising his arms, saying, "There is no need to count it, it is indeed a very large sum! This is a contest that will go down in the history of Telfar!" The tavern exploded in a raucous applause of hoots and hollers, and even more spectators flooded into the tavern, filling every inch of space as they pushed and fought for a spot to see the upcoming spectacle. In order to allow more people to see the ensuing contest, Tyberius and the monk agreed to move to the middle of the room, with the spectators forming a circle around the small wooden table. Brutal, Mikell, Bealty, Hammer, Julius, and Ariana were all in the front row standing behind Tyberius. Even Syd, the one-eyed owner of the Drip, came out from behind the bar to get a front row spot.

"What the hell are we going to do if, no, when he loses?" asked Hammer as the crowd began to form around the table. "It took me years to save up that much coin."

Mikell put his hand on Hammer's shoulder. "Let us deal with the known, not the unknown."

"What is that supposed to mean?" asked Hammer.

"It means," said Bealty, "we first see what happens, then we decide what is to be done."

"Exactly," said Mikell.

"When this is over, we need to have a talk with Tyberius -- this is not okay what he has done. Not by a long shot," said Hammer.

"It may be a setback, but it has made the evening more interesting," said Julius.

"Yeah, well, it may be interesting to you, but let Tyberius throw away your coin -- not mine," said Hammer, pointing to himself. As Hammer finished his sentence, Tyberius stood up from the table and turned around to face his friends.

"Hit me," said Tyberius to no one in particular.

"Holy shit, he really has lost his mind," said Hammer, raising his hand in disbelief.

"What do you mean?" asked Mikell.

"One of you, fucking hit me already -- right here," Tyberius said, pointing to his left cheek.

"Are you off your rocker?" asked Hammer. At that moment, Brutal stepped forward and swung a right hook, which landed on Tyberius's left cheek, snapping his head backwards and rocking the big man backward a half-step until finally regaining his balance. Tyberius straightened up and for a split second it seemed as if he might rush Brutal, but as blood began to drip down his chin, he raised his left hand to dab at the open cut on his lip.

York quickly moved between Brutal and Tyberius. "What is going on here? No interference! No interference! Tyberius, sit back down!"

Tyberius gave Brutal one more look and then returned to the table and sitting down, he put his left elbow on the table. "Okay motherfucker, let us get on with it."

York gave Brutal a reprimanding look but, quickly turning his smile back on, addressed the crowd, "Who here thinks Tyberius can beat the monk?!" A spattering number of voices cheered in support, and even his own friends, except for Bealty who shouted as loud as he could, remained silent. "How many believe the monk will prevail once again?!" This time the tavern exploded in applause and cheers, and even the sturdy Taper wood walls vibrated. York waved his arms, attempting to quiet the rowdy crowd, "It seems that the tide is against you Tyberius! But the fates have always favored those where the odds are stacked against them -- and those under-dogs are the foundation of the greatest stories of all time!"

The monk slowly reached up and grabbing the two sides of its hood, pulled it back, revealing its face, causing a collective gasp from the full room. The broad head, coarse braided hair, jutting lower jaw, and pronounced boar-like tusks curling upward outside its lips gave the once austere monk a sinister appearance.

Ariana felt her mouth drying up, and all she could manage to say was, "Oh my god."

Julius leaned forward to get the attention of his friends and, nodding in the direction of the monk, said, "Aye, that is a half-orc. A very strong half-orc, from the look of it, although most are I suppose."

Hammer groaned. "Oh shit...that son of a bitch just lost us all our coin -- all my coin!"

Ariana bristled. "How about we stop assuming he will lose. If we want our gold back, we had better start hoping he can win."

Mikell followed up. "Ariana is right, we need to give Tyberius our support right now."

"Fuck this," said Hammer as he turned around and started pushing his way through the crowd toward the door.

"Well, now we know who we can count on when the going gets a little rough," said Ariana loud enough to make sure Hammer could hear her, but he just kept on moving away.

Blood continued to dribble down Tyberius's lip, and small droplets fell onto the table. The monk leaned forward, putting his left elbow on the table. Taking hold of Tyberius's left hand, the half-orc smiled, as if it had a secret it was not sharing.

"You ain't gonna be smiling in a few minutes," Tyberius sneered through clenched teeth. They continued to maneuver and adjust their hands for another minute, then York came over and put his hands on top of theirs to hold them in place as best he could.

With York's hands still on theirs, Tyberius and the monk locked their eyes on each other. There was a brief pause and the crowd hushed in anticipation. During the brief, but relative quiet, the monk said clearly enough, at least for those near the front to hear, "Me, left-handed."

As if on cue, York released the combatant's hands and shouted "Pull!!" The air crackled with excitement and anticipation as York stepped backwards, watching, along with everyone else, and expecting an epic battle.

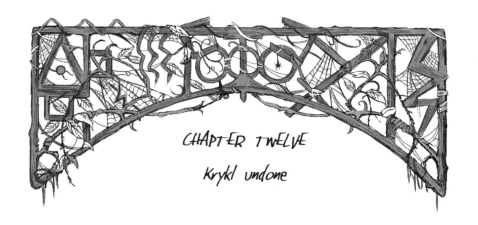

CHAPTER TWELVE
Krykl undone

YEAR: AG 1172, Month of Sepu

ANTHALL DID NOT FEEL ALIVE OR DEAD, he simply felt, and sensed, nothing. Then, like a distant sound, echoing through a canyon, he heard the familiar voice speaking to him. It was a simple command, repeated as each echo reached his consciousness: "Awaken...Awaken..." Anthall struggled to obey, using all the willpower he could muster, but it was unclear what he was struggling against. As hopelessness began to creep into his conscious, a small tingle in his right arm struck at his consciousness. The sensation began to spread across his body, going up his arm, into his torso and then down each leg. The tingle was followed by a burning sensation, which was then replaced with a feeling of wetness -- as if his body was soaked. Then the darkness began to fade, light flooding in to fill his vision, which at first it was blinding, but as it cleared, the battlefield came back into focus. Anthall blinked trying to clear his vision, and for the first time he felt back in control of his body as he brought a hand up to his face. To his surprise, his face and helmet were covered in a layer of melting ice. The ice fell away at his touch, and his vision cleared, revealing the bodies of his fallen soldiers littering the ground, some broken in half by the blast of cold, while some still lay in frozen in awkward poses, in the position they were in when the blast hit. Anthall swiveled his head around, looking for the ogre mage, hoping he was still near, when he heard the whip-like crack of the ogre's bow. Following the crack, the ogre blinked back into visibility forty yards beyond where he had cast his spell. Anthall's hand tightened around Slice, and he took comfort, as he always had, knowing it was with him. The voice telepathically urging him forward. "Attacksss...killssss the ogre."

Anthall rolled onto his front and pushed himself up into a standing position -- no small feat for a man in full-plate armor. Once back on his feet, he had a clear path to the ogre as Krykl and the bugbears had left nothing but death and desolation behind them. Anthall knew he was hurt badly, and he could easily escape to the west, but his men had sacrificed themselves and done exactly what he had asked them to do: get him to the ogre. 'No,' he thought to himself, he could not dishonor their sacrifice, and he began closing the distance to Krykl.

Slice, sensing Anthall's desire to kill, fed the urge. "Attack the ogre," he hissed, "Yesss, vengeance..."

"Soulmite, guide my strike," Anthall said out loud, feeling the adrenaline rushing through his body. Anthall's eyes glowed red from behind the mask, which as the sun sank lower in the sky, made him look like a demon walking on the surface of Kardoon. Raising Slice, Anthall began moving quickly toward where he had last seen the ogre. "Come on," urged Anthall in a whisper, "shoot your damn bow one more time..." A moment later, the air cracked with the sound of another massive arrow being shot by Krykl, and then the ogre blinked back into visibility. Anthall didn't waste any time. As Krykl reached toward the quiver of small javelins that hung by his side, Anthall struck, swinging Slice with all his might. The vorpal blade cleanly cut through the forearm of the ogre mage the dismembered limb falling to the ground. Before Krykl could react Anthall gracefully spun and swung another mighty blow, this time at the exposed leg of the ogre. The blade struck soundly with a thud as metal met bone, but it failed to sever the leg. Krykl growled in pain, his face contorting into a savage look of hatred. Krykl swung his huge bow but Anthall ducked and backed away, dodging the attack. The remaining bugbears that were still escorting the ogre turned to look back at what was happening and Anthall knew he did not have much time. Krykl's arm was no longer bleeding, and the wound on its leg was already starting to show signs of closing.

"Damn it to hell...regeneration," Anthall whispered to himself. These were creatures worthy of myth, he thought to himself. Without losing any more valuable time, Anthall charged, using his favorite technique of feinting low and attacking high. As he raised his blade and moved in he swung low which the ogre tried to parry with its bow, but as it maneuvered the bow to block the blow, there was nothing there but air, as Anthall arced his arm high striking at the ogre's chest. The blade tore a large hole in the light armor and cut into Krykl's flesh. Anthall pivoted on his right foot and stabbed Slice into Krykl's side. As he pulled the sword out, dark blood gushed from the wound and the large ogre mage sunk to one knee, but as it did so, he swung his bow in a low sweep, smashing into Anthall's side and knocking him back to the ground. As Anthall struggled back to his feet, he could see the ogre holding its side with its remaining hand, and curiously seemed to be looking for something on the ground.

Krykl searched the ground for his severed limb, since he could simply reattach it. The ogre cursed as he sifted and kicked dead bodies, both human and bugbear, out of the way, but the severed hand remained hidden. He could see Anthall getting back to his feet. "What do you think you are doing, General?" Krykl shouted in the common language at the mysterious human wearing the death mask helmet. "I was not supposed to be attacked like this...this was not the plan."

Anthall, now back on his feet, could see the bugbears were almost upon him. "I do not know what trickery you are speaking of, but I am going to make sure you do not outlive me today."

Krykl, still on one knee, glowered at Anthall, hatred contorting his face into pure evil. "You were supposed to be nothing more than a sacrifice today by Marshal Krugar, but instead, Anthall Mixnor, you have marked your family for death. I will track down anyone related to you and feed them to a pack of gnolls."

Anthall hesitated for a second when he heard his name. "How -- how do you know my name?" he asked.

Krykl let out a deep guttural laugh. "You really are a pawn, and a naive and stupid one as well. You will not survive the day, but you will die knowing that you have damned all your relations to a fate worse than death. I will see to that."

The rage boiled up inside Anthall and he resumed his charge. "I may die but I will wipe you from the face of Kardoon first!" In a flash he was on the ogre mage and Slice was in a high arc, on track for the ogre's neck. But just before the impact of the blade, Krykl vanished and was replaced by a greenish gaseous form. The blade passed harmlessly through it, sending ripples through the green gas like a pebble dropping into a pond. Anthall swung maniacally but the green gas coiled upwards in the air, hanging there for a moment, a small angry cloud above him, before flying off to the west.

Anthall spun around to see five bugbears, cautiously moving closer to him, spreading out to encircle him. "Your ogre is dead!" he yelled at them and made a threatening feint in their direction. The bugbears halted and moved backwards, a look of uncertainty on their bulldog-like faces. Anthall thought they might break and run, but their resolve stiffened and they began to close in on him again. Anthall raised Slice. 'I never did like defense,' he thought to himself.

Slice hissed his encouragement, "No defenssssse, attacksssssss."

Without hesitation, Anthall charged the two bugbears directly in front of him. Slice whirled in a deadly arc in front of him as he advanced. It wasn't an effective method of attack, but it was a good show of force that Anthall knew was liable to strike fear into weaker opponents. It worked! First, one bugbear fled in a panic, causing the others to halt their advance. At that moment, Anthall struck two quick and decisive blows to the bugbear nearest to him, the first blow disarming the bugbear of its ax, and Anthall's second attack successfully stabbing the bugbear through its heart. The large beast shuddered and fell as he withdrew Slice. The three remaining bugbears attacked simultaneously, swinging their large axes wildly but with so much power that it was difficult to parry. Anthall managed to deflect one blow with Slice and ducked underneath the second ax but the third bugbear struck him in the back with a downward strike. His armor dented in by the blow, punctured his back, but saved him from certain death. Spinning around Anthall swung Slice at the legs of the bugbear who had struck him. His first attack was parried by the bugbear's ax, but Anthall was too quick for the beast, and followed up with an overhand attack which managed to sever the bugbears head. The headless bugbear stood for a moment, took a half step, then crumpled to the ground next to its head. There were two bugbears left. One was taller and even bigger the rest, and it threw its ax onto the ground and charged Anthall with its bare hands. Surprised by the tactic, the bugbear caught Anthall off guard and easily tackled the smaller human. The bugbear grappled with Anthall and managed to get a hold of Anthall's arms, which he then pinned to the ground. Anthall was too restricted by his armor to do much in this position, and the bugbear was too heavy and strong to be moved. The remaining bugbear walked over to Anthall, an ugly grin on its face as it raised its ax, aiming for Anthall's neck. As it raised the ax to strike, Anthall's mind went to his family back in Telfar, and feared what Krykl had said to him. Was there nothing he could do? His mind raced as the ax had nearly reached its zenith. The blade hovered for a second, the bugbear savoring the moment, but just then Anthall could hear the sound of hooves beating the ground and the bugbear's expression changed from gloating to horror. The bugbear about to strike, bolted away at a sprint. The bugbear on top of Anthall swung a fist and clubbed Anthall's face and head several times before it too jumped up and sprinted to the west in retreat.

As Anthall struggled to sit up in his armor to see what was going on, a large force of human cavalry galloped around and past him, kicking up the ground and causing dirt to fly around him like an angry sandstorm. The soldiers were hooting and hollering, using their lances to drive the remaining bugbears to the west. Anthall, finally getting to his feet, could hardly believe it. Watching the cavalry chasing the bugbears, now in retreat, could feel that his jaw had been hurt very badly from the bugbear that had flailed on his head. Thankfully his helmet had saved him from a worse beating, but his jaw had been exposed, and he could taste the familiar and salty flavor of blood in his mouth. It hurt to spit the blood out, but he tried as best he could.

"Sir, we did it!" shouted an excited soldier from behind Anthall.

Anthall staggered a bit but managed to turn around and face the new voice, causing the soldier to take two steps backwards at the sight. The sun had almost set and Anthall presented a fearful sight, blood dripping from his battered face and mouth, the metal skull with the two fiery red eyes burning fiercely. Anthall's armor was coated with blood, some his own, and some from the ogre and bugbears. Slice was also covered in blood, with Anthall using it like a cane, the tip digging into the ground. Anthall could hardly speak, his jaw was broken and face was already swelling up.

"By the gods, sir, you need a cleric something awful," said the soldier. "Just...um, just relax and sit down there, and I will fetch one." The soldier turned to run and do as he had said, but then paused and said, "It is an honor, sir, to serve with you. We all saw what you and your soldiers did charging that...that thing. It was an incredible thing you did today. You won the battle for Kardoon!" Then the man turned again and raced back toward the human lines where a cleric could be found.

Anthall looked around and spotted a rock which was large enough to sit against. He limped his way over, continuing to use Slice for support. Once there, he gingerly lowered himself to one knee, then onto his rear, and sat down, grimacing as the armor irritated the gash in his back from the bugbear blow. One of his legs was bent, the other was straight on the ground and he rested his arm on his elevated knee. "How the hell did that ogre know my name?" Anthall asked himself. Then his thoughts turned to Telfar, 'I need to get home...to Fey,' he thought. Taking off the gauntlet from his left hand, he examined the clean platinum ring on his finger. As he did so, he began to feel light-headed, and he could feel the warm flow of blood running down his back. "I must stay awake," he said out loud to himself, but it was growing darker and as the sun set he could feel a chill taking hold of him. Anthall, fighting to keep his head up, tried to reach up and remove his helmet, but his arms were too heavy, and his head slowly bobbed down to his chest. Weary and bleeding, feeling his life force literally draining away, he could only stare at the ground as the light faded away. Barely conscious of the activity around him, his thoughts kept going back home. Anthall struggled to open his eyes one more time, but he could not lift his head, and as a result, he could only see the leather-booted feet of someone near him; the person knelt down onto one knee and began talking, whether to him or to someone else he could not tell. The words, although familiar, tumbled incomprehensibly through his mind. Summoning his last reserve of energy, Anthall managed to say in a choking voice, "Bring...me...to...Telfar." The darkness became complete, and he could feel his body sliding sideways, the metallic sound of his armor scraping the boulder behind him as he fell sideways toward the ground.

.

CHAPTER THIRTEEN
Isa

YEAR: AG 1175, Month of Sepu

THE DRIP ERUPTED IN A CHORUS OF SHOUTS, jeers, encouragements, and trash talking, resulting in a din that could be heard all throughout Telfar, a situation that the guards in the towers found concerning and eyed with a heightened level of scrutiny. Outside it was loud, but inside the Drip, the sound was deafening. Tyberius was the first to make his move, and pulling with all his might, he managed to get the monk's arm about halfway down to the table, but at that point, the monk began slowly forcing Tyberius's arm back up until their hands were back into the starting position.

"Good lord," said Mikell, "look at the face of the monk -- he looks like he is on a picnic -- or like he might start knitting a sweater or something."

"How can he be so calm and steady?" complained Ariana.

In stark contrast, Tyberius's face was already flushed red, with beads of sweat rolling down the sides of his face, stinging the open cut on his lip. "You..will...not...win," he said between breaths. But as he said so, the monk began to pull even harder, and Tyberius watched with horror as his arm slowly began to move downward toward the table.

Ariana moved closer, nearly shouting into Tyberius's ear, "Fight him, Ty, fight him!!"

York moved quickly to get between Ariana and Tyberius. "No touching, no interference!! Get back, get back!!" He grabbed Ariana by the shoulders and began to push her backwards toward Mikell.

The monk continued to effortlessly pull Tyberius's hand toward the table. As their hands neared the table, Tyberius saw York pushing a struggling Ariana backwards and he felt a rage growing inside himself, one which he had never felt before. With the salty taste of blood and sweat on his tongue, Tyberius felt his body start to quiver, his skin, already flushed began to develop blotches of purplish red as blood vessels burst, his skin seemed to visibly burn. Blood vessels in his eyes began to pop, causing large patches of red to appear in the corner of his narrowing eyes. The veins in his face and on his arms began to bulge and appeared where previously there were none.

"Oh, my god what is happening to him! Stop the fight! Stop the fight!" Screamed Ariana.

York looked over his shoulder, as he tried to restrain Ariana, and he could hardly believe what he was seeing. "No! The fight must go on!" he shouted, releasing Ariana and returning his attention to the match. At first, their hands just stopped moving, Tyberius's hand hovering an inch above the table, then to the amazement of everyone in the room, their hands began to move upwards again, ever so slowly and, for the first time, the monk's face was now beginning to show signs of the stress. It started with just a bead of sweat trickling down the side of his ashen face, then as their hands began to move closer and closer to the top position, the half-orc began to grit his teeth and growl.

The monk, taking a deep breath, let out a loud, "Ki-a!!" and with all his might, pulled on Tyberius's arm. But there was no effect, and Tyberius continued raising their entangled hands. Finally, at the top again, the monk summoned his strength again, with another loud "Ki-a!!" and their hands bobbed back and forth at the pinnacle of the arc.

It was almost imperceptible at first, but Tyberius began a low howl, and as he continued it became increasingly loud. As he howled with increasing rage, bloodstained tears began to drip from the inside of his eyes and trickle down his cheek, leaving a bloody trail. The monk, matched his howl, with his own deep-chested growl, and the two combatants' world narrowed to the small table where they each fought, as if their lives depended on the outcome. Their hands quivered for a moment at the top before Tyberius let out another blood-curdling howl, at which point blood began dripping from his left nostril, the droplets getting hung up in, and ricocheting through, the red hairs of his goatee. Feeling his hand begin to move the wrong way, the monk's eyes widened in disbelief, and in the next instant Tyberius smashed the monk's hand through the Taper wood table, shattering it. The half-orc, knocked off balance, was flung to the ground. Tyberius, releasing the half-orc's hand, leapt up, causing his chair to tumble backwards and what remained of the table was knocked over by his knees, raising two fists up in the air he let out another long howl of excitement. The blood vessels in his arms, having ruptured were creating large blotches of dark black circles under his skin and he stumbled forward a step causing the people in the crowd to fall back on each other in an attempt to get out of the way of the large, tall, crazed man before them. However, he didn't make it more than a step, before collapsing face first onto the floor of the tavern.

Mikell and Ariana ran forward, kneeling beside him. Brutal started to follow them, but Mikell shouted back at him, "No, go get our bag of coins!"

Brutal's head snapped backwards to look at the shattered table. The clay bowl lay broken on the floor, the gold pieces it once held were now scattered about the floor, and the bag was nowhere to be seen. The crowd was in a frenzy, not only from the spectacle of what had just happened, but folks were fighting over the gold coins that had spilled from the now shattered clay bowl. Brutal joined the melee ensuing in the room, and began pushing and punching people who would not get out of his way as he searched. Julius joined him and together they were able to clear out some space, but the bag was still nowhere to be found.

"Tyberius! Tyberius, are you okay?" shouted Ariana, grabbing his shoulder.

Tyberius rolled onto his back, his face streaked with blood, his red eyes presenting a gruesome sight, but his grin was back, exposing his teeth, which were normally pure white but were now tainted red with blood. "I knew...I could win..." he managed to say in a broken voice.

"Are you okay? What happened to you?" asked Mikell somewhat frantically.

Tyberius looked at Mikell and struggled to lean up on his elbows. "Ain't it obvious?" he said, and after a short coughing fit, finished, "I fuckin' won!"

"We know you won, but look at you -- you are a mess," said Mikell, touching Tyberius's left arm.

"This?" Tyberius said, using his right forearm to wipe some of the blood from his face. "This ain't nothing." Then something caught Tyberius's attention. Ariana and Mikell looked behind them and saw the monk, holding his left hand, sitting up. "Hey! Hey you!" Tyberius shouted.

The monk, hearing Tyberius, looked at him, his stoic expression once again on display.

Tyberius was still grinning, the blood in his mouth making his teeth look stained. "I am left handed, too," he said as he held up his left hand.

It took a second for the monk to register the comment, but finally comprehending, a semblance of a grin formed at the corner of his mouth, curling around his upward tusk-like teeth, and he nodded its head.

Meanwhile, York was going wild. "The greatest victory ever!! The greatest victory! Kings and queens will be paying me for years to retell this story!"

Brutal and Julius came over to join Mikell, Ariana, and Tyberius. "We cannot find the bag!" Brutal said in exasperation.

"I feared as much," said Mikell.

"We lost the gold?" asked Tyberius. Everyone turned to look at Tyberius, and he could tell right away the answer was 'yes.' It was gone... and it was his fault. "Shit...sorry, guys," he said.

Brutal, seeing Mikell looking around the room, said, "We looked everywhere, Mikell, it is not here."

"I am not looking for the bag," said Mikell.

"What are you looking then?" asked Brutal.

Ariana spoke first. "Not what...but who," she said.

"Aye," said Mikell.

That's when it dawned on Brutal. "Well, Bealty would not hang around at a tavern brawl. He probably took off once the chaos broke out," said Brutal.

"Nuh-uh," said Mikell. "I am thinking two things right now…"

Ariana cut Mikell off and said, "Missing halfling and missing bag of gold. That is no coincidence."

"Aye," said Mikell, grinning. "I…well, we, only have two gold pieces left," he said, tapping his belt pouch, "but since we are betting everything tonight, I bet these last two gold pieces that our bag is safe and sound. If you can call being in the hands of a halfling, safe and sound."

"I hope you are right," said Tyberius, who, feeling his strength beginning to return, started to stand up, whereupon Brutal helped lift him back to his feet. "Nice right hook, you have there," he said, patting Brutal on the side of the shoulder, and then rubbing his left chin.

"Believe me, it was my pleasure," Brutal said with his own grin. "By the way, why did you want to get punched?"

Tyberius winked at his friend. "I felt I needed a little incentive." Tyberius walked over to the monk, who was still sitting on the floor, and extended his right hand down, which the monk took. Tyberius helped him back onto his feet and while their hands were still clasped, gave it a friendly shake. "Well met, what is your name?"

"Me is Isa," the monk said, placing his hands over his chest and gave Tyberius a respectful nod.

"I am Tyberius…well, I guess you know that already," Tyberius said with a little laugh, thinking of all the times York had yelled it out. "This is Ariana, Mikell, Julius, and Brutal," he continued, pointing them out as he named them off. "They are my friends, and now you are, too."

"Yes," said Isa, with no perceptible emotion.

Ariana stepped forward. "If you do not mind me asking, but how did you and York become a team, I mean, no offense, but you seem like an odd couple."

Isa's brow furrowed trying to translate the question. "Let me answer that question for Isa," said York, who had apparently overheard the question and inserted himself into the middle of the group. "I did not even know his name until now, as we just met here at the Drip. In fact, I just took it upon myself to kind of help build up the intensity of the challenge," he said, balling up his fists in the air, then with one hand he cupped the side of his mouth as if telling a secret, "I mean, after all, it was just arm wrestling."

Ariana looked at Isa and asked, "You do not know York?"

"No," said Isa.

Ariana looked back at York. "So what is in this for you?"

"Is it not obvious?" asked York, smiling and holding out his arms dramatically. Not seeing any comprehension in their faces, his arms fell to his side, "I live in such an uncultured world," and after a short pause, he continued, "I am in it for the story -- for that is what I do," said York.

"You are a bard?" asked Mikell.

York's eyes sparkled at the recognition. "Aye, York O'Lurn, at your service!" he said with a deep bow, then continued, "Something about you all seems to scream 'story' to me -- so I must ask: what are your plans after today?" Nobody responded, creating an awkward silence. York looked at each of the companions, but no one answered his question. Smiling, he said, "Interesting -- well, that says a lot -- pun intended. Anyway, I am guessing you are not going home to farm potatoes or some such thing...If that is the case I will be heading somewhere else..." York paused, walking in and around, snakelike, amongst the small group, as he continued, "but something tells me that is not the case. I am guessing it is someplace much more interesting." Making his way full circle, saying, "If that were the case, I would like to join forces with you. I am good with my longsword," he said, patting the sword hanging at his side.

"Join forces?" asked Tyberius with a chuckle. "We are not an army."

York, ignoring the slight on his choice of words, responded quickly, "Yes, Tyberius! Join forces!" he said, raising his voice and fists as he said it.

"We appreciate the offer, York," said Mikell, folding his arms across his thick chest, "but let us think about it. We need to collect our thoughts after what has happened here."

"As you wish," said York with a dramatic wave of his hand, "you will find me here when you have your answer."

"Isa go with you," Isa said pointing to Tyberius. "Three ten day," he said, holding up three thick fingers.

"Sure," said Tyberius somewhat awkwardly, "glad to have you along."

Noticing the crowd within the Drip was beginning to thin out now that all the gold had been picked up, and that there would be no more arm wrestling matches, Mikell put his hand on the broad shoulder of Isa and said, "Sorry about your bowl of gold...."

"Oh shit, your gold!" interrupted Tyberius with a concerned look on his face.

Isa's stoic expression did not waver, and he said, "It be Craven's will," referring to the neutral god of combat. As with all eight of the domains, combat was covered by a good, neutral, and evil deity. While good and evil struggled against each other, Craven sought to maintain a balance.

Mikell, recognizing the reference to the neutral god, frowned at the monk's statement, and taking his hand off the monk's shoulder, said, "Isa, you should wait here with York while my friends and I go discuss what we need to do next," he said. motioning the others to leave the Drip. Isa looked at Tyberius, as if seeking his direction.

Tyberius, hesitating, earned a quick pinch in the back from Ariana. Seeing the look in her eyes, Tyberius said, "Ah, yes... Isa, you ought to wait here with York." With that, Isa folded his hands into his robe, picked up his chair that had tipped over, and sat back down, the broken table lying in pieces at his feet. York ventured back toward the bar and was soon speaking to Syd. The small group of friends headed out the north door of the Drip to find themselves in the street once again where the sun was getting close to setting and the chill of the night was starting to make its presence felt.

Hammer was outside waiting, and upon seeing Tyberius, he walked up and gave the tall warrior a shove, and said, "That was our fucking coin -- not yours to gamble away!"

Tyberius held his ground, the push not being very effective, and quickly straightened himself up and started to move toward Hammer threateningly. Brutal interposed himself between the two fighters and put a hand on each to keep them apart, saying, "Enough fighting already, save it for tomorrow!"

"Will there even be a tomorrow?" asked Hammer in a cynical tone. "How can we gear up with no coin? Or do we go into battle with sticks and stones?"

"He is right," said Mikell. "We need to find our bag of coins."

"But I thought I heard people coming out saying Tyberius won. Did he not?" asked Hammer.

Brutal replied, "Yes, he won, but the bag was lost during the confusion, when it was over."

Hammer gave Tyberius another menacing look and pointing his finger, said, "This is all your fault, Tyberius!"

"Bealty has the gold," interjected Ariana flatly, causing Hammer and the others to change their focus to her.

Mikell quickly added, "Well, we think he might have the bag, since he seems to have disappeared as well."

Ariana smiled, sure of herself, and said, "He has it," then pointing at the upstairs window of the temple down the street. "He's up there right now, with the bag...and probably snooping through all our stuff as well." She smiled, seeing everyone had the same quizzical expressions on their faces.

Mikell was the first to speak. "How do you know that?"

Ariana, still smiling, held out the open palm of her hand to Mikell, saying, "Give me the two gold pieces. Tyberius and I will head over to the Gustav. We will meet the rest of you there." There was a moment of hesitation, and then Mikell slowly handed Ariana the coins, and with that she turned and headed down the street alone.

Tyberius backed away from the group a step or two, saying, "Well, uh, I guess I will see y'all over at the Gustav," and then he turned, and with his typical speed, caught up to Ariana, and soon they were out of sight, turning down the main street heading toward the Gustav Inn.

Hammer broke the silence as Tyberius left. "So, summing up the situation: a halfling has our stash and he is rummaging through all our stuff as we speak?" Before anyone could answer, he added, "Wonderful."

* * * *

Ariana's prediction proved to be right. After a brief detour to collect the halfling from the upstairs of Mikell's temple, Brutal, Mikell, Bealty, Julius, and Hammer made their way to the Gustav Inn. The interior was similar to the Drip in size, but the atmosphere was much different. Whereas the Drip appealed to the more mercenary and adventurous, the Gustav Inn was more of a local favorite for getting a good simple meal or drink in a comparatively safer, if not slightly boring, environment. The tables were meticulously clean, and subdued conversations intermingled to create a steady, but soft buzz. There were eight circular tables, each with five finely crafted chairs -- all the wood had a dark stain giving the room an elegant appearance. Fine white curtains adorned the windows along the eastern wall, overlooking the street.

"Welcome to the Gustav Inn, Mikell," said a red-haired waitress carrying a tray with some empty mugs and plates. "Sit wherever you like." She motioned toward the empty tables.

"Hello, Jory," said Mikell. "Actually, those are my friends right over there," said Mikell, pointing.

Jory smiled. "Excellent, I will be right with you," she said as she disappeared through an opening protected by two swinging doors.

Tyberius waved as the others made their way to the table. Hammer and Brutal borrowed chairs from the empty table next to theirs and sat down. Bealty turned his chair sideways and sat on the arm of the chair, which lifted him up sufficiently to sit comfortably at the relatively gigantic table.

Mikell sat down, placing the missing bag of gold onto the table in front of him. "Thanks to Bealty, we have our gold back, plus he was able to contribute almost three hundred more gold," Mikell added with a pat on the halfling's back. Everyone at the table had a pleased look on their face, with the exception of Ariana, who sat with her arms crossed.

"Well, now that we have the extra gold from the victims in Whiteal," said Ariana, "we should head over to Boral's to get our equipment." Bealty sat quietly, ignoring her predictable jab.

"What victims?" asked Brutal. "You did not steal that money, did you?"

Bealty shook his head. "No. I helped my uncle do some extra work with his lock-smithy."

Brutal looked at Ariana. "See -- he did not steal it."

Ariana snorted. "Do not be so naive, Brutal."

"Yeah, well either way," added Hammer, "we better spend it before Tyberius finds some crazy nun sitting on a corner somewhere challenging folks to a push-up contest, or something."

"I did what I had to do," said Tyberius, his voice rising, as he stood up from the table. "If you have a problem with it, let us just settle it now." Seeing Tyberius stand up, Hammer, on the other side of the table, also rose from his chair, fists balled at his side. The chatter within the inn softened to whispers and the other patrons turned to look at the commotion.

"For the love of Zuel, sit your asses down," said Mikell, his voice gruff but hushed, motioning with his hands for his friends to take their seats, his balding forehead wrinkled from the frown on his face. "What is done is done, and it all worked out," then after a short pause, added, "some might even say for the best."

Jory, the waitress, hustled over to the table, deftly carrying seven mugs of ale on a tray. "Why not have a seat, boys?" she said as she handed out the mugs to everyone around the table. "If trouble is what you seek, you can find plenty of it elsewhere." On approaching Hammer, who was still standing, Jory held out a mug, which, after a moment, he took and then sat down, a pouty look lingering on his face. Tyberius also sat down, taking a long pull from his mug of ale, to help clear his mind. "Anything else I can get you?" asked Jory.

"No, I believe we are fine, for now. Thank you, Jory," said Mikell.

With that, Jory gave Mikell a wink and, tucking the platter under her arm, said, "You gents let me know if you need anything," and then took her leave to go help other patrons.

Mikell, sitting back down, folding his arms on the table in front of him, said, "We all need to calm down, we have a very big day ahead of us, and we still have an important decision to make -- today." Mikell made sure to make eye contact with everyone as he spoke, making sure everyone was listening. "The monk is apparently living up to his promise to serve Tyberius for winning his match, but the question is..."

"Can we trust a half-orc we just met?" interjected Ariana. "And the same goes for the creepy bard."

"I like the monk," said Bealty, leaning onto the table with both elbows, his forearms interlocked in front of him, "she is quiet, but obviously pretty strong, and she kept her word right away to Tyberius -- so she seems trustworthy to me." Bealty, seeing the quizzical expressions on everyone's face, looked over his shoulder to see if he was missing something going on behind him, but seeing nothing other than the other patrons enjoying their quiet meals, he looked back at his friends, "What?" he asked, one eyebrow elevating in curiosity.

Brutal broke the momentary silence. "Did you say she?"

The curiosity passing, Bealty's eyebrow returned to its resting position, and he chuckled a bit, saying, "Yeah...Isa is a girl." Then pausing for a second and sitting up straighter, a little doubt creeping into his voice, he asked, "So, you all think Isa is male?"

"There ain't no girl in all of Kardoon that is that strong," said Tyberius, "except maybe some damn giant or such -- and that ain't the same thing."

Mikell asked, "What makes you think Isa is a girl?"

Bealty considered that for a moment. "She looks like a girl," then quickly clarified, "well, a half-orc girl."

"So, you are an expert now of half-orcs?" asked Brutal somewhat skeptically. "I agree with Tyberius -- there is no way Isa is a girl...he is too strong."

"Gods, I wish I had not left -- I cannot believe I missed all this," said Hammer said, throwing his hands up in mock despair.

"I guess, in the end it does not matter," said Mikell, "although it seems odd now not to know, but it really has no bearing on whether we trust him," then looking at Bealty, added, "or her."

"We can debate this all day long, so I say we each say yea or nay to Isa being allowed to go with us," said Brutal, "then we each get our say and we live with the consequences." Everyone around the table nodded in agreement, and Brutal, nodding in accord as well, said, "Okay then, I will start. I say 'Aye' to Isa traveling with us."

Bealty, sitting to the left of Brutal, spoke next. "Aye. I like her," he said with a devilish smirk on his small face, then added with a wink, "alright. . . him."

"Aye, anyone that can beat Tyberius in arm wrestling," said Hammer next in turn, "man or woman, is welcome to fight with me."

Hammer, stressing the word 'woman,' drew a faint growl from Tyberius.

Julius, crossing his arms, sat back in his chair, saying, "I say 'Nay.' I have never trusted half-orcs, their orc blood taints all their decisions. You all would be wise to heed my advice."

Mikell squinted and rubbed his brow as the turn passed to him, "I must admit I am conflicted. I can read people pretty well, and I think Isa is trustworthy," Mikell paused, reflecting and uncertain, "but he mentioned Craven -- which is not a deity of the light -- but of the shadow."

"What the hell does that mean?" asked Tyberius.

Mikell, concern etching the corner of his eyes, said, "Those who worship the shadow gods exist between light and darkness. A shadow cannot exist without light, but neither can it exist in total darkness."

Seeing the confusion on Tyberius's face, Brutal said, "It means Isa worships a god who is neither good nor evil -- but neutral."

"Oh," said Tyberius, taking a long pull from his mug, leaving bubbles of foam in his red goatee.

Mikell covered his eyes with his hands and sat silently for a few seconds, deep in prayer. "People who live in the shadows live a life of balance, and for whatever reason, I believe our goals are complementary and that he can help us. He is strong and, at least for now, is bound to Tyberius by his oath, which I trust, coming from a monk." Mikell, with a slight grimace, finished, "So for now, I say 'Aye.'"

Tyberius, being next, began to speak, but Ariana cut him off. "I cannot believe you all are trusting Isa. We know nothing about him and we are going into a life and death situation tomorrow." Looking around the table, nobody, except Bealty, would make eye contact with her.

Tyberius, taking advantage of the interlude, asked, "Do I get to vote now?"

Ariana shifted her focus to Tyberius, sitting next to her. "Do not be a dolt, they already have four aye's -- so it does not matter what we say."

Tyberius hesitated, then complained, "What are you talking about -- but I have not voted yet."

Mikell put a friendly hand on Tyberius's shoulder and gave it a hard squeeze. "Say your piece, Ty, we want to hear it."

Tyberius smiled his big grin. "I say 'Aye,' I want Isa to come with us."

Ariana smoldered. "Oh, of course... You just want a slave for thirty days."

"Not true," said Tyberius, "if he can fight half as well as he wrestles, he will help us. I take it you are a 'Nay'?"

Ariana sat back in her chair, crossing her arms. "Julius and I are the only two sane ones here I think."

Mikell smiled at the comment, saying, "Then five to two, Isa will come with us."

Tyberius was still grinning, and, under his breath, he muttered, "Yes..."

"Now, how about York?" asked Brutal. "I will start again, and I say 'Aye,' we can use all the help we can get, and if money becomes tight, maybe he can help us earn some coin."

Bealty started to sit up, but Ariana jumped in, giving the halfling a defiant look, saying, "We will go this way around the table this time," she said, twirling her finger around the table in her direction. Bealty shrugged and put his arms back on the table. Pleased with her abduction of the process, using her index finger, pointing like a dart into the table, tapping it to make her points, she said, "York is not to be trusted and he does not have our interests at heart, so I vote 'Nay.'"

Tyberius put his arm around Ariana. "I do not trust him neither. Nay."

Interlocking his fingers on the table in front of him, Mikell said, "He seems opportunistic, and my gut is telling me, 'Nay.'" At the mention of the word gut, Brutal and Tyberius both snickered. Mikell gave them both a fatherly look and added, patting his large belly. "Very funny boys. It is big, but also, seldom wrong."

Julius was next and was still sitting cross-armed. "York is elven, and I will not judge him poorly just because he is a bard. He can be helpful, too. I vote 'Aye.'"

Hammer, pushing with his feet against the sturdy legs of the table, leaning back, his chair tottering on the back two legs, holding onto the mug of beer that was cradled in his lap, smiled and said, "I do not know what good a bard is in a fight, but the more the merrier. I say 'Aye.'"

Ariana's smile, which began when Mikell had voted 'Nay,' vanished when the vote, tied at 3-3, passed to Bealty for the deciding ballot. "You have to be kidding me," she said.

Bealty, never one to easily take offense, just smiled his boyish smile. "It may come as a surprise to most of you, but keep in mind I have spent more time in Whiteal, a larger city, than any of you." Bealty raised the gigantic looking mug to his lips and took a sip of the warm ale. Wiping his mouth with the sleeve of his shirt, he continued, "So I think I can say with some confidence that I may have the most knowledge of what a bard can do."

"Oh please, spare us the story," said Ariana, "just because you sit in taverns all day does not make you an expert on bards."

Bealty nodded, as if agreeing with her comment. "If I just sat in bars, that would be a great point," he said, pointing his small index finger upwards into the air, intentionally making sure it could not be interpreted as pointing in her direction. Ariana crossed her arms and sat back in her chair, purposefully looking away from the halfling. Bealty continued, "I watch people all the time, and you are right, Ariana," this caught her attention, and she looked back at the halfling as he continued, "bards probably should not be trusted. However, they are very resourceful, and their knowledge of lore is second to none, not to mention the music played by an experienced bard is magical. I know," he said, tapping his chest, "I have felt it."

Tyberius scratched his chin under his scruffy goatee. "So, what the hell are you saying? Is that a 'Nay'?"

Bealty smiled again. "I think we need to keep an eye on him, but I think he can help. I say 'Aye.'"

"There you have it," said Mikell, lightly pounding the table, like the gavel of a judge, with his fist. "They both will come with us." Folding his hands together in prayer, he said, "Praise Zuel. Bless us on our journey tomorrow and grant us your favor for what will be, no doubt, a trying day. Give us each the strength to overcome whatever evil we may face. In your name, we go forward, lovers of the light, with which we will stamp out the darkness."

"Shadows and darkness? I do not know about that mumbo jumbo," said Tyberius, "but I am ready to kick some serious ass tomorrow."

"I can see disappointment on some of your faces," said Brutal, "but they are volunteering to come along, and we need their help. If one, or both, of them does something that proves them to be untrustworthy, then we will deal with that then."

"I hope their deceit becomes apparent at an opportune time," said Ariana, "-- but I fear it will be at the most inopportune time."

Brutal sighed, the discontent weighing on him. "We will see... what is done is done. Let us finish our ale and head over to Boral's and get our equipment." The conversation around the table was minimal, but everyone was able to finally relax, sipping their ale and enjoying the calm, friendly atmosphere of the Gustav.

* * * *

Boral's Black-smithy was one of the oldest buildings in Telfar, having been built long before the walls were constructed. It was one of the few buildings not constructed of Taper wood -- but rather it was constructed of finely carved granite -- the rocks being taken from the banks of the Great White River -- giving the large shop a fortress-like appearance. As sturdy and strong as the construction was, it had an ugly, functional look. Combined with the ominous look, the almost continuous plume of dark, sooty, smoke wafting out of the chimney, located in the center of the structure, made it the most detested building by the inhabitants of Telfar. The Boral family had a long tradition of craftsmanship and was known for the lethally sharp blades that they produced -- necessary for the loggers to be able to cut the hard Taper wood trees down, and for the craftsman like bow makers, fletchers, and carpenters, to hone and work the wood into the useful buildings, ships, and weaponry. But the Boral family was most known, at least locally, not for their products or their uninviting architecture, but their dwarven ethnicity -- a race which was seldom encountered outside of the hills or mountainous regions of Kardoon. This made Boral and his small family, consisting of his wife, daughter, and son, an oddity, and at the same time a necessary component in the lifeblood of Telfar itself.

"I have everything I need already, so I am going to head back to the temple," said Julius.

"It is probably a good idea one of us is back there anyway, thanks for going, Julius," said Brutal. "Hammer, you are equipped, too, are you not?"

"Yeah, but I have never been inside Boral's before," said Hammer, "so I would like to see it -- I have heard a lot about it."

"In the years," said Julius, holding up the palm of his hand, citing an old elvish saying; because of their long life spans, which made them think in years, not days or hours, and their aversion to the finality of goodbyes, over time they adopted the abbreviated valediction. Without any further hesitation, Julius turned and began making his way back toward the Temple of Zuel.

"That was a strange thing to say," said Hammer, watching the half-elf moving away.

"That is just the elf in him," said Tyberius, "that is just his way of sayin' 'see you later.'"

"I ain't been around elves too much, so I do not know their ways," said Hammer as he and the others, Brutal, Mikell, Tyberius, Ariana, and Bealty made their way across the street to the door of Boral's Blacksmith. Looking up at the tall granite double doors, Hammer was expecting the doors to be heavy. He was surprised, grasping the door handle, at how easily, and quietly, the door swung open for him. "Whoa, that is amazing!" he exclaimed.

"Nobody makes a stone door better than a dwarf," said Bealty as he darted between Hammer's legs to be the first inside, easily squeezing between the small, initial, opening of the doors. The rest of the group followed. Inside, it was much darker since there were only slits in the walls to allow the fading sunlight inside -- most of the light coming from lanterns that hung along the walls and on the stone pillars holding up the massive stone ceiling. The flickering lanterns gave the space an unnatural feel, causing shadows to dance along the walls, as well as producing the acrid smell of burning oil. As large as the area was, it had the feeling of a cramped space, due to the massive number of items for sale which were hung, stacked, shelved, and piled along the walls and on the floor --

the pathway for customers to navigate the store consisted of well-worn granite tiles lined by a Taper wood railings.

Hammer stared around the vast store and the myriad of items it offered for sale -- almost any weapon or armor imaginable, and even some that were unimaginable. "By the gods, I have never seen such a sight," said Hammer, gently feeling the fabric of a cloak that was hanging on one of the stone pillars near the doors.

"My father is almost 130 years old now," said a low gruff voice from somewhere around the pillar, and from which appeared a stocky dwarf, just over four feet tall. His long orange beard was twisted into three rope-like braids, with colorful beads adorning it. Approaching Hammer, with both hands clasped behind his back and at ease, he continued, "and over that many years one acquires many things," then swinging an arm behind him in an arc, "in fact, all the things you see here today." The dwarf smiled at his new guests and, bowing his head slightly, said, "Well met, all of you, and welcome to Boral's. I am Kerkrand Whitrock, son of Boral Whitrock." Pointing to the cloak Hammer was touching, the dwarf continued, "You have fine taste, that cloak is magical and will help protect its wearer from melee blows of all kind."

Hammer let go of the cloak's sleeve. "No shit? It feels like a normal cloak to me, how much does it cost?"

Kerkrand took a step closer, looking up at the taller human. "For you, today, 950 gold." Kerkrand, seeing Hammer's eyebrows raise up, smiled. "Surprised, I see?" he asked rhetorically. "Well, maybe another day," he added to change the subject and save Hammer and the rest of the group any embarrassment. "Now you can see why we have accumulated so much over time...I wager that you all are probably interested in something more practical and," he said, holding up a finger in front of him, "functional."

Mikell stepped forward. "Excuse us," he said apologetically, "but we need to equip ourselves for a long journey, which will be dangerous."

Kerkrand, transforming his raised hand from just a finger to an open hand, waved it for Mikell to stop. "Say no more. Shall we start with armor or weapons?"

As Mikell began to turn, looking to see if his friends had a preference, Tyberius blurted out from the back of the group, "Weapons! We want to see the bad-ass weapons!"

Mikell smiled, turning back to Kerkrand, and clapped his hand in front of him, saying, "Well, weapons it is, please lead the way." As the rest of the group moved off to follow Kerkrand, nobody noticed Ariana, something catching her eye, move off in a different direction. Zig-zagging their way through the maze of items, Kerkrand took them to the back wall. Tyberius's eyes lit up, gawking at the vicious array of weaponry to choose from.

"Wow, this stuff is amazing," said Tyberius, still somewhat in awe of the display. "I thought I was going to just get a longsword, like Brutal," he said, pointing to his friend's weapon, "but now I do not think so."

Kerkrand smiled, pleased to see the positive reaction, "Do you have a preferred weapon?" he asked, straining to look up at the towering human.

Tyberius looked down and rubbed his chin through his scruffy beard. "Not really, I ain't had no call to arm myself, aside from my knife and bow for hunting."

"Hmmmm," said Kerkrand, "well, in that case, let me help you out, if I may." Walking over to a pile of weapons on a table, using two hands he hefted up a large, obviously heavy weapon. Carrying it back, he handed the weapon up to Tyberius. "Careful," he said, "this is a flail and has a ball attached to it which will fall when I let go." Tyberius grabbed the Taper wood handle, which had a leather grip, and with both hands lifted the flail out of Kerkrand's hands. The shaft was almost three feet long, the chain was another foot, and the spiked iron ball on the end was a little larger than a grapefruit. Kerkrand, backing up a step to give Tyberius a little extra room, said, "Being so tall, it would make sense for you to use a weapon that accentuates your reach." Pointing to a straw-stuffed dummy, he added, "There is a dummy target over in the corner if you want to take a few practice swings."

Tyberius, taking his eyes off the flail, looked up to see where the dwarf was pointing. "I do not know what ya just said about my reach, but I am going to take ya up on that -- and have a few swings at that thing," and with that, he took off down the aisle to the practice area.

Kerkrand turned his attention to Mikell. "Priest of Zuel, correct?"

Mikell smiled at the sound of his deity's name and nodded. "Yes, I will be needing..."

"A mace, most likely," Kerkrand interjected, finishing Mikell's sentence. "Of course, there are a variety of choices, but," pausing, he sized Mikell up while stroking his beard, "you look like a powerful fellow...yes, I do believe the heavy mace will be your best bet." Stepping past Mikell, Kerkrand pointed to a rack on the wall, which held more than a dozen heavy maces. "Try one of these."

Mikell looked over the inventory, but his eyes kept coming back to the same weapon. Unlike most of the weapons he could see, this one was entirely made of metal, even the handle. The intricately crafted handle had a woven pattern giving it a sticky texture that felt good to Mikell, while the shaft itself was solid metal, having three ring-like adornments spaced evenly along its length. The head of the mace was as destructive looking as it was beautiful -- the symmetry of the triangular knobs jutting outwardly that could deliver a punishing concussive blow while still piercing through armor. Mikell hefted the mace from its place on the wall with his right hand. Testing its balance by holding it at different angles, he took a few slow practice swings, then noticing the melancholy look on the dwarf's face, he stopped and asked, "Should I not practice here?"

Kerkrand composed himself, his smile returning. "This mace will serve you well, my father forged it twenty-five years ago -- I remember because he was very proud of it."

Mikell, taking a closer look at the mace, asked, "Is it special?"

Kerkrand smiled again. "Yes, in the sense that every now and then you just know when you have forged something...we call it Sundrudden -- which is difficult to translate," thinking for a brief moment, he continued, "well, I suppose it is best described as a combination of flawless and exceptional."

Mikell, stopping his inspection, let his arm with the mace glide back down to his side and, looking at Kerkrand, said, "We probably cannot afford what you are describing," and began putting the mace back onto the rack.

Kerkrand, putting his hands behind his back, shook his head side to side, saying, "Hold onto it, let us see what else is needed, and then we will negotiate the total purchase." Looking up, his eyes sparkling with the inherent stubbornness his race was known for, and brooking no argument, turned his attention to Brutal. "What do we have here?" asked Kerkrand rhetorically as he approached Brutal, and holding out his hand, asked, "May I see your blade?"

Brutal, lost in his thoughts as he looked around, was unable to conceal his surprise, snapping his head down at the expectant dwarf, "What -- me?" asked Brutal, "Ah, no, I already have a good weapon," he said, placing his hand on the hilt.

Kerkrand, continuing to hold out his hand, his smile returning, wrinkling the corners of his mouth, said, "Aye, I see ye have a longsword, would you let me give it a look?"

"Let him see it, he is the weapon expert," said Mikell. Brutal's fingers drummed hilt of his sword, but he did not draw the weapon. Seeing his friend hesitate, Mikell said, "He is not going to steal it, Brutal, he just wants to see it."

"Aye," said Kerkrand. "I have two reasons I would like to see it." The dwarf continued to stand, holding his hand out for the weapon, but said nothing more.

"What are the two reasons?" asked Brutal. The dwarf, flexing the fingers of his outstretched hand, silently urged Brutal to give him the sword. "Oh, fine, what do I care?" said Brutal, as he drew the sword from its scabbard and, turning it around, handed it to the dwarf hilt first.

"Thank you," said Kerkrand. The dwarf, reaching into a pouch on his belt and taking out a small glass eyepiece, examined the hilt closely, like a jeweler inspecting a diamond. After a few grunts, the dwarf moved his eyeglass to the blade. After drawing a few more ambiguous grunts, the dwarf turned around and began walking away from Brutal, heading toward the corner where Tyberius was still busy hitting the straw-stuffed dummy.

"Hey," said Brutal as he and his friends moved quickly to catch up to the dwarf, "where are you going?"

Kerkrand did not reply until they arrived outside the practice area, where he turned and offered the sword back to Brutal. Brutal took the weapon back, his eyebrows slightly furrowed, irritated by the dwarf. Kerkrand motioned with one arm for Brutal to enter the practice area. "Please, take your blade and strike the target."

Tyberius, seeing some of his friends watching, stopped swinging his huge flail. "I love this thing," he said, holding the weapon up in the air, his grin going from ear to ear.

"I am glad you like it, I thought you might," said Kerkrand. "Would you please allow your friend, here," he motioned to Brutal, "a turn attacking the dummy?"

"Oh," said Tyberius realizing they hadn't come down to watch him, "sure. I was done anyhow...I am kinda tuckered out," he added as he stepped out of the practice area, wiping some sweat off his face.

"I really do not need to practice here," said Brutal.

"Yes. Yes, you do," said Kerkrand matter-of-factly, then pointing into the practice area, continued, "give us three good slashing hits on the target."

"This is ridiculous," said Brutal as he began to sheath the sword, "all I need is some armor. Can you show us that now?"

Mikell stepped toward Brutal and put his hand on the big warrior's forearm, before he could slide the sword into the scabbard, "Brutal, give the target three hits -- Kerkrand is just trying to help. I am not sure what we can learn from three swings," he said, looking down at the dwarf, "but he is the expert."

At Mikell's touch, Brutal hesitated, the sword ready to be plunged back into the scabbard. Taking in a deep breath and releasing out a big sigh of frustration, he said, "Fine! Get out of my way," and he walked into the practice area. Unceremoniously, Brutal raised the longsword and slashed at the dummy half-heartedly, landing the blade with a dull thud.

"No!" said Kerkrand in a powerful voice, drawing looks from everyone. "Is that how you would swing if you were in a fight for your life-- and the life of your friends here?" he said, motioning to the group of friends standing near him.

Brutal's face flushed a light red at the criticism, and taking a tighter grip on his longsword, he brought the weapon back and with all his might he struck the target, landing the blade with a loud crack, the sword cutting into the dummy and hitting the Taper wood post underneath. "Was that hard enough?" he asked, frustration creeping into his tone.

"Aye," said Kerkrand, "that was splendid. Two more now," he added, putting his hands behind his back again, looking pleased, and relaxed.

Brutal, already sweating, wiped his brow with his forearm and brought the sword back, and again struck the target with all his might, as if to cut the Taper wood pole in two. The blade, first slicing through cloth and straw, struck the Taper wood post with so much force the weapon snapped into two pieces. The hilt and lower portion of the blade remained in Brutal's hand as he followed through his swing as the end of the blade flew off into the store, bouncing off the floor with a loud clang followed by a scraping noise. Everyone but Kerkrand ducked as the blade flew overhead, and Brutal almost lost his balance on the awkward follow-through.

Regaining his balance, Brutal looked at what was left of his sword: just the hilt and about a quarter of the original blade, making the sword look more like a large hilted dagger rather than a longsword. Kerkrand clapped loudly one time and let out a loud, "Whoa! Very nice, very nice!"

Brutal, still holding the hilt and flushing an even darker red, looked at the dwarf. "You knew this would happen!" he said.

"Actually, no, I thought it would take three swings," Kerkrand replied. "I must have underestimated your strength."

Brutal threw down the remnants of his broken sword, again causing a loud series of clanking noises as the metal struck the granite floor and bounced and spun briefly before coming to rest near the silhouette of the dummy. "Congratulations," Brutal said as he exited the practice area, "now I guess I do need a sword!"

"Brutal," Mikell said, this time grabbing the warrior's arm as he attempted to pass, "do you not see what Kerkrand has done?"

"Yes, he tricked me into ruining my sword-- so I would have to buy a new one," said Brutal, giving the dwarf an angry look.

Mikell shook his head. "No, I think he saved your life."

Brutal shifted his gaze from Kerkrand to Mikell. "What are you talking about?"

"Yeah, what are ya sayin'? Did that blade strike you in the head?" asked Tyberius, giving Mikell's head a gentle knock.

Brushing Tyberius's hand away, Mikell said, "No, I am serious. If you had taken that sword into battle, it would have broken and then what the hell would you be fighting with? Your fists?"

Brutal looked at Kerkrand again. "Is that true?"

"Aye, though I will not say that I saved your life," said the dwarf, placing his arms behind his back again and shrugging his shoulders, added, "Who could know that much? But your sword would have surely broken the first time the metal was truly tested."

Brutal's eyes narrowed, his face still flush from his anger. "Why, in the name of the gods, would you not have just told me the sword was no good?" asked Brutal. "Why make me put on such a spectacle?"

Kerkrand smiled politely, giving his red beard a quick stroke, then motioned for them. "Follow me. We have an excellent selection of longswords." Leading the group through the aisles, halfway turning his head, the dwarf said, "The longsword is a very good weapon. I have known many good warriors who swear by them -- and in the hands of a master, they are quite deadly."

"I am curious," said Mikell. "I have lived in Telfar for ten years now, and I do not recall ever seeing you, or anyone from your family out and about in the town. How is that?"

Kerkrand turned his head halfway, again, so as to keep one eye on where he was going. "We are self-sufficient here, there really is no need to go out." After a short pause, Kerkrand added, "Likewise, I am surprised, if you have been here ten years that you have not come into our shop." Stopping in front of a rack with dozens of longswords on display, Kerkrand turned completely around to once again see his guests, "Is it, indeed, your first time?"

"Yes," said Mikell, "actually it is."

"Ten years is a long time for a human, why have you not come in before?"

Mikell smiled. "Well, we are pretty self-sufficient out there," he said with a wide smile, motioning with a hand to the outside.

Kerkrand, his smile showing through his thick beard, nodded and waved a finger at the cleric. "Ah, very clever -- you make a strong point."

Brutal walked past Mikell and Kerkrand and began to peruse the multitude of longswords to choose from. Taking one off the rack he hefted it in his hand, testing its balance and feel as he put it through several different motions. Kerkrand turned his attention back to Brutal and moved closer, examining the warrior's testing of the weapon. Brutal swung the sword with ease, and his short-sleeved tunic showed the muscles in his arm flexing and bulging with each swing of the blade.

"It is not difficult to see that you are a very strong human," said Kerkrand.

Brutal stopped swinging the sword and put it back, and as he grabbed another from the rack asked, "Why do you say such a thing?"

"Do you plan to use a shield?" asked Kerkrand.

Brutal, towering over the dwarf, turned to give Kerkrand his full attention, "Enough with the cryptic questions, just say what you want to say."

Kerkrand stood his briefly, before sighing and taking one slow step backwards, his arms once again clasped behind his back. "My intentions are good. I want to see you armored and armed as best as your coin will allow."

Brutal face softened, his brow un-furrowing, the anger vanishing from his eyes. "Sorry...I am sorry."

"Do you plan to use a shield?" asked Kerkrand. Seeing the hesitation in Brutal's reaction, he said, "Have you used a shield before?"

Brutal shook his head. "No, never."

"I believe that with your strength, you will want a weapon that has a heavier blade; one which will be able to handle the hard blows you will be landing. The longsword is a great weapon, but unless you can afford a Juggredden blade," then correcting himself, "that is, a magical blade, then I think you would be wise to use something heavier -- not only to avoid damaging the weapon, but one that will allow you to use your strength as an advantage, rather than a weakness."

"What do you suggest?" asked Brutal as he placed the longsword he was holding, back onto the weapon rack.

Taking a few short-legged strides to the next rack of weapons,

Kerkrand conscientiously selected a sword from an adjoining rack. Walking back with the weapon, he carefully offered the hilt end to Brutal, saying, "This is a bastard sword -- give this a feel, I believe you will like it better."

Brutal grabbed the hilt with his right hand and examined the weapon. The metal had a darkened hue to it but was polished to the point that the lantern light danced off its reflective angles. The blade was slightly longer and heavier, but the biggest difference was the hilt, almost twice as long compared to the longsword. The hilt guard was also much larger, offering additional protection. The bottom of the hilt was shaped like a metal diamond to ensure that his hand would not slip off the end. Like pieces of a puzzle snapping together, Brutal placed both hands on the hilt, feeling the power and balance of the weapon. A smile crept across his face at the perfect fit.

"Yesss," said Kerkrand slowly, clasping his hands in front of him making a loud clap, a bit of pride in his voice, like an artist admiring his creation. "I can see you already feel the extra power. It feels good, does it not?"

The devilish smile on Brutal's face said it all, but he nodded affirmatively, "Yes, I can feel the difference. This sword has better balance, and with the bigger hilt, I can use my second hand, which gives me much more power in my swing." Brutal lowered the sword, and his smile disappeared. "But surely this sword is too expensive, the craftsmanship," he said as he stroked the flat edge of the blade with his left hand, "is superb -- and the metal seems unusual. Why is it so dark?"

"The darkness of the metal comes from a specific blend of coals my father used to forge this sword," said Kerkrand, then holding up both hands added, "unfortunately I cannot tell you more details than that -- family secrets, you know. However, as I told the priest," he said, motioning toward Mikell, "let us see if we can come to an agreement on price at the end for all the equipment rather than for each item."

"Wow, nice sword," said Ariana rejoining the group, who was now holding a light crossbow and a quiver of bolts, "but I thought you already had a sword?" she asked.

"The dwarf tricked Brutal into breaking it," announced the

familiar child-like voice from the shadows. Emerging into the light of the aisle-way near Ariana, Bealty said, holding up a short sword and dagger, "I found what I needed." Ariana, startled by the appearance of the halfling, gave him a glaring look.

Mikell, seeing the frown on Kerkrand's face, quickly interjected, "Well, he did not trick him into breaking it -- he did us a favor."

Bealty, carelessly shrugging his shoulders, said, "Yeah, okay, whatever," then added, "are we ready to go yet?"

"We still need to look at some armor," said Mikell, glad to change the subject. "Kerkrand, can you please show us the armor you have?"

Kerkrand, giving his braided beard a couple strokes, as if to make him forget Bealty's comment, turned on his heel and began to walk down the aisle, "Of course, follow me."

As the dwarf turned, Mikell gave Bealty a scolding look and in a hushed voice said, "You should wait outside. What were you thinking?"

Bealty, looking up at the priest, his dark eyes showing no remorse. "That is fine by me. I will head back to the temple then. Here," he said, handing up the short sword and dagger to Mikell. As soon as Mikell took the weapons, Bealty took a step backwards, quickly melding back into the shadows.

Mikell shook his head. "Can you not just use the paths?"

"Never waste a shadow," Bealty said, just above a whisper, his voice emanating from somewhere deep behind the piles and racks of weapons and armor strewn about the store. Mikell, looking back, could not see Kerkrand anymore, but fortunately Tyberius was easy to spot, his head bobbing along, above the piles of merchandise, with each step. Satisfied that Bealty was on his way out, he hurried to catch up with the rest of the group.

As Mikell neared the group, he could see that both Tyberius and Brutal were trying on chain mail shirts under Kerkrand's watchful eye. The dwarf handed each warrior a solid metal breastplate, saying "The chain mail will give you protection from slashing weapons, but not a whole lot from crushing blows. Here, try these on, they will give you some added protection, including from crushing weapons, like Mikell's mace." The breastplate armor protected both the front and back and slipped on over their heads, a strap with a buckle securing them to their waists. Both sets of armor were polished, giving them a mirror-like surface, the only difference was Brutal's had an engraving of two snakes, their bodies coiled together up the middle of the armor, with each snake lunging toward a different shoulder -- if seen from a distance, it might appear as if a "Y" had been etched into the armor.

"I feel like I am in a damn metal bubble!" said Tyberius as he stood there with his arms outstretched. "No, no, no..." Tyberius said, shaking his head and fidgeting with the buckles, "I-I cannot fight in this thing."

"I kind of like it," said Brutal as he slowly swung his sword in different directions and tried different positions. "It is a little restrictive, but I think it is worth the extra protection."

"And you never know where the blows will fall; not all will come from in front of you," said Kerkrand, knocking on Brutal's back, making two quick metallic thuds with his knuckles.

Finally getting the buckles undone, with some help from Ariana, Tyberius slid the breastplate off and set it back on the rack. "The only way somethin' is gonna get behind me is if I were wearin' an anchor like that there," he said, pointing to the breastplate. "No, the chain shirt is all I need," he added, touching the metal shirt he was wearing.

Kerkrand pointed to a stand behind Tyberius. "The chain shirt comes with a steel cap. Choose any of the styles you like."

Tyberius turned around to look, there were more than a dozen steel caps, but one caught his eye, and he immediately grabbed it. The helmet was shaped like the head of a bear, with eyes and rounded ears, the face was open, allowing for good vision, but it still offered good protection all around his head. Putting it on, Tyberius was beaming, his grin going from ear to ear. "Now this is a helmet." Turning to show Ariana, he said, "What do you think? This will scare the shit out of those dog people," he chuckled.

Ariana, crossing her arms, said, "You do not need to look fearsome -- you need to be protected," she said with a little reproach, then added, speaking to everyone, "You boys better remember the seriousness of what we are doing here." Ariana made sure she made eye contact with all of them, then, handing her crossbow and quiver of bolts to Tyberius, said,

"I am going back to the temple, this is all I need from here." Tyberius took the crossbow and quiver, and Ariana disappeared down the winding aisles, her leather boots clicking on the granite tiles. A short pause, and a moment later they all could hear the whump of the large stone door closing behind her.

"Man, who died and made her queen?" said Hammer rhetorically. "Why do you let her talk to you like that?" he asked Tyberius.

"Show a little respect," said Tyberius, adjusting the crossbow and quiver under one arm, and taking his helmet off with his free hand.

Mikell stepped between the two men. "You will learn that she is a very smart woman -- often someone to heed, as we should tonight. I think we are done here." Stepping to a table that still had some room on it, Mikell placed the heavy mace, a set of chain mail, and a medium-sized wooden shield onto it. Motioning to Brutal and Tyberius, he said, "Place your items on this table." Both men did as asked, with Kerkrand watching. Mikell sighed, looking at the size of their pile, wondering to himself if they had picked too much. But putting on his smile and game face, he turned to Kerkrand and asked, "It is quite a purchase, I would hope you would take that into consideration when considering your prices."

"Indeed, it is a good-sized purchase," said Kerkrand, and picking up the mace, he looked it over lovingly, almost as if it were a child. "Sundrudden," he said softly as he caressed the weapon. "It is always hard to part with such masterpieces. In some ways, they are even more precious to us than Juggredden -- because those weapons are the result of magical energy -- but Sundrudden is pure art and cannot be replicated."

"If it means that much to you," said Mikell, "then I will pick out another mace, as we cannot afford..."

Kerkrand put the mace back down on the table and raised his hand, interrupting, "No, you picked this mace out of all that were there, I will offer you a more than fair price for it." Then looking through the pile of goods, he started mumbling to himself, "Mace, flail, chain mail suit, dagger..." cataloging and adding up the sum in his head. After a moment, Kerkrand looked back up at Mikell, his face devoid of emotion, his voice deep a growly, and said, "750 gold pieces." Kerkrand, putting his hands behind his back once again, kept his eyes locked on Mikell's, like an owl on its prey just before it swooped down for the kill.

Brutal gasped and was about to say something, but Mikell gave him a look and shaking his head and said, "750 gold is a more than we had hoped to spend. We have a long journey ahead of us, and we need to have enough left over for supplies along the way. Can you not reduce your asking price a bit more?"

Kerkrand grimaced, the thought of a further price reduction being painful to him, like the stab of an unseen dagger. Rocking back and forth from his heels to his toes, he stroked his beard as he contemplated the request. He walked back to the pile of goods and re-examined some of the items, grumbling something under his breath. Looking up at Brutal, Tyberius, Hammer, and Mikell, Kerkrand said, "I hope all of you know what you are getting yourself into." They all looked at each other, not sure what to say, but Kerkrand did not wait, saying, "I know two things: one, Zuel is a good god, so I know whatever it is that you are doing will be for a righteous cause, and two, you need this equipment." His eyes narrowing behind his red, bushy, eyebrows, he continued, "But my price is my price." Mikell's shoulders slumped, and Brutal and Tyberius both swore under their breaths. Kerkrand continued, "But, as I said, you need these weapons, so I will sell them to you for five hundred gold pieces. However, I will expect you to bring me three hundred gold pieces whenever you return to pay off your debt. I know I can trust you," he said to Mikell, "seeing that you have a temple in town, and that you worship a good deity."

"What if we do not return?" asked Mikell.

"Then you will likely be dead," answered Kerkrand, "and your debt will be between you and your god, as our debt will be resolved."

"I cannot have you trying to get three hundred gold from my father," Mikell added.

"The debt is between the Boral family and your small group -- not your temple," said Kerkrand somewhat ominously, then added in a softer tone. "Your father will not be bothered. My word is my bond," Kerkrand added, placing a hand over his heart, citing a phrase that all followers of Yutrin, the good deity of wealth, use to consecrate a deal or oath.

Brutal stepped forward, saying, "We accept." Tyberius, Mikell, and Hammer all looked at Brutal, each thinking about the consequences of owing coin to the Boral family, but after a moment, they all nodded their heads in agreement.

"Excellent," said Kerkrand, smiling, and once again placing his hands behind his back, "who has the coin?"

* * * *

Kerkrand walked the small group to the front door, which swung quietly closed behind them, on it's massive, and well-oiled hinges. The only noise was the thud as the door finally closed, followed by a clang as the latch dropped into place, holding it firmly shut. Kerkrand stood for a moment holding the bag of five hundred gold pieces the group had paid, weighing it in his hand as if he could attest to the quantity by weight alone.

A slightly taller and more muscular dwarf appeared in the aisle behind Kerkrand, his face was smudged with soot, his hands were calloused, and his thick black hair was pulled back with leather strings, revealing the first traces of wrinkles beginning to take form around his deep-set eyes. "Ya let them walk away, still owing three hundred gold?" growled the dwarf, then after a disapproving grunt, added, "and to add insult to injury ye let him walk off with my Sundrudden mace?"

"Lambs to the slaughter, probably," replied Kerkrand. "I do not know where they are going, but they will need the equipment."

The older dwarf snorted derisively, "Well, that seals it -- ye have gone and lost yer mind," he said, throwing his arms up into the air. "We ain't no charity here, Kerkrand."

"One of them is a priest of Zuel," said Kerkrand, turning to face the taller dwarf, "from the temple here in town." Kerkrand handed the bag of coins to the older dwarf, but he held onto the bag before letting it go, and said, "Community counts, Father, how many times have I heard that growing up?"

"Bah, humans do not count as community -- only dwarves," said Boral, waving Kerkrand's comment away with one hand and yanking the bag from Kerkrand's grasp with the other. "Ye seem to have forgotten that part of the lesson." Looking up to catch his son's eyes, he said, "The most important part, too." Boral, not being able to help himself, also weighed the bag in his arm. "At least ye got five hundred gold -- so it is not a total loss."

"If they survive, especially the priest," said Kerkrand, "they will pay us the three hundred gp as well -- making it a very good sale."

Boral stared at his son for a brief moment, letting the silence change the subject, then he frowned, magnifying the wrinkles around his eyes. "The cursed halfling went downstairs, at least to the second level." Boral's free hand, at his side, tightened into a fist, "The little rodent was good, and I could not keep my eye on him the whole time. From what I seen, though, he was just looking around."

"His race cannot help but be disrespectful -- they are like cats and curiosity," said Kerkrand.

"Catsss," Boral growled, "do not steal."

Kerkrand, turning halfway, looking back at the now closed doors, gave his red beard a couple quick absentminded strokes, saying, "Where they are going, a thief might be a good thing to bring along."

* * * *

Returning to the temple, Tyberius, Mikell, Hammer, and Brutal placed all the weapons and armor into the corner by the backpacks. Bealty and Julius were sitting at the table, talking quietly, while Ariana was sitting on the floor, her back up against the wall, her backpack nestled by her side, her right arm resting on top of it.

"We are definitely armed now," said Tyberius with a large grin, showing off his new flail before setting it down in the pile of equipment.

"How much did we end up paying?" asked Ariana, looking up and watching the men.

Brutal, sitting down into one of the empty chairs at the table, placing his elbows on the table, said, "Five hundred gold pieces."

Ariana sat up a little, her eyebrows raising up quizzically. "Really? I am impressed -- you guys did a great job negotiating."

Mikell, who was partially sitting on the window sill by the table, said, "Well, we actually have to pay three hundred more when we come back."

"What?!" Ariana said, exasperated. "We had to pay eight hundred

185

gold for all this stuff?"

"He asked for 750 gold..." began Brutal.

"And you negotiated up to eight hundred?" Ariana interrupted. "I knew I should have stayed. Now we have nothing left for anything else."

"If you would let me finish," admonished Brutal, "we got him to take five hundred gold now, but we do need to pay another three hundred gold when we return," then giving Ariana a look added, "so we still have plenty of coin for traveling."

"Besides," said Hammer, "the gnolls will have a buncha coin," then rubbing his hands together greedily, "which will soon be our coin."

Ariana's eyes squinted slightly, questioning the truth of his statement. "That is a stunning display of optimism."

Hammer glared back at Ariana. "What is wrong with being optimistic?"

"As long as optimism does not cross into delusional or interfere with proper planning, I have no issue," said Ariana.

"And you think I am delusional or interfering with our planning?" asked Hammer, his voice rising a little.

"I think paying eight hundred gold for this equipment on the hope that these gnolls will have a lot of coin borders on stupid," said Ariana, her voice rising as well. "I do think that." Pointing in the direction of the hills, she continued, "What if the gnolls have nothing? Then what?" Before anyone could answer, she went on. "I will tell you what: we will have two options: one," she said, holding up one finger, "we will have to return to Telfar and pay off the three hundred gold with everything we have left -- and that is a great option," she added with sarcasm, "because then we get to walk into the hills with no provisions because all of our damn gold is gone." She took a quick breath, then holding up a second finger, her voice rising further, she said, "Or two, we have to avoid coming back to Telfar and we have to either walk to Whiteal to get provisions, or walk into the hills with no provisions and our lousy, useless, three hundred gold that we have left."

Hammer replied, "If we provision here, now, those are not even problems." He then crossed his arms as if proving her wrong.

Ariana smiled. "Why, thank you for pointing out option three," she said, holding up a third finger. "Option three is the riskiest of all, we buy our provisions now, leaving us no coin -- or at least not enough to pay off the dwarves. That is brilliant."

"Why is that risky? What is wrong with that plan?" asked Tyberius innocently.

Everyone looked at Tyberius, including Ariana. "Well, my dear, what if some of us are hurt badly and we need help? We will not be able to return to Telfar for healing or defense -- unless, of course, we do find enough coin to pay off the dwarves."

"We could always go to one of our farms," Brutal said.

"Brutal --" Ariana started to respond, but then she stopped herself, taking a deep breath, trying to calm her emotions. Her voice returning to a normal talking level, she continued, "What is done is done. We do not need horses or many provisions for tomorrow since we are within a day's walk, so we buy a couple lanterns and some limited provisions -- that way we will still have just enough to pay off the dwarves if we need to return to Telfar for help."

"That sounds like a good plan," said Mikell. "I also think we should leave the remaining gold here in the temple. That way if things do go wrong tomorrow," he gave Ariana a quick look, "any of us that can get back to Telfar will have the money waiting for them." A stillness settled over the group, as each person contemplated all the different kind of things that could go wrong.

Bealty, not interested in the what-if scenarios the others were thinking about, looked around the room, wondering what other little secret compartments Mikell and his father had created in this room. Not seeing anything obvious, his attention turned to Ariana, who was sitting quietly now, her head leaning back against the wall, and her eyes closed. Bealty, gracefully hopping down from the over-sized chair and landing with almost no sound on the soft soles of his leather boots, made his way over to Ariana. Because of his height, it was not necessary, but he squatted down to whisper into Ariana's ear.

Ariana's eyes popped open immediately, and she pulled her head away from the halfling, giving him a glare. "You little snoop," she said. This caught everyone's attention, and now all eyes were on the both of them.

"What is it?" asked Tyberius.

Bealty stood back up, a puzzled look on his face. "Sorry, I thought you would want to know, but I can see now you already did," he said to Ariana.

"Is that so surprising? Do you know what is in your little backpack?" she said, waving a finger toward the pile of backpacks. Before he could answer, she added like a jab, "I bet you do." Bealty squatted back down, motioning that he wanted to whisper something else to her. Ariana did not oblige, saying, "Just say what you need to say."

Bealty looked around the room, everyone was still watching them, then looking back at Ariana, asked, "What is it for?"

"What is what for?" asked Tyberius.

Ariana paused for a moment, still giving Bealty a dirty look. Then finally taking her eyes off the halfling, she waved him away. "Shoo, just get away from me."

Bealty stood up and took a couple steps backwards. "If it is your pet or something, we should know, otherwise it might get killed or something," then added quickly, "by accident."

"For the love of the gods, just tell us what is going on," said Hammer impatiently.

Ariana, her mind reaching out, connected telepathically with her target. "Foetore, when did he find you?"

Foetore, his mind now connected to Ariana, replied silently, "Do not know."

Ariana let out a long sigh as she untied the loose leather cords holding the flap shut on the front of her backpack. "Well," Ariana said out loud, "you may as well come out." Foetore, poking his head out of the bag, breathed in the cooler and fresher air, his nose immediately picking up many new scents.

"What in the eight hells is that? A skunk?" asked Hammer.

Tyberius moved closer to Ariana. "And what is it doin' in yer backpack?"

Foetore, seeing the movement, quickly scampered out of the confining backpack, and onto Ariana's shoulder. "I thought carrying a ferret," she said, giving Hammer a glance, "around town might cause a little more distraction and attention than we would want."

"Why carry a ferret around at all, is what I am wondering," asked Hammer -- though it seemed more like a statement.

"Is it a familiar?" asked Julius from his seat at the small table.

Ariana looked at Julius and nodded, her eyes could not quite conceal her surprise. "Yes, he is. Where did you learn of such a thing?"

"I have traveled some and have heard many stories about mages. Familiars were just another part of the myth -- well," he corrected himself, "in this case, it turns out to be a truth."

"What is a familiar?" asked Brutal.

"You would not understand the true connection -- suffice it to say he is my pet. But," she said, raising her voice to get everyone's attention, if she did not already have it. "He must be protected. Do you all understand?"

"Or what?" asked Hammer. "It is just a ferret," he said with a chuckle.

"He is NOT just another ferret, and this is no joking matter, Hammer. I mean it -- he is to be protected, the same as we all are," said Ariana.

Hammer lifted his hands in submission. "Okay, okay, we will protect it."

"He can take care of himself," said Ariana, "but he needs to be able to trust all of us -- just as we all need to trust one another."

"You do not need to worry, Ariana, you can count on us," said Brutal.

"Aye, ya can count on us," said Tyberius.

Mikell, sensing an opportunity to change the subject, said, "Brutal, we should go back to the Drip and let York and Isa know that they can come with us tomorrow." Brutal sighed, trying to muster up the energy. Standing up, he slid the chair back and joined Mikell on his way down the stairs.

* * * *

Stepping through the northern doorway into the tavern, Brutal and Mikell scanned the area. The Drip was considerably less noisy, but for most of its nightly patrons, the evening was still very young, and the tavern was alive with activity and quite full. The pair of friends made their way to the bar where they knew they would at least find Syd, but halfway there they spotted York -- he was already at the bar, sitting on a stool, talking to the one-eyed owner. Mikell tapped Brutal's shoulder and, getting his attention, pointed through the crowd. Brutal, looking in that direction, could see Isa was still sitting in the same chair, the shattered table at his feet. The monk was holding a long, sharp shard from the Taper wood table, examining it with some curiosity. Then as if sensing Brutal and Mikell's gaze was upon him, he slowly looked up, locking his eyes on theirs. After a few seconds, Isa stood up, letting the piece of wood fall back onto the floor, and started walking toward them. Isa's hood was down, revealing the square head, and sharp, tusk-like upward jutting teeth that curled just outside his upper lip -- and although Isa was slightly shorter than Brutal, the monk was much broader, making it feel like a huge boulder was bearing down on them. Isa, rising from his chair, caught York's attention, and the bard, looking to where the monk was heading, noticed Brutal and Mikell standing several yards behind him. Taking a long pull from his mug of ale, giving Syd a quick pat on the shoulder, he rose and started walking their way.

"Well, brave men, has your group made a decision?" asked York, slapping Brutal's back in a friendly manner.

"We have," said Brutal, who waited for just a moment, giving Isa a chance to get close enough to hear, then extending his hand out, said, "We have decided that we should welcome your company." York's face beamed, his smile going from ear to ear, and he eagerly shook Brutal's hand. Turning, Brutal extended his hand to Isa, who hesitated but eventually did grasp Brutal's hand. Brutal's hand was swallowed up by the half-orc's, like that of a child shaking hands with an adult, and he tried to pull away, but the monk's grip was like a vice. Brutal had a hard time imagining what it must have been like for Tyberius earlier -- especially if Isa had applied even more pressure -- but before his thoughts could continue, Isa let go, and their hands fell apart.

"You have made a wise choice, a wise choice indeed," said York. "When do we leave?"

"Tomorrow morning," said Mikell.

Putting his arm around Brutal's shoulders, leaning in a little closer, York lowered his voice. "And, uh, what exactly will we be doing?"

"You should come back to the temple with us, and we can talk about it there," said Mikell.

"Are we spending the night there?" asked York.

"That would be best," said Brutal.

"Let me get my stuff," said York. "I have a room here at the drip."

"Fine, but be quick," said Brutal. "Do you have anything?" he asked Isa.

Isa shook his head, saying, "No. Isa is ready." Then after a short pause, Isa added, "Thirty day."

Mikell nodded his head, saying, "We understand, Isa, thirty days."

"Wondrous!" said York, clapping his hands together, almost triumphantly, then he bounded toward the stairs leading up to the tavern's rooms.

Brutal, watching as the bard climbed the stairs, gave Mikell a quick look. Looking back at the bard, now at the top of the stairs, he said, to no one in particular, "Yeah, wondrous."

* * * *

Brutal, Mikell, Isa, and York climbed the stairs leading to the second level of the temple. Brutal looked around, and everyone had seemingly staked out a small plot of square footage in the room and were doing their own thing. Tyberius was sitting against the wall, his arm around Ariana who had her head on his shoulder, her eyes closed, with Foetore curled up in her lap. The little ferret's whiskers quivered, and one eye slowly opened -- seeing Brutal and the others his eye closed again. Tyberius gave a slight wave as they entered and then leaned his head on Ariana's and closed his eyes as well. Hammer and Julius each had a corner, on opposite sides of the window overlooking the street, and were talking quietly. The room was now beginning to feel a bit crowded, but Brutal admitted to himself that it felt good to have a strong group of people going with him. Mikell moved past Brutal and made his way to one of the straw mattresses and let out a long sigh as he sat down, propping a pillow between his head and the wall. Isa looked around the sparse living quarters and made his way toward the bookshelves along the north wall, running his fingers along the binders of the books, as if he was looking for a particular title. York also walked past Brutal, heading toward Julius and Hammer, the only two people talking at the moment. Brutal watched everyone getting settled, then noticing one conspicuous thing missing thing from the room, he scanned the room a second and third time.

"Where is Bealty?" asked Brutal to everyone. Mikell's head jerked up as he looked quickly around the room, concern on his face -- not for the safety of the halfling, but wondering what caused the rogue to go out again.

Tyberius, opening his eyes, lifting his head, and half-heartedly pointing toward the stairs, said, "He said he would go get some lanterns and torches for tomorrow."

Brutal's eyebrows raised. "And you let him go alone?"

"Why not?" asked Tyberius. "He travels to and from Whiteal on his own; I think he can handle buying some torches and such."

"You do not know Bealty very well," said Mikell, shaking his head.

"What do you mean?" asked Tyberius.

"Halflings are notorious spenders," chimed in York, who, pulling out two long pieces of a flute from his backpack, began fitting them together. As York finished his comment, a thud coming from the main floor of the temple below them announced the opening and closing of the temple doors. A moment later, the door at the bottom of the stairs leading up to where Brutal was standing creaked open. Bealty, barely opening the door, slid through the narrow crack and closed the door quietly behind him. Brutal, looking down the stairs, could see he was carrying a brown cloth sack, which was bulging with pointy objects.'Torches,' he thought to himself.

At the top of the stairs, standing by Brutal, Bealty gently set the bag down on the floor, the objects inside the bag rattling as they spread out in the bag. Always hyper aware of his surroundings, Bealty looked up at Brutal and said, "Oh, I see York and Isa have joined us."

"We just got back," replied Brutal. "What is in the sack?"

"Just some torches and a couple lanterns. I thought that would be enough -- I mean, they probably already have light in there anyway," Bealty said, shrugging his shoulders.

Brutal, opening up the sack, looked inside and nodded his head, saying, "Yeah, just torches and a couple lanterns."

"See, you all worry too much," said Tyberius.

Mikell, who was looking through a book, looked up, a skeptical look on his face, and asked the halfling, "Is that all you bought?"

"Well, I did buy this, too," said Bealty, fishing out a small brown bag from within one of his many hidden pockets. It was about the size of a grapefruit, the top was tied shut with some string, a large tight knot, making it almost impossible to open. Judging by the way the bag behaved, the contents, bulging here and there as he moved it around in his hand, seemed to be partially liquid.

Brutal, being the closest to the halfling, had the best look at the bag. "What in the eight hells is in that? Mud and rocks?" asked Brutal.

Bealty looked up at his friend, saying, "That is a very good question, but Harn warned me not to open the bag under any circumstances."

Mikell knew Andor Harn, the owner of the general store in Telfar, and although he knew him to be a good man, he knew that, like any merchant, he was driven, at least in some part, by greed. "What is it, Bealty, and how much did it cost?"

Before Bealty had a chance to respond, Tyberius scooched up to sit a little higher and get a better look at the bag. Scratching an itch on his head, Tyberius asked, "You crazy halfling, what good is a bag that you cannot open?"

Bealty started walking toward where Tyberius and Ariana were sitting on the floor, holding the bag out, giving him a better look, saying, "Because when you open the bag, the sticky stuff inside will glue you to the floor."

Tyberius started laughing, which was a contagious deep belly laugh. Catching his breath enough to speak, he said, "That is the silliest thing I have ever heard!" Ariana opened her eyes, taking a look at the bag, then closing her eyes again, she rested her head on Tyberius's shoulder. Foetore pointed his nose toward Bealty's outstretched hand, giving the bag a quick sniff, then rested his head back down on Ariana's lap. "How do you get the sticky stuff out if you cannot open the bag?" asked Tyberius, wiping away a tear of laughter.

Bealty smiled. "You throw it, and it explodes on whatever it hits."

"How much did it cost?" asked Mikell again.

"Harn wanted seventy-five gold, but I talked him down to fifty," said Bealty with pride in his voice.

Hammer, still sitting in the corner by the window, was wiping his hammer with a cloth. Looking up, he said, "Fifty gold? You just got robbed, little guy," said Hammer, matter-of-factly.

"You mean we got robbed," said Julius, correcting Hammer.

Hammer looked at Julius. "What do you mean?"

"I assume you used our stash of coins to pay for this trinket?" Julius asked Bealty. Everyone perked up a bit, even Ariana opened her eyes and sat up, looking at the halfling, waiting for his answer.

Bealty could feel all the eyes on him, but being the subject of mass suspicion was nothing new to him. "No, I had some coin left over from what I put into our pot," he said.

"What?" asked Ariana, sitting up further. "You withheld some gold from us?" Before he had a chance to reply, she added, "How much did you hold back?"

"Does it matter?" asked Bealty, then looking at Ariana, continued, "I gave three hundred gold to our cause -- how much did you give?" Ariana's eyes squinted in anger, and Foetore scurried off her lap, peeking at the halfling from behind Ariana.

Mikell stood up and quickly walked over, placing a hand on Bealty's small shoulder. "Ariana, you do not know Bealty very well yet. You will learn that his questions are just that -- questions of reason...they are not meant to be an insult."

"I do not know why we are even taking him along," Ariana said to Mikell, "we cannot even trust him to go buy torches," she said, emphasizing her point.

"You can always trust me, Ariana," said Bealty, his boyish voice obviously an irritation to Ariana, as he slipped the quivering bag into his backpack.

"I have not actually seen tanglefoot used in battle, but I have heard it is effective, even if just briefly," said York, just finishing up the assembly of his flute.

Tyberius looked at the bard. "You mean you know what that thing is?"

York chuckled, then said, "I have no idea what that thing is for sure, I suppose none of us will know until he throws it." York pulled a small white cloth out of his backpack lying next to him, and spitting lightly on the flute began to clean off a spot with the cloth, then looking back up, said, "But what he described is a known, well, weapon, I guess, for lack of a better word."

"We should all get some rest," said Mikell, "it has been a long day, and we are all tired. Not to mention, tomorrow is looming in all of our minds." Mikell walked back to where his small mattress was on the floor and said, "I would like to say a quick prayer." Everyone closed their eyes in respect, and Mikell, placing one hand over the holy symbol hanging around his neck, the other he outstretched to the heavens, said, "Zuel, blessed god of healing, bless us this night and let us carry that blessing with us tomorrow as we do your good work. Protect us and help guide us on our journey to find Brutal's father, wherever that may take us. As lovers of the light, watch over us and help us to be victorious over the forces of darkness." Mikell could feel the presence of Zuel as he spoke, it was a warmth, as if his soul was on fire within his body, but the feeling vanished as he finished up his prayer. Looking around, he knew nobody else in the group worshiped Zuel, but most of them worshiped Soulmite, who was also a good god of the light. Based on the few words Isa had spoken, he knew the monk worshiped Craven -- a deity that lived between the light and darkness -- a god of the shadows. That was a little concerning, but the monk seemed like a faithful and trustworthy person, even if he was a half-orc. Shifting his thoughts and gaze to the bard, who was still cleaning the flute, he studied the elf, concluding that he was probably the biggest mystery in the group. 'Who was he and why did he want to follow us,' thought Mikell to himself.

York, putting the flute to his lips, began playing a slow, soft melody. The music washed over the group like a warm, comforting wave and everyone, even Isa, found a comfortable spot on the floor. The room was dark now, the various candles around the room having been extinguished, the only light and sound coming in through the open windows. Listening to the gently swaying of the music, like being in a mystical hammock, the group soon found themselves fast asleep. York played the flute for a few more minutes, then re-lighting one candle on the table he sat down in a chair, and pulling out a bound book, unsnapped the clasp holding it shut. Taking out a pen and opening a small vial of ink, which he set on the table, he dabbed the tip into the ink and began writing in his book. He didn't get much written before he stopped, and absently scratching himself on the head with the dry end of the pen, said quietly to himself, "Hmm, damn, I do not even know where we are going tomorrow."

"To kill the gnolls," said the boyish, almost fiendish, whisper from the shadows. York, startled, dropped the pen, whipping his head around to look where the voice had come from, but he could see nothing other than the red shapes, provided by his infravision, of the sleeping bodies on the floor. Then from right beside him, "What'cha writing?" the voice asked again. This time Bealty stepped into the light, standing by the table, with the fallen pen in his hand. He held it out to York, who took it.

"I thought everyone was asleep," said York, with a mixture of embarrassment and a tinge of anger, then composing himself, added, "thank you, for retrieving my pen." York, closing the book, snapped its clasp, and asked, "to kill the gnolls you say? What gnolls, and where?"

Bealty climbed into a chair on the side of the rectangular table, and sitting on the arm of the chair, met York's eyes. "First, tell me what are you writing?"

York, pulling the closed book closer to himself, placed both hands over it, as if protecting it from the halfling. "It is no secret. I am a bard, I journal all my travels, noting who I meet, where I go," and then giving the halfling a hard look, "-- and what I do."

"You misspelled my name," said Bealty, pointing at the brown, worn journal.

York let a moment of silence hang in before answering, allowing his irritation to wane slightly. "Actually, no, I did not."

"I know my lettering. You wrote 'B-E-E-T-L-E,'" Bealty spelled out. "That is not my name. That is an insect."

York, the shadows from the flickering candle playing across the sharp, angular, elven features of his face, smiled. "Ahh, you are smart too, I see. Well, if you must know, Bealty is a dreadful name," said York. "While I was playing my song, I noticed where you had lain down..."

"I did not lie down," interrupted Bealty, "I was watching you the whole time."

York, still smiling, although it seemed forced now, gesturing toward a dark lump on the floor, said, "Yes, well, I thought you had lain down, which I now guess is probably a backpack with a blanket on it." York paused, to regain his line of thought, "anyway, dressed all in black, like you are, and you are small, no offense," he said, holding up a hand, "-- I thought you looked like a beetle. And that name has a better ring to it. When I retell the story, people will be intrigued by 'Beetle' the dazzling rogue." As York spoke, he looked off into the darkness, using his hands as if to lay out a scene before them, caught up in the drama of his own thoughts.

Bealty leaned forward, his elbows on his knees and, putting his chin in his hand, said, "But it is not true."

York, disturbed to have his imaginary scene interrupted, snorted dismissively, and looking back at Bealty saying, "Probably half the things you know are not true, you just do not know it." Bealty's thin eyebrows rose slightly, unconvinced, so York added, "I am not a historian. Besides, it is my story to tell, so I write it how it best suits me -- and my listeners."

"What else do you change in your stories?" asked Bealty.

The bard had a serious look on his face and said, "Nothing," followed by a moment of awkward silence as the two looked at each other. York broke the eye contact and leaned back in his chair, stretching his legs in front of him, under the table, "now, tell me about these gnolls."

Bealty explained what he knew, which wasn't much, but it was enough, so York now knew what they had planned for tomorrow, and that they were on a mission to find out what had happened to Brutal's father. After a few minutes of talking, Bealty yawing, hopped down from the chair. While he was in the process of picking up his blanket and backpack, he looked back at York still sitting in the candlelight of the table and gave him a mischievous smile, then, moving his possessions closer to where

Mikell was sleeping, lay down on the floor and curled up to get some sleep.

York watched the halfling for a moment. Making certain the halfling truly was asleep this time, he opened his journal and scribbled in the margin, 'Must keep an eye on the damned halfling.'

CHAPTER FOURTEEN
Bunker

BRUTAL PICKED A SPOT ON THE FLOOR along the western wall, opposite the window on the east wall, hoping the sunlight would wake him before the others. He used to have trouble sleeping all night because of disturbing dreams about his father -- not quite nightmares, but they were distorted, discomforting, and woke him frequently. But all that changed, when he made up his mind to search for his father, Soulmite now blessed him with a restful mind, allowing him to sleep through the nights just fine. The only downside was that he no longer dreamed about his father at all. On one hand, he was glad the distorted visions were gone, but on the other hand, he missed the glimpses of his father that they provided. Tonight was no different, he slept peacefully, and as the first rays of the sun bent their way through the eastern window, landing on his face, he slowly began to stir and wake. Rubbing his eyes, Brutal looked around, seeing that everyone else was still sleeping, Tyberius and Mikell snoring loudly, blissfully, he thought to himself. He couldn't help his eyes as they drifted to Ariana, who was lying on her side, her head still on Tyberius's arm. Brutal watched, her chest rising and falling with each breath, the rhythm and beauty sending his thoughts back many years, to a time when they were just young teenagers.

They had taken a walk together to the rim, as they called it, where the hills began their descent down to the Great White River. It was always a beautiful view of the river with small white caps appearing and disappearing, and a dazzling display of sparkles as the sun's rays danced on the surface of the water. He tried to remember why they had taken the walk, but as hard as he tried, the reason eluded him. But he could clearly remember her lying in the grass on the hill, on her side, and as she slept, he watched, entranced by her breathing. Overwhelmed by his emotions and the moment, he leaned down and gave her a kiss on the cheek, hoping not to wake her, but to his dismay, Ariana's eyes opened, and she turned to look at him.

Movement caught Brutal's eye, jarring him away from his memory, and bringing his attention back into the room. Foetore raised his head and was staring at him, his whiskers twitching in the early morning sunlight. Brutal, irritated by the small ferret's disruption of his thoughts, averted his eyes and quietly sat up. He was glad he had at least the first moments of the day to himself. Getting into a kneeling position, he said a quiet prayer to Soulmite. "Good and great goddess, thank you for bringing me all these good people into my life, to help me on my journey. Protect them today, as we head into what will surely be a fight where life and death will hang in the balance. Help guide our blows to strike true and help us destroy this evil lodge built midst our farms and gentle families. I do not see how destroying this den of creatures will bring me one step closer to my father, but I pray to you -- help me understand, show me the way. In your mighty name, Soulmite, I do your bidding." Finishing up his prayer, Brutal looked around the room, and aside from Foetore, who was still watching him, nobody seemed to be awake -- not even Julius, who he knew was an early riser. Getting up onto his feet, Brutal walked over to where Mikell was sleeping on the straw mattress. Bealty, who was lying nearby, rolled onto his back, stretching his small arms up over his head, and blinked his eyes open.

After his quick stretch, Bealty sat up, propping himself with his arms behind him. "Today is the day," said Bealty, his boyish voice, a mixture of tiredness, seriousness, and excitement.

Brutal, smiling at the halfling, bent down. Gently shaking Mikell, he said in a quiet voice, "Mikell... Mikell. Wake up."

Mikell groaned. His mattress, being on the eastern side of the room, was still relatively dark, even with the fresh sunlight streaming in through the window above him. Slowly opening his eyes, seeing Brutal standing above him, he said, "Good morning, Brutal." Mikell rubbed his eyes with palms of his hands, then looking back up at his friend, smiled and said, "Today is the day, my friend, the journey begins. Praise Zuel." Brutal looked over at Bealty, and both he and the halfling shared a laugh. Mikell, still smiling, looked quizzically back and forth between Brutal and Bealty. "What? What did I say?"

Brutal held out a hand to Mikell, saying, "Aye, Mikell, today is the day." Taking his hand, Brutal easily helped the priest to his feet.

Mikell, looking over his shoulder at the halfling, waggled a finger at him. "Whatever you two girls are giggling over, I know you were at the heart of it." Bealty was already up and starting to don the upper portion of his black leather armor, a sly grin on his face admitting at least partial guilt, but said nothing. With the increased commotion in the room, the others began to stir and awaken.

Bealty, tightening a clasp on his leather shirt, looked up at Mikell. "Where do you think Isa went?"

Mikell looked over to the north side of the room where the monk had been sleeping, but now he was gone. "Neither of you saw him leave?" Mikell asked Bealty and Brutal.

"No," said Brutal, "I thought I was the first one to get up," then looking over where the monk had slept, as if he might reappear, added, "I did not even notice he was missing."

Bealty shook his head while he finished buckling his belt, then he shoved his sheathed dagger between the belt and his thin waist, making sure it was snug. Picking up his short sword, which was also sheathed, he slung it onto his back and made sure it also was tied tightly so that it could not shift around while he was on the move. His one advantage in a fight was his quickness and agility, and he couldn't have a sword flopping around catching on things, or worse -- making noises that could give him away. All settled, he looked up at the tall pair of humans, saying, "Nope, I just woke up."

Mikell gave Bealty a look. "You are supposed to be our eyes and ears," he said, trying to bait the halfling.

"We were sleeping in your temple," said Bealty. "I did not realize sentry duty was necessary in the sacred house of Zuel."

Mikell crossed his arms. "Do not take Zuel's name in vain, you little pagan."

"I ain't no pagan," said Bealty, looking up to the heavens and clasping his hands together, he added, "Praise Graff!"

listening to the back and forth, Brutal could not help smiling and, walking over to where Bealty was standing, put a hand on the halfling's shoulder. "Mikell does have a point, I am surprised he could up and leave without you knowing." Stealthily moving his hand, Brutal began to stick his finger into Bealty's right ear, saying, "Maybe your keen ears are getting a little rusty in your old age."

Bealty jerked his head away from Brutal's intrusive finger and darted away from the warrior. "Keep your dirty hands out of my ear," he said, rubbing his ear, "-- or I surely will lose my hearing."

"He's sitting. Just outside of the temple, by the doors," said Ariana, who was still lying on the floor, covered by a brown canvas-like blanket, next to Tyberius, her head propped up by her backpack.

"Oh, good morning, I did not know you were awake," said Brutal. "Did you see him leave?"

Ariana hesitated, then as she sat up and stretched, said, "You might say that." Then she nudged Tyberius, who groaned and turned away from her onto his side.

Brutal's eyes narrowed a bit in frustration at the cryptic nature of her response. Seeing that everyone was either beginning to wake up or was in the process of preparing themselves for the day ahead, Brutal said to no one in particular, "I am going down to check on Isa," and with that, he bounded down the staircase multiple steps at a time, holding onto the railing with one hand and the wall with the other. Ariana was right, he found Isa sitting with his back to the temple wall, cross-legged, his eyes closed, and his large hands resting on his knees. Standing on the top step leading to the temple doors, Brutal enjoyed, for a moment, the quiet and the feel of the warm rays of sunlight on his face. The sun, slowly making its way up into the sky, was still not high enough to shine, with other buildings in the way, directly at ground level, thus keeping Isa in the darkened shadows of the dawn. "Everything okay, Isa?" Brutal asked, a little hesitantly, not sure if he should interrupt whatever the monk was doing.

Isa's eyes opened, and the half-orc looked up over his shoulder at Brutal. "Do we go?" Isa asked in a deep grumbly voice.

"Not yet. They are getting ready upstairs," Brutal said, motioning with a half-raised hand upwards. "We will be ready shortly." Isa nodded faintly, or maybe it was Brutal's own interpretation of a nod, and then the monk closed his eyes again, breathing deeply. Brutal looked at the monk for a moment longer, turned to go back inside, but was stopped by a nagging curiosity, and with his right hand still on the handle of the temple door, looked down at the monk and asked, "Why are you sitting down here?" Isa continued to sit motionless, but Brutal could hear the monk's deep breaths as he breathed in through his large nose, his large frame puffing up, and then, as he breathed out through pursed lips, his body slowly contracting. Brutal waited for a second, giving Isa a chance to reply, but the monk said nothing.

'Great,' Brutal thought to himself, 'Ariana answers in riddles, and Isa does not answer at all.' Giving the handle a quick turn, the door opened, and Brutal headed back inside. It was time, he thought, to get his own armor on and get ready himself.

* * * *

The mood on the second floor of the Temple of Zuel was one of quiet excitement, the air being charged with a mixture of anticipation and fear as everyone focused on their own tasks of preparation. Tyberius had it pretty simple, he slid his chain mail shirt over his padded tunic and attached his large flail to a clip on his thick brown belt. Slipping his leather boots on, and clipping his helmet to his backpack, he was done. Ariana also, had little to prepare, already wearing her leather shirt and leggings, she rolled up her blanket and affixed it to the top of her backpack, and adjusting two small bags on her belt, she was ready to go. Mikell was kneeling on his mattress, his hands folded in front of him, clasping his holy symbol of Zuel, as his body gently rocked back and forth as if in cadence to an unheard beat. Hammer and Julius were already finishing up getting their armor on.

Bealty, standing on a chair, helped buckle the straps of Brutal's breastplate. As Bealty finished up, Brutal looked around at everyone preparing for the upcoming day, impressed at how the group was forming up. Just an hour ago, everyone was lying around in a rag-tag assortment, but now they were beginning to take on a formidable look, and he smiled, feeling more confident than he ever had about the outcome of today. 'Thank you, mother of all battles, for bringing me such good companions,' he thought silently in gratitude to Soulmite. At the completion of his thought, as if on cue, the room grew darker. Brutal moved to the east facing window, near where Mikell was praying, and looking out saw a lone dark gray cloud obscuring the morning sun, creating a blood red sky between it and the horizon, as if blood were falling from the sky itself. Feeling his confidence shaken at the timing of the event, Brutal stepped away from the window, wiping his brow with the back of his hand; he had already worked up a sweat in the morning humidity and heat while putting his armor on.

"Are you okay?" asked Ariana, putting a soft hand on his shoulder, surprising him with how close she was.

"Oh...Oh yeah, I am fine," muttered Brutal, sneaking one more glance at the blood red sky, then regaining his composure, added, "It is going to be a hot day, I think."

"Yes," said Ariana, "hot and bloody, I fear."

Brutal looked into Ariana's eyes, his attention drawn to her choice of words. 'Bloody for damn sure,' he thought to himself, then nodding in agreement with her, he said, "Yeah. Bloody, too, I suspect."

Pardor, Mikell's father, who had slept near the altar during the night appeared at the top of the steps, carrying some loaves of bread and a hunk of ham. Isa was right behind him, carrying two jugs full of water, and they both walked over to the table by the southern window, stepping over and around all the gear scattered on the floor. Setting the food on the table, Pardor took a knife from his belt and began to cut pieces of the ham while the companions passed around the bread, each one ripping off a piece for themselves before passing it along.

"Sorry for not having a hot meal for you, but I do not usually cook, especially for so many," said Pardor waving the small knife clumsily in front of him, practically dropping it, "so I just picked up some food from Syd."

"Do not apologize," said Brutal. "Thank you for the meal. Can we repay you?"

The knife paused mid-cut in Pardor's hand and, without looking up, he said, "Well, just bring everyone home, that will be more than payment enough," then he continued his carving. Nobody seemed to know what to say further, or didn't have the confidence to reassure the older priest, except for Bealty, who, appearing next to Pardor, reached up and patted the priest on the back.

With their breakfast done, the companions gathered up all their equipment and, slinging their backpacks over their shoulders, began to assemble in the street outside the temple. Mikell gave his father a hug, and they exchanged a quiet word, and then Pardor went to all the others, and while shaking their hand, gave them each a quick blessing. As Pardor finished up, the group began the short walk to the town gates; the older priest watching his son walking away felt pride and fear. He, too, had adventured in his youth, but it seemed like simpler times and he always traveled with great numbers and well-organized formations. His son was going off to face an uncertain number of evil creatures, with, for the most part, untested companions. Holding onto his holy symbol of Zuel, he felt a pang of selfishness as he prayed, specifically, for his son's safe return.

* * * *

As the group neared the gate leading out of Telfar, Brutal hoped they wouldn't get harassed by the guards too much, but he also knew that seeing a large heavily armed group leaving the town, they would rouse a lot of questions. While they waited for their turn at the gate as other travelers were checked in and out of Telfar, Brutal, seeing the small wiry clerk that had given him a hard time before, let out a long groan, silently hoping the soldier would not remember him.

After a few moments, the sergeant waved the group forward. "Well, what have we here?" he asked as the group approached.

Brutal and Mikell were at the front of the group. Mikell, taking one step forward, raised his hand in greeting, saying, "Well met, Sergeant. We nine companions are heading to the north side, and then on our way to the Cruel Pass."

One of the sergeant's eyebrows tilted up in a mixture of curiosity, surprise, and disbelief. "What the hell are you going into the Cruel Pass for?" Before Mikell could answer, the sergeant added, "There ain't nothing up there except some bad shit. If you really are going that way, you best go to Whiteal first and find a caravan to ride along with." As the sergeant was talking, the clerk had picked up the large book and was walking closer to the group.

Brutal spoke up first. "No caravans will be going where we need to go, besides, as you can see," he said, gesturing to his companions behind him, "we are well equipped."

The sergeant let out a raspy laugh, which turned into a cough. Regaining his breath, a smile on his face, he looked Brutal in the eye and said, "Boy, if you run into one ogre up there, he would wipe out your entire crew here, and you could run into a clan of ogres in them hills," he said, pointing to the northeast, toward the distant pass. "The only thing that will keep you all safe is numbers." Looking past Brutal at the others standing behind him, he added coldly, "And nine ain't near enough."

"I recognize you," said the clerk to Brutal, pointing his feathered pen toward the warrior. "I remember all the liars."

Seeing Brutal's face flush red, Mikell put a hand on his friend's chest, holding him back. "I am not sure why you think us to be liars, but I assure you those are our plans."

The clerk, flipping a few pages backwards in the journal, ran his finger through the many entries, then said, "As I thought -- ten days ago your friend here came to get his hand healed so he could keep farming." Flipping all the pages back over to return to the present entry, the clerk's pursed smile was accentuated by his thin and spotty mustache clinging to his upper lip. "And now, here he is away on some grand, fool-hearty adventure. He was lyin' then and I thinks you's are lyin' now."

York made his way up next to Mikell. "I am York O'Lurn and can vouch for the truth of where we are going -- it is going to be a grand adventure indeed -- and I will make sure to note the very diligent guards of Telfar!"

"Like we would take the word of a bard, and an elf to boot, the biggest liars of them all," said the small clerk.

York, straightening up, gave the little man a defiant look. "I will have you know, my recountings are all true, good sir."

"I am sure they are," said the sergeant, regaining control of the conversation. "It does seem odd, but it is not against the laws of Telfar to get yourself killed in the hills. Give your names to Vindal here, and you can be on your way."

Everyone passed by, giving their names, and it was going well until Isa, the last in line of the group approached the little clerk. The short soldier with rat-like features looked up at the broad figure standing in front of him. "Pull your damn hood off," he said, pointing the pen at the monk's hooded head and flicking the feather end to gesture for the hood's removal. Isa stood there, unmoving. "Are you deaf under there?" asked Vindal. "Take. Off. Your. Hood," he said mockingly slow.

The sergeant's hand drifted down to the hilt of his sword as he moved closer to Isa. "Everyone must be seen, take off your hood," he commanded.

Isa's head turned to face the sergeant, then he slowly reached up and pulled it back, revealing his tusked half-orc face.

The sergeant's face did not change or show any visible surprise. "State your name," he said.

"Me is Isa," said the monk, then pulled his hood back up over his face.

Vindal wrote down the name and closed the journal. "Why, anyone would travel with a half-orc has got to be a fool -- he will surely kill you in your sleep," said the clerk.

Brutal, watching the procession, replied, "We will take our chances."

The sergeant looked at Brutal. "Vindal is a bit short on courtesy, but he is right about the half-orc. Have you known him for a long time?" he asked.

Brutal wanted to say yes, just to spite their little inquisition, but he did not want to lie to the man. "No, not long."

The sergeant smiled, an "I thought so" smile, then said, "Just be careful who you trust."

The sergeant's words struck Brutal like a punch to the gut, knocking the wind out of him, and he found himself speechless. Fey's warning rang out in his head: 'Trust only those who have proved themselves worthy of it.' A shiver ran down his spine. Giving the monk, who was already walking away with the rest of the group, a wary look -- Brutal could feel doubt creeping its way back into his mind. Still unable to speak, and not sure what he would say if he could, he nodded faintly to the sergeant, then giving the small clerk a final glance, he turned and began to walk away from the gates, and the safety of Telfar.

* * * *

On the ferry ride across the Great White River, everyone sat on the benches in the center of the ferry, except for Isa, who sat, cross-legged near the bow. Brutal, looking intently at the large half-orc, and feeling the pressure begin to build inside his head, rubbed his forehead with his left hand.

"Isa is a strange case," stated Mikell, sitting to the left of Brutal. "What are you thinking?"

Brutal blinked, embarrassed to be caught staring at the monk, and looked at his old friend. "I was wondering to myself: would I lay down my life for a group of people I had just met?" Brutal shifted his gaze back to the monk, who still sat unmoving. "I do not think I would."

"If you had promised to protect them, you might," said Mikell.

Brutal looked back at Mikell. "Maybe, but I worry about him," Brutal paused, contemplating if he should say what he was thinking.

"You are worried because he is half-orc?" Mikell asked before Brutal could continue.

Brutal, relieved his friend had said it first, let out a short breath through his nose. Lifting his right arm and gesturing to the monk at the bow, he said, "He will not even sit with us..." Brutal looked at his friend. "How do we expect him to fight for us?"

"He does not speak common very well, and he is a monk after all," said Mikell, "and perhaps he sits away to make us feel more comfortable."

Brutal chuckled. "You mean, like a favor to us?"

"Well, would you rather he sits on the bench across from us," Mikell said, pointing to the bench a few feet away, "staring at us?"

Brutal smiled again. "I suppose not."

Mikell gripped Brutal's knee. "Great things are happening, Brutal. I feel the power of Zuel more intensely than I ever have. I do not know what is in store for us on the other side of the river, but I do think Soulmite and Zuel want us to go there."

Brutal let his eyes drift back to Isa, his smile gone, asking, "Yeah, but you said Isa worships Craven?" Mikell nodded his head, and Brutal continued, "What does Craven have to do with this?"

Mikell shook his head. "I do not know. But the gods of the shadows dwell between good and evil," Mikell thought for a moment, "balance is the driving impetus for them and so they find themselves sometimes aligned with good...and sometimes evil." Seeing the skeptical look on Brutal's face, Mikell added, "Too much light or too much darkness, and the shadows disappear."

"If a gnoll had beaten Isa in that stupid arm wrestling match," Brutal said, "I wonder if he would be fighting on our side, or their side today?

Mikell let out a laugh. "Interesting question, I guess we will never know..."

* * * *

Delivered safely to the north bank of the river, Ariana, Tyberius, and Julius headed to the stables to get the horses while the others gathered near the gate, waiting. With the horses saddled and readied, Ariana and Julius mounted up, and the three companions joined the rest of the group at the gate.

A guard standing near them asked the group. "Are you ready to go?"

Everyone looked around at the faces of their companions. Ariana's pony neighed as if answering the question, and the group had a good laugh. Mikell, slinging a backpack over his shoulder, said, "We are ready, raise the gate."

The guard turned and yelled, "Raise 'er up boys!" And, with that, a whip cracked and the team of oxen started moving forward, lifting the portcullis open. Hammer, was the last one out, and as he passed the threshold of the gate, the soldier let out another command, "Close er down!" And the gate creaked downward, slamming with a dull thud into the hardened ground, compacted by thousands of poundings. Nobody looked back, and putting their heads down they began the zig-zagging climb up the bluffs overlooking the river.

Julius, trotting his brown horse toward the front of the group, turned in his saddle and said, "I am going to go up ahead and scout the area until you arrive. Wait for me at the turn."

"I will be going with ya," said Tyberius.

"That is a good idea," said Mikell, "it is better to stay in pairs."

Julius's thin elven-like lips widened into a smile. "Can you keep up with a horse, Tyberius?"

Tyberius, his own grin returning, and pointing at the brown horse, said, "What, that thing? You must be kidding." Looking back at Ariana, he said, "I will see you at the turn."

"I go with you," Isa said to Tyberius, grabbing everyone's attention with his first voluntary words of the day.

Tyberius looked skeptically at the monk. "Can you keep up?"

Isa nodded. "Yes."

"Well then, we will find out," said Tyberius, taking off up the hill at a blistering pace. Isa, who had always seemed to move at a deliberate pace, bolted into action, following close behind the warrior.

"Take me with you, Julius," said Bealty, I can help scout, too," then added, "that is my specialty."

"Among other things," said Ariana, her comment laced with sarcasm.

Notorious for being unable to discern or perhaps a stubborn unwillingness to acknowledge sarcasm -- an oft-used tactic by those traveling with halflings -- Bealty looked up at her and nodded in agreement. "Yes, among other things."

"Let us get going then, we cannot let Tyberius beat us to the turn," said Julius.

Bealty noticed that Mikell, taking the momentary respite in their journey to examine the leather boot on his right foot, had knelt down to one knee. Taking three quick steps and using Mikell's back like a springboard, the halfling sprang into the air doing a full somersault, and upon landing on the rump of Julius's horse, did a quick hop into a sitting position behind Julius, his short legs gripping the sides of the horse.

"Hey!" shouted Mikell, but it was too late to do anything about it, and looking up at the small halfling, he added, "Next time just ask."

Bealty shook his head and, looking over his shoulder, said, "You know better than that, Mikell." Julius, giving the horse a quick kick, took off at a trot, following the well-worn road. The brisk clop-clop of the trotting horse quickly faded into the distance, and the five remaining companions on the road, soon found themselves alone.

Hammer, his war hammer resting over his shoulder, gave Mikell a look. "What did the little guy mean by that?

Mikell, standing up, brushed his hands off. "Never ask for permission when you can ask for forgiveness," said Mikell, placing his hands on his hips, "it is a halfling mantra, if there ever was one." Brutal chuckled and, shaking his head, he started moving up the winding road, with the other four companions falling in behind him.

"I do not get it," said Hammer, scratching his chin.

＊ ＊ ＊ ＊

The Telfar road, winding its way up the steep bluffs overlooking the Great White River, straightens out upon reaching the flat plains above. Tyberius and Isa, with their direct route up the side of the bluff, managed to reach the top before Julius and Bealty. Once on the straight stretch, they began to lose ground and could first hear, and then see, Julius's approaching horse.

"Not even you can outdistance a horse, Tyberius," said Julius as they finally reached the walking pair.

Tyberius, looking up at the ranger smiled his grin and said, "Maybe, but we beat ya to the top though." After a short pause, he added, "I hate to tell ya this, but I think ya picked up a giant tick on the way."

Bealty leaned to look around Julius. "That is the second bug in two days that I have been compared to."

Tyberius, still grinning, asked, "Somebody else called ya a tick?"

"No," said Bealty, "last night York wrote my name down as Beetle in his journal thing. I ain't never been compared to a bug before, and now it is twice in two days."

"What is York writing about?" asked Tyberius.

"He is a bard," said Julius, "he is probably recording things to retell later."

"Yeah, that is what he said he was doing," confirmed Bealty.

"But he called you 'Beetle,' huh?" asked Tyberius.

"Yeah -- he said it had a better 'ring' to it," said Bealty, gesturing with his hands.

"A better ring?" asked Tyberius, suddenly thinking about the ring Fey had given him.

"You know -- he means it 'sounds' better," said Bealty.

"I think he is right...'Beetle' does have a better 'ring' to it," said Tyberius, parroting the new use of the word. After a few more steps, Tyberius asked, "What did he write about me?"

"I did not see what he wrote about you," said Bealty, "but I am sure he will be telling the story of your arm wrestling match with Isa for a long time." This seemed to please Tyberius, his grin returning.

"How far?" asked Isa in his gruff voice, jarring the others back to reality and the task at hand.

"About two miles up ahead on the left side of the road," said Julius, pointing up ahead.

"What is plan?" asked Isa.

"How about you and Isa approach the swale from the west side, and we," Julius said indicating Bealty and himself, "will approach from the east since we will be riding?"

"I work better alone," said Bealty. "I will ride with you to the east side, but once there I will go in on foot, by myself." Julius leaned to look down at his small passenger.

Bealty looked up. "No offense, Julius," he said, patting the ranger on the side, "the wilds may be your thing, but the whole world is mine -- they will never find me out there."

Julius turned around, saying, "Fine, you and Isa approach from the west, and Bealty and I will circle around to the east side." Half-turning to face Bealty, he added, "No gnoll is going to spot me in the wild unless

I want him to." Julius gave his horse a kick and moved down the road at a trot.

Tyberius slapped Isa's shoulder. "C'mon, we gotta start movin'." The two large companions began moving quickly down the road, their silhouettes in stark contrast to one another, one tall and lanky, the other shorter and much broader. After a few hundred feet, the two left the road and disappeared into the rolling plains alive with a mixture of green and brown grasses.

* * * *

About a mile away from the turn, Julius directed his mount into the grass on the southwest side of the road, away from the swale. "We should not ride directly to the turn," said Julius, "who knows what kind of lookouts they might have, and we cannot risk detection."

"Makes sense to me," agreed Bealty.

The two rode west a few hundred yards, then began going northwest, parallel to the main road. This allowed them to pass unnoticed by the swale to the north and stay concealed from the gnolls -- 'If they were looking,' thought Julius to himself. Once they reached the road to the farms, the ranger pulled on the reins of his horse and it came to a halt near a large outcrop of bushes, and said, "Alright, let us get down and go on foot from here." Instantly Bealty rolled off the side of the horse, landing on his feet like a cat. Julius was more cautious but also dismounted.

"Tyberius said the door was on the south side of the swale, so that is where I will approach," said Bealty.

"Are you sure about that?" asked Julius.

"I want to get a good look at the doorway from the top," replied Bealty.

"It could be dangerous," frowned Julius, "if something..."

Bealty cut him off with a wave of his tiny hand. "This whole thing is dangerous," then looking up at the half-elf, "I will be fine." And, with that, the halfling, in full daylight, disappeared into the tall grass.

Julius could hear Bealty moving, the swishing grass giving him away, but only for a moment, and then even that trace bit evidence, of his small friend's location, soon blended in with the rustling sound of the wind blowing through the grassy plain. Checking his gear one more time, the ranger removed his longbow from where it was attached to his mount and slinging the quiver of arrows over his shoulder, he too began heading toward the hidden entrance -- first heading due north, so he could circle around and approach the swale from the east. As he neared the Telfar road again, he began to move in a crouching position, using the grass for cover and not giving anyone looking a significant profile above the grass. At the edge of the grass along the road, Julius listened, using his elven ears to pick up the faintest sounds, but the wind was blowing fairly hard today and the grass was pretty noisy -- 'probably better for us,' he thought wryly to himself, but he could feel his heart begin to pump a little harder -- knowing that after he crossed the road, he was only a short distance from the swale, and things would become less predictable once contact was made with any gnoll. Taking a deep breath, in through his nose, and letting it out slowly from his mouth, he could feel his heart rate settle a little. He gave himself time for one more controlled breath, then quickly moved across the open road, still in a crouch. His eyes scanned the road in both directions for the few seconds it took him to cross, and thankfully he saw nothing -- and no one. Once back into the relative safety of the tall grass, he began to carefully move northwest until he felt that he was in position, then started moving directly west, as planned.

Julius knew he was getting close and allowed himself a quick peek above the top of the grass to get his bearings. There it was, just fifty more feet and he would be at the lip of the swale, where the ground began to dip down into the bowl. He got down onto his hands and knees and belly crawled the last ten feet, reaching the edge of the swale. He knew the entrance was to his left somewhere but still couldn't make it out. 'For gnolls, it is cleverly hid,' he thought to himself. As the wind swirled around in the bowl, he caught a whiff of the stinking carcasses that lay piled up, causing his nose to wrinkle up in disgust. 'Filthy pigs,' he thought, as he continued to scan the area for any activity, then he saw a head poke up from the grass on the other side of the swale -- a head that was not human or half-orc. "Oh, shit…" he whispered to himself, knowing that Tyberius and Isa would be heading right into that area. His mind raced, trying to figure out what he should do. He looked back to the south, where Bealty should be, but, of course, there was no sign of the little halfling. He looked back at the head across the swale, and it seemed to be looking directly at him, but there's no way it could see him. 'Could it?' he asked himself. If there was going to be a fight, he thought he better get moving around the north side of the swale so he could help. Having made up his mind, Julius was about to back up and start making his way around, when the sunlight glinted off the face of the gnoll, catching his eye. He stopped and looked at the face again. The distance made it difficult -- but there it was again! Each time the gnoll turned its head, the sunlight reflected off its head. "What the..." Julius whispered, unable to understand what he was seeing. The gnoll's head disappeared for a second back into the grass and then popped back up, but this time it was a human head, and the thin face and red hair gave it away. "Damn his stupid helmet," Julius whispered, now recognizing that it was Tyberius's helmet which was shaped like the head of some beast that had confused him. Carefully, Julius raised a hand above the grass. It took Tyberius a second to spot it, but then he too waived in acknowledgment.

Tyberius slunk back down into the grass. "What the hell took him so long?" he whispered to Isa, lying beside him. "He is the ranger..." He let the thought pass without finishing the sentence. He thought for a minute, then whispered somewhat rhetorically, "Well, now what the hell do we do? Maybe we should not have split up." Isa simply grunted. "What is that supposed to mean?" asked Tyberius but Isa did not respond further as the monk maintained his wary watch of the swale full of carcasses. The hood of his robe was pulled back, but his face still hid any sign of emotion, even when the breeze carried the smell of death over them. "I guess we will wait here and just keep an eye on things," Tyberius said, shrugging his shoulders, and proceeded to lay back down on his belly, propping himself up with his elbows.

After a while of watching nothing happen, Tyberius whispered, "This is bullshit, there ain't nobody around."

"Shhhhh..." hissed Isa.

Tyberius glanced over at the monk lying next to him, whispering, "You ain't said a damn thing all the way here, and the first thing you do is shush me?"

"The monk is right," came a whisper from behind the two prone companions. Tyberius and Isa both jerked their heads to look behind them, seeing Julius in a crouched position.

The ranger waived for them to follow him, and he slunk off to the west, a little way away from the swale. Once the other two had caught up to him, Julius said, "I made my way around the swale to the north to find you. I did not see lookouts, but I did see a fresh trail heading northeast. It is hard to say how many, but there were definitely more than just a few tracks."

"So, you think there ain't nobody inside there?" asked Tyberius.

Julius shrugged. "I do not know, all I know is that some of them look like they headed out, and not long ago."

"This is good," said Isa.

"How is this good?" asked Tyberius.

Isa put his hands together and then as he separated them, said, "they is divided now."

"There is some truth in that," said Julius, "but I am concerned that they could return while we are inside, and that could make things tricky."

"Where is Beetle?" asked Tyberius, using the bard's new nickname for their little companion.

"He wanted to check out the area above the entrance, and insisted he go alone," said Julius.

"Oh shit," said Tyberius, looking back toward the southern edge of the swale, "that could be bad..."

"I tried to argue with him, but he ran off into the grass before I could stop him," said Julius. "Look," he continued, "you should head back to the road and get the others to follow you here. Isa and I will stay back to make sure there are no surprises waiting for you."

Tyberius nodded. "Okay, we will meet you right here," he said, pointing to the ground. He gave the other two a quick look and said, "be careful," then taking off his helmet and handing it to Julius, he raced off to the southeast, toward the road, his large flail, bouncing against his back as he ran. He ran for about a half-mile when he first heard the faint sounds of voices coming from up ahead in the road, and, sure enough, it turned out to be Ariana, Brutal, Mikell, Hammer, and York. His large grin returned to his face at the sight of Ariana, and as he approached, he waved his hand. "Keep your voices down," he said. "It is not far now, and I could hear you from a long ways off."

"Did you see anything up there? Are there any lookouts?" asked Brutal.

"Nah," said Tyberius with a wave of his hand, "there ain't nothing up there except a pile of dead shit...and man does it reek."

"I forgot about that, but that is what drew me to the site in the first place: the smell," said Brutal.

"What do you mean...a pile of dead shit?" asked York.

Tyberius grinned again. "First, we gotta pick up the pace, cause we are in a bit of a race against time." As the group began to quicken their steps, Tyberius turned to the bard. "As for the pile, well, let me tell ya what gnolls do with their left-overs -- it ain't pretty..."

＊ ＊ ＊ ＊

Bealty had always felt more at home in the dark. The shadows had always been his friend, but the grassy plain was proving to be almost equally as good for concealment -- especially on a windy day like today with the grass in constant motion; it was like swimming underwater, unless you broke the surface, no one would know you were even there. Of course, this was better, he thought to himself, because he could breathe as he made his way under the surface of the grass, so to speak. It did not take him long to make his way to the top of the entrance. Whereas his taller companions had to crouch or crawl to stay below the tops of the grass, he was able to run, only slightly crouching, weaving his way through the thick cover. He slowed, figuring that the swale would open up just ahead, and even though his thirty-two pounds didn't create loud footfalls, taking chances at revealing his position to anything above ground or, in this case, possibly below ground, wasn't something he wanted to do. He listened carefully, but the one drawback to the wind was that it did make quite a bit of noise, and so he could only hear the rustling sound and occasional whistle of the wind making its way through the grass. Slowly, he made his way forward, examining the ground before each step, looking for anything out of the ordinary -- an odd shaped stone, an empty patch of ground -- anything that might hint at the location of a trap or anything else that looked man-made, or 'beast-made' thing, he reminded himself. Nothing caught his well-trained eye, so he kept inching forward, until finally he was at the edge of the grass, overlooking the swale. Taking his time, he examined the sides of the swale, looking for hints of other hidden clues to what might be below, or especially if there were other entrances -- 'If I lived in a hole in the ground, I would want more than one way out' he thought to himself. But the diameter of the swale was large enough that he couldn't see good detail all the way around. 'Well,' he thought to himself, 'I just need to make my way around.' So looking left and right, he decided to first try looking to the western side and began methodically moving around the edge, examining the steep slope below him as he went.

It had only been a few minutes, then Bealty stopped, an impish grin already starting to appear on his face. "Luck smiles on the faithful," he whispered to Graff, the good god of luck -- which was about as close as he ever came to saying an actual prayer. A faint, but altogether too straight, line ran vertically up the side of the slope below him. It would be easy to miss, but not to him -- this was not a natural feature of the land, and the hairs on the back of his neck stood up, knowing that he was sitting on top of the entrance. Bealty thoroughly looked the area over, but from his vantage point, he could not see any opening mechanism, 'I will have to go down to find it,' he thought, but he couldn't risk doing that alone, so he decided to wait for the others to show up.

* * * *

It took a little while, but keeping up a fast walking pace, Tyberius and the others finally joined Julius and Isa, near an old fallen tree, just west of the swale. Ariana, the only mounted person in the group, slid down the side of her pony, and tied Bella's reins to an old gnarled branch of the tree, next to Julius's gray mare which calmly chewed on a cud of grass.

Julius, stepping forward, said, "Let us rest for a moment, and discuss how we want to approach this."

"That is a good idea," said Mikell. "This kind of thing is new to all of us, so we need to make sure we all understand what we are about to do."

"We are gonna kill some damn gnolls," said Hammer, slapping the war hammer into the palm of his hand as punctuation.

"I like the enthusiasm, but we need to be smart here -- we cannot just go charging in there," said Mikell, pointing toward the swale -- then, looking around as if just remembering something, asked, "Where is Bealty?"

Julius nodded back toward the swale. "He insisted on going alone, he wanted to inspect the area around the entrance." Seeing Brutal and Mikell exchanging worried looks, the ranger added, "I tried to talk him out of it, but like I said, he insisted. He must be okay, we have not heard a peep from around the swale. If he had gotten into some trouble, we would know about it."

Trying to make eye contact with everyone, Brutal said, with some frustration, "We have been delaying this for too long, and I am ready to go in -- I mean what are we going to discuss? We do not know what is down there, so there is no preparing for it. Tyberius, Hammer, and myself will make the front line. Then you," he said, pointing to Mikell, "and Ariana, York, and Bealty will be in the middle, with Julius and Isa in the rear."

"What about traps?" asked Mikell. "Bealty will need to be in the front."

Brutal thought about that and nodded. "Aye, Bealty will be in the front with us, but he will have to, well," Brutal searched for the right words, but could not find them, "to do whatever halflings do during a fight."

"You might be surprised what a halfling can accomplish in a fight," added York. "What they lack in power, they make up for with ferocity, and shall we say -- placement."

"Yeah, multiple stab wounds to the ankle," chuckled Hammer. "He does his job with the traps -- and we will take care of the gnolls." Nobody laughed with him, everyone's face looked taught, the anticipation now that they were here, was hitting a crescendo.

"Let us move," said Brutal, who began walking toward the familiar swale. Everyone else followed. As they crested the top ridge, the bowl-shaped area appeared; carcasses, like bumps on the plains, littered the area.

"Oh, the smell is awful," said Ariana, placing a hand over her nose and mouth.

"You get used to it," said Tyberius. Ariana gave him a doubtful look but composed herself and, letting her hand drop to her side, she soldiered on, down the slope, the group following her into the base of the swale.

Seeing the group come over the ridge and into the base of the swale, Bealty hopped up from his sitting positing and carefully moved away from the entrance and descended the slope, and crossing the fifty yards, joined his companions. "I guess we are just going in then?" he asked as he approached the group. Everyone nodded in the affirmative. "Great -- I will lead the way."

"You found the door?" asked Brutal.

"Yep, I also think I figured out how to open it," said Bealty.

"Great," said Brutal, motioning with an outstretched hand, "lead the way." Without waiting for anything further, Bealty took off across the basin, dodging a carcass here and there, until he and the group were standing in front of what was seemingly just a steep part of the hill surrounding the depression.

"I do not see it," said Hammer. "There is a door there?"

"Uh-huh," said Bealty. Looking over his shoulder, he asked, "Are we ready?"

Brutal drew his new bastard sword. Tyberius unclipped the large flail from his back. Hammer already had his war hammer in hand and continued to lightly pat it into his other hand. Mikell unclipped the heavy mace clipped to his belt and, flexing his hand, tightened his grip on his wooden shield. Julius slung his longbow around his shoulder and drew his longsword from its scabbard. Isa flexed his hands and cracked a few of his knuckles. York, leaving his longsword sheathed, instead pulled out a small set of drums. Ariana opened her backpack, at which point Foetore leapt out onto her shoulder and scurried down her leather tunic, and settled into a pouch on her belt. After everyone seemed to be ready, Bealty drew out a dagger from his belt and, moving forward reached into what seemed like the side of the hill and pulled on a lever within. A loud click could be heard, and then a large door, covered with a layer of dirt and grass swung open, the hinges creaking loudly as it did so, sending shivers up everyone's spine.

"That is great," said Hammer, "now our best hope is that all the gnolls are deaf."

Bealty jumped onto the hill aside the doorway and quickly scrambled back to the top of the hill, right above the door. The rest of the group braced, expecting gnolls to come charging out -- but nothing else happened. The area inside the doorway was dark, even with the sun shining overhead. Brutal, Tyberius, and Hammer slowly made their way to the entrance. Once they were closer, they could see that a steep earthen staircase led downward. It was not completely dark -- several torches sat in sconces on the sides of the tunnel -- but they could not see all the way down as the passageway curved about thirty feet down.

Hammer let out a long whistle. "Damn, that goes a long way down!" he said, vocalizing a thought, unknown to him, that was also shared by Brutal and Tyberius, who both looked at each other.

Brutal looked back at the group, his eyes were steadfast, and motioning with his bastard sword in his right hand. "Time to do what we came here to do," and, with that, he stepped inside the entrance.

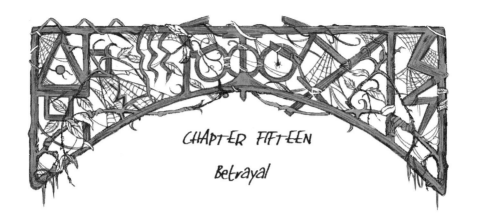

CHAPTER FIFTEEN
Betrayal

YEAR: AG 1172, Month of Sepu

ANTHALL FELT THE FAMILIAR TINGLE AND DISCOMFORT of the healing spell flow through his body -- he could feel bones setting and cuts closing; the process was always a little unnerving despite its positive effects. Despite the spell, Anthall did not feel even close to full health; he knew he had suffered a great deal of damage during the battle -- so much that it would take several powerful healing spells to mend all his wounds. However, the one spell was enough to bring him back from the brink of death -- 'if that's what that was,' he thought to himself. Anthall tried to push himself up from the ground, but found he still could not move his arms. 'Odd,' he thought to himself, finally opening his eyes.

It took a moment for his vision to come into focus, and when it did, he realized he was no longer outside, but rather inside a tent. He was lying down but quickly realized that his arms were shackled behind his back and around a thick pole which was no doubt dug deep enough into the ground to make breaking out of his predicament impossible. He looked around, confused -- the last thing he could remember were the bugbears running away. The tent didn't look like something a bugbear would use. 'So what could this be?' he wondered. The furnishings weren't lavish but did have some comfort to them -- including a large table that dominated the middle of the room, with a few chairs pushed in around it. Two smaller tables lined the side of the tent opposite from him: one had a large pitcher sitting on it with several mugs, and the other had a bowl of fruit and some bread, which looked fresh and untouched. With some effort, and quite a bit of discomfort, he was finally able to right himself, allowing him to lean back against the pole, offering him some relief and a better view of the tent. He could see the feet of two people standing outside, as the flaps of the tent doors lightly blew about in the wind.

Anthall tried to call the guards but found his throat intensely dry, and he croaked out a muffled and unintelligible sound. It took him a moment to work up a little saliva and swallow it. This time, he managed to raise his voice loud enough that the guards outside could hear him. "Hey... Hey, you!"

A hand reached in through the gap and pulled back one side of the doorway flap, poking his head inside, he gave Anthall a hard look. "The marshal will be with you shortly," the soldier said.

"What? Marshal Krugar?" asked Anthall, his bloody face contorted with confusion.

The soldier paused and looked away from Anthall, seemingly not wanting to make eye contact -- almost as if he was ashamed. "Yes," he said, looking back at Anthall. "Marshal Krugar."

"There must be some...some mistake -- I am General Mixnor, we are on the same side!" he said, exasperated.

The soldier, again looking uncomfortable, shook his head, saying, "I am sorry, sir, the marshal will be back shortly," and, with that, he turned his back on Anthall, letting the tent flap close behind him.

Anthall's mind raced, searching for the logical explanation for his predicament, but nothing made sense. Then he remembered the ogre mage saying something. 'What was it,' he thought to himself. 'A sacrifice?' he thought. 'By Marshal Krugar? ...No, it could not be true.' He rested his head against the pole, a sense of desperation beginning to creep into his being. The tent flap flew open abruptly, and Marshal Krugar and a priest he did not recognize entered the tent, the flap closing behind them, muffling the noise from outside. The marshal was wearing his familiar splint mail suit, and his black cape with gold trim was unmistakable. "What the hell is going on, Marshal?" Anthall asked, his confidence returning. Marshal Krugar slowly removed the gauntlet from his left hand; once it was off, he then began methodically pulling off the gauntlet from his right hand, ignoring Anthall's presence in the room. Anthall's voice now crackled with rage. "Krugar, what are you doing, and why am I shackled in this tent?"

Krugar glanced over at the priest standing silently, his hands clasped in front of him, and said, "Oh, how rude of me," Marshal Krugar said, placing a now open hand over his heart and setting the gauntlets down on the table next to him. "Anthall Mixnor, let me introduce you to High Priest Judar Ruverge," said Krugar, motioning to each man as he mentioned their names.

Anthall could see the holy symbol hanging around the high priest's neck and for the first time, he began to really worry. "The three circles," said Anthall, "I recognize the symbol of Blick." Then shifting his eyes to Krugar, he asked, "What are you up to? Theol, and certainly Bindal, were he still with us, would not look favorably upon a priest of Blick," he said the name of the evil god of spite and suffering with no small amount of distaste, "being used in his service."

"You are correct, General Mixnor. He really is fearless," Judar said as he took a step closer to Anthall and crouched down, letting his weight balance and rest on his toes -- his red robes, flecked with gold, covered what looked like chain mail underneath. Anthall recognized the boots from the battlefield, and looked at the priest, now almost eye level with himself.

"Let me go...I have done nothing but serve Kardoon here today," Anthall said.

Judar smiled, his teeth were white but small and jagged like a piranha and, looking back at Krugar, said, "He thinks it is the same day as the battle with Krykl." Turning his attention back to Anthall, the priest's smile faded, replaced by an evil careless stare. "You do not know where, or when, you are, do you?"

"Let me speak to Theol," said Anthall referring to Theol Kardoon, the current king and the son of Bindal Kardoon.

Krugar laughed. "You are right about one thing, my boy, I do not think Theol, praise the king, would approve of my associate, Judar, here," Krugar began moving around the table in the middle of the room to get closer to Anthall, "so I am afraid that is out of the question."

Anthall, again felt confusion setting in, but the mention of Krykl's name brought back with it the memory of the ogre-mage's threat to kill his family. That memory lit a flame inside his soul and burned away any other concern. He locked eyes with Marshal Krugar. "Krykl said he was going to kill my family -- just let me go back to Telfar," then looking at the priest crouched beside him, "I will never mention anything of this priest." Looking at the faces of his two captors, he could tell he would need to do better than that, "I promise, on Soulmite's honor, that I will not talk to anyone about this -- just let me go back to Telfar and live my life out peacefully."

Krugar sat on the edge of the table, taking some of the weight off his feet, the older marshal could still fight well but had gained more weight than he should have as he advanced in age, and the splint mail armor added that much more pressure onto his feet. "Ahhhh..." the marshal let out a relieved sigh, "it is no fun growing old, Anthall, let me assure you of that."

"Fuck growing old, Krugar, just let me go!" said Anthall.

"The odd thing is," said the Krugar, "I really believe you. I mean, you swear on Soulmite's honor, and if things were different, and I wish they were, I would just let you go. But," he continued, throwing up his palms waist high, "things are not that simple," then shaking his head, almost remorsefully, added, "they seldom are." Anthall strained with all his might on the metal shackles, but there was no give, and the metal bracers began to dig into his wrists, causing them to bleed. "Now, now," said Krugar, "do not go and injure yourself further -- it is really pointless, you cannot break these shackles."

Anthall, his face red from the exertion and rage, tried bashing the pole with his back while pushing with his legs, but the pole didn't budge. Judar and the marshal watched, entertained with his struggle. Finally calming down, his energy already low from his previous wounds, Anthall sat back against the pole. "You cannot just kill me -- Theol will want to know what happened to me... So we need to come to some agreement here."

A grin crept across Marshal Krugar's face, but it wasn't a friendly grin, it was something that came from the evil depths of hell. "You are right on both accounts," then the grin disappeared and the marshal's face darkened even further, "but it will not be the agreement you are hoping for."

Anthall's eyes hardened, locking in on Krugar's face, looking for some hint of vulnerability, but he could find none, and said, "Enough with the scare tactics, let me out of these shackles and let me be on my way."

Krugar just stared back at Anthall, their gazes locked together, neither man blinking until finally Marshal Krugar stood up and broke the silence. "The battle with Krykl and the bugbears was three days ago." Krugar started walking back around the table, turning his back to Anthall. "Your faith is strong, Anthall, and has saved you so far."

"What are you talking about, Krugar?" Anthall asked.

"Not too bright, are you Anthall," Judar said, more of a statement than a question.

"Now, now, Judar," said Krugar still making his way around to the other side, "he is just confused, and you would be, too," he said, wagging a finger at the priest, "if you had suffered the same injuries." Having made his way around the table, he now stood behind the crouching priest, both men now looking intently at Anthall. "You are right, we need to come to an agreement -- the three of us," he said, pointing his finger and using a circular motion.

"You let me go," Anthall stated again, "and you will never see, or hear from me again -- and I swear on Soulmite's honor that I will never see or tell Theol anything."

Krugar smiled again and let out a half-hearted laugh. "Theol would be most surprised to see you..."

"Why would that be?" asked Anthall.

Krugar frowned, irritated at being interrupted. Regaining his composure, he said, "Simple, my boy, because you are already dead."

Judar laughed, a croaky dismal cackle, and added, "You just do not know it."

CHAPTER SIXTEEN
Into The Lair

YEAR: AG 1175, Month of Sepu

BRUTAL BARELY PLACED HIS FOOT ONTO THE FIRST STEP, when Bealty leapt down from on top of the doorway. Landing with one foot on Brutal's right shoulder and his small hand on the warrior's head, he then proceeded to jump down the remaining six feet. Bealty did it in such a fluid motion, that Brutal wasn't sure what had just happened and flinched reflexively, albeit too late. Before the warrior knew it, the halfling had shot past him and was headed down the stairs. "Let me go first," Bealty whispered, dagger drawn.

"Yeah," Brutal whispered, "right, good idea." The hallway was cut out of the earth, had wooden supports, a curved ceiling, and was close to eight feet wide, comfortable enough for two people to walk side by side, but would force any fighting into a close quarter affair. As agreed, Bealty was first, then Brutal and Tyberius, with Hammer just behind them, and Mikell, Ariana, and York in the middle, and Isa and Julius bringing up the rear. Once they were all in, Julius grabbed hold of a crude handle on the inside of the door, and with a heave, pulled it shut -- creating a solid "whoomp" as it closed, as well as a softer metallic click as the door latched into place. With the sunlight gone, the descending hallway took on a much more menacing look -- the light from the torches dancing along the walls, creating moving shadows. Everyone stopped and looked up the stairs at Julius, and for the first time, they could hear noises coming from below -- and it sounded like voices.

Twenty feet down the stairs, at the point where the stairway began to curve, Bealty suddenly stopped, and without saying a word or looking back, he raised his hand, telling the others to stop. Bealty had found something along the floor. His little fingers traced a groove which led him to the wall. Continuing to trace a finger up the wall, he found several small holes. Brutal moved forward slowly until he was close to Bealty and whispered, "What the hell are you doing?"

"Found a trap," Bealty said, "some kind of dart I am guessing -- poisoned probably, but hard to tell until you see the dart." Finding the right tool, he pulled out what looked like a long, very skinny, set of tongs.

A concerned look came over Brutal's face. "Now, what are you doing? Cannot we just go around it?"

Bealty looked up at Brutal. "Well, we could -- but what if we have to come back this way in a hurry? We might forget it is here and then..." Bealty stopped talking and dramatically poked his finger into Brutal's thigh, adding, "Besides, I need the practice."

"This is no time for practice," said Brutal. A loud grunt followed by some guttural laughing came from below and was much louder than before -- either they were making more noise, or worse, getting closer. "Well, hurry up then," added Brutal.

Bealty took the tongs and shoved it down into one of the holes, fished around for a second, and pulled out a small dart. After examining the needle tip, he broke the sharp end off on a wooden beam along the wall. "Not poisoned...at least I do not think so," he said, and then taking what looked like little wooden wedges out of another pouch, he quickly and quietly pushed them into the holes -- plugging them. "There," he said, barely audible, and he put the little tongs back into one of his mysterious pouches. "The trap will still spring, but it will not hurt anyone now."

Brutal was impressed and, patting the halfling's shoulder, whispered, "Nicely done."

Tyberius moved closer to Brutal and Bealty, hugging the left side of the wall, being careful not to step on the pressure plate in the floor. He started to peer around the curving wall but stopped, "Damn this curving tunnel," he whispered to no one in particular, "I cannot see around it without exposing myself."

"That is what I am here for, Ty," said Bealty. "All of you stay here," he added, pointing a finger at the rest of the group. "I will go down first and see what is down there." Brutal had a concerned look on his face, but he didn't say anything, nor did anyone else, so the halfling got into a crouch and with his black leather armor, melded into the shadows, disappearing around the corner without a sound.

Hammer watched as Bealty disappeared around the bend in the hallway. He could feel his hands already begin to shake as the adrenaline was starting to flow through his body. Turning slightly to look behind him, he said to Mikell, "That little guy is one brave son of a bitch."

Mikell gave Hammer a quick look, their eyes meeting briefly. "While he does his part, get ready to do yours." Mikell, his mace already in hand, motioned for Hammer to keep his eyes forward.

Ariana glanced down at Foetore, their minds connecting. "Stay here and watch the door," she said telepathically, and Foetore immediately scampered out of the bag and leapt gracefully to the floor. Isa and Julius, who were in the rear of the group watched as the ferret ran between them and headed back up the stairs. Ariana could see the same curious look on each of their faces, "Foetore will let me know if anything comes through that door. Isa squinted in disbelief, distrust, or simply not understanding; which one Ariana could not tell. Julius nodded slightly. "We can count on Foetore," she said, turning her attention back down the stairs. Julius sheathed his longsword and taking the longbow slung around his shoulder, readied, nocking an arrow.

Bealty, crouching, was barely a foot and a half tall, and his movements like that of a cat stalking its prey -- each step slow and graceful. The tips of his toes were the only thing touching the ground, and he had one hand feeling the wall ahead of him. The hallway curved to the right, then back to the left making something of an 'S' shape -- with enough of a bend that one could not see past the slight curves. Inching his way around the second curve, the light was a little brighter and he could see the stairs ending at an archway leading into a room. He could hear several low guttural voices -- how many and what they were saying was difficult to determine, due to the distance and poor acoustics of the dirt walls. Although there was more light at the bottom of the stairs, there were still plenty of shadows to hide in, so he continued moving forward.

It didn't take him long to move the final twenty feet down the stairs. He continued to hug the right side of the wall, allowing him to see the western, left half, of the room. The construction seemed awfully good for gnolls, he thought to himself noting the arched ceiling of the room. Straight across from him, about thirty feet away was a closed, heavy wooden door. In the north-western corner, along the west wall, he could see a rack full of spears, and axes. The voices were clearer now, although they were coming from the eastern side of the room, which he could not see without peering around the corner. Taking a step backwards, Bealty moved to the other side of the hallway and using his hands as an extra set of feet, slunk forward so he could see the northeastern quarter of the room. Finally, he saw the source of the voices and froze: four large gnolls. They were sitting around a crude wooden table, using large, simple, logs as stools. Two were facing toward him and the open archway, and the two others had their backs to him. Each of the gnolls was armored with piecemeal bits of what looked like a mixture of chain mail and leather woven together, and each had a large war ax lying on the table in front of them. Several lanterns hung on the walls, making the room fairly well lit. The voices were clear now, but he could not understand the mixture of barks and grunts -- although they seemed animated about something. Having seen enough, Bealty crept backwards until he was out of their line of sight, then, feeling more confident, stood up and sprang softly and quietly back up the stairs.

Seeing Bealty walking normally around the corner, Brutal breathed a sigh of relief. "What took you so long," he whispered.

As Bealty approached, everyone crowded close so they could hear what he had to say. "There are four gnolls sitting around a table down there, in a room thirty or forty feet square."

"Is that all?" asked Mikell. "There is just one room?"

"No, there is a large wooden door," said Bealty, "directly across the room from where the stairs are."

"That is an important detail," said Mikell. "Anything else? What are they armed with?"

"Large axes, but there is a weapon rack in there as well," added the halfling, "and it was loaded with spears and axes."

"Do you think we could just rush them?" asked Brutal.

"They do not seem overly ready, so that might work well," Bealty responded.

"Okay, Ty, Hammer, Isa -- we will rush in and kill those fuckers hand to hand," Brutal said with conviction. "Mikell, York, and Ariana, you stay in the rear -- out of harm's way. Julius, stay in the rear with them -- and do not let anything get past you. If you can, use your bow to help out, but be careful. Bealty," Brutal finished, placing a hand on the halfling's head, "well, just do what you do." Everyone slowly nodded. There was a moment of silence that seemed to challenge the boundaries of time -- each companion realizing that their lives were about to change, one way or another, and there was no turning back.

Everyone took their positions as they began to make their way down the stairs, and around the curves. At first, they tried to be quiet, but the metal armor that many of them were wearing clanked or scraped as they moved, and when they got to within ten feet of the bottom, Brutal motioned forward and they all broke into a run, dashing into the room.

The gnolls, although surprised, were already up from their sitting positions with their weapons in hand. One of the gnolls, carrying a red buckler, was yelping what seemed to be orders to the others. The gnolls, gnashing their canine-like teeth, swarmed toward the companions, axes raised. A fifth gnoll, previously unseen, appeared from the southeast corner and also joined the fray. Being in the front right of the formation, Hammer was immediately confronted by gnolls on three sides, including the leader with the red buckler, who was directly in front of him.

The three gnolls surrounding Hammer screamed in rage as they each struck at the warrior. Hammer was able to duck the blow by the leader, and the ax blades of the other two glanced off this splint mail armor. Another gnoll rushed directly at Tyberius, who was in the middle of the front three of the companions, and made a high arcing swing that Tyberius, but the tall warrior was able to avoid the blow. The final gnoll headed for Brutal, who back-peddled at the sight of the large creature bearing down on him. The ax blade of the gnoll glanced off his breastplate -- jarring Brutal back to his senses.

Julius scanned the situation quickly and, seeing Hammer being ganged up on, drew an arrow and taking aim at the gnoll coming from the corner of the room, fired. The arrow glanced off the arm of the gnoll but managed to draw blood.

Bealty quickly made his way around the bunched-up mass of combatants and melded into the shadows near the weapons rack.

Hammer, surprised by the attack by the gnoll in the corner, reacted on instinct and swung his war hammer. The hammer struck the gnoll, who was flinching from the arrow that had just struck him, and it let out a loud yelp.

York, moving to the rear, started playing a song on his flute. The music at first was ordinary, but soon the air filled with a palpable energy that mingled with the soul of the eight other companions.

Isa moved up to the left of Brutal and kicked at the torso of the gnoll engaged there, but the gnoll saw the attack coming and using its buckler, intercepted the monk's leg. Brutal saw the opportunity when the gnoll extended its arm to block Isa's attack and stabbing with his bastard sword, sunk his blade through the gnoll's midsection. The gnoll screamed and, giving Brutal a terrified look and then going limp, slumped to the floor.

Ariana quickly moved to the western side of the room, well behind Isa and Brutal, but kept her eyes focused on Tyberius. There were two gnolls close enough to attack Tyberius, but she could also see that Hammer was in trouble. Not hesitating, she focused on the gnoll directly in front of Tyberius. Ariana opened her soul to the positive material plane, and tapping the energy she found there, she funneled it using the arcane verbal command. "Invoco missili di forza, infallibili nella loro volo." The verbal component required perfect annunciation, inflection, and timing, but once mastered, and combined with the fine motor skills required by the somatic portion of the spell, allowed her to channel the energy into her spells. Following her command, the energy funneled into her right hand which she held up, index finger extended, and as she finished the words, her hand glowed for a brief second and then two red bolts darted from her finger. Each bolt wound its own convoluted path, but unerringly struck the unsuspecting gnoll -- then as quickly as they appeared they vanished, the energy returning to its natural plane. The first bolt struck the gnoll in its right side and the second directly into its back. The gnoll recoiled at the strikes, yelping loudly in pain as blood began running out of each puncture.

Mikell, in the rear as planned, fought the strong urge to engage. He resisted as long as he could, but seeing Hammer surrounded, he decided he could not sit idly by. There was just enough room along the southern wall of the room for him to take a swing at the gnoll who had come from the corner. Rushing the gnoll, Mikell swung the Sundrudden mace with all his might, but the gnoll saw him coming and raised its buckler in time; the force of the impact jarred Mikell's arm and losing his grip on the weapon, it flew several feet behind where the gnoll was standing -- Mikell let out a shout as the reverberation coursed through his arm.

Tyberius, having just dodged the blow of the gnoll directly in front of him, raised his large flail and swung with all his might, but the blow was too slow and the gnoll, who had just been struck by the magic missiles, was able to back away in time.

York, finishing up his song, drew his longsword and with Brutal taking out the gnoll on the far left, was able to make his way around and attack the gnoll in front of Tyberius. The gnoll, noticing York approach was able to turn and, raising its buckler, block the blow, countered with its own attack, but the gnoll's swing was too slow and the bard easily side-stepped the attack.

The gnoll leader, with the red buckler, shouted something to the others, and while Hammer's attention was focused on the gnoll from the corner, swung his ax at the warrior, striking him hard on the left shoulder. Hammer's splint mail saved him from a worse blow, but the ax ripped through the armor, badly gashing his shoulder -- as evidenced by the large amount of blood running down his arm. The other two gnolls continued their focus on Hammer, and each one found an opportunity to strike at him, but each blow glanced off his armor, causing no real damage.

As the gnoll fell in front of him, from Brutal's attack, the monk quickly sprang onto the crude table and then back down to land behind the gnoll who had attacked Hammer. Isa punched the gnoll in the back, but the gnoll moved at the last second, causing his fist to glance off the improvised chain mail.

Julius was about to let loose another arrow at the gnoll from the corner, but Mikell, jumping into the fray, blocked his shot. However, when York moved around behind the gnolls, a new, albeit narrow, lane opened to the gnoll that Isa just attacked. Nocking the arrow, he let it fly before the combatants shifted again, and this time the arrow flew true, lodging itself deep into the right leg of the gnoll.

Mikell, horrified to see his mace go hurtling away, tried to take a step backwards, but the gnoll that he had just swung at saw the opportunity and stuck him in the chest as he retreated, the ax blade slicing through Mikell's chain mail, creating a deep bloody wound.

With York drawing the attention of the gnoll in front of him, Brutal swung his bastard sword low at the creature's legs. The gnoll didn't have time to react from blocking York's attack and Brutal's blade sliced deep into the back of its leg; the gnoll crumpled to the ground, unconscious and bleeding.

Hammer, recoiling from the blow to his back, stumbled as he tried to raise his hammer, the loss of blood beginning to take its toll on the warrior. The gnoll leader, was about to take another swing at Hammer, when Bealty appeared from out of nowhere. Running across the table and leaping off of it, the halfling tried stabbing the seven foot gnoll in the back, but the leader recognized the threat and was able lean out of the way of the deadly dagger, letting the airborne rogue sail past. Bealty, upon landing, gracefully rolled into a standing position.

With Tyberius out of harm's way for the moment, Ariana decided to unclasp her light crossbow, which was already cocked, and loaded it with a bolt. Raising it up to aim, she cursed, "Damn it!" as she couldn't find a safe angle to shoot. She could see Hammer was bleeding badly, but unless she wanted to cast another spell, there wasn't any way for her to take a shot -- not without risking hitting Hammer or Mikell. Watching as Mikell reeled backwards from the gnoll's blow, she said, "Aw, to hell with this," and taking the bolt out she dropped the crossbow to the ground, which made a loud twang as the force of hitting the ground caused the trigger to pull, releasing the bowstring. Tapping the distant plane once again, she focused on the gnoll from the corner, she uttered the words again. "Invoco missili di forza, infallibili nella loro volo." Two red bolts crackled forth from her finger -- both weaving through the combatants, and again, striking their intended target. The gnoll didn't see the bolts coming, and as it was pulling its ax back from hitting Mikell, the bolts struck, both sinking into its chest. The force of the impact knocked the gnoll backwards two steps before collapsing. "Take that you piece of shit!" she screamed even as the gnoll was falling.

Tyberius, seeing Brutal fell another gnoll gave his friend a quick smile then turned to his right, swinging his flail at the nearest gnoll, the same one Julius had just struck with an arrow. It was a powerful swing, but the gnoll was quicker and able to move out of the way of the massive spiked ball.

With Tyberius stepping in to attack the gnoll, there was no more room for anyone to maneuver for a melee strike, so York lowered his sword. "What the hell are you doing?" shouted Ariana at the bard.

"I cannot get in there!" he responded with an annoyed tone in his voice, gesturing with his left arm.

"Go fucking help Hammer!" she ordered, pointing at the stumbling warrior, still bleeding badly.

The bard gave Ariana a sideways look, then ran toward the bleeding fighter. As he made his way behind the front line of fighters, he took out his holy symbol, a square with a diagonal slash in the middle. Uttering the prayer, "Benedici il mio tocco con il potere di guarire le ferite lievi," he placed his hand on Hammer's back. The magical energy coursed through the warrior's body and the bleeding in his shoulder stopped, but it was only a minor heal.

Brutal, like York, found himself stuck behind Tyberius and Isa, with the large wooden table blocking his movement around the rear toward the lead gnoll. Isa and Bealty were able to leap up onto and over the table, but with his armor on, he was too heavy to do likewise, so he moved to the table and heaving, flipped it on its side, pushing it toward the north wall out of his way.

The smaller gnoll, with an arrow in its leg, swung its war ax at Isa. The blow was not a direct hit, but glancing off Isa's unarmored left shoulder, it still drew blood, which began to wick into his robe, creating a growing stain. The lead gnoll, having brushed off Bealty's dagger, turned back to Hammer who was still reeling and swung his ax at the warrior, but Hammer was able to parry it with his war hammer. After his quick parry, Hammer tried to reverse his swing, aiming for the gnoll's head, but the lead gnoll easily blocked the attack with its buckler.

With the gnoll, again, turning its back to him, Bealty swung his dagger toward the crotch of the towering creature, but the dagger deflected off the chain mail on the inside of its leg.

Isa waited for the right opportunity, and when the gnoll with the arrow in its leg leaned to dodge Tyberius's last attack, the monk twirled around with a circle kick, connecting cleanly with the gnoll's neck. The crack could be heard above the din of the battle and the gnoll spun backwards as it fell to the ground, dead.

Ariana, seeing all the gnolls fall except for the leader, leaned down and picked up her light crossbow and began readying it. As Brutal heaved the table out of the way, Julius quickly moved around to the northeast corner of the room to get a clean angle on the leader, "Now I have you," he said out loud as he nocked and let loose the arrow. The arrow struck the lead gnoll directly in the back -- and while it did not lodge itself, blood clearly began to seep out of the wound.

Mikell, finally recovering from being struck, and with all the gnolls near him now on the ground, ran to the southeast corner of the room and retrieved his mace. The heft of the mace in his hand helped return some confidence to the priest as he turned to face the remaining gnoll.

Julius quickly nocked another arrow and fired -- this time the arrow stuck into the back of the gnoll's knee, causing it to howl in pain and forcing it to hobble on its one good leg. Julius shouted in triumph as he again reached for another arrow.

Mikell, seeing the gnoll reel in pain, lunged forward swinging his mace, but the gnoll blocked it with its buckler.

Tyberius, yelling curses as he charged the gnoll leader, swung with all his might and this time the ball of the flail struck the gnoll squarely in the back, one of the spikes struck deep, crushing its spine in the process. The gnoll, its ax falling from its limp hand, sank to its knees and then, as if in slow motion, fell forward onto its face, gasping, and with one last whimper, hit the ground, dead. Tyberius whirled around, raising his flail, ready to strike again.

"Ty!" shouted Brutal trying to get the warrior's attention, but he could see Tyberius was not listening, the tall warrior's eyes were darting around frantically. "Ty!" he shouted again, taking a step toward his friend. This time the large warrior met his eyes and Brutal could see the recognition, and Tyberius let the flail drop to his side.

All of a sudden, it was quiet in the room, the sound only broken by the clanking of metal armor and heavy breathing. Hammer was the first one to move, taking a few steps to where he sat down on one of the log chairs, using his hammer as a cane to balance himself. The fighter tried to look at the gash, which was now mostly closed, but his body was still badly beat up. "Son of a bitch," Hammer said, "that plan sucked shit." Hammer looked behind him where Bealty was still standing. "I thought you said there were just four gnolls and that they were sitting at the table," he stated more than asked.

"Four were sitting around the table," answered Bealty, assuming it was a question. "I could not see into the corner, where the fifth one was." Without waiting to let the conversation go further, the halfling quickly ran to the door to the north.

"Wait," Mikell said, seeing Bealty moving toward the door, "we need a moment to regroup," and he also moved toward an open log chair where he sat down, laying his mace on the compacted dirt floor.

Brutal noticed the blood on the front of Mikell's armor. "Were you hit?"

"Yes, I --" Mikell started to respond then paused, "I lost my mace when the gnoll blocked my attack, and when I tried to back up he slashed me across the chest," he said, pointing to the gash in his chain mail.

"Well, heal yourself," said Brutal.

Mikell looked up at Brutal. "No, no, I must not waste a spell on myself. I consider it punishment for being a fool...I knew I was supposed to stay back, but when I saw Hammer surrounded, I thought I could help."

"You did help," said Hammer, "and I thank you for it. You too, Julius," he said, giving the ranger a nod. "Good shooting."

Julius was moving about the room, collecting the arrows he had fired, including the ones stuck in the dead gnolls. Pausing as he pulled the arrow out of the back of the gnoll leader, he looked over at the warrior. "You are most welcome, Hammer."

Hammer, looking back at Mikell, said, "Heal yourself...then if you could, please heal me as well, I am pretty beat up."

"I do not like doing this," said Mikell shaking his head slightly, "but I must heal my wound." Then, taking a deep breath, he focused on Zuel and, weaving his hands through the air to complete the somatic portion of the spell, he canted the verbal component. "Benedici il mio tocco con il potere di guarire le ferite lievi." Touching the wound on his chest, the gash closed and the bruising disappeared. Mikell closed his eyes for a moment, thanking Zuel for the blessing of his power. Opening his eyes, he couldn't help but smile. "Oh, that feels much better. Zuel is a great god." Standing up, he walked over to Hammer and performing the ritual again, cast the healing spell upon his wounded companion. The long, jagged wound on Hammer's shoulder completely healed and the color returned to his face.

"Holy shit, that felt weird, but I feel great now," said Hammer, flexing and rotating his previously injured arm. "I am ready to go again!"

Ariana, watching Mikell heal himself and Hammer, moved over near York. "You better not freeze up like that again when we are in a fight."

York, who was several inches shorter than Ariana, looked up at her standing beside him. "I did not freeze, my lady."

"Then what do you call it?" she asked with some iciness in her voice.

"I had no point of attack. I was simply waiting for an opening," said York.

"I will be keeping an eye on you," she said. After a short pause, she added, "Do not let me see you squirreling around in the back, doing nothing, again."

"I probably saved Hammer's life, you know," he said, crossing his arms in front of his chest.

"Bullshit. And even if you did, the only reason you went in was because I called you out," said Ariana.

York turned slightly to look at her. "We all must make our own decisions, my lady."

"What do you mean by that?" she asked. York just smiled and walked away, joining the rest of the group around Mikell.

Standing back up, Mikell looked at everyone. "Is anyone else hurt?" With nobody saying anything, he looked at Ariana. "The bolts you were casting were impressive -- I did not expect that from you." A half-smile formed around one side of Ariana's mouth, but she said nothing. Mikell continued, "Do you still have power left for more?"

"Of course, I do," Ariana said.

Mikell frowned slightly, Ariana's vague response not what he was hoping for. "I just want to make sure we are all ready to keep going, we do not know what is behind that door," he said, pointing to the heavy wooden door on the north wall.

Ariana's half-smile faded away. "How are your powers doing, Mikell?"

"I have plenty of healing left, thank you," Mikell answered. Looking toward the door, he could see Bealty was already inspecting the area around the door. Mikell made his way toward the halfling. "Finding anything?" he asked.

Bealty looked up and shook his head. "Nope. If this door is trapped, I cannot find it."

Brutal, moving toward the door, reached out for the door handle, but Bealty pushed his hand away. Brutal looked down at him, asking, "Hey, why did you do that?"

"I open the doors," Bealty said, pointing a small finger at his chest. "If there is a trap, I have the best chance of avoiding it. Besides," he said, looking up at the tall fighter, "I do not want anyone to get hurt from a trap I might have missed."

"Sounds fair to me," said Hammer. "So lead the way, little one."

Bealty reached up and slowly grabbed the handle, depressing the latch with his thumb as he did so. A metallic click, which seemed louder to the companions than it probably was, rang out. Bealty opened the door just enough for his slim body to squeeze through, then, looking back at the others, whispered, "Wait here, let me check it out first." Everyone's eyes were on him, but nobody said a word. The halfling hesitated for a second, then slipped through the crack and disappeared.

* * * *

Fortunately for Bealty, the doorway was slightly recessed into the wall, giving him a good hiding position once through the door. Easing his way to the edge of the doorway, he peeked around the corner and saw a hallway that ran east and west. To the west, forty feet down, he could see the hallway turned to the right, heading back north, but there was also another door at the corner, heading back south. Looking to the east, he could see the hallway opened into another room -- from which he could hear more voices -- the language and pitch of their voices were similar to the ones from the first room, Bealty figured it had to be more gnolls. Glancing down the westward passage one more time, Bealty hugged the south side of the wall, carefully making his way to the east, scanning the ground and wall for any telltale signs of a trap. Not seeing any, he continued twenty feet down the hallway, where it opened up into a large rectangular hall that looked to be about sixty feet long and forty feet wide, with two rows of wooden pillars running down the middle. He could see at least three gnolls standing near the south end of the large room, but thought for sure there were more. There was a pillar, offset from the rest, about ten feet from where he was -- if he could make it there, he would have a much better view of the room, but he would have to cross some open ground to get to it. 'Too risky,' he thought to himself, as there was another hallway coming into the room from the north, not to mention there could be a gnoll behind any of the thick wooden columns that he could not see. He was about to head back to the group when he heard a new voice -- this one was not a gnoll, or if it was, it sounded much different -- it was monotone and didn't have the yappiness and grunting characteristic of a gnoll -- yet it was speaking their language. Bealty took a long look at the pillar again, 'I could probably make it...' he thought to himself, feeling the familiar tug of curiosity.

* * * *

"Where the hell is he?" asked Tyberius, who was looking through the crack in the doorway that Bealty had slipped through.

Brutal put his hand on Tyberius's shoulder. "Just relax, he will be back shortly. If anything had gone wrong, we would have heard it."

"I suppose so, but I do not like sitting around not knowing what is happening," replied Tyberius.

"Brutal is right -- we just need to give Bealty a little more time," said Mikell. Just then, Bealty squirted back through the crack left by the open door, nearly bumping into Tyberius's leg.

"Ah -- Beetle, there you are -- what did you see?" he asked before the halfling could even come to a stop.

Bealty looked up, Tyberius was literally towering over him. "More gnolls, and someone or something else as well. I could not see the whole room, so I could not see who or what was the source of the other voice."

"What was different about it?" asked Ariana.

"The gnolls have a yip and growl to them. This was a much more natural voice -- like one of us," said Bealty.

"Maybe we should just rush them again," said Hammer, "that worked out well last time -- though this time I want to be in the center."

Tyberius's grin returned, the first time since they had descended. "Is it a little scary on the right side?" he asked in jest.

"Hey, I held my own against three of them damn gnolls," Hammer shot back.

"Enough," said Mikell, holding up a hand, "we need to be serious here. Bealty, did you see anything else?"

"The hallway goes left or right -- to the left there is another door where the hallway turns north. I followed the hallway as far as I could, but it opens up into a larger area, so I turned back. To the right is the large room with the gnolls and, well -- the other voice," he finished with a shrug. "I thought you guys could follow me to the edge of the room, and then I would try sneaking my way into the center of the room to get a better look. That way if I was discovered, you would be there to help out."

Mikell scratched his balding head. "I cannot believe gnolls built a structure this size. We are getting into something here we might not be able to get out of if we keep going." Mikell paused. "We should go back to Telfar and get help from Cragstaff."

"Fuck that," said Brutal, barely giving Mikell time to finish his sentence. "We handled those gnolls," he pointed to the dead carcasses in the room, "no problem -- and Soulmite brought us here for a reason." Brutal looked around at the faces of his companions. "If we go back now, we will miss something...I...I do not know what is down here, but we need to find it now -- today," his said with a point of his finger toward the ground.

"There are more than gnolls here, and who knows how big this complex is," Mikell said.

"Brutal is right -- we need to just keep on moving," said Tyberius. "I do not like sneaking around, we just need to go kick some ass."

"There is treasure down here for sure," said Hammer, "whatever, or whoever built this place -- has gold here."

Mikell looked around at all the faces. There was anxiousness, but not outright fear. "Alright, we keep going forward. May Zuel keep us safe," said Mikell, looking up to the heavens. Then he, turning to Bealty and motioning forward with his hand, said, "Lead the way."

* * * *

Bealty slipped through the narrow door opening again and looking to the left and right waved the others to follow him as he moved eastward down the corridor toward the opening into the large room. Bealty paused at the opening and peered around the corner, then, crouching, he moved silently across the dirt floor of the complex. Although there were lanterns along the walls, the halfling had an uncanny knack for finding shadows and staying concealed. After just a moment, Bealty was behind the first wooden pillar. Peaking around it, he could see six gnolls standing around what looked like a throne of some sort, and sitting in the chair was some sort of humanoid, but Bealty was not sure exactly what it was. It was relatively short, though much taller than himself, and had a bald head with thin, plain headband of some sort -- and was dressed in brown shirt and pants. The room, as he initially thought, was forty feet wide and sixty feet long, with eight large wooden columns, four on each side of the room with a wooden path running down the middle, leading to a chair, raised up on a dais. Having seen enough, Bealty moved back to the safety of the hallway with his companions.

"I do not know what the humanoid is," Bealty whispered with a shrug of his shoulders. "It could be a small human, skinny dwarf, or elf -- but it was bald and had grayish skin."

York squeezed his way between Mikell and Ariana. "Bald and grayish skin, you say?" Before anyone could answer, he continued, "Was it wearing dull and plain clothing?" Everyone looked at Bealty, who nodded affirmatively. "Ah, well, I cannot say for certain, but it sounds like a druegar."

Hammer squinted at the elf. "What the fuck is a druegar?" asking the question everyone else was thinking.

"Oh, well, I suppose the best way to sum it up would be an evil subterranean dwarf," replied York.

"A subter-what?" asked Tyberius.

York's mouth was half open, but Brutal replied before York had a chance. "A dwarf that lives underground."

"I thought they all lived fucking underground, no?" asked Tyberius.

York, closing his mouth, smiled a thin, wispy, polite smile. "Exactly," he said.

"Could druegar build a complex like this?" asked Mikell in a hushed voice.

York nodded. "Oh yes, all dwarves excel at construction. Although it seems like an odd mix -- druegar and gnolls, that is."

"A fucking gnoll could come around the corner down there," Ariana said, pointing to the west, where there was a door and the corridor turned north. "At any moment. We need to keep moving before we are discovered here." As if on cue, the latch to the door at the west end of the hallway clicked and the door began to open. Ariana gave Mikell and Bealty an angry look and then turned to see what was going to come through the door, her right hand slipping into a pouch on her belt where she grabbed a pinch of sand.

Julius and Isa, who were still holding up the rear of the group, quickly spun around, and Julius nocked an arrow while Isa slowly began to move down the corridor toward to the west.

"Oh shit," said Mikell, then looking back and pointing at Tyberius, Brutal, and Hammer, continued, "we are going to be attacked on both sides. You three need to hold off the gnolls from that room." The three warriors nodded and readied themselves near the opening to the east.

Tyberius put his hand on Brutal's shoulder, and he gave his friend his familiar grin. "Well, at least this beats harvesting wheat." Brutal's serious look faded for a brief moment, and he nodded. "But stick close," added Tyberius, slapping Brutal on his heavy breastplate. Just then, two gnolls appeared through the door to the west. Both were armed with war axes, but neither was prepared for what they encountered in the hallway, and their eyes widened in surprise at the sight of the group. Before they could react, Julius's longbow let out a loud twang as he loosed his arrow at the first gnoll through the door. The arrow zipped past the gnoll's head, smashing into the tunnel wall behind it.

Isa charged the second gnoll and attacked with a powerful front kick, but the gnoll, although surprised, was able to block the kick away. Ariana watched as her companions' attacks missed their mark and hesitated for just a moment before deciding to cast her spell. As she had practiced thousands of times, she let her mind reach into the positive plane, and pulling a sliver of energy back into the material plane, she pulled out the pinch of sand. As her hands gracefully wove the somatic component, she began to vocalize the spell. "Dalle sabbie del tempo, faccio piombare nel sonno i miei nemici." As she finished the verbal portion of the spell, she tossed the material component, the sand, into the air toward the two gnolls. The sand shimmered for a moment and then a shower of magical energy exploded silently around Isa and the two gnolls. The two gnolls had just begun to raise their axes in retaliation when the spell bust around them and unable to resist its effect, their axes fell out of their hands, their eyes closed, their bodies went limp, and they both crumpled to the floor in a magical sleep.

"Kill them before they wake up!" shouted Ariana to Isa and Julius.

Watching the action to the west, Brutal looked at Tyberius. "Did you know Ariana could do that?" he asked. Tyberius, putting on his bear-like helmet, gave his head a quick shake in the negative, but before he could say anything, a commanding shout came from the southern end of the large room where the six gnolls and druegar were talking. "Shit! They will be coming! Get ready!" said Brutal.

"This damn hallway is too narrow for me to stand next to you guys, move out into the room," said Hammer, urgency in his voice.

"He is right," said Brutal. "We need to move in so we can spread out." As the three fighters took their positions, Bealty disappeared into the shadows, making his way toward the eastern edge of the large room. Arriving at a pillar on the eastern side of the room, six gnolls ran toward the human wall Brutal, Tyberius, and Hammer had just formed.

The druegar ambled up to within twenty feet of the front line formed by the human warriors, and a mere fifteen feet from Bealty, who was still in the shadows of the northeastern most pillar, and now behind him. If the skinny dwarf saw him, he showed no signs of it. The dwarf uttered a command to a gnoll standing by his side, and the gangly creature readied itself to fight. Pulling out a miniature, empty, leather bag and an unlit candle he began to weave his hands, and the two components, through the air and canting the verbal component of his spell. "Invoco una creatura semplice in mia difesa!" He continued to chant, each time his voice getting louder and his arms and hands moving more vigorously.

"Shit," muttered Bealty under his breath, "a magic user." Neither the dwarf nor his gnoll guard were facing in his direction, but there was a lot of open ground between them, so he had to think quickly.

Back in the hallway, Julius set his bow down and drew out his longsword while he ran up to one of the sleeping gnolls, running his blade through the creature's chest. Its eyes shot open one last time, awakened by the pain as the blade punctured its heart. Reaching up, the gnoll grabbed the blade of the sword as if to pull it out, but its strength quickly faded and its arms fell to its side as the light went out of its eyes.

York pulled out his flute again and began to play a battle tune, which at first had the tinny empty sound of an ordinary flute, but as the song progressed, the air began to flux with energy, seeping into the souls of the companions.

Four gnolls engaged Brutal, Hammer, and Tyberius. One of the wooden beams split the gnolls into a northern couple and a southern couple, with Brutal on the southern end and Hammer on the northern end, and Tyberius in the middle. Being in the southern position, Brutal was the first companion the gnolls reached and, having readied himself, Brutal stabbed at the first gnoll to appear in front of him. The gnoll, carrying a blue-ish tinted buckler, tried to knock the blade away, but Brutal was too strong and the blade sliced through its patchwork armor, making a deep gash in its side, causing it to yelp in pain.

On the northern end, Hammer who also was ready, swung his war hammer at the left-most gnoll, its most distinguishing feature being a large snaggle tooth that protruded through its lower lip. Hammer's blow missed, the gnoll blocking the blow with the shaft of its war ax.

Back at the west end of the hallway, Isa, grabbing the head of the second sleeping gnoll applied a quick, jarring twist of the beast's neck, snuffing out its life before it even had a chance to wake up.

Tyberius found himself at the center of the battle, with one of the wooden beams inconveniently blocking him from pushing past the line of gnolls. The gnoll directly to his left, the largest of the bunch, carried no shield and wielded a large two-handed sword. His angle of attack was best against this gnoll, so raising his heavy flail, he swung. The large gnoll let out a snarl and leaning backwards, dodged the large spiked ball, missing its face by a few inches.

Ariana, seeing the gnolls dispatched to the west, turned her attention back to the east. She couldn't see past the front line of the battle, and even if she could, the wooden beam, and the corner leading into the room blocked her view of the dwarf. Cursing under her breath, she grabbed her crossbow and began loading a bolt into it. Mikell moved down the hallway to the west, joining Isa and looked through the now open door to the south. The room, like all the others was dimly lit by lanterns, which revealed the dominating feature of the room: a huge wooden table with forty or more wooden stools around it.

Mikell's eyes widened in horror and realization. "Zuel, protect us," he said as he scanned the room for any gnolls. He saw none, but there was a swinging door in the southeast corner of the room, and an archway opening into an adjoining room in the middle of the western wall. The room was a mess of dirty plates and half-eaten carcasses of poorly cooked animals littered around and on the table. Mikell's nose wrinkled in disgust as he absently put his hand up to cover his nose and mouth. He stepped into the room, conscious of his clanking chain mail, but he wanted to get a glimpse of what was in the adjoining room to the west, so he quickly, and as quietly as possible, made his way along the west wall, stopping as he neared the opening. His heart was pounding, he knew he was taking a risk, and hearing the sounds of battle, including shouting, coming from back in the hallway where his friends were, made him feel even more anxious to hurry. Taking a deep breath, tightening his grip on his mace, and whispering a short prayer to Zuel, he peeked around the corner of the open doorway. His heart sank at the sight, and the hairs on the back of his neck stood on end. "Oh...my...god," Mikell said, practically gasping. It was a huge cavernous room, with rows and rows of narrow, empty cots. The only positive thought running through his head is that it was empty... but if it was empty, that meant the occupants, likely gnolls, were out and about, and that meant they could return at any time. Being so absorbed by the sight, Mikell did not notice Isa following him and was surprised to see the monk also looking into the huge room, which could only be described as a barracks. Mikell, looking at Isa, said, "This place is home to a small army," not sure what the half-orc monk could understand, he continued, verbalizing what he now felt in his gut, "We need to get out. Come on," said the priest, and both companions moved quickly back into the hallway. Mikell, reaching back, pulled the door closed in case the barracks wasn't totally empty after all. 'As if that would help,' he thought to himself.

Back behind the pillar, Bealty watched as the battle ensued, and the dwarf continued to weave his spell. The small rogue, opening a small bag on his belt, pulled out a dart. Throwing came as easily to halflings as breathing, and many halfling traditions and games revolved around the sport, but that didn't mean the dwarf was an easy target. Not only was the dwarf was moving while casting the spell, but Bealty's line of sight was partially blocked by the gnoll acting as a bodyguard. Bealty whispered to himself, "I have to take a shot," and standing up the halfling drew back and hurled the dart.

It was a good throw, striking the mage in the back of his right shoulder, causing him to drop the small bag. The mage let out a loud growl as he spun around to see where the blow had come from, and pulling the dart out of his shoulder he threw it to the ground. His eyes were filled with rage as he spied Bealty by the pillar, in the common tongue, he said, "I should have known it would be a scumbag halfling in the shadows!

Fucking kill him," he said, pointing at Bealty. The gnoll either understood the command, or didn't need to, and charged at Bealty.

The gnoll, charging Bealty, swung its war ax and caught the small rogue across his chest, tearing through the black leather and leaving a bloody slash. The dwarf shouting another command, this time using the dark language, got the attention of another gnoll stuck behind the front lines. Immediately responding to the command, it ran to the eastern side of the room, directly toward Bealty, swinging its war ax and landing a solid blow into the rogue's back, leaving another deep gash.

Returning to the battle line, the gnoll with the blue buckler that Brutal had stabbed recovered from the blow and swung its battle-ax low at Brutal's legs. The low blow surprised Brutal and the ax blade caught him squarely on the right leg, sinking into his flesh. Brutal let out an angry shout, cursing at the gnoll, but as he reacted to the first blow, a second gnoll, south of the beam, struck at Brutal, hitting him on the breastplate, the blade penetrating the strong armor plate and cutting into deep into his side.

The snaggle-toothed gnoll at the northern end of the line, taking a heavy swing with its battle-ax, struck Hammer, cracking ribs as it sunk deep into his chest. Hammer let out a groan, blood already streaming down his chest as the gnoll pulled its ax out, readying for another blow. Hammer shouted, gasping, "Mikell!! Mikell!!" But before he could get another word out, the gnoll with the two-handed sword stabbed Hammer, its sword plunging into the warrior's side, going through the splint mail armor and sinking several inches into his stomach. Hammer fell backwards from the blow, his war hammer falling out of his hand as he hit the ground, blood seeping into the black dirt from both wounds.

Tyberius and Brutal yelled at the same time, "Mikell!"

"Mikell, get your ass up here!" yelled Ariana waving her arms. "Hammer is down!"

Mikell, having just closed the door and hearing his name being called multiple times, looked down the hallway. "Zuel, protect us!" He said, repeating the short prayer, as he raced, mace in hand, down the corridor to the east.

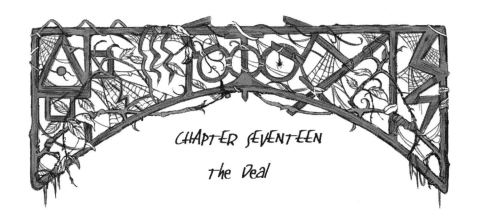

CHAPTER SEVENTEEN
The Deal

YEAR: AG 1172, Month of Sepu

ANTHALL GAVE JUDAR A COLD STARE, but he could not disguise the shiver that went down his spine and shook his very soul. "What the fuck are talking about, you bastard of evil?"

Marshal Krugar moved closer to Anthall and crouched down so their eyes were level. "Do you remember what happened in the battle, I mean, really remember?" Anthall continued to stare at the priest, ignoring the marshal and his questions. Krugar reached out and, grabbing Anthall's chin, forced his captive's head to turn and face him. "Anthall, you need to listen to me." Anthall jerked his chin out of the marshal's hand, his hatred beginning to boil, a fact his eyes could not hide. "Yes, let your hatred out, that will be valuable for you in the coming years and will serve you well." The marshal stood back up. "Now, do you remember everything that happened in the battle?"

"From what I remember, you led us into a trap and all our men were about to get killed," said Anthall.

"That was the plan, yes, but what really happened?" the marshal asked again.

Anthall's mind was spinning. "How could that have been the plan? Are you working for the ogre mage?" he asked with a perplexed look on his face, at which both Judar and Krugar let out a laugh, like it was an inside joke between them.

"You think I," said Krugar pointing to himself, "would work for a filthy ogre like Krykl? No, no, no," he continued wagging a finger in the air, "you have it all wrong, Anthall." The marshal's face darkened as he paused. "That stinking fuck of an ogre works for me," he said and, turning around, grabbing the pitcher from the table, pouring some water into a mug, he took a sip. Still facing away, he continued, "Well...at least he did work for me. He has not contacted me since the coward fled the battlefield."

Anthall licked his lips, which were cracked and dry, the sight of the water making him aware of how parched he felt. "Marshal, why would you have this ogre working for you? And, if that is the truth, why was he attacking us?"

The marshal turned back around and caught Anthall looking at the mug in his hand. "Oh, forgive me, Anthall, you must be thirsty," he said as he walked over and gently put the mug to Anthall's mouth. Anthall took several gulps of water before Krugar pulled the mug away. "Not too much at once, that will make you sick."

The feeling of the cool liquid going down his throat and into his stomach was heavenly, thought Anthall, as all the pain throughout his body subsided in the short-lived relief, but as Krugar pulled the mug away, the pains returned and he grimaced. Licking his cracked, but now moistened, lips, Anthall asked again, "Marshal, why is the ogre working for you?"

Krugar placed the mug back on the table, then turned back to face Anthall. "You have always been an excellent fighter, and a great soldier, but you have never had to deal with the court politics. No, you have been allowed to run away to Telfar and play daddy, as a Watcher, for many years while I have had to deal with Theol Kardoon and making sure our kingdom is safe."

"But why do you need Krykl?" asked Anthall again.

Krugar sighed. "You have no idea how fickle royalty can be; everyone wants to gain advantage in court and win the ear of the king, and it doesn't take much for the king to lose confidence in any one person, including his commanders."

"But you kept Kardoon safe from the orcs in '65, and the goblin raids in '69," said Anthall. "How could you think Theol would just abandon you?"

"After successes like those?" The marshal smiled. "After those wins, you are right, I felt very secure in my position."

Anthall shook his head. "Then why Krykl? What do you need the ogre for and why lead our troops into a losing battle with him?"

Judar let out a laugh. "I thought you said he was smart -- he is a fucking idiot." The priest gave Anthall's head a shove, and, turning around to Krugar, continued, "Just get to the point already."

Krugar's face reddened and, pointing at the doorway flap, said, "Get the fuck out of here, Judar. I will send for you when your services are needed."

Judar, his back stiffening at the rebuke, said, "Fine. Let me know when you are done playing around with this fool, and we can proceed." Judar gave Anthall a last glare, his prickly teeth flashing an evil grin. "Get ready to do the bidding of your new master," he stated, storming out of the tent.

Anthall looked at Krugar. "What is he talking about?"

Krugar paused for a moment. "I told you to hold your position in the rear, did I not?"

Anthall nodded. "But if I had not moved in, the bugbears would have overrun your left flank and rolled you up."

"Do not be such a dolt, Anthall," the marshal said, giving Anthall's outstretched foot a mild kick. "Krykl works for me," he said, slapping his own chest for emphasis, "and the battle would have been won by Kardoon -- just the way I had it planned!" His voice began to rise.

Anthall's face went white as the pieces started to finally fall into place. "The orcs and the goblins..." he began to say.

"Yes, Anthall, yes! Krykl led them as well. Now you are starting to see," said the marshal.

"You hired Krykl to create armies that you could defeat to save your position?" asked Anthall, knowing the answer. "All those men died so that you could remain Provost Marshal to Theol?

Krugar nodded. "I know it sounds terrible, but Kardoon is a safer place with me in charge of the army. We now have a reputation as never having lost a battle." Pointing to the north, the marshal went on. "Those barbarians from Thayol up north have not tried attacking Kardoon once since I have taken over the Provost position."

"You are a mass murderer, Krugar," admonished Anthall. "May Soulmite have mercy on your soul."

"How many more people would have died in a war with Thayol?" asked Krugar, "you just are not seeing the big picture, Anthall."

"I see the big picture, alright, the one you have created for yourself," said Anthall.

"That may be," said Krugar, shrugging his shoulder slightly, "but you still are not seeing the problem you have created for me."

"No, I see the problem. Krykl is gone," said Anthall.

Krugar cracked a half-smile. "That sip of water has helped clear up your mind. Yes, Krykl is gone, or so he seems to be, thanks to you." The marshal paused, allowing himself to half-sit on the large table. "Do you know how long it took me to find someone like Krykl? Someone willing to travel around the Cruel Pass and Doubtless Mountains for years at a time. And not only that -- but someone, or something, that is intimidating enough and tough enough to force these weaker races into servitude -- by sheer force of will alone," he said as he balled up a fist.

"Sorry I fucked up your big plans," Anthall sneered.

Marshal Krugar slowly nodded. "Yes, well, I know you are not...but you will be."

"So where is all this going, Marshal? We won the battle, so you can go home a hero again and sleep tight in your Provost bed for a few more years before you need to conjure up another 'war.'"

"Precisely," began Krugar, a finger pointing up in the air, "but who can I trust to build up a new force over the next few years, and then lead that force to their deaths against my army?" As he finished his statement, he locked eyes with Anthall.

Recognition of the implication lit up on Anthall's face and he laughed out loud, but stopped as his broken ribs sent a shock wave of pain throughout his body. Once the pain subsided, Anthall said, "You are crazy if you think I am going to do that for you."

"Maybe. But do you know what is on Krykl's mind right now?" asked Krugar. Anthall thought back to his battle with the ogre mage, and

Krugar could see the worry on the general's face. "Yes. Right now, this very moment, he is trying to figure out exactly who you are, and how to kill you and your family."

"And maybe you too," said Anthall.

"Hmmmm, well that is a possibility. He probably does feel betrayed by me to some degree, but my guess is, his first thought is to extinguish every relation you have in the world, and then yourself. If he were just an ordinary ogre, he would not even be a worry, but" the marshal made a clicking noise with his lips, "with an ogre mage -- now that is something to worry about. I mean, especially now that you are a hero of Kardoon. General Mixnor of Telfar," the marshal exaggerated the statement with his hands, as if highlighting his name in the air, "Savior of Kardoon! How hard will it be for an intelligent ogre mage to find the Mixnor farm near Telfar?" As he finished the statement, he let his hands fall to his thighs, making a light slapping noise on his armored legs.

Anthall thought back to the battle. The details were not clear, but he could remember Krykl calling him out by name. Anthall's heart sank. "He already knows my name."

"Ah, well, that is a pity. Then it is just a matter of time before he finds out where you are from, and then your family..." Krugar made a slicing motion across his neck.

"Marshal, I beg you -- release me!" Anthall pleaded, deep anguish in his voice.

"But who will raise my army?" asked Krugar.

"I will find you a replacement, I swear it," Anthall replied.

"I am afraid it is not that easy. The job I am asking you to do will require a lifetime commitment, and no matter how much I want to believe you will honor your word to Soulmite, I cannot take that risk."

Anthall let his body slump against the pole. "Fey...Brutal..." His voice trailed off.

"But there is a way, Anthall, that we can make this all work out," said Krugar, once again crouching down so that he was eye level with his prisoner, patting Anthall's outstretched leg, "you can save your family, and I get my new Krykl."

Anthall looked up at the marshal with hatred in his eyes. "The priest was right -- cut the shit, Krugar. How do we make this work?"

Marshal Krugar smiled again. "Ahhhh, I thought you would never ask." Then turning his head to look at the door flap, he shouted, "Guard!" The familiar face of the guard poked his head into the tent, and the marshal stood up and ordered, "Fetch Judar, we will be needing his services now." The guard looked down at Anthall, pity in his eyes, and then nodded before letting the tent flap close behind him, quenching the few rays of sunlight that had made their way through the opening.

CHAPTER EIGHTEEN
Bounty

YEAR: AG 1175, Month of Sepu

BEALTY REALIZED HE WAS IN TROUBLE, the last blow nearly knocking him off his feet. Fortunately, they were standing next to the large wooden beam, and he bolted away from the two gnolls. The first gnoll had no angle, it being blocked by the large beam, but the second gnoll snarled as the halfling sprinted away and swung its battle-ax, but it was a weak swing and missed completely. Having gotten away from the first two gnolls, the halfling continued his sprint right under the legs of the snaggle-toothed gnoll, who was surprised to see the appearance of the halfling. It took a wild swing as Bealty leapt right over Hammer's body. The gnoll's swing was off balance and its weapon slipped out of its hand and flew ten feet down the corridor leading northwest, as it roared in dismay. Bealty, landing right at Ariana's feet, tumbled to a few feet behind her.

"Where the hell are you going?" asked Ariana as the halfling rolled past her.

"Getting the hell out of there!" shouted the rogue, pointing to the east as he came to a knee out of his roll. Without wasting another breath, Bealty turned to face down the hallway. "Julius! You need to get up here! They have a magic user! You need to get some arrows flying in his direction!"

Tyberius, seeing Hammer go down and a bleeding Bealty sprinting his direction, began to feel the same rage he did back in the Drip. He could feel his blood beginning to boil, causing his skin to start turning a reddish-purple, and his arms flexed, bending the chain mail around his biceps. He let out a deep growl, his eyes glaring fiercely behind his helmet. Raising his flail, he swung with all his might at the gnoll with the two-handed sword, but the gnoll ducked and the ball of the flail screamed over its body.

Julius, hearing Bealty's call and seeing Hammer fall, raced back picking up his longbow and knocking an arrow took aim at the snaggle tooth gnoll who had just lost his weapon. With Hammer prone on the ground, he had a clear line of sight as he loosed the arrow. Aiming for the gnoll's chest, the missile zipped through the air, but, barely missing, sailed over its left shoulder.

Brutal could see that the gnoll he had hit earlier was bleeding badly and looked unstable on its feet. Brutal swung from below his hip and up at the head of the gnoll who didn't see it coming. The bastard sword slashed the gnoll diagonally across its face, cutting a deep gash and almost severing its muzzle. The gnoll spun backwards, collapsing into a heap on the dirt floor. Spurred on by seeing the first gnoll fall, Brutal continued his attack at the second gnoll on his side of the wooden beam. The gnoll was distracted and looking at Tyberius, who had just swung and missed at the gnoll with the two-handed sword. Brutal stabbed upwards at the midsection of the seven foot gnoll, who didn't have time to react. The blade penetrated the chain mail armor and skewered the gnoll through and through. The gnoll shrieked in pain, but the internal damage was too great, and it quickly lost consciousness. As Brutal retracted the sword, the gnoll fell, dead before it even hit the dirt.

The snaggle-toothed gnoll raced down the hallway to retrieve its ax. Meanwhile the gnoll with the two-handed sword swung right to left at Tyberius, who had abandoned any pretense of defense. The gnoll's blade gashed Tyberius's left arm, but the big warrior didn't seem to notice the hit. One of the gnolls attacking Bealty moved, with a noticeable limp, to where the snaggle-toothed gnoll had just been and swung its ax at Tyberius, but the warrior blocked the attack with the shaft of his flail.

The druegar, seeing the two gnolls fall on the southern side of the beam, near Brutal, shouted a command to the remaining gnoll, who responded quickly by charging Brutal and plugging the brief hole in the line. The gnoll swung its ax, but Brutal was able to raise his bastard sword and block the blow. The druegar, seeing Brutal almost break through the line, turned his attention to the burly looking human. Tracing a few lines into the air with his hands and pointing a finger in Brutal's direction, he uttered the command, "Invoco missili di forza, infallibili nella loro volo!" Three red bolts streaked from his outstretched finger, each striking Brutal with an incredible force, directly in the chest, sending him backwards a half step, nearly knocking him over.

The pain was excruciating, and blood began to run out of the three holes in his chest. "Mikell! I need help!" Brutal shouted, a feeling of panic washing over him.

Isa, hearing Brutal's plea coming from the eastern end of the hallway, sprinted the sixty feet, taking up a position just in front of Hammer's prone body, and kicked at the limping gnoll who had just taken up a position on the line but failed to make a good hit.

Ariana, looking back at York, said, "You better get in the fight, damn you!" Then, turning her attention back to the battle, Ariana reached into her pouch and grabbed another pinch of sand. Vocalizing the spell, as her hands wove the somatic portion, she said, "Dalle sabbie del tempo, faccio piombare nel sonno i miei nemici" and threw the sand into the air, and once again the shimmering magical energy blanketed the gnolls, causing three of them to shutter and sink to the floor, asleep. The only gnoll left standing was the one with the two-handed sword. Even the snaggle-toothed gnoll who was just returning from retrieving its fallen ax succumbed to the spell.

Mikell was torn, knowing that both Hammer and Brutal needed aid, but Hammer was on the ground and not moving, so Mikell first ran to him. Turning the fighter over, he could see that Hammer was still breathing but was losing a lot of blood from his chest where the gnoll's ax had split him open. Holding his holy symbol of Zuel, Mikell began the chant, using his free hand to complete the somatic portion of the spell. "Benedici il mio tocco con il potere di guarire le ferite lievi," he said. Finishing the spell, he reached out and touched Hammer's chest. The warrior's body convulsed for a brief second while his wounds closed, then

Hammer lurched upwards to a sitting position, gasping for air as his eyes shot wide open.

Ariana, having just finished her spell, looked back where York was still watching the events unfold. "Move your ass! Brutal needs help!"

York squeezed between Ariana and Julius making his way to just behind Brutal. "I guess it's not your time yet, Brutal!" shouted York above the din of the fighting. Grabbing the holy symbol hanging around his neck, a square with a diagonal line running from one corner to the other, he canted a healing spell. "Benedici il mio tocco con il potere di guarire le ferite lievi," he said as he wove the somatic portion and, touching Brutal's back, released the energy.

The odd sensation shot through Brutal's body, but he could immediately feel a drastic improvement. "Thank you, York!" Brutal shouted as he locked eyes on the gnoll in front of him.

The northwest area where the two hallways entered the large room was clogged with combatants. Isa, Tyberius, and Brutal essentially held the front line against the four gnolls, three of which were now asleep, and the druegar who was still over twenty feet away. Just behind them were York, Mikell, and Hammer, who was still prone on the ground. Julius, Ariana, and Bealty were holding the rear, but because of the congestion in the hallway, they could not advance.

"I do not have a shot!" shouted Julius, taking aim, then having to change targets as the combatants shifted around in the melee.

Bealty was leaning against the wall, one small hand clutching his chest where blood was trickling down his leather armor. The halfling pointed down the hallway to the west. "If you go that way, you can go around," after a short pause to catch his breath, he continued, "there is a passage that comes into the room from the north -- you will have a shot from there."

"Are you okay, Bealty?" asked Julius, concern in his voice. Bealty nodded and waved him away. "Get Mikell to tend to you," the ranger said, then sprinted away down the hallway, disappearing around the corner.

Hammer, having regained consciousness, scanned the confused state of the battle going on around him. Seeing his hammer lying near him, he reached out to grab it as he rolled over and pushed himself up to a standing position. "Thanks, Mikell," he said as he turned back to face the line of battle.

Brutal could not advance toward the druegar without exposing his back to the gnoll with the two-handed sword, but seeing one of the gnolls had fallen asleep at his feet, he raised his sword and rammed the blade through the slumbering gnoll's chest. The gnoll woke briefly as the blade skewered its body, but didn't even have time to let out a yelp as its life expired.

Seeing Brutal kill another gnoll, the druegar reached into a small pocket sewn into his gray pants and pulled out a small wispy strand of a spiderweb. An evil grin made its way onto the dwarf's ashen face as he mentally locked onto two points -- one was the northern wall just inside the passageway where the companions were, and the other was the corner of the wall where the passageway opened into the large room. The dwarf began weaving the somatic portion of the spell and throwing the web toward his target uttered the magical words, "Invoco un groviglio di ragnatele come quello che nasce dal ragno." The air crackled with magical energy as heavy sticky strands of a magical web materialized all around the companions.

Isa was getting ready to strike at the gnoll with the two-handed sword when the strands of web appeared all around him. One strand entangled his legs while another caught his arm in its sticky grip. Seeing the half-orc struggling to free himself, the gnoll with the two-handed sword stabbed at the monk. Isa was able to move his torso to avoid a direct hit, but the blade still caught him on the side, slicing through his cloth shirt and drawing blood.

York was pleased to find that none of the web's strands had entangled him, but they were all around him. Seeing that it was clear just beyond Brutal, he decided to try and make his way past, but as he tried stepping over one of the sticky strands, his left arm inadvertently touched the web and stuck fast. "Damn-it!" cursed York as he struggled to pull his arm free, but as he did so his left leg accidentally got stuck fast to another strand.

Back in the hallway, Mikell and Ariana were also entangled in the mass of the web. Mikell looked over at Ariana. "Do you know how to get out of this?"

Ariana, with both of her arms caught in the web, tried to pull them free but only managed to get herself more entangled as her torso bumped into another strand of web behind her. Unable to move, Ariana looked at Mikell, worry clearly written in her eyes, she shook her head, "No -- I have never seen this spell before."

"There was a table in the room down the hallway, it had over twenty chairs at it..." Mikell swallowed and looked around as best he could. "We have to get out of here, Ariana. If gnolls start pouring out of that doorway, we are all dead -- at the very least we will be cut off from getting out."

"I have seen this before," said Bealty.

Ariana could not turn to see Bealty but strained to see as much as she could. "What?!" she practically screamed. "You have seen this spell before? Is there a way to get out of the web?" she asked, almost out of breath from struggling.

"Aye," answered Bealty. "Fire."

"Well, what are you waiting for? Get a torch lit!" shouted Ariana.

"The web burns, but it will burn you too as it goes up in flame," explained Bealty patiently.

"Burn it!" commanded Ariana. "Get me out of this damn thing!"

Bealty looked at Mikell, who nodded in confirmation, although the priest lacked the same conviction as Ariana. "Okay, but I did warn you." The halfling took out a torch from his backpack and quickly lit it with a quick strike of his flint and dagger. The oiled rag on the torch burst into flames and Bealty paused for a second, looking at Mikell one more time. Mikell nodded again and the halfling shoved the burning torch into the web around Ariana. As the flame touched the web, all the stands flashed, creating a large, fiery, explosion, disintegrating in the process, and fading away into thin air. Ariana screamed as the flames engulfed her arms and legs, and as the web gave way, she fell to the ground, rolling away.

Mikell pulled with all his strength and was finally able to free himself from the web around him, but looking around he could not see an easy way out. Tyberius did not even pay attention to the web forming around him, his eyes were already bloodshot and crazed -- the only thing on his mind was the gnoll standing in front of him, who had just stabbed Isa. Heaving his flail, Tyberius swung, the muscles on his arms were bulging, bending the metal rings on his chain mail, the gnoll saw the attack coming and raised its small buckler to deflect the spiked ball, but the blow was too strong. Two spikes on the iron ball punctured the buckler and sunk deep into the gnoll's forearm, and as Tyberius followed through with his strike he ripped gnolls arm completely off. The gnoll stumbled, taking two awkward steps backwards, already going into shock, its strength gave out as it fell to the ground.

Isa continued to struggle against the strong strands of web, and with a loud grunt, the half-orc was able to rip his arms and legs free from the web. Looking down at the two remaining gnolls, both of which were fast asleep, the monk raised one of his think, trunk-like legs, and shouting a loud "Kiaaaa!" stomped his large booted foot, with all his might, onto the neck of the gnoll closest to him. The gnoll's neck made a noticeable cracking noise, like twig breaking into two.

The druegar snarled, showing his yellow, discolored teeth, and to Brutal's amazement, moved closer to the warrior. As he did so, the dwarf held both of his hands out in front of him, his thumbs touching and his fingers spread, almost as if playing an invisible piano, and as he canted the phrase, "Invoco pareti di fiamme," his hand burst into flames. The flames burst out into a ten-foot semi-circle in front the dwarf, engulfing Brutal, York, Tyberius, and Isa. Simultaneously, the strands of web also burst into flames creating a large, brief, explosion. The dwarf cackled in glee, watching the companions scream from the burning flames. York was able to duck under the sheet of flame, avoiding some of the damage, but the exploding web around him scorched him and his leather armor. Brutal and Tyberius felt the sheet of flame burn their midsection, then the force of the web exploding around them singed their entire bodies. Isa with his plain shirt and cloth leggings suffered the worst, the flames ripping into his midsection while the explosion knocked him backwards, and unconscious, his large body landing on top of the dead gnoll he had just stomped.

The flames from the dwarf's spell did not reach Mikell, but there was enough heat to set off the strands of web around him, and his arms

261

were burned badly in the ensuing explosion. As the flames vanished, Mikell opened his eyes in time to see Isa's body crumple on top of the dead gnoll. "Zuel -- help us!" shouted the cleric, his eyes darting to look around the corner to see the dwarf still cackling at the mayhem he had just caused.

Ariana and Bealty were just outside the area of the explosion but felt the wave of heat as the web went up in flames. "Oh my god!" Ariana shouted at the force of the spell. Her eyes immediately went to Tyberius, who looked even more demonic -- his head and face covered with the bestial helmet, and little wisps of smoke swirling around the tall warrior. She breathed a sigh of relief, seeing him still standing and looking into the large room, but she could not see what he was so focused on. Moving forward and rounding the corner, she spotted what Tyberius was looking at: the dwarf. Just as she saw the ashen-skinned dwarf, she heard a familiar twang from the hallway to her left. She could not see the attacker but knew it must be Julius. The arrow flew straight and true, glancing off the dwarf's shoulder but still opening a gash and drawing blood. The dwarf's grin disappeared as he instinctively reached to grab his wounded shoulder.

Mikell ran over to Isa and knelt beside him. Mikell could hear the half-orc's raspy and gurgled breathing and knew immediately that Isa was dying. Grabbing the holy symbol of Zuel, he canted the spell again. "Benedici il mio tocco con il potere di guarire le ferite lievi." Mikell tapped the power of his god and then touching Isa's head, completed the spell. The positive energy flowed into the monk, some of his wounds and burns magically healing in the process, but the monk was still badly hurt. However, Isa was able to open his eyes and look up at the priest. "You will be okay," said Mikell, patting the monk's large chest.

Nobody even seemed to notice Bealty moving through the bodies, until he appeared near Julius in the north hallway. Drawing out his dagger, he slammed it into the side of the last sleeping gnoll's neck. The gnoll died instantly. Julius looked down at the small rogue. "I thought it was already dead," said Julius. Bealty gave the ranger a glance, and quickly, but nonchalantly wiped the excess blood off dagger onto gnoll's leather armor, then after giving Julius a quick nod, slunk back into the shadows of the large room.

The dwarf, seeing that his spells hadn't dispatched the group, reached into a pouch and pulled out a small vial which he quickly gulped down. It only took a second, and the dwarf vanished from sight.

Tyberius had just started to move toward the dwarf when he disappeared. The big warrior growled loudly, his pupils were dilated and bloodshot, his breathing was rapid and heavy, and his arms and legs were blotchy where blood vessels had ruptured in his rage. He turned and spotted Brutal and began to advance on his friend.

Brutal backed up, holding up his free gauntleted hand. "Ty....snap out of it! It is me -- Brutal!" Tyberius didn't stop, the menacing look on his face, contorted by his rage, and bloodshot eyes made him look possessed as he continued to advance.

"Tyberius, no!" screamed Ariana, running into the room to insert herself between Brutal and Tyberius. This time, Tyberius paused, his eyes blinking, as if to get a better look at what was happening. His large flail was still raised, but his eyes met hers, and there was recognition. Ariana slowly approached him, her hands held out for him to see. Tyberius backed up a little. "Tyberius, it is me -- Ariana...put down your flail," she said in a soothing voice as she continued her cautious advance. Reaching the warrior, she placed her left hand on his right forearm, which was holding the flail. Finally recognizing her, he let out a long gasp, and his body crumpled, like air rushing out of a balloon; his arms dropping to his side, the spiked ball on his flail landing with a dull thud into the hardened dirt floor. The Taper wood shaft of the flail slipping out of his failing grip, Tyberius slumped to the ground, first on his knees, then, teetering for a moment, the tall warrior fell over onto his side before finally rolling onto his back. His breathing was rapid, as if he could not catch his breath, and blood began to seep out of the wounds and burns that he suffered during the fight. "Mikell!" Ariana shouted, "Tyberius needs you!"

Brutal knelt beside Tyberius, setting his bastard sword down onto the hard-packed dirt floor. "Hang in there Ty, Mikell is coming," said the warrior.

Ariana looked at Brutal. "Oh gods, you are hurt badly, too," she said, reaching out a hand and placing it gently on his forearm. She could see that Brutal's complexion was a blotchy mix of being pasty white from loss of blood mixed with patches of red, burnt, skin. Blood was trickling down his breastplate through three acorn-sized holes where the dwarf's magical bolts had struck.

Brutal managed a small smile and touched her hand, "I am fine..I will be okay."

Mikell, hearing Ariana call his name, stood up and surveyed the scene. Hammer and Isa were starting to get back on their feet -- knowing both had suffered more than enough damage to kill them, had it not been for Zuel's healing power. Tyberius was on the ground gasping, and Brutal looked half-dead. York looked like he was okay, although his armor was no longer in pristine condition -- some parts were blackened by the flames and his usually perfect hair was singed and matted with sweat. Julius seemed to be the only one not hurt and was standing alertly, an arrow nocked in his bow. Doing the quick math in his head, a feeling of panic hit him as he realized Bealty was nowhere to be seen, "Oh shit, where is Bealty?" he asked no one in particular as he spun around searching. "Bealty!" he shouted in a hushed voice.

"He slunk off that way," said Julius, pointing toward the southern end of the large room.

Mikell looked at Julius. "Go look for him and bring him back -- no matter what he says -- bring him back." The ranger nodded and immediately started moving to the south. As he moved away, Mikell added, "Be careful!"

"I always am," said Julius as he passed the group, crouching as he moved quickly to the south.

"Mikell," Ariana said with impatience in her voice, "get over here. Tyberius needs you."

Mikell made his way to Tyberius and by the time he was at his side, the warrior's breathing was already starting to ease, becoming more regular, and he opened his eyes, which were still tinged with red with blood. "Are you okay, brother?" asked Mikell.

"Of course, he is NOT okay," said Ariana. "Look at him."

Tyberius, still lying on his back, lifted his torso up, bracing himself with his elbows, into a half-sitting position. Then the grin appeared.

"Man, we fucked them up! Did we not?"

"Shhh," hissed Mikell. "Keep your voice down," he said, holding a finger up to his lips.

"What the hell happened there at the end?" Brutal asked, looking at Tyberius.

Tyberius gave his friend a smile. "What do you mean?"

"At the end there, it looked like you were going to start swinging at me," replied Brutal.

The smile faded a little and Tyberius squinted, thinking back. He shook his head. "I do not remember that. But I would not attack you."

Mikell stood up. "We can discuss that later. We have to get out of here."

"To hell with that," interjected Hammer, "we just reduced the population of gnolls down here to zero, I think -- and we need to find some loot."

"I do not know what this place is, but we are lucky to be alive," said Mikell as the group gathered closer to the priest. "There is a room back there," he pointed, "a barracks is the only word I can think to describe it. There were enough beds for fifty or more gnolls."

"Were there any in there?" asked York.

Mikell shook his head. "No, I did not see any. That is what I mean -- we are very lucky that they are not here." Mikell paused for a second. "But they could show up at any time, so we need to get out of here, quickly, and get back to Telfar."

York had a puzzled look. "I wonder where they are?" he asked no one in particular. The question hung in the air for a moment, but nobody ventured a guess.

"There could be a fortune down here," said Hammer, changing the subject, "all for the taking."

Mikell frowned. "You were practically a corpse a moment ago -- and now you want to risk our lives looting some coin?"

Hammer frowned back. "Hell yeah. That is why I came here with you. The main reason, really."

"I agree with Hammer," said York. "There is still some time to explore down here."

"Not to mention that little dwarven bastard is still down here somewhere," added Brutal.

Mikell looked down at Brutal, who was still kneeling. "Nothing good comes from vengeance, Brutal."

Grabbing the hilt of his sword, Brutal stood back up, but as he did, the blood rushed away from his head, and he nearly lost his balance. Stumbling backwards, the warrior dropped his sword and began to fall.

York, who was standing behind him, was able to reach out and catch the big warrior. "Careful there, my friend," the bard said. With one hand on Brutal's back, the bard reached down and picked up the fallen sword and handed it to him. "That is a heavy blade, no wonder you lost your balance."

"Thanks," Brutal said, accepting the hilt of the sword York offered, feeling a little embarrassed.

"You cannot even stand up," huffed Mikell.

"Bullshit, I am fine," said Brutal. Extending a hand down to Tyberius, the redheaded warrior grasped it and Brutal helped pull him back onto his feet. Giving Mikell a confident look, he said, "I just lost my balance."

"You do not look fine," said Mikell, walking over to him. "Let me see." Now that he was closer, Mikell could see the three acorn-sized holes in the breastplate with blood seeping out the holes, but he could also see where blood was trickling down from his waist, from underneath the breastplate. Mikell looked up into Brutal's eyes and could see the fatigue. "You will not last another fight," then looking back around the group added. "Please, friends, we need to leave. We still have our lives, and we need to alert Telfar about this place." Mikell looked around the group, hoping to find one person in agreement with him, but he could see the resolution on their faces. Raising his hands up he added, "What good will a few hundred gold pieces do us? Is it worth even one of our lives?"

"That is the risk we all decided to take, is it not?" asked Hammer rhetorically. "I say we keep searching this place. I think we killed most of the gnolls, if not all of them."

Mikell let his hands fall to his side, then raised them up again palms up. "My healing powers are not infinite -- I can only do so much. I only have a few spells left, then I will be helpless to heal any of us." Mikell looked back at Brutal. "But I can see you are gravely wounded, Brutal, you need some healing." Mikell quickly grabbed his holy symbol of Zuel, and canted the spell, "Benedici il mio tocco con il potere di guarire le ferite lievi," and, touching Brutal's forearm, funneled the positive energy into his friend.

The odd sensation flowed through his body, like thousands of ants crawling all over him, both inside and out, but the pain began to melt away and he could feel the stability and strength returning to his core which had been so damaged by the magic missiles. The color returned to his face, and he couldn't help but breathe a sigh of relief as the spell wore off. "Wow, that is amazing. Thank you, Mikell."

"Zuel is amazing," said Mikell softly and with some defeat in his voice.

"We know we need to get out of here, but we have fought too hard to leave empty-handed," said Ariana, stepping forward into the middle of the group. "Let us do a quick search and then get out of here."

Tyberius bent down and picked up the Taper wood handle of his flail and, standing back up, said, "Let us get moving." Looking around he frowned, "where be Julius and Bealty?"

Mikell pointed toward the southern end of the chamber. "Bealty went after the dwarf and I asked Julius to bring him back."

"I cannot wait to get my hands on that little bastard," said Brutal, then with a quick gesture in the southerly direction with his sword, he added, "Onward," and began moving down the middle of the columned room. There were eight columns, four on each side of the room, and the dirt floor was packed hard down the middle, like a dirty red carpet. At the southern end sat a plain but very large wooden chair.

"I guess this passes for a throne for these scum," said Ariana, walking up to the base of the chair. The ground was littered with small bones, trampled into the dirt around the chair, and they crunched lightly underneath her leather boots. Ariana snorted. "What beastly slobs..." she said to no one in particular as she used the toe of her boot to move a small bone still loose on the floor.

"Look," said York, "another door, that must be where Beetle and

Julius went."

"Beetle?" asked Mikell. "His name is Bealty," he said, emphasizing the 'E' sound at the end.

Tyberius, grinning and as he began moving toward the open door, quickly chimed in, "Beetle does have a better ring to it."

York was about to say something but just winked at Mikell and with a half-grin, said, "Tyberius is right." The bard then followed the group as they filed past Mikell toward the door.

The door on the eastern wall was already partially open, and Tyberius, raising his flail up into a ready position, gently pushed the door fully open. The hinges let out an awful metallic screech as it opened, making everyone cringe, and instantly tense. Everyone took a step backwards, including Tyberius -- readying themselves for combat.

"Well, get in here," squawked a familiar voice from inside.

Tyberius moved forward again, peering inside a small square room, each wall about thirty feet he guessed. There was a lit lantern on each wall, making the room much brighter than the large and dimly lit hall they were coming from. A large rectangular table dominated the room, surrounded by eight smaller chairs, and one large chair at the far end. Several coils of rolled up papers sat on the table, and a rack of weapons lined the eastern wall. Julius and Bealty were standing in the northeast corner of the room, watching him as he entered the room, shortly followed by the rest of the group.

"What are you two doing," asked Tyberius, his voice ringing off the walls of the room.

"Shhhhh," Mikell chided, "keep your voice down." Then turning his attention to Bealty, he asked, "Where is the dwarf?"

Bealty shrugged. "Not sure, but he did come in here -- I saw the door open. I suppose he could have doubled back, but I do not think so."

Tyberius chuckled. "What the hell are you talking about? He is not in here," he added, waving an extended arm around the room. "There is nowhere to hide."

"He turned invisible, so he could be in here --" Bealty said.

Tyberius cut him off. "Invisi-what?"

Ariana groaned impatiently. "Invisible -- you know, you cannot see him."

"Are you fucking kidding me?" Tyberius snorted. "You mean he can see us but we cannot see him?"

"Possibly," said Bealty, "but I do not think he is here." The small rogue pointed to the eastern wall. "Something is not right with this room, I think there is another way out."

A look of concern swept across Tyberius's face and his grip tightened around the Taper wood shaft of his flail. "Well, that is fucking great news," he said, then added with some sarcasm, "I suppose the door is invisible, too."

Bealty was examining the northeast corner again and, without turning around, said, "Possibly."

As the conversation went on, Brutal sheathed his sword and made his way to the large table and picked up one of the large coiled up rolls of parchment. The sheet of paper was over six feet wide, and Brutal had trouble keeping it open. Mikell, seeing Brutal trying to hold the paper down, walked over and set his mace on one side of the sheet, acting like a huge paperweight. "Thanks," said Brutal as he unrolled the sheet again, this time holding down the other end with his hand, and revealing its contents.

A frown crept across both Brutal and Mikell's faces and in unison said the same thing: "That is Telfar." Ariana, her interest piqued, walked to the other side of the table from Mikell and Brutal and began scanning through several of the scattered pieces of parchment.

"This is a pretty detailed map," said Brutal. "Why would they have a map of Telfar?"

Mikell pointed to some of the text on the map. "I cannot read the writing, but this is some sort of battle map...look at the X's -- those are garrison soldiers, if I am not mistaken."

"These gnolls could not raid Telfar, could they?" asked Brutal.

York, hearing the conversation, walked over next to Mikell. "Well, perhaps this is just a scouting outpost for a larger force." After a short pause, the bard pointed to the map. "Well, well, Mikell, it looks like they took an interest in your temple; look, someone circled it." Mikell had not even noticed, but sure enough, his temple was circled with dark ink several times. He scanned the map and did not see any other structures circled.

"Why would they circle my temple?" Mikell wondered out loud.

"What in the eight hells... Does anyone here know how to read this shit language?" asked Ariana, looking up from a letter-sized piece of paper in her hand.

"What is it?" asked Mikell, noting the concerned look on her face.

"What about you, Bealty? Can't you read this crap? Is that not part of your tradecraft?" asked Ariana.

"Speaking and writing are two different things," replied Bealty, who did not bother to turn around, as he continued to search the northern wall. "Unfortunately, I do not even speak the gnoll language, although it is similar to goblin and orc, which I do understand to a certain point."

"Why did we bring him along again?" Ariana asked in a disgusted voice. "Useless," she added after the fact, shaking her head.

"C'mon, Ariana," said Tyberius. "He scouts ahead, that is what he does."

Ariana, ignoring Tyberius, stared at York across the table. "Well, what about you bard-boy?" York looked up from the map on the table, making eye contact with her. "Do you know how to read this garbage?" Ariana asked again, holding the sheet of paper out.

Mikell, speaking before York could reply, asked, "What is in the letter that is catching your eye?"

Ariana shifted her gaze to the priest and tossed the paper across the table to him. "Take a look for yourself. Of course, I cannot read it, but it looks like 'Mixnor' and 'Telfar' are spelled out pretty clearly."

That caught Brutal's attention, and his head snapped to the parchment as it flew through the air, landing next to Mikell. "What? My name is on that sheet of paper?" asked Brutal with some surprise.

Mikell picked it up and looked it over, saying, "Indeed it is."

"Let me see that," said Brutal as he grabbed the sheet out of Mikell's hands. His eyes scoured the sheet, and sure enough, he too could quickly pick out the clear lettering of "Telfar" and further down the document, his name "Mixnor." Brutal nudged York, who was standing next to him, "So, can you read this?" he asked, handing the bard the paper.

York smiled politely and, taking the parchment from Brutal, said, "I am far from fluent in the Draconic language, especially in the writing, but let me take a look." York's eyes slowly scanned through the document.

"Well, what does it say?" asked Brutal impatiently.

York, saying nothing, continued to look over the writings. After another long moment, he looked up at Brutal and said, "I cannot read all the writing..."

"For the love of the gods, what does it say?" asked Ariana, interrupting the bard.

"If my lady would allow me to finish," York said in an icy tone. "I cannot comprehend every word, but my guess is this is a bounty document."

Brutal's eyes widened. "What? A fucking bounty? On me?"

York nodded. "As far as I can tell, yes. And it is no small sum," York looked back down at the paper and added, "I think the bounty is one thousand gold pieces..."

Brutal's voice grew louder. "One thousand gold pieces on my head," he said as he pointed at himself. "That cannot be, you must not know how to read this crap."

"Actually," York said with some sympathy in his voice, "I do not think it is confined to you alone. The bounty says one thousand gold per 'human.'"

Brutal squinted quizzically and shook his head. "What does that mean?"

"Could it mean your entire family?" asked Ariana, breaking the brief silence.

"No, no, no," Brutal continued to shake his head, "that cannot be. Why would they target me and my family? And how would they know my family name? We are missing something," he said and began to rifle through the remaining stacks of paper on the table. Unrolling another large coiled up piece of parchment, Brutal whispered, "Oh my god..." and he looked up at Tyberius and Ariana with horror in his eyes.

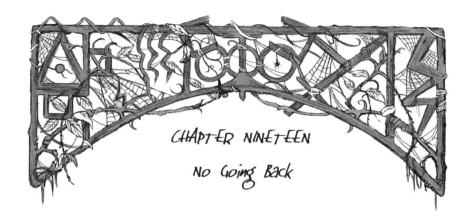

CHAPTER NINETEEN
No Going Back

YEAR: AG 1172, Month of Sepu

JUDAR, PUSHING THE TENT FLAP ASIDE, reentered the tent. "I assume he has agreed?" asked the evil cleric as he walked toward Anthall.

Marshal Krugar walked to the far side of the tent and grabbed an apple out of a bowl of fruit, and pulling out one of the chairs from the table, he sat down. "He does not know the details yet," said Krugar as he sliced an apple with a large knife he drew from his belt, "but he is ready to do what is necessary to get out of this tent."

"And back to my family," added Anthall.

The marshal shook his head. "No, we never agreed to that. But you will be able to save your family."

"How can I help them if I cannot return home?" asked Anthall.

Marshal Krugar let out a long sigh. "So many questions...I am beginning to think it would be easier to kill you and find another alternative."

Judar shook his head. "Where else will we find a warrior of his skill? He will be perfect, and once he is converted, he will be dependable, Marshal."

"Just tell me what you are talking about," said Anthall, losing his patience.

Judar looked at Krugar. "May I explain?" he asked. The marshal waved his hand for the cleric to proceed. Judar smiled, his pointy teeth jutting from between his red lips. "You see, Anthall, in order for this to work, you will need to renounce your faith from Soulmite and accept Blick as your new deity."

The request hit Anthall like a physical blow. "Why, what good will that do?" he asked.

Judar snorted derisively. "None, of course, but that is the whole point. I am not asking you to do a 'good' thing," said the cleric. "How do you think Soulmite would feel about you running around with evil hordes for the rest of your life?" Judar paused to let that sink in, then continued, "But really, we cannot trust you to live up to your word without a greater sacrifice."

Anthall felt the horror growing in the pit of his stomach. "What else would you have me do?"

Judar, still smiling, licked his lips, as if in anticipation of what he was about to say, "We are going to bind you to our will and cause -- through your death." Seeing the confused look on Anthall's face, the cleric nearly cackled with glee. "We are going to kill you, Anthall, there is no way around that now. The only choice left to you is whether you will use your death to help us," the cleric motioned toward Krugar, "or hinder us. Help us, and we will see that Krykl is hunted down and stopped before harming your family. Hinder us, and, well, I might even tell Krykl where to find your family, if he has not already figured that out for himself." Crouching down, Judar studied Anthall's face. "I can see you are still trying to figure out how to get out of this," Judar tsked three times, clicking his tongue and shaking a white bony finger at him. "There is no way out, Anthall." As he spoke, the cleric drew a long dagger from his belt. "I am going to plunge this dagger into your heart, and when I do -- you will die." Standing back up, the cleric continued to look down on the warrior. "When you pass, you will see or be confronted with some visage of Soulmite, and you will be tempted to follow her, but you need to be strong Anthall -- strong enough to turn from that being and accept Blick as your true savior. By doing that, Blick will return you to the material plane," then pointing to the ground, "here in Kardoon, with us."

"That is how we will know you have held up your end of the bargain, Anthall," said Krugar, putting his apple down on the table, and standing back up, continued, "if you come back to us, well, for lack of a better word, alive, then we will protect your family. If not, and you stay dead, then we know you chose to follow Soulmite. If you do that, you may live an eternity with your damned goddess, but your family will suffer greatly at the hands of Krykl before they become the main course."

"Nooooooo!" Anthall screamed with all the hatred and fury inside him. "Fuck you, Krugar! Fuck you and your fucking priest!"

Krugar walked behind Anthall and pulled on the shackles, pinning him tightly to the wooden beam. Anthall continued to curse them as he struggled to break free, but he had no leverage and was too weak to break the strong metal clasps or chains. Judar stepped to Anthall and placed a necklace with the holy symbol of Blick, three oval loops side by side, not overlapping but close together, around Anthall's neck.

"Take that fucking thing off me, you god-damned cleric!" Anthall continued to shout.

Judar then pulled two black candles from a bag on his belt and set one on each side of Anthall. Anthall tried to knock them over with his legs, but Krugar pulling on his chains, restricted his ability to move, and all his attempts failed. Judar lit each candle, and, closing his eyes, he began chanting in a language Anthall could not understand. The chanting lasted several minutes, until at last he stopped, and, opening his eyes, the cleric took the dagger and slowly, carefully, he cut his own right hand. Dabbing his left index finger into his own blood, using it like ink, he drew the three ovals of Blick onto Anthall's forehead.

"Guard! Guard!" Anthall shouted, his voice becoming hoarse. "Get me out of here!"

"Do not be a fool, Anthall," said Krugar. "No one can help you now -- but you can help yourself and your family, if you do the right thing."

Holding the dagger in front of Anthall's face, the cleric said, "Now, Anthall, the time has come. We have told you all you need to know. The life of your family depends on what you do next. Krugar and I will be waiting for you -- do not let us down...again," Judar added with derision.

"No, do not do it, Judar!" Anthall pleaded, but the cleric paused for only the briefest moment, then turning the dagger in his hand, he pressed the tip of the blade against Anthall's chest. Anthall met the cleric's gaze, and he shook his head, silently asking one more time for Judar to stop.

"On your way, Anthall," and, with that, Judar held the dagger straight with his left hand and with the palm of his right hand on the hilt, thrust the dagger forward with all his might. Anthall's eyes widened in horror as the dagger penetrated all the way through his body, a dull thud announcing the tip of the blade embedding itself into the wooden pole behind him. He let out a long gasp, blood gurgling up into his mouth, making breathing impossible. At first, the pain was excruciating, a terrible and frightening experience, but quickly all his feelings seemed to recede, replaced by a numbness, followed by the room fading to black. Anthall struggled to keep his eyes open, and, unknowingly he succeeded, but without even understanding what happened, his life slipped away and with it, all the pain and the weight of his being.

Krugar held onto the chains tightly, but soon he could feel Anthall's strength fade away. With the struggle over, he dropped the chains with a loud clanking and walked around the pole to get a view of Anthall from the front. His head hung down limply onto his chest, the dagger still pinning the warrior to the large pole. A copious amount of blood had washed over the dagger, acting like a facet, causing the formation of a large pool of blood on the ground between Anthall's legs which were spread apart during his struggle. A few drops of blood still fell from the hilt, landing with a plopping sound in the shallow pool which was already starting to soak into the dirt. "Will he really come back?" asked the marshal, with obvious skepticism in his voice. "I do not have to remind you that he is --" Krugar stopped himself, "was -- my best commander. So, for your sake, it had better work."

Judar, still crouching by Anthall, said, "Fetch me his sword, I need it to complete the ritual."

Krugar paused, an irritated look on his face, as he did not like his questions being ignored, or being given orders. "Answer my question first."

Judar turned his head to look at the marshal. "It is certain he will not, if you do not hand me his sword."

"Why does it have to be his sword? It is very valuable and I plan to sell it," said Krugar.

"Marshal, I was very specific about this point: he will be more powerful if he spilled blood in life with his soul sword, and," Judar added with emphasis, "time is critical right now -- so bring me his sword."

Krugar hesitated, as if pondering the pros and cons but finally relented, turning as he shouted, "Guards, bring us Anthall's sword.

"Yes, sir!" a voice could be heard outside and in just a few minutes the flap opened and a guard entered, carrying the sword, wrapped in cloth, placing it on the table in the center of the tent. The guard gave Anthall's body a quick, nervous, look, and then promptly turned and headed out, closing the flap behind him.

Judar stood up and moving to the table unwrapped the blade. Krugar was right, it was very well made and was sure it would be worth a lot of money on the black market, but no amount of coin could replace the suffering Anthall could cause with this blade -- a blade he had used, in life, to draw blood and cause so much suffering. Reaching down, his hand coiled around the fine leather wrapped hilt, his grip tightening, he lifted the bastard sword, which was unexpectedly light, effortlessly off the table.

"Leeeeaaavvvvve, meeee..." hissed Slice, "you are not worthy."

Judar flinched, as if from a physical blow, as Slice lashed out at the Priest's will. A cold sensation began creeping from his hand, up his arm, accompanied by the feeling of pins lightly poking at his mind. Judar's resolve stiffened. "I know one who is," Judar said defiantly.

Krugar frowned. "You know one who is what? What are you talking about?"

"Do not bind me to a corpse," hissed the voice again, "give me to Krugar and we can serve you well." Judar, already heading back to Anthall, stopped, and gave Marshal Krugar a look, weighing the proposal. "Yesss," the voice continued, "give me to Krugar....giiiiivvvvve me to him." Judar felt the urge to do as Slice was commanding and began to hand the sword to Krugar.

"What the hell are you doing, Judar?" asked Marshal Krugar.

Judar shook his head, in an attempt to wipe away the cobwebs forming in his mind. "No, you must be returned to Anthall," he answered, and, with that, he rested Slice across Anthall's legs, and taking Anthall's right hand, wrapped it around the hilt of the sword.

"Judar, you have made an error, and you will pay," seethed the voice just before Judar released the hilt of the blade. Judar gasped, as if breathing for the first time since he took hold of the blade, and quickly standing up, backing away, stumbling over the stool behind him, a look of fear and relief mixed across his face as he grasped his holy symbol for its comfort.

"Did something go wrong?" asked Krugar with concern in his voice, his hand reaching for his sword.

Judar, regaining his composure, put a hand on the table to steady himself. "The sword is cursed..."

"You idiot! You gave Anthall a cursed sword? What will that do?" asked Krugar, with even more concern.

Regaining his balance and composure, Judar straightened his cloak. "It will be fine. It...It could even be better this way. The curse can have no impact on Anthall, once he returns. And when he does, our problems will be solved for many years," Judar concluded with a devious smile, showing his spindly teeth.

* * * *

"Anthall," said a kind, whispery, but firm female voice. After a short pause, he heard the voice again. "Anthall, it is time to awaken."

Anthall's eyes felt very heavy, as if he had been in a very deep sleep, for a very long time. He tried to open them but could not. Thinking he could rub his eyes, he tried lifting his right arm up, but that too felt impossibly heavy and would not respond to his command. He tried to speak, but even that was too difficult. His mouth opened, but he could not vocalize any words.

"Anthall," said the voice firmly. "Rise and be seen."

Anthall could feel the touch of a soft hand brush cheek, and instantly he felt himself regain control over his body. He opened his eyes to see where he was and get his bearings, he thought hard but could not remember what he was just doing or where he might be -- and why he would be here. As his vision cleared, he recognized the room as a familiar place, but could not recall exactly where he was or what connection he had to it. He was in a small, but tidy, room in a cottage or small home. He was lying in the bed and slowly sat up, trying to get his bearings. He could hear a fire crackling in the room just outside his, but there were no other sounds, nor could he see the woman who had awoken him. Swinging his legs over the side of the bed, he noticed for the first time that he was wearing a pristine suit of chain mail. "Odd," he said out loud, examining his arms, extended out in front of him, which were also covered with chain mail. 'Why am I wearing armor to bed?' he thought to himself. Standing up, the wood flooring creaked under his weight as he moved into the larger room. Sure enough, there was the fire he had heard, crackling in the fireplace, and giving off a nice glow and warmth. There were three other smaller rooms that adjoined the main living space, and a large table dominated the room, which had seven places set. The walls were, unsurprisingly, bare; the only feature being a window over a basin on the counter, and a door leading out. "Where is everyone?" he asked quietly out loud. Looking around one more time and still finding the home empty, Anthall went to the door and opened it.

Anthall stepped out into the bright sunshine, causing him to squint. He still couldn't figure out where he was, although it felt like it was on the tip of his tongue. Looking around he could see a barn and a well. He already could picture the layout of the inside of the barn, but why could he not remember where this was?

"This is where your heart is," stated the familiar voice.

From out of nowhere it seemed, a figure of a woman in plate mail armor appeared, standing behind the well. She wore a longsword on her left hip and carried a shield on her left arm. He recognized the symbol on it, the three circles stacked in a triangle -- it was the symbol of Soulmite. Her face was difficult to see, it was like trying to look at the sun, you could see it out of the corner of your eye or in the periphery of your vision, but to look directly at it was difficult, if not painful. Anthall held his hand up to shield his eyes to see if he could get a better look, but it was no use. "This is where my heart is, eh?" he parroted.

"You are lucky. You might be surprised; most people's hearts are not at their home." Anthall could not see the woman's mouth move, but the voice definitely came from her direction.

'Home,' he thought to himself, with a chuckle and snort. Of course, this was Telfar! It was nagging at him, not knowing where he was, so it was a relief to be reminded. More worrisome, though, was how could he have forgotten?

"Do not worry yourself," said the woman, her voice firm and calming, "often our memories are different than the reality. It is difficult to reconcile, so the place seems familiar, but slightly off."

Her words struck Anthall as slightly disturbing, especially since he hadn't spoken his concern. "Wait, are you implying that this is not real?" he asked, holding up his arms in reference to their surroundings.

"Not implying, Anthall, simply stating the truth," the voice answered.

Anthall began to walk toward the well, and the figure standing behind it. "If this is not real, then where the hell are we?" he asked.

"I need warriors, Anthall, and you are a very good warrior. I have watched you your entire life and am pleased with your skills, loyalty, and devotion."

Standing on the opposite side of the well, Anthall stopped, not even attempting to go around to get closer. "Who are you?"

"You know who I am. It is time to accept your life and duty on the astral plane."

Anthall had heard of the astral plane, which was like another dimension, on which the gods resided. "How could I have gotten to the astral plane?" Anthall asked.

"We," the voice emphasized, "are on the astral plane. I am bound here in life, as you are in death," concluded the voice in a calm neutral tone.

"No, no, no," said Anthall. "That cannot be...that cannot be."

"It can be, and in fact: is," said the voice, then the voice continued in a more compassionate tone, "Do not be sad or fearful, this is where you were always meant to be some day, and that day is now. Your battles on the material plane have ended and have prepared you for your service here."

Anthall could feel the power and goodness flowing from the figure across from him and then he knew, "You are Soulmite?" he asked, somewhat rhetorically.

"Yes, Anthall. I have come to take you back to my domain," said the voice, pleased.

"Well, then let us be going," he replied, then looking down at his waist, he suddenly realized he was missing something. "Oh, I have no weapon. Where is my weapon?"

"We cannot go as you are, Anthall," the voice said, again in its neutral and calm voice.

"What? Why not?" asked Anthall.

"Raise the bucket of water from the well," commanded the figure. Anthall did not think twice and immediately began pulling on the rope to raise the bucket. "A true and faithful warrior -- with no hesitation...a true professional," she concluded as Anthall finished raising the bucket.

Grabbing the bucket, which was full of water, Anthall placed it on the edge of the well. "What shall I do now, m'lady?"

"Look into the water," she replied.

Anthall looked down at the bucket but saw nothing in it other than the reflection of the blue sky. "I see nothing in the bucket, m'lady," he said. As he finished his statement, a gauntleted hand grabbed the edge of the bucket and shifted it slightly, allowing himself to see his reflection. His face was immaculately clean and shaven, however, there were three distinct and interconnected circles drawn on his forehead. It took just a second, then he realized what he was looking at: the symbol of Blick. His memory came flooding back to him, but this time like a tsunami, crushing and drowning his very spirit. He looked up out of the water, searching frantically around and calling at the top of his lungs, "Fey! Fey! Kids!"

"Fey and your kids are not here, Anthall," said Soulmite.

Anthall stopped yelling and faced the figure of his deity. "You have to send me back to the material plane...just for a little while, please, then I can come back and I will serve you well."

Anthall could sense Soulmite shaking her head slowly, then he heard the voice. "I can do many things, but that I cannot do."

"But my family is in danger!" he gasped.

"I need you here, with me now. In time you will understand -- but right now I need you to do one thing: you must wash off the foul symbol of Blick on your forehead. That corrupt deity has no power over you here."

Anthall could sense the hatred in her voice at the mention of the evil god of suffering. Anthall's mind raced, trying to remember everything that Krugar and Judar had told him. Soulmite moved around the well, standing closer to Anthall, making her presence heavy and felt. "Wash the mark off, Anthall," she said, her voice was stern now.

Anthall cringed at her might and power, his hands moving, obeying her command, toward the bucket of water. Finally, plunging his hands into the cold water, he felt a chill run down his spine. "But if I do not return, my family will be killed...surely, you of all, can understand?"

"It is not a matter of my understanding," said Soulmite, her tone was harsh, "evil serves only itself; you cannot hope to save your family following a path of evil."

"But there is a chance I could...if...if I could just get back for a brief time...at least to warn them, if nothing else." Anthall said pleadingly.

"Neither you or I know what will happen in the future," said Soulmite, "and nothing you do here today will guarantee anything. Now, cleanse yourself of Blick's tainted symbol. I cannot accept your spirit in its foul state. If you do not -- you will have betrayed me."

Visions of gnolls and other beasts tearing his family apart, literally, made his stomach sick. "Please help me," he begged, getting down on his knees, "just give me one assurance that if I wash this filthy symbol off my head that my family will be safe." He paused for a second, then added, "Surely you can grant me that much?"

Soulmite backed up a step. Crossing her arms, she said, "I can say with certainty that your choice here will have little impact on your family. Blick does not care about your family, so your servitude to him, should you so unwisely choose that path, will not depend on, or ensure, their well-being." After a short pause, she added, "For the last time, Anthall, wash the mark off your forehead and join me in my good fight here," and, with that, she extended out her gauntleted hand.

Anthall's hands trembled, shaking in the cold water. Pulling them out, he looked at them, the water dripping off in slow motion, each drop hitting the dirt at his feet with a quiet tap, tap, tap, reminding him of the large branch of the oak tree that used to brush against his small home on windy nights. The thought of his house brought other memories of his family to mind, and he could picture them all sitting around the table sharing a meal. It was the simple things he missed most: a night around the hearth, telling of their day, a breakfast together, a hard day working in the fields, a clear starry night, or just the simple comfort of lying down next to Fey at the end of each day. Looking down, unable to look Soulmite in the eyes, his hands slowly fell to his side, the blowing wind already beginning to dry his hands. "Milady, I am sorry, I cannot...sacrifice my family." Sensing an absence, he looked up, and Soulmite was nowhere to be seen. Anthall spun around, looking desperately for the goddess, but as mysteriously as she had appeared, she was gone. The sky began to darken with black turbulent clouds off in the distance that began moving his way, flashes and streaks of lightning lighting up the sky, followed by ominous rumbles of thunder.

CHAPTER TWENTY
Unknown Losses

BRUTAL SET THE PARCHMENT DOWN on the table and held the edges down with two small stones that acted as paperweights that lay scattered about. "Look at that," said Brutal, pointing to the map. "It is a shitty map, but it is definitely a map of the surrounding area." Brutal pointed to each mark on the map. "Here is where we are, and here is my farm, Ariana's, and yours," he said to Tyberius.

Julius, listening to the conversation, walked over from the corner. "Is there any notation for my lodge?"

Brutal shook his head. "I do not think so. If there was it would be around here," Brutal used his finger to circle an area on the map, "but there is no marking."

"None of this makes any sense though," said Tyberius. "Why would these beasts have a bounty for any of us?"

"And why make this large base with so many gnolls?" added Ariana, shaking her head.

"I do not have any of those answers," said Mikell, "but I bet I know someone who does."

"Who?" asked Tyberius, his hand tightening around the Taper wood hilt of his flail.

"The fucking dwarf," said Brutal, "we have to find him." Turning, Brutal put his hand on the bard's shoulder. "No offense to your reading skills, but we need to find that son of a bitch to explain what in the eight hells is going on here." With that, Brutal shoved the piece of parchment with the bounty on it into his backpack. "Have you found anything yet, Bealty?" he asked as he tied his pack closed.

"We are wasting our time here," said Ariana. "That son of a bitch, if he is invisible, could already be out of this stinky pit of a base." Holding up her hand and gesturing toward the northern wall that Bealty was searching, she added, "Besides there is no door on that wall."

"Actually, I think you are wrong about that," said Bealty, turning a small stone in the wall, which gave off a small clicking sound. Bealty gave the wall a slight push and a section of it swung outward, revealing an adjoining room.

The room was briefly silent, interrupted by Tyberius letting out the laughter he was trying to suppress. Ariana gave her fiancé a cold hard look, and Tyberius managed to control his outburst. Then with his customary big grin, he put his arm around her. "See, it is like I said, he does what he does, and we do what we do."

"Well done, Beetle," said York with a quick clap of his hands.

"Yeah, way to go, little guy," said Hammer chiming in. Before anyone else could say a word, Bealty squirted through the new opening and disappeared beyond the door.

"Bealty, wait," said Mikell in his loudest hushed voice he could. Seeing that the halfling was already gone, he hefted his mace and started moving toward the door, "Well, we better follow."

Brutal, Hammer, and Tyberius were the first through the door, finding a well-lit room, with the finest furnishings they had yet to see in the bunker. There was an actual bed with pillows, and on the eastern wall there was a fireplace; there were logs in place, but the fire was not lit. Bealty was examining the fireplace when the warriors burst into the room, weapons drawn.

"How do you think they dug a chimney for this thing?" asked Bealty. "We must be twenty feet down and I cannot see a light up above."

"Quit screwing around with the fireplace, Bealty," said Brutal. "Only you would stop in the middle of all this to wonder such a weird question."

Bealty looked over his shoulder at Brutal. "Odd things always draw my attention, which is a good thing; I specialize in odd things. You know what else is odd?" the halfling baited the warrior.

"I am afraid to ask," Brutal responded, "but I have a feeling you are going to tell me anyway."

Bealty ran his hand underneath the fire grating that held the logs of wood, and then held up his hand, showing Brutal his palm, which aside from being a little dirty, was fairly clean. "This ain't no fireplace, it ain't never been used." Looking up what seemed to be a chimney of some sort, he added, "At least I do not think so."

The room was a small bedroom, about thirty feet by twenty feet, with the secret door in the middle of the south wall. The floor was still hardened dirt, but the furnishings gave the room a warmer feel than all the others. There was even a fine rug covering much of the floor in the middle of the room. The bed was made of wood, with a straw filled mattress on top of it. There was one small table with a chair. The chair was not pushed in, and the table had a basin full of dirty water, as well as a filthy piece of cloth resting on it. The only other item on the table was a small vial of black liquid, presumably ink.

Hammer walked to the bed and began pulling the one blanket off. "Just looking to see if there is anything here," the warrior said, but the bed turned out to be bare, aside from a few questionable stains all over the bedding. "Oh man, that smells awful, Hammer said, throwing the blanket into the corner of the room and covering up his nose.

Isa, lagging behind the rest of the group, shuffled into the small room. The large half-orc made his way to the bed and sat down, the wood creaking under his weight.

Mikell walked over to the monk. "Are you okay, Isa?" Isa nodded and waved him away. "I will not tolerate martyrs, let me take a look," said Mikell as he began to reach for the monk's shirt.

Isa pulled away, his face contorting into a grimace, then after a quick recovery said, "No hurt."

"Nonsense," retorted Mikell. "Now sit still," he said firmly, placing his left hand on the monk's shoulder, holding him in place. Mikell could see where the flames had scorched him completely around his abdomen, and he could also see the gash in his left side where the gnolls sword had barely missed skewering the half-orc. Mikell shook his head. "No, you need some help Isa, you are still losing blood... Hold still." Mikell, once again, grabbing his holy symbol, began the incantation. "Benedici il mio tocco con il potere di guarire le ferite lievi," then touching the monk's arm, he released the positive energy. Mikell watched as the gash in Isa's side knitted itself and some of the burn marks vanished from his torso. He still had wounds on his body but, overall, he could see the monk regain his lost strength.

Isa reached up and grabbed Mikell's shoulder, and pulling himself up to a standing position, grunted, "You thanks," and after a quick nod moved back toward the open secret door.

"Do not thank me yet," said Mikell, looking around the room at his beat-up band of friends. A loud screeching sound, reverberated around the room, startling Mikell and several others in the group. Mikell spun around to see Brutal jumping into action toward where Bealty had started to drag the iron grill from out of the fireplace.

"Bealty! Let me get that," shouted Brutal as he rushed to the fireplace and picked up the iron grill that was holding the logs.

"Oh thanks. Yeah, that was louder than I thought it would be," said Bealty as more a matter of fact than with any kind of apology, "but it also confirms my suspicions."

"What are you talking about Bealty?" asked Tyberius.

"There is something under the grate," answered Ariana, taking a couple steps toward the fireplace to get a better view.

"Indeed," said York, also moving closer to the halfling, who was busy brushing a thick layer of dirt out of the fireplace.

After a few moments, Bealty revealed a hatch with a small metal ring on the top of it. Bealty examined the hatch, the ring, and the fireplace. "Well, I do not see a trap, but I am concerned that something is going to fall from up there," he said, pointing up the supposed chimney.

"There could be treasure in there," said Hammer. "We need to open that thing."

Bealty looked up. "I would not advise it, my gut is telling me there is more to this, but I cannot seem to see the mechanism."

"If Bealty says it is probably trapped, I say we leave it be," said

Mikell.

"Man, if we listened to you we would never find anything," said Hammer, with some irritation in his voice. "Move aside, I will open that stupid hatch." Bealty and the others moved backwards, away from the fireplace as Hammer approached. Setting his hammer down and leaning it against the bed, he turned his attention to the metal ring. Looking around at the others who had moved away, Hammer grinned. "What a bunch of pussies," and reaching down, he pulled up on the ring. The hatch swung upward on its hinges revealing a small compartment below. "Fuck yeah," said the warrior, his eyes boggling, "there is a chest in there." Hammer bent down to pick up the chest.

"No, wait!" shouted Bealty, holding out his hands as if he could stop Hammer.

But it was too late, Hammer, paying no attention to the halfling, reached in and pulled out the chest. As he heaved on the chest, everyone took another step backwards, but to everyone's amazement he lifted the small wooden chest out of its hiding place and set it down in the dirt just outside of the fireplace. "Damn," said Hammer, grunting, "this sum'bitch is heavy," then looking up at the group a few steps away, added, "and you all wanted to leave it behind."

"Well, I would not say we wanted to leave it behind," said Brutal, "but I agree with Bealty it seemed suspicious."

"Damn, there is a lock on the chest," said Hammer, "well, I can break that thing off no problem."

Bealty sprang forward, placing a tiny hand on Hammer's arm. "Just wait, let me look it over. I would hate for you to break something inside by smashing it with your hammer."

Hammer stood up. "Yeah, good thinking, little buddy."

Bealty immediately began to look over the chest, which was wooden with metal bands reinforcing it. The clasp was held shut with a lock that had a small keyhole. "I still see no traps," said the halfling, shrugging his shoulders, "so I guess all there is to do is open it." Reaching into a pocket inside his leather armor, the halfling took out two small tools: one having a thin wire on the end of a Taper wood handle, and the other was a very thin, pencil-like metal instrument with a small hook at the end. Inserting both tools into the keyhole, Bealty began working on the lock, his small hands manipulating the tools inside the mechanism with practiced regularity.

Everyone was watching Bealty intently, including Ariana, who slowly was shaking her head. "I cannot believe my life has come to hoping for Bealty to pick a lock," she said, disbelief in her voice.

Tyberius grinned, putting his arm around her, giving her a quick squeeze, then gesturing with his flail in the halflings direction, said, "See…"

Ariana shook off his light embrace, interrupting, "I know…he does what he does, and we do what we do." Looking up at her tall fiancé, she said, "Just because you are right one time," she said, holding up one finger, "does not mean you can go on about it," then turning her attention back to the rogue, she added, "What a nag." Tyberius, still grinning, opted to say nothing more about it.

No sooner had Ariana finished talking when the lock clicked open, the latch almost falling off the hasp. "Aha, there we go," said Bealty. The various races across the world of Thran derive satisfaction from a wide array of activities. For some it's excavation, magic, construction, or tinkering, but for halflings, nothing is more rewarding than the click of a lock opening, or a disarmed trap, and like a druid honoring an animal they had just killed for sustenance, Bealty carefully took the lock of the hasp and laid it on the ground, admiring his work. However, not far behind the thrill of opening a lock on a halfling's list of favorite things to do, is to find out what the lock was protecting, so Bealty began examining the chest one more time for any signs of a trap, but seeing none, he slowly began to lift the lid open. The metal hinges creaked slightly, but it opened safely.

Hammer pushed his way to the chest. "I got first picks -- I was the one who took the risk opening it."

"We will divide any treasure later," said Mikell. "We cannot waste time here arguing about who gets what -- we must keep moving." As he spoke, everyone else moved forward, as well, to see into the chest.

"What the fuck is that?" asked Hammer with obvious disappointment, "It looks like an empty god-damned sack." Throwing up his free hand, he exclaimed, "Why would someone go to so much trouble to hide an empty sack?"

"Maybe they took whatever was in there and left already," said Brutal.

"Why would they lock it back up and put it back into the hiding place then?" asked Ariana. "That does not make any sense."

While the others were arguing, Mikell stepped forward, and tracing some divine runes into the air, canted a detect magic spell. "Concedimi il potere di vedere tutte le aure magiche." At the conclusion of the spell, Mikell could feel the presence of a sixth sense, and as he focused on the bag inside the small chest, which Bealty was already starting to lift out, he could sense a faint aura about it, which confirmed that it was indeed somehow magical. He was about to say something when his attention was unexpectedly drawn to Ariana. As the sorceress continued to debate the issue of the chest with Brutal and Hammer, Mikell kept being drawn to her. As Mikell continued to focus on Ariana, his sense was narrowing in on the source: the ring on her finger, the ring Tyberius had given her. 'Was it magical? How could that be?' he thought to himself.

"What the hell are you staring at?" said Tyberius with his wide grin, slapping the priest on the shoulder.

Mikell was startled by the friendly strike, snapped out of his self-induced trance, words stumbling to come out. "I, uh, yes -- sorry." Then recovering his composure, shaking his head, as Tyberius, Brutal, Hammer, and Ariana all looked at him, he said, "I, uh, cast a quick spell and the bag appears to be..."

"Hey, this bag is magical!" said Bealty in an excited voice as everyone quickly shifted their eyes back to the small rogue. "Look at this," he said as he lifted the apparently empty bag. "It looks empty, but there is some weight to it, and when I reach my hand in, I can feel coins." As if to confirm his words, he pulled out a handful of gold coins.

"So, there are a few coins at the bottom of the bag, so what," scoffed Hammer.

"Oh no, there are many more than a few coins," said Bealty.

Hammer took a step toward Bealty. "Let me see that thing," he said, holding out his hand. Bealty stood up and gave the bag to Hammer.

Despite the halfling's words, he was still shocked to feel the weight of the bag, "Damn, it does feel like something is in there," and upon reaching his hand inside, his face lit up in wonder and surprise. "No fucking way," he commented as he pulled out a large handful of coins, a couple of which fell onto the dirt floor.

"Hey, be careful," said Bealty, picking them up.

Ariana looked around for York and found him sitting on the bed, watching the group, writing in his small book. "York, have you ever seen anything like this before?"

"Aye, sorceress, I have," answered York. "Mostly I have heard of them referred to as a sack, or bag, of holding." After a brief pause, he added, "Quite a valuable item."

"We should dump it out and see how much is in there," said Hammer, a huge grin on his face.

"No!" shouted Mikell placing his hand on Hammer's shoulder. With everyone's attention, Mikell continued, "We have to keep moving, in fact it would be better if we got the hell out of here, right now."

"We just found a magical bag with a bunch of gold -- there could be a lot more treasure," said Hammer, "and that is why we are here."

"No," said Mikell, poking Hammer in the chest, "that is why you are here, most of us are here to help Brutal find his father."

"Well, in that case, what have we found out?" asked Hammer. "Exactly nothing, so if we leave now then we will have accomplished nothing."

"He is right, Mikell," said Brutal. "I know we are in danger while we are down here, but we must keep searching. That dwarf might have some information we need."

Mikell nodded. "Fine, but we must keep moving, we have already wasted too much time on this little room. Bealty," Mikell turned toward the halfling, "lead us out of here."

Bealty nodded and, snatching the bag from Hammer, stuffed it into his backpack. "Hey!" said Hammer, "I will hold onto that!" but it was far too late, as the rogue bounded out the secret door and through the map room, with everyone following close behind. Back in the great room, there was an odd silence.

"The hallway angling out of this room," said Julius pointing north, "leads to a hallway that runs east and west. We have not yet been to the eastern end of it."

"I know the way," said Bealty, who again began to slink down the middle of the great room, between the large wooden beams, some of which were charred from the fiery explosion. The angled hallway was only about twenty feet long, and opened into a wide hallway that indeed ran east and west. The western end of the hallway narrowed, and Bealty knew that it led back to the barracks. Julius was right, they had not been to the east, so the halfling began to move in that direction, but his movements were more careful and measured now, his eyes scanning the floor and walls for any peculiar signs of traps or even possibly another secret door. The hallway widened at the end, into a twenty foot by thirty foot wide room that was barren of any feature other than a single door on the southern wall, effectively at the end of the hallway.

Bealty moved to the door and scanned the immediate area for traps. Looking over his shoulder, he noted the rest of the group standing a safe distance behind him. The halfling nodded and waved. "It is okay, I do not see any traps."

"Well," said Hammer, "go on then, open it up -- we are all ready."

"Zuel, protect us," said Mikell quietly.

Bealty put his hand on the door handle and gave it a slight twist. The latch clicked and the door began to creak open, revealing another hallway, running further east. Peeking around the corner, Bealty could see that the hallway ran about twenty feet to the east and then turned north. Stepping into the hallway, he slowly made his way to the corner, where the passageway turned north, but rather than looking around the corner, Bealty was looking at the southern wall of the hallway.

"What is it," asked Mikell in a hushed voice.

"A door, I think," said Bealty. Turning his attention back to the hallway, he peeked around the corner, noting that the hallway went north for a ways, but otherwise was clear. The halfling moved closer to the southern wall and pushing a stone inward, sure enough a section of the wall swung open, the hinges creaking as it did so, causing everyone to cringe. Bealty slunk into a shadow, melding out of sight, as he looked northward, waiting to see if anyone or anything had heard and would come. But nothing did. The secret door only revealed a small ten by ten foot room.

"Tyberius and Hammer," said Mikell pointing to the north, "you both go up the hallway and make sure nothing surprises us from that direction."

Hammer and Tyberius, after taking a couple steps down the hallway, halted as Bealty spoke, "There may be traps down there, I have not checked that yet."

"Go on," said Mikell. "There will be no traps in this hallway."

"How do you know?" asked Tyberius.

"Yes, how can you be so certain?" asked Ariana with concern in her voice.

"Of course, I do not know, but why would they place traps so far into their bunker?" said Mikell.

"Fuck it, I am not afraid. C'mon, Tyberius," Hammer said, tugging lightly on the taller warrior's arm.

"Yeah, screw it, I am not afraid of a little dart," responded Tyberius.

"Okay, but be careful, it is not the dart, it is the poison on the dart, or it could be a pit, a spear, or even a gas," said Bealty in an informational tone of voice.

"What do you mean -- a 'gas'? What the hell is that?" asked Tyberius, stopping in his tracks.

Bealty thought for a second. "Like a puff of air that could be poisonous."

"A puff of fucking air?" asked Tyberius with skepticism. "You mean like a fart of air?"

"Somehow that puts a cruder touch to the explanation, but yeah, I suppose so," replied Bealty.

"That is just a bunch of bullshit to scare us," said Hammer, "I am going up there with or without you." Tyberius gave Ariana a quick look and then both he and Hammer started to make their way northward, up the hallway, lit by a few scattered lanterns that were hanging on the wall.

Turning his attention back to the small squarish room revealed by the secret door, Bealty first noticed the conspicuous wooden ladder that led upwards into a dark hole in the ceiling of the room. Aside from that, the room was empty, however, Bealty's keen eyes caught a subtlety on the south wall which he slowly moved to inspect. "It does not appear to be a trap...I think it is another door," said the halfling as he began to look around for any kind of mechanism to operate it. "Ah, there it is," he said with a little excitement in his voice, looking at a piece of the ground about one foot to the side of the door. Placing one of his small feet onto the suspicious patch of dirt, he heard the familiar click, and the door began to swing outward into another room. Everyone braced, waiting for a rush of gnolls or other enemies, but none came. As the door opened wider, it became obvious.

"Ah shit," said Brutal, lowering his sword, "this goes back into the bedroom." Indeed, the secret passages led back to the room where they had found the chest and the bag of holding.

"Well, now we know how the dwarf got away," said Bealty.

"The only question," added York from the rear of the party, "is whether he went up the ladder or down the hallway."

"Either way, he is on his way to get help," said Julius.

"Well, up surely leads back to the surface, and there is no sense in chasing him through the wilds at this point," said Mikell. "Besides, I bet he is still down here."

"I can climb up there lickity split," said Bealty, then we will at least know what is up there, for sure."

"It is dark up there, take this," said Ariana pulling out a small Taper wood stick, about six inches long. Reaching into one of the pouches on her belt, she revealed a small piece of lightly glowing moss, she canted the spell, "Invoco la luce," and touching the end of the stick, it burst into a bright light, which she handed to Bealty.

"Wow, Thank you, Ariana," said Bealty. Putting the stick between his teeth, like a dog with a bone, he launched himself onto the ladder, about six feet up and began bounding upwards.

Knowing her oft stated dislike for the rogue, Mikell and Brutal gave her a surprised look. Ariana, purposefully paying them no attention, watched Bealty scamper up the ladder with the grace and agility of a cat, but feeling their gaze linger on her, she said, without even a glance in their

293

direction, "I am beginning to see some usefulness in the little bastard," then with a slight wave of her hand, added, "now go make yourselves fucking useful or something." Mikell and Brutal grinned at each other, quickly shifting their eyes to the hole in the ceiling where the halfling was climbing.

Bealty figured there was just enough room for a gnoll-sized creature, but there was plenty of room for him. It was a thirty foot climb at least, he figured in his head, and peering back down the ladder, the small disk of light that was the opening to the room below was getting smaller and smaller. It was kind of Ariana, he thought to himself as he climbed, to give him the light, since halflings were not blessed with night vision, but, of course, he had some small candles that would have done the trick, but he still appreciated the gesture. Looking up again, he could see the top of the ladder. Once at the top, there was a small landing off to the side, about three feet long by four feet deep, and Bealty jumped onto the small ledge. Shining the light stick up, he immediately saw a problem. There was an obvious handle and latch which undoubtedly opened a hatch above, but it was about eight feet off the ground. Easy for a seven foot tall gnoll to operate, but not so much for a two foot ten inch halfling. Getting up there would not be the problem, he thought to himself. 'But how do I get the leverage to open the hatch?' he wondered out loud. Examining the small area, he noted that there were wooden beams supporting a wooden ceiling. "Ah, simple enough," he said quietly out loud. Pulling out a small grappling hook from his backpack, he tossed it up to catch on the handle of the hatch. His aim was perfect on his first attempt, and the hook caught the handle securely. The little halfling shimmied up the eight feet of rope like a monkey, then holding himself up with one hand, there were benefits to weighing just over thirty pounds, he used his other hand to screw in a little metal eye hook into the beam just under the hatch. With the hook firmly screwed into place, Bealty tied a small knot in his rope and fed it through the eye-hole, then made a loop and tied another knot at the other end. Placing one foot into the bottom loop, he tested his new foothold. It held firmly, the knot keeping the rope from getting through the eye of his hook above. Bealty gave the latch a twist and then pushing up with his back he was able to fully open the hatch.

* * * *

Back in the small room at the bottom of the ladder, everyone milled around nervously, occasionally looking up the hole for some sign of the little rogue. Tyberius and Hammer came back down the hallway with concerned looks on their faces. "I looked around the corner," said Hammer, "and could see another door further down the passage, as well as a large entryway into what looked like another room."

"Why do you both have that look on your faces?" asked Brutal.

"Something down there is making an awful noise," said Tyberius. "Like screaming and growling all mixed together."

Hammer nodded, silently confirming the report, then added, "A real raucous."

Tyberius gave Hammer a quizzical look. "What the hell did ya just say?"

Hammer, looking up at Tyberius, the taller warrior was almost a head taller, said, "A raucous...you know, a loud noise or something."

"Are you fucking with me?" snapped Tyberius.

"Calm down," said Mikell, addressing Tyberius. "Nobody is messing with you. Did you see any more gnolls or the dwarf?" Tyberius's face seemed to relax a little, and both warriors shook their head. "Something tells me he is down there."

"What is up there?" asked Tyberius, pointing to the hole in the ceiling.

"Right now, Beetle is," answered York, who was leaning against the wall in the small room and writing some notes into a small book.

Mikell looked at the bard, then did a double take. "Did you just call him 'Beetle'?" he asked.

York nodded. "I sure did."

"You know his name is Bealty, right?" Mikell asked, stressing the ending of the halfling's name.

"Ain't it got a better 'ring' to it?" asked Tyberius, his grin returning, a little pride showing on his face for remembering the term.

York smiled and pointed his small pen at the tall warrior. "Exactly, my tall friend -- it has an exceptional ring to it."

"How can you write at a time like this?" asked Mikell, annoyance in his voice.

York finished writing something in his little book, then snapping it shut, gave, what seemed to Mikell, a devilish grin. "Writing is what I do, my boy," said York, after which he tucked the book and pen into a side pocket of his backpack.

"What do you write in that book?" probed the cleric further.

"Names, dates, places -- things to jog my memory so I can write more detail later," York replied.

"But you make up different names?" asked Mikell.

"Names that capture the imagination make for better stories," said York.

"What else do you contrive to make your stories more interesting?" asked Mikell.

York stood up a little straighter. "My stories always tell the truth my friend, both the good and the unfortunate events."

"The truth is usually pretty boring," said Ariana, causing both men to look at her. Just then everyone felt a slight rush of air around them, as if they were suddenly in the middle of a small tornado, and simultaneously a bright light shone down through the shaft in the ceiling, creating a bright sunny spot on the dirt floor below the opening. They had all become accustomed to the stench in the complex, but the air funneling down from above was fresh and clean, and everyone took some deep breaths, as if they were surfacing from a long dive.

* * * *

The brilliance of the noon sun caught the halfling off guard, temporarily blinding him. Using his free hand like a visor, he allowed his eyes to adjust, then looked around to orient himself. The grass around the hatch door was too high to see over, so Bealty climbed out of the entrance and back onto solid ground. The grass was just about as tall as he was, so he took off his backpack and stood on top of it, which was just enough for him to see over the swaying field of brown and green grass. He could see the swale off to the south, maybe one hundred feet or so, he guessed, and the entrance to the stairs would be right there on the side of the swale. Hoping to get a better view, he picked up his backpack and slunk another fifty feet closer to the edge of the swale and placing his backpack down, he again perched on top of it. Looking around he saw no sign of more gnolls, or any other creatures for that matter, but there was one curious feature that now caught his attention, which he did not expect to see -- and that was a pillar of smoke rising into the sky to the west; it was impossible to tell from where he was if it was one large stream of smoke boiling up, or several smoke trails mingling into one large black cloud. "Grass fires to the west?" Bealty asked himself out loud in a curious manner. Halflings, by nature, are an optimistic race, being able to find the silver lining in most any situation, so dread and concern aren't a feeling that they cross paths with often, but as Bealty considered the geography a little more, his eyebrows raised, and his small oil drop pupils dilated slightly as he felt his heart rate step up a few beats per minute. As uncommon as it was, Bealty recognized the feeling immediately: the dread washed over him as if he had just stepped under a waterfall of the cold, numbing emotion. "Ohhh shit." The words dripped off his tongue slowly, sounding odd, like hearing a five year old cursing, but those were the first words that came to mind. "Graff, have mercy," he added, already turning around. Wasting no more time, the halfling hopped down off his backpack, and putting the light stick Ariana had given him back into his mouth, he quickly picked up the pack and slung it onto his shoulders. Sprinting through the grass back to the hatch, he leapt the last five feet, grabbing the handle, mid-flight, and letting the force of his weight rock the hatch cover backwards, causing it to rebound forward with enough inertia to fall shut with a loud 'whump.' Hanging by the hatch handle, Bealty grabbed his rope and slid down to the small landing. He did not bother to recover his hook, or the rope, but instead pulled some small black leather gloves out of a pocket. He barely had them on as he stepped into the hole in the floor and, grabbing the ladder by the sides, slid down at a very rapid pace. The acrid smell of burning leather stung Bealty's nose, but the descent was quick. The tiny circle of light that was the hole in the ceiling below him expanded rapidly as he plummeted, until, finally, he burst into the room.

CHAPTER TWENTY-ONE
Skik

BEALTY BARELY SLOWED HIS DESCENT as he shot through the hole in the ceiling, and, landing on the dirt floor, he rolled away from the ladder, negating most of the impact, and bouncing into a standing position after one quick revolution.

"Damn, are you okay little buddy?" asked Hammer, backing up a step as Bealty nearly ran into him through his roll, the warrior holding his hands out in front of him reflexively.

Mikell saw the worried look on the halfling's face immediately. "Did something chase you down?" he asked.

Bealty shook his head quickly side to side as he removed the singed gloves from his hands. "I cannot say for sure, but I think I know where the other gnolls went," he said, turning so he could see Brutal, Tyberius, and Ariana. "I saw black smoke rising from the west."

Brutal took a step toward the halfling. "Wait, what? The shaft went to the surface then, and you saw smoke to the west?" Seeing the halfling nod, Brutal rubbed his chin, thinking, then added, "I suppose it could have been smoke from chimneys."

"I do not think so, Brutal, it was..." Bealty paused for a second, swallowing hard, "it was thick black smoke -- too much for a fireplace."

"You think the gnolls from this place attacked our homes?" asked Ariana in an icy tone.

Bealty looked up at Ariana. "Yeah, I think so."

"I am going to kill all of those motherfuckers," said Tyberius, his face starting to turn red, his hand tightening around the shaft of his large flail.

"We have to get out of here and help them," said Brutal, his eyes widening in alarm as he began making his way toward the ladder leading up.

"We could split up," said Julius. "Some of us could head back to the homesteads while the rest continue on here."

"Splitting the group now would be a mistake," York stated. "It will make us all more vulnerable."

"He is right about that," said Mikell. "We should stick together -- we have no idea what is around that corner," he said, pointing down the corridor to the north.

"Every bit of time we waste down here means our families could be being kilt," said Tyberius.

"Then we need to make quick work down here and get out," said Hammer.

"You just want to find more treasure!" said Brutal, turning away from the ladder and pointing a finger at Hammer.

"They could already be dead, and the one shithead who might know what the hell is going on is probably right around that corner," Hammer retorted, his back stiffening.

Tyberius pushed Hammer backwards. "Do not say they are dead!"

"If they are -- that dwarf is our only chance of knowing why or who!" shouted Hammer.

"I do not need to know why if I get back in time to stop anything bad from happening!" Tyberius roared back.

"Ariana, how far can you communicate with Foetore?" asked Julius, this caused the rest of the group to fall silent.

"What?" replied Ariana, being caught off guard by the question. "I do not really know the limits, but certainly not from here to my homestead," she added, collecting her thoughts, knowing that her home was the closest to where they were.

Julius stepped forward. "We should not split the group, that would be too dangerous for those who remained here...but one of us could go and investigate. I have a horse and can travel quickly, so I propose I take Foetore with me to scout out what has happened...or is happening. Then, if I need all of you to come immediately, I can ride back toward the swale, and as soon as you can communicate, Foetore can call Ariana."

Tyberius roared, "Have your elf ears finally made you mad?"

Ariana put a hand on Tyberius's outstretched arm. "No, Julius has a decent plan." Turning, Ariana looked the half-elf in the eyes, noting his gray irises, common to most elves. "On one condition: you guard Foetore's life like it was any one of us."

"Of course," replied Julius. "No harm shall come to him, unless it is beyond my control."

Tyberius gave Ariana a concerned look, but she did not waiver. "We need to finish our business here, and Julius and Foetore can let us know quickly if we need to leave here."

"Are you sure about that?" asked Brutal.

Ariana, turning her head, could see the concern written on Brutal's face, and her stoic appearance softened, her eyes showing more compassion than they had a second before. "If you were on a raid, would you burn the homes before or after your raid?"

"You think we are too late, already?" asked Brutal, feeling his heart sink as her logic hit home.

"Of course, I do not know the answer to that, Brutal," she replied, "but Julius and Foetore will let us know very soon. This way we still have a chance to finish our business down here. If we all go up now and rush westward, maybe we get there in time, maybe we do not -- and maybe," she said, turning her attention to Bealty, "maybe the little runt is wrong, and someone is just burning some brush to the west. In all those scenarios, we will have lost our opportunity to find out anything down here. This place will be reinforced, or it will be abandoned -- either way, we cannot come back."

"For once, listen to the lady," said Hammer.

"Fuck you," said Tyberius and Brutal simultaneously, causing the two warriors to look at each other, wondering who Hammer was talking to.

"Well, that speaks volumes," said Hammer, shaking his head.

Ariana, ignoring the side conversation, walked over to Julius and whispered softly into his ear, "Take care of him. You know we are..."

"Bonded," said Julius, finishing her sentence. "I know, and I will protect him with all my ability to do so."

Ariana nodded and took a half step backwards. "He will be waiting for you at the turn, he is already on his way there."

Slinging his bow over his shoulder, he began climbing up the ladder, then stopped, hearing his name called out. "Julius, wait!" said Bealty, who quickly moved to the ladder and handed the ranger the little light stick. "It is pretty dang dark up there. You will need to use my rope to get the hatch open -- you will see it when you get up there."

Julius reaching down, took the light stick but tucked it into a pocket of his leather armor, smothering the light. "Thank you, Bealty, I do not think I will need it, but will take it just in case," and then he began the long climb, quickly disappearing into the darkness above.

"We have to move quickly now," said Brutal, drawing his bastard sword from its sheath.

"Bealty, get up there and see what is around that corner," ordered Mikell. The halfling didn't even wait for him to finish his sentence before he was bounding down the passageway to the north.

The hallway ran about sixty feet in length, then turned ninety degrees to the west. Bealty cautiously peered around the corner, knowing that, by now, whatever was out there was probably expecting them, which made the whole situation much more dangerous. 'As if it was not already dangerous enough,' he thought to himself. The hallway ran west thirty or forty feet before opening into an oddly shaped room, which had one door that he could see, on the north side of the room, but what was more peculiar, was the large opening further to the west that looked more roughly cut, or dug out, than the rest of the structure, but it was too far and too dark to see much more beyond the roughly hewn archway. There was no sign of any activity, but his keen ears picked up some noise coming from the darkness inside the rough cut room far to the west; it was a metallic sound, that was for sure, and had a jingling to it, like thousands of keys rattling together. But beyond that it was impossible to know exactly what it could be. Bealty waited one more second, then melded into the shadows as best he could and crept westward, scanning the floor, walls, and ceiling for any signs of a trap. This careful approach slowed him down, and he could hear the others were gathering behind him but staying safely around the corner.

"Psst. Psst! Why the hell are you moving so slow?" asked Hammer in a hushed voice.

Brutal lightly knocked Hammer on the side of his helmet. "Shhh, are you trying to get Bealty killed?"

"He is looking for traps," said Mikell. "Let him do his thing."

After watching Bealty creep a few feet further, making painfully slow progress, Tyberius stepped out into the hallway behind the small rogue, "Enough of this bullshit. Alright, Beetle," he said, using the halfling's nickname on purpose and talking in a voice loud enough to be heard by anyone or anything in the room to the west. "We do not have time for this now -- we need to get through here quickly and back up top," and, with that, he raised his flail and walked past Bealty and down the hallway.

"Tyberius," said Ariana, "get back here!" but it was too late -- the quick-footed warrior was already past Bealty and nearing the opening of the room, and as she spoke Isa had moved past her swiftly and silently, joining Tyberius.

"Oh shit, Tyberius, wait up!" hollered Brutal as both he and Hammer scrambled down the hallway trying to catch up, their armor clanking loudly as they ran.

Bealty stood up and still, being cautious, moved farther down the hallway to the west, and that's when he saw it: the dark circles on the dirt floor -- voids of some sort, and that meant trouble, but he had no time to inspect them and watched with painful helplessness as Tyberius and Isa stepped into the adjoining room. "Tyberius!" he shouted as loud as his small voice could muster. "Do not..." But as Tyberius and Isa stepped into the room, they all heard a loud thud, announcing something had just been released and a heavy metal portcullis came crashing down, trapping Tyberius and Isa on one side, and the rest of the group on the other. The spiked bars protruding from the bottom of the portcullis slipped snugly into the small round holes in the floor, and an audible click could be heard. Isa, fortunately, reacted quickly, leaping out from below the crushing metal barrier and rolling to a standing position a few feet away from Tyberius.

"No, no, no!" shouted Brutal, as if his words could reverse the last few seconds while he ran to the portcullis. Dropping his sword, he grabbed the bars and lifted with all his might, his face turning bright red from the effort. Then Hammer, Mikell, and York all grabbed hold and began heaving upwards, but the gate held firm. Tyberius and Isa joined from the other side, adding their combined strength to the task, but the gate wouldn't budge.

"It is locked somehow," said Bealty, examining the floor. "I heard something click into place when it closed."

Brutal looked at the Halfling. "Well, that is fucking great -- how do we get it unlocked?" he asked as sweat began to bead up and drip down his face. Reaching down, he retrieved and then sheathed his bastard sword, turning his attention back to the gate.

"By finding the locking mechanism," replied the halfling. "Unfortunately, it is most likely on their side of the gate," he said, pointing toward Tyberius and Isa.

Just then they all heard a loud creaking noise, exactly like the sound a large metal hinge on a large door might make. Everyone turned to look and watched as five large gnolls walked through the door on the north side of the room, the door continuing to creak as it opened wide. Their hyena-like dog jowls curled into a devilish smile while they yipped with what sounded like gleeful laughter at the situation. Readying their large war axes, the five gnolls started to spread out into a semi-circle, giving themselves more room to swing as they slowly and cautiously approached Isa and Tyberius.

Ariana, reaching through the bars and grabbing Tyberius's left arm, gasped. "No..."

The warrior paused briefly, looking back at his fiancée, saying, "Sorry my dove," then pulling his arm free, he gave her a wink and a flash of his renowned grin, then turning to meet the oncoming gnolls, raised his flail into a striking position. "C'mon you dog-fucking sons-a-bitches," he said in a growl of a voice, motioning to the gnolls with his free right hand for them to keep coming forward. The red-haired warrior could already feel his blood beginning to boil underneath his skin, his rage simmering in the anticipation.

＊ ＊ ＊ ＊

Julius climbed the ladder up the long shaft and, after a few minutes, reached the top. His eyesight was almost as impeccable in the dark as it was in the light, but here there was a true absence of light and he found himself in the unusual circumstance of being blind, so reaching into his pocket he pulled out the light stick. Even before removing the stick, light began gushing out of his pocket through the small opening, then finally pulling the stick out, the light spread 360 degrees from its tip, illuminating the small space completely. Seeing the small landing, he took a couple more steps up the ladder and carefully stepped up and over onto the landing. Grabbing the end of the dangling rope, Julius gave it a hard tug -- evaluating how much weight it could hold. Nothing budged, so feeling a little more confident, he pulled himself up off the ground a few inches and waited to see if it would hold his full weight. Once again, the rope held firm, so he began to pull himself up -- no easy task given the backpack and armor he was wearing, but once he got high enough he was able to slip his booted foot into the loop of the rope and take the weight off his arms. Reaching up he turned the latch and with a clank, the hatch opened to the fresh outside air, which once again rushed past him and back down into the bunker. He allowed himself a deep breath, letting the sweetness of the air fill his lungs, then he climbed out onto the solid ground above. The angst of the confining labyrinth, below, which constantly gnawed at his mind, vanished as the sun washed over his face and the wind blew the offensive odor of the gnolls away. Quickly gaining his bearings, he began running toward the fallen tree where the horses were tied up. Untying the reins from the tree, placing one foot into a stirrup, he swung up and kicked his mount into a quick trot, careful not to have the horse running over uneven ground he could not see, due to the thick grass. It did not take long for him to reach the turn, where he halted his gray mare and scanned the grassy edges of the road for any sign of Foetore. He only needed to wait a short while, when the white and black ferret scampered out of the grass, bolting in his direction. Julius was about to dismount so he could safely pick up Foetore, but the little ferret jumped high enough to grab onto his leather boot, quickly clawing its way up his chain mail armored leg, causing the half-elf to wince as its razor-sharp claws, small as they were, dug between the tightly woven loops of metal, into his flesh. Once up on the saddle, Julius opened the saddlebag on the right side of his mare, and Foetore made himself at home. With a wide open road ahead -- this time Julius kicked the mare into a gallop heading west, hoping to find nothing, but knowing in the back of his mind, where his hope could not quite reach, that the black smoke billowing, swirling, and rising ominously into the sky ahead of him, was not the result of any ordinary cooking fire.

* * * *

"Stay close to the gate!" shouted Mikell to Isa and Tyberius. "As long as I can touch you, I can still heal you." Neither Tyberius nor Isa acknowledged his advice, but the cleric knew it was not practical to hold the position by the gate during an open melee -- too much could happen.

"There has to be a way to open this fucking gate!" shouted Hammer as he tried vainly once again to lift it.

"I am sure there is," said Bealty, taking off his backpack and leaning it against the gate's bars. "Prepared for all but the smallest," Bealty muttered to no one in particular, recalling an old halfling proverb that described the tendency of most humanoids, when constructing buildings, defenses, or implements of bondage -- only to think in terms relative to their own kind -- or in terms of the those they plan to capture or defend against. The fortuitous aspect, in regard to halflings, was that nobody ever planned to defend against a horde of halflings, and that theory was once again proved by whoever had built this gate, allowing Bealty to easily squeeze through the small square of space created by the crisscrossing bars. On the other side, he reached through the bars and, pulling his backpack through the small gap, slung it onto his shoulders. "Mikell!" shouted the halfling, trying to get the cleric's attention, but everyone was fixated on the gnolls closing in on Tyberius and Isa. After a second failed attempt, he shrugged his shoulders and eyeing the shadows along the wall, parallel with the gate, he quickly melded out of view, moving silently along the perimeter of the room, searching for the release mechanism.

Pulling out a small finely crafted cylindrical case, York popped the end cap open and removed his rune encrusted flute. Putting it up to his lips, he began to play a fast tempo song. Everyone in the small group could feel the notes tugging at the inner being, causing their hearts to start beating a little faster, pounding a little harder, and heightening their senses.

"This damned gate cannot stop my magic," said Ariana watching, eyes wide as the gnolls closed in on Isa and her red-haired fiancé. Reaching into one of her pouches she grabbed a pinch of sand and began to intone her spell. "Dalle sabbie del tempo, faccio piombare nel sonno i miei nemici." Her hands were weaving in the familiar pattern as she canted; the sand, which she threw into the air at the end of her incantation, was promptly consumed by a magical force coming from within Ariana. She could feel the energy of the magic coursing through her veins, an exhilaration that she found herself craving more and more with each spell she cast, almost like an addiction -- but, as always, the feeling was fleeting as she released the pent-up energy, unleashing it on the gnolls. The air shimmered as a blanket of dull light hovered, ever so briefly, before falling over the five gnolls, causing two of them to fall to the ground, snoring in a deep slumber. Brutal watched in awe as Ariana cast her spell; the smooth cadence and inflections of the arcane words as they fell off her lips and the grace of her somatic motions.

"Nicely done, Ariana!" shouted Mikell, the others also cheering as the two gnolls fell to the ground.

Tyberius, aroused by the music of the bard, felt encouraged and ready for the fight. As Ariana's spell shimmered, dropping two of the gnolls, the remaining three lost their focus for just a split second as they staved off the spell's effect, which was just enough time for the tall warrior to spring into action. Rushing the gnoll to his right, he swung his flail at the head of the gnoll, but the creature was too quick, raising its shield up and deflecting the large spiked ball with a loud thud.

The other two gnolls continued advancing toward Isa, the monk stood as still as a statue, his hands held up in a defensive position. However, once they moved into striking distance, Isa lashed out with a flurry of punches forcing the left-most gnoll backwards. As the gnoll backed up, Isa crouched and spun around sweeping the legs out from under the gangly gnoll causing it to fall to the ground and knocking the air out of his lungs with an audible grunt. With practiced timing, as the gnoll hit the ground, Isa brought the back of his hand down on the beast's unprotected snout. The crack of bones was sickening, the gnoll rolled onto its side, tried to get up briefly, then sank back down to the dirt motionless.

Seeing his companion fall, the gnoll closest to Isa howled with rage, and raising its ax, swung down at the back of the monk just as Isa delivered the backhanded blow to his comrade. Isa turned, raising an arm to block the blow, partially parried the swing, but the ax blade still bit into the back of his exposed leg. Isa growled in pain and rolled backwards, out of the gnoll's immediate range.

After blocking Tyberius's attack with his old, battered shield, the gnoll swung clumsily at the warrior, missing by a wide margin, but causing Tyberius to take a step backwards. The gnoll, pressing its attack, closed the distance quickly, however Tyberius timed his counter-strike perfectly, the ball of his flail was already in motion as the gnoll entered his range. The ball landed with a crunch into the side of the gnoll's neck breaking bones while the spikes drove deep, severing its jugular vein. The creature crumpled to the ground, not even getting out a yelp.

The last gnoll standing, seeing his last pack-mate drop into a heap, ran toward his sleeping comrades, hoping to wake them up, but Isa was too fast. The monk sprinted after the gnoll, launching himself into the air and landed a flying kick to the gnoll's back. The blow was well placed, and the gnoll tumbled to the ground, its ax falling to the dirt floor. Unable to move its legs, paralyzed from the blow, the gnoll began clawing its way toward the sleeping gnolls, but Isa calmly walked, blood dripping down his leg from the gash made by the ax, and crushed the gnoll's neck with his foot. Tyberius and Isa dispatched the two sleeping gnolls and then looked around for any other dangers, but none were readily apparent.

"You have to find the release mechanism for this gate!" shouted Mikell.

"I know!" shouted Tyberius back. "But what the hell am I looking for?"

"Bealty, what should they be looking for?" asked Mikell, with some urgency in his voice, as he looked around. Noticing for the first time that the halfling was nowhere to be seen, he asked with some alarm, "Has anyone seen Bealty?"

"That little fucker," said Ariana. "He left!"

"No way," said Mikell. "He would not leave us down here."

"Yeah," added Brutal. "Beetle, would not do that."

"Well, where the fuck is he, then?" asked Ariana, her hands on her hips defiantly. Before anyone could answer, loud barking and growling noises came from the darkened area to the west, accompanied by the sound clinking metal, like that made by chains.

"Hurry, look along the walls for anything that looks like a release for this gate!" shouted Brutal, fear creeping into his voice as the sounds from the west were quickly growing louder.

"How are you doing for spells, Ariana?" asked Mikell, turning to face the sorceress.

Concern crept into her eyes. "Maybe one more spell, then I will need to rest to recover," she said, a little gloom in her voice.

"Make sure save it until there are no choices left..." Mikell began to say.

"What do you mean by that?" asked Ariana, her defenses going up.

Mikell put a hand on Ariana's shoulder. "They might have been able to fight off the five gnolls without your spell. It helped them no doubt, but you cast it before the fight even began."

"It was five on two, Mikell -- do not second guess my actions!" she shouted back.

"What the fuck is that?" asked Hammer, pointing to the west, his arm sticking completely through the gate.

Two sets of gleaming red eyes, like small flames, floated in the darkness to the west, blinking occasionally, watching them from a distance. Tyberius, who was moving along the southern wall of the room looking for any sign of a release lever, or something, stopped and turned around to look in the direction Hammer was pointing.

"Oh shit, what the hell?" asked Tyberius, as he started moving back toward the gate to be near the others. Isa remained in the center of the room, facing the approaching eyes calmly. "Isa!" Tyberius shouted in a hushed voice. "Isa, get over here!" Hearing his name, Isa looked at Tyberius and obeyed, moving to stand close to the gate.

The clanking metal noise began again, as the eyes started moving closer -- so did the growls. The lanterns hanging on the walls of the room gave off enough light to see, but light levels were still relatively low, making it hard to see what was approaching them. Mikell, reaching into his backpack pulled out the pouch with their remaining gold coins. Taking a coin out, he quickly said a prayer to Zuel, then canted the spell. "Invoco la luce." Touching the coin, it burst into a bright light. "Tyberius, toss this toward the creatures so we can get a good look at them."

Tyberius looked at the cleric's outstretched hand with the glowing coin as if he were holding a contagious and diseased rat. "No way, I am not touching that thing. I will fight whatever the hell those things are without touching that."

"Are you serious?" asked Ariana, not hiding her disgust.

"Isa," Mikell said, "can you throw this coin toward them?" Mikell pointed to the coin and then toward the approaching creatures.

Isa nodded and took the coin, which looked like a small pebble of gold in his large hand. Turning, the monk threw the coin to the west. It looked like a shooting star, flying through the semi-darkness of the room, lighting the area around it as it flew, arching its way toward the glowing eyes. The coin barely made a noise, landing on the dirt floor and skidding to a stop right in the midst of the approaching eyes.

The coin lit up an area in a twenty-foot radius, more than enough to see the group heading their way: two very large dogs, nearly four feet high at the shoulders, with arched backs, reddish-black fur, and tendrils of smoke blowing out of their noses with each breath. Holding them back with chain link leashes attached to spiked metal collars were two gnolls. Three other gnolls, ten feet behind the hounds, stood ready and just behind them was the dwarven mage, holding what looked like a scroll of some sort.

Tyberius slowly turned to look at his friends behind the gate, and he could see the horror written on all their faces, except York, who was scribbling notes into his little book as fast as he could. Tyberius, holding onto the gate with his free hand, pressed himself up close. "Get out of here," he said in a calm voice. "We will hold them off as long as possible."

"No!" shouted Ariana. "We are not leaving you."

"Get out, and get help while you still can," said Tyberius. "Better yet, get out of here and go help Julius -- make sure our families are safe."

"No fucking way -- we are not leaving here without you," said Brutal.

Giving the portcullis a light shake, Tyberius smiled at his friend, his grin still infectious, but in the present situation had transformed into a morose gesture. "No offense, but you ain't going to be much help from that side, Brutal. You have been a good friend, go find your father, it ain't over for you." Hearing an ominous low growl, this time much nearer, Tyberius glanced behind him to see the gnoll handlers manipulating the latches on the collars of the hounds, no doubt readying to release them. Looking back at his companions, he amended his previous statement. "It ain't over for any of you...as long as you move out now." Slowly taking one full deliberate step backwards, Tyberius looked at Ariana, her soft hands gripping two of the vertical metal bands of the portcullis, like a prisoner from behind jail-house bars, the ring that Fey had given him, which he had given to Ariana, sparkled in the flickering lantern light, sending a pang of regret down his spine that he had lied to her about it. Hearing a metallic clank, he spun around, assuming the hounds had just been released, but to his surprise the gnolls were still working on the collars. Raising his flail, once again he could feel his blood starting to boil through his veins. He was ready to strike down his enemies, one by one.

* * * *

Moments ago, as Isa and Tyberius began their fight with the first five gnolls entering the room, Bealty decided that, time being of the essence, he would need to risk missing something well hidden in order to move more quickly in the hopes that whatever mechanism controlled the gate wouldn't be too difficult to spot. With that in mind, staying in his crouched position, the halfling moved swiftly along the eastern wall, the same wall containing the closed gate. As he reached the northeast corner of the room, Bealty heard a cheer erupt from his companions behind the gate, and risking a quick look up, he saw two of the gnolls fall down, asleep. Unfortunately, there was a gnoll between him and where he needed to go, along the northern wall of the room, but Tyberius charged the gnoll, distracting it enough for him to bolt past and back into the shadows, continuing his search. He made his way along the northern wall until he arrived at the door the five gnolls had come out of, which was still open. 'A good thing,' he thought to himself, 'the hinges were really loud.' Being more than fifty feet away from the fight still going on behind him, he felt safe from them -- but there was no telling what was in the adjoining room, so drawing his two daggers, the halfling quickly rounded the open door and darted into the room. He scanned the room, as any expert rogue was trained to do, looking for dangers, hiding spots, and, of course, valuables.

The room appeared to be devoid of any enemies, hesitating only for a second before moving into the shadows along the southern wall of the room. Once hidden, he waited a split-second, listening and looking. The only sounds were coming from the battle going on in the room to the south, but being patient by nature, he lingered in the shadows, giving his senses a little more time as he scanned the room. The room was roughly square, about fifty by fifty feet...maybe sixty feet east to west, he revised in his mind. It contained six large cot-like beds, a large round table with six wooden chairs, a rack of weapons, all axes and shields, on the west wall. There were two decent-sized wooden chests, he figured three feet by two feet, and maybe two feet high, each with metal reinforcing bands. Again, the main lighting in the area came from lanterns hung on the walls at what seemed like random intervals. "Ah-ha," he whispered to himself, spying in the southeast corner of the room what he was looking for: a large vertical wheel with wooden bars sticking out to the side to grab onto -- in order to wind up a rope, which was currently completely unwound -- it trailed off to the south toward the gate blocking his friends. The rope ran up and through a pulley fastened to the ceiling and then through a small hole at the top of the wall. The wheel was just forty feet to the east of where he was, and as he was about to move when his instincts sent a warning down his spine and he froze, his mind flashing back to the cots. Six cots, but only five gnolls had come out of the room; that math did not work in his favor, so he immediately hunkered down again. The sounds of fighting had stopped in the room to the south, and he wondered if his friends were dead or were still trying to figure out a way to open the portcullis. Not a race to dwell on the negatives, he quickly decided he needed to continue his mission, of unlocking that gate, but there was a gnoll in here, somewhere... 'How could such a large creature stay hidden,' he wondered to himself.

Reaching into his backpack he pulled out a medium-sized black bag, and carefully he reached in and pulled out a handful of Taper wood caltrops, each side being about the length of Bealty's pinky finger -- not enough to kill, but a damn sight enough to lame creatures even as large as a gnoll. Despite the packed dirt floor, it was not ideal for driving a spike into the foot of an unsuspecting creature, but it might slow the damn thing down, which is all he would need. Bealty created a spread of caltrops that covered a small three foot area along the southern wall in front of him. Then reaching into a small pouch under his armor pulled out a small empty glass vial and taking aim at one of the wooden beams along the eastern wall, threw it with all his might. His aim was true and the glass vial shattered, releasing a nasty smelling gas. Whether it was the smell or the sound, a gnoll quickly stood up near where he had thrown the vial. The gnoll's dark vision was superb, and scanning the room, it immediately locked eyes with Bealty. "Uh-oh, here we go," said the halfling, who also stood up, a dagger in each hand, their blades glinting in the flickering light of the lanterns..

The gnoll jabbered something in its own language as it charged the small halfling, its ax raised and ready to strike. Bealty waited patiently, hoping to draw the gnoll into the caltrop trap he had created, and at the last moment, abandoned his spot, rolling backwards, and then bolting toward the cots along the northern side of the room. With one large foot, the gnoll stepped right into the heart of the area with the caltrops, but somehow managed to miss all of them and bounded after the dodgy halfling. Using his small size to an advantage, Bealty rolled under the first cot just as the gnoll struck down at him, his ax blade slicing the end cross beam of the cot into two pieces. Bealty continued his roll and, bounding up to his feet, jumped onto the next cot over. The gnoll, enraged, began swinging wildly, but Bealty was able to duck and leap from one cot to another while the gnoll kept trying to get into a good position to strike the halfling. Running out of cots to jump to, he spied the only other large piece of furniture in the room: the large circular table. Sizing it up, Bealty figure he could fully stand underneath it, and somersaulting off the last cot as the gnoll's ax cut the air where he was just standing, the rogue landed lightly on his feet and ran underneath the table. He could hear the gnoll chortle like a hyena that had finally cornered its weakened prey, but without bending down, it could not see the small halfling under the table.

"Day One," whispered Bealty to himself, as he readied his daggers -- acting as a reminder to himself of the location of critical areas on most creature's bodies, something most halflings are taught on the first day of any combat training: groin, inner thighs, back of the heel, lower back, armpits, solar plexus, throat, eyes, and ears. This was going to be perfect, he thought, assuming the gnoll would cooperate. Sure enough, rather than bend down into an awkward position the gnoll, using its free hand, lifted the table up; as he did so Bealty shot out from under the table striking twice, like a coiled snake, his first dagger plunging up and into the gnoll's groin, his second dagger, deviating from his Day One training, but still very effective, plunging into the back of the gnoll's right knee, its blade piercing all the way through, tearing and pushing the kneecap out of its leg. The dagger in the gnoll's knee was stuck, so he let go of it, but Bealty was able to pull the other dagger out of the gnoll's groin as he continued his sprint between its legs. Not stopping for even a second to see the condition of the gnoll, he rolled back underneath the nearest cot, expecting the gnoll's ax to come crashing down on him, but no blow came and as he lay motionless under the large structure of the bed, his eyes darting every which way looking for danger, he heard a low groan, the table dropping back down onto its legs, followed by the gnoll falling, landing squarely on its back, motionless.

Scurrying out from underneath the cot, Bealty eyed the large body of the gnoll lying on the ground, giving it a wide berth, then stopped in his tracks, his eyes locking onto the two large chests in the northeast corner of the room. His mind ached to know what was inside, and unconsciously he took one step toward them, his right hand instinctively reaching for his lock picking tools. "The gate," he said softly to himself, shaking his head. "First the gate." He sprinted to the southeast corner and realized the first handle of the wheel was too high for him to reach. Looking around, he spied the chairs. "That will do," he muttered, sprinting toward the table. The large chair proved awkward to move for his small stature, but the halfling managed to drag it across the hard-packed dirt. Placing it near the large wheel, he jumped up and grabbed hold of the nearest bar and heaved with all his might...nothing; he could not budge the wheel. "The lock," he thought. Examining the wheel, he found a cog on the other side of the wheel that kept the wheel from being turned. Lifting the locking mechanism out of the way and using another small lever to keep it from re-locking, Bealty again reached and heaved on the wheel, but it still would not move. Grabbing his head with both of his gloved hands, he muttered, "Dammit, what in the eight hells?" Hopping down again, he looked around the area of the wheel again and this time saw another bolt-like slide lever cleverly constructed into the floor. Twisting the metal of the lever back and forth, he was able to slowly work the bolt out, which emitted a loud metallic clicking noise. "There!" he exclaimed a little louder than he had meant to but, wasting no time, leapt back onto the chair and heaved on the bar. It moved slightly this time, but Bealty could feel the weight of the wheel was still too much for him. "Son of a bitch," he whispered under his breath, then giving it another thought, he climbed up onto the wheel itself and, bracing his back against the south wall of the room and placing his feet on the handle to give him the best leverage, pushed with all his might. This time the wheel turned a quarter turn, but he quickly realized he did not have enough strength with one leg to hold the wheel in position, making it impossible to turn it further.

Holding the wheel in place, he considered his options, scanning the room for any other tools that might help him, but as he did so the wheel lost all its tension, causing a chain reaction: first his legs shot out away from his body, which in turn released the pressure he was using to brace his back against the wall, causing him to fall backwards, head first to the ground. It all happened in a split second, but that was enough for the halfling's cat-like reflexes to twist his body around and get his arms and hands out in front of him to soften the awkward fall. Unfortunately as his body twisted around, his left foot got caught in the hand bars of the turning wheel, giving it a nasty twist, to which he let out a loud yelp of pain before his foot was released and he finally fell. Using his arms, he was able to soften his landing enough to avoid any further injury, but as he stood up, he knew he was in trouble, wincing in pain as he tried placing a little pressure on his injured ankle. Leg or foot injuries were a halfling's worst nightmare since it often negated their one advantage: mobility. "Shit," he muttered under his breath, slapping his thigh in frustration -- then, as if on his cue, the rope connected to the wheel snapped back to full tension, accompanied by a loud crashing sound and all hell break loose in the room to the south.

* * * *

As Tyberius turned to face the threat, the others could only watch in horror as the gnolls and hellhounds readied themselves, making their infernal yipping sounds, as if talking to each other. As their feelings of helplessness mounted, the portcullis raised ever so slightly, just a hair, and then set back down. Had they not been holding onto it, it might have gone by unnoticed, everyone behind the gate was looking at each other, all wondering if that really just happened.

"The gate just moved!" shouted Ariana in astonishment, "The gate moved!"

"I felt it, too," said Brutal. "Quick everyone, give it another lift!" Everyone grabbed hold of a crossbar while Brutal counted off, "One, two, lift!" With their combined strength the gate quickly lifted up, and they were able to hold it about three feet off the ground. "Mikell, Ariana, go under!" commanded Brutal. "Hammer, York, and I can hold it." Ariana easily rolled under and through the gate, but Mikell took a little longer, his size and armor making it difficult to maneuver, but he, too, made it to the other side. York did not listen, however, as he too quickly dropped and rolled to the other side, well ahead of Mikell, leaving just Brutal and Hammer holding the gate. "York!" Brutal shouted angrily, straining to hold the heavy metal structure. "What the hell are you doing?!"

Isa, hearing the commotion behind him, turned in time to see Ariana, York, and Mikell pass under the gate, and noticing Brutal and Hammer struggling to hold it up, sprinted the short distance, grabbing onto the gate as well. "I hold," the monk stated calmly, "you come."

Brutal looked questioningly at the monk and was about to argue

-- but with Isa now helping, he could feel the weight of the gate relax on his arms, and he nodded. "Okay, Hammer, you go first," commanded Brutal. Hammer let go of the bar he was holding, then waited a second to make sure Brutal and Isa were able to hold it. "We got it, get the fuck through!" shouted Brutal, then to his amazement, Isa grunted and lifted the gate up above his head, which was high enough for both Brutal and Hammer to simply duck underneath and walk into the room. Once on the other side, Isa let the gate go, and it came crashing back down, sending a reverberation throughout the complex.

Tyberius looked back. "Glad to have you back -- at least being sort-a useful," he said to Brutal.

"Shit," Brutal responded, "you think I am going to let you have all the fun? Much less die like some martyr?"

"Now that we are all here, we cannot wait for them to make the first move," said Mikell.

"Oh, I have just the thing to get the party going," said York, pulling out a miniature one string guitar-like instrument.

"We do not have time for your bullshit," said Brutal, eyeing the toy-like instrument, still incensed that the bard had disregarded him at the gate.

York, looking up at the taller warrior, a mischievous smile creeping into one corner of his pursed lips, took a step past Brutal. "Ready yourselves."

* * * *

Approaching a path leading south, which would take him to Ariana's home farm, Julius slowed the gray mare down, and finally stopped at the intersection. There was no question, the smoke was coming from Brutal's farm, off to the east, but looking at the path to the south, which led to Ariana's farm, the numerous tracks left no doubt that gnolls had taken it. Foetore squeaked, drawing the ranger's attention. Patting the ferret's head, he said, "Evil is out and about today, Foetore." As he continued to stroke the ferret's head, he added, "Let us go see what they are up to." Guiding the gray mare off the path, the ranger cautiously made his way toward Ariana's farmstead. Reaching a small rise, knowing

Ariana's farmhouse would be visible from the other side, Julius halted his horse and, climbing down, tied the horse to a small brush tree. The horse was breathing hard from the run and began eating some of the tall grass around the tree as it took the respite to recover. Julius picked up the ferret and placed him on the ground. "I suspect we both work better alone, but for now stick close to me, so we do not get separated. We need you," the half-elf paused and, squatting down, gave the ferret a look, "you do understand me?" Foetore squeaked and stood up on his hind legs. "Can you still communicate with Ariana?" Foetore rested back down onto all four of his legs and shook his head side to side. "Okay, we are too far, good to know. Stay close, but out of sight. If anything happens to me, you need to head back to the swale -- but do not tell them about what you see up here -- especially if things go badly. They will be too late to do any good up here, and they may lose their only chance down there." Standing back up, he asked, "Did you understand all that?" Foetore's squeak had a hint of distress to it, Julius thought, but before he could say anything else, the little white and black ferret disappeared into the tall grass.

Julius took the quiver of twenty arrows and slung it over his shoulder, then unhitching his bow from the mare's saddle, checked to make sure the bowstring was still tight and ready for use. Taking off the dark brown cloak he wore over his chain mail, which served him well in the bunker, he pulled out and adorned a light sandy-colored cloak that blended in well with the tall grasses of the plain. Satisfied that his equipment was ready, he patted the gray mare on the neck and made his way to the crest of the small rise, crawling the last few feet to stay concealed.

Cresting the peak, he could see the small farmhouse and barn. The home was typical for the residents of the plain: barely large enough to house the family, of moderate craftsmanship, but very functional. The barn was a large two-story structure, slightly larger in dimensions than the house, and had large double doors that were currently closed. There was no sign of activity anywhere around either building, but the front door to the home was slightly open. 'Not completely out of the ordinary,' thought Julius to himself, given the heat of the day, but still a little odd. His sixth sense was telling him not all was right here, but then again he was on edge, and he knew the mind could play tricks. Action always helped distract from uncertainty, so Julius backed down the hill out of sight and started circling in a wide arc around the house and barn. Time was of the essence, he knew, but he was out here alone, so he needed to be careful. Safely on the other side of the property, he was able to get closer to the house, he figured about fifty yards or so. There was no back door, but there were two windows, both open. He watched for a moment but, still seeing no movement inside, decided he would get closer yet. The tall grass ended around thirty feet from the house, and giving the area one more careful scan, he left his concealment and ran, still crouching, to the side of the house, where, standing up, he flattened himself against the wall.

The wind was blowing through the tall grass, creating a low but constant rustling noise, however the half-elf's keen ears could hear the front door creaking, accompanied by light, rhythmic banging. Julius noted that the ground around the back of the house looked undisturbed. 'But why would it be?' he asked himself. There was no need for the gnolls to sneak up on the farm from the rear. Risking a glance inside, Julius could see into the main living area, including the eating table and the front door, which was swinging in the wind as he had thought. Only allowing himself the quick glance, he pulled back and straightened against the side of the home, waiting and listening, but still there was nothing. Julius, drawing an arrow from his quiver, readied his bow and began to slowly make his way around the eastern side of the house. At the southeast corner, Julius peeked to see if anything was there and, seeing nothing, continued along the side of the house, heading toward the front. Reaching the corner of the house, he allowed himself a quick glance at the front of the home, but it was still very quiet except for the wind, the door creaking, and the sound of the grass rustling. Warily, the ranger turned the corner and began making his way to the front door but stopped just to the side of it, leaning his longbow against the house. Placing the arrow back in his quiver, he drew out his longsword, using the tip of it to push the door all the way open. He paused to see if anything jumped at the door opening, but still -- nothing. Julius looked inside, noting some disarray, one of the seven chairs was tipped over, a mug with some spilled water lying on the floor of the home. The fire was all but out, a small, single trickle of smoke whisking up the chimney. There were four rooms along the north wall, and he checked each one, but they were all empty. He gave the main room one more quick scan and noticed several small drops of blood on the table. "Savages," Julius whispered out loud to himself.

Standing outside the front door, Julius could see enough tracks in the ground outside the house that there must have been four or five gnolls. Following the trail, it was also obvious that the gnolls had some humans with them; it looked like there were a couple gnolls in front, with one on each side, maybe one in the rear, but it was difficult to tell. One thing the matted down grass left no doubt about was where they were heading: the clear trail they left could be seen going over a hundred yards out until finally disappearing over a small hill to the east, directly toward Brutal's farm.

Foetore emerged out of the grass where the gnolls had matted it down and stood on his hind legs. The ferret squeaked, looking at the ranger towering above him.

"Ah, there you are," said Julius, "follow me, we must hurry," as he sheathed his sword, heading back to the house to retrieve his longbow before beginning the short run back to his mount. Foetore was surprisingly quick and kept up easily over the short distance, and as Julius mounted the gray mare, the ferret again dashed up the ranger's leg and found his way back into the saddlebag. Julius gave the horse a quick kick and clicked twice with his tongue, urging it forward at a fast-paced trot, clearing Ariana's farmhouse, he led the horse straight down the path the gnolls had left in their wake.

* * * *

York stood poised for a brief second, his finger hovering just over the lone string of the ridiculously small instrument. The other companions stood, looking at him with a mixture of doubt and expectation, not sure what the bard was up to.

"For the love of our lady, pluck the damn tune already!" exclaimed Hammer, referring to his goddess Soulmite, as he stood just behind and to the right of York, nervously fingering his grip on the shaft of his raised war hammer.

York paid him no attention but began to cant while weaving the tiny instrument through an arcane pattern in the air. "Invoco una cacofonia dai piani magici per stordire e disabilitare!" Simultaneously with the verbalizing of the last word, the bard plucked the lonely string on the tiny instrument, resulting in no sound whatsoever from where they were standing -- but from where the gnolls were readying themselves, multiple cracks of thunder combined with what could only be described as a myriad of bells and gongs sounded off. The sound caused everyone in the small party to reflexively jump back and cover their heads, but York stood firm, not flinching in the least. Being at the epicenter of the spell, the gnolls and hellhounds were not so fortunate, the sudden and deafening sound sent a shock wave through the beasts and their handlers, blowing out ear drums as evidenced by trickles of blood running down their earlobes. The two gnolls regained their balance, but the two hounds reeled backwards, throwing their front paws over their heads to block the brief but intense noise.

Ariana, recovering quickly, stood back up and, seeing both the hounds on the ground covering their heads, aimed her light crossbow at the nearest one, thirty feet away, pulling the trigger. The string gave off a sharp twang and the bolt hurled with great accuracy and lodged itself with a dull thud into the side of the hellhound, which yelped at the impact.

Tyberius, characteristically using his absurd speed rushed ahead of the rest of the group, brought his large flail down at the other hellhound, but the beast, in its thrashing, rolled to its side just as Tyberius brought the ball of the flail down, narrowly missing.

One of the gnolls in the back, outside of York's spell, seeing Tyberius sprinting up, also ran up, meeting Tyberius just as the tall warrior strike hit the dirt floor next to the hound. Raising its ax, the gnoll swung across Tyberius's body. The warrior was able to turn slightly, avoiding a critical blow, but the ax blade cut deeply into his left arm and blood began to run down his chain mail.

"Argh!" yelled Tyberius in pain as he reeled backwards, beginning to feel the now familiar rush of adrenaline coursing through his veins -- like vinegar he could feel its sting, and the rage began to boil within. His arms began to bulk and his face visible contorted into a bestial look, his eyes losing their focus, except for one thing: to kill. As his face and body flushed red with anger, he began cursing the gnoll that had struck him, but his words quickly turned into a garbled, jumbled, mess of vulgarity that was unintelligible, only understood by his own berserking brain.

The remaining two gnolls standing in the rear, close to the dwarf, ran forward. The first one to the front took up a defensive position in front of the hellhound Ariana had just shot and readied its ax and buckler. The last gnoll, coming up from the rear, ran between the two gnoll handlers, who were still recovering from the spell, and took a swing at Tyberius's exposed flank, the ax slicing through the chain mail on the warrior's back, the blade sinking into his flesh.

Brutal, seeing his friend getting battered, charged screaming at the gnolls, and raising the bastard sword, swung at the gnoll on Tyberius's flank. The gnoll was too quick, raising its buckler up in time to deflect the blow.

The gnoll handler, seeing Ariana unleash a bolt into the side of his hound, screamed in rage and, running around the wounded beast and the gnoll that had charged forward to guard it, headed straight toward the sorceress. Isa, seeing the attack, was able to insert himself between Ariana and the charging gnoll, but the gnoll paid the monk no attention and continued to run toward his initial target. Ariana's eyes widened in horror as the seven foot tall beast raised its ax to strike, raising her left arm in front of her defensively. But the gnoll, as it past Isa, gave the monk too much time, and the monk spun around with a kick, using the forward momentum of the charging gnoll against itself, the heel of his foot catching the gnoll squarely in the stomach. The gnoll crumpled over, letting out a gush of air from its lungs, but it did not stop, and recovering, raised its ax again, swinging with blind rage. Ariana stepped backwards, but she was already close to the eastern wall of the room and flattened herself against the wall, the ax blade swinging perilously close to the exposed midsection, but yet still managed to miss her completely.

The dark dwarf, emerging from the shadows of the hallway leading west, scroll in hand, began reading, "Invoco una sfera di calde fiamme bianche per ustionare i miei nemici." The written arcane words on the scroll began to snake, as if alive, the magical energy being called forth, releasing from, and finally consuming the paper in a flash and puff of smoke. Simultaneously, a ball of fire blinked into existence behind Brutal. The ball was four feet in diameter and looked like a small sun, white-hot, bluish flames leaping and flickering off its gelatinous, orange outer skin. The dark dwarf grinned evilly, considering where to send his ball of destruction, then seeing the sorceress with her back against the wall, made his decision; the sphere raced at a rapid speed, rolling easily between York and Isa, missing the gnoll that had just attacked Ariana.

"Ariana! Look out!" cried Mikell, standing ten feet away, watching the ball as it weaved through the traffic in her direction. Having just watched the gnoll's blade pass less than an inch from her stomach, she looked up just in time to see the fiery ball dashing between Isa and York and heading directly toward her. Ducking and diving to her left, rolling onto the ground along the eastern wall, she was able to dodge the licking flames, which singed and then lit the wooden beam she was just standing next to on fire. As the sorceress was diving out of the way, Isa turned and punched at the back of gnoll he had just kicked, but his fist glanced off the leather armor.

Hammer, being on the right-most side of the room, hesitated. He could see Ariana and Isa struggling against the gnoll and the dwarf's ball of flame, but he was more concerned seeing Tyberius being ganged up on. Making up his mind, he sprinted, his armor clanking as he ran to the aid of the redheaded warrior. Reaching the gnoll that had just struck Tyberius's arm, the former caravan guard swung his mighty war hammer, but the gnoll was able to deftly knock it aside with its ax, growling and snarling as it did so.

The remaining gnoll handler, still recovering from York's spell, shook its head to clear the disorientation and charged around the northern flank of the party's line, attacking Hammer. The gnoll's ax blade came crashing down on Hammer's right arm, but the metal plates of his banded armor deflected the blade, spewing a few sparks in the process.

Mikell, seeing the large force arrayed against Tyberius, Brutal, and Hammer, charged toward the front line. "York, you help Isa and Ariana!" he said, pointing in the direction of the monk and sorceress.

Seeing York nod, the cleric continued his sprint, his chain mail jingling as he ran, and saying a small prayer, "Benedici il mio tocco con il potere di guarire le ferite lievi," timing it so he finished just as he neared Tyberius, and reaching out with his hand holding the mace, touched Tyberius's back, releasing the magical energy into his friend. Tyberius, his eyes already looking crazed, did not acknowledge the cleric's actions, but the blood stopped seeping down his arm and a little vigor returned to the tall warrior who was already preparing for another swing of his flail.

Just then, Bealty appeared in the doorway on the north side of the room, scanning the ensuing battle. Limping severely, the halfling melded back into the shadows and began to slink his way eastward, behind the line being made by the group of fighters.

Diving to the ground, Ariana spun around to a sitting position and drew out her dagger, throwing it at the gnoll. Though the gnoll didn't see the weapon hurtling through the air, it was a poor, awkward throw, and the weapon bounced, hilt-first, off the surprised gnoll's chest, causing the gnoll to hesitate and flinch and allowing York enough time to draw his longsword and close the distance. The gnoll was raising its ax to strike, as Ariana again, defensively, put her left arm up from her sitting position, but the blow never fell, as York's blade pierced the gnoll from behind and skewered the dog-like warrior. The gnoll's ax hung in the air above its head as its eyes widened in horror. With its strength draining away, the ax fell from the gnoll's hand while its legs gave way, falling forward, right on top of Ariana.

Holding the far northern end of the line, Hammer squared away with the gnoll directly opposite him and both combatants made several feints and small attacks, like boxers jabbing, until Hammer thought he saw an opening. Making a full swing, his hammer was blocked high by the gnoll's buckler, leaving his front exposed. Taking advantage of the opportunity, the gnoll swung at Hammer, its ax blade hitting the warrior in the stomach. Hammer's banded armor blunted the blow, but the ax blade still penetrated, leaving a wide cut in his abdomen. The armor had saved him from a critical blow, but he could feel the warmth of the blood as it trickled down his belly, underneath his armor.

Brutal tried to push the gnoll backwards by advancing, to get it away from Tyberius's flank, but the gnoll wouldn't budge, and finally Brutal gave an enraged yell as he stabbed with all his strength to try and force the issue, but the gnoll was too quick and it parried the strike away.

The gnoll facing Tyberius, looking to follow up its successful first blow, watched as Tyberius began to transform into a crazed human. Trying to strike before the redheaded warrior regained his focus, the gnoll swung weakly, its blade deflecting off the chain mail armor protecting Tyberius.

Bealty, safely in the rear of the main battle, hobbled out of the shadows and walked toward the cleric. "Mikell," the halfling said but did not get his friend's attention. "Mikell!" he shouted a little louder, his child-like voice lacking the force it was intended to carry, but the cleric spun, mace in hand to the voice from behind. "I am hurt and need your help!"

"Bealty! Where have you been?!" asked Mikell astonished to see the rogue appearing from nowhere.

"Just heal me, quickly!" the halfling replied.

"My powers are almost gone, are you sure you need it?" Mikell responded with worry in his voice.

Bealty nodded. "I can barely move."

"Fine -- but you need to get behind the gnolls and take down that damned dwarf," Mikell stated. Bealty nodded. Mikell stepped toward the halfling, canting the spell, "Benedici il mio tocco con il potere di guarire le ferite lievi," then touching the halfling on the forehead, released the healing energy.

Bealty felt the energy flow through his body like a mystical wave and instantly he could feel the swelling in his ankle subside, the bones knitting together while simultaneously the other bumps and bruises he had suffered earlier faded away. Quickly, the rogue began twisting his ankle around in a circle, testing its mobility, then gave Mikell a wink. "One dwarf coming up," he said before dashing back into the shadows with his usual uncanny grace and speed.

The hellhound with the bolt in its side finally recovered, and being on the southern flank of the line, rolled back onto its feet and quickly made its way to Brutal's left flank. Brutal turned just in time to see the lanky beast take a deep breath and exhale a sheet of flame that engulfed both Brutal and Mikell, who happened to be standing just to Brutal's right. Brutal was able to step forward, dodging a significant portion of the flames, but Mikell did not see the attack coming, as he had just finished healing Bealty and was facing the wrong way. The flames scorched the exposed skin of the cleric, leaving red sores and some seeping wounds as he screamed in agony.

Tyberius, oblivious to all the activity going on around him, was solely focused on gnoll that had struck his arm. Charging the gnoll as he yelled garbled curses, he forced the gnoll to back up and then, swinging his flail, managed to strike the gnoll on its right shoulder, the spikes of the ball sinking deep into the dog-man's fleshy bicep, causing it to yelp in pain.

As Tyberius pushed the gnoll back, Tyberius left his rear exposed to the second hellhound, which, finally recovering from the bard's spell, lunged at the warrior's left leg, but its timing was off, and Tyberius moved just as its jaw snapped shut, empty.

Isa, seeing York fell the gnoll he was engaged with, turned and charged the nearest enemy -- which was the hellhound on the southern flank. It had just used its breath weapon on Brutal and Mikell when the monk came sprinting into its flank. Using his momentum, and being that the beast was broadside to his approach, he kicked upwards with all his might, shouting a loud "Kia!" and catching the hound squarely underneath its rib cage. The snapping of bones was quite audible and clear, and despite the weight of the six foot hound, the monk's strong kick sent it tumbling limply through the air, five feet backwards, where it landed on its side, motionless, the bolt from Ariana, still protruding from its side.

The gnoll trying to protect the hound Isa had just kicked, stepped forward, growling with rage, and struck at the monk. Isa spun to face the new threat, raising his arm to block the gnoll's swing, but the gnoll changed the angle of its attack and the ax blade swept down and to the side of the monk's defense and sunk deep into Isa's thigh, his thick femur the only thing stopping the blade from slicing his leg completely in two. Isa roared in pain, the force of the blow knocking the monk to one knee, when the gnoll followed up, kicking Isa in the chest, knocking him prone onto his back, his leg resting at an absurd angle, with blood pumping steadily out of the half-orc's exposed and severed veins.

Pleased to see the monk dealt with, the dwarf, still concentrating on the sphere, again had it roll toward the sorceress, who was now in a more vulnerable position on the ground. The sphere rolled too quickly for Ariana to move out of its way, and the fiery ball slammed into her, its white-hot flames scorching her exposed flesh and knocking her flat to the ground, unmoving. The dwarf seeing his success, cackled in glee and, emboldened, braved taking a few steps closer to get a better vantage of his handiwork.

Tyberius, seeing the gnoll backpedaling after the vicious blow, pressed his advantage, but he was hasty, and by not taking his time to get the heavy flail into a good position, his attack was weak and sloppy, and the gnoll easily knocked it away with its buckler. Meanwhile the remaining hellhound now had a perfect line of attack against Tyberius and Hammer and, taking a deep breath, let out a snarl and a wave of flames that shot out burning both fighters.

Brutal, first ecstatic to see one of the hellhounds taken down, was quickly horrified seeing Isa fall to the gnoll, but there wasn't much he could do at the moment with a gnoll still facing him, the two combatants squaring off, each looking for an opening in the other's defenses. The gnoll attacked first, trying cut at Brutal's legs, but the fighter was able to parry the ax with his own blade and then countering, was able to follow through, turning the blade toward the gnoll, successfully stabbing the gnoll in the side. It would have been a much more grievous wound, but the gnoll, yelping as it did so, was able to quickly step backwards, avoiding a deeper penetration.

The gnoll engaged with Hammer turned slightly as if to strike Tyberius since the tall warrior's flank was now almost completely exposed to it. Hammer, sensing an opportunity, lunged forward bringing his hammer down hard, but the gnoll saw the attack coming and knocked the hammer away with its buckler. No longer in a position to strike Tyberius, the gnoll lashed out at Hammer with a flurry of wild swings, none actually doing any damage but managing to drive the human backwards and into a defensive posture.

York, seeing Ariana fall, and burning, ran forward, grabbed one of her limp arms, dragging her away from the burning ball of flame. "Mikell!" he shouted. "Ariana is hurt badly!"

Mikell spun around, mostly because his backside had just been scorched, but he was always listening for the needs of his companions, and hearing York, he scanned the battle quickly. "Zuel, help us," he whispered into the dank air, noticing that Isa and Ariana were both down and looked to be unconscious. The monk was the closest, and looked to be the worst off -- his leg practically torn off, his life's blood pouring out of him. Ariana was another twenty feet away, and he could not see her very well, the flaming orb obscuring most of her body, like a giant solar eclipse. "Guide me, Zuel," he said out loud and then decided to take care of the monk, since getting to Ariana could be problematic. Mikell's ability to call on Zuel's healing was limited and required rest and prayer each day to replenish his powers. Only having enough mana for three more spells, he needed to be very prudent, but it was clear Isa was dying, and without further hesitation, canted the spell, "Benedici il mio tocco con il potere di guarire le ferite lievi." Upon completion, he touched Isa's head. The monk's body convulsed and, in doing so, his leg returned to a more natural position and the wound closed completely, leaving a scar that navigated halfway around his thick thigh. The color returning to his bluish skin, the monk's eyes snapped open, looking around frantically, as he tried to figure out what had just happened.

"Get up! Get up!" yelled Mikell lifting the monk's shoulders, trying to get the half-orc back on his feet.

The gnoll that had almost taken off Isa's leg had turned, looking for another target when he heard Mikell's shout. Turning back around the looming beast snarled, in broken common tongue, "Fucking shaaa-man," and advanced again toward Mikell and the monk. The gnoll's eyes zeroed in on Mikell and with greyhound-like speed, quickly closed the distance. Mikell was caught in a vulnerable position, not able to lift his shield or mace in defense as he was lifting the monk. The gnoll brought the ax down at an angle as if to sever Mikell's neck, but Isa, regaining his senses at the last moment, spun out of Mikell's grasp, intercepting the ax blade. The blade bit deep into Isa's back -- the crack of the blade on Isa's backbone was loud enough to be heard, and the monk grunted as the air was knocked out of his lungs and he toppled forward, unconscious and bleeding once again, on top of Mikell, who was now pinned in a prone position on the ground.

With practiced ease, Bealty was able to make his way behind the gnolls as he slunk through the shadows along the walls. Knowing they may want the dwarf alive, to question, Bealty switched his dagger to his off hand and armed his right hand with a sap from inside his leather armor. Eyeing the dwarf, whose attention was on his ball of fire, the rogue found it easy to flank the evil mage. Once in position, Bealty quickly closed the distance and, raising the sap, the halfling struck at the back of the dwarf's head, but the dwarf unexpectedly moved forward as he swung and the lead-weighted end of the sap merely brushed the nape of the dwarf's neck, causing him to spin around to see what had just happened.

Spotting the rogue, the dwarf's face curled into disgust, and he cursed, "You little, useless fucker!" Looking back at his ball of fire, he motioned for it to roll at the bard, who was dragging the sorceress. The ball responded immediately and, rolling rapidly, struck the half-elf, engulfing him. The bard screamed in agony as the flames singed his exposed skin and blackened parts of his once pristine leather armor. Dropping Ariana, he batted at the flames, which, after a moment, blinked out of sight -- at which point, his spell complete, the dwarf returned his attention back to Bealty.

While that was happening, the gnoll Tyberius had been backing up finally stood his ground and began a flurry of attacks itself. Tyberius, already in a mindless rage, paid the attacks no heed, but fortunately his armor was sturdy enough to deflect all the blows but one, which cut through the chain mail in his right side, leaving a deep cut. Tyberius roared in pure rage and, raising his flail, swung left to right with his left hand. Being focused on his own flurry of swings the beast did not see the attack, the spiked ball striking the gnoll squarely on the side with enough force to knock it off its feet. Landing on the ground, it squirmed for a moment, then succumbing to the loss of blood gushing out of the multiple spike wounds, it went limp.

The remaining hellhound growled and jumped at Tyberius's back, biting and clawing in rapid succession, but the chain mail armor kept the evil hound's teeth and claws from penetrating, and the big warrior spun around swinging his free right arm, knocking the animal back to the ground.

Mikell scrambled to push Isa as gently as possible to the side and then, using his shield, tried to keep the seven foot tall gnoll at bay, but it was too difficult, and in the process of getting to his feet, the gnoll struck him a vicious blow across the side of the head, leaving a cut that went from his left ear to his chin.

With the ball of fire winking out of existence, York had a moment to collect his thoughts. Surveying the scene, he could see Mikell was in no position to help Ariana, who, it seemed, was bleeding to death at his feet. "Only Linkal knows your fate," said York as he took out a worn coin from a small pocket in his leather armor. "With your beauty, the face must be your fate." The face referred to the side of the coin with a bust of a hooded face, on which only a grinning mouth could be seen. "The swords are not for you," he concluded, flipping the coin, tumbling into the air before catching it again. Turning his closed fist over, he opened his fingers, revealing the crossed swords of the platinum piece. "Kindness begets kind fate," said York, shaking his head, watching the pool of blood slowly growing around the sorceress, then stuffing the coin back into his pocket, added, "I shall write about your magnificent death," and, with that, he drew his sword and charged the gnoll who had just struck Mikell. Taking a full swing, the blade bounced off the hardened leather armor of the gnoll, not doing any significant damage, but it did manage to gain its full attention. The gnoll looked down at the bard, over its lanky snout as its lips curled into a snarl, baring its teeth. Recognizing York as an elf, a hated race, the gnoll turned its body around to face the new attacker.

Bealty backed up a couple steps, looking for a place to run if he had to. The ashen-skinned dwarf cackled. "Yours is a race of cowards." Then quickly tracing his hands through the air, he canted, "Invoco missili di forza, infallibili nella loro volo!" Three glimmering bolts arced the short distance between the dwarf and Bealty, all striking the halfling, two in the gut and one in the right shoulder.

It felt like being punched and stabbed, all at the same time, and the quick succession of blows nearly knocked him off of his feet, but the halfling did not fall, and more than holding his ground, the little rogue dashed toward the taller dwarf, causing the ashen mage to backpedal a few steps and draw his dagger for some kind of protection, but as Bealty neared him, the halfling leapt into the air, doing a somersault over his opponent's head and, at the crest of the vertical, struck with his sap, connecting with the very top of the dwarf's head. The clap of the leather-clad iron plate on the bare skull of the dwarf was like a small thunderclap, and the evil dwarf crumpled to the ground, his dagger falling out of his debilitated hand. Bealty, landing the somersault behind the dwarf, found himself back to back with the remaining hellhound.

As the dwarf was falling, Brutal continued his struggle with the gnoll guard, each combatant feinting, striking, parrying, while looking for the opening. Noticing that the gnoll liked to strike high if he struck low, Brutal used that piece of insight to his advantage, and striking low at the gnoll, which the gnoll easily parried, Brutal took a chance and ducked low while bringing his bastard sword back for another swing. Sure enough, the gnoll's ax cut the air above his head and Brutal was able to bring the blade of his sword up and across his body, landing a devastating blow to the gnoll's exposed midsection. The blade cut through the hardened leather armor and sank several inches into the creature's flesh. It yelped in pain and shock as it stumbled backwards, sinking to one knee, then falling over onto its side.

Hammer was still battling the same gnoll he had been during the entire fight, neither combatant being able to land a telling blow. They both exchanged blows again, the gnoll's ax bouncing of the banded metal plates of Hammer's armor, and the gnoll used its buckler with great effectiveness, blocking all the blows that Hammer tried to land.

Tyberius, turning to face the hellhound that had just clawed at his back, roared incoherent obscenities. Raising his massive flail again, he brought it down, trying to crush the hounds back, but the infernal animal was too quick and darted out of the way, the ball of the flail striking the hardened dirt floor with a dull thud.

Brutal was standing between the remaining hellhound and the gnoll that had turned to face York, presenting its back to him. Remembering how Tyberius almost had attacked him earlier, he quickly made up his mind to take the opportunity to attack the gnoll from behind when he saw Ariana's crumpled body on the floor in the southeastern corner, small trails of smoke wafting up into the air from parts of her leather tunic that had been scorched. "Oh my god -- Ariana!" he called out, hoping she would acknowledge him, but there was no movement.

"Brutal, help York with the gnoll!" commanded Mikell. 'I will see to Ariana!"

"You fucking bastards!" shouted Brutal, raising his bastard sword and charging the gnoll. The gnoll turned tried to raise its buckler to parry the unexpected blow, but it was too late, the bastard sword sunk into the gnoll's back, causing it to yelp in pain.

York, taking advantage of the distracted Gnoll, tried stabbing it through the gut, but this time the beast was able to swing its bucklered arm around and knock the blade away. With York's blade parried, the gnoll brought its ax down hard onto the bard's shoulder, cutting deeply. York cried out, taking a step backwards as the gnoll raised its ax to strike again.

After dodging Tyberius's last blow, the hound again lunged at the warrior, raking and biting, but this time it drew blood, it's teeth and claws finding their way past the torn chain mail armor. Tyberius didn't even flinch at the small wounds, and sidestepping, was able to swing his flail, striking the side of the hellhound, knocking it back to the ground on all fours. The beast snarling in defiance, crouched, preparing for its next attack.

Mikell, giving the gnoll, Brutal, and York a wide berth, made his way to Ariana, where, kneeling beside her, he was able to assess her condition. She was still alive, he could see her chest weakly expand and contract at a sporadic interval, but she was losing blood as it seeped through the various burns, pooling around her. "Zuel, what have we done here?" Mikell asked softly to himself. Canting his prayer, he traced the mystical patterns with his free hand. "Benedici il mio tocco con il potere di guarire le ferite lievi." Touching her bare shoulder with the two forefingers of his right hand, he released the healing energy of Zuel into her body. Immediately her red and blistered skin began morphing back to its normal pinkish hue, her internal broken blood vessels began repairing themselves, stopping her blood loss, and within a few seconds of his touch, she gulped in a breath of air as her eyes snapped open -- searching frantically for something familiar. There wasn't much around her except for the wooden ceiling and reinforced dirt walls of the bunker, but her eyes finally locked onto Mikell's face and she felt comforted briefly, but the expression on the cleric's face, although calm, was stern and serious -- not to mention the cut on his face was bleeding enough that some of his blood was dripping onto her shoulder. "Welcome back, Ariana," Mikell said loud enough to be heard above the din of combat behind them.

Ariana bolted upright into a sitting position and looking around could see the fallen gnolls, hellhound, and even Isa was on the ground, not moving. "What-what, happened?" she asked, putting one hand on Mikell's chain mail covered knee, which was covered on blood, and pushing herself to a standing position.

Mikell rose to his feet with her. "I did not see exactly, but the dwarf caught you in some sort of rolling ball of fire."

That missing piece of information opened the floodgates in her mind, and her short term memory came gushing back to her. Whipping her head around to see the southwestern area of the room where the dwarf and others had emerged, she was glad to see the body of the dwarf lying on the ground. Turning her attention to Mikell, she placed a hand on his thick forearm and said, "My magic is gone, Mikell..."

"I feel drained as well," said Mikell in a tired voice, "although I can still cast one more spell before I, too, will need to pray and rest." Putting his hand on her shoulder, he said, raising his heavy mace, "But I can fight as well."

As Ariana was standing up, Tyberius continued his duel with the hellhound, who was coiled and ready to spring, but disregarding that fact, the warrior charged the large beast. The hellhound leapt at the same time, both combatants ignoring the dangers, the hellhound struck first, its toothy maw closing on Tyberius's free right forearm, which he had raised to protect himself. Taking the easy bait, the fiery hound clamped its jaws down on his arm, sinking into flesh, but as it did so, Tyberius brought his large flail down upon the beast's back, the spikes plunging deep and the metal ball breaking bones on contact. The hound yelped, fire and blood spewing from its mouth and nose, briefly, as it crumpled to the ground.

There were two gnolls still standing, the one facing Hammer swung several times in rapid succession, more with the intent of keeping Hammer at bay than inflicting damage, but was successful in pushing Hammer back a few more steps.

Ariana, feeling the blood flowing again, nodded at Mikell as she loaded a bolt into her crossbow. "We can both fight," she said, emphasizing the word "both," and taking aim at the closest gnoll, which was engaged with Brutal and York, she fired her round. The bolt shot out of her light crossbow and whistled through the air, missing the gnoll and lodging itself in the wall on the eastern side of the room. "Damn!" she exclaimed as she began to load another bolt.

York was startled by the bolt, which streaked between him and the gnoll, and looking to see who had fired the shot, frowned, noting the source, but continued his attack on the large gnoll. Distracted by the blow to its back from Brutal, the gnoll's guard was down, and York plunged his longsword into the gut of the gnoll, his blade running deep. The gnoll gurgled a foul sounding curse in its dark language, as it sank to its knees, after dropping its ax, the gnoll grabbed the blade with both its hands to steady itself. York withdrew the sword, and the gnoll tipped over onto its side.

As York felled the beast next to him, Brutal turned and sprinted over to help Hammer, who was fending of the flurry of blows from the last remaining gnoll. Swinging his bastard sword low, he sliced into the gnoll's right leg severely enough to break the creature's Femur. Howling in pain, the gnoll dropped its ax and sank to one knee, giving Hammer an opening. He swung his hammer down and connected on the top of the gnoll's head, creating a sickening sound as the gnoll's skull fractured, and the creature fell backwards, dead.

"Fuck yeah!" shouted Hammer, excited at the spectacular hit.

Tyberius spun around, looking for something to attack, but all the gnolls and hounds were motionless on the ground. Brutal was the closest ally, and his crazed eyes locked onto his friend.

Hammer saw the look and pointed behind Brutal. "Brutal, look out!"

Brutal spun around in time to see the tall red-haired warrior moving closer, and raising a hand while he took a step backward, said, "Tyberius! Tyberius! It is me -- Brutal! Put down your flail!"

The warrior hesitated, looked around, confused, but then refocused on Brutal.

"Tyberius! Stop!" shouted Ariana, the familiar voice again causing the redheaded warrior to hesitate. This time seeing Ariana, he reached up and removed the metal bear-faced helmet and lowered his flail. As before, his strength gave way as his rage subsided, and he staggered a few steps to the east and leaned against the dirt wall, slowly sliding down until he was in a sitting position. As the adrenaline receded, his various wounds opened up and Tyberius began to bleed an alarming amount of blood, even coughing up blood as he tried to catch his breath.

Disregarding all that, Mikell rushed over to Isa's body. The monk was still alive, but barely. "Are you going to be okay, Tyberius?" shouted Mikell. "I have to know, right now!"

Brutal and Ariana rushed to Tyberius, who, head down, raised up a bloodied hand. "I...will," he coughed up some more blood, "be okay," he concluded in a gurgled voice.

"You had better be certain, I only have enough power for one more spell," Mikell shot back.

"I do not," Tyberius coughed some more, weakly holding up one hand, "want any spells." Ariana and Brutal, looking at Tyberius weren't convinced, there was so much blood it was hard to tell where his worst wounds were that needed attention.

"Help Isa!" shouted Brutal, finally.

Wasting no more time, Mikell canted the prayer as he fluidly traced the somatic pattern in the air, calling down the power of his god. "Zuel, Benedici il mio tocco con il potere di guarire le ferite lievi," and finally touching the monk's forehead, releasing the spell. The monk was too severely injured for all his injuries to be healed, but some of the wounds sealed themselves, his bones mended, and he groaned as consciousness returned.

Isa blinked a few times, then realizing he was on the ground, rolled over and pushed himself to a sitting position. Looking around, he relaxed, noting that all the gnolls and the two hounds were lying motionless on the ground. He looked at Mikell. "You save Isa..."

Mikell said dismissively, and in a tired voice, placing a hand on the Isa's shoulder, "You do the fighting, I will do the healing. That is the deal." Looking around, Mikell could see the exhaustion on all their faces -- Brutal, Ariana, and Tyberius were sitting on the ground close to each other, Hammer was still standing, his armor covered in blood, and using his war hammer more like a walking stick. York slowly walked to the southern wall and also sat down, and even Bealty, who seemed to have boundless energy, stood over the dwarf, his shoulders slouching. "So much destruction and death," whispered Mikell to his god. "Zuel, get us out of here."

"So, is the dwarf dead?" asked Hammer, breaking the brief silence, walking toward the fallen mage.

Bealty, who was standing near the dwarf raised the sap so everyone could see. "Nope, I knocked him out with my sap."

"Nicely done!" said Brutal, slowly standing back up and sheathing his sword.

"We have the dwarf, now we need to get out of here," said Mikell.

"But there are two pretty large chests in that room," said Bealty, miming the dimensions with his hands and pointing to the door to the north. "Can we open them first?"

"We will not survive another fight like this," said Mikell, "I have no healing left, and Ariana is also out of spells."

Everyone looked at the sorceress, and she nodded, "He is right. I must rest."

"There is no time for resting," said Mikell. "Not only do we have to get out of here, but we need to get to your homes and help Julius."

Tyberius looked up for the first time. "Shit...I forgot about the smoke." Then clawing at the dirt wall, the tall warrior managed to get to his feet. "Mikell is right, we need to keep moving."

"We cannot leave without opening those chests, have you all gone crazy," asked Hammer in a mixture of amazement and incredulity. Looking at Bealty, he continued, "Beetle, c'mon, I will check the chests out with you," and the warrior began walking toward the door.

"We are choosing treasure over lives right now," said Mikell, in a scolding tone, "ours, and possibly your families!"

"It will only take a few moments," said Ariana, also standing up with Tyberius. "We may need the extra coin if we have to travel from here."

"Quickly then," said Brutal. "Mikell is right, we do not know what will come out of that tunnel to the west." Stopping to consider that, Brutal looked at Mikell. "In fact, you and I should at least look down there to make sure a hundred gnolls are not camped out."

Mikell nodded. "Good idea. Isa, you grab the dwarf and go with the others." Isa looked at Mikell, not quite understanding. Mikell pointed to the dwarf on the ground and mimicked the motion of lifting the dwarf up. "Pick up dwarf," he said again.

Isa nodded this time and walking over, easily picked up the limp dwarf with one muscular arm and threw him over his shoulder like a rag doll, then followed the others into the room to the north.

Mikell and Brutal, taking a lantern off the wall, used it to light the way to the west. The construction was much more rudimentary in this part of the lair, the walls were rough-hewn, and the floor was not as compacted as the other areas, but for whatever reason the ceiling was a little higher.

Mikell walked behind Brutal, resting a hand on the warrior's shoulder. "Be careful Brutal," Mikell warned. "If we see anything, we need to head back."

"You don't need to convince me," responded Brutal. "If there is so much as a gnoll baby, we are out of here."

As the two slowly moved forward, they found a wall that did not go all the way to the ceiling blocking their way, forcing them to go around it to the north. Looking around the corner of the wall, Brutal could see two lengths of chains, now lying motionless, the collars attached to each end lying open. Along the eastern wall, he could see another set of bars.

"Well, what do you see?" asked Mikell in a hushed, impatient voice.

"Sorry," said Brutal, "nothing much," he added as he walked around the corner and into the adjoining room, with Mikell following him.

"What is that?" asked Mikell, pointing at the bars. The two

companions walked cautiously toward the ten foot wide section of bars, but Brutal stopped, abruptly, about five feet away. "What is it, why did you stop?" asked Mikell.

Brutal pointed toward the center of the cell, where a human-like leg was sticking out from behind the bars. "A foot...a human foot, I think."

"No," said Mikell. "Let it not be so."

The two continued forward and, reaching the bars, looked inside. Indeed, there were several humans inside. Brutal, handing the lantern to Mikell, tried to open the cell door, but it was locked and, though he tried, he could not budge the bars. Mikell held up the light to get a better look at some of the faces, "They could not have been dead for long," Mikell looked at Brutal, sadness in his eyes, "they probably killed them because of us," then, shaking his head added, "Zuel, bless these souls, help them find their way home."

Brutal, resting his forehead on one of the jail door bars, gasped as Mikell's light passed over the dead bodies. "Wait, I know that man," he said, pointing to a corpse on the ground. "That is Jarrious, and that is his wife," he said, pointing to another body. "I cannot see her face, but the blue lace on her dress gives her away. Their farm was to the west of Tyberius's. These fucking bastards kidnapped them...and then killed them. That means the smoke Bealty saw can mean only one thing..."

"We need to get moving," Mikell said, lowering the lantern and already heading back toward the others, Brutal following right behind.

Bealty was the first one through the door heading back into the room with chests. Eyeing the chests like a lion would an antelope, the halfling started walking toward them, but upon seeing the gnoll lying on the ground, he remembered he had left one of his daggers in the fight and decided he wanted it back. A pool of blood, slowly soaking into the dirt floor, surrounded the gnoll, and stepping lightly trying to avoid the blood, the halfling navigated his way close enough to retrieve the dagger still lodged in the back of the gnoll's knee. It took a few tugs and twists, but finally the blade slid free, and wiping the dagger on the gnoll's leather armor, the rogue sheathed the blade back into its small scabbard at his side. "Sorry, but I am sure I will be needing this more than you," he said to the dead gnoll.

The others shuffled in, forming a small semi-circle around the two chests as Isa set the dwarf down roughly on the ground in front of him.

Ariana watched, an irritated look on her face, as the rogue retrieved his dagger. "Forget your damned dagger, we need to get out of here."

Bealty, sheathing his dagger and hustling back toward the chest, a slight limp still noticeable in his stride, replied, "I need my dagger, Ariana." As Bealty neared the two chests, the dwarf slowly rolled onto his side and looked up at Isa and the rest of the group, first coughing, then laughing.

Hammer, standing close to the dwarf, gave him a hard kick in back. "What do you have to be laughing about, you piece of shit?"

"Stop that!" shouted Mikell. "We are not going to abuse him while he is in our custody."

"Custody," harrumphed Hammer, "this asshole nearly killed Ariana," pointing at the sorceress, "and did a pretty nice job on all of us back there in the great room."

The dwarf, coughing some more after the kick, looked up at Ariana, "Ah yes, the ball of flame engulfed you." The dwarf cackled again. "I wonder: did it hurt?" he asked with a bloody grin.

Ariana, still blistered where she had been burned, drew out her dagger, but Tyberius and Brutal each grabbed an arm. "Let me go!" she screamed at the two warriors. "I am gonna shove this dagger into his god-dammed eye!"

"That is what he wants you to do," said Mikell. "We cannot abuse him while he is in our control. Besides we need to get more information out of him."

Ariana struggled for a moment more, then relaxed, saying, "Okay," but when Brutal and Tyberius didn't let go immediately, her eyes lit up again. "Okay, dammit! Let me go!" The two men looked at each other and slowly let her go.

The dwarf, fighting through another spasm of coughing, blood running down his chin, looked up at the warriors holding Ariana back,

"Are you the one they call Brutal?" Brutal's name coming out of the dwarf's mouth riveted everyone's attention, even Bealty stopped his work on the first chest, turning to look at the dwarf. The dwarf half cackled, half gurgled. "Yesss, so you are."

Brutal, letting go of Ariana's arm, stepped closer to the dwarf. "Who are you and how do you know my name?"

The pale dwarf, looking up, a trickle of blood still running down the side of his bald head where Bealty had struck him, squinted, as if looking into the sun. "My name is Skik Drukkofen," the dwarf paused, as if considering his next words, "and which one of you is Elgar?" he asked, looking around.

Tyberius's eyes widened in surprise. "I am, ya little rodent. How do you know ours names?"

The dwarf coughed again, then wagging an ashen finger at Brutal and Tyberius, he continued, "Whatever you have done, you have aroused, and angered, some powerful forces against you..." The dwarf began coughing some more.

"What forces do you speak of?" demanded Brutal.

The dwarf studied Brutal's face. "You do not even know you are being hunted, do you?"

"Hunted?" asked Brutal, stepping nearer the dwarf. "For what reason?"

Skik smiled, wiping blood from his chin with his shoulder. "We will have to work out a deal for more information; I need to get out of this alive...somehow," he said, looking around the room.

Brutal was about to ask another question, but Mikell interjected, "Perhaps the appropriate question is: why do you know his name?"

The pale dwarf pushed himself up into a sitting position, leaning back against the legs of a cot, and pointed a bloodied finger at Mikell, "Ahh, leave it to the wise priest to ask the right questions." Looking around at his captors, he added in a louder, more firm voice, "But unless this whore of Zuel promises me my safety and to let me go, I will not say another word -- and fuck all you and your families."

"Okay, fuck that," Hammer said incredulously, "I will make you talk the old fashioned way," and lifting up his hammer, which was resting on the ground near the dwarf, he brought it back down hard onto the dwarf's right hand, which the gray-skinned dwarf was using to prop himself up. The dwarf screamed in pain, trying to pull his now pinned hand back. Blood and spittle sprayed from his mouth as he gasped in pain. "Try casting your miserable spells with a stump," Hammer added as an exclamation point.

"Hammer, stop it!" shouted Mikell. "I will not stand for this kind of brutality for a prisoner!"

Hammer turned his attention to the priest. "Are you kidding me, Mikell? You are not in charge here."

The dwarf, his one hand still pinned to the ground by the hammer, used his other hand to pull a dart from his belt. "Human scum," he said through his blackened, bloodied, and gritted teeth, and using all his strength, the dwarf plunged the dart into Hammer's left calf, the needle sliding through the chain mail links and past the banded plates, sinking deep into the warrior's muscle. Hammer leapt backwards, his leg flailing from the sting, the dart still firmly lodged in place. Reaching down, he yanked the dart out and threw it on the ground.

Brutal leapt into action, kicking the dwarf on the side of the head and knocking him over back onto his side, where he once again lay motionless.

As the dwarf was swinging the dart, Bealty was already springing into action, but was too late as well. Seeing Hammer throw the dart to the ground, the halfling moved quickly and, carefully picking it up, inspected the tip.

"That does it, now I really am going to crush that son of a bitch's skull," said Hammer, but he stopped when he saw Bealty looking at the dart. "I ain't never seen someone so anxious to get a dart before."

"It is not the dart, it is what might be on the dart that has Bealty worried," said Mikell.

Hammer looked at Mikell, concern on his face. "What, you think it might be poisoned or something?"

Bealty dropped the dart back onto the ground. "There is a foul-smelling green liquid on it, but it is not familiar to me." Looking up at Hammer, he continued, "How do you feel?"

Hammer, looking down at the small halfling, said, "I feel fine right now, but you can fix this, right?" he asked, looking back at Mikell.

Everyone looked at Mikell, but the priest slowly shook his head, holding his hands out by his side. "I am afraid, I cannot. If it is a poison, you will have to fight for your life." Mikell instinctively reached for the holy symbol around his neck, and in a tired voice added, "I need to rest, I have no energy left for more spells right now."

A look of concern washed over Hammer's face and he quickly swiveled around. "York, you can help this, right?"

York was sitting on the east-most cot, leaning back against the wall, his pen was out and he was writing in his traveling book, but he stopped when he heard his name, and looked up. "I cannot cure poison, if that is what it is."

"So you are just gonna sit there and write about it?" Hammer said angrily.

"I cannot help," replied the bard, "would it please you if I stand up while you die?" The sarcasm dripped off his words, like a poison of their own.

"Fuck you, you damn elf! You are useless anyway!" Hammer roared back, but just at that moment, a spasm racked his body, nearly knocking him over. Managing to drop to one knee, he hacked, coughed, and suffered through a bout of dry heaves.

Mikell ran over to him and steadied the warrior. "Hold on Hammer, we will get you out of here...you will be okay."

The attack subsided in less than a minute, but in that short time, Hammer was already sweating, and his skin was beginning to take on an ashen look. Despite all that, he was able to stand back up and, leaning on his war hammer like a walking stick, said, "Let us get this damn treasure and get out of here."

Bealty was already back at the first chest and plying his lock picking tools to the lock. "No traps...at least there does not appear to be any," the halfling commented in case anyone was listening. No one replied, but everyone took a noticeable step backwards. Bealty's small hands moved gracefully as he maneuvered the lock picks into place, and then the gratifying click of the locking mechanism letting go rang out with a hollow sound in the confines of the room. Before Bealty could even open the chest, those who had taken a step backwards returned to their original positions around the chest. Halting only to give the lid one more quick check for a trap, Bealty slowly opened it, the hinges creaking as he did so.

* * * *

Julius, glimpsing Brutal's home a few hundred yards away, pulled on the reins of his horse, who slowed to a trot. Finding a small group of bushes, he tied up the horse, and let Foetore climb up onto his shoulder. "You can hitch a ride until we get closer, then we will have to split up again." The ranger quickly made his way through the grass, keeping a keen eye out for any danger. Around a hundred yards out, he knelt down and let Foetore down onto the ground. "I do not know what is up there, so I just want you to observe. I do not want you to get involved if there is any fighting," Julius said, holding out the palm of his hand, hoping the gesture would help reinforce the concept, not being sure what the little ferret could or could not understand. To his amazement, the little guy waited until he was done talking, then flicked his tail in the air and took off toward the house.

Julius waited a short bit, observing the farmstead, hoping beyond hope that one of Brutal's family members would show themselves, and everything would be okay, but the scene in front of him almost certainly excluded that as a possibility. The black smoke was coming from two places: somewhere in front of the house, which he could not see, and the second source, the barn, looked to be half-burned down and still smoldering. Seeing no movement, he began to creep forward, crouching to keep as much of his body below the grass as possible while still being able to walk. Nearing the house, a horrible stench began to fill the air as the breeze shifted directions briefly, sending the smoke his way. Arriving at the back of the house, Julius looked in the window of Brutal's room. Seeing no one, he carefully crawled into the small room. The metal interlocking rings of his chainmail shirt made a light clinking noise, but Julius did not think it was enough for even a gnoll to hear, unless there was one inside the house. Once inside, he slung his bow over his shoulder and drew out his longsword. Peeking into the main room, he could see it was in complete disarray. The table was tipped on its side, and the chairs we scattered about the room, some even broken. Crouching once again, he made his way to the window on the east side of the house, overlooking the barn, the well, and the wheat fields. Looking out the window, his fears were realized; a pile of bodies were stacked up in front of the house, near the table by the well, but the worst part of the scene were body parts on the table itself. Slowly standing up, the half-elf walked to the doorway of the home and walked outside to get a closer look. There was an arm, a small leg, and the partial remains of a hand, all with what looked like bite marks. "Animals," Julius seethed through pursed lips, feeling outrage. Thud. It wasn't a loud noise, but Julius's keen ears couldn't miss the sound that came from the direction of the barn. The doors to the barn were off their hinges and laying flat on the ground on either side of the barn entrance. The back half of the structure was burned out, allowing light to illuminate the inside, but there was a lot of rubble and places to hide if that was what you were trying to do. Making his way to the doorway, his sword at the ready, Julius peered around the rubble of the barn, but there was no sign of a gnoll, or any other evil creature. Foetore came running around the southeast corner of the barn and chirped at Julius, startling the ranger. Taking a half step backward, the ranger turned to face the unexpected friend who was now standing on his back feet and waving a front paw -- indicating for him to follow. Running around to the back side of the barn, Foetore led Julius to a pile of partially burned hay. Underneath the smoldering pile, the ranger could see a body underneath: a human body.

Sheathing his sword, Julius quickly ran into the smoldering ruins and brushed aside the hay, uncovering Percival's body, burned, but intact. Reaching down, he picked up the young human, who although just seventeen years old, was already physically larger than himself. Carrying the boy on his shoulder, Julius laid him down gently next to the well and immediately sent the bucket down to get some water. Retrieving a mug from the ground near the outside table, Julius used it to splash a little water onto the boy's face. To his surprise, Percival flinched and brought his hands up to his burned face, which was streaked with a mixture of soot and blood. Julius grabbed his hands, holding them down. "Take it easy Percival, you do not want to touch your face right now, you need some help."

"Who...who are you?" asked the boy, his eyes unable to open and see clearly.

Julius pulled a rag of cloth from his backpack and dabbed Percival's face, careful to avoid what looked like burnt skin. "It is Julius, and you are going to be okay now."

"Julius? Why are you here?"

"I was with Brutal and the others when we saw the smoke coming from your farm," answered Julius.

"Why did Brutal not come, too?" Percival asked, some pain in his voice.

"Just rest for now," responded Julius. "All your questions will be answered in time."

Percival began to sob. "I...I am a coward."

"No, Percival, you are not," Julius began to say.

"I am," interrupted Percival, "I did nothing, I hid while the creatures killed my whole family!"

"If you had done anything else, you too would be dead...or captured," said Julius.

"Captured? You think they took some of them away, alive?" asked Percival, desperation in his voice.

"I am not certain yet, but I believe so," answered Julius. "You stay here and rest, the others will be here in a while. I am going to do some cleaning up...there is no need for anyone else to see this scene."

"Julius, do not leave me here," pleaded Percival.

"I will not leave you," assured Julius, "if you need me just holler." He patted the boy on his leg and then stood up. He wasn't sure how much time he had before the others would get here, assuming they got out of the bunker alive, of course. It was grisly work, but Julius did the best he could to sort the bodies and parts so that each person was as whole as possible, then he covered them up with sheets from inside the house and the used pieces of wood to hold them down. He watched as Foetore sniffed at the bodies, knowing that Ariana's family was among the dead.

As Foetore sniffed, Julius walked to the front of the barn and, finding a shovel, began digging a hole in the ground near where the doors lay next to the barn. He dug it about three feet deep, by about two feet in length, and one foot wide. Walking back toward where he had lined up the bodies, Julius approached Foetore, who was lying by the head of one of the bodies, curled up into a small black and white ball. As the ranger neared, the ferret rose onto his back feet, gesturing with a small paw to himself and then pointed in the direction of the swale.

Julius shook his head. "No, it will do them no good for you to tell Ariana anything right now. We need to wait here for them."

Foetore shook his head back and forth and gestured again, his whiskers folding back along his face.

Julius smiled. "You care deeply, I can tell. Okay, let me take you back, it will be quicker," said the ranger, bending down and holding out his arm for the ferret to climb up, which it did, Foetore's claws, as usual, finding their way through his armor and scratching his shoulder. Standing up, Julius reached up and grabbed the ferret around the waist, pulling him off his shoulder. Foetore squawked, hissed, and clawed as Julius carried him toward the fresh hole in the ground. "I am sorry, little fellow, but I cannot allow you to alarm Ariana -- that would truly do no good." Once there, he carefully dropped Foetore into the small pit before covering it up with one of the wooden doors from the barn, trapping the ferret. "Once the others return, I will let you out. I am truly sorry for this, my little friend."

Julius sighed, knowing that Ariana would be upset about many things, including this act, but hopefully, he thought, she would agree with his logic. Grabbing the shovel again, he walked to the south side of the house and began the arduous chore of digging a grave for each person. By his count, there were twelve bodies; it was going to be a terrible shock for Tyberius, Brutal, and Ariana.

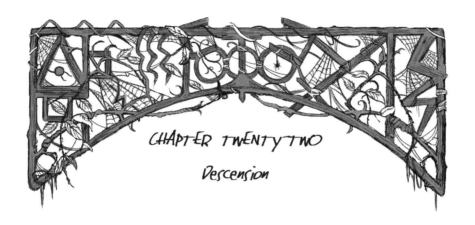

CHAPTER TWENTY TWO
Descension

YEAR: AG 1172, Month of Sepu

ANTHALL COULD FEEL THE POUND OF THE THUNDER in his chest, which grew more intense as the clouds moved closer and closer. As the darkness grew more intense, the distinguishing features of his surroundings faded into nothingness, first the buildings, his home, the barn, then the fields themselves faded into the void. The well was the only feature left, and Anthall sank down to a sitting position, his legs outstretched in front of him, his back against the rocks that they had used to build the well years ago. Closing his eyes, he kept repeating, over and over, out loud to himself, "For Fey and the kids... For Fey and the kids..." as if the repetition could grant him some comfort, despite his decision to abandon Soulmite.

"The great Anthall Mixnor," said a raspy voice in front of Anthall. Looking up, he expected to see a great demon, but to his surprise he saw an old man, dressed in shabby, torn, and bloodied clothing, with many lesions and wounds about his body, most of which oozed trickles of blood and pus, who was leaning on a gnarled walking stick. "I see the surprise on your face but, one must lead by example, no? Who has suffered more than I?" Anthall, still shocked, did not answer. "I asked you a question," his voice, still raspy, had a tinge more power behind it, "who has suffered more than I?"

Anthall did not know what to say. "I do not know..."

The old man moved closer to Anthall, his walking stick making a dull thud with every other step, until he was standing right in front of the seated warrior. Leaning on the walking stick again and looking down, he asked, "Who am I, Anthall?"

"I assume you are Blick," Anthall responded, searching the man's clothing for the three ringed symbol of the evil god, but not seeing it, he lost some of his confidence, "but I am not certain of anything here," he added, looking around at the darkness surrounding them, noticing that even the clouds were gone, only the well, still propping him up, remained as a reminder of where he was.

"What were you saying as I approached? You were chanting something," inquired the old man. Anthall thought hard, but his mind was becoming as blank as the landscape around him, and he could not remember. "Was it something about your family?"

The memory flooded back into his mind, like a beacon of light in the darkness. Anthall stood back up. "Yes! Yes, my family! You are to allow me to go back and save my family!"

The old man smiled, his yellow and blackened teeth showing. "Now why would we want to avoid all that suffering?"

Anthall, frustrated by the response, stood up, and being a few inches taller than the old man, looked down at him. "Because that is what was promised to me."

"Promised, you say? Promised by who?" asked the old man.

Anthall searched his mind for the name, this time remembering. "Judar Ruverge, your stinking priest, promised me that if I served you, if you are Blick, that you would allow me to return."

"Yes, Judar, he is a loyal priest and has made many suffer in my name...including you." Meeting Anthall's gaze, he added, "And yes, I am Blick." Speaking his own name, the old man grew in size, until he was more than a foot taller than Anthall. Towering over the warrior, Blick began moving even closer, backing Anthall up until the warrior was pressed against the well. With no place left to go, their bodies almost touching, Blick leaned down, face to face, his outward breath wafting a horrid odor, Blick continued, "And make no mistake: now you serve me."

Anthall did not shrink away but stood his ground, eye to eye with the god. "Only after I have saved my family -- that was the deal."

Blick stood up to his full height. "There is only one problem with that plan." As he spoke, he saw Anthall's hand drifting reflexively to his hip, where Slice would normally have been, but the sword was not there, and the evil god grinned again. "You have a nasty temper, do you not, Anthall Mixnor?"

Anthall, though surprised that Slice was not there, stood undeterred. "What problem could there be that you, a god, cannot resolve?"

"I am not in the business of saving families, but I do enjoy seeing them torn apart," as he spoke, Anthall reached up with lightning speed, grabbing Blick by the throat with his right hand. Anthall was about to say something, when Blick, raising his left hand and opening his palm, released an invisible force that easily pushed Anthall away. Anthall lost his grip on Blick's neck as his whole body slid backwards, slamming him against the side of the well and pinning him in place. "Saving your family, even if I could, would not serve my interest, surely you can see that much Anthall."

"Fuck you then," Anthall said through gritted teeth, his whole body still being pressed backwards against the well. "Kill me then, or do whatever you do in this shit-hole afterlife."

Lowering his hand, Blick released the power holding Anthall back. "You strike me as someone who could be quite vengeful." Placing his hands behind his back, the battered-looking old man eyed Anthall. "Now that could be of use to me." Anthall did not respond, returning the old man's gaze with a look of hatred in his eyes. "It must be quite upsetting to know that Marshal Krugar and Judar have tricked you into the position you now find yourself."

"Why the questions and the games? I do not care about you, your plans, and your reasons. Just tell me what I need to do to go back," Anthall said, straightening his posture again now that he had been released from the force holding him back.

"You should care," Blick snarled, "your soul is mine. You can suffer here, or you can suffer there, it makes no difference to me," he added, gesturing with his arms. "Judar, by performing your ritual killing and committing to his own sacrifice, has given us -- yes, you and I -- an opportunity to create much suffering together."

Anthall, turning his back on Blick and crossing his arms, interrupted, "You bore me with your intrigue, for which I care none."

Blick laughed, a low rumble in his throat. "Judar did well to send you to me. You have no idea what a great servant you will be for me."

Anthall turned around, arms still crossed. "Send me back then..."

Blick didn't let him finish. "Oh, you will go back, but first you must learn the joy of real suffering. Krykl will see to that," at the mention of the ogre mage, Anthall's eyebrows shot up as horror and anger swept across his face, and once again the warrior rushed at the old man, this time swinging a closed fist. Blick stiffened and stuck out his jaw, inviting the blow, which landed with a loud crack, splitting the god's lip and opening a wide gash on his chin. Anthall followed with a left-handed uppercut, that landed solidly, again crushing Blick's jaw and sending the god falling backwards, landing on his back with a grunt. Anthall leapt, pouncing onto the god, but Blick again held up a single hand, and Anthall froze in midair. "Physical pain," Blick began, his free hand coming up to his face and wiping the dripping blood from his lip, leaving a smear of read across his face, "although it does have the benefit of immediate gratification when it comes to suffering, it is not as effective, lasting, or rewarding as emotional suffering. Unfortunately, I have never felt the despair associated with emotional suffering, a curse of being a god, I suppose. I wonder if your previous bitch-goddess, really knows what it is like to love? I doubt it, what would she know of love?" Blick effortlessly raised himself back up, as if an invisible hand lifted him to his feet, and walking to Anthall, his walking stick thudding on the hallow ground, reached up and gently grabbed Anthall's chin. "But you -- ohhhh, you can feel deep, true, existential suffering. Consider it a gift from me to you, a blessing delivered unto you by way of our good ally, Krykl."

"Noooooo!" screamed Anthall through his frozen jaw, his eyes darting wildly as he tried to fight his way out of the god's spell.

"Once you have truly suffered, then I will consider fulfilling Judar's ritual promise to you, for only then can you serve me properly on Thran." Taking his hand away from Anthall's chin, leaving smudges of his own blood, he continued, "For now, I sentence you to the well at your farmhouse. You will be bound to within three paces of the well, and from there you can watch your family die at the hands of Krykl. You will not know what day or time, but you will see them die. Only once the hope within you is dead will you be useful to me." With that, Blick vanished, and Anthall, released from the spell, fell to the ground next to the well.

Opening his eyes, Anthall looked up. The darkness was gone, replaced by the sight of his home, once again, and Fey was standing at the well, drawing a bucket of water, filling a jug. Judging by the sun, it was still morning, as it slowly rose over the plains east of the farm. Jumping to his feet, he ran over to her. "Fey! Fey! It is me!" and as he neared her, he tried to reach out and touch her, but his hands passed right through her. Fey, looking up from pouring the water from the bucket into the jug, flinched, as if a chill ran down her spine, spilling some water as she did so.

"Oh, damn," she murmured as the cold water splashed onto her feet. Then dropping the bucket back down into the well, she turned and began walking back to the house.

"No, Fey -- wait, you have to get out of here!" Anthall desperately tried to get her attention, waving his hands in front of her face and trying to grab at her arm, but she paid it no attention and after a few steps, Anthall felt a searing pain, as if he had run into an invisible wall of knives, stopping him in his tracks and cutting his body in multiple places, including several deep cuts crisscrossing his face. He fell backwards, landing on his rear, unable to go any farther, he could only watch as Fey went inside their old house. Tears began to well up in his eyes and one, running down his left cheek, crossed one of his open cuts, adding a little extra sting as the salt entered the wound. "No, there must be a way," he said out loud, the conversation with himself somehow offering some reassurance.

After a little while, the door to the home creaked open again, and one by one his family exited, heading for their daily chores. First Nicholas and Percival, both heading to the fields, then Trinity and Lila heading to the chicken coop behind the barn, then Brutal, pausing at the doorway, said something Anthall couldn't hear to Fey inside, then his tall son slowly trod to the barn. "Brutal!" Anthall called several times but could get no response.

The days passed by, and no matter what he tried, he could find no way to communicate with his family. As happy as he was, at first, to see them, he could feel the hope draining from his body, like a boat with a slow leak and no way to plug the hole. Knowing that one day the boat will sink, and there is nothing he can do about it. Despair began to settle in, every dark cloud in the sky heightening his fear that one day Krykl and his hordes would come riding from the Cruel Pass and descend onto his farm.

The nights were the worst, since he never slept, the time creeping by and making him feel conflicted and guilty, wishing on one hand for the next morning to come, bringing with it the stimulation and activity of the farm, but on the other hand, he also knew that it was one day closer to their death. Many times, he would pray to Soulmite to deliver him from this cursed situation, but he felt no relief when he did so, his words feeling empty, hallow, self-serving, but most of all, unheard. The only interactive part of his existence was the invisible wall of blades that bound him to the well. If he was feeling particularly miserable, he would even find himself running into the wall on purpose; the cuts, the pain, and the ensuing suffering that it caused, he thought to himself, laughing at the irony, although not pleasant, provided some feeling of being alive, and that feeling became oddly comforting and seductive. The only other thing that stimulated his mind during the long and tedious hours of the night were his thoughts of Krykl, Judar, and Krugar, and to some extent Blick himself. His hatred, growing each day, was another emotion that seemed to become a source of nourishment. The love he felt for his family, as he watched them every day, made him feel vulnerable and helpless -- and over time thoughts began creeping into his mind: 'just let it end, so I can seek my revenge.' But when a thought like that came to his consciousness, he would immediately abuse himself against the wall of knives as punishment and -- in a sickening new way -- as a reward.

Anthall's world revolved around the vicious cycle of events: the days, the nights, the wall of knives, his continual self-abuse and loathing, the certainty of his family's death, and his deteriorating thoughts, which went on for what seemed like an eternity.

⋆ ⋆ ⋆

"When will we know if it worked or not?" asked Marshal Krugar, already impatient with the process, minutes after the murderous act was complete, as he looked down at Anthall's pale and motionless body.

Judar inspected his cut hand and, wrapping it with the now bloodied white cloth, said, "I do not know, Krugar, there are many variables...it depends on what Anthall does initially, and then after that it depends on our lord of suffering and how he decides that Anthall can best serve him."

"He is not my lord, you sniveling priest -- remember that," said Krugar, pushing a thick finger into Judar's chest. "Craven," he continued, referring to the neutral god of war, "has brought you into my plans, only because our purposes are aligned at the moment."

"I do not forget, but do not treat me as one of your servants," said Judar, knocking the marshal's hand away, "as I am not yours to command."

The two men stood nose to nose, for a moment, then Krugar turned away. "So, we just sit here with his corpse rotting away for an indefinite period of time?"

"I must keep the candles burning," said Judar, "if either one was to go out, then the spell will be broken, and my master will no longer have the option to return Anthall to us. Also, no one can be allowed to touch the body, and only I can place new candles, so keep everyone out of this tent."

"How many of those cursed candles do you have?" asked Krugar.

"Enough to allow for fourteen days," said Judar.

"Fourteen days?!" Krugar shouted. "Hell no...we cannot keep our army in the field for fourteen more days."

"There is no need for your army to be here," said Judar, "nor you for that matter. You can pick up and go right now. Take your forces back to Bindal, or wherever you plan to go," he added with a wave of his hand.

Krugar let out a belly laugh and turned to face Judar. "No fucking way -- you dodgy priest. If and when Anthall wakes up, I will be here to make sure he gets the right instructions."

"He will be serving Blick, through my instruction, not yours," said Judar. Reaching down, he picked up the stool he had tripped over earlier and, righting it, sat down. "As you said, our goals align for now."

"All the more reason I need to be here," said Krugar, making his way around the table, sitting on a stool opposite Judar. "I will give you and your god four days to complete your horrid ritual, then we are moving on -- even if I have to find another way. Already I am beginning to regret going down this path."

Judar pursed his already thin lips. "I sacrificed some of my own life force to cast this spell, I will not abandon the task until I run out of candles."

"After four days," Krugar said, leaning forward, his elbows on the table. "I will snuff out your precious candles and piss on his body, and then I will take my army back to Castor, in the north."

"You could not possibly find a better champion than what Anthall will become..." began Judar.

"If he returns at all!" interrupted Krugar, holding up four fingers. "Four days, that is all you get."

Judar sat, fuming, his mind racing as to what he could do, but he was currently surrounded by over one thousand of Krugar's men. "Very well," Judar said with some disgust in his voice, "we will wait up to four days, then we will talk again about your lack of faith."

Later that evening, Judar sat on the ground near Anthall's rigid corpse and said a prayer to Blick. "God of Suffering, I have made a substantial sacrifice so that you could return a powerful force to Thran -- a force capable of causing great suffering in your name. Marshal Krugar has threatened to cut short our time to complete the process, and I pray to you to make him suffer the next four days, and even greater suffering should he interrupt our work."

With his eyes closed, a voice crept into Judar's mind, which he had never experienced before, accompanied by a vision of a black spirit in his presence that spoke to him. "Your planning was flawed, your punishment, should you fail, will be great. It is unknown how long the false visions will take to corrupt his mind and more importantly his soul." The voice paused, the spirit drifting closer to Judar, whispering as if it were next to his ear. "Time waits for no man...or god." A shiver ran down Judar's spine, his eyes snapping open, only to see the two black candles flickering in the night, casting shadows on the walls of the tent, illuminating little more than Anthall's body, which was already beginning to attract flies.

CHAPTER TWENTY-THREE
Daylight

YEAR: AG 1175, Month of Sepu

THANKFULLY THE TWO CHESTS WERE NOT TRAPPED, and Bealty was able to make quick work of each lock. The first was about a quarter full of a mixture of gold and platinum pieces, enough so that it was more coin than any of them had ever seen, except for perhaps the rogue himself. The second chest had a mixture of silver and copper pieces in it, which although looked like a lot of coin, the denominations were much smaller. However, there were a set of bracers at the bottom of the coins, made out of steel and with fine etchings engraved into each one.

"I can carry the coin," offered Tyberius, starting to take off his pack.

"No need," said Bealty, taking out the bag of holding that they had found and opening it up.

Tyberius laughed. "That little bag ain't gonna hold all this coin, besides it weighs more than you."

"It can hold it, it is magical," said Bealty as he took a handful of coins and dumped them in. As he dumped more and more coins in, the bag did seem to fill up, but not to the extent of the coin that was being put in, and the little rogue continued to hold the bag easily with one arm.

Tyberius stopped laughing and took a handful of gold and platinum out of the chest and put it into his backpack. "I ain't puttin nothing into that damn thing."

"But we split all the coin, so it is better to keep it all together, in

355

the bag -- we can divide it up later," said Mikell.

Tyberius shook his head. "No fucking way, I ain't taking any coin that has been sitting in a sack of cursed magic. I took one handful, that can be my portion," then he backed away from the bag as if it contained a contagious disease.

Brutal, reaching in, grabbed the two bracers. "These look like they were made for smaller wrists, perhaps you should try them on," he added, extending the bracers to Ariana.

She was about to take them from Brutal when Bealty piped in. "I would not put those on until we get them identified."

"What do you mean, identified?" asked Brutal, pulling them back.

"He is right," said York from where he was sitting, still writing in his journal. "They could be cursed."

"Just put them in the bag for now," Bealty said, holding the bag open and moving closer to Brutal, who looked the bracers over for a second, then dropped them into the bag, where they promptly disappeared into the impenetrable blackness within.

Before Bealty could even cinch the bag closed, Mikell, placing a hand on Hammer's shoulder, asked, "Finally, now can we get the hell out of here?" Before anyone could even respond, the cleric began moving toward the open door on the southeast side of the room. Hammer, looking even more pale, followed quickly behind Mikell while the others gathered up their gear, also making their way out. Nobody volunteered to pick up the dwarf, so rather than leaving him there, Isa grabbed the back of the dwarf's tunic and, once again, callously slung the limp mage over his shoulder, and, out of habit, closed the door behind him.

* * * *

The trek out was uneventful, everyone walking at a brisk pace, aware that they needed to get Hammer out, as well as to get back to the surface and find out what was happening at their farmsteads. No one spoke, the silence only being broken by Hammer, who every now and then coughed or gagged, and the further they went the worse he seemed to get. Back in the small secret room, the companions began the long climb up the ladder, Brutal leading the way. At the top, Brutal opened the heavy hatch. Climbing up the rope, made difficult by his heavy armor, he was finally able to pull himself out. With his feet once again on firm ground, Brutal helped the others with the short climb.

Tyberius was the last one out, and as his head broke out into the fresh air, he couldn't help but grin. "Ahhhh, the fresh air. I never thought nothing could smell so good!" Brutal gave the warrior a hand, pulling him up out of the foul-smelling bunker. Standing up, Tyberius tuned back and, with no small amount of relief and satisfaction at being out, slammed the secret hatch down, the metallic click from below announcing the locking mechanism sliding back into place.

Tyberius and Ariana made their way back to the fallen log where they had tied up her pony while the others headed straight toward the road heading west to the farms. Once back together as a group, they decided to stay on the road, since it would be the fastest way, and the plains didn't offer much of a place to hide, especially with a horse in the group. After a quarter of a mile, Hammer began to stumble and would have fallen if Mikell had not quickly caught him by the arm.

"Hold on for a moment, Hammer cannot continue like this," began Mikell. "Ariana, can you allow Hammer to ride the rest of the way?"

"No, no," Hammer growled between coughs, "I can make it."

Ariana pulled on the reins and slid down the side of the pony. "Well, we cannot afford to stop every five hundred feet to wait for him, so I suppose we have no choice."

"Brutal, Ty, help me get him up onto the horse," said Mikell. The two warriors quickly moved and helped to lift the warrior onto the back of the horse.

"I...I do not need to ride," said Hammer weakly, holding onto the horse's mane for balance.

"We know you do not, we just want to keep moving and get you someplace to rest quickly," said Mikell. Tyberius and Brutal gave each other a look, deep concern on their faces, as Hammer's condition was looking very serious. Once in place, Mikell took the reins from Ariana and began walking the pony down the road, the others following behind.

"Shit, B, he looked pretty much damn dead already," said Tyberius quietly.

Brutal swallowed hard. "Mikell can fix him, we just need to get some rest."

"Mikell will need to pray and rest, too, before he will be able to help," added Ariana, listening to the conversation. "Hammer will be dead before that happens."

"How the hell would you know?" snapped Brutal. "What do you know about priestly spells?"

"I know more than you think," said Ariana, and giving Brutal a hard shove, pushing him backwards, she brushed past him, fuming, following Mikell down the road.

"Oh, nicely done," said Tyberius, throwing his hands up slightly, turning to follow Ariana. He gave his long-time friend a quick look that silently asked, 'Did you have to do that?'

"She is right, you know," said York.

Brutal, turning around to see the bard walking behind him, who was still writing in his journal as he walked, admonished the bard. "Just because it may be so, does not mean it should be said."

Putting his pen down for a second, the bard looked up and, in a matter of fact tone, asked, "Does pretending he will survive make it easier for you?"

Brutal eyed the bard, there was a callousness about him, but he couldn't determine if it was the elven blood flowing through his veins, or something else. "Does writing all this down, like it was some storybook, make it easier for you?" the warrior shot back.

York smiled, his thin elven lips curling around and upwards, revealing small dimples in his cheeks, and said, "No, his death is mostly irrelevant to me, although he fought well for the brief time I knew him. The writing does not make anything easier or more difficult, but it is essential because it immortalizes all the people I write about."

"That is a heartless thing to say," said Brutal.

"Maybe to you," said York, "but Hammer, if he does die, will come back to life every time I tell his story. What would be truly terrible is if the memory and the story of Hammer dies with his physical body."

"We are all nothing more than a story to you, is that it?" asked Brutal with disgust in his voice.

"All life is, is a story -- and someone has to tell it," said York.

Brutal did not know what to say to that and let himself drift to the back of the group and collect his thoughts. The group made better time with Hammer riding, as they didn't have to keep stopping, and after another two miles, they neared the small road that led to Ariana's farmstead.

"We should go make sure everything is okay at Ariana's home," said Mikell.

"No," said Ariana, sadness in her voice.

"Why not, what is wrong?" asked Tyberius.

"There is no need. Julius and Foetore are waiting for us at Brutal's home," Ariana said.

"What, how do you know?" asked Brutal.

"Like I told you, Brutal, I know more than you think," Ariana caught herself, her tone was sharp with Brutal, and she took a deep breath before continuing. "Brutal, Tyberius, there is not good news awaiting us, you must use what little time there is left, before we get there, to prepare yourself."

Brutal moved forward, grabbing Ariana gently by the forearm. "What do you mean? Prepare for what, Ariana?"

Placing her hand on his, she pulled her arm away, breaking his light grip, and looked him in the eyes. "For the worst, Brutal. Prepare for the worst." Turning, she let his hand go and began walking down the road she had walked so many times in her life. 'Maybe this was the last time,' she thought to herself.

* * * *

The sun was beginning to get low in the western sky when the group crested the small hill and Brutal's home first came into view. A small trail of white smoke still wafted occasionally from the charred remains of the barn, and they could see someone, presumably Julius, doing something near the house. The dread was unbearable, so Brutal and Tyberius quickened their pace and soon were quite a distance ahead of the others.

Julius heard the pony's hoofs lightly beating the ground and leaned the shovel on the side of the house. He had only been able to dig three and a half graves; there was a soft layer of topsoil, but it was only a foot deep and below that the ground became hard and difficult to move. Walking out into the open courtyard of the home, he could see Brutal and Tyberius making their way quickly down the road to the house. While they approached, Julius walked over to the barn door lying on the ground and lifted it up partially -- just enough for Foetore to quickly squirt out from underneath. "Sorry about that, Foetore," said the ranger. The ferret squawked harshly as it took off toward Ariana and the rest of the group. Dropping the door back down, the half-elf went and sat down at the table.

Tyberius and Brutal's eyes were wide open as they walked into the courtyard, taking in the horrid scenery: the burnt out barn, the bloodied ground around the outside table, and most noticeably, the line of bodies lying motionless, covered up, near the house and the newly dug graves. They started heading toward the bodies, but Julius gracefully stood up, intercepting their path and holding out his arms. "I would not go there, my friends, there is no need."

Brutal's mind was spinning out of control, a mixture of rage and sadness screaming inside his head. "I...I have to see..."

"Yeah, me, too, step aside Julius," said Tyberius, with similar thoughts careening around his head.

"Please, let me assure you -- you do not want to look -- I would spare you that much," said Julius.

Brutal stopped and looked at the blood soaked wood of the outdoor table just behind Julius. "What... Who..." Brutal stumbled to find the words to formulate all the questions going through his mind.

"Gnolls, of course," said Julius, "it was as cruel and vicious as you can imagine, which is why we should focus on burying the dead, then move out of here," Julius paused for a brief second, then added, "to kill those responsible and, with Soulmite's blessing, save those they took." The last part of Julius's sentence, the realization that some of their family were taken prisoner, was like a gut-punch to both warriors.

"Why th'fuck would they take prisoners?" asked Tyberius, beginning to feel the rage stirring within himself.

"We should make camp in the field to the north," Julius said, putting a hand on the shoulder of each of his friends. "We do not want to be sitting around here, surrounded by all this. We have much to talk about, and there will be plenty of time to answer all your questions tonight."

"At least tell us who is lyin' over there," said Tyberius, his eyes turning red, tears welling up, half with rage and half with sadness.

"Can it be enough, just for the moment, to say that you, Brutal, and Ariana all have slain family members," Julius paused again, "the curs brought them all here, for what reason, I do not know."

"Oh, blessed father, Zuel, what has happened here?" asked Mikell, as he came into the courtyard, Ariana's pony snorting as if in agreement with the cleric's disgust.

Julius stepped past the two warriors, addressing Mikell. "Take Tyberius and Brutal and the others and make camp fifty yards into the field there," Julius said pointing north. "Isa, York, you two help me dig some of these graves."

York looked surprised. "What, me? Oh no, no, I do not dig, my hands," he said, showing his palms, "are my livelihood. I will help make camp, and my music will help everyone calm their nerves."

Tyberius, turning around, faced the bard. "Ya gotta be shittin' me, you little elf bastard."

"It is okay, Tyberius," Mikell interjected. "I will help dig the graves, I can help more doing that, and York may be a better service to the group doing as he suggests."

Ariana moved to Tyberius, taking his arm. "Come along, Ty, let us help make camp, and tomorrow we will head out of here...for good." Tyberius, wiping away the tears running down his reddened cheeks, acquiesced, and the pair walked slowly to the north side of the property.

York turned to follow but was caught short of his turn, as Mikell, reaching out, grabbed the bard's forearm with a very firm grip, enough to make the elf grimace. Mikell, holding on long enough to get his point across, took the reins of the pony and, with some force, stuffed them into York's hand. "Take good care of Hammer."

"I am no cleric, but I will do my best, of course," said York, grasping the reins. "That reminds me, should you not be resting and praying to Zuel for some kind of cure for Hammer?" York could see Mikell's face soften at the mention of Hammer's name, and the cleric's head and eyes dropped slightly, as if ashamed. "You cannot stop the poison, even when rested, can you?"

Mikell let out a deep sigh. "We live by the will of the gods, and this is no different." Looking up with renewed vigor in his eyes, he continued, "So I place him in your care and expect you to be attentive to his needs while I help bury the others." With that, Mikell let the bard's arm go.

As Mikell was turning away, York said, "Why not dig an extra one... you know -- just in case." The cold nature of the comment, despite the hint of logical truth, sent a chill down Mikell's spine, and he was about to say something, but the bard had already turned and was moving away.

* * * *

Julius, Mikell, Isa, and even Tyberius and Brutal helped dig the graves, fifteen in all, the last one being empty. The work continued into the night, by torchlight, and for those still sitting around the campfire, the methodical sound of the shovels repeatedly slicing into the dirt, followed by the 'whump' of the dirt being thrown to the side, or thrown back into a newly filled grave, could be heard in the background of the night. Surprisingly, York played his cittern long into the night, the sound washing over the group, helping ease the tension everyone was feeling. The camp wasn't much, just a cleared out area, with a fire in the middle, the flames casting their mystical, dancing, shadows around the group of adventurers.

Finishing up the last grave, the four companions rejoined the group around the fire. There was not much talking, everyone being dog-tired and wounded. Looking around at each of his companions, aside from Julius, they were all bloodied and moving gingerly, each nursing serious wounds. Mikell would need time to pray and rest before he could cast another spell, so that meant everyone would have to make it through the night with no help from him, or Zuel. However, that was only part of the problem, Mikell thought, absently smoothing out his thick, ruffled mustache. With a full night's rest, he might be able to heal all their wounds, but in so doing, he would expend all his spells, leaving him powerless to heal anyone during the upcoming day's events. Given the amount of damage they had just sustained in the bunker, that would make venturing off after an unknown number of gnolls a very risky proposition, but he also knew they had no choice now – time was not on their side, and they could ill afford to wait an extra eight hours for him to pray, again. Letting out a deep sigh, Mikell went over to Hammer, who was lying down on one of the hay-filled mattresses from Brutal's house. They had taken the warrior's armor off, and he was now wearing some of Brutal's old farming pants and a dirty white work shirt that had fresh blood stains from his coughing fits. Mikell had no spells left to offer but placed a hand on the top of Hammer's head and said a silent prayer to Zuel to help his friend survive the night. It felt good to pray, he could feel Zuel's touch on his soul which was refreshing, and reassuring. Finishing the prayer, the cleric took a seat on the ground next to Hammer, comfortably near the fire burning in the middle of the camp. He looked around at the faces of the small group, and they all looked haggard. Even the elven bard, who they had made fun of due to his pristine leather armor and well-groomed golden hair, with a streak of gray, now looked weary. The elf's armor was now scuffed, torn, and bloodied, and his hair was spattered with dirt and dried blood. Somehow, even in that condition, York continued to scribble notes when he wasn't playing an instrument. Ariana and Tyberius leaned against each other, Tyberius's long arm wrapped around her shoulder, holding her close, while Foetore lay curled up in Ariana's lap. Brutal sat near Ariana, he had taken off his armor, like everyone else, and now sat comfortably around the fire, nursing the cuts and bruises he had suffered during the rough day -- but there was a deep sadness on the warrior's face, as if he was holding something back. Percival, lay on the ground asleep, with Brutal resting an arm gently on the young man's shoulder. Julius and Bealty sat near Brutal, quietly talking, as sitting in silence would have been too much to ask of the halfling. Isa sat cross-legged, in a state of meditation, with the dwarf tied up and lying motionless on the ground behind him. 'What have we gotten ourselves into?' Mikell wondered to himself.

Brutal broke the silence, slowly standing up. "This is all my fault. I mean, all the deaths today are my fault -- I know that."

"No, Brutal, it is not your fault," said Mikell, interrupting.

"Aye, it is not your fault," said Julius. "If you, or any of us, had been home, we would have been killed or captured as well."

"No," said Brutal, shaking his head. "For whatever reason, they were looking for me. It was my name in the documents down there," he said with emphasis, "and the damned dwarf knew my name. I believe my father has something to do with this, I feel it in my bones -- there can be no other explanation. Which means I plan to continue my search, but I do not expect any of you to join me, as I have brought this evil upon you and your families."

"Do not be such a fucking martyr, Brutal, and a bad one at that," said Ariana, her tone cutting and unsympathetic. "Now that our families are dead, or captured, you expect us to curl up here and cry, doing nothing? Do not forget, Tyberius's name was also in the letters.

"That is not what I meant..." started Brutal.

"No? Then what? We go our separate ways and see what happens?" asked Ariana. "No fucking way -- our paths are joined -- now more than ever."

"Aye, I agree," said Tyberius. "We are going with you. There is nothing here for us now, and, b'sides, those sons of bitches that did this are still out there, and they need to pay."

Bealty, reaching into the bag of holding, pulled out a platinum coin, which he tumbled between his fingers with great dexterity, and, in his boyish voice, said, "Did you know that platinum pieces are not a very common currency?"

Everyone looked at the halfling, Ariana saying what everyone was thinking, albeit, not her specific words: "What are you babbling about?"

"Well, it is interesting how much platinum the gnolls had down there. Where did they get it?" asked the small rogue. "Farmers and common folk have no need for platinum."

"I think you got hit on the head a little too hard today, Beetle," said Tyberius.

Bealty rubbed his head unconsciously. "No, I speak the truth. Platinum is a currency favored by merchants, and especially by traveling merchants. They prefer the platinum because they have to carry less of it."

"The fuck you say," said Tyberius, interrupting again.

"Ten copper to one silver, ten silver to one gold, ten gold to one platinum. That is a lot less coin to carry around, so that makes sense," said Ariana, "but what the hell is your point?" Tyberius gave Ariana a look, surprised that she agreed with the halfling.

"They did not get the platinum from Telfar, obviously, so they must have stolen it from traveling merchants. Being on the north side of the Great White River, the only place they would find merchants carrying this kind of coin would be on the Cruel Road between Whiteal and Castor. Being that Brutal's pa was killed..."

"We do not know he was killed," said Brutal.

"Sorry, you are right," said Bealty, still flipping the coin between his fingers, "being that Brutal's pa disappeared in the Cruel Pass somewhere, it is possible that this gang of gnolls had something to do with it...and why they came looking for Brutal."

"That does make sense," said Julius. "The gnoll tracks came from the bunker to Ariana's home, and then to Tyberius's home, and then here to Brutal's home. An odd order, especially being that their tracks from here head northwest. They chose Brutal's home to be the last one sacked. And they either, coincidentally, have a camp that direction, or they are taking them to the Cruel Pass."

"None of that matters. Once we catch them assholes tomorrow, they will all be dead," offered Tyberius.

"What if we did not kill them? Right away, that is," said Bealty.

"Yes, I see it now," said Ariana, then giving the halfling a mixed look of scorn and respect, continued, "you have a devious mind, but I see where you are going."

"We are just gonna let them go? Have you lost your damned minds?" asked Tyberius indignantly. "They just kilt or kidnapped three entire families!"

"We follow the gnolls back to their camp, wherever it is," said Mikell with the realization.

"It could be a trap to follow them," added Julius. "They may be stupid beasts, but they are survivors and have evil cunning."

"Maybe that is why they took prisoners," added Ariana, "to get us to follow."

"Well, it worked!" Tyberius said, his voice filled with anger. "We follow them in the morning and kill all of them. Hell, if we sit here and listen to all the great minds talking about fucking coins and traps -- and we do not follow -- then the people they took are gonna die, that is for damn sure!" Nobody said anything for quite a while. Even Bealty, putting the platinum coin back into the bag of holding, said nothing, simply warming his hands by the fire.

"Tyberius is right," said Mikell, breaking the quietude of the moment. "We need to do everything in our power to help those they took." The cleric sighed and added, "I am sorry I cannot help any of you tonight -- I must pray and rest, in order to recover my spells, so I must bid you all a good night, may Zuel watch over us and our families." And, with that, he closed his eyes, losing himself deep in prayer, shutting out the outside world and focusing on Zuel's power that resided deep within his soul.

"I need to rest as well," said Ariana, giving Tyberius a quick kiss on the cheek before lying down and pulling a woolen blanket over her.

Closing his small book, capping the inkwell, and carefully placing the pen and the other writing components into his backpack, the bard lay down as well. "Aye, I must rest as well to recover my spells, please do not disturb me."

"I will take the first watch," offered Bealty.

Brutal smiled at the small halfling, shaking his head. "You surprise me at every turn, Beetle," Brutal said, using the new nickname for the first time. "Thank you."

"I will take the second watch," said Brutal.

"I take three," announced Isa, his gravelly voice surprising everyone.

"I will relieve Isa," offered Julius.

"I guess that leaves me with the last shift," said Tyberius, already trying to find a comfortable position on the soft layer of dirt that made up the field.

With that decided, Brutal finally let the fatigue he had been holding at bay overtake him and, lying back down on the ground, it did not take long before he was fast asleep.

Bealty watched as everyone settled in around the fire, and in a short while, everyone was lying down asleep, except the monk who continued to sit cross-legged, his hands resting on his knees. Fascinated, Bealty got up and as quietly as possible walked over to the monk and waved his hand in front of the monk's face, but got no reaction. Turning to go back, the halfling walked gingerly, his ankle still hurting, back to his spot, whispering to himself, "Hmm, never seen that before." It was difficult finding a comfortable position, his shoulder and stomach still had wounds where the dwarf's missiles had struck him, but like everyone else, his fatigue was greater than anything else he might be feeling. His eyes were growing heavy, so he pinched his arm, the pain shocking him back awake. He even tried talking to himself, but the night, and the crackling fire, slowly seduced him into a sleep, his eyes growing heavier and heavier until finally they closed one final time.

* * * *

Tyberius twitched in his sleep, his elbow bumping Ariana in the back, the sharp jolt jarring the sorceress from her rest. Her eyes snapped open, and she sat up quickly, wincing in pain as her burns rubbed against her clothing. Looking around, she quickly realized that Tyberius had awoken her, and she was just about to lie back down when it occurred to her that nobody noticed her abruptly sitting up. Looking around again, this time with more clarity in her mind, she noted that everyone was asleep. "Oh shit," she whispered to herself, then quickly looked to see if the dwarf was still on the ground behind Isa and felt comforted to see the bald, ashen-skinned dwarf still lying in the same spot and position she remembered him being when she fell asleep. She began to reach for Tyberius, to wake him up to keep watch, but stopped short of touching him as she glanced back toward the dwarf. Pulling her hand back, she slowly stood up, partly to help ease the pain, but also to do it quietly so that she wouldn't wake anyone else. Taking measured steps, trying to avoid stepping on dried out hay which crackled lightly, she made her way over to the dwarf. Lightly she began patting down the dwarf, who was lying on his left side, starting with his back and working her way up his side. It didn't take long until she felt something under his clothing, near

367

the small of his back. Not wanting to wake the dwarf by pulling the shirt up, which was pinned down underneath him, she drew her dagger and cut the back of the dwarf's shirt until she could see what he was hiding. It was dark and hard to see, but she couldn't risk casting her light spell, so she simply kept cutting the shirt, almost from his waist to his shoulders, and then felt the object. It felt like more cloth. 'An undershirt, perhaps,' she thought to herself, but as she continued to probe, she could feel the outline of something...something inside the cloth, and that brought a smile to her face. But her smile quickly vanished. As she started to move the dagger to cut the cloth open, the dwarf rolled over onto his right side; his eyes were wide open and glaring at her.

"You are pretty -- for a human," the dwarf practically spat out in a hushed tone.

"Fuck you," Ariana whispered back. "What are you hiding back there? I bet I know."

"Hmm, why are you whispering, I wonder," said Skik. "What is it you are trying to hide?"

Ariana stood up. "I am trying to hide nothing, but I want that book." She pointed the tip of her dagger in his direction.

"Take it then, it will be no use to you," Skik said, then paused, "unless I help you."

The dwarf's hands were now tied behind his back, but Ariana saw the damage he had done to Hammer, and so approached cautiously. Kneeling next to Skik, they both watched each other closely, but the dwarf made no attempt to move, and she easily cut the cloth strap. The inner garment slipped around the dwarf's sides and she pulled it away. Standing up, her nose recoiled at the smell of the cloth, which was damp with blood and sweat, causing her to slightly gag as she pulled the soft leather-bound book from the soiled garment, which she tossed to the ground. The book felt solid in her hands, and her fingers traced the cracks in the leather cover before releasing the small clasp holding it shut. Opening the book, she flipped through the pages, which were obviously written in magic.

Skik snorted an evil little giggle. "You cannot read it, can you?" Before she could even answer, he added, "I thought as much; you are weak."

"You are gonna teach me these spells," Ariana knelt back down, "or I will slit your throat."

Skik shook his head. "That is not possible."

"Why?" asked Ariana, her voice rising a little louder than she meant to, so she quickly looked around to make sure no one woke up. Bealty moved a little. Reaching a small hand, he scratched his head and then settled back down.

"Some spells are too advanced for you," Skik said in a scolding voice, "and you could not absorb all the knowledge."

Ariana thought for a second. "Then at least teach me the verbal component of the web spell I saw you cast."

Skik, using his elbows, was able to get into a sitting position. "I will do that, but we will need to move a little further away from the others if you do not want them to awaken."

Ariana contemplated the request. On the one hand, she thought, if the others woke up, they would probably be irritated that she was interacting with the dwarf at all, and would probably tell her to wait until morning, but they would be packing up in the morning and there wouldn't be time to concentrate and learn the spell. "Fine, we will go over there," she said, pointing with the dagger toward Brutal's burnt out barn. Skik, using his eyes to direct Ariana's attention to the rope restraints around his ankles. Ariana hesitated, looking around at her sleeping companions, they really wouldn't like her undoing the restraints, but he couldn't run his way to freedom, she thought to herself. Feeling justified, she was about to cut the rope when she stopped, realizing she would have to put them back. So sheathing her dagger, she was able to undo the knot and free his legs. Helping him up to his feet, she held onto his arm as they walked toward the old house.

Near the barn, Skik stopped. "I have already cast the spell, so it is no longer committed to my memory, you will need to show me the page with the spell on it."

"This better not be some god-damned trick," Ariana said.

"We can stand here all night if you like, but I need to see the page," Skik said, his gravelly voice still whispering.

"Are we going to need light?" asked Ariana. Skik shook his head.

He must have night vision, Ariana thought. "Fine, which page?" asked Ariana, flipping through the pages.

"There," Skik said as she reached the middle of the book, "that is the one. Hold it a little closer." Ariana put the point of the dagger up to his throat, gave him a look, and then moved the book closer. The dwarven mage's eyes began scouring the page, he murmured as he did so for what seemed like an eternity. Ariana's arm was beginning to hurt from holding the book up, but she did not say anything, so as not to disturb his concentration. The first hints of the sky beginning to lighten created a growing concern for what she was doing, but just before she was about to put the book away, the dwarf smiled and looked at her and said, "Ready."

The dwarf spent the next hour or so working with her to get the intonations and verbiage correct, Ariana keeping the point of her dagger firmly pressed against his side. When she felt she had it memorized and correct, Ariana asked one last question, "What is the component?"

"Spiderweb, of course," answered the dwarf.

Ariana looked around, the barn was just a few steps away. "C'mon then," she said, leading Skik to the barn where she inspected a corner, easily finding a web. Tucking the spell book under the belt on her leather pants, she sheathed the dagger. "This better work," she said with iciness in her voice.

She was about to try the spell when suddenly Skik leapt into the air, somehow passing his bound arms underneath his legs. As soon as his feet were on the ground, he brought up his bound hands, in which he held what looked like a torn piece of wool clothing he had ripped from his shirt. "Stordisci il mio nemico," said Skik, and despite his bindings, he was able to trace the necessary somatic symbol for the simple cantrip. The small torn piece of cloth vanished, and suddenly Ariana felt her mind spinning, not sure what had just happened. Skik quickly moved to Ariana, pulling the leather spell book out from where she had tucked it, and with practiced rapidity, flipped to the back of the book and tore out a page. "I would stab thee if I had the time," Skik said with venom in his voice, "but we will meet again." Ariana could hear his voice, she even could see what he was doing, but she couldn't formulate any coherent action in her mind -- all she could do was watch in confused horror. The dwarf held up the torn page and read the magic words. "Faccio appello alle forze magiche affinché pieghino il tempo e la distanza, trasportandomi alla destinazione che ho scelto -- Gilcurr." At the conclusion of his reading, the page vanished, the air crackled with magic, like static charges being released, and Ariana could feel the hair on her arms and the back of her neck stand on end. Skik let his arms fall to his side, an evil smirk wrinkled the corners of his ashen lips, then closing his eyes as if in anticipation, the static energy consumed him in flash of darkness. What followed was like a miniature thunderclap following a bolt of lightning, the parted atmosphere crashing back together, reclaiming the void the dwarf left behind. He was gone, and all the was left was silence.

"Noooo..." she managed to breathe out weakly, watching the events unfolding, a second later, she felt her mind snap back into clarity, and drawing her dagger, she lunged at the dwarf, the blade hitting nothing but air. "Oh my god," she whispered to herself, spinning around, half expecting the dwarf to come lurching out from somewhere, but after a moment she realized he was truly gone -- the silence of the night was too pervasive for him to be anywhere near -- it was as if everything had just stopped, leaving no sounds left in the night. Glancing back at the camp, she sheathed her dagger, noticing for the first time that they were shaking slightly. "Take a deep breath," she whispered to herself as she clasped her hands together, giving them something to do. Closing her eyes, she obeyed her own advice and took a deep breath. "Just relax..." she murmured under her breath. Letting her thoughts clear again, she could feel her body settling down, then opening her eyes, she held out her hands which held steady as a rock. "Okay," she said to herself as she began to make her way back to the camp, eventually finding her spot around the fire, and carefully lying down next to Tyberius, she took a few more deep breaths. Once she felt ready, she strategically nudged Tyberius with her elbow and then turned back, closing her eyes.

Tyberius groaned at the jab, his eyes slowly blinking open. "C'mon Julius, let me sleep just a bit longer," he managed to say through a long yawn. Waiting, but hearing no response, he rubbed his eyes, saying, "Alright, you bastard half-elf, I will get up." Sitting up, he looked around with a confused look on his face and with growing concern. The fire was reduced to a pile of coals, still smoldering but certainly not giving off much heat, and everyone, even Julius, was sound asleep. "Julius!" Tyberius shouted in a hushed voice. Seeing no reaction, Tyberius stood up, noticing the dawn light starting to show on the eastern horizon. "What the hell?" he mumbled to himself as he approached the ranger. Tyberius kicked the half-elf in the shin lightly. "Hey -- Julius!" he said. The ranger turned over looking up at him confusion on his face as well, and Tyberius burst out, "Julius, what the hell happened?" he said, gesturing at the camp. "You dumb ass, you fell asleep?"

"What?" said the ranger, bolting up into a sitting position. "No, I never was awoken." Both men's gaze shifted to the monk, still sitting cross-legged with his eyes closed, his breathing as regular as a heartbeat. Tyberius walked over, crouched down in front of the half-orc, and tapped Isa's shoulder, at which the monk opened his eyes.

"I ready to watch," said Isa, cracking the knuckles of his large hands.

Tyberius's eyes tracked behind the monk, and the tall redheaded warrior stood up. "Oh shit, where is the fuck'n dwarf?" he said, pointing at the tangle of rope lying on the ground.

Isa's head spun around, and the monk jumped up to a standing position, scanning the area. As part of his orcish heritage, he retained the ability to see well in the dark; even absolute darkness was no issue for him. Julius also stood up, scanning the campsite area with his elven vision, which allowed him to see very clearly in low light conditions. It didn't take the pair long to figure out that the dwarf was nowhere to be seen.

"Everybody wake up!" shouted Tyberius at the top of his lungs, anger tinged in his voice. Everyone jerked awake in the camp, sitting up at the sound of the harsh voice, their hands going for the weapons lying near them.

"What is it!?" asked Mikell and Brutal simultaneously.

"The dwarf is flam'in gone!" said Tyberius.

"What? No...how?" asked Brutal, his mind stumbling, trying to wake up, to process what was going on.

"Somebody fell asleep while on watch," Tyberius growled, "and I am guessing by the way ya is actin' that it ain't you." Turning to glare at the halfling, he continued, "That leaves only one sum'bitch left -- Beetle."

"You let a halfling stand watch?" asked Mikell in a scolding tone, wiping a hand over his eyes.

Tyberius turned his head to see the cleric. "Well, yeah, we all did."

Mikell shook his head. "Then it is our own fault."

"No, it is my fault," said Bealty. "I tried to stay awake, but it was so boring." Tyberius and Brutal both let out a gasp of air, as if in disbelief of what the halfling had just said.

"You are damn right it is your fault!" shouted Brutal. "Now who is going to show us where the gnolls are?"

Julius continued to search the area around where the dwarf had been tied up, his keen eyes piecing together the only things left to help them figure out what happened: the tracks. He could see footprints coming from the area around the campfire to the dwarf, then two sets of footprints leading away, toward Brutal's house, which he began to follow.

"Hey -- where are you going?" asked Tyberius, watching Julius heading toward the house, but when the ranger did not answer, the tall warrior quickly followed the half-elf.

Mikell gave Bealty a look. "You know your limitations better than to volunteer to stand watch alone."

Bealty shrugged his shoulders. "I thought I could do it."

Mikell shook his head. "Your lack of good judgment allowed the dwarf to get away, and Zuel only knows where he is now, or who he is talking to."

Bealty placed a piece of wood onto the coals and stoked a small fire back to life. "Well, I am not worried about it."

Brutal snorted, throwing up his hands. "Well, of course you are not, why would you be? Skik and his buddies only managed to kill our families, and maybe Hammer." At the mention of their stricken friend, both Mikell and Brutal looked at their friend, who was lying, covered by several blankets, between York and Mikell.

York was sitting up, writing in his journal as usual. "I believe our young warrior may have passed, he has not made any noise for quite some time."

"What?" exclaimed Mikell, hurriedly moving to his friend. "Why did you now wake me if you thought he was in trouble?"

"You know as well as I do, there was nothing we could do," said York, "and I was not going to interrupt your rest."

"That is a bullshit excuse, York," Mikell said, giving the bard a glare as he knelt on one knee next to Hammer. Placing a hand on the warrior's forehead, the cold skin sent a shiver down his spine. "Zuel, have mercy," he whispered to himself. It was too dark for his human eyes to see any details, but he felt again, this time with both hands; his friend's body was too cold. "Well, you are right, York -- Hammer is dead," he announced loud enough for everyone to hear, then added more quietly, "Zuel, protect him. Soulmite, please accept his soul." While he spoke, Mikell crossed Hammer's arms over his chest and, pulling a blanket up, covered up his face. Mikell shifted to a kneeling position and his head sank, chin to chest, closing his eyes.

Brutal walked over and crouched down, placing a hand on the cleric's broad shoulder. "I am sorry, Mikell."

Mikell, still looking down, sighed. "Will you help me bury him?" Brutal did not answer, he didn't need to.

* * * *

Meanwhile, Julius and Tyberius followed the tracks which led to the corner of the burned out barn. "Something happened here, but what I cannot tell," said Julius. "The dwarf's tracks simply vanish right here," he added, pointing to where the dwarf, unbeknown to him, had been standing when he cast the spell.

"What do you mean, vanished?" asked Tyberius, not understanding.

"The dwarf just, well, disappeared," said Julius. "I do not see him moving from this spot."

"How could he do that?" asked Tyberius.

"I do not know," Julius said. The dawn sky was beginning to brighten a little further, and Julius gave Tyberius a look, his angular elven features beginning to take on a more distinct form to Tyberius's human eyes in the burgeoning daylight. "But someone does. There are two sets of tracks leading here. One seems to vanish, but there is one set heading back to camp."

"Back to camp?" asked Tyberius, surprised. "Why would they go back to camp?"

"Someone let him go, Tyberius," Julius replied.

"What do you mean, someone?" asked Tyberius.

"I know who it was, the tracks are easy to read," the ranger said, crouching down and tracing a hand inside a small heel mark.

Tyberius crouched down as well, the increasing light now allowing him to see the detail of the track better. "Shit," he said as he ran a hand through his red hair, smoothing it backwards as he did so. Letting out a long breath of air, his head dropped. "I know that foot mark."

"I thought you might," said Julius, and after a short pause asked, "What do you want to do?"

Tyberius began to stand up, causing Julius to do likewise, the half-elf looking like a child next to the six foot seven warrior. "C'mon, let us walk and talk," said Tyberius already striding toward the small camp.

* * * *

Back at camp, Ariana sat quietly, her mind racing. 'How stupid,' she thought to herself as she watched Tyberius and Julius easily following her and Skik's tracks to the barn. Her mind turned to Foetore. "Go...follow them but stay out of sight if you can." The little ferret bolted out from camp, heading toward the barn. He covered the ground quickly, arriving before Tyberius and Julius. Surveying the scene, it was open ground in front of the barn, where the tracks would lead them, near the northwest corner of the burned structure. Running around to the back, Foetore made his way through the rubble, entering the barn through gaps in the boards of the northwest corner. Easily maneuvering his way through the maze of twisted, broken, and burnt boards of the barn, he curled up close enough to hear the two men talking.

Ariana closed her eyes and concentrated on her link to Foetore, feeling the life force of the small animal intermixing with her own. The men's voices were as clear as if they were standing in front of her as she eavesdropped on their conversation. She listened intently, but the outcome was clear. "Dammit," she whispered to herself, knowing they knew it was her. Opening her eyes, she watched the two men stand up from their crouching position and start walking back toward camp. "Come on back, little one," she said telepathically; she could feel Foetore's quickening heart rate as he responded, quickly working his way back through the rubble of the barn before turning back toward the small camp.

* * * *

"Let me talk to her first and find out what happened before we tell the others," said Tyberius.

"The others will be angry, Ty," said the half-elf.

"Yeah, I know," said Tyberius. "Hell, I am, too."

"Do you still trust her?" asked Julius.

Tyberius stopped and gave the ranger a look. "Hell yeah, I trust her, I am sure it is not what it looks like, which is why I want to talk to her first."

Julius put a hand on the side of Tyberius's arm. "I trust her, too. All I meant was, find out what happened, then if we need to tell the others, we will."

Tyberius looked surprised. "You mean you ain't gonna say anything?"

"If we need to, yes," Julius let his arm fall back to his side, "but only if we need to. From what I can tell, we have a long way to go here, and shattering trust within the group is not what I want to do."

Tyberius grinned, his white teeth showing behind his red goatee. "Thank you, Julius." Reaching out, the two men exchanged a warrior's handshake, grabbing the other's forearm firmly. "I will let you know what happened, and then me and you will decide together what the right thing t'do is."

* * * *

Walking back into the small camp, Julius and Tyberius were intercepted by Isa, the monk rising to his feet, quickly closed the distance and addressed Tyberius. "I not let dwarf go."

"Well, we never said ya did," said Tyberius.

Isa's face looked serious, but it always kind of had a scowl. "I woke, dwarf gone."

376

"Do not worry, Isa, we do not think it was you," said Julius.

"Oh," said York, suddenly joining the conversation, "but you think it was one of us then? Who?"

Tyberius turned to look at York. "We ain't sure. The tracks just up and disappear, like, like," he thought hard, trying to find the right words, "like he flew away or somethin'," his face twisted into a scowl, "probly some magic crap or somethin'."

York, pulling out his traveling book and a pen, jotted some notes into the small and growing tome. "Interesting, he must be a very powerful mage if he is able to cast spells that can do that. Perhaps a spell of flying, or even teleportation." Turning back to look at Ariana, he said, "It is too bad he is gone; perhaps he could have been convinced to share knowledge with you, Ariana."

Ariana, who was rearranging some things in her backpack, didn't even look up. "That dwarven scum could not teach me anything. My power does not come from books."

"Magic is all interconnected, I am sure you know that much," said York.

"Maybe," she replied, "but I want nothing from him. The next time I see him, I am going to put a missile right into his heart."

"You are a very vengeful person," York said, jotting some more into his book.

Ariana stopped rearranging and gave the bard her icy stare. "He fucking burned me," she said, pointing to the blisters along her exposed arms and neck, still red and seeping, "not to mention he killed Hammer... I would think we all would feel the way I do...or are we all just expendable characters in your god-damned story?" she said, pointing at his pen and book.

York stopped writing and held up his free hand. "I am not trying to anger you Ariana, but I do try to understand motives. I like to know what drives people."

Ariana's eyes lingered on the bard for a moment longer, then she went back to packing her backpack, shaking her head. "Honestly, I do not know why we let you come along, you are useless."

"It might seem that way to you now," said York, "but you are shortsighted. Vengeance has that effect on a person."

Seeing faint red blotches began appearing on Ariana's face, Tyberius quickly closed the distance and put a hand on her shoulder. "Let it go, Ariana, he ain't worth it."

Gritting her teeth, she seethed, knocking Tyberius's hand off her shoulder she stood up, but Tyberius inserted himself between her and the bard. "C'mon, let us go for a walk." York started to say something, but, somehow sensing it, Tyberius, turning his head to see the bard out of one eye, quickly said, "Shut it, York!" He turned back to Ariana. "Now, let us take some air together," he said as he put an arm around her, guiding her away from the camp, heading back toward the main road.

"Why did you do that?" Julius asked the bard. York's eyes glanced at Julius, a half smile flashing in the corner of his mouth, but he said nothing, returning his attention to his writing. "We're trying to create bonds here, not break them, you might want to try to keep that in mind before you push her too far."

York put his pen down and looked up at Julius. "I know her better than you think I do, I have traveled all over Thran, and I have seen her type before." The bard seemed to be looking past the ranger, and his voice grew softer. "She is driven by a rage, but the source of that rage, I do not know...yet."

"You may think you know her," said Julius, "but we all do not fit neatly into your types, and she might surprise you." York's eyes returned to meet Julius's and, for a second, it looked as if he was going to say something, but then changing his mind, he picked his pen up and returned to writing in his journal.

"As well as you may know Ariana," said Bealty in his small voice, "you may want to keep an eye on Tyberius, because I have known Tyberius for years and he does things I would not expect all the time-- and if you push Ariana, you are pushing Tyberius."

"And Brutal, too, do you not think?" said York, not looking up from his writing. "He seems rather fond of her, too."

Julius cocked his head. "What do you mean?"

"I have seen the way he looks at her," said York. "There are some feelings there."

"Brutal and Ariana grew up together, they are like brother and sister, and you are misinterpreting Brutal's feelings."

York, still writing in his journal, let out a little sigh and replied, "Yes, I am sure you are correct."

Julius took a step closer toward the bard. "Like I said before, York, we are trying to build something here and do something for our friend, so be careful how you stir the pot." With no response from the bard, Julius shook his head slightly and turned around, heading back toward the house where Mikell and Brutal were preparing to bury Hammer.

* * * *

Tyberius, practically pulling Ariana, led her away from the small little camp. It helped to get her little ways away as he could feel her emotions starting to settle down as the distance to the camp increased. The tall warrior, with his arms still around her, said in a calm voice, "Do not let that stupid bard get you riled up."

Ariana stopped, this time forcing Tyberius to halt with her. "If he were talking to you like that, you would have had your flail out already, so do not tell me to calm down!"

Tyberius let out a low chuckle, and his famous grin reappeared on his face. "Yeah, you are probably right about that." Tyberius took a step in front of Ariana and turned to face her. "Look, forget about the stupid bard, what the hell happened last night?"

The smoldering fire and Ariana's eyes went out, and she looked away. "When I woke up this morning, I noticed that nobody was on guard. My first instinct was to wake you up, but then I thought, that damned dwarf must have a spellbook somewhere." She looked back up at Tyberius, the fire starting to burn again inside eyes. "So I went to the dwarf and searched his stinky body to see if I could find it. And I did find it, he had it strapped to his body underneath his clothing, and I almost had it, but he woke up before I could get it."

Tyberius's grin faded away. "Why did you not just wake me up, you could have had the spellbook."

Ariana shook her head. "It does not work that way. I needed him to show me how to cast the spell."

"So, what, you let him go just to show you a spell?" asked Tyberius.

Ariana growled. "No, no, I knew you would not understand." Ariana held up her hands questioningly. "Where would I find another opportunity like this? I mean, even if I did take the spellbook, there was no way he would show me how to cast the spell unless he thought he was going to be freed."

Tyberius crossed his arms across his chest. "So what happened?"

"I cut the bonds at his feet, and we walked to the barn. He showed me a new spell, but as I turned to cast it, he somehow got his hands in front of him and he cast a spell on me, which somehow confused me. I," Ariana fumbled for the right words, "I do not know why I did not stop him...but before I could do anything, he snatched the spell book and cast another spell..."

Tyberius waited a second for her to continue, but she just looked away. Unfolding his arms, Tyberius held her shoulders. "Ariana, what happened then?"

Ariana, still looking away, said, "Julius was right."

"What do you mean?" asked Tyberius. "Right about what?"

Ariana looked up into Tyberius's eyes, her own filled with a burning hatred mixed with regret. "He vanished."

* * * *

It took them a while, but Mikell and Brutal managed to get Hammer's scale mail armor back on him, preparing him for the battles that lay ahead at the side of Soulmite in the afterlife. Brutal, still resting on one knee, looked up at Mikell and said, "He fought well down there, and I'm sure he will fight well up there with Soulmite." Brutal looked up at the heavens. "Poison is the tool of a coward, and Hammer did not deserve to die that way."

"Nobody deserves to die," said Mikell, in a slightly scolding tone, then, leaning on his shovel, added in a softer tone, "but he was called home and it was his time."

Brutal gave Mikell a look. "When I started this, I thought it was going to be something I did alone, I...I Did not want others to die for something I have been called to do."

Mikell let out a sigh. "Hammer was a good man, but he was not here to help you find your father, do not make that mistake. He was here for one thing, he was here for the gold, and the adventure, and he knew there were risks. Unfortunately, he made a mistake and paid for it with his life, and that is not on you or me, or anyone else."

"You may be right, but nobody would be out here if it was not for me," said Brutal.

Mikell crouched down to be eye level with Brutal. "Do not deceive yourself, everyone is here for their own reasons, it just so happens that your effort to find your father suits their reasoning."

Brutal scoffed in dissent. "What are you talking about? Tyberius, Ariana, Julius, yourself, Bealty... Well, maybe Bealty is here for the adventure, but you and the others are here only because of me. York and Isa, they are not here for me, I know that, but they are still risking their lives for my cause, even if it is of their own choosing."

"You are confusing the mission with the responsibility," Mikell said, putting a hand on Brutal's knee. "Just because we are out here for you, does not make you responsible for us."

Before Brutal could think of a reply, Julius approached from the small camp. "I thought perhaps you two could use some more help," he said, giving Hammer's corpse a long look. When neither Brutal nor Mikell immediately responded, Julius stopped. "Am I interrupting? Should I come back later?"

Mikell stood up, dusting off his hands, his already gruff voice rumbling in the morning air as he said, "No, your help is much appreciated...please help us lower his body into the grave." The three men, carefully picking up Hammer's body, lowered it into the shallow grave. Mikell stepped into the shallow hole, placing the large hammer on his friend's chest with the shaft pointing toward his feet. Taking Hammer's hands, he wrapped them around the shaft, as if by doing so would help the warrior take his weapon with him into the afterlife. Turning around, Brutal and Julius each gave him a hand stepping out of the three-foot-deep grave. Turning around, standing on the edge of the grave, Mikell's hand absentmindedly drifted up to his holy symbol of Zuel.

"I know how you feel, Brutal," said Mikell, his eyes still lingering on Hammer's body. "I invited Hammer to come along on this journey. I could feel responsible for his death," Mikell paused, changing his gaze to Brutal, "but he chose to come, and Soulmite called him home." Grabbing hold of his holy symbol, Mikell closed his eyes, allowing for a moment of silence in honor his lost friend. Opening his eyes, he said, "Julius, please go tell the others that Hammer is ready to continue his journey, and they should come pay their final respects."

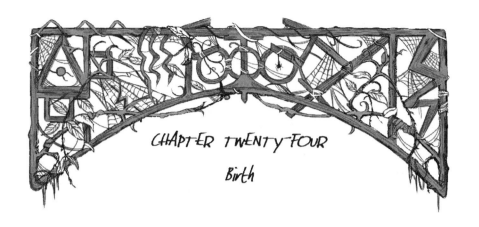

CHAPTER TWENTY FOUR
Birth

YEAR: AG 1172, Month of Sepu

ANTHALL SAT WITH HIS BACK AGAINST THE WELL. It was the middle of the night, the hours seemingly stretching into days, where he found himself wishing for sleep, but it continued to elude him. In the beginning, he would pray to Soulmite for sleep to come, but that never worked, and his sleeplessness continued, never-ending. Eventually losing track of the days, 'or had it been years?' he wondered. He finally gave up on Soulmite and found himself resorting to praying to Blick to grant him some sleep, but even that desperate attempt went unheard, or at the very least, unanswered. With no distractions that the daytime activity offered, his thoughts were hard to control and he often found his mind wandering, sometimes to memories of past times, but often he thought of the future and the horror that always loomed around the corner when his family would be killed. Anthall held up his hands turning them over, analyzing the scars that crisscrossed his skin, where the knives of his invisible cell had cut and mended, only to be cut again. Touching his face, he could feel the raised skin of the scars that ran, like rivers of memories, across his face.

Tonight seemed to be no different, his family slept inside the small house, the stars slowly migrating across the sky, the wind rustling through the wheat fields, the occasional chirp, grunt, howl, screech, or other animal noise being the only distraction. But then he saw it, a twinkle in the night: it was a short figure in black leather armor skulking up to the edge of the house. Anthall leapt to his feet, his hand reaching for where Slice used to be, but when his hand touched his hip, his heart sank, knowing the sword was not there. He moved to the edge of his prison, where he could feel the blades touching his face and hands. All he could do was watch as the figure slipped gracefully through the front door, not even a creak of wood to give away its passing.

"No," Anthall said softly, then began pounding on his prison wall, the blades cutting into his hands. He began shouting louder and louder, hoping somehow his voice could reach through the walls and warn his family inside. Blood was already running down his forearms, dripping off his elbows into the dirt at his feet, when the shadowy figure came back out the door, closing it as quietly as it had opened it. Then the figure reached into a pocket and took something out and placed it on the base of the wooden door frame. Turning, the figure paused, quickly scanning the area. In that briefest of moments, Anthall caught a glimpse behind the intruder's hood, and although he could not see the person's face, he knew enough to recognize a dark elf when he saw one. Before he could make out any more features, the figure darted across the small courtyard with cat-like grace, disappearing behind the barn. "I will kill you! I will kill you!" he hollered with all his being, hoping the figure would hear his shouts in its nightmares. Anthall turned his attention back to the little house, wondering what had happened inside, hoping whatever had happened had been quick and painless. Once again, he had to wait for the nighttime hours to pass by but the anticipation, horror, and longing for the moring to come, made the moments tick by at a painfully slow pace.

Fey was almost always the first one awake, and this morning was no different. To Anthall's amazement, the door creaked open, with Fey appearing with her empty jug in the crook of her arm. "Hmm, what is this?" she asked, bending over she reached down and picked up the object that the figure had left behind and examined it as she walked over to the well. Setting it down on top of the stone wall of the well, she lowered the bucket to fetch a pail of water for the morning breakfast. Anthall quickly moved to stand next to her and examined the object, which appeared to be a well-polished black stone or marble of some sort, oval in shape, and so pitch black that the morning rays bent around it rather than bouncing off its surface, as if it was a drop of darkness. Having collected the water, she picked the black stone up and slid it into a large pocket on her apron, and picking the now full pitcher up, she headed back into the house. After a few minutes, Anthall began to hear the regular morning sounds of the family waking up and gathering around the breakfast table, and a feeling of relief washed over him. "Thank the gods," Anthall said to himself. Closing his eyes, he slumped onto the ground, leaning against the well wall --- and he felt ashamed. Deep down, within the core of his being, he found himself wishing they were dead, and that it would all be over.

But it wasn't over, and the cycle began again, days turning into nights, and nights turning into new days. Anthall knew that the appearance of the dark elf meant that the time was drawing near and could only be a matter of days perhaps a couple weeks before an evil descended upon his family. He found himself praying to Blick more and more as the hours ticked by, praying for deliverance from this place so that he could protect his family, but his prayers went unanswered.

Time was a meaningless thing to Anthall, all he knew was that it was the middle of the night when he saw the first tall form come over the hill, the silhouettes being outlined by the stars behind them. The shapes were unmistakable: tall, lanky, fleet of foot, and slightly bent at the waist as they moved. It was a troop of gnolls, by his count nine or ten and in the middle was an even larger figure, wider and taller, its movements more akin to lumbering than the fleet-footed gnolls around it. Anthall searched his memory, which had already faded, making it difficult to retrieve past events, but in this instance his memory served him well, the picture being burned in his mind, he recognized Krykl.

The troop moved in silently, surrounding the small house, Krykl placing himself outside the front, facing the door. Krykl made a sharp snapping noise with the fingers on his left hand. Anthall couldn't help but notice that Krykl's right hand was still missing. At the signal, a gnoll on each side of the house struck a flint, lighting a torch. Once all four torches were alight, Krykl snapped his fingers again and the four gnolls threw their torches through the windows, into the house. It only took a moment until the first screams came from the house, the flames spreading from the floor to the bedding, from the bedding to the walls, and from the walls to the ceiling. At first, there was a lot of commotion within the house as the family tried to put out some of the flames, but the fire spread too quickly, and the family started to come out the front door, one by one. The first one out was Trinity, the youngest daughter. She opened the door, immediately heading to the well to get some water, but stopped in her tracks, letting out a scream as she saw the figures surrounding the house. Brutal came out second, beads of sweat streaming down his horror-stricken face, seeing the figures he raced back into the house, reappearing, sword in hand. By the time he had gotten back, a gnoll already had his sister in a bear hug, squeezing her as she screamed.

"You bastards! What do you want?" asked Brutal as the flames grew within the house.

Krykl laughed, his deep voice rumbling. "Your father is Anthall, yes?"

Brutal looked confused at the question and took a few steps closer to the Ogre Mage. "Yes, yes! What do you know?" At that moment, Nicholas, Percival, Lila, and Fey all came out of the house, standing behind Brutal.

Krykl laughed again. "Your father brings this misery upon you. He took something of mine," Krykl held up his stump of an arm, "and now I'm going to take something of his."

Brutal raised up his sword. "I'll take some of you with me, I promise you that!"

"You are an insect, you can do nothing," snarled Krykl, "and just so you know, after you're dead, you will get no burial: the kin of Anthall Mixnor will provide a feast for my troop, and we will shit your family out while on our return through the Cruel Pass." Raising his hand and extending his index finger of his left hand, pointing it directly at the family, the ogre's eyes narrowed, feeling the flood of magic being drawn into his body, the ecstasy of the energy as it briefly resided within him. But even for a powerful mage, trying to contain the magical energy too long is unwise as it needs to be released, and the ogre did so, using the ancient words he was taught long ago. "Invoco un cono di morte gelata." The cone of cold was immediate, racing from the tip of the ogre's finger, the cone rotating like a sideways tornado, widening the farther it reached until it was a large enough to engulf Brutal and his entire family. The force of the spell toppled the family members, throwing them like rag dolls, and even extinguishing the flames within the house with a loud hiss, as trails of steam rose into the night sky.

Trinity screamed, having just witnessed her entire family killed in a single moment. The gnoll's bear hug was too tight for her to move her arms, and with tears streaming down her face, she bit into the gnoll's forearm. The gnoll winced but did not let go. Instead, turning the child sideways, the gnoll snarled, revealing his canine teeth hiding behind his jowls, and in one swift movement, he snapped down on the girl's neck. The sound of bones breaking cracked in the night and the gnoll ripped her flesh as he pulled away, chomping and swallowing the bite. Blood spurted and ran down the gnoll's face, as he dropped the lifeless child to the dirt at his feet, using his now free hand to wipe a grungy, bloody, path across his face.

Anthall tried to look away, but an unseen force wouldn't allow him to close his eyes or turn away, forcing him to watch as the troop of gnolls gathered the bodies, started a fire, and began roasting their feast. Anthall couldn't scream anymore, he lost his voice during the events leading up to their death, so all he could do was pound on the invisible bladed wall and croak unintelligible words, tears streaming down his bloodied and ravaged face.

Krykl and the gnolls spent a horrifying three days at the farm, killing and consuming all the living creatures, including the horse, the chickens, and his family. At the end of the third day, Krykl led the troop away, disappearing over the same hill from which they appeared, heading back into the Cruel Pass. All that remained was the charred structure of the small home, and the bones and bits of grizzled flesh that lay scattered about the courtyard. Anthall sat on the ground his back against the wall, his hands limply lying at his side, palms up, his eyes wide, unable to close, unable to look away.

"Tsk, tsk, tsk," said a voice from behind Anthall, but he did not move or turn to look. The familiar thud, thud, thud of Blick's cane pounding the ground reached Anthall's ears, and the warrior, able to take his eyes off the carnage for the first time, turned to see the evil God approaching him.

Anthall, with a sudden rush of adrenaline and hatred, jumped to his feet. "You murdering bastard! I could have saved them!" he shouted as he charged the old figure, tackling Blick to the ground. Anthall pinned the god's arms beneath his knees as his hands flailed away against Blick's face, each blow opening new wounds on the god's face, breaking bones and chipping teeth. Blick did not struggle but emitted a mixture of groans and laughter with each blow. Anthall continued to strike in a frenzy, cursing the God with a stream of vulgar language, but as the minutes wore on, he could feel the strength siphoning away until he could barely lift his arms for the next blow. Finally, with no strength left, his arms too weak to even brace his fall, his hands bloodied and broken, tears making trails through the spattered blood on his face, he fell to the ground, mumbling curses as he toppled.

With Anthall no longer on top of him, Blick slowly stood up, again as if an unseen hand helped him back to his feet, his disfigured face already starting to mend. "Your rage will serve you well, but it is misplaced with me for I am not responsible for this, and you could not have prevented it. I must admit, it was such wonderful suffering, it would have been a shame if you or anyone else had prevented it. They suffered so well, my only criticism is that Krykl could have taken longer to kill your family, but still, being frozen to death is a most terrible way to die, suffocating under a shroud of ice," Blick shivered, "a nasty way to go."

Anthall crawled toward the god, wrapping his arms around the god's legs. "Blick, have mercy on me, destroy my soul, or do what you will with me, but do not leave me here any longer!"

"You have suffered greatly, and that is pleasing to me," the god said, placing a hand on Anthall's sweaty and bloodied head, "but perhaps not yet enough."

"No, no, no...I have suffered...enough," croaked Anthall in his raspy voice.

"I do not know," said Blick, rubbing his chin with one hand. After a moment of thought, he continued, "I truly do not want to destroy your soul, but your lack of faith is disturbing. Serving me, you could be a very powerful force on Thran."

Anthall, letting go of the deity's feet, looked up, and asked, "By serving you, will I be able to go back...to seek my revenge?"

Blick smiled. "Revenge on who?"

Anthall sat up a little, propping himself on one elbow. "You know who!"

Blick smiled again. "Indulge me."

Anthall reached up and tried to wipe the blood away from his eyes. "Krykl must pay."

Blick nodded. "Krykl is a very loyal servant to me. Why would I send you back just to seek revenge on Krykl? How would that create more misery and pain in the world?"

Anthall slowly stood up, grabbing the edge of the well to help himself to his feet. "If you release me from this place, allow me to take my revenge, then I will serve you," Anthall said, slowly nodding his head, his voice was still raspy, giving it a sinister tone. "You do this for me, and I will serve you, and I will create the kind of suffering the likes of which even you have never seen before."

Blick's eyes narrowed. "What would you know about what I have seen? And what could you, a mortal, show me that I have not seen before?"

"I do not know, but I will find a way to make the entire world suffer," said Anthall.

Blick stood motionless for a moment, considering Anthall's words, and chuckled. "You never have lacked ambition, but you did show a lack of loyalty. For the mere lives of the few humans, you were willing to forsake that bitch goddess Soulmite. What pittance would it take for you to forsake me?" Blick's face darkened.

"That whore, who I served my whole life, would not help me," Anthall took a step closer to Blick, using a hand to wipe away blood from the cuts on his forehead that was dripping into his eyes, "but you will." He tapped a finger on Blick's chest.

Blick looked down at Anthall's finger tapping his chest, then looked back up at the warrior's face, which, from his time at the well had become crisscrossed with scars. There was no sense of pity, but there was satisfaction in Blick's voice. "You may think I have taken away everything from you, but I have not. You will do my bidding, and if you displease me, or fail me, I will bring your soul back here," Blick drew Anthall closer, until their faces were inches apart, "to this exact place, and I will make your suffering a masterpiece, a thing of the ages, a thing even unimaginable for a god."

Anthall did not flinch or move. "I do not fail, and I will not fail you."

Blick reached out, grabbing Anthall's shoulders, forcing him into a kneeling position and reaching inside his dirty and bloodied shirt, the god pulled out a platinum necklace with the three touching circles, his unholy symbol, and placed it over Anthall's head. The chain felt cold on his neck, the tingle feeling refreshing, and the platinum holy symbol felt heavy as it rested on his chest, those simple sensations sent a thrill through his body -- being the first time he felt anything, aside from the pain and misery, that he had felt since having been sentenced to the well... it was exhilarating.

"You will be my servant on Thran. Know that your power comes from me, and me alone, and without my power, your soul cannot remain on the prime material plane -- your body would disintegrate into dust and be scattered by the wind. But your soul will return to me, and if it does, then I will know you have forsaken me or failed me, and neither will be tolerated. Rise up," said Blick, helping Anthall to his feet. "You will no longer recognize the name Anthall Mixnor, that is not who you are anymore, he was mortal, you are not. I will know you, and the world will know you, and all mortals on Thran will tremble at hearing your name, which will be as simple as it is terrible. From the bottomless depths of suffering, sorrow, pitilessness, dread, and hatred, I raise up your broken flesh and return you to the mortal world from whence you came, immortal to the effects of time, to be known and feared as my dark disciple, my death knight. Forevermore you shall be known as Kord, Lord of Suffering. Rise and do my work.

Anthall felt his spirit infused with strength, and his soul burned within him, feeling as if it was on fire. "Yes...yes...I feel the power, I feel my strength returning." Anthall's eyes, once emerald green, were replaced with an emptiness, a void, a blackness with tendrils that reached out grabbing at the light. "Send me back, Dark Lord, I am ready."

* * * *

"You damn priest, you never mentioned anything about having to wait so long for this accursed ritual to take place," Marshal Krugar said, slamming his fist on the table causing his mug of ale to tip over.

"Marshal, be patient, I beg you to be patient," said Judar, sitting across from Marshal Krugar.

Krugar picked up the fallen mug and threw it against the side of the tent, enraged as the ale spilled over the edge and into his lap. "Argh! Damn this ale, and damn you and your wretched ritual. We have waited six days now, two more days than I had planned," Krugar said, holding up two fingers. "The army is getting restless, and everyone is asking why we are just sitting here, and I'm running out of good reasons," he said, glaring at Judar, his eyes then switching to the corpse of Anthall's body. Krugar started to walk around the table. "Screw this, Judar, I am gonna snuff those candles and we are going to be on our way, we will have to find another way to raise an army." Judar jumped up from the bench, intercepting Krugar, grabbing him by the shoulders. "Get out of my way, priest! Do not make me kill you, that will set me back even further than your foolish ritual already has."

"No, please, Krugar, just give me one more day!" said Judar, desperately trying to hold onto Krugar.

Krugar lifted his arms and forcefully brought them down on top of Judar's, breaking the priest grip on his shoulders, and in a swift follow-up motion kicked the priest in the gut, knocking him backwards into the side of the tent. "No more of your bullshit, Judar, you have run out of time." Krugar, making his way over to Anthall, glared down at the corpse and covered his nose with his hand, the smell of the decaying body and the buzz of the flies making it a sickening scene. "I cannot believe I even thought this could work, that this wretched corpse could be of any use whatsoever." Krugar, raising up his metal boot, poised to crush one of the black candles, saying, "Enough is enough," as he brought his foot down, but before his foot reached the candle, the corpse's hand shot upwards, grabbing the marshal's heel, stopping it instantly.

"No," Kord, formerly known as Anthall, rasped, his lungs drawing in air, while his slumping head slowly raised up, his black eye sockets, locking onto the marshal's eyes. "Do not do that," and, with that, Kord threw the marshal backwards, causing him to topple onto his back, his legs flailing in the air.

Kord's other hand, already wrapped around Slice's hilt by Judar, tightened its grip, bringing with it a familiar presence, but being like a distant acquaintance Kord could not remember more. "What magic is this?" Kord silently asked in his mind, connecting with the sword.

Slice hissed in his drawl, once again awakened by a handler. "Youuu awaken...I thoughtsssss you had been killlllllled." Slice reached out with its will, to where it knew Anthall's subconscious used to be, in an attempt to use its domination, but as soon as it began its search, a weight like Slice had never felt before pushed its own will backwards, suppressing it completely. "It isss you, but yet not youuuu."

Kord tightened his grip even tighter, as if to crush the sword's will even further. "You are bound to me now by the godly power of Blick. As I serve him, you will serve me, whatever you are."

Slice, if it could, would have cringed, the weight of Kord's will crushing its own, the only relief to be had was through submittal, which it quickly did, "Yessss, massssster."

Kord, in an unnatural looking move, drew his feet underneath him and raised up to a standing position, taking two steps toward Marshal Krugar."

Krugar held up his left arm as if to ward off a coming blow. "Stay back, you fiend! Judar! Judar! Take control of this...this thing!"

Kord slowly turned his head to look behind him, spotting the priest. The death knight's eyes were drawn to the intersecting three-circled symbol of Blick on the priest's chest. "Ah, a true believer."

"Put your weapon away; Marshal Krugar is a friend," said Judar.

Kord tilted his head. "Who is it that you think I am to be commanded by you?"

Judar took a step forward holding out his hand as if to keep Kord at arm's length. "Do you not know who we are?" he said, motioning to Krugar and himself. Kord looked back and forth between Krugar and Judar but said nothing. Judar licked his lips, uncertain what was happening. "I brought you back to serve me."

Kord turned to face the priest, his grizzled face menacing, as he pointed the bastard sword's tip at the priest. "You are quite mistaken, I do not serve you," Kord looked back at Krugar still on the ground, "and I find it most unlikely that he is a friend." Looking back at the priest, Kord continued, "You, however," Kord reached out with his free hand, grabbing Blick's symbol hanging on the priest's neck, "you might be an ally." Judar could see the massive amount of scarring on Kord's hand and arm, scars upon scars where the wall of blades had cut him countless times, his skin still ashen and sickly colored. Kord heard Krugar moving behind him, and letting go of the priest's holy symbol, he spun with unnatural speed, raising Slice, to face the marshal who was trying to get up. Kord, stepping toward the marshal, prepared to strike downward on Krugar.

"Hold! I command you!" said Judar.

Kord felt an invisible grip in his mind, preventing him from striking. Looking back at the priest, Kord rasped, "Who are you to command me?"

"No, I think the question now is, who are you?" asked Judar, his confidence growing now that he seemed to have control.

Kord tried to resist, not wanting to tell the priest anything, but he felt obliged. "I am Kord, Lord of Suffering."

"A new name, this is unexpected," said Judar, raising a hand to his chin in contemplation.

Marshal Krugar clambered to his feet, brushing the dirt off his armor as best he could, "Well, Kord, you have a lot of work to do."

Kord turned around slowly, Slice still his hand. "If not for his bidding, I should like to kill you."

Ignoring Kord, Krugar looked at Judar. "Why does he not listen to me?"

Judar chuckled, his pointy teeth exposed by his grin. "Because only I am his master." Then added quickly, "I and Blick, of course."

Kord glanced back at Judar and then looked back at Krugar, an idea already forming in his mind. "However, were you to kill the priest, I would be forced to serve you."

"No! That is not true," Judar said quickly, taking a step to the side to get a better view of Marshal Krugar. "If you kill me, Kord will be free to do as he will."

Kord shook his head. "No," he said in his unearthly voice, "the priest lies, he knows nothing and does not want you in control."

Marshal Krugar looked between the two, irritation showing on his face. "It does not matter, I am not going to kill Judar. We have much work to do back in Bindal, and you, my friend," he emphasized the word, pointing at Kord, "have an army to raise."

Kord glared at Judar, saying calmly, "For your own sake, you would be wise to kill me now, and put me back in a grave."

Judar continued to smile his pointy smile and shook a finger at Kord. "No, no, we have much suffering to create in this world, and we must please Blick."

The thought of creating suffering pleased him, but Kord did not return the smile, his thoughts already turning toward other ideas, ideas of how he would destroy this mortal. It was, he thought confidently, just a matter of time before he would throw off this mortal shackle standing in front of him. He glared with his black eyes, voids, at the priest. "That is a predictable, yet unwise decision, but for now I will do as you command." Sheathing Slice, Kord finally noticed the dagger that Judar had killed him with was still stuck hilt-deep into his chest. "What is this?" he asked as he grabbed the hilt and pulled out the blade, small bits of his flesh ripping off as he did so, leaving a sickening looking wound, a gap really, in his chest. Kord looked the blade over. "A very fine blade," he said, tucking it inside his belt while walking over to the table. Glancing down, he surveyed the maps laid out on the table. The geography looked familiar, like deja vu, and looking back up at Marshal Krugar, asked, his voice raspy and ominous, "Where shall the suffering begin?"

CHAPTER TWENTY-FIVE
Into The Cruel Pass

YEAR: AG 1175, Month of Sepu

AFTER EVERYONE PAID THEIR RESPECTS to hammer, the group once again found themselves sitting around the campfire, the morning fog already beginning to dissipate with the rising sun. Mikell had done his best to heal the group one by one, but their wounds were too numerous and severe for everyone to fully recuperate. Despite Mikell's efforts to heal the group, everyone was still dog tired from the exertions of the previous day, and, not being used to combat, their muscles were sore and burned with every movement.

"I have done the best I can," said Mikell, sitting around the morning campfire, "most of you are only left with scrapes and bruises, but I have no power left without resting more, and resting more will just give the gnolls that much more time to get away." Mikell looked down at his feet, where he was tracing a circle in the dirt with the tip of his mace. "But if we venture out today, I will not be able to heal anyone, and that seems quite dangerous. It is a difficult choice." Reaching up with his left hand, Mikell smooth out his thick mustache, wrinkles of concern creasing his forehead.

Brutal was the first one to speak. "I think we need to head out now so we can catch the gnolls," he said, stabbing a finger toward the ground.

"I am sure I can track them," said Julius, "so they will not be able to elude us, regardless of how far they go, but it will make it harder to catch them, just due to the distance."

"We cannot let them damn gnolls get away!" said Tyberius. "We should get moving now, we will not need any healing."

"How can you say that, Tyberius?" asked Mikell. "Each one of us came close to death yesterday and I did not have enough power to heal all of us today!"

"Yeah, but that was a whole bunker full gnolls This is just a few stragglers," responded Tyberius.

Mikell shook his head. "We do not know anything about this group of gnolls. For all we know this is an elite group, and who knows what manner of surprises wait for us when we find them?"

Tyberius frowned, sitting back. "Bah, it be just a few mangy -- cowardly -- gnolls!"

"Mikell is right to be concerned," said Ariana, speaking up, "but we cannot let fear stop us from acting."

Mikell, still fidgeting with his mustache, growled, "You say fear, I say common sense."

Ariana bristled. "So, if common sense dictates friends and family should die, your advice is to let them die?"

Mikell stopped fidgeting, crossing his arms across his barreled chest. "You know that is not what I meant. What good is it to chase them, find them, only to be killed for lack of healing?" Mikell motioned at everyone around the campfire. "Which one of us is willing to die for lack of healing, when all I need is eight more hours to regain my spells?"

Brutal looked at Mikell. "Being that it is our family members out there," he motioned to Tyberius and Ariana, "I guess we look at it a little bit differently and feel our lives would be a worthy sacrifice for them."

"Aye, I agree," added Tyberius.

Mikell looked at Bealty. "What are you thinking?"

Bealty was rubbing his hands by the fire, the flames casting shadows on his face in the dawn light. "I say we get moving," he said, shrugging nonchalantly.

Mikell smiled, it was not an unexpected response, as he knew halflings hated being idle, it just wasn't in their nature. Turning his attention to York, Mikell was about to ask the bard for his opinion, but as usual the bard was busy writing in his journal, transforming Mikell's smile to a slight frown. Changing his mind, the priest stood up, letting out a sigh. "Well then, it is settled, and we should get moving -- Zuel help us," he said, raising his hands waist high, palms up, asking for his deity's blessing.

Everyone began moving with quiet efficiency, packing up their gear, readying the horses, and cleaning up the campsite. After getting his gear packed, Brutal allowed himself a tired look at the small house he grew up in, hoping that he could yet save some of his family so they could return. Brutal put his arm around his little brother. "Percival, come with me to the house."

Percival looked up at his brother and asked, "Why?"

Brutal began walking toward the house, giving his brother a slight tug on his shoulder before letting go. "You will see when we get there." The two brothers made the short walk to the house. Once there, Brutal led him inside. "Have a seat, little brother," he said as he picked up the chairs and repositioned them around the table.

Percival did as he was asked and took a seat. "What are we doing in here?"

Brutal sat down across the table from Percival and, leaning one elbow on the table, looked his brother in the eyes. "You need to stay here, little brother," to which Percival immediately began to say something, but Brutal held up a hand to silence his little brother. "No, no, we have lost too much already, and someone has to stay back to take care of this farm."

Percival leaned back in the chair, his face full of doubt. "I cannot tend the farm alone, besides the barn is half burned and I do not even have a horse to help me with the fields in the spring."

"We will not argue about this," said Brutal, "and we have enough money to give you so that you can go to Telfar and purchase a horse, a few chickens, and some food to get you through Darkal, by which time I expect to be back."

Percival shook his head. "What if you do not come back? What then?"

Brutal let the question hang in the air for a few seconds, then stood up and took a few steps to his old room where he looked up at his old nemesis, the knot in the beam above his old bed. "I will be back for you, my old friend," whispered Brutal into the empty room. The knot, of course, could not reply but simply continued its ceaseless stare, seemingly to focus on Brutal.

"What?" asked Percival, not able to hear the comment.

Brutal turned around on his heel. "Nothing...Just something between two old friends," Brutal said as he reached into a pocket, pulling out a small bag that jingled with coins. "Here, take this to Telfar and get the horse and the supplies that you need to get you through the cold months of Darkal."

Percival stood up, sliding the chair back into place around the table. Nearly as tall as his older brother, he reached out, exchanging a warrior's handshake. "Take care, brother, and see that you return, as you have promised."

Brutal said nothing but let the handshake linger, nodding and politely smiling before letting go and walking out the door, where he paused, taking in a deep breath, finally taking the two steps down from the small porch and making his way back to the others. He did not, could not, look back, otherwise he would have seen Percival on the porch, watching him leave.

* * * *

By the time Brutal returned to the group, everyone was ready to go, small tendrils of smoke slowly rising into the morning air being the only sign that they had camped there for the night. Reaching down, Brutal picked up his heavy backpack and slung it over his shoulders and, jerking his body to get it into position, said, "Okay, let us get moving, daylight is already burning." The group made their way down the small path until eventually finding themselves on the Telfar road. So many times, they had found themselves on this road but until today, almost always taking the southwest course to Telfar. But today, they stopped for just a moment, nobody needing to say a word, before heading northeast, along the Telfar road, unsure of what was waiting for them in that direction.

Julius trotted his horse up to the front of the group. "This road will end ten miles to the north..."

Mikell frowned, interrupting with, "It just ends? I thought this went all the way to the Cruel Pass?"

Brutal patted the priest on the shoulder. "No, you're thinking of the Cruel Road," pointing down the road he continued, "this is but a mere path, you forget that we live on the edge of civilization out here."

Mikell looked back and forth between Brutal and Julius. "I hope you guys know where we are going."

Tyberius let out a short laugh, his large grin showing from behind his red goatee. "Mikell, we grew up here, we know this area like the back of our hand," the tall warrior paused for a moment, "although I have not gone all the way to the Cruel Road. But hell, finding the Cruel Road cannot be too hard - I am thinking it is a damn big road."

Julius smiled. "Yes, it is a big damn road. Do not worry Mikell, we will not get lost. When you get to the end of this path, simply head northwest and eventually you will run into the Cruel Road."

Mikell looked at the ranger, asking, "What do you mean 'you'? Where are you going?"

"I will scout the way, staying a quarter mile or so ahead of you," the half-elf took a small whistle out of pocket showing it to the group, "if there is trouble ahead and I cannot get back to you in time, listen for three quick shrills of my whistle."

Mikell nodded. "Very good, but make sure you do not need to blow that whistle, do not let yourself get into that situation."

Julius's lip curled into a half smile. "This is my element," he said, holding up his hands, palms of the sky, "but I always like to have a backup plan." With that, Julius lightly kicked his horse into a trot and soon disappeared over the rolling hills of the plain.

The remaining seven companions began their journey down the road. Ariana, being the only one with a mount, she slowly walked her horse down the middle of the path, with the others finding a spot surrounding her. As they made their way down the path, Brutal noticed that Bealty, being less than three feet tall, had to take about two steps for every one of theirs, and so he was almost in a light jog to keep up. "Hey, Beetle," said Brutal, "perhaps you should ride on the horse."

Ariana, hearing the suggestion, bristled. "Look, I will admit that the little shit was more helpful than I thought he would be, but there is no way in hell that he will be riding with me." Tyberius was about to say something, but Ariana's gaze quickly darted in his direction, and he held his tongue. Ariana smiled, less from a sense of humor than a sense of control. "Wise decision, Tyberius, a very wise decision."

"Why would I want to ride on the horse?" asked Bealty.

The question caught Brutal off guard. "Well, I, just thought you might like to," he said, hiding his true reasoning.

Bealty looked up at Brutal for the first time during their conversation, his expression serious, as it usually was, his brown eyes tucked below thin eyebrows, his thick brown hair parted and hanging down the sides of his face, the tips of his pointed ears, similar to an elf, poking through. "Look at all the crap you have," Bealty gestured at Brutal's backpack and armor, "I bet you a gold piece you ask to stop before I do."

Brutal was about to answer, but Tyberius jumped into the conversation. "Hot damn! I want in on that bet!" he said, clapping his hands together with a loud crack.

Brutal's eyes squinted a little, doubting that the halfling's stamina could outlast his, but answered, with a little suspicion, "You have a bet."

Mikell let out a little chuckle, like a deep rumble. "When will you two learn? You are fools to make wagers with a halfling," he said, shaking his head.

Bealty gave the cleric a sideways look. "Mind your own beeswax, Mikell -- just because you do not enjoy a good bet does not mean the rest of us cannot." Turning his attention back to Brutal, he announced, "You have yourself a bet -- and you too, Ty." Barely finishing his agreement, the halfling sped up and was shortly out in front of the group. "I think it is time to quicken the pace." Looking back, the halfling waved his small arms, urging his companions forward. "Come along now, we have some gnolls to catch."

Tyberius and Brutal exchanged worried looks. Mikell reached out and roughly shoved each of them to the side, his low voice rumbling as he walked between, and past, his two friends. "Oh, well done, well done...now we will have to run the whole way."

Tyberius, recovering his balance from the shove, reached out and patted the priest on the belly as he walked past. "Look at it as a chance to lose a couple pounds!"

Mikell swatted Tyberius's hand away, waving a finger. "Keep your hands off me, string bean...this," he said, patting his own bellow, "is pure muscle."

Brutal smiled for the first time in what seemed like a long time, but before he could let out a laugh, thoughts of his family and friends that had been killed just the day before came rushing back into his mind, smothering the light moment with a renewed heaviness, and his smile disappeared.

* * * *

'A blind man could track these gnolls,' thought Julius to himself as he trotted his horse along the clearly disturbed earth, where he could see paw prints from the gnolls and footprints from the prisoners. It was difficult to gauge the size of the entire force, but Julius figured there were six or seven gnolls and three or four prisoners, humans. They had about a full day's head start, but the tracks were getting fresher and he knew they were closing the distance which seemed unusual for tracking a pack of gnolls. The only logical explanation being that the prisoners, the humans, were slowing them down. On one hand that was a good thing, on the other hand, it worried him because the gnolls could kill and eat whoever was slowing them down the most. 'Where are you going?' Julius wondered to himself, 'if they came for Brutal, why would they leave without Brutal?' Questions like that nagged at him, but trying to figure out gnoll logic was bound to be a fruitless task, since food and fear were usually the primary considerations for a gnoll's next move. In this case, it must be fear, he thought to himself, feeling confident.

* * * *

It took most of the morning, and was almost midday, when the companions reached the end of the path. Tyberius glanced up in the sky noting the location of the sun and pointing said, "Julius said to head northwest, so this be the direction." The group made good time, in part, helped by the pace that Bealty set, but it was starting to show its effect on some of the companions. Isa and the York seemed to have no problem keeping up, and of course, Ariana, who was mounted, had it the easiest.

Tyberius, long known for his running stamina, also seemed to be largely unaffected, although he wasn't used to lugging fifty pounds of equipment, including his chain mail shirt. Brutal, breathing heavily, was showing signs that his load was, in fact, starting to take its toll, just as Bealty had predicted. The worst off, however, was the priest, as beads of sweat glistened on Mikell's forehead, dripping down the side of his face, crossing his flushed cheeks, and disappearing into his thick black mustache. At different times, both Brutal and Tyberius offered to carry Mikell's shield but, in each case, were rebuffed with an angry grunt, bordering on a growl, after which both warriors tried to keep their distance, which wasn't too hard as the Mikell was almost always at the back of the line, muttering something under his breath.

Although it was easy to follow the path left by Julius and the gnolls, the virgin ground made traversing the grassy plain much more difficult. The tall grass made it difficult to see each footfall and soon the unmounted companions began to miss the hardened and trodden path which they had left behind. Their pace didn't slow, but their progress did as each person meandered through the grass, finding the best footing.

After another hour of walking, Julius and his mount appeared, cresting a hill a short distance off, and soon the ranger closed the distance. Bealty, being out in front, was the first to greet him. "Well met, Julius!" said Bealty waving at the ranger, his hands barely rising above the flowing grass, and had they not been following the tracks where some of the grass had been trampled down, the ranger might well not have seen him.

"Well met, little Beetle," said Julius, sliding down the side of his mount and taking hold of the reins, joined the companions in their walk. "I must admit, I am surprised to see you out in front."

Bealty was about to answer, but Brutal made a quick shushing sound. "Julius," he said under his breath, waving his hand as a slashing motion at his neck and shaking his head, but it was too late.

Mikell, huffing and puffing, his chain mail armor clinking as he walked up to the front, gasped out in his gravelly voice, "Oh, yes...Bealty, tell Julius why you are out in front." Julius could see Mikell's face was red and flushed, unsure if it was from fatigue, or anger...or both.

"I have a wager with Brutal and Ty," the halfling said, gesturing toward the two warriors, now standing next to each other, "that they will need to rest before me." Bealty looked at the two warriors and, without a smile, gave them a confident wink.

Finally sensing the lightness of the affair, Julius handed the reins to Mikell, "Here, Mikell, why don't you ride Jasper for a bit? It looks like you might be getting the worst end of the deal."

"Aye," Mikell gave the two warriors standing behind him a quick glare. "thank you, I think I will," Mikell said as he pulled himself up into the saddle. "Zuel bless your strength, Jasper," Mikell said, patting the horse's neck.

Julius fell back into the middle of the group as they continued to walk to the northwest. "We are definitely gaining on them, the humans must be slowing them down. At this rate, I believe we will catch them about two days from now, unless, of course, something changes."

"Do you think they know we are following them?" asked Ariana.

"It is impossible to know for sure, but I doubt it," Julius said without looking back at Ariana. "Gnolls are wary by nature, so we likely won't surprise them regardless of whether or not they know we are following them."

"How many gnolls do you figure are up there?" asked Brutal.

"Six or seven gnolls," Julius paused for a second uncomfortably then added, "and a few prisoners." The mention of the prisoners caused the hole in the conversation, as everyone reflected on yesterday's events.

"I cannot wait to get my hands on those damn gnolls and break their necks," said Tyberius interrupting the silence.

* * * *

The rest of the day was uneventful, the group walking mostly in silence. As the sun sank lower and lower on the horizon, the temperature began to fall as well, and this time Julius broke the silence. "We have very little daylight left, so we need to start preparing for the night." Everyone looked around, but all they could see were rolling hills and grass in every direction, except for a few small trees here are their jutting out of the ground at varying distances away. "There," said Julius, pointing to a larger tree to the north, "we will make camp there, at the base of that tree, where we have a chance to find a little firewood." Nobody said anything, they didn't have to, as everyone started moving in that direction. It had been a long day. Tyberius was able to keep up, but Brutal lost his bet with Bealty hours earlier, after asking for a short rest. Now, at the end of their hard walk for the day, even Bealty was starting to limp a little bit on the ankle that had broken the previous day, and so even the little halfling was glad when they finally reached the tree.

Fortunately, there were some fallen limbs and other bits of wood for Julius to put together a small fire, which helped keep the cold at bay. There was no time to hunt, so everyone dug out some of the iron rations they had bought back in Telfar and quietly nibbled on the crackers and dried pieces of pork. Julius was the only one standing, pacing a little as he ate some of the rations.

"Why do you not sit and relax?" asked Tyberius.

Julius gestured out into the darkness. "The fire, while it is keeping us warm, is also like a beacon for anything out there."

"Bah! There is nothing out there," Tyberius said, waving his hand, dismissing the ranger's concern.

Julius stopped pacing for a moment and gave the warrior a hard look. "We are not in Telfar anymore," the half-elf rebuked, "we are not even in the Cruel Pass yet, just in the hills leading up to it, but it is dangerous out here, and," Julius looked away from the warrior and back out into the darkness, "attracting whatever is lurking out there is not wise."

Tyberius laughed, still unconvinced, but it was enough to give Brutal pause. "Perhaps we should put out the fire then," said Brutal.

"Fire is protection," said Tyberius firmly. "Maybe there is a risk of attracting something, but it is better than freezing to death."

"There are trade-offs for everything," said Julius. "I was just telling you my concern." The group again fell silent, deciding by a lack of action to keep the fire going. After finishing the rations, everyone began to relax a little, glad for the warmth of the fire and for being able to rest their sore feet.

"Three hundred and eighty-two," said Bealty.

Everyone gave the halfling a tired look, but Ariana asked the question everyone was thinking, "What did you say?"

"Three hundred and eighty-two," said Bealty again.

"I thought that was what you said. So, what the hell are you talking about?" asked Ariana.

"That is how many gold pieces we have," said the rogue, holding up the bag of holding, "and better yet, we have two hundred and fifty-three platinum pieces."

Tyberius chuckled, his white teeth reflecting the light from the fire. "You daft halfling, since when is two hundred whatever better than three hundred whatever?" Now it was everyone else's turn to have a laugh, except Isa who couldn't quite follow the conversation completely. Tyberius cocked his head a little, asking, "What?" but nobody answered, not even Ariana. Realizing he might not be fully understanding the issue, the red-haired warrior shifted how he was sitting. "Aye, to the abyss with all of you!" The comment, of course, only incited more laughter, and soon even Tyberius was grinning again, although still unsure why.

Isa suddenly stood up and pointed to the northwest. "People coming." The laughing immediately stopped, and the others quickly stood up as well. It was a cloudy night, and the waxing moon provided little light, creating a very dark night. The half-orc's dark vision painted a colorless but clear picture of his surroundings, like a pencil drawing, but the halfling and human eyes had no special gift for night time vision.

Julius looked to the northwest. "Damn the fire, it is hindering my infravision." Elves, and some half-elves were gifted with infravision; sight that illuminated heat signatures from living creatures. Taking a few steps away from the flickering fire and placing a hand up near his eyes to shield them from the blinding heat source, he squinted into the darkness. "Are you sure, Isa? I do not see anything."

"Four come," Isa said, holding up four fingers.

Brutal drew his bastard sword. "Nobody would be wandering around at night, so this is going to be trouble."

"Aye," said Tyberius, picking up his large flail, the chain connecting the ball to the shaft clinking in the night. "Time to start crushing things," he added.

Ariana turned to Bealty, holding out the empty palm of her hand. "Hand me one of your darts."

Bealty hesitated just for a second, then reached to his belt where several darts were attached. "Uh, okay, here you go."

"What are you going to do with that?" asked Mikell.

Ariana closed her eyes, just for a second, to gather her thoughts and focus, as her eyes reopened she uttered a quick spell. "Invoco la luce." As she finished the cant, the wings of the dart burst into a bright light. Everyone reacted with the same groan as the pure light bathed a large radius around the group.

"Have you gone mad!?" exclaimed Tyberius, "put that out!"

Ariana handed the dart to Isa. "Throw it to where you see the people."

Isa, trying not to look at the dart's bright light, reached out and took the dart from Ariana. Winding up, the half-orc heaved the dart, which arced through the night sky like a flare and, after cresting, fell to the earth with a thud, its tip burying in the ground. The shifting grasses blowing in the wind gave the light the dart emitted an eerie look, but it was enough to catch several glimpses of the four slightly hunched figures walking toward them, about one hundred paces out, before they moved out of the light's radius and back into the darkness.

"I am not sure why," said Julius, "but I cannot see them with my infravision."

The small group began to form a line, with Brutal on the far left, then Tyberius, Isa and finally Mikell on the far right. York, Ariana, Bealty, and Julius took positions behind the others, as they all began readying themselves for the unknown that was coming toward them.

"There is something odd about this group. They move swiftly enough, but it is more like a shuffle," stated Mikell.

"Perhaps they are not alive," said York.

Tyberius snorted. "What are you talking about? They are walking right toward us."

"Some things come back from the dead and walk the surface of Thran," answered York.

Mikell put his hand over his heart feeling the cool touch of his holy symbol. "Zuel, protect us." The thought of something undead sent a shiver through the spines of the inexperienced group as they braced themselves for the upcoming encounter. It only took a few more moments until they could hear the footsteps of the figures approaching in the darkness.

"Who goes there?!" demanded Mikell.

The four figures moved to the outer edge of the firelight, standing about ten paces away. One of the figures took a step forward. "Who are you, and where are you going?" a male sounding voice asked. His voice sounded cracked and parched, as if he had just come out of the desert.

"You have it wrong, mister, we are the ones asking the questions here," said Tyberius, half growling.

Mikell took a step forward holding up a hand. "Forgive my friend here, but it is odd that you are traveling at night, and to come upon us as you have. We mean you no harm and will not hinder you on your way."

The lead figure let out a sickly sounding cough. "No, I think you should not," he paused, "in fact, I dare say you could not. We have traveled a long way, and now that I see you, it reminds me of a hunger I had previously ignored."

Mikell glanced back at his companions, now a step behind him, then turning his attention back to the figure, said, "We can share some food, but we ask that you eat it on your way."

The lead figure paused, letting the silence hang in the air for a few seconds as if he was contemplating, but eventually he shook his head. "No, our hunger will have to wait." The figure held up a hand, slightly waving it. "We will pass around you tonight, you shall not be bothered." The four figures began to shuffle around the edge of the firelight as they moved their way around the small camp, keeping a guarded eye on the companions.

As they were making their way around, Ariana took one step forward and asked, "What do you know of Gilcurr?"

It was hard to tell who was more surprised, her companions or the cloaked figure. The lead figure halted, then turned and took another step closer to the fire, allowing the light of the flames to illuminate his face a little more. It was obvious even in the low light that he was disfigured and most obviously not human, or if he was human, death had robbed him of those features.

His parched voice still crackled, but whereas before it seemed feeble it now seemed menacing. "How do you come to know this place of which you speak?"

Everyone was now looking at her, wondering the same question. Ariana wasn't sure what to expect by asking a question, she wasn't sure if it was a place or person, but now she had that answer: it was a place. Ariana stood her ground firmly, replying "We are heading there."

The figure hacked and coughed in what was most likely a fit of laughter. It did not last long, and as his coughing subsided, he said, "And why would you be heading to Gilcurr? What is your business there?"

Tyberius now took another step forward. "Forget it, pal, like I said we are the ones asking questions here, now be on your way!" the tall warrior gestured with his large flail for them to continue.

The lead figure hissed as if drawing in a deep breath, the sound sending shivers down everyone spine. "I must know your business. What, or who, are you seeking in Gilcurr?"

"What is it to you, what our businesses is? Are you from Gilcurr?" Ariana shot back.

"I am from nowhere, somewhere lost meaning to me a long time ago," answered the lead figure.

"How do you know where Gilcurr is then?" asked Ariana.

"You are a persistent creature, it would be a shame to have to snuff out your life, but that is what will happen unless you begin answering my questions. How do you know of Gilcurr?"

Ariana did not hesitate, replying, "Skik told us about it." She said it like a dagger, pointed and sharp.

"Persistent and surprising," said the lead figure as he raised his fleshy hand and pointed a finger at Ariana. "You seem to know a lot more than you should. Why would Skik tell you about Gilcurr? And where did you have this...discussion?"

Ariana could feel herself being pulled into some sort of trap. "Perhaps I should ask you the same questions. How do you know Skik?"

"Clever girl, you will get no information for me. Now answer my question," said the lead figure.

All her companions were looking at her with curious stares as she contemplated her options. "We met at the Telfar bunker."

"Oh my," crackled the lead figure's voice, "this is most interesting." He and his three companions took another step closer, advancing a little further into the firelight. All the companions gasped as the additional light not only fully revealed the tortured faces of the three figures, but also their filthy clothing, which was little more than tatters held together by strands of thread.

"Ready yourselves," York said in a hushed voice. "The undead are before us."

The lead figure cackled. "Yes, yes, we are beyond our mortal lives, but we have business to attend to here. I would wager that if you were the bunker, and now you are here, Skik most likely talked to you, as you held a dagger at his throat, and that Skik is now most likely dead."

"That little dwarven son of a bitch is not dead, but I'm gonna make him dead soon enough," said Tyberius, raising his flail.

Ariana put a hand on Tyberius's arm. "Everyone just relax." Turning her attention back to lead figure, she asked, "Can you take us to Gilcurr?"

The lead figure snickered again. "You are all fools, and you are the most foolish of them all, little girl," he said, emphasizing 'little girl.' "Kord would have no use for the likes of all you and you will take whatever little knowledge you have learned to your graves tonight." With a speed not before seen, the four figures rushed into the midst of the group, and as they did so, a stench the likes of which none of them ever smelled overwhelmed their senses, it rolled in and over them like an ocean wave, engulfing them, and making each breath difficult, oppressive, and utterly detestable. Brutal, Mikell, York, and Julius were the most affected their eyes began to water and the urge to gag and wretch was formidable.

Julius was the first to react, and although tears were streaming from his eyes and he was fighting back the urge to vomit, he was still able to fire two arrows at the lead figure. The first arrow flew past the lead figure's head, but his second arrow lodged solidly into the creature's shoulder, but the impact did not slow it down.

Tyberius was already struggling to restrain his aggression, and when the undead began to charge, he himself flew into a frenzy, racing directly at the lead figure, unknown to him, a ghast. With a great roar, ignoring the rancid stench, he swung the flail with all his strength, the spiked ball nearly ripping the ghast's arm clean off.

Brutal, feeling off balance, his eyes were watering heavily, and gasping for air, was still able to muster the strength to swing his bastard sword. It was a weak strike and the ghast easily batted it aside. As Brutal was taking his swing, Ariana focused her mind, feeling herself reaching out and drawing in the magical energy surrounding her, she canted the magical phrase. "Invoco missili di forza, infallibili nella loro volo." Releasing her spell at the ghast, the three red magical bolts of energy flew from her pointed index finger, each bolt taking its own unique path and arcing through the night sky, weaving their way through the combatants, and striking without error. The ghast let out a sinister hissing sound as it collapsed to the ground, its forward momentum causing it to roll into heap at Tyberius's feet.

The ghoul directly behind the ghast croaked in rage and, stepping on the body of the ghast, lunged at Tyberius. The tall warrior was able to knock aside the ghoul's left-handed clawing attack, but its right hand scratched his hand holding the flail, cause a deep cut with its razor-sharp nails. The cut itself was mostly ineffective, but its poisonous touch plagued his nervous system and Tyberius felt his muscles locking up, leaving him frozen in place. The ghoul's third attack was a snapping bite at Tyberius's arm, but the chain mail kept its sharp teeth from puncturing his skin underneath.

Bealty reached to his belt and took a dart from its strap and eyeing up the ghoul charging at Brutal on the left side of the line, he hurled the dart but the ghoul deftly ducked out of the way, the dart sailing harmlessly into the grassy plain.

York began chanting a battle hymn, his voice resonating and encouraging his companions. While he began his chant, a second ghoul wearing tattered armor charged at Brutal, its arms flailing at the warrior with a ferocity spawned from deep seeded evil. It's left hand scraping Brutal's right shoulder, but its right hand did most of the damage, landing a lucky strike right across Brutal's face and nicking his left eye. The ghoul also tried biting his left arm but his snapping jaws missed the mark. Missing its bite didn't matter much, however, as the same poison that paralyzed Tyberius, also coursed through Brutal's veins and quickly paralyzed him as well. The ghoul's blow landing with enough force to knock Brutal over, like a tree being felled, onto his side, frozen like a statue.

The last ghoul charged Mikell, clawing and scraping Mikell twice, not causing a lot of damage but once again the poison proved too much, causing Mikell to freeze in place.

Isa, standing next to Mikell, reacted just as the ghoul finished striking the priest. Isa moved forward and unleashed a powerful roundhouse kick that landed squarely on the ghoul's head, caving it in, resulting in the creature crumpling to the ground. Isa immediately spun around, attacking the ghoul that paralyzed Tyberius, but the foul creature turned to face the monk and the two quick punches that Isa threw both missed.

York, continuing to chant his song, drew his longsword advanced at the ghoul Isa had just attacked. He stabbed at the undead creature, but missed, almost wounding Isa in the process. His poor attack left him in an undefended position, and the ghoul savagely struck at the bard. His clawing attacks glanced off the bard's leather armor, but it managed to bite him squarely on the neck, causing a jagged gash. As the ghoul released the bard from its jaws, York toppled backwards, frozen in an awkward position.

Bealty threw another dart at the ghoul attacking Brutal, but the dart glanced off the ghoul's tough skin, doing no damage. With Brutal on the ground and Tyberius frozen, Julius had a good line of sight to the ghoul that Bealty just missed and loosed two arrows at the creature, both striking deep into its chest and with a gasp, it fell into a heap on top of Brutal.

Ariana focused in on the only ghoul left, but being surrounded by Tyberius, Isa, and York, it made taking a shot with her crossbow risky. Once again, she reached out, absorbing the magical energy around her, and canting her spell once more, "Invoco missili di forza, infallibili nella loro volo," she pointed her finger at her target and unleashed the energy. The three magical bolts, once again dodging their way through the traffic, thumped unerringly into the ghoul who immediately flopped to the ground, death reclaiming it once again.

As quickly as the battle started, it had ended. Ariana immediately ran to Tyberius who was still frozen in place. "Tyberius! Can you hear me?!" but the tall warrior did not respond, his body seemingly locked in place by whatever evil had overtaken him.

Isa moved quickly, reaching down and picking up the fallen ghoul that was on top Brutal, and flung it aside. With the last ghoul falling, Bealty also moved in quickly, checking Mikell to make sure he was okay, but like the others, he remained frozen, his eyes wide open in terror. Julius slung his bow over his shoulders and moved in to kneel beside York, but there was little he could do.

"What is wrong with them?!" asked Ariana, worry and a little desperation in her voice. She looked around at those who remained unaffected, but Bealty, Julius, and Isa said nothing, everyone had the same bewildered look. Sitting down on the ground, she put Tyberius's head on her lap, her arms over his shoulder.

Just as Ariana was sitting down, Mikell felt the grip of whatever had seized him, loosen, and he stumbled backwards, once again in control of his muscles. "Zuel protect us!" said Mikell, looking around. Mikell first glanced at York, near his feet, but seeing Tyberius on the ground and Brutal still immobile, he quickly moved toward the two warriors, looking over their wounds. Their injuries weren't severe, but a black pus oozed from each cut and bite mark.

Tyberius could feel his muscles finally relax and his head sank into Ariana's lap. "What happened?" asked the confused redheaded warrior.

"Thank the gods," said Ariana, letting out a breath as if she'd been holding it for a while, "those -- things -- somehow paralyzed you."

"What do ya mean: paralyzed me?" asked Tyberius.

Brutal began coughing, and, stumbling forward, was also released from his paralysis. Barely recovered from catching his balance, he immediately felt the stinging pain in his left eye. Bringing his left hand up to gently touch it, he was horrified to see blood on his hand as he pulled it away. "Shit, I cannot see out of my left eye!" he stated with urgency and fear in his voice. Looking around, and noticing for the first time, so many of his companions on the ground and not moving, he asked, "By the gods, what just happened?"

Before anyone could respond, York also recovered, Julius helping the bard back to his feet. With everyone now moving once again, relief washed over the small group.

Tyberius, sitting up, asked again, "What do ya mean he paralyzed me?" Everyone let out a nervous laugh, letting the tension of the moment ease.

"Thank Zuel, everyone is alive," said Mikell, making his way to Brutal. "Let me see your eye."

Brutal, gingerly removing his hand, said, "It hurts like a son of a bitch." Mikell did not want to alarm Brutal, but he could see significant damage to his friend's eye. Fortunately, it wasn't out of the socket, but there was a significant tear in the sclera of his eyeball, causing bleeding in his eye, and his iris was surrounded by a deep red shade. "Well, is it bad?" asked Brutal. "Can you heal it?" Brutal tried to put his hand back up, but Mikell stopped him, continuing to look at it.

Seeing blood on Brutal's hand that he was using to cover his eye, Mikell finally spoke. "The blood on your hand is not from your eye, it is from a deep cut above your eyebrow, and just under your left eye. He got you good, there is no doubt about that."

"But you can fix it, right?" asked Brutal, a second time.

Mikell shook his head. "Not right now, I told all of you that I had to use all my spells just to get us healed from yesterday." Mikell pulled out a clean strip of cloth from a pouch on his belt and gave it to Brutal. "Keep this on your eye, for now. I will pray tonight to Zuel and, in the morning, we will see if he can help you."

The stench, although still potent, was beginning to dissipate. Julius looked down at the pile of undead. "York, have you come across these creatures before?"

The bard, standing but still weak, leaned on Julius as he caught his breath. He shook his head. "No, but I do know what they were." He let the statement hang there in the air, not voluntarily continuing.

Ariana, still sitting on the ground next to Tyberius, gave the bard a cold look. "What the hell, York? Tell us what you know!"

York raised up a hand. "Let me catch my breath while we gather around the campfire." The bard turned, and with Julius's help, made his way back to the fire, lying down on his side, leaning on one elbow.

Mikell shouted at the bard as he was being helped away. "At least tell us what we should do with these bodies. We cannot just let them sit here stinking up the place," then added, "they cannot come back to life, can they?"

"I do not know what they were, and I do not know the answers to your questions, but I say we move them further away from camp and burn them," said Bealty breaking the silence.

Mikell nodded. "Yeah, that is a good idea, but how can we burn them? We barely have enough wood for the fire."

Bealty winked at Mikell. "You move the bodies, and I will see to burning them."

"Okay," Mikell said, then turning his attention to the monk and Tyberius, asked, "will you two carry the bodies over there a ways?"

The big monk's expression was stoic, and he did not say a word, but he leaned down and grabbed the arms of the now dead ghast. It was awful work, the stench almost unbearable, and no matter what limb or part of the body they grabbed, the skin tore away and what flesh remained ripped, making the bodies difficult to move. Although difficult and unpleasant, the two companions made quick work, moving the bodies about a hundred feet away and downwind. Tyberius and Isa returned to the camp, their eyes watering in their noses running as they took their seats around the fire.

Pouring some water onto his hands from his canteen, Tyberius washed his hands as best he could, then pouring some water onto a cloth, he washed his face. "Gods, those things are awful." Giving Bealty a look, he said, "Alright Beetle, your turn, go burn them...them...things." Hopping up, the rogue grabbed his backpack and slung it onto his back and wasn't more than a couple steps away from the fire before he disappeared into the night. Tyberius shook his head. "How does he do that?" referring to the halfling as he squinted into the night, trying to spot the rogue who was only a few feet away.

"So, York, what the hell were those...things?" asked Ariana.

York, still lying down, was wiping his face with a cloth, like Brutal, trying to get the stench out of his nostrils. "Undead, most obviously. The talkative one was most likely a ghast," the bard paused to cough while suppressing a gag, "I have never been paralyzed before, I thought my elvish blood was immune to such magic."

Tyberius looked up at the mention of magic. "You think it was magic they used?" he said as he apprehensively gave the ring on Ariana's finger a quick glance.

"Aye, their touch is magical, and obviously deadly," responded the bard.

That fact sent a shiver down Tyberius's spine. "Damn...fucking magic. What good comes of magic anyway?"

Ariana elbowed Tyberius in the arm. "Magic saved your life tonight, that is what."

Tyberius gave his fiancée a questioning look, and Julius chimed in, "She is right, her missiles took at least two of them down, including the gas-thing."

Tyberius's face softened. "Well, your magic is okay, I guess."

"You better get used to it, too," Ariana replied, again resting her head on Tyberius's shoulder.

"What were the other ones?" asked Mikell.

"Ghouls," said York, sounding tired.

"Ghouls," said Mikell, repeating the name, then after a moment, asked, "where do they come from?"

"Evil priests, evil ceremonies," York replied, turning onto his back, he covered his eyes with his right forearm, his head resting on a bedroll, using it as a pillow.

"Zuel protect us," Mikell said. "It must be powerful evil magic that can create such creatures -- binding them to an afterlife here." There was a long silence, then off in the distance, Mikell could see a large blaze building in intensity. "It looks like Beetle found the bodies."

"So, what the hell is 'Gilcurr' and where did you hear that name?" asked Brutal, changing the subject and looking at Ariana with his one good eye.

Ariana sat up. She had heard Skik say the word when he cast his last spell, but she used the brief time that sitting up afforded her to think of another scenario. "I…I saw that name a couple times in the documents that we found in the bunker."

Brutal immediately shot back, "You told the…" he searched for the word, "the ghost that the dwarf told you. So, which is it, Ariana?"

Ariana gave Brutal an icy stare. "I was trying to get as much information from him as possible. Do not forget, I am on your side, Brutal. Why are you questioning me like this? While your paralyzed ass was lying on the ground, the rest of us were defending you and killing those fuckers."

"Everyone calm down," said Mikell, his gruff voice ringing with a parental tone, "no one is accusing anyone of anything here."

"You could fool me," said Ariana, to which Julius gave Tyberius a look and raised a thin eyebrow. Tyberius saw the knowing look the ranger gave him and looked away.

* * * *

While the others were discussing the encounter, Bealty made his way to the stack of bodies. It wasn't hard to find, regardless of the wind direction, all Bealty had to do was follow the horrid stench. The bodies were beginning to decompose at a rapid rate, the magical and evil force that held them together and gave them re-life was gone, and now nature was reclaiming their physical bodies. Regardless of the stench, as bad as it was, Bealty couldn't resist the urge to see if any of the creatures had anything interesting or useful. Arriving at the pile of dead bodies, he felt a pang of guilt, like he was a grave robber, but such thoughts were fleeting, and soon the little rogue was rifling through what remained of their tattered clothing. Not surprisingly, the three ghouls had nothing; their clothing was so deteriorated that only one of them even had a pocket left, and it was empty. Bealty got to the ghast last, his clothing was at least in moderately good shape, albeit disgustingly filthy, damp, and, of course, outrageously noxious. An expert in lifting, some might say pick-pocketing, his nimble hands made short work of the ghast and soon pulled out a scroll case. Wiping his now filthy right hand on the ground to remove bits of flesh that were sticking to his skin, he examined the case. It was intricately crafted, octagonal in shape, with a small keyhole presenting itself on one side. Bealty carefully set it down and then, turning back to the pile of bodies, went through the ghast's clothing one more time, sure that there must be a key, but if there was, he could not find it. "Damn," he muttered to himself, but in reality he was already feeling the pleasant anticipation of picking the lock. Using his short sword like a scythe, he cut some of the drier tall grass and stuffed it underneath and around the pile of bodies. Reaching into his backpack he pulled out a vial, and popping the top off, he poured some of the liquid onto each of the bodies and some on the grass he had just cut and placed. Putting the top back on the vial, he placed it into his backpack while taking out a flint, and with a practiced stroke, using the blade of his dagger, he sent two sparks into the odorous pile. The grass quickly caught on fire, the flames quickly spreading across the bodies. Bealty stood, watching the fire build for a moment, pouring some water from his small canteen over his hands, he washed off the blood, pus, and pieces of flesh. Giving the burning heap one more look, he turned on his heel and, scooping up the scroll case, headed back to the small camp, glad to be away from the smell.

* * * *

Bealty walked back into the camp, the silence magnifying the tension in the air. "Hey, look what I found on the ghast," he said, holding up the scroll case. Everyone looked up, but nobody said anything. "It is locked, so I will have to pick it," he said with scholarly interest as he took a seat next to Ariana and Tyberius on a root sticking out of the ground.

"If that thing is trapped, and it goes off next to me, you are a dead halfling," Ariana said without looking at the rogue.

Bealty examined the scroll case from every possible angle and distance while using his small hands to feel the wood for any defects or abnormalities that might betray the presence of a trap. "There are no traps," but after a short pause, added, "at least not one that I can find -- and I am pretty good at this stuff." With one hand, Bealty brushed his long black bangs away from his face and tucked them behind his pointy ears.

"Why not just bust it open?" asked Tyberius, growing impatient as Bealty continued to investigate the case.

Bealty lowered the case slightly, looking over the top of it, giving

Tyberius a serious look. "Why would you swim across a river, when you could just walk across the bridge?"

"What in the eight hells are you talking about?" asked Tyberius, unsure of the analogy.

Bealty set the case down on the ground, and reaching into his black leather armor, he pulled out a set of lock picking tools. Selecting a small s-rake pick, Bealty carefully slipped the pick into the small keyhole and, as if the pick was an extension of his hand, began feeling around the inside of the lock. It took only a few seconds, and if the smile on Bealty's face didn't announce his success, the audible click did. Pulling the s-rake out, he slid it lovingly back into the black case, which he closed and placed back inside one of his many pockets. Bealty gave the case one more quick look for anything that might hint at a trap, but seeing nothing, he slowly opened the case, feeling the adrenaline rush of cracking a lock and the anticipation of finding out what was inside. Not surprisingly, there was a scroll inside, which he immediately pulled out and unrolled.

"Well, can you read it?" asked Ariana, hardly giving him a chance to get it unrolled.

Bealty didn't answer right away, taking his time to look the scroll over. After a moment, he rolled it back up and, looking at the others in the group, replied matter-of-factly, "Nope. It is written in a language, like the papers we found in the bunker. I do not understand it." Looking over at the bard, Bealty was about to say something, but it seemed that York was either asleep or not paying attention. "Is he asleep?" asked Bealty using the scroll to point at the bard.

Mikell spoke up first. "The undead seemed to have taken a toll on him, and, yes, he does appear to be asleep."

"Are you serious?" Ariana scoffed. "Wake his ass up. Time is not on our side and we cannot just sit here while he sleeps."

"What was the name the ghast mentioned?" asked Mikell, trying to change the subject.

"Kord," said Bealty, as he placed the scroll back into the case.

"Does that name mean anything to anyone? Brutal?" asked Mikell.

"No, I have never heard that name before," said Brutal, scratching an itch on his head. Everyone else shook their heads or kept silent.

"Well, would it not be nice if we had a bard, an elf no less, who has traveled Kardoon for hundreds of years, with us to ask this question?" asked Ariana rhetorically, her tone dripping with sarcasm.

"For the sake of Zuel, Ariana, let York have a few moments of rest," said Mikell, his gruff voice laden with parental chiding. Ariana, surprised by the rebuke, her face flushing red, eyes narrowing, looked to be on the verge of saying something, but she simply turned away from the cleric and, lying back, using her bedroll as a pillow, closed her eyes. Tyberius gave Mikell a look that said, 'Sorry,' but was careful not to verbalize it, then lay down on his side next to Ariana, protectively draping his long left arm over his fiancée.

"Well, we know that this undead fellow knew about both Gilcurr and Skik...and he knew about the bunker, too. In fact, I bet they were heading there with instructions," Bealty said, holding up the scroll case, its intricate carvings visible in the firelight.

"That is true," said Brutal. "Somehow we need to read this scroll."

"Let me see it," said Julius, standing up and walking around the fire to Bealty, his hand outstretched.

"Sure," said Bealty, handing him the scroll case.

Taking the case, Julius moved back to his spot and sat back down at his place, and carefully opening it, removed the parchment. Unrolling the scroll and turning it to better catch the firelight, he looked over the scrawled writing. After a few moments, Julius rolled the scroll back up and placed it into the case once again. Shaking his head, he said, "I too cannot read this writing, hopefully York will have better luck," said Julius, tossing the case over the fire to Bealty, who deftly nabbed the case out of midair.

Brutal shook his head, disbelief showing on his face. "How is all this possible? Gnolls, ghasts, ghouls, undead..." Brutal looked up to the heavens. "Soulmite, help me understand -- how does this bring me closer to my father?" There was, of course, no response, just the quiet night breeze on swishing the grass and the crackle of the fire. Brutal's head sank into the palm of his hands, covering his face, discovering for the first time the stubble of stiff whiskers, and realizing he hadn't shaved in three days. Rubbing his face, trying to regain his composure, he leaned backwards, clasping his hands in his lap, and looking up to the heavens said, "I did not think it would be this hard...what are we doing here?" he asked the night air, with a mixture of grief and uncertainty in his hushed voice.

"Druegar," said Bealty.

"What?" asked Brutal, a little surprised.

"Gnolls, ghasts, ghouls -- and druegar." He added with emphasis, "Do not forget to account for Skik."

"Yeah, I guess he slipped my mind," said Brutal.

"You are breaking the first rule of adventuring," said the halfling. "You gotta stick to the rules."

Brutal took a drink of water from his canteen, swallowing the cool liquid, hoping it would help to calm his emotions. "What rules would that be?" he asked, feeling a little refreshed, his question coming across a little light-hearted.

"It is a set of rules, and it ain't a joke," said Bealty matter-of-factly, his tone still in a helpful nature, like that of a school teacher.

Brutal, sensing the halfling's seriousness, asked again, "Well then, tell us what rule we have broken?"

"Not 'we,' you broke it, just now," replied Bealty, pointing a small finger in his direction.

"Okay, okay. What rule have I broken?" asked Brutal a third time.

Bealty was about to speak, but Mikell beat him to it. "Never ask why."

"Hey --" said Bealty. "I wanted to tell him."

"What do you mean, 'never ask why'?" asked Brutal, not sure, now, who he should be asking.

"Because," replied Bealty quickly, making sure Mikell couldn't answer this time.

Brutal waited a moment, expecting more of an explanation, but neither Bealty nor Mikell expounded further. "Well, go on, because why...?" he asked.

"I just told you why," said Bealty. "If you do not understand, then you think about it for a while."

"We are all tired," Mikell said, his gravelly voice stretching out with weariness. "It has been an exhausting two days -- both in our minds and our bodies, and we will not solve any problems tonight. We need to get some sleep. I, for one, need to pray for a while, and cannot be disturbed." Mikell gave Bealty a look. "We need to keep a watch, but this time, Beetle," the gruff cleric continued with a half-smile underneath his thick, broad mustache, "you can sleep through the night without an expected shift."

Bealty, not smiling, cocked his head. "Beetle? Really? You, too, now?" he asked.

"What?" asked Mikell. "That is your new nickname, is it not? I mean, it does have a clever ring to it."

"Yeah," said Tyberius in a hushed voice, barging into the conversation. "It gots a nice ring to it."

The little halfling gave Mikell a wry smile, then lying down, he covered himself with a blanket. Closing his eyes as he rolled onto his side and faced away from the cleric, he said, "Whatever."

"I will take the first watch tonight," said Brutal, shifting his weight to get into a more comfortable position. Even Isa looked thankful, the half-orc's face looking haggard, as even he lay down, rather than sitting in his usual meditative position. It wasn't long, and the large half-orc, who, in the dark, looked like a mound of earth under his brown robes, fell asleep, snoring loudly. Despite the grating sounds coming from Isa, the others also soon drifted off, leaving Brutal alone with his thoughts, 'just like at home,' he thought to himself, the only thing missing was the eyeless knot, ever watching him, on the beam above his bed.

The night was cold, a harsh reminder that Darkal, the coldest season, was not far off. Everyone recognized this was not an ideal time to be heading into a region, unforgiving by its very nature; known for its rugged terrain and forbidding inhabitants. Caravans traveling through the Cruel Pass did so with heavy escorts, and even that was sometimes not enough to stave off disaster. They weren't, technically, even on the Cruel Road, or even in the Cruel Pass, thought Brutal to himself, and they had already encountered creatures that could only come out of a nightmare. "Soulmite, please, help us," Brutal whispered in prayer, looking up at the heavens. "We are doing your bidding, but we are lost out here..." Brutal felt no response, like his prayer had not been heard, which made his heart sink. Unrolling his blanket, Brutal threw it around his shoulders and head, turning it into a cloak-like garment, and he scooched a little closer to the fire, enjoying the extra warmth it provided. It was difficult to stay awake, but the pain in his eye and the effort of keeping the fire going kept sleep at bay. After a couple hours, he awoke Julius to take the next shift, and despite the pain, his complete exhaustion finally led to sleep, and his tired body and mind finally got some rest. Fortunately, for all the companions, the rest of the night passed by in peace.

* * * *

Bealty was the first one up, just as the first glow of the sun began to show over the horizon. The sky had cleared off during the night, augmenting the cold, but it also allowed the near full moon, missing just a small corner, to light up the sky. Tyberius was awake, standing near the fire, his hands extended over the flames to capture more of the warmth it was casting off. Bealty was still fully clothed and armored, one of the benefits of wearing padded leather armor, allowing him to slowly and silently slide out from underneath his blanket and roll away from the firelight. Glancing once more at Tyberius, who seemingly did not notice the movement, Bealty gracefully rolled over and up onto his feet and hands, like a cat, disappearing into the grass. Once he was several yards away, he was able to stand up fully, which still did not get his head above most of the blades of grass, and he continued his walk, heading to where he had burned the undead bodies. The combined and now competing light of the moon and the brightening skyline provided just enough light for the halfling to see well enough. Arriving at the small patch of scorched ground, he was surprised to see no trace of the bodies: not a tooth, or piece of bone, just a couple fragments of their tattered garments, blown by the wind and hung up in the tall grass surrounding the burned and blackened area, remained. 'No stench,' either, he thought to himself. He looked around the blackened ground, using the toe of his boot to dig through the soot and debris of burnt grass.

Feeling mother nature call, Tyberius stood up, yawing, and moved a little way away from camp to relieve himself. While doing so, he surveyed the campsite, noticing, with some alarm, that Bealty was nowhere to be seen. "Shit," he whispered, finishing up his business. With the dawn light shedding some light, it wasn't hard to find the little rogue, who was standing in the blackened ashes, where the ghouls had been. Curious, he decided to go see what the halfling was up to, and in no time, his large strides closed the distance. "What are ya doing, Beetle?" asked Tyberius, emphasizing the rogue's new nickname both in tone and with his large grin.

"Nothing," said Bealty, not even looking up.

"Aw, bullshit -- you be looking for something, what is it?" Tyberius said, continuing to pry.

"Where is Ariana?" asked Beetle, hoping to change the subject.

"Back by the fire..." said Tyberius, glancing and nodding back in the direction of the camp.

Before Tyberius could finish, Bealty interrupted, "Is York awake?"

"Nah, he still be sleeping," answered Tyberius, then added, "but Isa is up. Doin' some kind of weird stretching or something." Tyberius snickered a little. "Ain't he the damnedest sight -- a huge half-orc prancing around all monk like? I ain't sure what is more surprising so far, seeing dead corpses walking around like they was alive, or watching a huge half-orc stretching in the morning?"

"What to do you mean, 'monk like'?" asked Bealty, looking up for the first time, "He is a monk."

"Well, c'mon, do you believe he is a real monk?" Tyberius said, putting his hands on his hips. "What kind of moneferry, or whatever the hell you call it, would take him as a member?"

"You mean as a brother?" asked Bealty, correcting his tall friend.

"No, ya little bastard, a member of the clan...or whatever," said Tyberius, irritation beginning to creep into his tone. "I came over here to see if I could help you," he began, gesturing with his arms, "with, well... whatever the hell ya were doin' here, but fuck that, I can tell ya ain't wanting my help." Tyberius waved a hand as he walked away, his brisk steps taking him back to the little camp a short distance away.

Bealty poked his toe around the soot and ashes for another minute, relying on his keen eye for detail and finding things that didn't belong, but he found nothing. "Hmmm, maybe Skik has the key," he said, speaking his thoughts out loud while one of his small hands scratched his chin.

* * * *

Everyone was waking up as Bealty walked back into camp, some were still sitting, but others were up and already starting the ritual of getting ready for the next day's travel, which by all accounts would likely be more treacherous, and difficult, than the day before. Everyone, except Brutal, who still was lying on his side. "C'mon, B," said Tyberius, giving his friend a light kick in the butt, literally. "We gotta get moving, we have family to rescue and some damn gnolls to kill."

Brutal rolled over onto his back, his left arm draped over his eyes. "I...I cannot go."

Tyberius looked over at Mikell, concern in his voice as he said, "I think you better get over here, Brutal needs your help."

Mikell did not have his chain mail on yet but stood up and walked over to Brutal. Kneeling next to his friend, he placed a gentle touch on Brutal's arm that was covering his eyes. "Remove your arm, Brutal, so I can see what is going on."

Brutal did not move his arm. "I am totally blind, Mikell. I...I opened my eyes a few minutes ago. The pain in my left eye is almost unbearable, and now I cannot see out of my right eye -- it was just a foggy blackness." Brutal paused for a second, taking a deep breath, trying to collect himself. "That god-damned thing blinded me."

"Zuel is powerful, Brutal, have some faith." Mikell's voice was gruff as always, but it could be comforting when he needed it to be.

"This is not a cut, I am fucking blind." Brutal's voice was getting louder.

"Take your arm away," commanded Mikell, tightening his grip on Brutal's forearm and raising his voice to match Brutal's, "and let me do my job, so you can do yours." Everyone was awake now, sitting up to see what was going on, watching the back and forth. Brutal felt Mikell's powerful grip on his forearm, he was picturing the cleric's bushy black eyebrows furrowed into a frown, his thick black mustache, his pursed lips, and a concerned but slightly agitated expression on his face. In all this, he would be correct. Slowly, Brutal moved his arm away. It took all

424

Mikell's constitution and self-control not to gasp at the gruesome sight. Brutal's left eye had been overtaken by coagulated pools of blood, his eye had turned a deep dark red, almost black, and although his right eye had not sustained any injury that he could see, the same thing was starting to happen. "I am not sure what is happening here," said Mikell, "so I will need to do two things."

"What two things?" asked Brutal.

Mikell took a deep breath and placed Brutal's arm back over his eyes. "You may be afflicted with something...a disease, or something, I am not sure -- but whatever happened to your left eye is now happening to your right eye, so first I want to have Zuel purify your body. Once that is done, I will attempt to restore your sight."

"No fuck'n way.... You can do all that?" asked Tyberius in a hushed voice mixed with mystification.

"Shhh, let Mikell do his thing," scolded Ariana, not taking her focus off the cleric as she watched intently.

Mikell, not allowing or showing any distraction from Tyberius's comments, knelt on both knees, grasping his holy symbol in his left hand, raising his right hand to the heavens, his face bowed in prayer. After a brief pause, he began to cant his prayer, his right hand extended, moving and tracing symbols over Brutal's body. As the long, complicated, prayer progressed, Brutal could feel a warm sensation creeping up his body. The feeling started in his toes, then washing up through his legs, into his abdomen, then into his chest, then out through his arms, and into his hands, until finally his head felt light. He had the feeling that his body was floating. To those watching, they could see a visible light flowing from Mikell's hand, gushing into Brutal's body, and when Mikell finally laid his hands on the warrior's body, Brutal lit up in a flash and his body convulsed. Mikell held onto Brutal's arms through the whole process and repeated the canting more than a few times, the process taking what seemed like a long time to the onlookers. Upon completion of the spell, Mikell stood up. "Take your arm away from your face," he commanded, his voice gruff and edgy, as he could still feel the remnants of the holiness that had passed through him, and into his friend.

Brutal could still feel the warmth flowing through his veins, but

425

he no longer felt light-headed. Taking his arm away, he slowly sat up, propping himself with his arms behind him. He looked around. "The pain is gone, but I still only see darkness...is that supposed to happen?" he asked, concern and fear still in his voice.

Mikell looked at Brutal's face and was pleased. The gruesome visage that was there just moments before was gone, replaced by Brutal's normal eyes, both in structure and color. "Zuel is amazing!" said Mikell, clapping his hands together. "The good news is your eyes look normal once again -- Zuel has purified the disease from your body. You have a new scar, which makes you slightly uglier than before, if that is possible, but Zuel cannot be expected to solve all your problems." Everyone let out a collective, if not reserved chuckle, at the priest's small joke, except Brutal. Even York, who didn't seem to laugh at much, smiled, as he recorded the events in his journal.

"But you can still fix my sight, right?" asked Brutal, hope creeping into his tone.

"Well, I guess, we should not expect gratitude quite yet," said Mikell, using his right hand to smooth out his thick mustache, "perhaps we should proceed before you lose total faith." Mikell reached down and grabbed Brutal by his armpits. "Stand up and receive Zuel's touch," he said as he helped the warrior to his feet. Mikell held the holy symbol with his left hand and began to cant the spell while tracing holy symbols in the air around Brutal's head and face. Once again, Mikell's prayer was a long, complex, crescendo and with the spell's completion, Mikell touched Brutal's forehead with a quick tap of his index finger. Upon his touch, a vibrant light leapt from Mikell's hand and was absorbed into Brutal's head. Pulling his hand away from Brutal, Mikell looked into the warrior's eyes.

Brutal blinked, the darkness was replaced by a light, that ironically was blinding at first, but very quickly receded, and as it did so, his vision came back. First it was lights, then shapes, and then it all came back into focus, and he could see! Mikell was standing in front of him, still holding his holy symbol, an expectant look on his face. "I have never felt such warm energy flowing in my body, and yes, I can see again. Thank you, Mikell, you have grown very powerful!" Brutal stepped forward and gave the priest a warrior handshake. "I am lucky to count you as a friend!"

Mikell beamed with pride, the rising sun glinting off the bald, slightly reddened skin on his head, and a broad smile showing underneath his thick black mustache. "No need to thank me... Praise be to Zuel -- I am just a vessel for his greatness."

"That was amazing, Mikell," Ariana said, truly impressed by the display of magic.

"Wow, yeah, that was pretty incredible," Bealty said, missing the matching enthusiasm or conviction, before continuing, "Well, now that that is all out of the way, we do have the matter of a scroll we cannot read." As he spoke, the halfling walked over to York, who was still sitting down, and extended the scroll case to the bard.

"You truly are an irreverent breed," said Mikell, a chuckle in his tone.

"What?" Bealty shrugged, giving Mikell a quick, respectful look. "Zuel is great, what more do we need to know?" Bealty turned his attention back to York, who still had not taken the case. "It is time we find out what this scroll says, unless you are still too tired?"

York put his pen and journal down on his blanket, which was over his lap, and reaching out took the case. "Hmm, exquisite workmanship on the case," York said as he clicked open the latch, and, lifting the lid back, revealed the parchment inside. Taking it out, he unrolled the paper and examined the writing, saying, "Hmmm, interestingly good penmanship... Fellpon... Krykl... Mixnor... Elgar."

"What did you just say?" asked Tyberius, interrupting York.

York looked up. "Elgar," he replied.

"My name is in there? Can you actually read that crap?" asked Tyberius.

York breathed a heavy sigh. "Yes, my good man, I can read this 'crap,'" he said with disdain in his voice. "Well, admittedly, maybe not every word, but I can read enough to know what it says."

"What language is it written in?" asked Mikell.

"A dialect known and used by evil..." York started.

"Are you saying it is written in an 'evil' language?" asked Julius, interrupting.

"Ah, well, that is a bit of a simplistic way of putting it," York replied, with unusual patience, "-- kind of like saying all things round are wheels. Are all wheels round, yes, but to describe them as just being round, is simplistic and not enough to capture the essence of what makes it a wheel."

"What in the eight hells are you talkin' about?" asked Tyberius. "And who cares anyway what damn language it is -- what does it say?"

"The language might tell us something about who wrote it," Mikell answered.

"Aha," York said, pointing a finger at the cleric. "Mikell is correct; it does tell me something about the author of this note." York paused, lending a little tension to the moment. "The author signed the note 'K,' and if I remember correctly, the ghast may have told us his name, quite nice of him, but then he thought we would be dead by now..."

"Go on, dammit!" said Tyberius impatiently.

York cleared his throat. "No appreciation for a good telling... Anyway, the ghast told us a name last night: Kord, I believe it was, and this is signed 'K,' so I can only imagine that Kord authored the letter. The impeccable penmanship, and," York continued, giving Mikell a nod of recognition, "the language it is written in, I am guessing Kord is wealthy, educated, and of course, evil. It seems 'K' is directing some sort of war against Kardoon, so that means he could be a warrior, a priest, or perhaps even undead himself."

"Zuel protect us," said Mikell, unconsciously grabbing his holy symbol with his right hand, taking comfort in its cool silver. "What kind of power does this Kord have to control wights, ghouls, gnolls, dwarves..."

"That may not be the worst news," said York interrupting Mikell. "This note confirms," York paused again, letting the comment settle in, "that Brutal's family was targeted to be killed, but that is not all." York looked at Tyberius. "It says the Elgar family was the primary target, and Brutal's was secondary."

"What?" asked Tyberius, shocked. "How could those...those," Tyberius stumbled, looking for the right words and names, finally pointing toward the burned patch of grass, "those evil sons of bitches even know about us?" Before anyone could answer, he went on. "And why

428

would they want me and my family dead? For what purpose?" Nobody said anything, but Ariana ran her hand through Tyberius's short red hair, putting her arm around his shoulder. The silence hung uncomfortably.

"Perhaps," said the bard, breaking into everyone's dark thoughts, "the only good news, is it sounds like they are behind schedule in completing the bunker."

"If there are more bunkers," said Julius, "there could be a hundred or maybe even more gnolls, and the gods only know what else, being lodged within a day or two of Telfar."

"Julius is right," said Ariana. "It is an army -- building up right under the nose of Theol Kardoon and his forces."

"But why attack Telfar?" asked Mikell to no one in particular. "What, or who, does that gain? We are missing something."

"Maybe this is part of Soulmite's plan -- that we need to find this Kord and kill him," stated Brutal. "Maybe everything, all these other plans, just fall apart."

"Yeah -- cut off the head of the snake," added Tyberius, making a hacking motion with his hand.

"We do know where Kord is," said York, "or at least was: Gilcurr."

"Yeah, great, but where is Gilcurr?" asked Ariana, throwing up her arms.

"I am sure I can track them, for quite a distance," said Julius, "but after a couple days, nature tends to start covering the tracks."

"I bet I know," said Bealty, causing everyone to look at him. "It is as simple as Straight time...Crooked time."

"Please, Beetle, no riddles right now," said Mikell, speaking, he was sure, for everyone. "Just tell us what you are suggesting."

Beetle stood up and drew his dagger. "It is not a riddle, it is years of common sense condensed into those two little statements." Bealty drew a straight line into the dirt and next to that, a line that zig-zagged. Pointing to the line that zig-zagged, he continued. "Plenty of time," then pointing to the straight line, "short on time." Bealty looked up, but he could tell by the looks on their faces, that they were not getting his point. "The letter said Skik was behind schedule." Bealty pointed to the straight line again. "Those undead were not taking the scenic route, I guarantee you that, which means they were doing straight time. Meaning they moved in a straight line from where they came from. Given the letter was from Kord, and assuming Kord was in Gilcurr at the time, all we have to do is have Julius track their movement for a while, and I bet you they walked in a straight line to right here." Bealty stabbed the ground with his dagger, punctuating his point.

"That is very clever, Bealty, but what about the gnolls that have our family prisoner?" Ariana asked, her tone cold. "We must find them first."

"She is right," said Brutal. "We cannot abandon the gnolls, we have to find them first."

"If we can catch them today, we should be able to make it back to this spot," Julius said, "and still track the undead far enough to give Bealty's logic a chance."

"Good, let us get moving then, we have no time to lose..." Mikell said, then turning to Bealty, he put a firm hand on his little companion's shoulder. "We are on 'straight time.'"

"Shit, yeah, straight time!" said Tyberius, his wide grin accompanied also by a look of anticipation.

* * * *

Julius rode Jasper on ahead, following the easy and obvious trail left by the gnolls. They were much closer than he had thought, and by late morning, he caught up with the motley band of humanoids. His first glimpse was that of the gnolls ascending a small hill and going over the other side, each silhouette vanishing over the crest of the hill. He waited a few minutes before trotting Jasper to the base of the hill, where he dismounted. Making his way up the hill and nearing the crest, he got down onto his stomach and began to crawl through the grass. Finally at the top of the hill, he could see a long distance, the plains spreading out before him, with even larger hills on the horizon, and even further in the distance, loomed the white peaks of the Doubtless Mountains. The view was breathtaking, but he did not enjoy it for long, as the sight below him on the plain made his heart sink. The party of gnolls they had been seeking -- eight in all, pulling along three prisoners, was halted at the base of the hill -- but the truly horrifying, and unexpected part of what he saw, were the two approaching giants from the north, hill giants if he had to guess. Each wore simple hides and carried a club that was actually a small tree. They took long slow strides, heading right toward the gnolls. Julius wondered, as he watched, if the giants were about to attack the gnolls, but the gnolls were not acting or doing anything to indicate they were preparing for a fight. Sure enough, the giants met up with the gnolls, and the two groups appeared to be communicating, not fighting. He was too far away to hear the conversations, even with his keen elven ears, but when one of the gnolls pointed in his direction, the two giants nodded their large heads and began walking in his direction. After the brief meeting, the gnolls continued hauling their prisoners away to the north while the giants began rapidly closing the distance to his position with their long strides.

"Notria, protect us," Julius said in a hushed voice as he quickly crawled back down the hill. Once he knew he could stand up, he began running to Jasper, who was casually munching on some grass. Placing a foot into a stirrup, he practically jumped into the saddle, and giving the horse a quick kick, galloped off, retracing his path back to his friends. Julius glanced back over his shoulder periodically, and he was surprised at how soon he was able to see the heads of the giants bobbing up and down as they had already made their way up the large hill he had just left. The great length of their strides more than made up for their plodding gait and resulted in a deceptively fast pace -- at least over long distances. Jasper's speed slowly outdistanced the giants, but only marginally, and Julius knew that once he got back to his companions, there would be precious little time to prepare, so he had Jasper gallop for short intervals, hoping the extra distance created would provide some additional, and valuable, time.

CHAPTER TWENTY SIX

Two Tasks

YEAR: AG 1172, Month of Sepu

"SINCE YOU HAVE SCATTERED KRYKL'S ARMY to the four winds, the current objective will be to rebuild another insurgent force, here," Marshal Krugar stabbed his finger on the map, indicating a position in the hills of the Cruel Pass, marked with the name: Gilcurr.

Kord looked up from the map to eye the marshal. "Why do you implicate me in your failure?"

Krugar stood up, his back stiffening. "You piece of shit -- you know you disobeyed my orders!"

"Who are you talking to? Ghosts?" asked Kord.

"He does not remember, Marshal, and I would advise you to leave the past in the past, like water under the bridge," said Judar.

Kord took a couple steps around the large table, dragging his fingers along its finely sanded surface. "No, tell me more, Marshal, I want to know what happened -- how I scattered, this Krykl's, forces."

"No, that is not necessary information," said Judar, his voice firm. "You are here to serve me, and that is all you need to know, right now..."

"Blick," said Kord, interrupting the cleric. "I am here to serve Blick."

"I serve Blick, which means you serve Blick, but make no mistake," Judar grinned his toothy grin, "you serve me first."

"I will make you suffer, you unbeliever," Kord said, giving the marshal a discomforting glare, taking a few more steps around the table, nearing Krugar.

"Stop, I command you!" said Judar. Kord's feet betrayed him, it was as if his feet were bolted to the ground, no matter how hard he tried, he could not take another step. "Get on your knees," Judar ordered. Kord fought the compulsion to obey, but it was a short battle, and he soon found himself kneeling, the hatred he felt for both these men went to his very core, and he wished to strike out, but his arms felt weak, and he could not. "You see, I am your master -- it was my life force that has been imbued into you -- and you will always be a slave for me alone to command."

"He is more dangerous now than he ever was alive -- he will kill us the first chance he has," Krugar said through clenched teeth.

"Nonsense," Judar said with a wave of his hand. "He cannot harm either of us, is that understood, Kord?"

"I shall not harm either of you -- that is understood," replied Kord, emotionless, as if it were scripted.

"Then rise and listen to what you must do," said Judar. Kord did as he was commanded, rising effortlessly, supernaturally, to his feet.

Krugar pointed again to the map. "You will go to the ogre village of Gilcurr, and use that as your base of operations. From there you will need to muster all the lower humanoid races you can. They will follow you if they fear you enough," Krugar paused for a second, giving the Death Knight a look, noting the black, soulless pits of his eyes, and his already decaying features, "and that should not be a problem."

"Krykl will be there, waiting for you, he will do as you ask," said Judar. "He knows you are in command."

"But, do not let your guard down, Krykl will not like the change," warned Marshal Krugar. "He will destroy you if he thinks he can."

Kord looked at the marshal. "I will slaughter him then."

Marshal Krugar laughed, gesturing at Kord but talking to Judar, he said, "This is what I am telling you. He will want to kill everything -- he cannot lead an army."

Judar nodded, conceding that it could be a problem. "You need to pick and choose when you kill. If you kill everything, you will have no leaders or followers left, and although Krykl is very dangerous, that also makes him very useful."

"He is like a babe in the woods here -- with his memory gone, he has no life experience to draw from," said Krugar.

"You are partially right, he does not remember details of his past, but he does retain his life experiences," said Judar. "When he fights, it will be like a learned reflex, when he commands the army, it will be like an invisible hand guiding him. He will not know how or why he knows -- but he will know."

"You speak of me like I am an infant," Kord said with a gravelly hiss, pounding his fist on the table.

"Yes, in a few ways you are...but in more ways, you are not," said Judar. "You are more powerful than anything else on Thran."

"I can create much more suffering if you simply let me loose into this world of weaklings," said Kord, gesturing with a wave of his hand at the map on the table.

"I am sure you could. But you forget your whole purpose here: me," Krugar said, stabbing a finger into his own chest. "What good would that do me, to have some rogue, undead, lunatic terrorizing Kardoon?"

Kord's empty sockets narrowed, the black voids burrowing into the marshal, his gravelly voice etched with eternity. "I will bring no good to anyone, you can count on that, Marshal."

Marshal Krugar looked at Judar, the priest interjected, "It was a very poor choice of words, what the marshal meant was benefit. There must be an end to the means, meaning, there must be a reason for all that we do, including you."

Cocking his head slightly, Kord asked, "And to what end does the suffering I will inflict serve you?"

"It keeps Marshal Krugar and myself in positions of power within the Bindal court," answered Judar.

Kord let out a raspy hiss, the closest thing he could muster to a chuckle. "And what do mortal positions matter to Blick? What do I care what positions you hold?"

"The only reason you exist is to benefit the two of us," Krugar said, pointing to Judar and then himself, "and the day that is not true is the day you go back to the hell you came from."

There was a short pause before Kord responded, as if he were contemplating something, but then quickly moved on. "We shall see. For now, I will do as you bid -- if for no other reason, than to see what possibilities exist outside this damnable tent."

"I expect you to have at least five thousand humanoids, no less, ready to fight in three years. Nobody ventures into the hills around the Cruel Pass, so if you keep your main force in Gilcurr, you will not be discovered. Also in this time frame, you will need to construct bunkers near Westal, Whiteal, Telfar, Castor, and, of course, Bindal. It is from these underground bunkers that we will harass and fight Theol's forces."

"Only five thousand?" asked Kord.

Now it was Marshal Krugar's turn to laugh. "You are an ambitious son of a bitch, just like Anthall, I will grant you that. Maybe, after all, there is some of him buried in your carcass." Judar looked uncomfortable at the mention of Anthall's name, which Krugar noticed, and pausing very briefly, pondering that statement, the marshal concluded, "Five thousand will be plenty to do what we need."

"Why not raise forty thousand and kill everyone in all these cities?" Kord asked.

"Ah, well, then that comes back to the benefit discussion we just had," Krugar was careful to enunciate the word 'benefit.' "It would not benefit Judar or myself for you to kill every fucking person!"

Kord was about to respond when he heard words whispering in his mind, 'Physical punishment, while amusing, is the cheapest form of suffering.' The voice was so familiar, fatherly, but he could not place it. He looked at Judar to see if somehow it was him, but the priest was not looking at him. Kord stood up straight. "Five thousand, in three years. I will not fail."

"Well, thank the gods... Hopefully you will obey orders this time," said Krugar.

"The gods have nothing to do with this," said Kord, interrupting, "nor will they be able to stop me."

"Do not speak such heresy," scolded Judar, "you are indeed powerful on Thran, but do not presume to defeat gods. We serve Blick, never forget that."

"Blick will not be the one trying to stop me," said Kord, his scratchy voice deep with sincerity.

"Now that you know what you must do, it is time that we tell you what happens next," said Judar, looking at Kord from across the table. Kord looked up, and Judar continued, "You cannot be seen with us, so you will need to follow along with the next part of the plan."

"We have been telling the troops that the reason we have not been able to leave, is that you were too badly injured to move, and Judar has been trying to save your life," Krugar paused, "but now we will tell them that you died, which, ironically, is the truth. We will bury you, fully armored and with your weapons, as a true warrior and general should be."

"Once we are gone, you can dig yourself out and begin your mission," said Judar, who began rolling up one of the maps. "We will leave you with several maps to help you with your planning, although Krykl will have some as well, back in Gilcurr."

"Is that going to be a problem?" asked Krugar.

Kord wanted to ask what general he was supposed to be, he craved the information, but instead, he just shook his head. "No. When do we begin?"

"Right now," replied Krugar.

Judar and the marshal helped put Anthall's armor onto Kord, each piece fitting perfectly. With each piece of armor that was attached, Kord felt like a piece of himself was being returned and awoken. Once they had his armor on, they handed him his skull-shaped helmet. Taking it in his hand, he felt its familiar weight and slowly placed it on his head.

"Magnificent," said Judar, "just magnificent."

"What are you now, his fucking girlfriend?" asked Krugar, some irritation in his voice, causing Judar's face to flush red with anger. "This is not a beauty contest, we need to bury him and get this damn army moving."

Judar was about to say something, but Kord spoke first. "Yes, the sooner we get the army away, the sooner I can begin."

"You should show me more respect, Marshal," Judar said through his pointy teeth, "your plans depend heavily on me, and Kord, now."

Krugar turned to face the evil priest of Blick. "Is that a threat, Judar? Are you threatening me?" Krugar took a few steps closer to the priest until he was within a sword's length, his face was dark and menacing. "How many of my men do you think you can kill before you and your undead nightmare here," Krugar motioned toward Kord, "are overcome? Fifty? One Hundred? Two hundred?" Krugar took another step closer. "Kord may serve you, but you serve me." Krugar pushed a sturdy finger into the chain mail shirt of the priest, who defiantly returned the marshal's stare, but after a few seconds Judar looked away. "Yes, yes, look away little priest -- and do not forget your place -- which is below me." Kord watched the exchange, his burning eyes, hidden behind his helmet, but the lower half of his face was still exposed, and one corner of his mouth curled upwards, ever so slightly.

"Where shall I lay?" asked Kord.

Krugar's gaze lingered momentarily on Judar, then he turned to face the Death Knight and pointed at a stretcher leaning against the south side of the tent. "Put that stretcher on the ground and lay on it."

Kord did as he was told, and as he lay down, he closed his eyes and crossed his arms across his chest. While he lay there, he searched his mind, for what he did not know, but his mind was so...so blank. Anthall was the name Krugar had mentioned, so he searched his mind, but although the name sounded familiar, he could not place it in his mind. It was just another name...yet it held some importance, he was sure, so, 'task two,' he thought to himself, was to find out why it was important and what the hell it meant to him.

* * * *

The procession was not grand, and he never once opened his eyes, but he could feel a light rain pattering down onto his helmet and face and his exposed chin, making little pinging sounds as larger drops bounced off his armor, or the armor of the people around him. There was no service, no one spoke, and no eulogy, although every now and then he would hear a voice as his body passed by saying something like, "May Soulmite bless you, General," or "Rest in peace, General." Kord wanted to rise and strike them all down, the mention of Soulmite's name burned in his blood. He was barely able to control the anger and hatred he felt welling up inside of him, but he did as he was commanded by Judar: to lie motionless, to allow himself to be buried, and then wait at least a full day before trying to make his way out of the grave. Soon enough, he felt himself being lowered into the grave, quickly followed by dirt and rocks being shoveled on top of him, until at last he was completely buried, the weight of the dirt and rocks, conveying an odd feeling of comfort to him. Of course, he did not sleep, that mortal requirement no longer was necessary for him, and so he bided his time, slowly counting in his head to one hundred thousand, which he did by counting to ten thousand ten times, focusing on a finger each time he did.

* * * *

Much time passed, and Kord was about halfway through his counting, just finishing up his right hand, when the silence was broken by the sound of digging from above. 'What is this?' he wondered to himself as the weight of the dirt was beginning to lessen, and the sounds, and voices started to become clearer.

"Boys, we ain't gonna have to work another day in our life," said an excited, commanding male sounding voice as the sound of shovel pierced the dirt above Kord. "Honestly, I thought we might have to kill some other fuckers who had the same idea we did."

"Oh yeah! I git his sword, that thing is worth a bunch of gold I bet!" said another higher pitched voice that sounded farther away.

"Shut up, you idiots. We stick to the plan, we take all the shit, and we sell it all in Erdeep, and then we split the gold," said the commanding voice, followed by another dig with the spade.

'Erdeep,' Kord thought to himself, the place was familiar, like it was from a dream long ago, but the memory was too clouded. After a few more shovels of digging, his thoughts returned to the moment at hand. 'Grave robbers,' thought Kord to himself, the marshal's plans were already falling apart, 'so I will have to improvise.'

The men kept talking until finally a spade clanked into Kord's breastplate. "Hot shit, boys, we just hit the general and his money load!" Kord could hear several voices above snicker with excitement.

* * * *

Up on top were six men. Each taking turns at digging, except

Kirsh, who was an officer in the Kardoon army who sat on his warhorse, supervising the excavation. Two spears were struck into the ground by the edge of the grave, each with a lantern hanging from the end of the spear, illuminating the digging operation. At the moment, Tyree and Greggory, two peasant soldiers, were standing almost shoulder deep in the grave, digging, and it was Tyree's shovel that first struck Kord. Wagard, Soxust, and Pex, also peasant soldiers, were sitting, resting, leaning their backs against the tall rock outcropping that Kord had stood upon days earlier.

"Well, keep fucking digging!" said Kirsh. "And be careful not to fucking dent the shit or break anything -- if ya do it will come out of your end of the cut!"

"It ain't my fault, boss!" said Tyree, being more careful now with his shovel.

"Oh yeah? Why not get your ass down here and dig if ya's so worried!" said Greggory, defiance in his voice.

"I am an officer, remember who you are talking to, soldier!" said Kirsh angrily.

"Not no more," said Greggory. "The way I see it we all just quit the army when we came back here." Wiping sweat and dirt from his face with his forearm, Greggory looked up at Kirsh. "Now we is all the same."

"This was my idea," said Kirsh, "and I am still the leader of this group, do not forget your place. Remember, we have a nice fresh grave we can fill with however many bodies that disagree with me!"

"Shut up, Greggory!" said Tyree. "Just dig like you were told and we will all be rich."

"Fuck you, Tyree, I will say whatever I want," said Greggory, who began digging again, this time more carefully.

Tyree carefully shoved the spade into the dirt again, but this time Kord reached his right hand up and grabbed the shovel just above the spade, his gauntleted fist wrapping tightly around the shaft. The lanterns still left much of the pit dark and shadows bounced around the bottom of the grave, making it difficult to see anything with great detail. "What da hell?" said Tyree, as he tried to pull the shovel up to throw the dirt over the lip of the grave. He pulled as hard as he could, but the shovel wouldn't budge. "Aw, fuck'n hell, my shovel is stuck, somehow, in the son of a bitch!

This ain't coming out of my cut neither!" said Tyree.

Greggory laughed. "You weakling, give me that thing." Tyree switched places with Greggory. Greggory was slightly bigger than Tyree, and sure of himself as he grabbed the long shaft of the shovel, but, heaving with all his might, the shovel still would not budge. After grunting and groaning through a few tries, Greggory stopped, saying, "Hand me the dang lantern so I can get a better look at what is goin' on here."

Nobody moved, so Kirsh shot a look at Pex. "Well, get him a damn lantern!" Pex hopped up and lighting an extra lantern, handed it down to Greggory. Taking it, Greggory leaned down, holding the lantern next to the spade of the shovel, which was only about halfway dug into the dirt. The light of the lantern illuminated an even more surprising, confusing, and ominous picture. "Well, what the hell?" asked Kirsh from above impatiently.

"How the hell?" asked Greggory to himself, looking quizzically at the scene before him. "It looks like..." He ran his fingers through his hair, thinking what he was about to say next sounded idiotic and unbelievable. "It looks like the fucker's hand somehow got wrapped around the shaft of the shovel..." Greggory paused again. "And ain't letting let go."

"What kind of stupid games are you two playing down there?" asked Kirsh.

"No game," said Tyree, crouched down, looking at the strange scene: a gauntleted hand sticking up through the dirt, holding onto the bottom of the shovel's handle. Looking at Greggory standing in the grave next to him, he asked more quietly, "Ain't that fucking somthin'? How is that possible?"

Greggory hesitantly reached out and touched the gauntleted fingers. Nothing happened. With a little more confidence, he grabbed at the fingers, trying to pry open the hand, but he could not and gave up. "I ain't never seen something like that," then looking at Tyree with fear in his eyes, added, "It ain't..." he searched for the right word, "natural -- that is for damn sure."

Seeing the fear in Greggory's eyes, for the first time Tyree felt a gnawing fear grasping at his own soul and whispered, "Screw this, I am done with this shit. Ain't no coin worth this kind of demon-ation." As Tyree finished his statement, Kord, using the dagger that Judar had plunged into his chest, thrust his arm and hand above ground and stabbed Greggory through and through in the neck. Greggory immediately went into shock, not even realizing what had just happened, as blood gurgled and spurted from his mouth, his eyes wide in horror, the lantern dropping from his hand, so close to the ground that it landed upright. Tyree, who was very near Greggory's when the strike landed, felt warm blood spatter his face from the initial blow and, for a second, thought he had been struck. Tyree felt his voice box clench from fear, and, gulping for air, vainly trying to scream, stumbling backwards. With his back against the wall of the grave, Tyree's eyes widened in horror as he watched Kord sit up. To Tyree, it all happened in slow motion, the dirt sliding away, like water off the armor and face, as Kord's torso raised up. From his sitting position, Kord looked at Tyree, the glowing red eyes created by the skull helmet, zeroing in on the frightened man.

Pex, who was still up on top, saw it all happen up close as well. When Kord struck, it took a second for his mind to comprehend what he had just witnessed, and after that brief second, he screamed, jumping to his feet and stumbling backwards, falling onto his back, still screaming. Pex's scream startled Kirsh's horse, who was very near, and the warhorse reacted on instinct, raising up on its hind legs, and coming down, crushed Pex's chest, who let out a final gurgling gasp as his midsection was crushed. The whole chain reaction of events confused Soxust and Wagard, who were still resting by the rock outcropping, and they each leapt to their feet, drawing their swords, which were resting nearby.

"What the hell just happened?!" demanded Wagard with fear in his voice.

While Kirsh was trying to regain control of the warhorse, Kord grabbed Slice, which had slid off his chest as he sat up and, in a fluid motion, rammed the blade through Tyree's chest, piercing his heart and pinning him to the earthen wall behind him. Again, Tyree did not let out a sound as blood filled his lungs and gurgled up through his mouth, but not dying instantly, he looked at Kord, wondering what had just happened, and what kind of monster was now sitting in front of him, with its glowing red eyes, and fearsome aura. While Tyree looked on, the light fading from his eyes, Kord rose to his feet, aided by some unseen force. Despite his full plate armor, he felt extremely agile and light, and once standing, he looked at Tyree, who had tears streaming down his face, the light beginning to die in his eyes, as blood seeped out of both sides of his wound, front and back. The wounded soldier mouthed the only word he could think of as darkness began to shroud his consciousness. Kord watched as the dying man mouthed the word, "What..."

"What am I?" asked Kord, sliding the dagger back into the small scabbard on the left side of his belt and leaning in, his face was now very close to the dying soldier. Grinning, the ashen flesh of his face was already like that of a corpse. His teeth, once white, were already yellowing, the gums red and swollen, he hissed in his gravelly voice, "Unstoppable." Without waiting for the man to die, Kord reached up with his gauntleted hands and heaving, pulled himself partially out of the grave, then using Slice, which was still pinning Tyree to the side of the grave, like a ladder rung, he easily exited the grave with two quick steps. Getting on his knees and reaching down, he retrieved Slice. Tyree, finally unpinned, fell face first into the bottom of the grave. Standing up and turning around, Kord held Slice at the ready, taking a step forward as he observed the three remaining men, who were dumbstruck, having just watched their fallen general crawling out of the grave.

"Thank gods you are alive!" said Kirsh, still sitting on his horse. "We...we came back for you, General!"

Soxust blinked hard a couple times, being a little farther away, the soldier took a few steps closer, straining in the darkness to see what, exactly, was going on. "What the hell is going on Kirsh?" he asked, hesitation in his voice.

"It looks like I was right, boys," Kirsh said loudly, ensuring Soxust and Wagard could hear him. "The general is not dead after all," the officer's voice was shaky, but he continued, "I...I knew the others were lying -- Marshal Krugar is a traitor!" Kord stood still, saying nothing, as the others slowly moved in closer, for a better look.

Wagard tapped Soxust on the shoulder and whispered, "That ain't the fucking general, though it do look like him..." The soldier paused as Kord looked in their direction, his fiery red eyes glowing in the night. "Oh shit, we gotta git out of here."

Soxust stopped in his tracks. "Relax, that is just his helmet -- I seen it on the battlefield."

"I got a very bad feeling about this..." Wagard said. "That son of a bitch just came out of a six-foot grave after being in there for almost half a god-damned day. And where are Tyree and Greggory? Fuckin' dead, I say."

"Keep coming, boys," said Kord, his voice scratchy and low, motioning with his right hand as he continued to hold Slice in his left hand.

"You heard the general: you two, get your lazy asses in here," Kirsh commanded.

The two soldiers looked at each other, hesitated, then Wagard shouted, "Get the fuck out of here!" as he turned and ran. Soxust, startled by the shout, also turned and ran.

Kord outstretched his right hand, pointing his index finger in the direction of the fleeing soldiers, and spoke the words, as familiar and fluently, as if he had spoken them for centuries, "Invoco le tenebre affinché distruggano tutta la vita intorno a me." Although it was already dark, at Kord's command, a palpable heaviness descended. Kord's body acted as a conduit for an evil, malignant, and powerful negative energy that rushed at and enveloped the two soldiers. Unable to outrun the dark magic, the vengeful darkness swirled around them for a brief moment, then each of the men screamed in horror as they felt their souls being rendered from their bodies. Their faces twisted in agony as two silvery souls, like ghosts, peeled away from their bodies. It all happened very quickly, and their screaming stopped as suddenly as it had started, each man's body going limp and crumpling to the ground; the ghostly visages hovered for a split second, then vanished in a silent white explosion, then implosion of light, leaving only darkness and their lifeless bodies behind. Although casting the spell came naturally to him, Kord looked at his still outstretched hand, one corner of his mouth curled slightly into an arrogant and evil grin.

Kord, lowering his arm and closing his hand into a fist, turned and began walking toward Kirsh, whose horse reeled backwards, fear in its eyes. "Get off the horse, and I will spare your life," Kord's voice crackled and grated, "flee and I will skin you alive."

Kirsh's eyes darted around, wondering if he could still escape, but after seeing what this, this, thing, had done to the others, running didn't seem like a plausible, or successful decision. Finally regaining control of the animal, Kirsh was able to dismount, but as he did so, the horse again bucked and ripped the reins out of his hands. Not wasting second, the horse turned and bolted, running away before Kirsh could react.

Kord closed the remaining distance quickly between himself and Kirsh, plunging the blade completely through the officer's chest, just underneath his heart. Kirsh grabbed Kord's forearm with both his hands, trying to pull the sword out, but his strength quickly drained away, and he could feel the darkness closing in around him. "No matter about the horse," Kord said, "you were dead either way." Kirsh coughed, trying to grab a few last breaths, but Kord pulled Slice out, and as he did so, he heard a familiar, yet distant voice, ringing in his head. "Yessss...blood and death." Kirsh, groaning as he fell, clawed at the ground weakly, but soon stopped moving, his blood soaking into the plains. Kord slid Slice back into its scabbard, hanging on his belt, then knelt beside Kirsh's body. Removing Kirsh's helmet and grabbing a fistful of hair with his gauntleted hand, he lifted Kirsh's head to see if he was still alive. The officer's eyes were wide open, but it was a blank stare into emptiness. Kord could sense, like a pulsation, the absence of the man's spirit, leaving no doubt that Kirsh was, indeed, dead. Still holding Kirsh's head, Kord, closing his eyes and bowing his head, said a prayer, "Invoco le tenebre affinché leghino le anime ai morti e servano la mia volontà su Thran." Kord didn't know how he knew those words, but knew the spell might be able to recall the man's spirit and thus bind it to the corpse forever. Kord opened his eyes but nothing happened; Kirsh's body simply lay there, motionless. Dropping the corpse's head, Kord stood back up, surveying his handiwork. "Judar was right...I will create much suffering here," he said. As he finished his sentence, Kirsh's body convulsed violently, went limp again, and then after a few seconds, the officer slowly stood up.

"What is thy bidding?" Kirsh asked, his voice filled with eagerness, his face now pale and ashen. As Kirsh asked his question, Pex's body rolled over, and despite his crushed chest, he also stood up, and from within the grave, two more figures clawed their way to the surface and began lumbering their way toward Kord.

Kord nodded in approval, again, of his handiwork and, looking at the dead officer, now standing next to him, said, "You shall be known as Kijjit."

CHAPTER TWENTY-SEVEN
The Stream

YEAR: AG 1175, Month of Sepu

EARLY INDICATIONS WERE THAT IT WOULD BE VERY HOT despite the normally cool temperatures of Octu, and so the companions were walking at a brisk pace, hoping to make up ground before the midday sun began to beat down on them in full force. The companions fell into a long line, Bealty was alone about a hundred feet in front of the group, followed by Tyberius and Ariana, the tall warrior walking next to the pony. Isa tended to stay near Tyberius, and the case was no different now, the monk walking closely behind the couple. Brutal and Mikell were fifty feet behind Isa, sweat already beading on their foreheads, provoking complaints about the heat to one another. York held up the rear of the small column, plucking away at his cittern, and every now and then singing a short tune to go along with it, the notes carrying with them a small amount of magical energy that helped make the hard walk a little more manageable.

"What do you think of York so far?" Mikell asked Brutal.

"He seems a little arrogant and is a bit of a loner, but then again he is an elf," Brutal responded, then added, "He has helped so far. Why, did he do something?"

Mikell shook his head. "No... No, nothing overt." Mikell reached into a side pocket in his backpack, pulled out a piece of cloth, and wiped his brow and head. Putting it away, he continued, "I just do not see why he chose to come with us. I mean, I cannot recall an elf ever coming to Telfar, and the first true elf that does somehow ends up traveling with us. Does that not seem odd to you?"

Brutal half snorted. "What the hell is usual about the last two days? That is the better question."

"Aye, you have a point," Mikell conceded, letting out a brief and low chuckle at the reversed logic. "Still, I am missing something. I can usually sniff out the charlatans, yet York seems to have a veil about him, which I cannot see through."

They walked a little further, both pondering the issue. Brutal walking with his head down, examined the ground around each footstep and kicked at any stone that stood out. After a short distance, Brutal looked at his long-time friend. "Perhaps, you can read humans because you are around them every day, but with an elf, how do you know if his behavior is strange or normal?"

Mikell, smoothing out his thick mustache, gave the idea some thought. "I am sure you are right about that...but we all have motives, regardless of race. What is his?" he asked somewhat rhetorically. "Greed? Ambition? Revenge? Fame?" Mikell paused. "I just do not see it yet, and that makes me nervous."

"My dear boy, you missed the most important motive of all: Love," said York, suddenly behind them. Mikell and Brutal both were surprised to see the bard walking directly behind them, immediately creating an awkward moment, but York didn't let the silence linger. "But as I have told you before, I am here for the story," he said, holding up his right hand, which was stained black in places from the ink he was always using.

"But, why were you in Telfar?" asked Mikell. "I have never seen an elf in the town before, and I have been there for over ten years."

"It is all about perspective, my young friend," said York, still lightly strumming his Cittern. "The last time I was this far south, Telfar was not even there. In fact, Kardoon was not even a country yet. You humans tend to create a lot of change wherever you go." York stopped playing his instrument. "Your race tends to burn the candle brightly, no doubt, but, alas, a human life is more like a forked flash of lightning: bright, narrow, powerful, concentrated, and leaves a ripple of thunder that can still be felt after it is gone." York began playing again. "Oh, did I forget to mention, the most notable characteristic of lightning?" Answering his own question, he said, "It is oh so brief."

Mikell frowned. "You did not answer my question: why were you in Telfar?"

York continued to play, walking a step or two behind Brutal and Mikell. "Have you ever sat somewhere and watched a thunderstorm?"

"Just answer the question," Brutal said, raising his tone and growing impatient.

"I have already answered your question," said York in his usual casual tone. "I am simply trying to put it in a perspective you might actually understand."

"Yes, of course, I have watched a thunderstorm," Mikell said. "How does that answer my question?"

York, still strumming a pleasant tune, said, "Being an elf amongst humans is like watching a thunderstorm -- of human activity. Humans run here and there, desperate to make an impact -- never content to just 'be.'" York stopped playing his cittern again. "I have been alive for almost 350 years, and I wander Thran looking for interesting adventures, especially things I have never seen before. Mostly, elves are content to just watch the storm from a distance, but sometimes, you get caught in the storm, in which case you get wet and must act. You created this storm, which happened to cross my path directly, so here I am."

Mikell thought for a moment while they walked. "That is not entirely true, you still chose to come with us," Mikell said, and, after a short pause, added, "you could have easily 'watched us leave.'"

York began playing the music again, a gentle tune whose notes seemed to wrap themselves around the companions, invigorating them and urging them onward. "How astute of you, my priestly friend," said York. "I was just trying to paint the perspective of most elves. I," he said with a slight bow, "am a bard by profession, something not common to my kin-folk, so I am drawn to the storms more than an average elf, I suppose. I like to record events, and where better to do that than on, well, an adventure, such as this?"

"You have a risky profession, I think," said Brutal, "always putting yourself in harm's way to simply get a 'story.' You are lucky to have survived 350 years doing so."

"I have plainly told you why I have chosen to be here, although you may still not understand, I cannot tell you any plainer," said York as he changed the tune he was playing. Giving Brutal and Mikell another small bow, he slowed his pace, falling back to the rear, alone again.

The two friends continued walking in silence for a ways, when Mikell finally spoke, asking, "He talks in riddles and half-truths, does he not?"

"He is a bard, y'know, maybe riddles, poetry, music," Brutal paused and then added, "and half-truths are how he communicates. I guess I believe him when he says he is here for the story -- I mean, the guy cannot stop writing in his damn journal."

"Maybe," said Mikell. "Maybe..."

* * * *

The companions walked through the mid-morning, Bealty still out front. With the grass being almost as tall as the halfling, the downside was that he couldn't see very far, but the upside was that nothing could see him, either. Following the gnoll's trail -- evidenced by the trodden, broken, and otherwise disturbed grass that they left in their wake, was obvious and easy and it also made traveling a little easier for the small halfling, since he could easily weave a path through the trail to avoid having to constantly brush grass away from his face.

By this time, Mikell and Brutal had caught up with Tyberius and Ariana, while Isa was walking in the rear with York where the bard was having a one-sided conversation with the monk. Mid-sentence, York stopped talking and looked up, cocking his head a little, both ways. They all walked a little farther, when York broke into a light run to catch up with the rest of the group, followed easily, and closely, by Isa. "Julius is coming, and there must be some danger," York said, a little out of breath from the jog.

Everyone stopped except Bealty, who was too far away to hear the conversation. Tyberius put his fingers into his mouth and let out a loud whistle, which the rogue did hear, causing him to turn and look back. Seeing the group stopped, and huddled together, he began jogging back to find out what was going on.

"How do you know Julius is on his way back?" asked Brutal.

"I can hear his whistle; it is still faint, but getting louder," answered York.

"Damn, I guess those pointy ears are pretty good -- I hear nothin' but the wind in the grass," said Tyberius.

"Me hear it, too," said Isa, tapping his large ear with a bulky finger.

Brutal quickly looked around, but there was no cover to be seen, just the rolling plains and tall grass. "Ty and Ariana," Brutal said, "you should go off the trail and hide yourselves in the grass, but stay together. That way if there is trouble, at least we may have one surprise up our sleeve. The rest of us will stay here, on the trail, and see what the whistle is about and if something is following him."

"I will go into the grass on the other side of Ty. I will not be much use standing in the trail," said Bealty.

"Sure, good idea," said Brutal.

Ariana slid down from her pony, whereupon Foetore scampered out of a saddlebag and onto her shoulder. Handing the reins to Brutal, she said, "Be careful, Brutal -- no heroics."

Brutal smiled a polite smile and nodded. "I will be." Ty and Ariana walked out into the plain, found a sunken area in the grass, and hunkered down, disappearing from view. Bealty vanished almost instantly upon entering the grass, and where he went from there, Brutal could not tell. Looking at Mikell, who was standing just behind him, he said, "When we were back in Telfar, I thought Bealty would be a burden, you know? Someone we would always have to be taking care of -- I mean, he is so small..." Brutal stumbled to find the right words.

Mikell smiled, something that seemed reassuring and comforting to Brutal. "Relax, you do not have to tell me. Shit, I knew him the best out of all of us, and I had the same thoughts," he continued in his deep voice, "but now, sometimes I am embarrassed to think the reverse is true." Mikell chuckled. "I think he takes care of us. I know I would not want to be out here without him."

Brutal felt relief that he was not alone in misjudging his small friend's value to the group, and he returned the smile, "Yeah, I feel the same..." but his sentence was interrupted, hearing it for the first time -- a shrill whistle, faintly carried on the wind, instantly sending a shiver down his spine. The sound, wiping away all smiles, brought everyone back to the seriousness of the moment. "Trouble is coming people," Brutal said ominously. "Do what you need to do to ready yourself." No one spoke while everyone readied their weapons, adjusted their armor, and some even said prayers.

* * * *

Julius and his horse appeared over the nearest rise, two hundred yards ahead, at a full gallop. Brutal pointed. "There! There he is!"

"I do not see anything following him," said York, his elven eyesight allowing him to see clearly over long distances.

The next few moments were tense as the companions watched Julius getting closer, expecting at any moment a horde of gnolls to crest the hill behind the ranger. Julius finally arrived. Jasper was exhausted and breathing heavily -- a thick bead of sweat wetting down the animal's coat.

"What is wrong, Julius?" asked Brutal as the ranger hopped down from the horse, then added in rapid succession, "Did you see the gnolls? Did you see the prisoners?"

Mikell had his shield readied on his left arm and, using his left hand, grabbed Brutal's shoulder. "Give him just a moment -- he will tell us...Let Julius tell us."

Julius took a long pull on his water flask, then took a deep breath, looking around, a worried expression came over his face. "Where is everyone else?"

"We were not sure what to expect when you arrived, so we had them conceal themselves in the grass," said Brutal, who then whistled loudly. "Everyone! Come back here!" he shouted as loud as he could.

"So, they are here -- thank the gods, as we will need everyone," said Julius, pausing to catch his breath. "We do not have much time, there are two hill giants following me," he gulped some more air, "and they will be here soon." While Julius was talking, Tyberius, Ariana, and Bealty all made their way back to the trail where the others were talking.

"What is going on?" asked Tyberius as they neared.

"There are two hill giants following Julius," said Brutal. "They will be here soon."

"Fucking giants?!" asked Tyberius. "Ain't they just child tales?"

"I am afraid not," said York. "They are quite real, and quite deadly -- especially so with the large rocks they throw, well, 'boulder' would be a better description. They can hurl them a great distance."

"Zuel, protect us," said Mikell reverently.

Julius looked at York, it was strange to have someone in the group so much older than himself, and with so much more knowledge of lore. "That is good information. So we need to fight close in. We need to find a place where we can take away their ranged advantage," but as he spoke, they all looked around, and aside from the occasional hill, rise, or tree, it was rolling open plains.

"What if we all hide in the grass and let them pass?" asked Ariana.

Julius shook his head. "The horses cannot be concealed, and we may need them later to help carry things, or maybe even..." Julius stopped himself mid-sentence.

"Bodies," Ariana finished the sentence for him.

"People," Julius quickly corrected, "was what I was about to say."

"If we cannot lose the horses, and we cannot hide the horses, then I say we use them to our advantage," said Bealty.

"Great idea," said Ariana. "Please, enlighten us on how we are to do that?"

Bealty, as always, ignored the sarcasm. "Okay," he said, pointing to a tree off in the distance. "We take the horses and tie them up to that tree over there..."

"How is that an advantage?" interrupted Ariana.

Julius raised a hand, as if to silence her. "Ariana, he has a good idea... I think I see where you are going with this."

"Yeah, especially if the giants are on 'Straight Time,'" said Bealty, matter-of-factly, his hands on his hips.

* * * *

The two giants walked over a small hill, and upon cresting it, they each spotted what they were looking for, the gray mare that the human

452

had been riding. Aside from their enormous height, each giant standing a little over eleven feet, disheveled appearance, and their similarly poorly sewn leather armor, they looked quite different. One was a little heavier, with thinning red hair and a full red beard, while the second giant was much thinner and had long black hair tied into a tight ponytail that pulled his filthy, matted hair back away from his face, which had tufts of stubble dabbling his cheeks and neck.

"Look, two horses now," said Wachog, the red-haired giant, pointing in the direction of the tree where the two horses were now tied up.

"He not ride that fast forever," replied Gebank, an evil chuckle of anticipation in his voice as he hefted his large club to rest on his right shoulder. "What you look forward to more? Horse meat or the human meat?"

"Do not be a dumb ass, Gebank," said Wachog. "Of course, human is better than horse, but they ain't dead yet, so quit droolin' and keep ya'r eyes open. Them humans may be small, but they is crafty."

"Not crafty enough -- me gonna' crush them easy," Gebank said, his voice a low rumble.

As they continued to walk toward the tree, Wachog kept scanning the fields, his brow furrowed. "Do you see anyone?"

"No, they is so scared, they left they's horses," said Gebank, "hoping we just stop and eat them...or somethin.'"

"Or they is hiding in the grass," said Wachog, slowing his pace.

"Come on out, little ones! We just want talk!" shouted Gebank at the top of his lungs, his voice booming.

Wachog backhanded his thinner companion in the chest. "Shut up -- ya fucking idiot," giving the other giant an evil glare, "you moron -- they not understand what you say. Ya have to use the common."

"I do not know the common," said Gebank, irritated at being hit and admonished.

"You never fought a human before?" Wachog asked, snorting scornfully before his companion could even answer.

"No -- but I have ate one once," Gebank said defiantly.

Wachog stopped and gave his companion a look of rebuke. "Eating ain't same as fighting. I fought them before," said Wachog, "an' armed ones, like these here...are dangerous. We not even know how many there is yet, so shut ya'r fucking yap and keep eyes open."

Gebank growled, hating his older companion, thinking one day how he would like to crush his ugly red head. But now was not the time, and he knew it, so heeding the advice, he followed closely behind Wachog as they both eyed the surrounding grassy plain warily, continuing their slow and careful walk toward the tree and the horses.

"Get ready with rock," said Wachog, switching the club into his left hand, reaching into a large pouch hanging on his belt with his other hand, and pulling out a small boulder-sized rock that fit neatly into his hand. Gebank did not argue, doing the same as they slowly closed the distance.

* * * *

"Damn, that was loud. What the fuck did he say?" asked Tyberius. Mikell and Ariana both shushed him, and even Isa, who was lying down in the grass next to Tyberius, gave the tall warrior an angry look. The companions had split up, with half the group on the east side of the path they figured the giants would take, and the other half, Brutal, Julius, York, and Bealty on the west side of the "straight line" path. The only exception was that Bealty, as he preferred to do, took off on his own -- but presumably he stayed on the west side of the path somewhere. As they lay low in the grass, they watched the two giants walking, then stopping for a bit. It looked like they were suspicious of something, but eventually they did continue, albeit, at a slower, more careful pace. As they drew closer, everyone was awed by the sheer size of the two giants approaching them, unsure how to fight such behemoths without getting kicked, or god forbid, hit by the small tree trunks that they were using as clubs.

"Stay calm," whispered Mikell, sensing the growing fear. "Zuel will protect us," he said as he kissed his holy symbol gently, then letting it fall and dangle around his neck, he tightened his grip on his mace, his face full of intensity as his thoughts turned back to the giants.

* * * *

On the west side of the expected path, Brutal, Julius, and York lay on their bellies, watching the same scene unfold, and were experiencing the same anxiety. At the sound of one of the giants yelling, Brutal immediately looked at York with a questioning look, silently asking if the bard understood what he had said. York knew they were looking to him to translate, but the bard simply shrugged his shoulders and shook his head. Brutal, turning his attention back to the giants, watched as they slowly proceeded, as expected, toward the tree where they had tied up the horses. So far Bealty's plan was working well -- to use the horses as bait to draw the giants into a close quarter fight, where they could attack the giants from both sides. The plan was to wait for Brutal, Julius, and York to attack first, then once the giants turned to meet that threat, for Tyberius, Ariana, Mikell, and Isa to attack them from the rear. The giants were very close to entering the space between the two groups when the red-haired giant suddenly stopped, and, holding out his arm with the club, barred the other giant from moving forward.

* * * *

"Look at grass there," said Wachog, now pointing at a spot where there seemed to be no grass to the south and west of them, about fifty feet away. The giant's height allowed them a different perspective of the world, and it was obvious from their vantage point that something wasn't right about the grass in front of them -- it was like a hole in an ocean of grass.

"There, too," said Gebank, nodding to the east.

"See, I told ya -- they is crafty," said Wachog.

* * * *

"What the fuck?" whispered Tyberius. "They seen us for sure, they are almost looking right down at us."

"Wait for the signal," whispered Mikell through gritted teeth.

"I ain't waiting for those fuckers to hurl them boulders at us," said Tyberius in a hushed but determined whisper. "Screw that."

Ariana put her hand on Tyberius's forearm. "Just wait, Ty..."

* * * *

"The red-haired one just pointed at us, I think," said Brutal in a hushed voice. "They must see us."

455

"But they are not yet between our groups, and we will have to cover a lot of ground to get to them," said Julius, eyeing the huge rocks each of the giants now held in their hands.

"We will have to take our chances," said Brutal. "If we wait much longer they may just start hurling their damn rocks right..." Before Brutal could finish his sentence, he heard a loud howl from across the plain, and he didn't need to look to know that it was Tyberius.

"Shit, Ty is charging them," said Julius in a loud voice.

* * * *

"No!" screamed Ariana as Tyberius easily broke her grip on his arm. Leaping to his feet, he charged the giants, flail in full swing.

"Ty!" shouted Mikell, standing up and running through the grass but unable to keep up with the quick-footed warrior.

Isa sprang to his feet as well, and although he was a couple steps behind Tyberius, he was able to keep up, closing the distance to the giants very quickly.

* * * *

The giants, still a little startled to see three humanoids jumping up and charging them, hesitated for a second, then hurled their huge, fifty pound, rocks at Tyberius -- the human they first saw charging. The human was quicker than they thought and both of their initial throws sailed long, over his head.

"Him fast!" said Wachog, reaching into his bag for another rock. As he did so, he noticed three more humanoids popping up from the hole in the grass where he suspected someone might be hiding. "More over there!" he said as Julius, Brutal, and York stood up.

Gebank grabbed another rock and readied himself to throw it at Tyberius who was rapidly getting closer, but his nerves got the better of him, and he dropped the stone onto his foot. "Argh!" he yelled in pain as the stone rolled away from his foot.

Wachog didn't see Gebank drop the rock as he was focusing on the three men to the west. The taller dark-haired one began running his way, a large bastard sword in his hand. Taking aim, he threw his stone at the human. Not as quick as Tyberius, Brutal made for an easier target, and Wachog's aim was right on, the fifty-five pound rock slamming into Brutal, glancing off his breastplate and left shoulder, knocking him off balance momentarily. Thankfully, Brutal's breastplate deflected some of the stone's energy, although it managed to leave a large dent in the armor that cut into his chest, causing some blood to trickle through a small crack in the plate. Barely avoiding being knocked off his feet, Brutal continued his charge at the large redheaded giant, roaring in pain and anger as he rushed to close the distance.

Reaching Gebank, Tyberius, using the momentum of his charge, swung with all his might, but the giant stepped out the way easily, the ball of his flail missing entirely.

Seeing Brutal get hit by the rock, Julius, pulling an arrow from his quiver, loosed it at Wachog. The arrow arced gracefully through the air, striking the giant, piercing through the hide armor, and lodging itself briefly in Wachog's belly. The giant seemed to barely notice the sting, and as he wound up to throw another rock, the arrow worked its way out and fell to the ground. Targeting Brutal again, Wachog hurled another rock at the charging human, but this time the boulder went just a hair wide, missing.

York, running a short distance behind Brutal, drew his longsword and began singing a fight song he had learned over time, the unusual magical notes he was able to hit washing over his companions, invigorating them both physically and mentally.

Gebank, now engaged by Tyberius, gave up on the rocks and, grabbing his club with both hands, swung it downward at the warrior. Tyberius saw the blow coming and, quickly backing up, was able to dodge the swinging club which swooshed loudly as it passed in front of him so close that could feel the gust of wind created by the club.

Ariana, now standing, began walking in the direction of the giants. Eyeing Gebank, as his club whistled past her fiancé, she raised her right hand, and pointing her index finger at the giant, canted the magic words, "Invoco missili di forza, infallibili nella loro volo." Finishing the somatic tracing with her left hand, three bolts sprung from her index finger and silently raced through the intervening space, each bolt taking a unique path, but all three striking Gebank with a loud thud, thud, thud. The red bolts, easily piercing the hide armor, lodging themselves into the belly and side of the enormous giant, vanished, leaving gaping wounds that immediately began to bleed.

"Arrrgghh!" roared Gebank as the bolts struck home. "They has fucking wizard!" he said in his native tongue, pointing at Ariana.

Wachog looked at Gebank and, following his companion's finger, spotted Ariana, "Kill the mage!" he shouted as he began moving rapidly in her direction.

Seeing the redheaded giant start running her way, Ariana looked around, but there was nothing but open plains and nowhere to run. Mikell, seeing the redheaded giant moving directly toward the sorceress, changed the direction he was running and veered toward the new threat. "Run, Ariana! Run to get behind us! I will do what I can to buy you some time!" shouted Mikell. Ariana, not having to be convinced, broke into a run northward, trying to keep Tyberius, Isa, and Mikell between her and the redheaded giant now tracking her down. Feeling the ground shake with each heavy footfall of the giant and the loud thumping sound getting louder and louder as he closed the distance, a rush of adrenaline began coursing through her body, urging her on.

Isa, now joining Tyberius, lashed with a hard kick to the Gebank's left knee, but his foot glanced off the giant's think skin and bone, not doing any noticeable damage.

Bealty, still hidden in the grass, watched the scene as it unfolded. Being just two and a half feet tall, he would barely be able to reach the giant's knees, but thinking back to his Day One training, there was still one vulnerable point on the giant's body that he could effectively target: the back of the giant's heel. It wouldn't be easy, but as he moved through the grass, he locked on the thinner, giant, who was being distracted by Tyberius and Isa. He was able to move pretty quickly through the grass, since he had many favorable circumstances going for him: one, the grass was slightly taller than his head, so his movement was effectively concealed, two, the giant's back was to him, so concealment was almost unnecessary, and third, the noise of the battle would wash out any slight noise he might make running through the grass. Feeling confident, the little rogue drew his short sword and dagger, closing the distance to

Gebank.

Julius, now in the rhythm of shooting, quickly launched two more arrows at the redheaded giant. The first arrow struck Wachog in the right thigh, easily punching through the giant's skin and lodging itself deeply, but the giant seemed to pay it no heed and continued his sprint toward Ariana. The second arrow hit Wachog in the right side but glanced harmlessly off the thick hide armor.

Ariana was beginning to really worry -- the giant was much quicker than her and was closing rapidly. Mikell was trying help by blocking it, but she wasn't convinced he could do that in the open field. If she stopped to cast another spell, he would catch her sooner, but she wasn't certain continuing to run was going to do her any good anyway. Every step the giant took in her direction was another step farther for Brutal and Mikell to try and make up. "Maybe we can slow him down, Foetore," she said, reaching into a small pouch on her belt and pulling out a piece of spiderweb. Turning around to face the oncoming giant, she canted her spell, "Invoco un groviglio di ragnatele come quello che nasce dal ragno." Completing the somatic portion of the spell with her free hand, she filled her body with magical energy, sucked in from the positive plane, then unleashed it into the small material piece of web. Focusing on the area right in front of the giant, the web shot out of her hand, expanding rapidly in size until it hit the grass, where it was forty yards wide and twenty yards deep. Wachog ran right into the sticky strands, which did slow him down, but because the web wasn't anchored to anything solid, he was able to power through it, as if he were wading through waist-deep water.

Seeing the giant slowed, she turned and began running again, able to put a little distance between her and Wachog, but it wasn't long before the giant had broken through and was again running full speed. Feeling a rage welling up within her, and with the bard's song encouraging her, she halted once again, and turning, she gave the pursuing giant an icy stare. "You want me? Come and get me asshole!" she shouted, motioning for him to come closer.

"No! No! Keep running Ariana!" shouted Mikell, waving his left arm with the shield, motioning for her to keep moving while he continued running to try and intercept the giant, but seeing her stop, his heart sank, knowing the angle wasn't good, and he wasn't sure he could get to her in time.

Ariana heard Mikell but paid Mikell's pleas no heed. Holding her ground, she mentally cleared her mind, closing out all other thoughts and, reaching out with her mind, she tapped the positive material plane once again. She felt the rush of energy, sucking in as much as her body could hold, like taking a deep breath until your lungs were full, then canting the spell once again, she let her missiles fly. The three red bolts, homing in like bees returning to their hive, struck the redheaded giant without error, puncturing his left leg, left arm, and the front of his belly.

Both Brutal and York were running to catch up with the redheaded giant now chasing Ariana, but they could not keep up, and Wachog was getting away from them. Mikell, spurred on by his fear for Ariana, interposed himself between the sorceress and the giant. Mikell swung his mace and connected with the giant's leg, but it was a glancing blow, not doing any damage, but worst of all, it didn't even slow the monstrous giant. Completely ignoring the priest, Wachog raced past, giving Mikell another opportunity to take a swing, but his timing was off, and he missed the giant with his second swing as well.

Tyberius and Isa circled the thinner giant, looking for the opportune moment to strike. Seeing Gebank turn his attention to Isa, Tyberius moved in, swinging his flail. The ball struck the gut of the giant, bouncing off the hard leather hide, but although it didn't do much damage, it did get Gebank's attention long enough for Isa to also move in and strike. Moving in, Isa punched Gebank, landing a hard fist on the giant's exposed left leg. The giant roared in pain, then turned just in time to see Isa also in the middle of a roundhouse kick that he easily dodged. Seeing the monk in an exposed position, Gebank swung his club at the monk, but he lost his grip on the club and it flew out of his hands landing about fifty feet behind him.

Wachog was bleeding from multiple locations on his body and by the time he made to Ariana, he was thoroughly enraged. "Fuckin' wizard!" he shouted at the top of his lungs in the common tongue. Ariana tried to back away, but Wachog swung his club with good accuracy, slamming into Ariana's left side as she tried to somehow shield her body. It wasn't a direct hit, but it was more than enough to knock her down, screaming, to the ground, the knots in the club gashing her left arm, both in the forearm, and the shoulder.

"Ariana!" shouted Mikell, horrified and running as fast as he could toward her, but he was not fast enough to stop the giant. Mikell watched in slow motion horror as the redheaded giant, raising his club to strike again, brought it down on Ariana, who, looking up at the last moment, was barely able to raise her battered arm up to defend herself. The blow had so much force that Mikell felt the ground reverberate. She didn't even have time to scream. Caught between the ground and the powerful blow, which landed along the entire left side of her body, she was crushed into the ground, creating a small, shallow crater. "Noooo!" shouted Mikell, still racing toward the sorceress.

"Oh my god, Notria, help her..." Julius said to himself, seeing the sorceress fall, and then receive the crushing blow. Even from a distance, the blow looked...un-survivable.

Brutal and York both caught up with Wachog, but not in time to stop the horrendous blows he had delivered to Ariana. "Die you motherfucker!" shouted Brutal swinging his bastard sword -- the blow glancing off the giant's leather armor. York was more delicate and graceful, slashing at the giant's exposed leg, but it too was deflected by the giant's thick skin.

Mikell arrived as Brutal and York engaged Wachog, but he disregarded the danger the giant posed, running right to Ariana. Without checking to see if she was even still alive, which seemed doubtful, looking at the extensive damage: broken bones all along the left side of her body, and the amount of blood that she had already lost. Mikell reached out to Zuel, and canting the healing prayer, "Benedici il mio tocco con il potere di guarire le ferite lievi," he touched her body. The positive energy glowed in his hands for just moment, then at his touch, absorbed into her body. Although some of her wounds had closed, and some of her bones had mended, she still lay motionless. Mikell bent further over, pressing his head against her bloodied chest, and placing a hand, ever so lightly, over her mouth and nose, as he listened for a heartbeat, and felt for breathing -- but there was just too much noise and commotion going on right around them. The giant was practically trampling them, each time he moved, a heavy foot pounded the ground around the priest and fallen sorceress.

Isa, still trying to recover from the awkward kick, regained his balance. Seeing Gebank reeling from the loss of his club, Isa charged in, and leaping into the air, unleashed a flying kick, delivering a compound fracture to the giant's knee. The leg, breaking into two pieces, was only held together by the skin and sinew alone, but the broken bone was not the real injury, as the bones splintered apart, his femoral artery was severed, and Gebank fell over, onto his side. He squirmed for a moment, grabbing at his leg, but the loss of blood was too much, and he quickly lost his strength. He felt the numbness in his leg traveling up his body, which was followed by a chill, and soon he found his arms going limp. In the last moment, all he could do was stare, with hatred in his eyes, at the half-orc standing near him, looking down at him. His eyes, one second filled with hatred, the next second, emptiness, as his life finally passed, leaving his corpse staring at his killer.

Bealty was about ready to strike when he saw Isa fell the thinner giant. Never having been able to attack a giant before, he felt a little disappointed, but he didn't linger on that point for long, as he began running again, this time toward the redheaded giant.

"Fuck yeah -- nice kick!" shouted Tyberius, seeing the giant fall. Spinning around, he found the other giant behind him, near the area where Ariana should have been. "Where is Ariana?" he asked Isa.

Isa shrugged, saying, "Not know," as he took off running toward the remaining giant, quickly followed by Tyberius.

It was a little riskier shot, with so many of his companions around the last giant, but he shot anyway, the arrow flying wide and high. Reproaching himself for not trusting his ability more, he started running to move closer for his next shot. Feeling more confident, he quickly loosed two arrows. His first arrow struck the giant in the neck, but glanced off, leaving a nice cut, but his second arrow again went high and wide. "Sindu!" he shouted, directing the comment at himself -- using the vulgar slang term used by elves to describe someone as weak and unworthy. Frustrated, he pulled another arrow from his quiver as he began moving still closer to the fray.

A worried expression came over Wachog's face, surveying the forces now arrayed against him; this group turned out to be larger, and much more powerful than they had been led to believe, and now he was surrounded, like being swarmed by little humanoid bees. Seeing Gebank's large body motionless on the ground, Wachog made up his mind. Roaring in rage, he swung his great club, aiming at Brutal and York, in a wide low arc, but it was not as much an attack as it was to force the small human, and even smaller cursed elf, backwards, giving himself enough room to disengage. As expected, the dark-haired human warrior and fair-haired elf jumped backwards, avoiding the club, and as soon as they did that, Wachog turned and bolted. Seeing the giant turn, Mikell ducked, covering Ariana with his body as the Wachog's huge foot landed just inches away from the prone companions. Inadvertently, stepping right over both Mikell and Ariana, Wachog began running with amazing speed and quickly began putting distance between himself and the companions.

Julius, now close to Mikell and Ariana, and seeing the giant making a break for it, loosed another arrow. This time the arrow flew straight into the back of Wachog's right shoulder. Each second, the giant got further away, making his shots less lethal and more difficult, but he took aim again. Firing, the arrow hit the center of the giant's back, but the hide armor deflected the missile. Julius looked back at the tree where Jasper, his light warhorse, was still tied.

"Do not go after him alone," said Mikell, holding up a hand, seeing the ranger contemplating the notion.

"I can catch him," said Julius, a frenzied look on his face. "He is hurt very badly. Two of us could go after him, we have two horses."

"Yeah -- we could catch him," said Brutal, and after taking a couple deep breaths, added, "and kill him."

Tyberius, now arriving on the scene, noticed Ariana for the first time. "What...what happened? Ariana!" he shouted, dropping his flail and hurrying to her, kneeling by her side. Seeing she was covered with blood and had multiple obvious fractures, he wasn't sure where to touch his fiancée without hurting her.

"That one," said Mikell, pointing to the Wachog, still running off in the distance, "rushed right for her after she cast her missile spell on the other one." Mikell, looking back down at Ariana, continued, "I tried to stop him, but he was too fast and he ran right past me." Mikell paused. "I have never seen a more vicious blow. I cannot believe she is still alive."

"Wha? Wha? What the hell are you waiting for? Cast your damned spells!" stammered Tyberius. "Cast your fucking spells to make her better!"

Mikell nodded. "I can cast another spell, but I think she will need time, not more healing."

"Are you fucking kiddin' me? Cast the damn spell!" roared the redheaded warrior.

"Okay, okay, Tyberius, I will," said Mikell, closing his eyes and grabbing hold of his holy symbol, he said his prayer to Zuel one more time. "Benedici il mio tocco con il potere di guarire le ferite lievi." Finishing the somatic portion pf the spell, his hands began to glow with the light and power of Zuel. Gently touching her shoulders, the light immediately began flowing from his hands into her body. As the spell took effect, more of her wounds closed and her bones reset, but she still did not regain consciousness.

"Dammit, priest, do it again!" roared Tyberius, grabbing Mikell by the shoulders and shaking him.

Mikell, grabbing Tyberius's forearms, firmly held his ground. "No, it is beyond me now. That final blow brought her too close to death, she is in the hands of the gods now." As he spoke, Foetore crawled out of Ariana's backpack. The final blow also crushed the little ferret. It had broken its two back legs, but, nevertheless, it hobbled and dragged its rear to lie on top of Ariana's stomach, curling up as best he could. "Oh no, he is hurt badly," said Mikell, watching him struggle to climb up the side of her body. "It may help her if I heal him as well..."

"Then do it! Heal it!" said Tyberius, anger in his voice and vengeance in his eyes as he watched the giant getting farther away.

"Benedici il mio tocco con il potere di guarire le ferite lievi," canted Mikell, calling upon Zuel's power. Placing his hand on the little ferret, he felt the energy leave his body and enter Foetore's. The ferret's back legs straightened out, and he looked up at Mikell, gave a squeak, then rested his head back down onto Ariana. "That will have to do," said Mikell.

Bealty finally joined the companions now clustered around Ariana. "What is going on?" he asked, stopping next to Brutal. "Oh, damn, is she okay?" he asked, true concern in his voice.

"We do not know yet," answered Brutal, "but at least for now, she is alive...Soulmite, protect her," he added at the end.

"The giant is probably heading back to the gnolls," said Julius. "Those are his nearest allies -- that we know of anyway."

"Ariana should not travel in her condition," said Mikell, his hand unconsciously petting Foetore gently.

"We can tie her to her pony..." Tyberius started to say, still watching the giant, its huge body getting smaller and smaller as the distance increased.

"No!" Mikell said firmly, his voice deep, gruff, and commanding. "She is barely alive, Tyberius -- if you truly care for her you will leave her be."

"We cannot just let that son of a bitch run away!" Tyberius shouted, pointing in the direction of the giant.

"I will stay back and protect her," said a small but firm voice. Bealty's arms were crossed, and with a flick of his wrist, he continued, "I hate to miss a good fight, but if one of us has to stay back, it should be me -- stealth will not be a factor in what we need to do today."

"Yeah. Yeah, that is a good idea, Beetle," said Tyberius, jumping on the offer. "Brutal, help me carry her back to the tree."

Brutal looked at Mikell. "Is that okay, Mikell?"

Mikell nodded. "Yes... I suppose we cannot just leave her lying in the middle of the plains." Brutal, Tyberius, and even Isa jumped into action, helping gently carry Ariana back to the lone tree. Bealty ran ahead and made some improvised bedding by cutting some of the nearby grass and forming it into a small mattress. The three men carefully laid the sorceress on the hastily made bed, on her back. Structurally, she looked okay, but she still looked like a bloody mess, with blades of grass sticking to her skin in various places, and blood matting her hair down.

Tyberius knelt down and gave her bloody forehead a kiss. "We will be right back," he said, then looking around, a little embarrassed, added, "my love."

"We should be back before dark," said Julius. "I know right where the giant is heading, it is not far."

Bealty sat down, leaning back against the tree with his arms resting on his bent knees. "Better get going, do not worry about us," he said with a flick of his hand.

"Mikell, you take Ariana's pony," said Brutal. "She will not be needing it, and we need to move quickly."

Mikell did not argue, but for the first time he noticed the large dent in Brutal's armor, with dried blood running down the front. "Are you okay," he said, putting his finger into the center of the large dent and wiping a little of the blood away, showing it to the warrior.

"It hurts, I cannot lie, but I am okay," said Brutal. "Save your spells -- we will need them, I am sure."

Mikell frowned but did not push the subject, and he began to quickly untie the pony. Once the reins were free of the tree, he pulled himself up into the saddle while Julius did the same with Jasper. The horses, neighed while the riders mounted them, but soon they were off, following the large tracks left by the fleeing giant.

Bealty watched them move quickly away, chasing down their quarry. Playing with a long, thin, green blade of grass, Bealty practiced making knots with it. Once the group was out of sight, the little rogue stood up, stretching his left ankle, which still gave him some discomfort, and taking out a small piece of black cloth, Bealty poured a little water from his flask onto it. Gently, he wiped away the blood, dirt, and grass, that was on her face. He continued to rinse, dab, and repeat until he had cleaned her face. The rest of her body was still a bloody mess, but they would need more water to clean her up than he had in his flask, so he rung the piece of cloth out one more time, and stuffed it back into a hidden pouch within his armor. He was about to put the flask away but decided to take a small sip of water before doing so. Already starting to feel boredom creep into his consciousness, he looked around but could see nothing but the tree and the surrounding grass. "Gotta go up," he said to himself. Easily scaling the thick trunk of the tree, Bealty perched himself on a branch seven feet off the ground and surveyed the plains to the north, which were now empty, with the exception for one feature: a large lump, rising above the grassy plain, almost like a boulder jutting out the plain. But he knew it was no boulder. "Aha, there you are," said Bealty out loud to himself. Unable to resist his curiosity, Bealty, looking down at Ariana, noticed that Foetore, was looking back up at him. He wasn't sure who he was talking to, the unconscious woman, or the ferret, but just in case somehow one, or both, of them might understand, he said, "Well, you both look like you are doing fine. Do not worry, I will be back before you know it," and, with that, the halfling sprang from the branch like a leopard leaping down onto its prey, and after a quick tuck and roll, absorbing the impact of the fall, he began moving quickly toward the lifeless body of Gebank. Foetore looked around nervously, giving a little squeak of disapproval, but the halfling quickly disappeared into the grass, and the small black and white ferret, resting its head, which was still sore from the crushing blow the giant had delivered, closed its eyes.

* * * *

The six companions moved as quickly as they could, but after a few miles, Julius raised a hand, calling for a halt. "This is not going to work," he said. "I fear that once the giant rejoins the gnolls, they will kill the remaining prisoners."

"Why in the eight hells would they do that?" asked Tyberius, anger in his voice.

"Because gnolls are cowards," answered York, who, taking the stoppage as a chance to pull out his journal, began jotting some notes down.

Julius nodded. "Yes, exactly -- they will know we are coming after them, and they know the prisoners are slowing them down, so..."

"I know I can move a lot faster than we are going right now," Tyberius said, then hesitated before continuing, "but B, you are really slowing us down."

Brutal bristled at the statement. "Screw you! I cannot run the whole way, I am going as fast as I can!"

Mikell quickly interjected himself. "We know, Brutal, we know. Believe me, if I were walking and you were riding, he would be calling me out. Julius is right," said Mikell, getting down from the pony, "the way I see it, Tyberius and Isa are setting the pace -- and we have two horses, so that means only four of us can continue."

"I am gonna be one of the four, that is for god-damned sure," said Brutal.

"Fine," said Mikell, "then who is the other?"

"Since it will be a fight, I should go," said Julius, tapping the bow slung over his shoulders.

"No, my dear boy," said York, "I will be the fourth."

Mikell gave the bard a sideways glance, his thick bushy eyebrows, angling in a mixture of surprise and suspicion. "Julius is much more of a physical threat, I think he should go."

"Ah, well, yes, in that regard, I cannot make a good counter argument," York began as he tucked the notebook, pen, and small ink vial back into his backpack, "but I do have spells that could be useful in this situation."

"What spells?" asked Tyberius, giving the bard a wary look.

"How come we have not seen you cast these spells before?" asked Brutal.

The elf ran a hand through his thick blond hair, pulling it back. "There has been no need, or more precisely, no use for my spells, until now."

"This better not some bullshit about wanting to see the battle so you can write it down in your book," said Brutal, waving a finger at York's backpack.

"Heavens no," York began, "well, of course, I want to see the battle -- but that is not my only motivation." Seeing the skeptical looks on the other faces, he quickly added, "In this particular case, I am the better choice to go along."

"What spells can you cast?" asked Mikell.

"Out here, in nature," York said, gesturing to the fields surrounding them. "I can use the vegetation to our advantage." Still seeing the skepticism on their faces, he again added, "I can also heal minor wounds."

"Really?" asked Mikell, crossing his arms over his thick chest. "Now, why have you not offered to help in that regard before?"

"I have helped, if Hammer were alive, he could tell you, as I healed him in the bunker," said York.

"By what power do you call on to heal?" asked Mikell, his gruff voice deepening.

York met the cleric's stare directly. "Linkal answers my prayers for healing."

"I knew it," said Mikell, jabbing a finger toward the bard. "You worship a god that lives in the shadows."

"What do ya mean, the shadows?" asked Tyberius.

"I seek a balance, nothing more, and right now, I see the balance shifting out of alignment," said York, a seriousness in his voice that the others had not heard from him before.

Mikell and York locked stares, neither yielding. Julius stepped between the two of them. "Easy, we are all on the same side here."

"Maybe, for now," growled Mikell, finally turning his back on Julius and York and walking over to Brutal. His expression softened, and his voice, gruff as usual, returned to a more normal tone. "Since I will not be coming along, I want to heal you now." Brutal was about to say something, but Mikell held up a hand to silence him. "Not negotiable," he said, then canted the spell, "Benedici il mio tocco con il potere di guarire le ferite lievi." As he finished, the positive energy drawn into his body illuminated his hands. Mikell, reaching out, touched Brutal's shoulder allowing the energy to flow into his friend's body. Brutal felt the warm sensation spread throughout his body, healing injuries as it spread, but as quickly as it began, it faded away, leaving him feeling refreshed.

"Thank you, Mikell," he said, placing a hand on Mikell's shoulder.

"It is settled then, no?" asked York, the cheerfulness back in his voice.

Julius gave the elven bard, who was an inch shorter than himself, a hard look. "Yes, it is agreed," he said, handing Jasper's reins to York, who reached out to take them, but when York tried to pull them away, Julius held on, catching the bard's attention as their matching green eyes locked on one another.

Not backing down from Julius's stare, York said, "The sands of time are slipping away," as he lightly pulled on the reins again, but Julius held on tightly.

"No betrayals," whispered Julius, inching closer to York.

"Of course not," said York, smiling. Julius held the reins a second longer then let them go. York smiled again and then swung himself up onto the light warhorse, which he quickly turned and giving it a slight kick, sent the animal into a quick trot, motioned for the others. "Come on, gents!" Without any hesitation, Tyberius and Isa began running after the bard.

Brutal, using the stirrup, pulled himself up onto the pony's back. "We will meet you back at the tree," he said, "if we do not return within two days, we are likely dead. In which case, you should head back to Telfar, and warn them of the bunkers. Well met, brothers!" he said with a wave, and then sent the pony into a gallop, to catch up with the others.

"Do you trust the elf?" asked Mikell, stepping forward to stand by Julius's side, both men still watching Brutal ride away.

"For now... Yes," said Julius, caution in his voice, "but it seems we have little choice at the moment."

Glancing at Julius out of the corner of his eye, Mikell noted the half-elf was still fixated on their companions and had a dour look. The weathered creases forming on the cleric's forehead, narrowing eyes, and pursed lips, belied his own distrust and apprehension. "Zuel will protect us," he said, his right hand clutching the holy symbol attached to the chain around his neck, taking comfort, and confidence, in its sturdiness and heft. His fingers traced the textured engraving, written on the outside circumference of the symbol, which he knew so well: 'The Light Shines On the Faithful, Keeping Darkness at Bay.'

* * * *

The four companions made excellent time. Tyberius and Isa, displaying amazing speed and fortitude, pushed through any thought of rest, and as a result they began to close the distance to the giant. "There! Right there!" shouted Tyberius, excitement in his voice, pointing at the giant now visible, ascending a large hill in the distance. "We is get'in close now!" Even from a distance, it was obvious the giant was limping and moving much more slowly, perhaps it was the uphill climb, but whatever the reason, they were now closing the gap quickly.

Halfway up the hill, Wachog turned around and, sitting down to rest for a moment, immediately spied the four small humanoids moving rapidly and directly toward him. His red eyebrows raised in surprise. "Fucking littlelings," he muttered to himself. Taking a deep breath and wincing in pain as he stood back up, he bellowed in his evil tongue, his booming voice ringing out below him, "Come and get Wachog!" Turning, he started making his way up the side of the hill, until finally he was at the top, where, once again, he turned around, and pulling a large stone out of a bag hanging on his belt, he sat down, and watched the companions as they neared.

"What did he say?" asked Brutal as the giant's shout rang out from the hill.

"It ain't 'hello, how ya doing,' I can tell ya that much!" said Tyberius, still jogging by the side of Brutal's pony, and between deep breaths.

"York, what did he say?" asked Brutal again.

"Some vulgar challenge, most likely," said York, "I am sure he is none too pleased to see us tracking him down."

"He is moving again!" said Brutal, watching the giant begin to climb the hill again. "We need to keep pressing!"

The companions continued their chase until they neared the base of the hill the giant was climbing. It was here that they saw the giant turn around and sit at the top, after having taken out a large rock. "Shit!" shouted Brutal. "We need to stop and think this through, he is going to hurl those damned rocks at us from up there." Pulling on the reins, the pony came to a halt, as well as everyone else. "Anyone have any ideas?"

"Did you see the bee-line that redheaded giant made for Ariana?" asked York.

"Bee-line? Me not know this," asked Isa.

"Right," said York, smiling. "Anyway, my point is -- as soon as Ariana cast her first spell, both of the giants immediately reacted. You two had the dark haired one pretty tied up," he gestured to Tyberius and Isa, "so he could not get to her..."

"Yeah, now that you mention it, that makes sense -- that bastard," Brutal interrupted, pointing up the hill, "charged right at her after she hit the other one with her missiles."

"Precisely," said York, a little miffed at the interruption. "I think if he sees me use my magic, that he will focus on me, allowing you three to make a good run at him."

"No offense, but all it will take is one rock to take you out, then what?" said Tyberius, skepticism in his voice.

"Very astute," York began, then seeing the lack of comprehension on Tyberius and Isa's faces, paused and began again. "Very true, however, hitting me may prove to be more difficult than one might think," he said, finishing with a wink.

* * * *

The hill was perhaps two hundred feet high, with a consistent and medium slope, making the climb far from easy. But the real problem was the intervening three hundred feet they would have to navigate, all the while, under a hail of rocks from the giant, but York had a decent plan, as long as he didn't get crushed on the giant's first couple throws. The companions left the horses at the bottom of the hill, not wanting to risk their loss, and given the uphill situation, everyone felt more comfortable on foot. The companions lined up at the base of the hill, in a straight line across, with York far out to the left of the other three. Closest to York was Brutal, then Tyberius, and Isa took up the right side of the line.

"Alright, gents, we walk until he throws his first rock," said York, and everyone began moving up the hill in unison, maintaining their spacing and formation.

The hill turned out to be more difficult than they had planned, the ascent being steeper than it looked from the bottom, and it began taking a toll on everyone, especially Brutal, who was wearing his heavy breastplate armor. About a third of the way up, Wachog stood up and hefting the rock in his hand looked at the four littlelings coming up the hill, and deciding the half-orc looked the most formidable, took aim and let the rock fly. The speed and accuracy of the throw was shocking to all four of the companions. Isa saw the throw and tried to dodge the fifty pound rock, but he misjudged the arc and was barely able to get his hands up and turn his thick body when the stone slammed into the back of his left shoulder. The monk let out a roar of pain, the force of the blow knocking him down and backwards. The monk rolled uncontrollably twenty feet down the side of the hill until finally catching himself by grabbing a fistful of grass.

"Isa!" Tyberius shouted, turning and running toward the half-orc, but just as Tyberius began to run, Isa looked at Tyberius and held up his hand.

"I is okay!" the monk hollered and hopped back to his feet, rubbing his shoulder with his right hand, an evil, toothy scowl now on his face. "Craven's balance will be restored," he growled in his native Orcish language.

Seeing the rock strike the monk and sending him reeling backwards, Wachog let out a loud whoop of delight as he reached into his bag for another stone. He was about to throw it but stopped, noting that the littlelings had retreated down the hill a little distance. "No! You come here to fight Wachog!" hollered the giant.

Having found the giant's range, the group moved back down the hill, as planned. Once back in line, York nodded at the others, "I am going to begin -- as soon as you see me casting, start your charge," then added, as if a second thought, "good luck."

"You, too," said Brutal, drawing his bastard sword and looking up the hill. "Ready when you are."

York took a deep breath, and then began casting his spell. While his hands traced the necessary magic symbols in the air, he canted the spell, "Invoco immagini del mio aspetto, che rispecchino la mia carne mortale."

Wachog watched, unsure of what they were doing, then he saw the small elf begin doing something, but he could not tell what. Considering what he should do next, he took a few steps down the hill, closing distance to his targets...then he recognized what was happening. "Fucking scum of a mage!" he roared. Hefting the rock in his hand, he wanted to target the elf -- but now he was confused, uncertain at what he was now seeing.

At the completion of the spell, four mirror images of himself burst into being around York -- each one an exact, three dimensional, replica, and all of them mimicking his every move, making it nearly impossible to know which image was the real person. Everyone was now charging up the hill, including York, and everyone was yelling and screaming as they did so, creating a fearsome sight.

Wachog's elation just a second before quickly morphed into fear, but not before he threw the rock in his hand. Picking out one of the elves, he hurled the stone, which went right through the image and rolled harmlessly down the hill -- however, the image, shimmered, then wavered as the rock passed through it and finally blinked out of sight, leaving just three images left and, of course, York himself. Wachog roared in anger, cussing the magic user, as he pulled out another stone. Looking at the rate the littlelings were moving up the hill, he figured he had two, maybe three more throws before they would be on him. Turning his attention back to the elf, he decided on the leftmost elf and, taking aim, hurled the rock. Once again, the rock passed through the image, causing it to blink out of sight, leaving just three possible targets for the elf. The littlelings continued their frenzied rush up the hill, their voices getting louder as they drew closer. Reaching for another stone, he didn't waste any time throwing another rock down the hill, this time aiming at the rightmost elven figure. But once again, the rock sailed through an image, destroying it, but wasting precious time he did not have. The humanoids would be on him soon. Figuring he had one more opportunity, he picked the left image of the elf and hurled another rock with all his might, but the stone sailed high, missing both visages of the elf. Growling in rage, and in disgust at himself, he picked up his club and readied for the imminent assault.

Staying in formation on their way up, all four of the companions arrived at the crest of the hill at about the same time. Wachog snarled, waving the club in a wide arc in front of him, daring one of them to come closer. "Surround him!" shouted Brutal, and each of them moved around the giant, making a large box. The giant focused on Isa and Tyberius, who formed one side, but that left Brutal and York on his flank.

Brutal took advantage of the situation and moved in, slashing at the giant's mid-section, but the giant saw the attack coming with his peripheral vision, blocking the blow with his club. However, turning to block Brutal's attack created an opening for Isa who ran forward, and kicked the back of Wachog's knee, cracking bone and tearing tendons. In the process, Wachog dropped to his broken knee, which buckled under his own weight. With the giant's neck now within reach, Isa quickly followed up, striking the giant in the throat, just under the chin, with the back of his fist, crushing Wachog's larynx and windpipe. Wachog reached up to his throat with both hands, his eyes wide with horror, gasping to draw a breath. Despite being utterly helpless and already on death's door, Tyberius, letting out a guttural war cry, releasing a day's worth of pent-up anger, swung his flail. The large spiked ball solidly struck the giant on the side of the head, causing a loud cracking sound and toppling the giant awkwardly backwards into a position only possible due to his shattered leg. Wachog moaned for a second on his back, weakly trying to right himself until at last his arms gave out, and he stopped moving.

The four companions waited a moment to see if the giant would move again, but he continued to lie motionless in the awkward position. Isa cautiously walked up and checked the giant more closely, even feeling its chest for movement, but feeling none, the half-orc brought his hand up to his neck and, shaking his head, made a slashing motion at his neck. The others finally let their guard down, Brutal sheathed his sword, and Tyberius let the ball of his heavy flail rest on the ground.

"Are you alright?" Brutal asked Isa, seeing a large cut on the left side of the monk's cheek, "that was some hit you took from that rock."

"Me okay," said Isa.

"That was nice work, York," Brutal said, turning his attention to the bard, who still had a twin image mimicking his moves, causing him to be unsure of which one to look at.

"I thought it might come in handy," said York, "although we were very lucky, too." The bard already had sheathed his sword and had his notebook in hand and was jotting something down.

"We need to keep moving, we do not have time to rest," said Brutal, "one of you two," he said, indicating Tyberius or Isa, "run down there and bring back the horses. We need to catch those gnolls before they somehow get more help -- or get to wherever they are going." Tyberius, not waiting to see what Isa would do, took off back down the hill toward the horses. Brutal looked at the others, and sheathing his sword, started down the other side of the hill, with Isa and York.

* * * *

Back near the companion's camp, Bealty approached the fallen giant, walking up to his head, which was almost the size of his whole body. Gebank's face was still frozen in his final hateful stare, peering up at an empty sky. Bealty lingered for another moment, studying the large brown glazed eyes of the giant. Flies and other insects were already being drawn to the decaying flesh, and Bealty tried vainly to shoo them away with a wave of his small hand. Sighing, he switched his focus to look down the long length of the giant's body where he could see three large brown leather bags attached to the giant's belt. If there was a fourth bag, the giant must be lying on top of it, he thought to himself, and that would be a shame as he knew he did not have the strength to budge the giant. 'Not dwelling on the not,' as halflings were apt to say and live by, he put the possibility of a fourth bag out of his mind and, drawing his dagger, he closed in on the first bag and began cutting it open. Slitting the first bag open, he was surprised to see what looked like parts of animals -- mixed with human remains -- hacked to pieces, fall out of the bag at his feet, causing him to jump backwards to avoid them piling up against him. "Where would they get humans from, around here?" Bealty asked himself out loud, but softly to himself, then, slowly, a thought crept into his mind. "Oh no," he said, looking at the bloody limbs now lying on the ground in front of him. He searched the other two bags, but they only contained rocks. Giving the giant one last look-over but finding nothing, the little rogue waded back into the tall grass, and after a few moments, rejoined Ariana back at the tree, where he sat, his back leaning against the thick trunk and his arms hugging his knees up against his chest. "That is not what I was hoping to find, Ariana," he said, as if she were listening, but the sorceress, still lying motionless on the hastily built bed of grass, showed no sign recognition, her chest rising and falling with each breath being the only sign she was even still alive. Foetore, however, looked up and gave the halfling a squeak, before going back to sleep.

Bealty tried to stay awake, but keeping watch was always a problem, so he occupied his mind by climbing the tree. He went up and down many times, trying to see how quickly he could make the ascent and descent, counting in his head, like a ticking clock. But eventually he got tired and decided to stay up in the tree, selecting a comfortable spot where he could relax that still provided him with an excellent vantage of the plains, in all directions. He could easily see the path he and his companions created getting here, and he could also see the swath of disturbed grass heading north, making him wonder what was happening. 'The world looks a lot different, from up here,' he thought to himself, but his thoughts were interrupted by an unexpected sight: two individuals were walking back his way, coming right down the path that would lead them to the tree. Bealty watched as they neared, and it soon became obvious that the two individuals were Mikell and Julius. "Gods, what happened?" he said out loud to himself with a mixture of dread, hoping the giant didn't kill the others or something, and partial relief that he didn't have to watch Ariana alone, which would have been a mighty expectation for a race prone to distraction.

Fifty yards away from the tree, Mikell looked at Julius. "Please tell me you see Bealty somewhere near Ariana," the cleric said, remembering the fiasco the last time they had relied on Bealty to stand guard.

"Up in the tree," Julius nodded with his head, urging the cleric to look up, "a smart place to be, I am sure he saw us coming from miles away."

Mikell growled, tugging on the lower earring in his right ear. "Well, he is a resourceful friend," then giving the ranger his fatherly glare, "just a horrible guard."

Julius let out a little laugh. "That he is, Mikell, let us hope this will be the last of his guarding duties for a while."

Arriving at the base of the tree, Bealty yelled down. "Why did you come back?!"

Mikell, looking up, used his hand to shield his eyes from the sun. "Get your arse down here and talk to us like a normal person!" Bealty did as was asked, quickly leaping from one branch to the next, Mikell wincing with each leap. "Be careful! If you fall -- I will not be able to help you!" but Bealty did not fall and soon he was practically sliding down the trunk of the tree, landing at their feet.

Not even out of breath, Bealty looked up. "So why are you back so soon? Are the others dead?"

"Dead?" Mikell said taken aback. "Why, no -- at least I certainly hope not."

Julius, walking closer, knelt next to Ariana. "We could not all catch up with the giant, so the others took the horses and kept chasing him down."

Bealty nodded, and crossing his arms, leaned against the tree. "Ahh, that makes sense," he said, giving Mikell a quick glance.

Mikell, seeing the look, stood a little straighter, puffing out his chest. "Oh -- go ahead, Bealty -- say it, I dare you," he said his arms on his hips.

"I just wish I could have gone with them, instead..." began Bealty.

"Instead of being here?" asked Mikell, interrupting.

"Well, yeah," said Bealty, "but it ain't no big deal. The die is cast."

Hearing the familiar halfling-ism phrase, stolen right out of Graff's small prayer book, which was more like a list of rules and mottoes to live by, Mikell's face softened. Remembering who he was talking to, and feeling a little ashamed of himself, the cleric let out a tired groan as he sat down, leaning his back against the tree, "Of course, you are right Bealty, the die is cast," he parroted as he unclipped his mace and set it on the ground next to him. Leaning his head back, Mikell closed his eyes. "All there is to do now is pray for their safety."

The blanket covering Ariana had blown off a little, and Julius tucked it back in place, then he too sat down, leaning against the tree, placing his sword, bow, and quiver on the ground next to him. "The die is cast," he said, accepting the finality of the phrase. "May Notria protect and guide them," he said, referring to the good goddess of nature.

Bealty thought about the human remains he found in the giant's possession and wondered if he should tell his friends. Most likely, he thought to himself, the gnolls had given some, or all, of their prisoners to the giants as a bribe, but he couldn't be sure. If he was right, what could they do from here? If he was wrong, then he was worrying his friends for nothing. Either way, the right thing seemed to be to say nothing, so the halfling scrambled, once again, up the tree, and after lodging himself into his comfortable spot, he gazed around the plain, wishing his friends somewhere over the horizon, the best of all things: luck.

* * * *

The Octu sun was beating down on them, making for an unusually hot day, and even though Brutal was riding, he found himself having to mop his brow with a cloth, the breastplate making him feel like he was traveling with a small oven strapped to his body. The heat didn't seem to be bothering the others, and he was truly amazed at the endurance of Tyberius and Isa, who kept up with the trot of the horses. The trail left by the gnolls was easy to follow, and soon they found themselves at the crest of the hill where Julius had first spied the gnolls and the giants together. The small group of companions paused at the top, looking down. They could see a large area of the grassy plain, where it had been trodden down by a large group, but what really caught their attention was the large amount of red that colored the area.

Tyberius looked up at Brutal. "Shit, B, I hope that ain't what I think it is," he said, pointing down the hill.

Brutal's face darkened, a mixture of concern and anger. "I hope not, too...let us go see it up close," he said, his voice taught, then clicking his tongue, he urged Jasper, the light warhorse, onward. The group quickly made their way to the trodden area, and it looked far worse up close than it had from high up on the top of the hill. The gore was unimaginable -- there seemed to be blood everywhere, and the innards that littered the ground made it obvious that a massive butchering had taken place. Flies infested the area, and the smell was awful. Brutal slid down off Jasper's back and slowly looked around the scene, taking it all in. "We are too late..." he managed to croak out, his voice failing him, then he saw the hat, and his heart sank. Brutal started walking toward it, his legs feeling weaker with each step, while an anger welled up inside of him, along with a hatred he had never known could exist. The little leather hat, hung up on the tall grass, lightly waving in the wind as if a last call for help, drew Brutal to it. Nearing the dreaded object, he reached out and grabbed it. Holding the hat gingerly, he turned it around, seeing what he already knew would be there: two wolf's teeth sewn into the front, above the rim of the hat. Brutal sank to his knees, tears first welling up, then dripping down the side of his face, mixing with beads of sweat.

Tyberius, seeing his friends sink to his knees, quickly ran over to him. "B, what is it?" he asked but stopped in his tracks when he saw the familiar hat that Brutal's youngest brother used to wear -- the two teeth making it unmistakable. Tyberius could feel the surging anger, his blood feeling hot in his veins, his hands balling up into tight fists, "Those god-damned, sum-bitches, are gonna pay for all of this," he said through clenched teeth.

"We should keep moving," said York, breaking the short, uncomfortable, heartbreaking silence.

Tyberius noticed the bard seated on Ariana's pony thirty feet away. Seeing the bard, writing in his book, he lost control over his emotions. "Put that fucking pen down, put it down right now!" he hollered, pointing and moving briskly with purposeful strides toward York. "You ain't write'in any of this shit down, or I will be wipin' my ass with the pages of yer little book!"

York closed the book immediately and tucked it away with the pen, then holding up his empty hands, quickly replied, "Done -- see, not writing!"

Tyberius stopped next to the bard. "Make sure this shit stays out of yer damned book."

"Oh, absolutely, Ty," said York. Seeing the tall redheaded warrior's face relax a bit, he added, "We really should keep moving, there is nothing more we can do here."

"He right," said Isa, his deep voice devoid of compassion.

It was unusual for the monk to talk, much less give an opinion, so the comment caught Tyberius's attention. The tall warrior's face was grim, and he gave the monk a hard look before walking back over to Brutal, who was still kneeling. Tyberius put a hand on his friend's shoulder. "C'mon, B, it ain't just Nicholas's blood out here, we gotta go get some fucking revenge for this, and right now, they be putting more distance between us and them while we sit here. Isa and York are right -- we gotta get movin'."

Brutal, looking down and away from his friend, wiped his face with the small hat. Looking back at his friend, he stood up. "I am going to kill every fucking gnoll on Thran if I have to, just so I know I killed the mangy cowards who did this."

"It be easier than that, B, they be just down the way," Tyberius said, pointing at the obvious trail cut through the grass. "If we kill them sons of bitches, then we got the ones who did all this shit, and at the homesteads, too."

Brutal nodded and clasped the side of his friend's shoulder. "I am glad you are here with me for this..." he started.

"Yeah, well, there ain't no damn way I would be lettin' you do somethin' like this without me," Tyberius said, poking himself in the chest. "Now, can we go kill some no-good, god-damned, gnolls?"

Brutal, still holding on to the hat, trying to control the rage and hatred he could feel coursing through his body, nodded and remounted the light warhorse. Closing his eyes and wiping away his tears, he gave the warhorse a light kick, spurring it to a trot as the group began following the well-worn trail of the gnolls once again.

* * * *

"Look," said Huppkif, pointing a hairy hand up ahead, his canine teeth showing as he talked, "there be the crick, it not far now."

Vilnesk looked at his Huppkif and snarled, "I can see, you dumb ass, I know where we is, and it be a cr-eee-k, not a crick, you mangy mutt."

Huppkif's lip curled back, irritated at the insult. "No need to be an asshole."

Vilnesk, ignoring the comment, looked behind him. His nine gnoll pack looked worn down and beat from traveling hard over the last two days. "We will rest when we get up there, I could use a drink and a break -- my feet are killing me -- I hope those fucking humans got what they deserved for chasing us so damned far."

"You think Wachog killed all of them?" asked Huppkif.

Vilnesk gave his cohort a glaring look. "Of course, he did -- they probably crushed them with the damn rocks they throw, an' did not even have to bloody their clubs."

"Yeah," said Huppkif. "Did you see them clubs -- they was like trees."

Vilnesk, shaking his head, kept on walking. Finally reaching the creek, fifteen feet wide at this point, and three or four feet deep, he bent down, lapping up a large amount of water. Enjoying the cool liquid running down his throat, he plunged his entire head into the creek, cooling himself off. The rest of the pack also began refreshing themselves, some even going into the middle and submerging their entire bodies. After drinking and cooling themselves off, the gnolls finally lay down in the grass, panting in the late afternoon heat. Vilnesk let them all rest for a little while, but as he watched the sun slowly getting lower in the sky, he stood up. "Alright you lazy curs -- get on your feet. We gotta get to Gilcurr, and we can just make it tonight if we hurry."

The other gnolls, not budging, all looked at Huppkif, who seemed to be the most capable and diplomatic of the bunch when it came to convincing Vilnesk of something. Huppkif stood up. "Hey, Vil, c'mon, we is all beat, and you said yourself," he said, pointing at Vilnesk, "them giants killed those human scum, so what is the rush? We can get to Gilcurr tomorrow."

Vilnesk hesitated, then looked past Huppkif to the horizon and the hills hiding any potential threats. "If I was not saddled with such lazy curs like you, I would have made it back to Gilcurr already. Fellpon and Krykl will want to hear what happened." After a short pause, he added, "And he will want to know tonight, not tomorrow, you lazy curr."

Huppkif straightened up, holding his ground. "Well, me and the rest of the pack are gonna spend the night here. If you want to go back tonight, go on ahead," he said, gesturing to the north.

Vilnesk reached for the ax tucked into his belt. "You disobedient mongrel, I ought to break your head open."

Huppkif raised a hand, motioning for Vilnesk to stop while the other hand drifted to his own ax. "Now hold on, Vil, this ain't worth one of us getting kilt over. Just go on your way. If them humans somehow got passed old Wachog, we will finish them off for ya."

Vilnesk did not draw his ax but kept walking until his snout was inches away from Huppkif's, the two gnolls' eyes being locked in a duel, neither blinking, until finally Huppkif looked away. "You are pathetic, Huppkif, you always have been." Looking around at the rest of the gnolls lying on the ground, he said, "And so are the rest of you useless curs." Seeing none of the pack move, Vilnesk snarled, saying, "Fine, if you all want to waste your time whoring each other all night, I do not care a shit." Turning to Huppkif, he pushed the gnoll backwards. "And you, you mangy dog, get these assholes moving at first light, and when you do finally get back to Gilcurr, the first thing you fucking do better be finding me." Huppkif nodded. Vilnesk shook his head in disgust, his voice returning to a calm level. "Those giants could have easily just taken our human offering and walked away. Hill giants are fucking tough, I will give them that, but they are also crazy, selfish, and untrustworthy. So, you all better keep one eye open. Those scumbag humans could be on their way here right now. They were moving quickly, so if they did get past Wachog and Gebank, or if those damn giants never even tried to hunt the humans, they will be coming over those hills before sundown," he finished, pointing into the hills now behind them.

"If they come here, we will kills them all," said Huppkif defiantly.

Vilnesk gave the pack one last evil look. "Fine, I will see you idiots tomorrow." Turning, the gnoll pack leader waded across the creek and disappeared at a quick pace into the undulating hills of the Cruel Pass.

"Do you think them giants kill't them stinkin' humans?" asked a gnoll with a large scar on the side of his face.

Huppkif kicked the gnoll in the chest, knocking him flat onto the ground. "Dumb ass. Of course, they did. You is so stupid," he chided. Ignoring the injured yelp from his prone pack-mate, Huppkif allowed himself a long look at the hills on the southern horizon, but seeing nothing, he sat down, glad to finally be able to relax.

* * * *

"We are very near the gnolls now," Tyberius said, kneeling, looking at a large paw-print in the ground. "These tracks are so fresh, they could be over the next hill for all I know." He paused, contemplating, then looking up, added, "I wish Julius was here, he is a much better tracker than me."

"If that is the case, we must be ready," said York. "Remember the plan." Everyone nodded.

"I will go out front and scout ahead," said Tyberius, "if they is as close as I think, we do not want to get ambushed coming over the crest of a hill or somthin'."

"Good idea," said Brutal. "Let us get moving, we still need to get back to Ariana and the others before dark, if we can." Nobody said a word as they began moving, with Tyberius moving out ahead, almost at a sprint.

After an hour of traveling north, Tyberius crouched as he crested another hill. He was surprised to see the hills give way to a large, almost valley like flat area, with a creek, almost a small river, running through the middle of it -- and camping right along the bank, perhaps three hundred yards away, was the group of gnolls. Tyberius backed down the hill a little way before standing up and waving the others to come up. "There are seven or eight gnolls resting near a creek on the other side of this hill. They are a ways off, and I do not see how we can get near them without them seein' us."

"In this case, it is probably a good thing they will see us coming," said York, a smile on his face as he wrote down some notes in his journal.

* * * *

Dox, a brutish looking gnoll even by gnoll standards, was sleeping, worn out from the forced march. Not only was it a grueling pace, but he also had to carry one of the child prisoners, which was easy at first, but with each mile, the little son of a bitch got heavier. He was on the verge of welcomed sleep when his chin slipped off his forearm, on which it was resting, and slammed rudely into the ground, causing him to bite his tongue, jarring him awake. He growled in anger, tasting the fresh blood, his eyes opening to see what had just happened. It was still bright out, and the gnoll squinted, trying to block out some of the sun. Catching a glimpse of movement in the distance, he jerked his head up and opened his eyes completely, now fully awake. Off in the distance, he saw three humanoids, one riding a horse coming down the hill, three hundred yards off. "Wake up, you dogs!" he barked in their draconic tongue and pointed to the hill, shouting, "Humans are coming!"

Huppkif jumped to his feet, his ax already in hand. Looking off to the south, he saw the small force of humans, but he also spotted a lone rider separated from the others, riding toward them as well. "There is a fourth, riding alone," he barked and pointed. The other gnolls all looked, then looked back at Huppkif, waiting for orders. "We got screwed out of the human flesh by the giants -- but today," Huppkif said, raising his ax above his head, "it will be a human feast!" The other gnolls all let out loud barks and yelps, whipping themselves up into a frenzy. "Dox," Huppkif said, yipping out the orders quickly, pointing to the large gnoll. "Take Karig and Gauth with you and go kill the lone rider, then come help us finish off the other three. The rest of you dogs, come with me!" he added as he began running toward the small group of humans, closely followed by five of his pack-mates. Dox and two other gnolls took off, yipping and howling, in the direction of the lone rider.

* * * *

Seeing the gnolls finally take notice of their approach, Brutal lifted his right leg over Jaspers head, and he slid down off the warhorse. Trusting in the horse's extensive training, not to run away, he let go of the reins, watching as the gnolls broke off into two groups: three heading toward York, and the other five heading directly toward himself, Isa, and Tyberius. "I hope he knows what the hell he is doing," he said, watching the three gnolls quickly closing in on the bard.

Tyberius, watching with concern as well, nodded, saying, "Yeah -- there ain't no way I am going to depend on magic to save my arse...no fucking way," he added as a shiver ran up his spine thinking about it.

"Ariana and Mikell have already saved us more than once with magic, Tyberius," said Brutal.

Tyberius looked down at his shorter companion, his face serious, "Yeah, tho' I ain't talkin' about priest magic -- that comes from the gods and all...but the shit York and Ariana is doin'? Shit, B, who knows where that kind of magic comes from," Tyberius said as a statement, not a question, then added, "it makes my skin crawl."

Brutal wanted to continue the conversation, but the gnolls were advancing rapidly, so he changed the subject. "They are going to be on us pretty quick," said Brutal, drawing his bastard sword, its long, thick, dark blade glinting in the sun. "It is two to one, so try to keep our backs to each other so they cannot get behind us." Tyberius nodded and Isa grunted with what Brutal hoped was understanding as they each took a few steps, forming a small protective triangle.

"These gnolls is about to pay up for what they done," said Tyberius, pulling his flail from his belt, the large ball jangling at the end of its chain while he flexed his fingers around the Taper wood shaft, finding the right grip. He could already begin to feel the blood in his veins starting to tingle and burn, in what was becoming a familiar, and welcomed, feeling. Reaching back, he pulled the shield from his back and slid his right arm through the straps, grabbing the handle firmly. His eyes darkened into a frown, as he thought of how the gnolls had killed their families, and he began bashing his shield with the Taper wood handle of the flail, "C'mon ye dogs -- c'mon!"

* * * *

York watched as the three gnolls broke off in his direction. "Damn," he said into the wind, having hoped one or two more would have come his way, "but this will have to do." Still sitting on Ariana's pony, the bard reached into a small pouch on his belt and, pulling out a small amount of mistletoe, he began readying himself. "Good," he said under his breath, seeing the gnolls sticking together, not spreading out, and coming directly for him. When they were about eighty yards away, he held up the small twig of mistletoe and began chanting the spell. "Albero, erba, cespuglio, albero, erba, cespuglio: svegliatevi per difendere il vostro protettore. Intrappolate, irretite e legate il nemic." Finishing the verbal and somatic portions of the spell, he focused on the area around the gnolls. As he did so, the twig in his hand disintegrated. Following the sacrifice of the mistletoe, the grassy plain around the gnolls erupted into life -- every blade of grass, every weed, and every piece of vegetation began groping, twisting, and entangling the gnolls. Karig tripped and landed on his stomach, where the grass immediately engulfed his body, blades wrapping themselves around his arms, legs, torso, and neck. Squirming, he cried out for help, yelping to his companions for aid, but Dox and Gauth, although they had not fallen, found themselves busy using their axes to cut and beat away the aggressive foliage.

"Forget Karig," screamed Dox, "and keep moving out of this mess, toward the wizard!" Gauth, slicing, stepping, slicing, stepping, yipped that he understood, and the two gnolls continued moving toward York, albeit slowly.

Seeing the spell take effect, he was surprised to see two of the gnolls continue making progress, but there was nothing he could do about that, so giving the pony a kick and shouting a quick, "He-ya!" he began galloping toward Brutal and the others, who were already surrounded, engaged with the other six gnolls.

* * * *

Huppkif slowed down as he approached the three companions and hollered, "Dest and Camich, you take the orc-man! Narsdil and Futhi, the tall one!" Looking at the gnoll standing next to him, who stood a couple inches taller than himself, making him almost seven and a half feet tall. "Custog, you and me will kill the dark-haired one!" With their orders, they split up, surrounding their quarry, slowly inching in for the kill.

Camich was an average seven feet for a gnoll, but was battle hardened, as evidenced by a long scar that snaked its way down his left jowl, creating what looked like a cleft lip. He and Dest, the only gnoll with a chainmail shirt, closed in on the large half-orc, cautiously stabbing and feinting, looking for an opening. Thinking he saw one, Camich swung his ax low, trying to clip the monk's left knee, but Isa easily moved out of the way. Seeing the monk dodge Camich's swing, Dest, swung his ax high, at Isa's neck. Isa blocked the shaft of the ax with his thick right forearm, following it up with a hard left punch straight into Dest's solar plexus. The chainmail shirt, designed to deflect bladed weapons, did nothing to soften the crushing impact of Isa's fist, as evidenced by the cracking and snapping of the gnoll's bones ringing out. Isa's blow knocked Dest off his feet and backwards several feet. Landing on his back, Dest lay there in shock, unaware that the broken bones in his chest had punctured his heart. All he knew was that he could not catch his breath, and as he tried to roll over to get up, he found he was already too weak. As the world faded from his vision, he lapsed into unconsciousness.

Narsdil was a short gnoll, known for his vicious scrappiness in battle. Futhi was a veteran warrior, having seen many battles, making him was old by gnoll standards, and was missing his left eye. They each looked at the large spiked ball dangling behind the tall redheaded warrior and weren't too eager to get close, but they could smell the human flesh, and their instinct was to kill. Following that instinct, they began harassing the warrior with quick strikes, high and low, trying to get the tall human to commit to an action.

"C'mon and fight me!" Tyberius growled at the gnolls, urging them closer.

Narsdil and Futhi growled back, exposing their fangs as their jowls pulled back; their teeth, while not clean, looked viciously sharp. They both attacked simultaneously, howling as they did so. Tyberius blocked Narsdil's ax with his shield while using the Taper wood shaft of his flail to block the Futhi's ax. Tyberius roared, pushing Narsdil backwards with his shield, as he took a quick swing at Futhi with the flail, but it was a weak, awkward strike, missing widely.

Huppkif and Custog moved in on Brutal, making swift thrusts, not so much to kill but to wear down the dark-haired human. Huppkif did not recognize the human at first, but now that he was up close, the pieces of the puzzle were falling into place: dark hair, muscular, fairly tall...then it dawned on him, lighting up his face with an evil grin, exposing his sharp canine teeth. "Brutal Mixnor," Huppkif said in his best common tongue, pointing his ax at Brutal. "Custog," he continued, back in his yipping gnoll language, "this is no mercenary group -- this is the family of the humans we took!"

Hearing his name, Brutal did a double take, then swatted the ax away with his bastard sword. "That is right, I am Brutal, and we are going to kill all of you!"

Huppkif knew enough common tongue to understand the threat and yipped as he lunged in for his first serious assault. He unleashed a high arcing swing but Brutal, raising his bastard sword, cross blocked the descending ax blade. Custog, taking advantage of Brutal's distraction, swung laterally, aiming for Brutal's chest. Although the human was quick enough to repurpose his bastard sword, partially deflecting the blow, the ax still managed to clang off the lower part of Brutal's breastplate, slashing his hip, doing minor damage, and drawing blood.

＊ ＊ ＊ ＊

Brutal flinched at the pain, moving his body away from the sharp blade of the ax. The gnoll, Custog, with a bulldog-looking face, looked different than the rest of the troop, and his pudgy, loose jowls flapped with his every move. The gnoll was grinning as his ax drew blood, but although Brutal hadn't been able to fully defend the gnoll's attack, he was able to redirect his own blade, stabbing at the exposed belly of the gnoll. The gnoll's leather armor couldn't stop the blade as it slid into Custog's left side. Letting out a loud yelp of pain, the bulldog-faced gnoll jumped backwards, saving his life in the process. Despite the gnoll's attempts to put pressure on it with his free hand, a thick stream of blood immediately began flowing down his belly. "C'mon!" shouted Brutal, motioning with his left hand for the wounded gnoll to get back in the fight.

The short, beefy Narsdil moved in again on Tyberius, this time rushing in close to the tall redheaded warrior, slashing as he did so with the ax. The gnoll's attack got inside Tyberius's shield, cutting into the tall warrior's left thigh, inflicting a minor wound. Tyberius initially felt the pain, but the pain quickly subsided, replaced with the now familiar burning sensation of adrenaline pumping throughout his body, his muscles beginning to bulge with the new, refreshing, and abundant blood flow. At the same time, however, his mind, starved of the blood being diverted to the rest of his body, was becoming clouded, as all thoughts beyond killing what was in front of him became secondary.

Brutal, meanwhile, sensing some hesitation on the part of Custog and Huppkif, surged forward, attacking quickly, swinging in quick succession at Huppkif, but the pack leader was too quick and was able to dodge the well-placed strikes.

"Get your ass back in here!" Huppkif yipped, cursing his wounded pack-mate. Snarling, Huppkif gnashed his teeth and, jumping toward Brutal, lashed out with his clawed hand, ripping at Brutal's chest, but the solid breastplate easily protected him from the blow.

Custog quickly eyed the river, then looking back at Brutal, he also rushed in, slashing downward with a hard blow, landing on the top of Brutal's right shoulder. Brutal's breastplate was held together on top by two hardened leather clasps, and while the metal armor was able to deflect the main force of the blow, the ax blade bounced into the side of his neck, causing a serious gash. Huppkif and Custog, barking furiously, pressed their attack.

Isa, staring down Camich, flashed his own teeth, his lips curling back in hatred of his opponent. Even at rest, Isa's lower fangs protruded outside of his mouth due his large underbite, but with his face twisted in anger, his large teeth were fearsome. Camich was used to orcs, and although this one was unusually large, he showed no outward sign of fear. The two combatants sparred, neither committing until Camich slashed his ax in front of Isa, trying to drive the monk backwards. It worked momentarily, but as soon as the ax had passed, Isa charged the gnoll. Surprised, Camich took a step backward and tried to reverse his swing, striking with the spiked back of the ax, but Isa got inside his swing and tackled the large gnoll, first picking him up in a large bear hug, then pile driving the gnoll into the ground. Placing his shoulder across the gnoll's stomach, he could hear the air rushing out of the gnoll's lungs mingled with the snapping sound of the beast's ribs, followed by the cracking sound of the gnoll's head bouncing violently off the hard ground, knocking him senseless. He groaned for a second under the weight of the half-orc, but the force of the blow to his head, and the internal damage from Isa's shoulder, left the gnoll unmoving and unconscious.

Futhi had been around a long time, and he was beginning to realize that this battle was not as lopsided as it initially looked. The gnoll, already seeing two of his pack-mates disabled by the half-orc now warily eyed what had to be a mage that was now on his way into the battle. Returning his attention to the redheaded warrior in front of him, his doubts only increased as the redheaded human with crazy eyes waved the spiked ball in his direction. Seeing Narsdil rush the human, he thought it was a good time to make a run for it, and he broke off running as fast as he could back toward the creek. York saw the gnoll make a break for it but decided not to alter his course, keeping the pony galloping toward the main battle.

"Your friend is a coward!" roared Tyberius at Narsdil, seeing Futhi running away. Semi-understanding, Narsdil glanced backwards to see his pack-mate heading away. The gnoll's glance was all the opening Tyberius needed, raising the flail he swung it downward at the gnoll, who looked back just in time, allowing him to knock the flail away with his ax. Reversing his block, he swung his ax back at Tyberius, the blade whizzing by the warrior's neck, leaving a small scrape, but was mere inches from a death blow.

Custog could see the blood running down Brutal's breastplate, but it was the smell of the human blood that was driving him into a frenzy. Howling, the gnoll jabbed the pointed end of his ax at Brutal, the tip glancing off the breastplate. Brutal swung his sword at Custog, but the swing was too slow and had no effect. Isa rolled off Camich, and flipping back on to his feet, he rushed Huppkif's right flank, throwing a flurry of punches. Huppkif saw the monk coming and blocked the punches with his free arm, then chopped down with his ax, striking the monk across the chest, ripping through the cloth fabric and cutting into the half-orc's greenish flesh, blood quickly wicking into the brown robes.

Karig still lay prone, immobilized by the grass, but Dox and Gauth were finally making it to the outer edge of the area of the spell, hacking and slashing the grass is they moved. "Keep moving, you dog!" Dox said, barking at Gauth.

York was close enough now, and pulling back on the reins, he quickly dismounted.

Huppkif, inspired by his successful blow, pressed his attack, striking again at the monk, but this time Isa raised his arm to block the strike, the shaft of the ax slamming into the monk's forearm. Isa, counter-striking, spun around with a wheelhouse kick that struck the gnoll in the chest. Huppkif, barely managing to keep his feet under him, was forced to take a couple steps backwards before catching himself.

Brutal swung again at Custog, but although badly hurt, the gnoll still showed amazing speed and easily blocked the sword strike. Taking a quick step back, the Gnoll immediately struck back at Brutal, the ax blade slamming into the breastplate, but deflected without doing any serious damage.

Narsdil and Tyberius continued to spar, trading blows, trying to find a weakness in their opponent's defenses, but with no real damage being done until Tyberius stumbled on a loose stone hidden in the grass. Narsdil saw the misstep and immediately rushed in, hacking with his ax. Tyberius tried to raise his shield up to block the blow, but as he did so, Narsdil altered his attack and the ax struck Tyberius in the left thigh, slicing through the tough leather armor, resulting in a gaping wound. The tall warrior stumbled backwards a step. In his enraged state, all concern for his physical well-being was long gone and his vision tunneled in on the only thing in front of him: Narsdil. Roaring like a madman, Tyberius began swing his flail madly, pushing the gnoll backwards with each mighty swing, the solid, spiked, ball humming through the air.

Brutal paid no attention to the shouting going on behind him, he remained focused on Custog, the bulldog-faced gnoll that continued to harry him despite the gaping, bleeding wound Brutal had delivered. But now it seemed Custog had gained the upper hand, his quick decisive blows scoring multiple hits. This time Custog feinted high and Brutal took the bait, raising his sword, which was getting heavier with each passing minute, to block the ax, but the gnoll was too quick. Rather than continuing the high attack, Custog ducked, spun around, and struck a hard blow to Brutal's right calf. Too slow to avoid the ax blade, Brutal gave into the blow, but with his bastard sword already high, he brought it down with all his might. Custog was yipping and howling, thinking for a moment he was about to fell the human, until his peripheral vision caught the descending bastard sword. Custog raised his ax to block the blow, but Brutal's blade sliced right through the shaft, embedding itself deep into Custog's neck, nearly decapitating the gnoll. Custog let out an abbreviated yelp of pain before slumping to the ground, his lifeblood pumping out onto the matted grass.

Just as Custog was falling, Huppkif attacked Isa with a flurry of swings with his ax. The monk was unusually quick, thought Huppkif, as the large half-orc blocked each successive strike with his thick forearms. But Huppkif continued pressing his attack, and Isa finally misjudged the angle of the incoming blow, resulting in the blade sinking into his left forearm. Isa winced in pain, then quickly went on his own offensive with punches and kicks, but Huppkif simply backed up, dodging the attacks.

Tyberius continued his rapid swings, sending the large spiked ball left to right, then right to left, howling in rage with each swing. Narsdil, ducking, dodging, and moving backwards was able to successfully avoid the wide arcing swings and, in the process, began measuring the timing in his mind. If he could get inside the reach of the tall human, it would be hard for the flail to hit him with much force, if at all. As the spiked ball went sailing past him again, Narsdil jumped inside, hacking with his ax and successfully striking the tall human directly in the chest, but Tyberius's chain mail armor stopped the blade from penetrating. Tyberius's eyes glared up at the gnoll now practically in his face, and leaping up and into the gnoll, delivered a head-butt to Narsdil's snout, causing the gnoll to take a half step backwards, right in the path of Tyberius's back-swing. The spiked ball slammed into the right side of Narsdil's head, the spikes burying themselves deep into the gnoll's skull. Narsdil's eyes went out of focus and he stood still for a second, in a coma-like trance, until Tyberius punched him directly in the face with his free right hand, felling the seven foot gnoll backwards, like a small tree. Tyberius didn't pause to gloat but immediately began looking around to find his next target.

York, now dismounted, was able to approach Huppkif from the rear and, drawing his longsword, stabbed at the gnoll's back but missed when the squad leader sidestepped, barely avoiding the jabbing blade via sheer luck. Isa, seeing York's attack miss, jumped into the air with a spinning roundhouse kick, but Huppkif, leaning backwards, narrowly avoided the powerful attack. Brutal, seeing the gnoll getting overwhelmed, also joined in the gang-style attack, slashing with his bastard sword and scoring a hit on Huppkif's left side, the blade slicing through the tough leather hide and drawing blood. Huppkif yelped at the blow, immediately swinging his ax at Brutal, who ducked in time to avoid the head shot.

Huppkif, seeing that he was now surrounded, dropped his ax and, getting down on one knee, raised his hands in the air. "Me give! Me give!" he yipped in the best common tongue he could muster under the difficult moment.

"My spell will not last much longer," said York, pushing the tip of his longsword into the back of Huppkif's neck. "We should kill him now..."

"No kill...no kill!" shouted Huppkif, recognizing the common tongue word.

Brutal, stepping to the kneeling gnoll, grabbing a handful of the gnoll's leather armor, yanked the gnoll to get his attention. Brutal's face was inches from the muzzle of the gnoll, "Did you kill all the prisoners?!" he shouted, half crazed with anger.

Huppkif looked into Brutal's eyes. "I live," he gestured to himself,

"Huppkif tell you all!"

"Tell me now!" Brutal shouted again, shaking the gnoll.

"We do not have time for this!" warned York.

"Child killer!! You kilt your last human!" yelled Tyberius, raising his flail and moving toward the groveling gnoll.

"No!" shouted Brutal, but Tyberius paid him no heed. "Tyberius, no!" he shouted again. Letting go of the gnoll, he raised his hand to stop his friend. Tyberius looked like a wild man, his eyes darting back and forth between Brutal and Huppkif, breathing heavily from all his exertion and blood streaking down his face. "He has information!" Brutal shouted, readying himself to react if his friend would not, or could not, listen.

Tyberius paused for a second, looking at Brutal as if he were trying to consider what his friend was saying, but it was a fleeting effort, and the words were lost on the warrior. Roaring, Tyberius's face twisted into an angry mass of hatred. Brutal tried holding him back, but Tyberius's enraged strength was too much. Using his shield, he easily bashed Brutal out of the way, knocking him to the ground. With a mad growl, Tyberius brought the flail down on the Huppkif. The spiked ball cracked the gnoll's skull and broke his neck simultaneously, and with a swift kick in the chest, Tyberius knocked Huppkif over onto his back, blood spilling out onto the ground.

As he was falling to the ground, Brutal heard the blow followed by the sickening crack of bones coming from the gnoll. Pushing himself back to a sitting position, he looked up just in time to see the gnoll, already lifeless, land on its back. "Nooo!" he gasped.

"They come!" said Isa, growling and pointing toward the other gnolls, who were now moving quickly, closing the distance.

"The spell has worn off," confirmed York. "Everyone get behind me."

"Why?" asked Brutal, standing back up.

"I have another spell up my sleeve, but you will not want to be in front of me when I cast it."

Isa and Brutal did as he asked, but Tyberius, seeing the gnolls, shot out in a sprint to engage them. "Tyberius! Wait!" shouted Brutal, but it was no use, his friend didn't miss a stride. "Now what?" asked Brutal, looking at York.

The bard shrugged. "I can still cast the spell, but he might be affected," said York. As they were talking, Isa ran after Tyberius, the two companions closing the gap together, leaving York and Brutal standing there.

"Shit!" said Brutal, giving the bard a look. "Hold off on the spell!" And he also began running to join his two friends. York nodded and, drawing his longsword, also began moving toward the imminent battle.

* * * *

The gnolls, seeing the humans running toward them, howled and yipped as the distance closed. Dox was now the lead gnoll, his wolf-like appearance struck fear into many of his pack-mates, and usually into his prey, but unfortunately, it seemed to have no effect on these humans. Growling as he neared the tall redheaded warrior, he leapt the last bit of distance, swinging his ax, but Tyberius saw the attack coming and easily blocked the blow with his shield. Gauth was right behind Dox, and the light red-haired gnoll moved around to Tyberius's left side, where there was no shield, and struck the warrior with a quick slash, but the chain mail shirt deflected the sharp blade.

Gauth was so focused on Tyberius that he momentarily lost track of Isa as he swung his ax at Tyberius. Seeing the gnoll give him his flank, Isa, still running, used his forward momentum and delivered a massive punch to Gauth's lower spine, right above his waist. Gauth felt the blow only for an instant, as his spine was fractured, then he felt nothing as his legs gave out from underneath him, and he fell forward into Tyberius, then finally into a small heap on the ground.

Tyberius, being buffeted from all sides, swung his flail at Dox, but as he was swinging, Gauth fell into him, disrupting his attack and allowing Dox to easily side-step the blow.

Karig was a scrawny, relatively shorter gnoll, but he was also quick and scrappy. Seeing Gauth fall, he zeroed in on the monk and struck a slashing blow with his ax. Isa tried to block the attack, but the ax blade sunk into his right bicep, drawing blood. Ignoring the wound, Isa grabbed the ax and ripped it from Karig's grasp, then with his left hand he struck the gnoll in the neck, shattering his windpipe. Karig stumbled backwards, his hands going to his throat, his eyes wide in terror, as he gasped for the air he desperately needed.

Tyberius swung his flail again, but Dox ducked underneath the swing and as he stood back up swung his ax upwards, slashing Tyberius's left arm, and although the padded armor was not strong enough to stop the blow, it still lessened the damage, resulting in a gash to his triceps.

Brutal, finally arriving on the scene, swung his sword with an upward thrust, catching Dox on his exposed right side -- the blade cutting through the hard leather armor, cutting the gnoll with a gash all the way to his right ribs.

York, seeing that it was now three on one, sheathed his sword and began chanting a battle hymn, creating a field of magical energy around the three fighters.

Brutal, seeing the wolf-like gnoll reeling, tried to quickly follow up his successful blow with a life-ending stab but the gnoll was too quick and, bringing its ax down, blocked the blade. Following up from parrying Brutal's attack, the gnoll, using the curved edge of the ax, ripped the bastard sword from Brutal's grip, tossing the weapon ten feet away. Tyberius swung his flail, the large spiked ball missing but driving the gnoll back a step, allowing Isa to engage the overwhelmed gnoll with a strong punch right into the center of the gnoll's chest. Dox yelped in pain at the crushing force and stumbled backwards a couple steps, holding his chest as he sank to his knees, before falling forward onto his face.

Tyberius looked around frantically, his eyes still darting back and forth, trying to figure out what to attack next. Not seeing any gnolls, he took a step toward Isa, who moved back maintaining his distance from the berserked warrior. Tyberius took another staggering step toward Isa but let the ball of his flail drop to the ground with a thud. Tyberius wobbled for another second before sinking down to the ground in a sitting position, his right arm propping him up. As his muscles relaxed, his capillaries expanded and blood began seeping out of every wound.

"Are you okay, Ty?" asked Brutal, taking a cautious step toward his friend.

"Aye," Tyberius rasped, lightly nodding his head, as if it were hard to hold up now, "I...I just need a bit to rest."

Brutal breathed a sigh of relief, but as he did, he began to feel the pain in his shoulder and neck where he had been badly cut. Reaching up with his gloved left hand, he felt around and, wincing in pain, pulled it quickly way, noting that his gauntlet was stained red with blood. Looking toward the creek, his eyes following the path the one-eyed gnoll had taken as he ran away, he sheathed his sword. "We gotta catch that gnoll," he said in a tired voice.

Tyberius looked up, blood dripping down his left cheek. "Hell yeah, we do...just...I need a little bit more time..." he said as he lay onto his back, his knees still up in the air.

"I hate to break it to you boys," said York, already writing in his journal, "but we cannot go after that gnoll."

"The fuck we ain't," said Tyberius, mustering some strength, which he put into his voice.

"Are you serious?" York asked rhetorically. Before anyone could answer, he continued, "All three of you are about dead yourself. No, no, no," he said, waving his pen at them, "not only could we not catch him at this point, but who knows where the next lair or pack is."

"I thought you told Mikell you can heal? Or was that bullshit?" asked Brutal.

"Of course, I can heal," said York, not even looking up, but again waving his pen around, "but for this kind of carnage we need a cleric." Looking up, he added, "You need Mikell."

"But we cannot let that son of a bitch get away!" shouted Brutal, gesturing toward the hills with his hand.

York shook his head. "You do not get it, he already got away," he said, stressing the word, "and that means we only have a little time before he comes back with reinforcements."

Brutal seemed to finally accept the bard's logic, sitting down on the grass next to Tyberius. It felt good to take the weight off his feet, but the relief was quickly replaced with frustration as he thought back to the gnoll who had surrendered. "Why did you have to kill that gnoll, back there?!" Brutal shouted at Tyberius, pointing in the direction of its fallen body. "He surrendered! He had information we need! And he could speak some common!"

Tyberius, still on his back, raised an arm up slightly, gesturing. "I do not remember," then after a short pause, "but that fucker deserved to die."

"Well, now we will never fucking know if there were any survivors, or whatever else he might have been able to tell us," Brutal commented in an angry tone. Tyberius did not answer, or comment, continuing to lie on the ground, with his hands on his head.

"Isa, would you be a help and go fetch Jasper over there," York asked, pointing to Julius's warhorse that was still grazing where Brutal had left him, then offered, "I will go get the pony." Isa nodded and took off at a sprint.

Brutal rested a hand on his friend's shoulder. "Ty -- we needed that gnoll alive."

"Sorry, B, I do not remember you try'in to stop me," Tyberius replied, moving his right hand away from his head to get a look at Brutal. "I just remember a gnoll that needed kill'in...and that is what I did." He gave Brutal a hard and unapologetic stare, and added with emphasis, "He needed to die."

Brutal could see the honesty in his good friend's face and let out a long sigh. "Well, what do we do now?" asked Brutal.

"What do ya mean?" Tyberius asked right back, sitting up on his elbows.

"We cannot go after that gnoll, and we cannot go back to Telfar." Feeling sweat running down his face, Brutal used a hand to wipe the numerous beads away. "I do not know what to do next."

"Mikell will know," said Tyberius, "he always knows the right thing."

Brutal sighed again, feeling terribly tired, and looking off into the direction the gnoll had run, took a deep breath. "I hope so."

* * * *

The sun was dipping dangerously close to the horizon, and as the light began to fade, so did everyone's hope for a good outcome to the day. The only good news was that Ariana had finally awoken. Mikell's healing had taken care of the damage, but she was confused, sore, and had little strength. Mikell stayed close to her, trying to keep her comfortable on the bed of grass Bealty had made for her.

"There is something terrible out there..." Ariana said, her voice barely above a whisper, as she looked up at Mikell's face. "I...I felt it, like... like we were connected."

"Nah, what you felt was the giant's club crushing you into the ground," said Bealty, still perched up in the tree.

Looking up, Mikell gave Bealty a quick, disapproving glare before turning his focus back to the sorceress. Putting a hand on her forehead, he whispered reassuringly, "Rest now, Ariana, you were on the doorstep of death, and your mind is just playing tricks on you."

"Where is Tyberius?" she asked, licking her lips, which she noticed, for the first time, were parched.

"Let me get you some water," Mikell said, reaching into his backpack and pulling out a flask, he helped hold her head up so she could take a sip. Mikell, putting the flask away, glanced at the tattoo on her shoulder of the two parallel arrows, pointing in opposite directions. Axis, a shadow god, he thought to himself, then recounted that York worshiped Linkal and Isa was a follower of Craven -- both also deities of the shadow. He always remembered his father saying, 'You cannot have a shadow without light,' but for Mikell, that felt like the glass was half full perspective, and he worried about the flip side of that, you couldn't have a shadow without darkness, either. Being the neutral god of magic, Axis was a legitimate choice for a magic user or sorceress, but why was she drawn to Axis and not Serrendal -- the good god of magic? The question nagged at him ever since he noticed her tattoo back at the Drip, in Telfar. He only knew Ariana through Brutal and Tyberius and had only seen her a few times before... 'Before all this,' he thought to himself, letting out a sigh. Either she wore clothes that concealed the mark, or it wasn't there, he could not remember which it was. Normally, with Ariana's defenses up, he didn't feel he could talk to her about it, but right now her defenses seemed down. Perhaps, he thought, he was taking advantage of her momentary weakness, but taking a calculated risk, he lowered his voice so others could not hear, and leaning in closer to Ariana, said, "You were so close to death, perhaps you encountered Axis," Mikell's eyes narrowed a bit as he talked, "perhaps that is what you sensed."

Ariana half-opened her eyes, the effort seemingly great. "No," she whispered, "when Axis appeared to me, the feeling went...away."

"He appeared to you? How can you be sure?" Mikell pressed, a little too eagerly, he thought to himself.

Ariana closed her eyes, the task of keeping them open seemed unnecessary and difficult to her. "I have seen Axis before. He appeared to me again," she said, swallowing and taking a deep breath. "He said..."

Mikell drew even closer, his ear very close to her mouth. "What, Ariana, what did he say?"

"What he said, made no sense..." her voice trailed off.

Putting a hand on her arm, he shook her very lightly. "Ariana... Ariana, what did he say?" Foetore, who was still lying curled up like a ball of fur, uncoiled and squawked right near Mikell's face, but Mikell did not flinch.

"Queen..." Ariana said, her voice trailing off.

Before Mikell could decide what to do next, Bealty broke the calm of the early evening. "They return!" he shouted, still sitting high up in the tree and pointing to the northwest. "It looks like all four, and both horses!"

Mikell was irritated by the timing, but Ariana's head had turned to the side, and she breathed softly in and out, so he carefully backed away. "Thank Zuel they are okay," said Mikell, clasping his hands together in thanks, then grunting as he stood up, every muscle in his body, unaccustomed to the grueling activity of the past two days, had tightened up from the few hours of rest.

The small group moved slowly, all their previous energy used up in the chase and the battle, leaving them exhausted for the journey back. Arriving at the tree, Tyberius walked purposefully to where Ariana still was lying. "Has she awoken?" he asked, looking at Mikell.

"You bet she has, Ty!" said Bealty, jumping down from the tree branch.

"Thank Soulmite!" said Tyberius, his eyes showing a hint of the tears he was holding back, then turning to Mikell, added, "and Zuel...and you, too, Mikell."

"The light protects us all," said Mikell. Looking down at Ariana, he continued, "But she is still very weak."

"We can rest here until she gets better," said Tyberius.

"There will not be time for that luxury," said York, still sitting atop Ariana's pony.

"Why do you say that? What happened out there?" asked Julius.

"We found the pack of gnolls camping on the bank of a creek," said Brutal. "They engaged us, and we were able to kill all but one of them."

"All but one?" asked Julius, some alarm in his voice.

"Yeah, all but one," said Brutal, and before Julius could speak, he continued, "I know -- likely that means more gnolls are going to be coming after us."

"Gnolls," said Mikell, concerned. "If we are lucky, it will just be gnolls."

"What do ya mean?" asked Tyberius, who was now sitting by Ariana, leaning his back against the large tree, one hand touching Ariana's forearm.

Mikell looked at the returning companions, they were all bloodied and moving about gingerly -- each nursing severe wounds, except for York, he noticed. "Julius, can you get a fire going?"

Julius nodded. "Of course." His backpack was lying on the ground near the tree, and the ranger went to it and pulled a hatchet that was clipped onto it. Tucking it into his belt, he climbed up the tree and began hacking some of the smaller branches off and dropping them down.

"You may be right, York," said Mikell. "Time may not be on our side, but we are not going anywhere tonight... We have at least that much time."

York, flashing his elvish, condescending half-smile, said, "Those undead knew who Skik was, and the undead never stop to rest, so the night is not necessarily our friend." After brief pause, he added, "Certainly, it is far from safe."

"Have a seat, York," said Mikell, giving the bard a stern glance, the glint of the dying sunlight bouncing off his earrings and bald head. Using the gruffness of his voice to communicate there was nothing left to argue, he added, "Take out a pen and that journal of yours -- I am sure you have a lot of writing to catch up on."

"Of course," said York, swinging his left leg over the pony's head and sliding down the other side, landing nimbly on his feet. Finding a good spot on the ground, he laid his backpack down, and sitting next to it, he began writing in his journal.

CHAPTER TWENTY-EIGHT

Reunion

YEAR: AG 1172, Month of Sepu

IT TOOK KORD AND HIS UNDEAD MINIONS FIVE DAYS of straight walking to find Gilcurr, arriving just before noon. The makeshift city rested in a wooded valley, lying at the very foothills of the Doubtless Mountains. The city's outer defenses consisted of a fortified, double-thick layer of log walls, each carved to a fine point at the top. A river, flowing from the nearby mountains, entered underneath the west wall of the city and served as a source of drinking water and as a sewer before exiting under the wall on the south side of the town. From his vantage point, Kord could see all manner of humanoids inside the city, there was even a squad of frost giants working on the outside wall. How he knew they were frost giants, like everything else he knew, was a mystery to him, but he was growing accustomed to the feeling and accepted that he had a wealth of knowledge that he could recall, but which was only useful to him when confronted with a pertinent situation. Another frustrating aspect was that the memories, when they did return, weren't linked to any other memories, just as he knew he was looking at frost giants, but he had no access to where he had gained that knowledge -- who he was with, what he was doing, or how he had encountered them in the past. But he knew their behavior and customs well. Standing over fifteen feet tall, they were hardened warriors, known for their ferocity in battle. Although not all frost giants were highly intelligent, there always seemed to be a capable leader, clever enough to make his clan an opponent to be avoided, or, at the very least, to be dealt with carefully.

"Let me do the talking when we get down there," Kord hissed, addressing Kijjit, who was jabbering with the three ghouls.

Hearing Kord speak, Kijjit immediately stopped talking and hastened to Kord's side. "Yes, yes, of course."

"When we get down there, we will need to make an example, so those wretches know who they now serve," Kord continued to stare at the town. Long rows of barracks made up the majority of the buildings, Gilcurr being more of a marshaling area than a town, but there were quite a few other buildings constructed in the middle of the town, the largest and tallest, being in the dead center, with seven roads leading to it: a large keep that went up seven stories. "That building," Kord pointed to it, "in the middle, that is where we will find Krykl."

Kijjit rubbed his hands together. "Of course, master." Then he cackled. "Shall we kill him and eat him as an example?"

"No," said Kord, causing a disappointed look to wash across Kijjit's sore-pocked face, making it look even more pathetic and horrifying. "Krykl will live, but we will slay some of his minions, which you can devour."

"Oh, thank you, master!" Kijjit's face brightened, showing his true excitement. "We are all so hungry."

* * * *

Walking into the forest surrounding the town, he lost sight of the walls but somehow he could sense the direction, he could feel the energy of its inhabitants. Descending into the valley through the wooded approaches, Kord could feel that there were eyes on him, but he continued on a course taking him directly toward the large eastern gates. Following what seemed to be a natural path through the woods, a squad of seven bugbears appeared ahead of Kord on the path. Six of them held their halberds at the ready, but the seventh, who was in front, carried a shield and sword.

"Halt, who goes there?" said Keckdoz, the lead bugbear, in his native draconic tongue, holding his shield and sword up.

Once again, not sure how, but he understood the bugbear. Stopping as asked, Kord said, his voice crackling with an eerie, grating tone, "I stop only to allow you the chance to take us to see Krykl."

Keckdoz let out a nervous snort. "Krykl ain't gonna see no stragglers, and how do ya know his name, anyhows?"

Kord moved his hand to rest on Slice's hilt. "Kiiiillill themmm," the weapon hissed in his head, its voice, as always, containing a seductive, convincing element.

It was hard to resist the sword's urging, but Kord managed to restrain himself. "One more question from you, and I will alter my course of action to plan B." Keckdoz was about to say something, but before he could, Kord held up his hand to stop him. "Before you ask what Plan B is, let me tell you: plan A, which we are currently on, is the one where you and your entire troop take me and my companions to see Krykl. Plan B is, I only need one of you, half alive, to do the same task." Kord waited a second for this to sink in, his gauntleted hand rapping, with a metallic rhythm, on the Slice's hilt, as he asked, "Which shall it be? Plan A..." Kord took his helmet off, revealing his face and the advanced decay already starting to ravage it, and finished his question. "Or plan B?" Keckdoz looked in horror at the scabbed, scarred, and cut up flesh that covered Kord's face, but the most fearsome part was Kord's eyes: pitch black voids, as if they were pulling all the surrounding light into them.

Keckdoz, taking a step back, tried to say something, but his voice cracked. The bugbear, swallowing hard, tried to get it back, but before he could, another bugbear named Futhagog stepped forward, elbowing Keckdoz to the side. "You mangy fuck'n skunk, shut yer damn yap." Then the smell hit him. Kijjit's foul odor almost had a life its own, oozing into the air, adding a heaviness to it. Covering his face with one hand, Futhagog wretched a dry heave. "By Falmas, what a stench," the bugbear uttered, invoking the evil god of hate's name.

Kord shrugged his shoulders. "I smell nothing."

Recovering, except for his watering eyes, Futhagog looked right at Kord. "Well -- count yer'self lucky for that," and, giving Keckdoz a sideways glance, continued, "forget about him, we wills take ya, but Krykl ain't likely to treat you good. And keep your stinking scumbag away from us," he said, pointing at Kijjit.

"How I am treated will not be a problem, I assure you," said Kord, putting his helmet back on.

* * * *

Approaching the front gates of Gilcurr, the troop of frost giants paused in their work, repairing the wooden wall just to the left of the front gate. The wood was scorched and badly broken, the giants were pulling the large logs, the size of trees, and replacing them with new ones. The five giants each turned, looking at the Kord, their faces serious and scornful, but they said nothing. The main gates of the city were of interesting architecture, with the huge double doors leaning outward, enough so that they created an angle to the ground. From inside came a loud screeching of metal straining as the huge double doors began to swing up and open, like a gigantic mouth, but they soon stopped, parting only wide enough for the group to enter single file. Once inside, the doors began to swing back to their closed position. There were two large towers on each side of the entrance, and Kord could see large chains and pulleys that were opening the doors, but not who, or what, was operating them.

"Interesting," said Kord, following the small contingent of bugbears down the main road leading into the heart of the city. They passed row after row of basic barracks, their long rectangular structure not conducive to much more than sleeping, and housing thousands of troops. The main contingent seemed to be gnolls, which wandered around as far as the eye could see, but bugbears also seemed numerous. The streets weren't empty, by any means, but given the volume of barracks, and their size, the town seemed ghostly empty. The gnolls and bugbears they did pass on the street, gave them wide berth, and those that didn't were overcome by Kijjit's stench, some even falling to the ground vomiting. The deeper they went, the structures changed, becoming smaller, more numerous, more personalized and, as they neared the dominating keep, more civilized such as temples, taverns, and forges where blacksmiths hammered away at weapons and armor. One smithy stood out in particular due to its sheer size, and as the small party made its way past its front, which was open to the air, Kord could see a fire giant, hammering away at a large halberd.

The giant looked up, pausing mid-swing. Standing fully upright, his lip curled into a sneer. "Fuck off," he said, his voice crackling, deep, and resounding.

Kord, never slowing, ignoring the vulgar giant, continued his walk toward the keep until they reached the end of the edge of the twenty-foot wide moat. Looking down, it was apparent that some sort of creature, or creatures, lived below its murky surface, stirring the water with its, or their, movement. The surface of the water was about ten feet below the road on which they stood, but its murky nature hid whatever was lurking.

"Well..." said Kord, impatient at the delay, giving Futhagog a glance.

"They will lowers it," said Futhagog. "Now that they sees us," he said, pointing to a large opening three stories up, where three dark elves stood. The three figures stayed in the shade of the tower, avoiding the sunlight, watching Kord and his four companions. Two had bows in hand, but not readied, the third stood, arms crossed, with no visible weapon. Once again, he recognized the elves for what they were and understood their nature, but wracking his mind, he could find no answers to the source of his knowledge -- the white hair, red eyes, dull black, ashen, skin and their narrow, sharp, facial features were unmistakable. After a moment, the dark elf with his arms crossed, waved to someone Kord could not see, and the twenty-foot drawbridge began a noiseless, smooth descent until landing with a loud 'whumpf.' The heavy wooden bridge fit neatly, snugly, into place, making the road look almost contiguous.

"Right, on you go now," said Futhagog, waving Kord onward.

"Kijjit," said Kord, "stay here with the others."

"Oh no, master, that is unwise," hissed Kijjit, "we should go with you."

"No, Kijjit, what is unwise is disagreeing with me," Kord said in a collected tone, then added, "stay here." Kijjit backed away a step, slightly bowing. Turning his attention to the bridge, Kord took one step, then in a quick fluid motion charged and pushed Futhagog backwards. The bugbear was not expecting the attack, and his eyes shot open wide as he tried to grab onto Kord's arms as he fell backwards. But it all happened too fast, and in his panic, Futhagog's groping efforts were uncoordinated and in vain. The helpless bugbear plummeted toward the murky liquid, but even before he hit the surface, a large tentacle shot up out of the water, coiling around the bugbear's body and yanking him underneath the surface. As the tentacle and Futhagog disappeared, there was a momentary disturbance in the water, followed by . . . nothing. The surface of the water quickly returned to its placid, foreboding state.

Keckdoz raised his axe, as did the other five bugbears, just as Kijjit closed the distance, his foul stench overcoming three of them. Kord drew Slice in a smooth motion, eyeing the bugbear leader who had seemed to reclaim his place from Futhagog's quick demise.

"Yessss, killll the bugbear!" said Slice, telepathically urging Kord.

Kord's will fought Slice's temptation, and as he did so, he took a menacing step toward the bugbear. Recovering control, Kord stopped his advance. "No need to die today, the creature in the moat looked hungry, and I need to cross the bridge -- it is as simple as that," said Kord, spreading his arms in a gesture of peace. Kord paused, allowing Keckdoz to retreat backwards, keeping his distance from the Death Knight. "Now I will pass across," Kord said, sheathing Slice.

"Cowwwward..." Slice scolded.

Kijjit and the three ghouls were in a frenzy, wanting to engage the bugbears, but Kord held out his hand. "Settle down, little ones, wait for me here." Seeing them relax at his command, Kord turned and began walking across the long wooden bridge, his metal boots thumping with each step. The weaponless Drow, still watching him from above as he made his way across, crossed his arms. Kord, halfway across, noticed the bridge start back up at a slow pace, halting about a third of the way up as Kord stepped off the wooden planks and onto the stone floor of the keep. The masonry was excellent, the stone structure being supported by hand crafted archways and pillars, reaching up to a thirty foot ceiling. Two rows of columns ran down the middle of the enormous room, creating a clear, red carpeted path to the far end of the one hundred foot chamber. The chamber had small slits in the walls, allowing in some light, but huge chandeliers and torches held in sconces, provided most of the light deep into the chamber.

Kord walked down the center of the carpet, surprised to note the lack of activity within the hall. Coming to the end, a large rectangular table dominated the area. Standing in two groups were a large pack of twenty bugbears to the left and thirty or more gnolls to the right of the carpet. Standing in the middle was a huge ogre, over twelve feet tall. One eye was glazed over, and it appeared that his right hand was a stump. Aside from those defects, he was an imposing figure.

"That is close enough," said Krykl, holding up his left hand. The two groups of humanoids on either side were bristling, the tension and hatred in the air being palpable. "Well, if it ain't like a family reunion right now -- forgive me if I do not shed a tear."

Kord stopped, paused, then took one more step, ratcheting the unease in the air another notch. "You are Krykl, I assume."

"Do not think you can fuck with me, General Mixnor, you know who I am, and I do not give two shits why Krugar sent you here, but you are most egregiously not welcome here -- nor needed. Eh, boys?" the ogre added with disdain, giving each group of humanoids a sideways glance, eliciting their response. The hall erupted in laughter, taunts, and jeers of the most sordid nature. As the laughter began to die down, Krykl continued, "In fact, I have a pack of gnolls, at this very moment, hunting down your family. It will be a Mixnor feast!" Again the hall erupted into a cacophony of laughter and insults.

Kord reached up, causing the laughter to abruptly stop, each group readying for an attack, but Kord simply removed his helmet, revealing his sickly, ashen, decaying face, his eyes of impenetrable darkness. Holding the skull-faced helmet in the crook of his right arm, he took another step forward, leaving him about ten feet from Krykl. "I am not General Mixnor, that name is unfamiliar to me. I am Kord, Lord of Suffering himself, and I am here on behalf of Marshal Krugar. If I understand the circumstances correctly, I am here because you have failed in your duty."

Krykl stood a little taller, prickling at the suggestion of his failure, his greenish face flushing with a tinge of red. "Marshal Krugar is the one who failed -- by trusting worthless humans..." Krykl paused, taking in Kord's grizzly face, confusion and uncertainty about the thing standing before him, but continued his line of accusation. "Humans like you... foolish generals like yourself." He pointed at Kord. "You did not follow the plan and used your knowledge to turn the battle against us. You are the traitor and have set us back years with your soft sentimentality."

"Your confusion about who I am will be your undoing," Kord said, taking another step closer.

"One more step, and you will die," said Krykl, but then, cocking his head to one side slightly, he seemed to reconsider. "Ah fuck it boys -- this human ain't got a clue where he is, and Marshal Krugar is gonna have to get by with little old me."

"Most unwise," said Kord, his left hand sliding down to rest on Slice's pommel.

"Well, my momma always said I was too impulsive, but I fucking killed her, too," said Krykl, a malicious grin on his tattooed face as he raised his finger, saying the command, "Invoco un cono di morte gelata." The cone of cold leapt from his finger, spreading outward like a cyclone of freezing destruction, enveloping Kord, who turned his face, raising an arm as if that could somehow block the spell. The roar and rush of the air, the sting of the cold, and the stabbing shards of ice all stirred within Kord, a feeling of deja vu. As the spell faded away, Kord remained standing, encased by a layer of ice, as the two groups of humanoids descended on him from both sides.

Kord felt the rage swell within him, along with the anticipation of knowing that he was about to inflict a massive amount of suffering. The fools did not know what they were up against, he thought to himself, a wry smile forming beneath the layer of ice. Once again, he felt powers, previously unknown to him, welling up from a dark source. This was a power he could only tap so often, but it was perfect for the moment, with so many souls descending on him. Reaching out into the negative plane, he tapped the energy, drawing it into his being, containing it as long as possible, allowing the crescendo of pressure to build until, finally, as a tea kettle whistles, he released the force by canting the spell, "Dal mio centro, invoco fiamme esplosive di sofferenza!" The fireball, centered on his body, erupted in a mighty explosion, tearing through flesh and scorching the pillars and table nearby. The front line of bugbears and gnolls were incinerated, their ashes covering the ranks behind them, creating odd shadows on the keep walls on either side as. The beasts that were not cremated outright were thrown backwards, their fur igniting in a fiery blaze as they landed in random heaps upon each other. Krykl, knocked backwards off his feet, landed on the table behind him, the force of the fireball blowing him across its smooth surface and tumbling over the other side, crushing several chairs as he fell back onto the floor.

Kord, released from the ice, drew Slice and, with unnatural speed, closed the distance to Krykl, who was already trying to right himself. Kord leapt onto the table, took two quick strides, and then, in one fluid motion, dropped onto Krykl. The ogre was twice Kord's size, dwarfing him, but the Death Knight was still able to straddle Krykl's torso, stabbing Slice through the ogre mage's gut and pinning him to the stone floor. Kord's pitch black eyes narrowed. "No more tricks, Krykl. I know yours, now you know one of mine," Kord hissed.

Krykl tried to squirm free, even trying to push Kord away. "Get... off...me..." gasped the ogre.

Kord could feel the awesome strength of the ogre but was able to hold his position. Angling Slice so the blade was almost parallel with the ogre's body, he slid the blade deeper into Krykl's torso, coming perilously close to the ogre's heart, causing the beast to howl in pain. Kord could hear Slice practically purr with joy. "Finishhhh himmm."

Kord had other plans and, using his will, silenced Slice. Drawing his dagger, he put it up to Krykl's throat. "There is no escape for you, other than servitude."

Krykl looked at the face, now just inches away from his: so many scars, there were scars upon scars, leaving no part of his face untouched. With the mask on, he thought for sure this had been Anthall Mixnor, but this couldn't have been the human on the battlefield. 'Could it?' he wondered to himself. The pain, mixed with confusion, was making it hard to think coherently, but Krykl was able to croak out between gasps of air, "Who...what are you?"

"I ask the questions," Kord said, driving the point of the dagger several inches into the ogre's throat, causing a stream of blood to start running down its blade.

Krykl didn't flinch. "Okay...Okay..." He gasped, trying to catch a breath.

Kord could smell the blood on the dagger, intriguing him. His face was close but not quite close enough, so he leaned in, giving the blade a long lick. The blood was wet and warm on his sickly tongue but being flavorless to him, it gave him no particular pleasure so he stopped. "Lucky for you, I feed on suffering, not flesh," said Kord, blood still dripping down his horrifying face, some parts of which were still blue and frozen.

Krykl, horrified as Kord tasted his blood, gasped for air again. "What...what do you want?"

"What I want, you alone cannot give me," said Kord, sliding the dagger deeper into Krykl's throat. "But you can still help me. Are you interested in that opportunity?" Kord asked with derision in his voice.

Krykl tried to nod but couldn't with the dagger so far into his neck. "Yes...yes! I will help!"

"For now, I must help Judar and Krugar with their pathetic," Kord paused, jiggling the dagger in the ogre's throat to cause more discomfort, "no...with your pathetic plans of building this army once again. But fortunately for me, I have...you," he said, jamming the dagger further into the ogre's throat, causing blood to spurt out of the wound, and run rapidly down the blade. Krykl's eyes went wide, then he began to lose the sparkle of life as the dagger nicked an artery. "Fortunately for you and me, this is a win-fucking-win. I will leave you here to raise the army while I take care of other, more important, matters." Kord paused, watching Krykl's eyelids growing heavier. Krykl weakly raised his left arm, grabbing Kord's arm, engulfing it in his huge hand, trying to pull the dagger out, but his strength was all but gone and it was a feeble attempt. Kord shook his head. "There is no escape, not even for you, unless you submit right now and never forget that you answer to me." Kord paused again before finally asking, "Does that sound agreeable to you?"

Krykl said nothing for a second, then weakly mouthed something, struggling to get the words out. Finally, with great effort, his voice croaked, barely a whisper. "Yes..."

Kord could sense the ogre's suffering and it sent a warm, exhilarating feeling through his body. The new sensation, heightened by a general void of any feeling, created a sense of longing for it to continue and a desire to feel it again. It was the suffering, he realized, the suffering in others that evoked it -- and the feeling made him feel almost...almost alive again. But Krugar was right, he thought to himself. He could cause so much more suffering with Krykl alive, and so with some regret, and applying a significant amount of self-control, Kord pulled the dagger out of the ogre's throat. Standing up, he pulled Slice out as well, sheathing both weapons. As soon as the weapons were out, Krykl's regeneration immediately started taking effect and his wounds began to heal. First the bleeding stopped, then the internal wounds knitted themselves, followed finally by the gashes in his skin, slowly sealing the wounds. Kord surveyed the scene, the pile of dead gnolls and bugbears, not one of which seemed to have survived the blast, were strewn about the large room. Looking back down the hall toward the gate, three stories up above the entrance stood the three dark elves, watching him, and presumably the event that had just unfolded. After a few more minutes, Krykl began to groan and stir, showing signs of life returning to his massive body.

* * * *

Kord stood over the prone body of the ogre mage. "Feeling better now?" asked Kord rhetorically.

Krykl looked up at the Death Knight while his innate ability to regenerate continued making progress on his burns and horrific wounds, both internal and external. Reaching his good left hand up to his neck, the ogre rubbed the gashed leathery skin as the wound continued to knit itself closed, leaving a long scar. "Repeat to me what you remember. We cannot have any confusion over what we discussed," stated Kord.

Krykl didn't answer right away, still allowing his throat to recover. Finally, the ogre mage sat up, then, grabbing onto the table, pulled himself up to a standing position. Looking down at Kord, then looking away, a mixture of anger, hatred, shame, and respect showing through in his demeanor, he said, "I answer to you alone. I will continue to build the army here, as I have been, while you..." he looked back at Kord, his milky white eye and good eye locking with Kord's empty black sockets, "while you take care of whatever the fuck it is you need to take care of."

Kord smiled, spatters of Krykl's purplish blood still fresh on this face. "Excellent. I will leave Kijjit here with you as your lieutenant, shall we say, just to make sure things are progressing as planned. We cannot disappoint the marshal, now can we?" Kord asked, a mischievous grin flashing across his sickening face. Krykl, still swaying on his feet slightly, grabbed the back of a chair to steady himself but said nothing. "Who are the dark elves? What is their purpose here?"

Krykl grimaced in pain as his body continued to patch itself back together. "We hire them for many purposes: as assassins, spies, recon, intimidation, or for any manner of special projects." Krykl groaned from some internal pain, before adding, "How do you think we find and convince all these clans of gnolls, bugbears, and even giants to join our cause? Nothing is better than a fucking dark elf for those kinds of tasks."

"Indeed, I can imagine their usefulness," responded Kord.

"Where are you going to go?" asked Krykl, growing steadier on his feet now, releasing his hold on the large chair.

Kord, turning, began walking away. On his way out, he bent down, picking up his skull-shaped helmet which had been blown out of his grasp by Krykl's cone of cold spell. Placing it back on his head, his dark eyes, replaced by the fiery red sockets that the helmet emitted, looked back at Krykl, "Gather the forces, Krykl...do not get ahead of yourself," he warned. Giving Krykl a last look, Kord turned, walking the rest of the way down the red carpet, half of which had been seared by his fireball, the edges still smoldering. Back by the gate of the keep, he paused, looking up at the three dark elves, still watching him. "Come down to me," Kord ordered, his words echoing around the large chamber.

The dark elf with no visible weapon placed his hands on the balcony railing. "If you have need of a service, state what it is or be on your way, dark knight."

"Why are you here?" asked Kord.

Krykl, having made his way down the corridor, closer to Kord, answered before the dark elf could speak. "They are here, reporting on the whereabouts of humanoid clans located in the farther regions of the hills. I have even spent extra coin to explore some areas of the Doubtless Mountains -- but it is pricey, as not even the dark elves explore the mountains lightly."

"Gilcurr looks empty. Where are all the humanoids that live in the barracks here?" asked Kord.

Krykl stood up a little straighter, a scowl quickly forming on his face. "Are you really fucking asking me that?" Seeing no reaction from Kord, he continued, "You," he said, gesturing at Kord, "and your fucking 'heroic' actions," he used the word derisively, "led to the destruction and scattering of our whole god-damned army. So now we have to gather up all the stragglers, and in order to replace all the ones that died, we have to search and find clans that live farther away." Krykl waited a second, then added, "It is a real pain in the ass finding..."

Kord waved his hand, hushing the ogre. "Enough. I do not care about your inconveniences." Then turning back to the elves, he said, "I do require your services."

"We will meet you in the audience chamber. I am sure Krykl can show you the way," said the unarmed dark elf as the trio quickly disappeared behind the walls of the keep, heading into a passageway to the north.

Krykl grunted in irritation. "Filthy god-damned dark elf. I am no errand boy."

"Today you are. Show me the way, then you can be leave," said Kord. "You have much work to do."

Krykl, outraged at the comment, seemed to weigh his options very briefly but resigned, nodding his large head. "Fucking elves," he said as he led Kord to the northwestern corner of the keep's main hall. There were six large doors lining the chamber, and opening the large double doors set into the corner of the hall, Krykl motioned for Kord to enter. The audience chamber was another large room, but as with the rest of the keep, it was dirty and not well kept. A large throne-like chair was the main feature, sitting on a dais, surrounded by four steps leading up to it. There was an old, red, tattered rug with a pattern of faded black triangles sewn into it.

"You can leave now," Kord said, and without waiting for Krykl to respond, he stepped into the room and pulled the double doors closed. Kord waited, like a statue, for several minutes until the door on the eastern side of the room opened, the three dark elves walking in, single file, the unarmed elf in the middle.

"I wish to speak to you alone," said Kord as they approached, "that

515

way if what I ask of you is leaked out, I will know who to kill."

"I assure you, Azelli and Tint'ian," the dark elf motioned to each of his companions as he said their names, "would never reveal anything we discuss."

"Never the less, have them leave," Kord insisted.

"No," said the dark elf. "They will stay, like they always do."

A sickly, evil smile formed on Kord's cracked and split lips. "If I wanted you dead, you would be dead, and there is nothing these two could do to stop me."

The dark elf did not hesitate, crossing his arms. "Perhaps... But you should know, I have been on Thran for over 320 years, and my guild has been around for thousands of years. If you are what I believe you are, then I know your weakness." The dark elf let that comment hover in the air for a moment, then added, "But I have no interest in destroying you, because our interests are aligned - at least for the moment."

"Is that so? And how would you know what my interests are?" asked Kord, still standing statue like still. He could feel the tension in the air.

"You being here means you bear the interests of Marshal Krugar. I do not know what services you are needing from me, but I have need of a service from you," said the dark elf. "The fact that we need each other, means we are aligned -- at least for now."

"Hmm," Kord growled. "So very logical. What is your name?"

"You may call me Lyr'ifol," said the dark elf.

"Lyr'ifol...Lyr'ifol," said Kord, placing his hands behind his back, searching the unlabeled archives of his memories. "That name means nothing to me."

Lyr'ifol smiled, a sliver of his bright white teeth showing, contrasting with his dark skin and ashen lips. "As it should be, you are not meant to."

"What do you require for your services, from me? Coin?" asked Kord.

Lyr'ifol laughed, his perfect white teeth fully visible. "Forgive me, Kord," he said, trying to regain his composure, "but coin is left to the little people to worry about." He waved his right hand in a gesture of contempt.

"What I need is access and immunity."

"Do not toy with me, Lyr'ifol, or we will find out if what you think you know about me is true: if I have a weakness, or if you will be dead." Kord took a step closer, watching the two Drow on either side of Lyr'ifol place their hands on the hilts of their sheathed swords.

"Forgive me. Of course, you are correct," said Lyr'ifol, holding out his hands in front of the other two Drow. "What I want from you is to convince Marshal Krugar to allow my guild to place a clerk in the Bindal palace, and I need the Bindal militia to leave my organization alone inside their city -- within reason of course."

Kord retraced backwards his one step, easing the tension. "And what organization is this that you speak of?"

Lyr'ifol slowly, non-threateningly, reached into a pouch on his belt and pulled out a small round, black, stone and extended it to Kord. "I represent the Penumbra guild. You will know our work when you find a stone of shadow left behind."

Kord reached out and let the Drow drop the stone into his gauntleted palm with a small clank. Seeing the smooth black pebble resting in his palm brought back a wave of grief, a feeling of loss washing through his soul, causing a shiver to run down his spine. He searched his mind but could not locate the memory of where he had seen this stone before, or why it affected him as it did. The feeling was fleeting, but the guild name did ring a bell in his memories. "Penumbra...an assassin's guild?"

Lyr'ifol grimaced. "Certainly, that is one aspect of what we do, but the Penumbra network of activity is much more complex than merely a group of thugs running around killing people." He paused for a second before continuing, as if he was cleansing the air of the disdainful thought. "Which brings me back to my request, we need access to the Bindal court and, of course, a modicum of freedom to conduct business there."

"Your request will not be a problem," said Kord.

"In six years, Krykl has been unable to accomplish this for us. Marshal Krugar does not realize the setback he has just suffered and the difficulty it has caused in rebuilding the army here. He, of course, does not want our guild to have a significant presence in Bindal, so it will be no small task to convince him," responded Lyr'ifol.

"Your request," Kord repeated, pausing for emphasis, "will not be a problem."

"Well then, excellent," said Lyr'ifol. Switching gears, he asked, "What is it that you require of my guild?"

Kord knew where he wanted to go and why, but once again, his mind was like a wide pool of knowledge but lacked depth. Windred was the capital city of the Kingdom of Thayol, which lay to the north and shared a narrow stretch of border, an isthmus, with Kardoon. The unusual feature of the isthmus gave rise to two huge walls: one on the south side controlled by Kardoon, and another on the north side, controlled by Thayol. A two hundred mile strip of land, fifty to seventy five miles wide, called No Land by the locals, lay between the mammoth structures. Some people did choose to inhabit the fertile ground of No Land and formed themselves into two towns: Erdeep was located nearer to the north wall and was situated on the western coast, while Pergate was kitty-corner, nearer the southern wall and settled on the eastern coastline. Thayol was the elder of the two kingdoms, and although Bindal Kardoon was the first human to settle the large peninsula, the Thayol monarchy had always viewed the land to the south as an extension of their rule. But by the time King Vosun Thayol, in AG 1125, was made aware of the settlements Bindal Kardoon was building, it was too late. The cities of Bindal, Whiteal, and Westal had been settled, built, and fortified. King Vosun Thayol sent a small contingent to the city of Bindal, demanding that Bindal Kardoon pay homage, but Bindal refused. Trying to appease Vosun, Bindal sent the envoys back with a proposal for a thousand-year treaty of peace between their two kingdoms. Vosun Thayol was outraged, seeing the act as a form of treason, and shortly thereafter skirmishes began to break out along the isthmus dividing the two kingdoms. Over time the walls were built, and the land between the walls settled and farmed to feed the two large cities that were forming for each country. Feldor, on the Thayol side of the North Wall, was located along the coast of Cray Bay, while Castor, of similar size, was located on the Kardoon side of the South Wall, on the coast of the Gulf of Thayol. Thus, the stalemate was created. Even with Vosun Thayol passing in AG1140, and Bindal Kardoon soon following in

AG1145, their sons and heirs, Cayux Thayol and Theol Kardoon, continued the feud to the present day.

"I need someone skilled at gathering information," said Kord. "I will be heading to Windred and will need to know everything -- all the nuances -- that is going on in the Thayol court before I get there."

"That is also excellent news. Being on the edge of the Maldore forest, our network in Thayol is much more established, and I know just the person," said Lyr'ifol.

"May I assume that your guild can get me through No Land and the walls between Thayol and Kardoon?" asked Kord.

Lyr'ifol waved a hand. "You will not be an easy 'package,'" he said, "to get smuggled across No Land, but what kind of guild would we be if we could not get through the walls?"

"Time is of the essence, I will need your services to begin immediately," said Kord. "I will be leaving after our conversation here ends."

"What about Bindal?" asked Tint'ian, the Drow standing to the right of Lyr'ifol, his face was serious, his amber eyes nearly glowing in the torch-lit room, his white hair was neatly braided and tightly pulled back away from his face, revealing a scar running down his right cheek, almost as if a tear had fallen from his eye once, leaving the scar in its wake, all the way down to his jaw line.

Lyr'ifol glared at his companion. "Hold your tongue Tint'ian, and know your place." The two Drow glared at each other, longer than seemed appropriate, but Tint'ian eventually took a step backwards, a slight bow of his head to show that he understood.

"He cannot keep his mouth shut here," Kord said, pointing a finger at the ground, "yet you trust him to control himself outside of your presence?"

"Tint'ian will say nothing of our conversations to anyone. Our word is our bond," said Lyr'ifol. "But he asks a good question. If you are going to Windred first, when can we expect delivery on your end of the bargain?" Kord glared at Tint'ian, his eyes glowing red from behind the helmet, but the Drow did not back down, meeting Kord's stare without a blink. Lyr'ifol moved between the two staring combatants. "Kord, what about your commitment?"

Kord looked down at Lyr'ifol. "I will take care of that after I get things moving in Thayol. You have been without access for years, what are a few more tendays to an elf?"

"Give me a time frame, so we both know the expectation," said Lyr'ifol, a demanding note in his voice.

"You will have your access within three tendays," replied Kord.

Lyr'ifol scoffed in disbelief. "It will take you three tendays to get from here to Windred, and it is triple that to go from Windred back to Bindal."

Kord removed his helmet, revealing his grizzly face, and black void-filled eyes to the elves. "Do not forget who you are dealing with. I am Kord, Lord of Suffering." His voice crackled inhumanly. "I do not live by the same mortal constraints that you do." The three Drow took a step backwards in unison. "Keeping your end of the bargain is all you need to worry yourself with."

"Of course, your travel is your concern," said Lyr'ifol, holding his ground now. "If you would like to be teleported to Windred, that can be arranged and solves many logistical problems."

Kord smiled, revealing his swollen gums and blackening teeth, his pale and scarred face twisting as he did so. "Never will my existence depend on your skill, much less on understanding your loyalties," Kord hissed, and turning over his hand, he dropped the jet-black pebble to the floor of the keep, the little stone bouncing, clicking, several times on the stone floor, before finally coming to rest near the feet of Lyr'ifol. "Do not forget your little pebble," said Kord, turning away and walking down the hall, where he opened the doors back into the main hall. Pausing there, he looked back at the trio of dark elves. "I will be in Castor in three days; I will await your envoy just after dark, just outside the main gates."

"We are already waiting for you," said Lyr'ifol with a slight bow and nod of the head.

* * * *

Back outside, Kord found Kijjit and the ghouls just where he had left them. A semicircular ring of bugbears and gnolls had formed around the small contingent of undead, keeping them hemmed in by the moat, where the drawbridge connected to the road. Nearing the end of the bridge, Kord said, "I see you are making new friends already."

Kijjit cackled. "Yes, yes, we have become very popular guests." But the wight's mood changed quickly. "I heard two loud explosions. is Krykl still alive?"

"Indeed he is," Kord replied, "but he understands his position now. Speaking of which, I will need you to stay here and keep an eye on Krykl and make sure he continues his work here, building the army back up. For now, you do as he asks and report back to me. There is a dark elf in there named Lyr'ifol; he can get your messages to me."

"Where are you going?" asked Kijjit.

Kord didn't answer right away as he eyed the troops surrounding them. "Windred," Kord finally replied.

"Why, master?" asked Kijjit. The wight looked at Kord, who continued scanning the crowd of humanoids, a small grin creeping into the corner of the Death Knight's mouth, which the skull helmet left exposed.

"For two very good reasons," Kord's voice was low and scratchy, "to create suffering in this world, and at the same time regain my freedom."

The slack sickening skin covering Kijjit's face, mottled with sores, squished into a perplexed expression. "Freedom, master? Freedom from what?"

Kord shook his head ever so subtly. "Not what, Kijjit," Kord paused, then lowered his voice into a low growl, adding even more emphasis as he said, "but who."

"Who is this person, master?" asked Kijjit, but Kord did not respond or acknowledge the question. After waiting a few seconds, Kijjit's face relaxed, a smile exposing his rotting teeth. "How will you accomplish both of these great things in Windred?"

Kord's hands slowly tightened into balled up fists. "War," he said, his voice grating and unnatural, "and not a phony war, like the charade you see going on here. Real. Total. Fucking. War."

CHAPTER TWENTY-NINE
Waiting

YEAR: AG 1175, Month of Sepu

FUTHI RAN AS FAST AS HE COULD, splashing across the stream, pausing only for a second to look back, and seeing no one was pursuing him, he lapped up some water before continuing his retreat. Being a gnoll, and half canine, his stamina was immense, allowing him to run late into the night until, finally, he crested the hill at the top of the valley. Below he could see the sprawling walled town of Gilcurr nestled in the very foothills of the Doubtless Mountains. The city was bright, in the dark night, lanterns, torches, and other instruments lit the streets and complexes. Feeling safe from the humans for the first time, he let out a sigh of relief, but that feeling didn't last long as the dread began to set in for the task now in front of him -- delivering bad news to Fellpon, the commander of all the gnoll troops. Futhi was an old veteran and had been in this situation many times before. Summing up his courage, he began moving with some urgency down the slope of the hill leading into the valley below.

Finally, at the large main gates, he called out, and the oddly angled gate opened like a gigantic mouth, the portcullis behind it rising, like jagged teeth, just high enough for the tall gnoll to scamper underneath. Just as he cleared the metal gate, the portcullis dropped back into place, and the large door began to be pulled upward, closing, the ropes straining as it did so. Futhi did not wait around to watch that spectacle but took off down the main road, dodging the other denizens of Gilcurr as he headed directly for barracks #128, which he considered the closest thing to home he ever knew.

Opening the large double doors to the barracks, Futhi burst in. The barrack was one hundred feet long and thirty feet wide. The first twenty feet of the barracks had a large table around which the troop leaders would conduct business throughout the day. The remaining eighty feet were lined with cots, with about one cot every four feet, allowing the barracks to house forty gnolls. Normally at this time, the barracks would be full of sleeping gnolls, but since Vilnesk's troop of gnolls had been deployed to Telfar, it now was empty, save for four figures standing near the command table, as they called it. Seeing the four figures sent a shiver of fear down Futhi's spine, immediately recognizing all of them. Vilnesk was there, along with Fellpon, Skik, and even Krykl. Fellpon was an incredibly large gnoll, even by their standards, and not only large, but smart as well. Standing over nine feet tall, his black furred body and legs contrasted by his silver, wolf-like head. Every gnoll in the company was terrified of him, including the troop leaders. But their fear of Fellpon was dwarfed by their fear of Krykl, who was well known for his fits of rage and spite, especially at hearing bad news. Skik was an oddity to the gnolls since he wasn't in the command structure that they knew of, but he was still avoided and viewed with suspicion. All four turned to look at him, as he stood in the doorway, a lump forming in his throat.

"Futhi?" asked Vilnesk, surprised to see the old veteran gnoll, but continued, not giving his subordinate a chance to answer. "Where the fuck is Huppkif? He better not be at the damn tavern, and sending your sorry ass in here." Seeing the gnoll cower, Vilnesk waved him in. "Well, get your carcass over here and tell us what the hell you are doing here and what news you have. I figured you would be licking Huppkif's ass right about now!" All three of the leaders had a good laugh at Futhi's expense.

Leaving the doors to the barracks open, Futhi meekly began to move toward his three intimidating superiors. Once he felt close enough, but left just enough room so he thought he might at least be able to make a break for the open door, he looked up at Vilnesk, "It... It..." he began, but the lump in his throat choked him.

"For fuck sake, spit it out, you fool!" said Fellpon, his voice a growl of hatred, even for his own kin.

Futhi swallowed hard, mustering the courage to speak, "Them humans found us at the stream, and…"

"And what, you mutt?!" asked Vilnesk, taking a step toward Futhi, who backed up, maintaining his distance.

"They's kilt them," said Futhi, finally spitting it out in a single breath.

There was a pause, then Vilnesk clapped his hands with one loud crack. "Well, that is fucking great news! I guess we are done here then, eh, Fellpon?"

Fellpon wasn't so sure. The stench of fear coming from Futhi and his cowering posture wasn't that of someone bringing good news. Krykl felt it, too, and crossed his large arms as he observed Fellpon, who took a couple steps toward the cowering gnoll, but Futhi retreated, step-for-step, in response. "The next step you take will be your last, you mutt," said Fellpon, his voice commanding and harsh, closing the distance. Towering over his subordinate, looking down, he placed his large hand on Futhi's shoulder, forcing him to look up. "Who killed who, you son of a bitch?" he said.

Futhi shook his head. "We did everything we could, but they was too tough and they had a damnable elf wizard…"

Vilnesk felt the hackles on his back go up. "You mean Huppkif and the others are dead?" he said, his anger growing, and his voice rising with each word.

"Yes, boss, yes…" pleaded Futhi, shaking with fear now, his voice quavering. "But please I can take you to them, I knew you would want to know, and Huppkif told me to stay back and if things took a bad turn to get back here to you. I swear he did."

Fellpon pushed Futhi backwards. "You idiots!" Turning around to face Krykl, Vilnesk, and Skik, he continued, "Well, what does it matter now anyway? They cannot do anything. Troop 125 is almost to bunker 24, and they will regain control of the hill overlooking Telfar. If they head back that way, our scouts will pick them up."

There was a long silence, until Krykl broke it. "What does it matter? Is that your optimistic conclusion, Fellpon?"

"Well, what can they do? Go back to Telfar and tell Strix Cragstaff about the 'army' of gnolls they encountered?" asked the gnoll leader sarcastically.

"Well thought out, as always, Fellpon," said Skik, materializing from the shadows, his dark gray robes lightly dragging along the wooden floorboards. Barely five feet tall, the druegar looked like a tiny child amongst his towering allies, but his presence was larger than his stature, and he pointed up at them. "The only detail unaccounted for is: which one of you is going to tell Kord that his instruction to kill the Elgar and Mixnor families," Skik paused, feigning to think, "how did you so eloquently put it? Something along the lines of 'not mattering' anymore." Nobody said a word, but Krykl continued to give Fellpon a hard, contemptuous stare.

"First your compound is breached, then you fail to kill the eldest..." Krykl began but was cut off.

"And the bitch Mixnor mother," added Skik. "Where is she now?"

Fellpon wasn't one to get intimidated, but he did fear Krykl, and the dwarf was a bit of a mystery, he wasn't sure where he fit into Kord's plans, so he was always cautious not to offend, but he didn't fear the dwarf physically. "That is all bad fucking timing and not my fault," he said, crossing his arms, and returning the hard stares, a snarl on his wolf-like face, "and you," he said to the dwarf, "not only did they breach the complex you designed, but you got captured for fuck's sake! If anyone is to blame..."

"Enough!" shouted Krykl, silencing the gnoll leader. "You both fucked this up," he said, pointing to Fellpon and Skik, "so both of you will fix it. Once and for all."

"I have work to do on the other complexes," said Skik matter-of-factly, with a wave of his hand. "I do not have time for that kind of grunt work. It was Fellpon's assignment, let him finish what was assigned to him."

"No, we have underestimated this group for the last time," said Krykl. "Fellpon, you will take Jumdug and his troop, along with Harpajash." Looking down at the druegar, he added, "And Skik. This time there will be no excuses for failure. If you do fail, you had better hope you die out there." He let the impact of the warning sink in, but as he did so, Futhi took off running out of the barracks.

Vilnesk, reaching for his axe, started to move, going after the fleeing gnoll, but Fellpon held up a hand, halting the troop leader. "Let that filth go for now, we have more important work to do."

"Not Vilnesk," said Krykl, his voice commanding. "He will be heading out to the Telfar bunkers and will oversee their completion while you clean up your mess." Fellpon's mouth curled into a snarl at the rebuke, the hackles of white hair on the back of his head and neck standing up straight. Despite the gnoll's unusual height, Krykl still towered over the gnoll commander, and moving closer, made his physical presence felt. "Do you have a problem with that, Commander?"

Fellpon glared upwards at the ogre mage, holding his ground long enough that both Skik and Vilnesk each took two steps backwards, clearing the immediate space around the two powerful leaders. Before the situation exploded, Fellpon broke eye contact with Krykl and backed away. "Not problem," he snarled, unable to conceal the hatred he felt toward the ogre mage.

"Just like the obedient dog I trained you to be," Krykl said, still glaring at the gnoll commander, trying to incite him further.

Fellpon knew he had pushed the envelope too far already, and didn't take the bait. Ignoring the insult, he looked at the druegar. "C'mon, you mangy fucking dwarf. I will track down Jumdug and his crew and meet you and Harpajash at the front gate at first light. Do not make me wait."

Skik gave both Krykl and Fellpon a nasty look as he considered whether or not to argue the ogre's command, but finally relented, letting out a hiss of displeasure. "Only because Kord ordered the deaths, will I go with you," then added with some derision, "to make sure it gets done right this time."

* * * *

"Where is that son of a bitch? I told him not to keep me waiting," said Fellpon, leaning against the inner wall of the south tower guarding the main gate of Gilcurr.

Jumdug, an eight foot tall Minotaur, snorted out of his nose.

"Me think the dwarf does it on purpose -- to piss you off." The six other Minotaurs that followed Jumdug all snorted and nodded in agreement, mixed in were a couple hints of laughter, as they enjoyed the slight at Fellpon's expense.

Fellpon stood up straight, using his height advantage to remind them who was in charge. "Shut your fucking cud-eating mouths," he said, glaring at the group of Minotaurs, his warning heeded as the snickering immediately stopped.

"There he be," said Jumdug, pointing into the town. Skik was making his way through the street toward them, riding a pony.

The Minotaur troop broke out laughing, and even Fellpon cracked a smile, forgetting his anger about the dwarf not being there on time. The gnoll commander stepped out in front of the others. "I did not think dwarves rode horses," he said with laughter in his voice, adding fuel to the others levity.

"It was either a horse, or being carried by one of you idiots," he said, waving an ashen finger in the darkness, lit only by the torches resting in their sconces along the wall of the tower and the light of the half-moon now high in the sky.

"Fuck if any of us is carrying you around," said Jumdug, still chuckling a little.

"Yes, well, I would rather be carried around by a halfling than the likes of any of you," Skik said. Midst the chuckles still coming from the brutish group, he continued, "Well, what are we waiting for?"

Fellpon was not laughing anymore, his white, wolf-like face showing clearly in the moonlight had a snarly look. "Where is Harpajash? We obviously need him." Skik didn't say a word, but lazily pointed a finger upwards, causing everyone to look up into the sky. It was impossible to see anything clearly, but there seemed to be a shadow moving amongst the stars. "What did you tell him?" asked Fellpon.

"Find and then guide us to the group of humans," said Skik.

"He better not screw around with his task, do you trust him?" asked Fellpon.

"In this case, yes -- he told me more than once that he needs the heart of one of them, he did not care which," Skik paused, "so he seems properly motivated."

"Good, we will head southeast until Harpajash can start guiding us to the human scum," said Fellpon and, without waiting any longer, moved toward the gate. "Open the damn gate already!" he shouted in a commanding voice that was quickly followed by noises in the towers. The chains soon began creaking as the unusual drawbridge slowly lowered. The thick wooden bridge had barely touched the ground before Fellpon and his powerful group moved out, immediately setting their course to the southeast. It would be over an hour before the sun would make its debut for the day, but even in the dark of the early morning hours they moved at a brisk pace.

* * * *

As the first glow began to appear on the horizon to the east, Tyberius sat upright, leaning against the tree, using a long stick to poke at the small fire, its flickering flames still sending some warmth outward on the cold night. No frost yet, he thought to himself, but damn close, and cold enough to make him miss his warm house...but then he shut his thoughts down. Home. It wasn't even there anymore, and his family was gone. A mixture of sadness, anger, and hatred washed over him. Putting the stick down, he reached into his backpack and pulled out the small scroll case that Fey had given him. He looked it over, fascinated by the intricate design crafted into the metal case. Mikell, who was sleeping next to him and Ariana, let out a low growl and then mumbled something as he shifted on the hard ground. Tyberius quickly started to hide the scroll, but seeing that Mikell was still sleeping, he hesitated, looking around at the others, including Bealty, who was still nestled on his perch up in the tree, like a damned squirrel or something, he mused to himself. But everyone still seemed to be asleep, so he went back to examining it, wondering what the scroll inside said. For the first time in his life, he wished he could read; that thought made him think of his father, who had often said, "If wishes were horses, beggars would ride." Tyberius smiled at the memory, then tucked the scroll back into the backpack and leaned down to give Ariana a kiss on her forehead.

Bealty watched the whole thing. It was an uncanny knack, some would say luck, which was likely in part the truth -- he did, after all, worship Graff, the good god of luck and fate, so that was definitely on his side. In this instance, the halfling opened his eyes just as Tyberius was taking the scroll case out of his backpack. 'Why does a man who cannot read keep a scroll?' he wondered to himself. 'What an excellent question,' he commended himself, thoughtfully, and began to try and reason out all the possibilities in his head. He would not buy such a thing...unless it was a gift for Ariana. Could he have found it? Why would someone give it to him? Better yet, why would Tyberius not show it to them? His thoughts kept spinning around, but nothing seemed to quite make sense, and soon he found his eyes growing heavy again. Taking advantage of the little time remaining before the sun came up, he fell back to sleep, losing track of his thoughts and time.

* * * *

The morning sun silently snuck up over the horizon. The temperature was still very cool, and Tyberius welcomed even the small warmth the first rays of the sun provided. Standing up, the tall warrior grimaced. He awoke to find his body was stiff and sore from all the wounds he had sustained, so he gingerly began to stretch and work the pain out. The stretching helped, but after a few minutes, he gave up despite the remaining dull soreness that permeated throughout his body. Looking around the camp, everyone was still asleep and looked dead tired, making him feel like he should let them sleep a little longer, but he knew time was not a luxury they had right now. Enjoying the quiet moment, Tyberius scanned the horizon to the northwest for any signs of danger, but all he could see was the grassy plain that, with no wind to speak of, stood still in the brisk morning air.

"Alright, you lazy butts, time to start wake'in up," Tyberius said using a normal talking voice, but nobody moved, except for a noise up in the tree, causing Tyberius to turn and look upwards.

Bealty was sitting up on his branch, his left boot off, and rubbing his ankle. "Dang, morning already?" he asked.

"Yeah, time to get moving," Tyberius paused to think for a second, "get moving to wherever the hell we are going." He chuckled lightly at the thought -- they were in a rush to get moving, but where to -- nobody probably really knew that answer. Seeing that nobody was yet moving, aside from Bealty, he raised his voice, not quite yelling. "Time to git up! Git up!" he said again, this time going around nudging everyone. Finally, everyone began to stir and wake, a mixture of groans and yawns ringing out into the morning air. Stopping by Mikell, Tyberius knelt on one knee beside the cleric. "Where we goin' today?"

Rubbing the sleep out of his eyes, Mikell yawned, "I...I think I have one thing to try, but it could be dangerous, if only because it brings us closer to those that might be hunting us down now."

"Well, we ain't gonna be out-run'in anyone," Tyberius said, gesturing at the rest of the group, "so we may as well go right at 'em," he finished, flashing his grin.

It took only a short while for everyone to wake up and begin organizing and readying their backpacks for travel. Even Ariana was able to sit up and begin preparing herself for the day, albeit a little more slowly than usual, and perhaps a little more quietly. Mikell, who had been sleeping next to her and Tyberius, asked the sorceress, "How are you feeling today?"

Foetore was on her shoulder, watching Mikell, but Ariana, without giving him the courtesy of looking at him, answered in an icy tone, "Like some fucker hit me with a tree." Letting out a sigh, she looked up, revealing her bruised face, continuing in a softer tone, "Look...I know you saved my life. I..." she paused trying to control her emotions, "I cannot remember what all happened, but nobody could have saved me but you, so for that I thank you." She reached out and put her delicate right hand on Mikell's thick left forearm. "But, I do not want to talk about it further."

"I know it is not my business, but what did Axis tell you?" asked Mikell, unable to resist the urge of his curiosity.

Ariana smiled, despite the pain it caused. "Trying to take advantage of me while I was dazed, Mikell? What would Zuel think of that?" She let her rebuke hang in the air, before letting it go. "You best be getting ready, Mikell, today could be another busy day."

Mikell knew better than to push now, but she had some explaining to do. He felt like she was holding something back. 'Why would she not explain?' he wondered as he watched her for a second before turning his attention to his own gear and needs.

* * * *

"Well, where are we heading today?" asked Brutal, now that everyone was up and ready to go. Ariana was already mounted on her pony, as was Julius on Jasper. "Mikell, Tyberius mentioned you might have a plan?"

Mikell straightened his posture, his commanding presence a comfort to those around him, "You mentioned there was one gnoll who might have had information, is that true?"

"Aye," said Brutal, giving Tyberius a look, "but he died."

"He deserved to die!" said Tyberius defensively.

"I am sure he did," said Mikell, holding up a hand to calm the redheaded warrior. "We are not trying to argue that, but," Mikell paused to get everyone's attention, "I may be able to speak with him yet, if we can still find his body."

"What?" asked Tyberius. "What do ya mean?"

"Zuel has shown me how to speak with the dead," said Mikell.

"Are you serious?" asked Brutal. "If that is true, can you speak to Nicholas?"

Mikell shook his head. "I would need a part of his body. But even if I could, I am afraid he would have little to tell us. Besides, even though you found his hat, we do not know for sure he is dead, and I only have one shot at this today. No, the gnoll is our best hope for information. We know he is dead, we know where his body is, and he has the best shot at having information that could be helpful to us."

"As soon as the gnolls organize a hunting party, they will head directly for that spot, for sure, since that is where we were last seen," said Julius.

"He is right," said York, adding weight to that argument, "we could be walking right into another fight."

"What is our objective?" asked Mikell.

"It used to be finding my father, but for now it has become to rescue our families," answered Brutal.

"Exactly," said Mikell, pointing a thick finger at Brutal. "Who is the only person," Mikell quickly corrected himself, "thing, that we know -- who might have that information?" The question was rhetorical, of course, and no one said anything. "Right. So, unless someone else has a better plan, that is our only option."

"I am sure I could track the gnoll that ran away, to wherever he went," said Julius, offering a possible second option.

"You could," said Ariana, "but how do we know he would be taking us to the captives?" Before anyone could answer, she continued, "He will more than likely lead us to some other pack, or whatever the hell you call a bunch of gnolls."

"Mikell is right, as usual," said Brutal. "Let us go back and find that damned gnoll."

* * * *

The morning started off cool, but as the sun rose, the dew on the grass began to evaporate, adding to the humidity as the temperature rose. By late morning the companions were cresting the final hill, overlooking the stream, where the fight took place. They couldn't see the bodies, but the birds circling overhead were a good sign that they were still down there. The group paused, taking in the scenic view and catching their breath, before heading down the hill.

"It is a pretty view," said Ariana, her pony pawing at the ground and giving out a snort. "She remembers and smells the death," she added, patting her pony on the neck reassuringly.

"Aye, it is pretty -- from here," said Tyberius. "it will not be so pretty up close."

"C'mon," said Brutal, "we need to keep moving," as he began moving down the hill, followed by everyone else. It did not take the companions long to close the distance, and soon they found the scattered bodies of the gnolls.

"Do you remember which one it was?" asked Mikell.

"Yeah, the one with the crushed skull," said Tyberius, a little pride in his voice.

Brutal recognized the gnoll, still lying awkwardly on his back, the top of his skull cracked, blackened, coagulated blood covering its head. "This is the one," he said, pointing to Huppkif's lifeless body.

Mikell walked up to the body and, looking down at it, felt his stomach knot up nervously. He had never tried this before, and he wasn't sure about what to expect. Talking to a dead gnoll was a discomforting thought, but he also had his faith, which was stronger than his uncertainty, and he knew Zuel would protect him through the process. "Make yourselves comfortable, this will take a little bit for me to prepare." Everyone heeded his advice, except Julius and Bealty. Julius stayed mounted and rode off toward the edge of the stream, over one hundred yards away. Bealty began walking around the battlefield, inspecting the fallen gnolls. As the two companions wandered off, Mikell pulled out a stick of incense and placed it into an incense holder. The ground around the fallen gnolls was still partially matted down, but nature was already trying to repair itself, so Mikell cleared a small area for him to sit and to place the incense holder securely on the ground. Using a piece of flint, he lit the stick of incense and breathed in its relaxing aroma, which he allowed himself a brief moment to enjoy, but then put his mind and spirit to work. Giving up his conscious awareness of his surroundings, he placed himself at the mercy of Zuel and his friends, closing his eyes and beginning the long chanting prayer, "Concedimi il potere di parlare a coloro che sono nell'oltretomba." Mikell repeated that short prayer over and over, his hands weaving an intricate, somatic, arcane script in the air. As the others watched, nothing seemed to be happening at first, but as the chant went on, Ariana could feel the energy in the air intensifying as she intently watched Mikell's every movement.

"I do not think it is working," said Tyberius, breaking the silence.

"Be quiet," Ariana whispered, "something is happening, I can feel it."

York, sitting on the ground, also was watching intently, jotting down his version of the events into his journal.

Bealty, after pocketing a few copper coins he had found among the gnolls, returned to see what, if anything, was happening. Walking back into the trodden area, he asked, "Well, did I miss it?" He was immediately shushed by Ariana and Brutal. Completely used to that reaction and not taking any offense, he sat down, cross-legged, watching and listening to Mikell as he rubbed his ankle, which was still sore.

It seemed like a long time to those sitting around as the chanting took over ten minutes. As Mikell's chant started out softly, but by the end, his voice was booming, commanding, as if he were demanding that the spirit return. And then it happened. A small sparkle of light appeared above the body, no larger than the flame on a candle, hovering in midair -- but then it flashed into a ghostly form of the gnoll, clearly recognizable as a duplicate of the shattered gnoll on the ground, but no wounds were visible on the spirit. The gnoll's dog face contorted into a snarl, its canines showing as it looked around at each of the companions. Everyone stood up and took a step backwards, not quite believing what was happening. Everyone except for Bealty and York. York was writing frantically to capture the scene, and Bealty stayed seated, taking it all in.

"Human trash…" the spirit growled, its voice hollow and distant.

Mikell stayed seated, but opened his eyes. "Zuel compels you to answer my questions."

"No, he does not. Fuck you, yours god, and yours questions," the spirit shot back in broken common language.

"Did you kill all the prisoners you captured from the farms around the Mixnor home?"

At first, Huppkif's spirit jerked and convulsed, as if he were trying to fight off some invisible force, then he calmed down, smiling, as if remembering a good time. "One go free," he said, holding up a single shadowy finger. Ariana, Tyberius, and Brutal gasped at the revelation.

"What?! Who?!" shouted Brutal, his mind reeling.

"No, ask 'im how they got free!" said Tyberius, louder than Brutal.

"Ask him why they attacked our homes -- who ordered it?" said Ariana. "That will be more important information!"

"There is only time for one more question," said Mikell, his face turning a faint shade of red, beads of sweat beginning to trickle down his forehead as he struggled to maintain control of the spirit. Turning back to the gnoll's ghostly form, he quickly asked, "Who was the prisoner that escaped?"

Again, the spirit fought the urge to answer the question, its ghostly shape spinning and lashing out around it, but once again, it suddenly stopped fighting. Looking down, its eyes burning white globes locked onto Mikell. "You assume wrong." Then the spirit turned its attention to Brutal, pointing a glimmering, transparent finger at the warrior. "Mixnor...bitch...mother."

Brutal sprang at the spirit. "Where is she, you son of a bitch! Where is she?" But as soon as the spirit gave its answer, it smiled an evil grin, cackled, and blinked out of existence, leaving Brutal shouting at the empty air.

Everyone sat silently for a moment, experiencing a mixture of shock at what the gnoll had told them and amazement at having just witnessed Mikell summon a ghost and spoken to it. They were in awe of Mikell's growing power -- but the mood was quickly snuffed out by the halfling, his boyish voice cutting through the silence. "Now what?"

Brutal, a rage still on his face, looked down at the rogue and was about to say something, but York beat him to it. The bard, pen still in hand, said, "Beetle asks a very good question. We know your mother is alive, thank goodness," he added as an afterthought, "but we do not know anything more about where she went or could be, nor do we know exactly where the gnolls were planning on taking them."

"I bet ten silver that they were taking them to that place called Gilcurr," said Bealty, "and I bet if we follow the gnoll that ran away, he will take us right to it."

"How would you know?" asked Ariana.

"Is that a bet?" asked Bealty, seriousness in his voice.

"I trust his instincts, as you should by now, Ariana," said Mikell.

In the middle of their discussion, Julius came galloping back. "We are being watched, I am sure of it."

"What? How?" asked Brutal and Tyberius, simultaneously, in rapid succession.

Julius pointed upwards. "That thing flew in from the southwest; I saw it come over the hills." They all looked up. The first thing they all noticed was the flock of carrion birds, that had gathered to feast on the dead gnolls, were gone. In their place was a solitary creature, what looked like a huge bird of some sort, circling very high in the sky above.

York looked up as well, shielding his eyes from the sun, using his far-sighted elven vision to see what it was. "It is flying too high, I cannot quite make it out."

"That is one hell of a big ass bird," said Tyberius. "You really think it be watching us?"

"Is it a dragon?" asked Brutal.

"No," said York, then changed his mind. "Well, I suppose it could be a very young dragon."

"Why a young one?" asked Tyberius. "The old ones cannot fly or something?"

York took his hand away from his eyes and looked at the tall warrior. "No, Tyberius, whatever that is up there, is too small to be an aged dragon," he said.

"Have you ever seen a dragon?" asked Bealty.

"Yes, little Beetle, I have," York said with a smile, looking down at the halfling. "I have seen two adult dragons in my life. I saw a Golden Dragon when I was still a boy, in Oak Grove." York's voice seemed to trail off, as if recalling a distant, fond memory. "Magnificent creature. A pure creature. Gepavithrex was his name."

"Was it attacking your town? Did you kill it?" asked Tyberius.

"Gold Dragons are good, Ty," answered Ariana.

"There are good dragons?" Tyberius asked, astonishment in his voice. "I ain't never heard of that."

"Indeed, they are the epitome of good," said York.

"What was the other dragon?" asked Bealty. York's distant stare vanished, a darkness washing over his face -- perhaps a sadness, thought Bealty.

"Well, we had best figure out what we are doing," said York, dodging the question. "That thing up there knows where we are."

"And probably directing a group on the ground," added Julius with a concerned look on his face.

"Well, there is no place to hide out here," said Mikell, looking around at the rolling hills of grass, the doubtless mountains in the background, still distant, but close enough and foreboding enough to add to his uneasiness. "So I say we follow Beetle's advice and let Julius track the gnoll if he can."

"I can track it, but I fear it will lead us right to whatever is hunting us," said Julius. "I can see where he came out on the other side of the stream."

Tyberius growled. "Fuck that. Whatever is out there, we is the hunters and they is the prey."

"I suggest we head west," said Julius. "Judging by the mountains in the distance, if we head west now, we will run into the eastern shore of White Lake."

"What good will the lake do us?" asked Ariana.

"First, by not following the gnoll, it will give us more time to find favorable ground." Julius pointed upward. "It is only a matter of time before that thing leads whatever is on the ground to us. Secondly, the lake protects our back, preventing us from getting surrounded, which means we have a chance to keep you safe from direct attack when we do finally engage."

Ariana nodded slightly. "That is good thinking, Julius."

Brutal sunk down to his knees on the ground, placing his hands on his head. "First my father disappeared into these hills, and now my mother? How will we ever find her?" Brutal said, sadness in his voice.

Mikell snuffed out the incense stick and tucked it back into a small case before putting it into his backpack, then standing up, he walked over to Brutal, placing a hand on his friend's shoulder. "Let us focus on the task at hand -- surviving today and the next day. Soulmite has led you, and us this far, do not lose faith now."

Brutal looked up, his eyes red, holding back his tears. "You are right," he said with sudden realization, the doubt receding. He continued, stronger, as he stood back up. "I cannot lose faith... Soulmite will not let me down."

"Lose faith, never," said Isa, his gruff voice oddly comforting despite his stiff cross-armed resolute stance. Brutal gave monk a quick look and a thankful nod.

"It sounds like we ought to be heading toward the White Lake, no?" asked Brutal rhetorically, and before anyone could answer, he looked, gauging the sun, and began walking away from the group.

Brutal didn't get far before Julius let out a little cough, but Brutal did not stop. "Brutal," Julius said a little more forcefully. This time the warrior looked back over his shoulder, seeing Julius pointing west, the opposite direction from which Brutal was walking. "Let us try this way."

Everyone let out a much needed laugh, and although at first a little embarrassed, even Brutal cracked a smile and laughed, adding, as he turned around, "Damn rangers..."

* * * *

The little, ashen dwarf said they were powerful and that more than one of them could cast spells, so Harpajash watched the group of humans from high in the sky as he had been instructed. 'Spell casters,' he thought to himself in disgust. If there was one thing he hated, it was spell casters. From up high, the group of humans didn't look powerful at all, more like little ants that he wanted to squash, but he had his orders, and he wasn't going to cross Skik, at least not now. Surprisingly, the group was heading right toward Gilcurr and straight into Skik, Fellpon, and the Minotaurs. What he couldn't understand was why they rested at the stream and then changed their course. They turned around, heading west, slightly backtracking, away from their pursuers. It was an odd decision, he thought, to head in that direction since there wasn't anything that way aside from the forked river that fed into the White Lake. And there was no way for them to cross that deep, wide, cold, and swift river, at least that he could see. "What is your play?" he questioned in his mind, but he could not formulate a good answer.

Harpajash continued circling, watching the group of humans plod to the west for a while longer, making sure they were really committed to their course. Satisfied that they were going to keep moving in that direction, he tucked his wings back and began descending rapidly, heading toward Fellpon and the others.

It didn't take long to find Fellpon and his group, and at his rate of speed it didn't take long for Harpajash to swoop down on them. Extending his wings outward, rearing back, and giving two mighty flaps, the air noisily slowed his descent and made his landing look graceful and easy. "They changed direction," Harpajash said as he folded his wings back in tightly against his sides.

Fellpon, Skik, and the others gathered near the Peryton, an odd creature, to say the least. The bottom three quarters of its body was that of a giant eagle, but its head was that of a large elk. However, the most notable feature was the large, jagged, and deadly rack of antlers that adorned its head. "Are they heading back toward Telfar?" asked Skik.

"No." Harpajash chuckled, in an evil bleating voice. "The idiots are heading due west from the stream crossing."

"Why would they head west?" Fellpon asked, then thinking about the geography, said, "they will run into the forked river, no?"

"Can they cross the river somehow?" asked Skik.

"How in the eight hells would I know? You have me flying so high, they look like ants to me," snapped Harpajash.

"And you keep it that way," Skik snapped back. "We do not need you getting shot out of the sky."

"Bah," Harpajash snorted, ruffling his wings, adding with confidence, "they cannot hurt me."

"Shut your damn mouths," Fellpon scolded. "And you," he said, pointing at Harpajash, "do as you are told. How many are there, and are they mounted?"

"Eight, and two are riding," answered Harpajash.

Looking around, Fellpon did a quick count; there were eight of them, nine if he counted Harpajash. "That useless piece of shit Futhi could have at least told us there were that many of them," Fellpon said, curling his hand into a fist.

"What you worried about?" asked Jumdug, the large Minotaur leader growled. "We will crush them," he added with a snort out of his bullish nose, sparking his troop to snort as well.

Jabbing a finger into the chest of Jumdug, Fellpon stepped close in to the Minotaur. "I am not fucking around with those human scum -- stay sharp and do not forget they are dangerous."

"Maybe to you," said Harpajash, scratching at the ground with the razor sharp talons of his right foot.

Fellpon turned his head to give the Peryton a glare. "Why are you still here? Get back up there and let us know if they change course again."

Harpajash eyed the large gnoll, the hatred in his heart feeding his desire to kill, but he knew better. He knew Fellpon was armed with magic weapons, and that made him vulnerable. Besides, he needed a human heart, and this mission was his best chance to get his claws on one. Letting out a disgruntled snort, the Peryton unfolded his wings and, with a mighty push from his muscular legs and clawed feet, lurched his heavy body into the air. The first few flaps of his wings struggled to lift his heavy frame off the ground, buffeting his companions below him. He rose slowly at first, but, with each flap, rose higher and higher, flying faster and faster, and soon he was high in the sky, flying off to the southwest.

"Fucking Peryton; he thinks he is invulnerable," said Fellpon. "Did you see the look he gave me?"

Skik grunted, watching Harpajash fly off. "To most," he paused before completing his thought, "they are."

* * * *

"He is back," said Bealty, pointing up into the sky.

"Damn," said Julius, "for a while there, I thought maybe I was wrong -- that he was not following us after all."

"Well, we know now for certain it is," said Brutal, craning his neck to look upwards, using his hand to shield his eyes from the sun.

"The good news is, I watched it as it left, and it headed over the horizon to the northeast, which means whatever is chasing us is, indeed, directly behind us."

"That will give us more time to get to White Lake," said Mikell. "And with Zuel's blessing, we will find a good defensive position. How far do you think it is to the lake?"

"At least another day's travel," Julius frowned. "But I am not certain. I have not traveled this deep into the hills before."

"What?" asked Ariana, perking up. "I thought you knew where you were going?"

"No one travels out here -- not even the caravans that have tens, if not hundreds, of foot guards," said Julius. "I am doing my best to help us find better ground -- to protect you, I might add." His last statement came out sharp and defensive, and he immediately regretted it.

Ariana's face flushed red. "Aside from a fucking giant running me down, I can take care of myself...I have so far."

"You are right, of course, I am sorry, Ariana," Julius said. "I did not mean it as if to imply you are weak. We," he said, gesturing with his hand to his chest, "need your magic, and we need to make sure you have a chance to use it." Ariana didn't reply but gave her pony a light kick, making it break into a trot, putting a little distance between her and the rest of the group.

Tyberius ran a hand through his red hair that was slick with sweat. "Sorry, Julius, she still ain't quite recovered yet. We knows you is doing your best to help us find better ground." Tyberius gave the ranger a quick pat on the thigh before jogging ahead to catch up with Ariana.

"You should not be apologizing to her, Julius, she has the patience of an angry bee," said York, looking up from his journal, pen in hand.

Brutal, walking just ahead of York, turned around, "We are the ones who failed her, York," he said, causing the bard to halt in his tracks. "She does not need to apologize to any of us."

"If it was not for Julius here," said York, pointing with the pen up at the mounted ranger, "we would be heading blindly into an ambush."

Sensing the tension, Mikell inserted himself between Brutal and York. "You are both right." Putting his arm around Brutal's shoulder, Mikell turned the warrior around and got him walking again. "No need to fight amongst ourselves; there will be plenty of fighting to do ahead of us."

* * * *

The companions pushed hard, even past dark, unsure whether or not what was following them would need to rest or not, until finally Mikell convinced Brutal and Julius that the group needed to rest. The risk ended up paying off as it allowed Mikell to cast his healing spells, bringing the group back up to full strength for the first time since they had entered the bunker. Despite the chill air in the night, they decided to forgo even trying to make a fire. Luck was on their side, and the night passed quietly, and although sleep came hard to most of them due to the hard ground and cold, they all felt better the next day for it. Ariana especially looked better; she had her edge back and was moving about more decisively.

At the first light of dawn the companions were ready to go, and moving out, continued moving west away from the rising sun. The sky started out clear of their high-flying spy, but not long after sunrise, the familiar shape returned, circling high overhead. Despite the gnawing feeling of being watched, there was nothing to be done, so they continued their westerly course.

It was well past mid-day, the sun having already made its way halfway down the sky toward the horizon when the group crested one of what seemed like hundreds of hills they had climbed and descended. But this hill was different. "What the hell is that?" asked Brutal, the group pausing to catch their breath, taking in the new sight. Some ways off in the distance, a wide chasm that stretched as far as they could see to the north and to the south.

"Sounds like rushing water," said York, his elven ears hard at work. "I believe we have found a river."

"A river?" asked Tyberius. "Where is White Lake?"

"Dammit, we must have been farther north than I thought," said Julius.

"So much for finding better ground," said Ariana.

"We still have the river to guard our backs," said Julius, "it will work just as well as the lake."

"C'mon," said Mikell, his voice deep and fatherly. "Let us keep moving and see what we have before us." No one argued, although a sense of unease permeated the group. They covered the distance quickly, and soon the found themselves standing at the edge of the plains, looking down a steep, nearly vertical slope, to the river below. The river stretched as far as they could see to the north and to the south. The particular area they stood in now jutted out forty feet, like a small peninsula, creating a pocket of land surrounded by the steep cliffs. The sound of the rushing water below, now plainly audible to everyone, added an ominous touch, immediately intensifying their unease for everyone except Bealty.

"Damn!" Bealty exclaimed, his voice echoing off the canyon walls below. "That must be two hundred feet down, maybe more!"

"Very perceptive," said Ariana, peeking over the edge, then added as she took a step backwards, "I am not sure I want my back up against this."

"We should head south and see if there is a better position," said Julius.

"No," said Brutal. "No," he said again, shaking his head and drawing his sword. "We aren't running anymore. We fight here."

"Fuck yeah!" chimed in Tyberius. "That is the Brutal I know!"

"I agree with Julius," said Mikell. "This does not feel like a good place to me."

"There is no good place, Mikell," Brutal said, his voice calm. "There is no element of surprise with that...that thing up there," he said, pointing up into the sky with the tip of his sword, the shape slowly circling, like a scavenger waiting to feast on a kill. "This is good flat ground, and with this area right here," he said, gesturing to the peninsula of land, "they cannot get around us, they will have to get through us -- and I ain't gonna let that happen, not this time."

Isa grunted, interlocking his fingers and stretching them outwardly, cracking his knuckles. "No get pass, Isa," he said as he laid his backpack down, near the edge of the cliff, the act akin to putting a stake in the ground.

Mikell sighed, accepting the decision. "Very well." He patted Isa's huge shoulder. "We will fight here." Isa looked at the priest, the whites of his eyes were actually a soft yellow, an orcish trait, but his green irises, making a sharp contrast, were part of his human ancestry, not black like a true orc. Isa nodded and grunted agreement.

* * * *

Harpajash streaked out of the sky once again, breaking his descent by extending his large wings and gracefully landing ten feet in front of Fellpon. "Well, what are they doing now?" asked Fellpon.

Harpajash barely had time to furl his wings into position, the gnoll's impatience and belittling attitude irritating the Peryton. Instead of answering right away, he took his time recovering from the landing, but just as Fellpon was about to say something else, Harpajash looked up at the gnoll. "They have stopped at the edge of the forked river."

"What do you mean they stopped?" asked Skik, walking his pony out from behind Fellpon.

Harpajash did not like the bossy little dwarf and wasn't sure why he had been sent along or what role he even had in relation to Kord, but as much as he would have liked to spear the druegar with his antlers, he controlled the urge and responded without giving him the satisfaction of looking at him. "A silly question, from a silly dwarf," spat Harpajash. "Stopped means stopped -- meaning they got to the canyon edge and stopped traveling. From what I can tell, they are camped out in that spot."

"Why would they do that?" wondered Fellpon out loud.

Skik interrupted the momentary silence, as everyone was thinking about the question, "Either they know they are being followed and have decided to stand and fight, or they do not know they are being followed and are not sure where to go next."

"Either way, we have them," said Fellpon, completing Skik's line of thought.

"Exactly," said Skik, bothered by the stolen thought.

"How far are they from here?" asked Fellpon.

Being a creature of the air, Harpajash had a knack for judging distance. "Ten miles to the southwest."

Jumdug snorted, flexing his large arms. "We can still get there in light today! We are gonna crush them!" The other Minotaurs also began snorting in anticipation.

Fellpon's mouth curled into an evil grin and couldn't help but lick his jowls, at the thought of human flesh, his favorite. "Alright, you dogs, we need to keep moving, they could decide to start heading south at any moment." Turning to Harpajash, he continued, "You, get back in the air and let us know if they start moving again."

* * * *

"He be back," said Tyberius, pointing up at the large dot in the sky.

"Most likely," said Julius, "letting someone, or something, know that we have stopped."

"I hope it be more gnolls," said Tyberius. "I am getting a real knack for killing them." The group had stomped down a large patch of the grass and had all sat down, finally being able to rest a little from the hard last few days. It was a strange reprieve since time was working against them, knowing their foes were closing in, but the intervening period seemed calm, like that just before a storm.

"What if it is a hundred gnolls?" asked York.

Tyberius looked stunned. "I ain't thought of that," he started out, then regained his confidence. "They ain't gonna send a hundred damn gnolls after us!"

"How many did we kill in the bunker? And how many were in the troop you killed?" York continued to probe.

"There were nine gnolls at the river; we killed eight," said Brutal. "I bet we killed twenty or more between the bunker and the stream," added Brutal, then after a second, added, "not to mention the undead we happened upon."

"York is right," said Mikell. "They will send a much larger force, or a force that is much stronger."

"We are stronger now than we were before, too," said Brutal. "Whatever they send at us, we will kill, then we will head north to find this Gilcurr." Looking around, he noticed one person missing. "Hey, where is Beetle?"

Ariana perked up and looked around. "He better not have left -- not now!"

"Ariana," said Mikell, "give him a break, he made a damn bed for you when you were hurt. He is not going to abandon us." He paused, letting that sink in for a moment, then answered her question with a nod of his head, motioning out into the grassy plain. "When that thing up there left the last time, he took off into the grass." A smile crept across Mikell's face. "He told me, 'at least they will have one surprise waiting for them.'"

"Smart," said Julius, "not even that thing up there will be able to spot him."

York was writing in his journal, his stained fingers hard at work, capturing notes that caught his interest. Looking up from his writing, he said, "Indeed, Beetle can be a crafty and dangerous opponent. I am glad he is on our side, would you not agree, Ariana?" The sorceress gave the bard an icy look, but said nothing. "I would take that as a 'yes,' would you not, Julius?"

Julius, startled by his sudden inclusion, scrambled to figure out a response, but Tyberius saved the ranger further discomfort, growling, "She likes Beetle as much as any of us, so leave her out of it, York. Jot that down in your damn book," he flicked a finger, gesturing at the bard and his book. York smiled, as only elves could do, mixing a large amount of arrogance and condescension into an otherwise friendly gesture.

Mikell, shifting his sitting position, looked around the small group. "No need to get testy with each other now," his voice was low and serious, "get your rest, be prepared, because trouble is coming, and I have a feeling we will be sorely tested...very soon." Nobody said a word, they didn't need to, each heeding the cleric's advice as they quietly went about their preparations.

* * * *

Jumdug, the lead Minotaur paused, lifting his large bull head up into the air, catching a scent. "Ahhh, me smell the human flesh. It be not far now," he added with anticipation in his voice.

Fellpon lifted his snout as well but could not yet catch the scent that Jumdug had sensed. That was not unusual, however, as he knew the Minotaurs had a very keen sense of smell, even better than his very capable wolf-like sense could detect. "Good, then we must be careful going forward -- keep you damn eyes and ears open, too."

The small hunting party continued for another five miles when they saw the first indication that someone had passed through the grassy fields. A faint path of bent grass could be seen, easily if you were looking for it, off to the west. Even Fellpon could now smell the human flesh, and it was difficult to control the urge to charge forward, but he knew that would be foolish.

"The smell is strong," said Jumdug as they reached the beaten trail. "They very close."

Fellpon nodded. "Yes, I can smell them now as well." The gnoll leader's ears swiveled around picking up faint sounds. "The river is very close, too, I can hear the water flowing."

"Yes, I smell the water, too...It be very, very, close." The Minotaurs all reached behind their backs and pulled out their large double-bladed axes, hefting them, their arms bulging, showing off their mythical strength.

"If you can get to the spell casters, do so. They will be our biggest threat," said Skik, halting the pony next to Fellpon. "They have a sorceress and a cleric of Zuel." Folding his hands over each other and resting them on the back of the pony's neck, he continued, "They will be well defended, and now I can see why they headed to the river."

"For protection, of course," said Fellpon, "but they will not be able to protect their magic users."

"How do you propose to break through their fighters?" asked Skik.

"I will use what they perceive as an asset to their defense against them," Fellpon said, an evil grin spreading across his jowls, which were already starting to drool.

* * * *

York, holding the feather pen under his nose, akin to a mustache, thinking about what he had just written, looked up, scanning the looming hills to the east from which they had come. Movement caught his keen elven eyes, and that's when he saw the troop. "There they are!" he said, some excitement in his voice, using the feather to point at the approaching enemy, atop a distant hill. Despite the distance, the large humanoids were easy to spot, their silhouettes clear against the sky behind them as they crested the hill.

Everyone bolted upright and looked in the direction York had indicated. Sure enough, they could make out the forms coming down a distant hill to the east. Brutal stood up, holding a hand over his eyes to help him focus. "Can you tell what they are?" he asked.

"Can you see them, Julius? Do you know what approaches?" York asked.

"Yes," said the ranger, concern in his voice.

"Well, what be it?" asked Tyberius, short on patience.

"I count seven Minotaurs, a gnoll, and something else on horseback," said Julius.

"Yes, yes, that is right. The only thing you missed is our old friend Skik, he is the one on horseback," said York, nodding in approval of Julius's eyesight, who had obviously been gifted with elvish sight. The bard, writing it all down, looked up from his journal, tapping the feather end of his pen on his bony chin. "Too bad he got away from us, he is a dangerous spell caster."

Tyberius and Julius both looked at each other, then at Ariana, who seemed to pay the comment no mind, but just as they were about to breathe a sigh of relief, she spoke up. "I am glad he is back, I want to kill the little bastard myself."

"Yes, well, they will be here very soon, and they do not seem to care that we know it," said Mikell, standing up and unhitching his mace from his belt. He lifted it, feeling the extraordinary balanced weight of the weapon. Taking the shield, which he wore on his back while traveling, and slipping his large forearm through the leather straps, he grabbed the handle with his hand, securing the shield on his arm.

Likewise, Tyberius donned his shield on his right arm. Hefting his flail, he could feel the blood flowing through his body, the burning sensation fueled by his anticipation. Setting his flail down for a moment, unclasping his bear-faced helmet from his backpack, he put it on. He didn't particularly like the restrictive feeling and vision limitation, but he wanted the added protection, and he liked the fearsome look it presented.

Brutal, with help from Julius, donned his breastplate, the ranger tightening the leather straps holding the two large pieces of metal snugly in place. Earlier, Brutal pounded out the large dent left by the boulder, and although it was a sloppy job, it was effective. The intertwining snakes once again looking as they should. He didn't draw his bastard sword yet, deciding to leave it in the scabbard on his back until he really needed it.

Isa did some stretching and cracked his knuckles, his yellowish eyes looking determined and fierce. Julius was already prepared, standing with his longbow in hand, and Ariana, standing near Tyberius, her hands on her hips, looked determined and ready as well. York, looking comfortable and relaxed, was the only one to remain seated and continued to write in his journal.

Mikell looked around; it made him nervous not to know where Bealty was, but he knew the halfling was out there somewhere, and he took some comfort in that. Now all they could do was wait.

* * * *

"They are coming straight at us," Julius commented as the companions watched the gnoll and Minotaurs cautiously closing the distance between them.

"That was the whole point of coming here and putting the river to our backs. We did not give them many options," said Brutal.

"Or, they are confident in their ability to dispatch us all," said York, then, after a moment's thought, added, "perhaps, overconfident." York, for once, wasn't writing in his journal, instead, he was playing an energetic tune on his flute when he wasn't talking. The magical tunes surrounded the companions and they could feel the energy, like prickles on their skin, heightening their senses and reflexes.

"Where is that little dwarf? I do not see him," asked Tyberius in a low voice, practically a growl.

Julius pointed toward the oncoming group. "He is there, in the back, but he is hard to see behind the others, and, of course, the grass is half as tall as him, helping hide him."

"We are counting on you, Julius, to take him out as quickly as possible," said Mikell. "We will not be able to engage him with all those Minotaurs in front of him."

Julius nodded, confident in his ability. "Out in the open like this, with nowhere to hide, he will be dead very quickly."

Mikell surveyed their formation, one more time, checking for weaknesses. Isa, Brutal, and Tyberius made up the front line of defense, with himself and York just behind them, offering support: Mikell with healing, and York with his offensive spells. Julius and Ariana made up the third row and stood well back within the small peninsula for their protection, allowing Julius to freely fire his arrows and Ariana to cast her spells. That left Bealty. Mikell looked out into the grassy plains in front of them, hoping he'd see a sign of the little halfling, if only to reassure himself of where he was, but he knew it was futile.

* * * *

"Spread out a little more!" barked Fellpon, looking at the Minotaurs in front of him. "Do not forget they have magic users!" The formation was simple, the Minotaurs in front, with Fellpon and Skik in the back.

Jumdug grinned, already salivating at the thought of the human flesh awaiting them. "We is gonna knock them backwards -- right off the fucking cliff!"

"Do whatever you have to, but make sure they are killed -- or you will be climbing down the cliff after them," said Fellpon with pure sincerity.

"We is gonna feast tonight!" howled Magzig, literally licking his chops. He wasn't the tallest Minotaur in the group, but he was the strongest, as evidenced by his thick broad shoulders and body.

Skik snorted derisively. "Just remember, you oafs, they have killed everyone else they have encountered, except me, of course. So, before you start thinking about the menu, you better start thinking about killing them first."

"They is already fucking dead," grunted Rusta, the smallest Minotaur, only standing a mere seven feet tall, but he was also the quickest and most agile, fighting with a bastard sword in one hand and a longsword in the other. All the others, including Jumdug, hefted huge double-bladed battle axes.

"We will see," said Skik, not convinced. The group continued until they were about two hundred yards away. "Stop," said Skik, raising his hand. "Give me a moment."

"What the hell for?" asked Fellpon.

Skik gave the gnoll a fuck-you look but said nothing as he reached into his backpack, pulling out a scroll case. Taking out three sheets of vellum paper, he flipped through them, finding the one he was looking for in the middle. Carefully rolling up the other two, he placed them back in the case and resealed it. Finally, focusing on the sheet in his left hand, he read the magic words written down on the sheet. "Invoco una barriera per respingere tutti i missili naturali." As he traced the air with his right index finger, precisely as mandated by the spell, the air crackled around the druegar, encasing him, briefly with a shimmering dome around his body, but as quickly as it appeared, it vanished -- as did the inscriptions on the vellum page.

"Did you see that?" asked Julius.

York stopped playing his music for a second. "Yes, I did."

"What do you make of it?" Julius asked again.

"Too hard to tell, but it is certain he cast a spell of some sort," answered York, "and being that far away, it must have been some kind of protection."

"Then it is time we start our own protecting," said Mikell. "Everyone, gather in closer to me." As everyone moved closer, Mikell held out a hand. "That is good enough," and everyone halted. Touching the platinum holy symbol around his neck, he began the spell. "Zuel, benedici tutti i miei amici donando loro grazia e vitalità; colpisci tutti i miei nemici rendendoli vittime di errori e debolezza." At the conclusion, everyone felt the tingle of energy as if a blanket had been laid over them very briefly.

"Oh shit! What was that?" asked Tyberius, a shiver of distaste running down his spine. "That magic stuff makes me queasy."

"I said a prayer for our good fortune today," Mikell said with a smile, which quickly turned into a scowl, "and their misfortune." As everyone returned to their position, he walked back to Ariana. "I am guessing the dwarf will want to use his magic against you, as he did last time, with that ball of fire." As he spoke, he could see a defiant look in Ariana's eyes, as if to say, "not this time," but he didn't want to take any chances. "I want to cast a protection spell on you that will help you resist fire -- will you allow it?"

Ariana smiled and nodded. "You can do that?"

"No, but Zuel can," said Mikell with a twinkle in his eye. Taking out a small metal vial from a pouch on his belt, he unscrewed the cap, which had a rubber top and turned out to be a dropper. Squeezing out a tiny droplet of mercury into his cupped hand, Mikell invoked the spell. "Benedici il mio tocco con la protezione da ogni forma di calore." As he said the last word, the drop of mercury, which had been rolling around in the palm of his hand, vanished, and reaching out, he touched Ariana on the right shoulder. Ariana felt the sudden, but brief, surge of magic course through her body, binding to her skin like an invisible film.

"It feels strange," Ariana said.

"The feeling will subside, but the protection will be there for quite some time." Mikell paused. "Enough, anyway, to see us through this fight."

"Thank you, Mikell," Ariana said. "You are a good friend, and a true companion." Mikell blushed a bit, not used to being complimented, but also because it felt like a sincere and heartfelt comment coming from Ariana, who usually had her guard up. Mikell nodded and winked before turning and walking back to his position as he screwed the dropper back on and tucked the vial into the pouch on his belt.

"They are moving again!" shouted Brutal.

"I will stall them as best I can just in front of us, as I did with the gnolls," said York. "So be careful you do not step into the moving grass, or it will try to entangle you as well."

"But all the grass is moving from the wind!" snapped Tyberius. "How..."

"You will know," interrupted York, "the grass will look alive."

"Fucking great..." said Tyberius, shaking his head, but deep down, although the magic made him uncomfortable, he took comfort knowing they were on his side.

"Soulmite brought us here, there is a reason for it. I know it!" Brutal said with confidence. "She will see us through this as well!"

"Brutal is right," Mikell responded. "The good gods are on our side, but they," Mikell pointed at the approaching Minotaurs, "have evil forces at their back as well. This is a true test of will... But today, lovers of the light and shadows will prevail!" Mikell didn't like it, but Ariana, York, and Isa all worshiped shadow gods of neutrality, and he didn't want to risk offending them or their gods just before the fight, as they would all need the aid of the shadows today. It made him uneasy, depending on the shadows, but he thought the end justified the means...then felt a little guilt, wondering how many other people had used that same logic only to find themselves morally lost. But surely, he would not get lost, he told himself, saying a little prayer to Zuel for strength today. He could now hear the grunting of the Minotaurs approaching, and the tall gnoll in the back seemed to be shouting commands. Mikell looked around at his companions, and he could feel everyone's nervous energy. "Hold fast, all of you! Watch the back of your neighbor, and for god's sake -- strike to kill with all your might!" The foul smell of the Minotaurs now washed over them, and as they closed to within twenty yards, the enormity of the Minotaurs' size, now becoming evident, began to feel overpowering. Then, as if on cue to add to the intimidation, all six of the bullish beasts, in unison, let out a terrible deafening roar as they began charging, at full speed, and with a massive amount of momentum, directly at the front line of the companions.

Tyberius, nearly twitching with agitation at hearing the Minotaur battle cry, let out his own howl of pent up rage, matching the Minotaurs' intensity. At first, it surprised Brutal, but then he too joined in, followed by Isa -- all three bracing to receive the charge. The Minotaurs, about to slam into the companions' defensive wall and blinded by their rage, paid no attention to the elf finishing his spell. The tall grass around the Minotaurs instantly erupted into a writhing mass of aggressive vegetation, wrapping and coiling its reeds around any limbs it could find, the hindrance further enraging the charging Minotaurs as evidenced by their growls, snorts, and curses in their dark, unfamiliar, language.

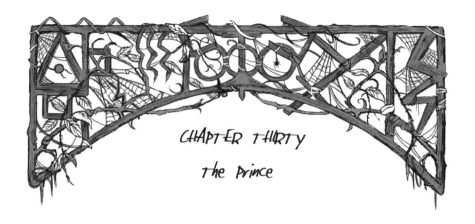

CHAPTER THIRTY
The Prince

YEAR: AG 1172, Month of Sepu

KORD DIDN'T WASTE ANY TIME. After stopping to talk with Kijjit briefly outside the keep, he immediately headed toward the outer gates of Gilcurr. As he made his way through the somewhat vacant city, the few bugbears, gnolls, and other assorted creatures kept their distance, unsure of who or what he was and what he was doing there. As he neared the outer gate, he didn't even have to say a word before the oddly angled door began lowering, allowing him to walk straight through without altering his pace or course. Once outside, the mechanism operating the gates creaked back to life, raising the door and closing it behind him with a resounding thud. He paused, only for a moment, wishing he had a faster mode of transportation, but horses weren't needed by the likes of those inhabiting Gilcurr, so he had no other option than to walk. The sun was already descending, each day growing shorter than the last, but, being mid-day now, it was still bright and although the brightness didn't have a negative effect on him, he was already, instinctively, beginning to feel more comfortable in the darkness. He needed to head due north, but the Doubtless Mountains would delay him too much, so he decided to head east until he reached the Cruel Road, then head north from there. Resuming his brisk walk, the only sound was the clanking of his full-plate armor, but he noticed for the first time he had a slight limp to his gait. He didn't feel any pain, yet he, unconsciously, was favoring his right leg. "What weakness is this?" he asked himself out loud, irritated by the nuisance. It didn't slow him down, and it was a minor limp, but he was annoyed at its introduction. He tried to remember more about it, but nothing came to mind, and he cursed his tarnished memory that kept his past hidden. As he walked through the forest that shrouded the valley, nature seemed to take notice of his presence, and either the natural inhabitants sensed his negative energy and fled before him, or they remained still and silent as he passed.

He walked, nonstop, for a full day, until, finally cresting a hill, he caught a glimpse of the Cruel Road. Descending the hill and crossing the last mile of rough terrain, Kord finally stepped onto the rough road that was more of a rutted trail than a road. Wagons, people, horses, oxen, donkeys, and whatever else traveled the road, wearing a weaving path of trodden dirt through the grassy hills, leaving behind wheel tracks and footprints scattered along its dusty, dirty surface. Kord smiled to himself, the obvious signs of recent footprints and wagon wheels, heading north, meant that a caravan had passed through this spot not too long ago. "Blick will provide," he said reverently as he turned to start heading north.

* * * *

Kord walked, his lifeless body not needing a moment's rest, for another two days, and still no creature, large or small, dared interrupt his travels through the notorious Cruel Pass. As he progressed, the signs of the caravan grew fresher with every step, until around dusk on the third day since he had left Gilcurr, he caught his first glimpse of the large group. It was a rear guard of ten humans, all on horseback and all but one were armored with chain mail and carried long spears. The only exception was a robed human, possibly an elf, but likely a human, he thought to himself. Kord decided to follow them at a distance until darkness truly set in; being outnumbered, the darkness favored him.

Kord patiently watched from a distance as the caravan halted and started to set up camp for the night. As darkness settled, the caravan began to light up with a very large fire in the center while armored wagons formed a circle around the camp, each with two large torches lighting up the perimeter. Kord waited longer than he had intended, but found himself admiring the tactical thought that went into the formation. As the activity within the camp settled down, he finally decided to make his move, but before he could start moving, he heard the familiar voice, the same one he had heard in Krugar's tent; it sounded like an old man, and it whispered to him, "Sacrifice a heart of a good cleric to me, and I shall provide what you seek." He couldn't tell if the voice was in his head or was truly audible. As the voice receded, a jolt of pain ran up and down his body, causing him to fall to his knees. "Never forget who you serve . . ." he heard the voice say, this time using a firmer tone. Kord lost control of his body, falling to the ground, as it contorted through the stabbing, wrenching, and searing pains. "Remember your suffering . . ." the voice hissed, conjuring up flashes of memories from his time at the solitary well and the grief associated with it. The pain shooting throughout his body was debilitating, but the sorrow he felt was intolerable and yet, despite his suffering, his mind still defied him as he could not pinpoint what, or who, he was grieving for. This went on for some tim; how long Kord could not be sure, but as quickly as the pain and feelings of grief took over his body and mind, they ceased, replaced by the fatherly voice, presumably in his head, trailing away, "Bring me the heart . . ." Regaining his senses, he realized that, in his agony, he had been screaming out loud, and his shouts were still echoing through the hills. His helmet, granting him the benefit of infravision, highlighted the ten humans he had been trailing, who now had him surrounded. The ten riders, still mounted, had him encircled, watching as he writhed on the ground.

"Be careful, Ledi," said Pel, the only non-armored rider now surrounding Kord. Pel was a middle-aged human with black hair, which was pulled back and tied to keep it out of his face. But he, like many of his companions, looked dirty and tired from the already long ride. "He is obviously crazed," he added, his hands resting on the pommel of his saddle.

"You, sir!" said Ledi, a stocky, well-built man still in his early thirties, holding his spear in a readied position. "What are you doing there?!" he asked in a firm voice, once Kord stopped shouting. Kord, on his back when he regained his senses, sat up onto his elbows, looking around. The riders were ten yards away, creating a full circle around him, the horses pawing at the ground nervously.

"Holy shit!" said Wedu, a rider next to Ledi. "His eyes glow red!" he said, pointing, the light from the half-moon being just enough for the humans to see Kord's dark shape, but the glowing eyes stood out starkly. The others, already seeing the oddity, raised their spears.

Kord rolled over to his stomach and, pushing himself to one knee, rose to both feet, the act looking unnatural, as no man would have been able to do that in full battle armor, drawing gasps from several of the riders. "That ain't right...he ain't right!" shouted Pase, a tall fair, haired human from behind Kord, and not waiting any longer, he charged his horse, attempting to knock Kord back down, but Kord side-stepped and in a smooth motion, drew Slice and in one swing the vorpal blade severed the head of the horse, which crumpled to the ground, sending Pase flying, landing hard on his right shoulder.

"Yesssss! Killllll them allll..." hissed Slice telepathically to Kord, reveling in the warm blood of the animal on its blade.

The eight remaining fighters charged their horses in, jabbing their spears at Kord. All but one glanced off the plate armor, but Ledi, ramming his spear at a steeper downward angle, landed his blow between Kord's helmet and chest plate. The spear tip got stuck, pinned between Kord's armor and his right shoulder. While that was happening, Pel canted a quick spell, releasing two magic missiles, which raced toward Kord, striking him in the chest with two solid thuds.

Kord relished the pain from the bolts and spears, but could not afford to waste time. With the group descending on him, he seized the opportunity, and recalling the power he had used while fighting Krykl, he reached out to the negative plane and drew in a tremendous amount of raw energy while he canted the spell. "Dal mio centro, invoco fiamme esplosive di sofferenza!!" The fireball, centered on himself, erupted around him, the explosion knocking both horses and riders backwards, with three of the riders being completely vaporized, while the others were simply charred to death. Even Ledi, the most experienced of the small troop, was blown backwards, dead before he hit the ground with a loud thud. Pel, seeing the fireball, turned his horse and sent it into a gallop, heading northward, back toward the caravan.

"No, no, no," said Kord, shaking his head. Leveling his free left hand, he pointed at the fleeing mage as he said the prayer to Blick. "Invoco le tenebre affinché distruggano tutta la vita intorno a me." For Pel, it felt as if someone had just reached inside of his body and pulled out his spine -- the pain was so intense, but it wasn't his spine, it was his soul that Kord ripped from Pel's mortal flesh. The white, luminescent spirit hung in the air for just a moment as Pel's lifeless body fell off the galloping horse, crashing head first to the ground and rolling several yards away. Before his body had even come to rest, Pel's soul blinked out of sight, forever gone. "It is a shame I could not have had you as well," said Kord in the darkness alone. "I could have used a mage." Looking around at the casualties, he was pleased with himself, and, raising Slice and his empty left hand to the sky, he said one more prayer to Blick. "Invoco le tenebre affinché leghino le anime ai morti e servano la mia volontà su Thran." After completing the prayer, he watched and waited. At first nothing happened, as before, but just as he was about to move on, three of the riders rolled over and stood up. Ledi, Wedu, and Pase, each terribly burned, their faces and legs black and charred, missing chunks of flesh, shuffled to Kord.

"Master," said Ledi. "What is your command?"

* * * *

"The night camp is now set up," said Ropels, a medium-sized human, wearing banded armor and carrying a shield that bore the insignia of the Hunting Herd mercenary group, which was the face of a snarling, black-furred wolf. "The goods wagons be in the middle, with the armored wagons forming the outer line," continued Ropels, "with three warriors in each armored wagon." Ropels took off a gauntleted hand, and although the night was cool, he wiped away a muddy mix of sweat and dirt from the hard day of walking and riding. "The mages and clerics are in the middle, with the civ'es -- along with yourselves."

"Very good Ropels," said Saxick, standing up from his comfortable-looking chair set around a large fire. His platemail armor looked worn but was still a fine suit and had the wolf insignia etched into the breastplate. "See that you and the others get some food to eat, it has been a hard day," he added with compassion in his voice.

"Thank ye, sir, we will in just a short bit," said Ropels gratefully,

558

"but I sent Ledi and a group back along the road, as we had a couple reports of a figure being spotted a couple times."

"What kind of figure?" asked Kanatars, a tall human with straight black hair that fell to his shoulders. Dressed in blood-red robes and adorned with a multitude of small pouches along his belt, his attire sold him out professionally as a wizard.

Ropels eyed the wizard warily, never trusting that sort. "Oh, well," he waved his bare hand, "nothing to worry about, most likely, sir. People 'see' all manner of things on the Cruel Road -- the myths of the Cruel Pass tend to get everyone on edge, it is most likely nothing."

"I did not ask for a lecture, Ropels, I asked: what kind of figure?" Kanatars asked again.

"Sorry, sir," Ropels nodded his head submissively. "An armored figure of some sort."

"A solitary armored figure...roaming around the Cruel Pass?" asked Sestisa, the firelight reflecting off her black skin as she spoke. She too stood up, her fine platemail armor clanking as she did so, her heavy mace, clipped at her side, lightly bouncing against her right thigh. A thin golden necklace hung around her neck, holding a medallion of Equis, the neutral shadow god of comfort and suffering. "This would be a most dangerous person," she added with a slight drawl in her speech, belying a distant heritage.

Saxick was about to say something, when a loud explosion rocked the night air to the south of the caravan. Everyone looked southward, seeing a large fireball lighting up the night sky. Kanatars now stood up as well, the hems of his robe brushing the dusty ground, hiding his leather-booted feet. "Pels could not have done that," he said, vouching for his young pupil.

"Aye, that can only portent bad news," said Saxick. "Ropels, how many soldiers did you send?"

"Ten," replied the sergeant. "A regular contingent for a scouting party."

"Damn these hills," said Saxick, true worry on his face -- not for his safety but rather the safety of his troops.

"What are you waiting for?" asked Kanatars, looking at Saxick, his hands gesturing out into the darkness.

"Do not be a fool, Kanatars. Whatever happened out there is already done..." began Saxick.

"Are you fucking serious?" the mage asked incredulously. "We need to go out there and help them!" he continued, his voice rising.

"Sit down!" ordered Saxick, his face darkening, his mouth tightening behind his thick brown mustache. "You are out of your depth here." Kanatars's eyes went wide at the rebuke, and although he did not respond back, he didn't sit down, either. Taking a whistle hanging around his neck, he blew three short blasts, notifying his mercenaries to be on high alert -- if the fireball explosion hadn't been enough of a warning. "We will wait here and defend from this lighted and fortified position," Saxick said, drawing his longsword, its long blade emitting a soft white glow. As he did so, Pel's horse came running into the inner circle of the camp, riderless.

"Son of a bitch," said Kanatars under his breath through clenched teeth, recognizing the horse with the white marking on its nose, and its absent rider.

* * * *

"I need a horse," said Kord, looking at the carnage around him, lit by the half moon, but nothing was moving. "How well defended is the caravan?" he asked.

Ledi, his face half-burned, let out a half groan. "It be well defended, m'lord."

"Explain yourself further," said Kord in a raspy tone.

"M'lord, there be around fifty mercenaries, but that ain't gonna be your main worry," said Ledi. "Saxick, Kanatars, and Sestisa are most formidable."

Kord looked back at Ledi, the enchanted eyes of the skull helmet glowing red in the darkness. "Who are they to stop me?"

Ledi snorted derisively. "They are very powerful. A warrior, a mage, and a cleric...I have seen Kanatars and Sestisa cast powerful spells."

Kord let out a low growl, irritated at the news. "You and the other two," he pointed at Pase and Wedu, who were already munching on the dead corpses, "head back to a fortified town called Gilcurr. Head west until you get to the foothills of the mountains and then head south. Ask for a servant of mine named Kijjit."

Ledi bowed, "Yes, m'lord, we will be waiting for you there."

* * * *

The fireball not only lit up the night sky, but Rasan, Pohut, and Faldar, situated in the southernmost armored wagon guarding the perimeter of the caravan, felt the tremble of the blast, ever so slightly, resonate from the ground up into the wooden frame. "It is awfully quiet out there," said Pohut, his eyes meticulously searching the darkness beyond.

"Shut up, Po," said Rasan, standing next to Pohut as they both looked over the barbed wall of the wagon.

"What be out there, you think?" asked Faldar, standing near the locked exit of the wagon. "I ain't know of any weak creatures that can be casting that kind of magic."

"Whatever it be, it kilt all of them -- even Ledi," said Pohut.

"Aw, shut it -- you ain't knowing that, youse wernt there," said Rasan.

"Hey! What be that?" asked Pohut, pointing at a figure approaching on foot.

"Look at his eyes!" said Faldar, in a hushed shout. "He be a demon from hell!"

"Halt, mister!" shouted Rasan, holding a hand out over the side of the wagon, while Pohut and Faldar aimed crossbows at the darkened figure.

Kord took a few steps closer, then stopped as requested. "All I require is a horse, and I will be on my way -- no bother to you or your caravan," said Kord.

"Sounds like you already went and created a problem," said Rasan, "and give'en you a horse ain't a likely outcome. It would be best if you just turned aroun' and go back from wherever the hell you came."

"Ledi said I should speak to Saxick," said Kord, his voice relaxed. "Take me to him." This statement caused a small commotion inside the

561

locked wagon, and Kord could hear whispering, but not the content.

The whispering stopped. "Where is Ledi and the others?" asked Rasan.

"Back there, over that small hill," said Kord.

"Why would he be back there, fella? Why ain't he here with you?" asked Rasan.

"His group attacked me, and they all died," replied Kord without a hint of emotion.

"You son of a bitch, you kilt Ledi and all the others?" Shouted Pohut, angered by Kord's coldness.

Rasan elbowed his companion. "Let me do the talkin'," he scolded. Turning his attention back to the figure outside, Rasan asked, "If he and all them are dead, how did he tell you to seek out Saxick?". The young mercenary smiled in the darkness, thinking he had just outsmarted the intruder.

"You would not believe the truth, if you heard it," answered Kord evasively, before continuing, with a more menacing tone. "I have lost my patience with you; go fetch Saxick."

Rasan looked at Pohut. "Alright, you go get the boss."

"You got it!" responded Pohut, glad to be getting out of the wagon and away from the dark figure. Sliding the large deadbolt out of its clasp, Pohut opened the door and jumped down, not even bothering with the small steps attached to the backside of the wagon. Faldar quickly closed the door and reinserted the bolt, locking the door shut.

* * * *

Saxick, Kanatars, and Sestisa were standing at the ready, with fifteen other mercenary fighters in the middle of the caravan camp, the wagons and merchants tucked into a tight grouping inside the well-lit area. Pohut came running from the darkness of the outer ring of fortified wagons, stopping breathless in front of Saxick.

"Sir, there is a man who claims Ledi told him to seek you out," stammered Pohut in a stream of words, one fumbling over the other.

"One man, you say?" asked Saxick.

"Yes, sir, dressed in battle armor and carrying one hell of a big sword," answered Pohut, "but that was all I could make out." Then he remembered the eyes. "'Cept for the eyes, sir -- they glowed red!" he added with some drama.

"What about Ledi and the others?" asked Saxick.

Pohut's face went from an urgent look to a dismayed look in an instant. "He says he kilt them on account of they attacked him."

"All of them?" asked Kanatars, a sliver of hope in his voice for his apprentice, Pel.

"Yes, sir, he said all of them," answered Pohut.

"Bring him here then, and let us see what parlay he offers," ordered Saxick.

"Yes sir!" said Pohut before turning and running back. As he ran back to the wagon, a feeling of dread crept into his soul, something he had never felt before. Knocking on the door of the wagon, he yelled, "Saxick said to bring him on in!" he yelled.

Rasan looked down at the figure, still standing there, statue like. "Alright, mister, sounds like you can go on in. Pohut, there, will take you to Saxick."

"What?!" exclaimed Pohut. "I ain't going alone!" he complained.

Rasan raised his voice, carefully eyeing Kord as he walked around the wagon. "You do as you is told, boy. Now take him on in."

Pohut drew out his longsword, watching with terrified eyes as the dark figure appeared from around the corner of the wagon. "No fun-funny business now, mister," he managed to get out, practically choking on the words and not sounding nearly as confident as he was hoping to convey.

Kord ignored the mercenary's comment. "Take me to him," he said plainly. Pohut started moving quickly, keeping an eye on Kord over his shoulder, ready to run if the powerful figure made a move.

Kord surveyed the scene as it unfolded. It was a tight perimeter, and a well-defended area, with the supply wagons neatly tucked into the middle. Whoever was running the caravan knew how to defend it. He could feel that his powers were drained at the moment and regretted using the power-word kill on the solitary fleeing human. 'Should have let him go... too impulsive,' he thought to himself and tucked away the experience for later benefit. It was a brief walk into the middle, well-lighted area, and he noticed once again that his gait had reverted to the limp. In front of the supply wagons, a multitude of mercenaries stood on either side of three figures, with one figure, dressed in platemail, out front, his longsword drawn, the blade giving off a dim light of its own.

As Kord approached, Sestisa leaned and whispered to Saxick, "Be careful with this one, he wears a symbol of Blick plainly on his armor." The mercenary leader nodded, showing he had heard the advice.

Once Kord was about fifteen feet away, Saxick held up his left hand. "That is close enough," he said as a chill ran down his spine. Inspecting the man, he couldn't see much past the armor, as only the bottom half of the man's face was visible -- and that looked -- 'What?' he thought to himself -- mangled was a word that came to mind, but despite the large fire and being well lit, it was still night and he could not see the man's face with any great detail. "What is your business here, and what have you to say about killing ten of my men?"

"They attacked me, not the other way around," said Kord, "It was unfortunate that they did not parlay first. My mount stumbled and broke its leg two days ago, so I have been walking since. I only ask for one horse, so I can be on my way."

"You will suffer for what you have done!" shouted Kanatars, his arms still folded underneath his robes, but the spells he had memorized were already coming to mind.

Kord shifted his gaze to the red-robed wizard. "I suffer every day." His voice grated, but his lips curled into a smile. "That is my lot now." Then his gaze shifted to Sestisa, seeing the symbol of Equis, an 'X' with two dots. "And what do we have here? A shadow sister of suffering? Well met," said Kord with a slight nod of his head.

"No sister of yours," hissed Sestisa, her northern drawl obvious. "I see no balance in you whatever."

"Well," said Kord, shrugging his shoulders, "you are right, I do not pretend to seek a balance," he continued looking at the cleric, "but I know you touch the darkness when it suits you."

"Enough," said Saxick. "Take off your helmet, I want to see your face." Then added quickly, "Your whole face."

Kord made no effort to take his helmet off. "All I need is a horse, and you have plenty, even a few extra now, I suppose. Think of it as the silver lining to this whole...situation," he said, gesturing around the camp.

"You are very bold, indeed, to make light of the death of my men. Before we talk further, I will know who I am dealing with," said Saxick. "Take it off," he said in a more commanding tone, pointing to Kord's helmeted head.

"I am Kord, Lord of Suffering," answered the Death Knight.

"Lord of what realm?" asked Saxick skeptically.

Kord let the question hang in the air for a moment, then answered, "Thran."

"Lord of the world, you say?" asked Saxick skeptically. Pointing again at Kord's head, he added, "The helmet."

Kord debated what to do next and could sense the tension in the air, as well as the fear and weakness in the mercenaries, but there was no fear from the three leaders directly in front of him. They simply looked... ready. "As you wish," said Kord, and, reaching up with his left hand, he removed the skull helmet. A gasp went through the mercenaries as he revealed his scarred, marred, and rotting flesh -- but what struck them most of all was his dark, voided, unnatural eye sockets.

"By the gods," said Sestisa, holding up her holy symbol.

"That really is not necessary," said Kord, tucking the helmet under his left arm and waving his hand dismissively at the cleric, "nor effective."

Saxick, sensing his companions were about to unleash their spells, held his hand up. "Hold..." he said, a carefulness and calculation in his voice.

"A wise man, you are, Saxick, to hold your attack," said Kord. "All this can be done and over. All that you need to do is give me a horse and no one else dies tonight. Simple and, regrettably, painless."

"What are you?" asked Saxick.

Kord chuckled. "A blunt, but eloquent question. Unfortunately, one I cannot answer with the specificity you desire." After a short pause, he continued, his voice hissing and cracking unnaturally, "Now, give me, a fucking horse."

Saxick could feel the weight of the decision, as if a hundred-pound boulder was sitting on each of his shoulders. Looking around, he could see the fear in many of his mercenaries' eyes. Taking notice of Pel's horse standing near a wagon where a merchant was holding onto its reins, Saxick made his difficult decision. "Give him Pel's horse," he said, motioning to the merchant with his hand. But nobody moved. "Damn you, Theold, give him the horse!"

The merchant looked around, surprised he was being asked to do anything, but slowly and reluctantly got down from the wagon. The short, skinny, aged merchant nervously walked the beast over to the Death Knight. Kord watched with disdain as the feeble, trembling, merchant approached. Kord, only taking his eyes off the old human long enough to slip his helmet back on, snatched the reins from Theold, who was nearly collapsing, due to his knees shaking so badly. Kord, using his free hand, pulled himself up onto the steed in an easy fluid motion; something no man could possibly have done alone wearing full battle armor. "Well met, Saxick," Kord said, "perhaps we will meet again."

"I hope not. The next time we will come to blows -- regardless of my duties and the dependents in my care at the time," said Saxick, locking his eyes onto glowing red orbs behind Kord's helmet.

"I would doubt any man who said that to me...but I do believe you," said Kord with a slight nod of his head, respecting the man's confidence, but also accepting of the challenge. "Very well then," he continued, "to blows then, when we next meet." Leaning down low from his saddle, addressing Saxick directly, the distance between the two seemingly shrinking, he asked, "Who, I wonder, shall suffer the most? You?" Then switching his gaze to the people behind Saxick with a slight nod of his skull-faced helmet, his malevolent red eyes glowing, he said, "Or your people?" Saxick's face flushed red with anger, but before he could answer, Kord let out a crude, crusty laugh and, sitting back up, urged the horse northward, leaving the caravan behind.

* * * *

The rest of the journey northward was uneventful for Kord. The inhabitants that made the journey through the Cruel Pass, so deadly for most travelers, were either fortunate enough to have truly missed Kord as he passed through or, seeing him, chose to steer clear of the lone rider. Either way, he traveled unimpeded, with the horse greatly increasing his speed. He couldn't care less about the life of the horse, but he needed to make better time than he could walking, so the only time he stopped was to occasionally let the horse rest, eat, and drink -- lest he ride it to death. Even with the horse, it took over three full days to reach Castor -- the fortified city of Northern Kardoon. The Cruel Pass emptied out into flat plains as the Cruel Road wound its way through the otherwise grassy fields for the last one hundred miles. Ten miles away, the thick fifty-foot walls of Castor started to loom on the horizon, and at night the torches could be clearly seen atop the battlements. The timing worked out well for Kord, riding his horse into the surrounding settlements, which were mostly traders and a large contingent of bivouacked Kardoon regulars. The soldiers' tents were lined neatly, but the merchant and other structures were scattered around, most of them in rough shape. Not wanting to draw attention to himself, he had taken his helmet off so his eyes wouldn't stand out like a beacon in the night. Of course, if there were elves or other humanoids along the way that had infravision, the ability to see heat in the night, he would stand out anyway, as a cold black shadow atop the horse -- but he would have to risk that much, and besides, he could feel the power of his abilities welling inside of him, and he felt much more confident to be able to handle a crowd, if it came to that. As enjoyable as that would be, to kill a multitude of people, it would hinder and delay his ability to get through the city and into Thayol, so once again he had to fight back the primal urges that were compelling him to simply start inflicting as much pain as possible on everyone around him. He fought to remember what the old man had said: "Pain is the simplest of all suffering, immediately gratifying, but the shortest in duration." He smiled a sickly smile to himself, his split lips curling upwards, thinking of the suffering he could cause once he was free of the two mortal idiots, Judar and Krugar.

"You there!" said a female voice from the side of the road, near a small tent-like structure. "It looks like you might be looking for someone."

Kord stopped the tired horse and glanced over his shoulder. The figure was svelte and was wearing a cloak that hid most of her features, but not the fine black leather boots. Kord was amazed, his night vision was almost as good as his day vision, although some colors were still hard to distinguish, but the boots were definitely black. "Maybe I am," he answered back, in his gravelly, unnatural voice.

"Hop down and join me inside my tent." The figure waved a gloved hand, motioning for him to follow her. Kord looked around, noting the regular flow of people going both directions on the road, which was steady, even at this hour, but saw nothing out of the ordinary. "C'mon, nothing to be afraid of," she urged, her face hidden from behind the hood. Kord dismounted, taking his helmet out of a saddlebag that had been conveniently left by its former owner and placing the it on his head. He led the horse over to the tent, but the figure waved it away. "Never mind the horse, you will not be needing that anymore."

"We will see," said Kord, unconvinced, as he tied the reins to one of the ropes holding up the tent.

"Suit yourself," she said with a chuckle.

"You go in first," said Kord, standing in front of the flap.

"Not the trusting type, eh?" she said, again with a short chuckle. "Well, okay…" and she pushed the flap aside and went in, and as she did so, light from inside the tent poured out into the road.

Kord followed her in. It was a small ten by ten foot tent, and about seven feet high, just enough for a normal-sized human to stand comfortably. There were two other cloaked humanoids in the room, along with the female who had flagged him down. They all removed their hoods. The female had dark metallic skin, certainly a Drow, or dark elf, just as Lyr'ifol and his companions were back in Gilcurr. The other two were human men, each of average height and build, although one had brown hair and was clean shaven, while the other had dark black hair and a bushy beard. The only other remarkable feature was the coffin along the eastern wall.

The dark elf walked up to stand directly in front of Kord, looking him up and down, and, with a gloved finger, began to trace the circles of Blick's symbol that had been engraved into his armor. "If I asked how your trip was from Gilcurr," she said in a seemingly seductive voice, "would that be enough to convince you we are here for your purposes?"

Kord looked down at the fine and delicate features of the Drow's face. "Lyr'ifol sent you then?" he asked.

Taking her finger off his armor, she shook it at him, audibly tsking him with a few clicks of her tongue. "Names mean nothing, but that does not mean you should go throwing them about, either. Be a champ and do as we say, and you will see the other side of the North Wall in no time."

Kord did not like the feeling of being in someone else's care, but he had no alternative. "What would you have me do?" he asked, his voice crackling. "Let me guess, you want me to get into that coffin?"

"Sounds like we have a clever one here, boys," the Drow said, turning to face the two men. "I guess we are not as creative as our guest was hoping!" The two men let out a hearty laugh. Gracefully spinning around to face Kord, the Drow looked up at his glowing eyes. "No magic, I was told," she said, tapping his armor with her finger again. "No magic means you gotta perform."

"What do you mean, perform?" asked Kord, his patience growing thin.

"You gotta play dead," she answered with a smile, her white teeth a sharp contrast to her dark complexion. "But that should be easy for you, no?" she asked, but Kord did not reply. "Well, you are on a tight timeline, you have some business in Bindal, down south, I understand?" she asked rhetorically. "So if you would," she said, gesturing to the coffin, "hop in, and we will get moving right away."

"Tell me what is going to happen after I get in the coffin," demanded Kord.

"I can see patience is not your long suit, but that is what you must be today: patient," answered the dark elf, "as it will take a few days to transport you where you want to be. Think of it as...a vacation." Once again motioning to the coffin, she added, "Time is a-wasting."

Kord studied the Drow's face carefully, then those of the two humans, but he could not read any deceit, if there was any. "If names mean nothing, tell me yours," he asked, addressing the dark elf.

"Names only add complications, and I know you want to avoid any of those," dodged the Drow. "Now, get in the coffin, or our business is concluded," she said, crossing her arms for emphasis.

Every fiber of Kord's being was urging him to kill the Drow and the two hapless humans. He could feel the powerful emotion of hatred burning through his body, but he knew he could not go that far. Raising his finger, he pointed it at the clean-shaven human, then the bearded one.

"Hey! What are you doing there?" asked the clean-shaven man, drawing his weapon.

The dark elf quickly clapped her hands twice in Kord's line of vision, trying to draw Kord's attention. "Friend, we do not have time for these..."

Before the elf could finish her sentence, Kord tapped the negative plane, sucking the dark energy into his being, reveling in the surge before he released it with the simple cant, "Invoco le tenebre affinché distruggano tutta la vita intorno a me." The result was immediate, as the bodies of the two men convulsed in painful, unnatural jerky movements. It only took a few agonizing seconds before their souls were rent from their bodies; the white light of their inner life force hovering for an instant over the mortal shells they had just vacated, watching helplessly. Ending their misery, the two men's eyes rolled back in their heads as their bodies crumpled to the ground. A second later, the whispery souls blinked out of sight, returning to whatever god they worshiped for final judgment.

The dark elf felt the brush of death, felt the pull on her soul as well, but she resisted. Seeing her companions drop, she drew a dagger that was hidden in the small of her back and rammed it into Kord's side, but the blade deflected off the hardened steel of his armor. Kord grabbed the back of the dark elf's neck with his left hand and, drawing his own dagger, pushed it up to her throat, holding it there, the sharpened blade cutting her skin, but just barely. "You were about to tell me your name," his voice crackled. The Drow grabbed Kord's forearm, holding the dagger, and tried to move it, but the Death Knight's strength was too much. Kord tightened his grip on the dark elf's neck and watched as she grimaced in pain. "Your name," he commanded again.

Her expression went from grimace to frown, her own anger welling up, but she relented. "Shimeq'ena," she said through gritted teeth.

Kord squeezed tighter again. "Full name."

"Shimeq'ena Remerendil," she said, then spat in Kord's face.

"Plaguess will defile you," she cursed, invoking the vengeance of the evil god of Death.

Kord released her with a low chuckle. "Do I look like someone who fears death?" Kord said, pointing the tip of the dagger at his face, before sliding it back into its scabbard on his right side. "You do not know it, but I believe we could be great allies in the future, if you keep an open mind."

Shimeq'ena rubbed her neck and backed away. "I always keep an open mind," she said, then pointing to the coffin, continued, "now, get the fuck in there."

Kord smiled and nodded. "But of course." Kord drew Slice from the scabbard on his back and stepped into the box. Lying down, he held the sword on his chest.

"Killlllsssss her, tooooo," Slice's hissing voice slithered into Kord's consciousness, but the Death Knight willed the sword into silence, which it begrudgingly obeyed.

Shimeq'ena walked over and, looking down, reached for Kord's helmet, but the Death Knight reached up and grabbed her arm, halting it in mid-reach. "Your eyes are glowing red with that on, and that will not do," she said. Kord continued to hold her arm in his iron grip. "The coffin will be searched before it goes through each wall. If your eyes are glowing red, it will raise suspicion." Kord held on for a few more painful seconds, then let her arm go, allowing Shimeq'ena to take off his helmet where she set it in the corner of the coffin, near his head; its skull face still dreadful, even when it was empty. As a Drow, Shimeq'ena had seen many horrors, inflicting some of them, but she was struck by the Death Knight's face and the depth of his wounds: his skin was torn asunder, with scars crisscrossing his whole head, and where his eyes had been were now voids of darkness. She reached out and touched the flesh of his forehead, which was ashen colored, with mottles of red blood under the skin. He was so cold to the touch, like touching an icicle, she thought. "What happened to you?" she asked.

Kord hated the question as he spent most of his time asking himself the very same thing. Searching his mind, he hoped for hints and clues to his past and what brought him to this point. But his mind was a blank slate to him, only serving him situationally, like a deep set of instincts. Shimeq'ena couldn't see Kord looking at her, the dark voids revealing nothing, but without turning his head, he did. "I do not know," he said, his voice sounding almost normal. After a moment of reflection, he continued, his voice once again scratchy and unnatural. "Now move along, as you pointed out, time is fucking wasting." He gestured for her to leave with a gauntleted hand.

Shimeq'ena nodded and placed the cover on the coffin, then using some nails and a hammer, sealed the lid. Looking at the crumpled bodies of her guild-mates, she shook her head, whispering to herself, "Shit..." knowing she would need to get some new help to move Kord's body. Pulling her hood back over her head, she exited the tent and was surprised to see a crowd had gathered along the road.

"Are you alright?" asked a decently dressed middle-aged human, an obvious merchant.

"Of course, I am, what is everyone doing?" asked Shimeq'ena. As she looked around, it began to dawn on her as her infravision, despite the darkness, helped her piece together what was happening. She could see a dozen bodies on the ground, already beginning to cool from death.

"People just fell over dead -- their...their...spirits... just flew away!" the merchantman explained, gesturing with both hands up to the heavens.

"Thank you for your concern, I am fine, but two of my companions inside my tent also perished. It was horrible," said Shimeq'ena, feigning as if she were about to break down crying. "Would you mind keeping an eye on my tent for a moment? I need to go find my brothers to help me," she said pleadingly to the man.

"I 'spect I will be around for a while anyway, so sure, I can keep an eye on it for you, young lady," the merchantman answered, trying to get a look under her hood.

Turning so the man could not get a look at her face, she began moving away. "Oh thank you, mister, I shall return quickly! Thank you!" she said, still pretending to be on the verge of tears. With a few graceful strides and years of practice, she quickly melded into the darkness and the gathering crowd, hurrying to get more help from her guild -- cursing under her breath, along the way.

* * * *

Shimeq'ena spent most of her time in Thayol's capital of Windred, having been sent down to Castor to help a "friend" of the guild through the fortified walls of Castor and Feldor. No simple task, as suspicion ran deep between the two kingdoms. Usually the task was smuggling some object or person from one side to the other, but this time it was a body. A most unusual request. There were much easier ways to get from one side to the other, and, in fact, trying to pass through the damn walls was the hardest option. But after her brief, and deadly, encounter with 'the body,' she thought to herself, perhaps there were good reasons they didn't exercise those better options. Not being from Castor presented her with a bit of a problem, so she brought two of her most dependable shitbirds for the very purpose of avoiding any complications or setback on this mission. Despite her confidence in the small team she brought, she always had a contingency plan, which included having another capo named Beshin, who was intimately familiar with Castor, available to her should she need it. Her pride prickled at the thought of seeking assistance, which although available, always came with a price. With no apparent alternative, she made up her mind and, cursing under her breath, she moved at a brisk pace to the prearranged location where she knew Beshin would be waiting. The Penumbra guild had safe houses located all over Castor, both inside and outside the city, which typically consisted of a legitimate business acting as a front for the guild's illegal behavior. Shimeq'ena was given the name of a blacksmith and farrier shop not far away, that was connected to the guild. "Building" was too strong a term for the structure, which was half tent and half wooden walls, a hodgepodge of construction like everything else in the outer city. To do anything more would have drawn attention, and that isn't what the guild wanted. But it did draw travelers coming into, and some leaving, the city to get their horses' shoes checked out, or have their equipment repaired, prior to the long journey ahead of them. As a source of information on the coming and going, and who was worth robbing, it was priceless.

Shimeq'ena went in the back way, a wooden door along the eastern wall of the building. Barely opening the door, she slid inside. The interior was one big room, but a large curtain was hung across the thirty foot width, essentially making two rooms: the front of the smithy where

Corso, the blacksmith, handled the legitimate side of the business, and the back where the guild could hide, meet, or conduct whatever business they needed, but also served as Corso's living quarters. It was dark in the room, and Corso was asleep, snoring in his bed. Shimeq'ena's infravision showed two heat signatures: one in the bed and the other being a human-sized person sitting in a chair at the small kitchen table. Quietly, she moved over to the table.

"I was not expecting the great Shimeq'ena to need my help tonight," said Beshin, lighting a small lamp on the table before Shimeq'ena could close the distance. The yellow flame did little more than illuminate the immediate area around the table, and of course, ruined the Drow's infravision. Beshin was human, with short brown hair, of medium height, and though he wasn't the most handsome man, he did have dazzling blue eyes, which seemed to be highlighted by the dancing yellow flame of the lantern. Shimeq'ena noted that he was rather physical in nature, not slender or agile looking, making her think he might be more of a thug than a thief. Shimeq'ena shielded her sensitive eyes as she sat down, giving them a second to adjust to the unwelcome light.

"Damn, Beshin, you humans and your constant need for light," Shimeq'ena complained.

"I wanted to see your pretty face," he said, trying to peek behind the hood. "I hear you are quite the beauty," he said with a smile.

Shimeq'ena didn't smile. "Shut up," she said. "We have a problem."

Holding up the index finger on his left hand, he quickly responded, "Ah, no -- you mean to say, you have a problem," he said, leveling his finger and jabbing it in her direction, emphasizing his statement.

"Do not be difficult with me," Shimeq'ena said, somewhat annoyed. "I just lost the brothers, Turmi and Tund."

"What? You lost two of your shitbirds?" asked Beshin, using jargon to refer to the lowest level members of the Penumbra Thieves Guild. Shimeq'ena and Beshin had attained the rank of capo, which means they each had up to ten shitbirds reporting to them. Beshin chuckled unsympathetically, followed by a hushed whistle. "Damn, your agent is going to be pissed," said Beshin. Getting more serious, leaning forward on the table with both elbows, he continued, "You are gonna lose points on this, ya'know." Every guild member earned points, or lost points, based on their performance of the tasks given to them -- and the bosses kept track. Points equaled rank, and rank equaled more coin and more power, and for Shimeq'ena, it was the power that she sought. This was a decent job, points wise, and reporting back to her agent, Claffum, after having botched the job and losing two shitbirds in the process, could end up costing her twice as many points as she stood to gain.

"Only if he finds out," said Shimeq'ena, also leaning forward despite the light of the lantern hurting her eyes, her red irises reflecting the soft glow back at Beshin. Beshin gave Shimeq'ena a skeptical look, so the dark elf added, "Help me move the package through the Dragon Wall, that is all I ask. But we must be quick about it." The Dragon Wall, referred to the massive northern wall and gate that led out of Castor into No Land, the land between the two great walls of Kardoon and Thayol.

Skeptical, Beshin sat back in his chair. "Shit, Shimeq'ena, the bosses always find out." He threw his hands up in the air. "Hell, that is what they do. I mean, the guild has agents watching agents that watch those agents and capos to watch the capos that watch the capos watching those capos." He chuckled again. "You know the saying, they have eyes on eyes all the time."

Shimeq'ena didn't hesitate. "It just happened, literally a moment ago, in a tent with only me, the two shitbirds, and the package in it. So, there is no way..." Then her mind went back to the moment she came out of the tent: the merchantman. 'No,' she thought to herself, the merchantman couldn't have been a guild member, it all happened too fast.

Beshin caught her pausing to think. "What? Do you think they know?"

Shimeq'ena shook her head. "No, no way."

Beshin leaned forward again, elbows back on the table, his blue eyes piercing. "What is the package?" he asked.

"First you need to commit your help to me, then you find out what the package is," responded Shimeq'ena.

Beshin looked at Shimeq'ena, her face now more visible. She was indeed beautiful, by any measure, as most elves were, even dark elves. Her red eyes practically glowing int the dim light of the lamp. Her small, delicate, mouth was highlighted by her dark red - almost black - lips. A thin nose complimented the smooth, well defined cheekbones of her face -- but he couldn't let her beauty distract him from reality; he had his own career in the Penumbra guild and was inching his way closer to the rank of agent, and he wouldn't gain any points helping Shimeq'ena on her task -- a mission he had been instructed to observe, not assist, much less cover up. "Look, I want to help, but there ain't nothing in it for me, just a lot of risk and no reward."

"I will give you an oath stone in return," said Shimeq'ena, referring to an oath debt. While the thieves held nothing sacred outside of their guild, and not much sacred within it, there was honor among thieves -- but it came at cost, and that was a guild oath. The thieves traded oath debts carefully and wisely, using and caching them in only after careful consideration.

Beshin scratched his chin, considering the offer. It wasn't every day you could collect an oath debt.... In fact he had never been offered one, and he found the idea intriguing. "Okay, I will do it, but give me your oath stone first," he said, holding out his left hand.

Shimeq'ena smiled. Reaching into a hidden pouch she pulled out a small black pebble and, pressing her thumb to it, left a metallic print on its smooth surface. She held it for a second, examining it, before dropping it into Beshin's waiting palm. "There, it is done. The package is some undead motherfucker -- he is the one who killed the brothers."

Beshin's face blanched, closing his palm and pocketing the stone. "Undead? I do not like dealing with their kind. What kind of undead?"

Shimeq'ena smiled again. "I do not know; I have never come across something like him before."

Beshin frowned. Figuring Shimeq'ena must be hundreds of years old, it was concerning that she didn't recognize the creature. "How old are you?" asked Beshin, curious and alarmed by her admission. That, or she was lying about the true nature of the package.

Shimeq'ena smiled. "Long enough to know we better get moving. He is in a coffin, just down the road a bit, all we need to do is get the coffin to the Castorian undertaker, to get his body through the Dragon Wall, then I will take it from there."

"Why not just teleport the son of a bitch across?" asked Beshin.

"Look, how do I know?" said Shimeq'ena, gesturing with her arms. "We just complete our tasks and move on to the next one, right?" Beshin didn't argue, so she continued, "Now, we need to get moving."

"You go back to the tent and keep people out of there, and I will round up a couple shitbirds for you," offered Beshin.

"No fucking way -- me and you can do it," said Shimeq'ena.

"That ain't the deal -- I said I would help, and I will get you two of my best shitbirds," said Beshin.

"No, the oath stone was for your help, not more shitbirds," huffed Shimeq'ena. "Besides, this calls for more discretion. No one else can know, or I will just take my lumps with my agent."

"That is bullshit, and you know it. Go ahead, take your lumps, see if I care, but you already gave me the oath stone, so it is mine." Beshin leaned back in his plain wooden chair. "Now, do you want my help or not?"

Shimeq'ena waited a moment, trying to control her rage. Buying herself some time, she snuffed the lantern and turned away so the human could not see her face, which was flushing a rosy hue due to her spiking anger, but an instant later she had regained her composure, and, masking her true feelings, she calmly said, "Fine, have them meet me in the white tent, just five blocks from here, north toward the city. It will be the one surrounded by all the dead people." She paused. "They cannot miss it -- oh and be a doll, and have them bring two extra coffins while they are at it."

In the darkness, Beshin smiled, tucking the stone safely away into a deep hidden pocket. "No problem." Shimeq'ena, her infravision having returned, saw the heat signature around his lips curl upwards in a smile and witnessed the action of tucking away the stone; now it was her turn to smile.

* * * *

Shimeq'ena hurried back to the tent, anxious to stave off any further setbacks during this damned mission. Leaning against the sealed coffin, her arms crossed, she silently cursed Claffum, her agent, for giving this assignment to her. She couldn't help but crack a devious half-smile, the points Claffum, that human son of a bitch, had offered for this task were too many, and now she understood why. 'Dammit,' she scolded herself, pounding a closed fist on her leg. This had gone from a straightforward task to a complicated one in a hurry, and now she had an oath stone in play. 'That has to come back,' she thought to herself, her mind spinning on what to do over the next several hours. Interrupting her thoughts, the tent flap opened and two young humans, in their late teens, walked in. Shimeq'ena recognized them both, the slightly taller one was called Tenz. She was never certain if that was a real name or a nickname, but it didn't matter to her, so she never asked. The shorter one was Kermair. Light skinned, not quite albino, and more intelligent than Tenz. Both were proving to be capable shitbirds, but she didn't think Kermair would make it. Too soft, too...what was it about him, she wondered...too nice might be the way to put it.

"Well met, Ms. Shimeq'ena," said Tenz in an obnoxious manner; not unlike many humans, the Drow thought to herself, hearing the greeting. Tenz continued, "Beshin said you could use some help on a task." Looking in the corner, he saw the two dead bodies. "Oh damn, are they..." he paused, looking questionably at Shimeq'ena, "dead?"

"Oh shit!" exclaimed Kermair in a half-excited, half-surprised giggle. "How did they bite it?"

Shimeq'ena frowned. "Fuck both of you," she said in a serious tone, "and wipe those shitty smiles off your face. Where are the two extra coffins I asked for?" Tenz and Kermair both whipped into shape immediately, both knowing they had points to earn as well, not to mention, a Drow was nothing to trifle with, and Shimeq'ena had a reputation for being particularly apt at the art of assassination. Her race, combined with her reputation, made her someone to be respected -- at least by two shitbirds.

"Sorry Shimeq'ena," said Tenz, holding up a hand in apology, "but we have no extra coffins." He looked nervously over at Kermair. "Beshin said nothing about that." Shimeq'ena's face, still hidden behind the hood of her cloak, darkened further, but she said nothing, letting the silence hang, uncomfortably, for what seemed to Tenz and Kermair like an eternity.

As the tension mounted, Kermair finally broke the silence. "But I know where we can get 'em," he offered.

Shimeq'ena seethed. Pulling out a small, hourglass-shaped timer, she set it on the coffin. Flipping it over, the sand began trickling through the small connecting tube of glass, slowing filling the bottom. "You two have exactly three flips of this glass to get your asses back here with two coffins." The two young men looked at each other, but before they could say or do anything, Shimeq'ena raised her voice, a melodic hiss, and dangerous sounding. "Get the fuck out of here," she said, pointing at the tent's door flap. Needing no more encouragement, the two shitbirds took off.

Outside the tent Tenz grabbed Kermair's shoulder. "You better have not been lying in there."

Kermair knocked Tenz's hand off his shoulder. "Ain't you heard of old Sedric?" he said. Tenz gave his guild-mate a doubtful look. "Shit man, Beshin has this old coot under his protection -- he does carpentry, so I bet he could make two boxes lickity-split."

Tenz relaxed a bit, asking, "Who knows how long we have with that stupid hourglass. Is he close by?"

"Yeah, not too far," said Kermair pointing toward the city. "he gots a shack in the outer city, near the wall over there, but how are we gonna haul the boxes, not to mention the boxes with bodies in them?"

Tenz, looking behind Kermair, pointed to the horse, still tied up to the tent rope line. "Looks like this one is ours to use," he said, grabbing the reins. "I will follow you to the carpenter, then I will go get a damned cart or something while you make sure this Sedric fool builds us two boxes." Kermair nodded, and the two thieves scampered off into the night with the horse.

* * * *

The boxes weren't masterpieces, neither had a flush cut or joint, but they were, by definition, boxes. Tenz found a decent two-wheeled cart and while its owner slept in a nearby pitched tent, he hitched it to his horse and pulled it away. Taking it back to the carpenter, Tenz and Kermair loaded the make-shift coffins on the cart and headed back. Arriving at Shimeq'ena's tent, they carried the first box inside.

Seeing the tent flap open and the two boys walk in with the

first coffin, Shimeq'ena, who was sitting on Kord's coffin, hopped down, snatching the hourglass as she did so, tucking it into a hidden pocket. Seeing the craftsmanship, or lack thereof, the Drow snickered in disbelief. "This is what you call a coffin? Where did you get it from? A blind, one-armed halfling?"

Kermair shrugged. "It is true," he couldn't help but chuckle in agreement, "it looks like a piece of shit." Pausing half a second, he added in a more serious tone, "but it will git the job done, right?"

Shimeq'ena looked the sassy rogue up and down, her voice strangely calm. "Yes, it will work, now go fetch the other one."

* * * *

It didn't take them long to get the two bodies into the coffins, nail them shut, and then load the three coffins onto the cart. With that done, Shimeq'ena began leading the small company down the road, with the horse and the cart in tow, Tenz holding onto the reins. They passed the enormous South Gate, which, for many travelers, signaled the end of their long journey, no matter if they came to Castor through the Cruel Pass and Whiteal, or the Long Road, which ran from the capital of Kardoon itself, Bindal. It was heavily guarded, with hundreds of Kardoon troops out front, and up on the parapets, their crossbows at the ready, as they scanned the crowd illuminated by a mixture of moonlight and firelight.

"Goddamn, we gotta go all the way around to the eastern door?" complained Tenz. Shimeq'ena glanced back, and Tenz waved half-heartedly to the Drow, understanding her unspoken command -- shut up -- which he did as they bypassed the main gate and started heading north along the eastern side of the city's fifty-foot walls. Castor was an enormous city, being four miles wide, east to west, and almost three miles deep, north to south. The cart was slow and it took them almost an hour to get around the wall and finish the final two miles to the eastern gate. Of the four main entrances to Castor, the east and west gates were well fortified, but smaller than the north and south gates, which were the primary entrances and exits to the city. Of all the gates, the north gate, the Dragon Wall, dwarfed them all, in both fortification and the number of soldiers guarding it. Still, each entrance had a burgeoning community of tents, shanties, and small buildings, and the eastern gate was no different. As they made their way through the maze of temporary structures, Shimeq'ena paid the merchants and peddlers no attention despite their impassioned pitches for whatever odd trinkets they were selling. Entering the well-lit and cleared area in front of the gate, which was closed at night, Shimeq'ena walked up to the portcullis. There were several guards on the other side, all watching as she neared the gate. The closest one moved toward her, the tip of his spear jutting through the square gaps between the heavy metal, overlapping bands of the door.

"No entry or exit until dawn," said the husky voice of the guard.

"Of course, Officer," said Shimeq'ena in the meekest voice she could muster. As she reached into a pocket, the guard jabbed the point of the spear into her chest. "Careful now," he warned.

Shimeq'ena slowed down her movements and pulled out a scroll. "I just want to give you this," she said, adding a little fear into her voice with the spear point pressing against her, and held the parchment up to the gate, half of it sticking through to the other side.

The guard pulled the spear back and snatched the scroll away from her. "Stay here, I will give it to our officer," he said, and, with that, he disappeared into the southern fortified tower that overlooked the gate.

"Damn, what did you give him?" asked Tenz in a hushed whisper, eyeing the guards still standing watch on the other side. Shimeq'ena didn't answer.

"Obviously it is some sort of pass or order from someone to let us in," whispered Kermair, making an assumption.

"It better be good, cause if it ain't, they ain't just gonna let us go," said Tenz, some concern in his voice, "this ain't right."

"Shhhhh," Shimeq'ena scolded, not even looking back, her voice sounding like that of snake, about ready to strike. The two shitbirds looked at each other but fell silent. Tenz tightened his grip on the reins of the horse, and Kermair was already scoping out his escape route. After an agonizing few moments, a new guard appeared on the other side of the gate, except this time it was an officer of some sort, her plate mail was spotless, shimmering in the firelight, and her short brown hair was neatly trimmed, while one gauntleted hand rested on the hilt of her longsword.

The officer warily eyed Shimeq'ena for a moment before handing the note back through the gate to the Drow.

"This is most unusual, what business do you have going through the wall at night?" the officer asked, her voice pleasant but stern.

"Call it an exchange," answered Shimeq'ena curtly.

"An exchange?" asked the officer skeptically, one eyebrow lifting upwards. Peering behind the hooded Drow, she looked at the two boys standing by the cart carrying the caskets. "An exchange of bodies?" she asked, her eyes shifting back to Shimeq'ena, trying to see past the hood. "And pull your hood back while we are talking," she added, gesturing with a flick of her hand.

"I know it is strange," answered Shimeq'ena, "but who really knows the mind of generals and kings?"

"The hood," the officer responded immediately, hardly letting Shimeq'ena finish, again gesturing with her hand.

Shimeq'ena cursed the officer in her mind. 'Who was she to ask all these questions?' The written order was simple: let them pass. 'Dammit,' she cursed again, silently. Reaching up, she pulled the hood back, revealing her dark skin, elven features, and shoulder-length white hair that was pulled back into a tight braided ponytail.

The officer looked surprised but not shocked, and Shimeq'ena detected even, perhaps, a hint of amusement. "Since when do Drow work in the service of Kardoon?" asked the officer plainly.

"Just let us pass, like the order commands you to do," said Shimeq'ena calmly, but behind her, Tenz and Kermair were getting much more anxious. "Or, I suppose you could force us to wait until morning, and then you can explain to your commander why you disobeyed an order from Marshal Krugar himself."

The officer didn't blink twice. "So it would seem," she said, then fell silent, the hand resting on the hilt of her sword gently fidgeted with it as she looked over the peculiar and very suspicious trio, with dead bodies no less. Nothing about this was right, but it looked like a valid order. It had the right seal and code word for their shift, which 'changed every damned night,' she thought to herself. It was correct...but how could these three misfits have broken the code and forged a waxed seal with such skill? All these questions rattled around her mind.

The silence was foreboding, and for the first time, the thought crossed Shimeq'ena's mind that the officer might not let her pass, or worse. "Alright, boys," said Shimeq'ena, breaking the silence and turning around. "It looks like we will need to camp out here with the bodies tonight, until we can get this mess sorted out." Tenz and Kermair looked at each other, not sure what to do.

"No delays," said a firm but muffled voice from within the coffin. Kermair, standing the closest, was the only one who seemed to hear the eerie command, and he felt a chill go down his spine.

"What in the eight hells?" Kermair asked under his breath, stepping away from the cart.

Shimeq'ena turned back to the officer, still standing impassively, saying and doing nothing. "Tomorrow, you will be sorry you delayed us," warned Shimeq'ena. "We were ordered to deliver these bodies to a Feldor undertaker four days from today, on the sixth day of Otu. You know and I know, it is a hard four day journey across No Land, which means if you hold us up, we will miss the delivery, and I do not know what the consequences will be -- but it is important enough that Marshal Krugar gave us an order to pass through your gates, night or day."

The officer remained silent for another minute, then finally relented. "Operator, have your crew open the gate. Half high," she commanded, her voice firm and forceful.

"Aye commander, opening half-high!" came a gruff disciplined reply from above. It took a few more moments, but the heavy metal gate began to lift upward, and while it did so, the officer remained where she was, watching the Drow. Once the gate was about seven feet high, it halted.

"Come through," said the officer, with a wave of her hand. Several other people lined up, hoping to gain entrance as well, but a group of armed guards stepped forward and pushed them back. "Only the three tonight, the rest of you will have to wait. Step back or the gate will crush you." Shimeq'ena, Tenz, and Kermair all got through with the horse and cart. As soon as they were clear of the gate, the officer shouted out another order. "The gate is clear! Close the gate!"

"Aye, commander, closing the gate!" came the familiar voice, and the solid metal gate slid back down, the massive pyramid-like points on the bottom slamming home perfectly into pre-fit holes, creating a tight seal.

"You may be going through, but I am damn sure looking in those boxes," said the officer, "and you better hope it is nothing other than bodies in there."

"Go ahead and look," said Shimeq'ena.

The officer walked to the cart and could see easily enough in the well-lit tunnel, under the great city wall, that the caskets were nailed shut. "Derg, fetch a crow and hustle," commanded the officer, glancing behind her. One of the soldiers ran down the thirty foot tunnel, his armor clanking, disappearing around the corner.

"None of this is necessary," said Shimeq'ena, trying to strike up a conversation, but the officer didn't reply. Taking a different, more direct and aggressive tact, Shimeq'ena asked, "What is your name, Commander?"

That got her attention, and the officer turned to face the Drow, who was several inches shorter. "I am Commander Erinalia," she replied evenly. "I would ask your name, but I know it would be untrue."

"Well, that seems a bit presumptuous," said Shimeq'ena, feigning hurt feelings. "We are on the same side, you know."

"I highly doubt that," said Erinalia, her right eyebrow lifting in skepticism and arrogance. "I admit, I do not know exactly what you are up to, or how you came to possess an order like that, but when I figure it out, you three will be in the Castor prison," Erinalia looked at all three of them, "where you will be interrogated. Then we will find out your true names, and much more."

"Here you go, Commander," said Derg, finally returning and handing Erinalia the crow.

"Thank you, Derg, stay here and keep an eye on these three while I open these coffins," she said.

"Yes, ma'am," he replied, his hand drifting to the sheathed sword belted to his hip.

"Why are two of the coffins pieces of shit, and one is well made?" asked Erinalia.

"One for the master, and two for the squires," said Shimeq'ena, thinking quickly on her feet.

Erinalia paused, then cracked the first coffin open with the crow. Lifting up the lid, she peered in, seeing the body of Tund. Placing the crow on the boy's chest, she felt around his body. "How did he die? I see no wound."

Shimeq'ena's mind raced, the order was supposed to get them through the wall, no questions asked. The Drow could feel time running out, her hesitation to answer becoming obvious. "Some kind of pox, I believe," said Shimeq'ena, going with the only thing that came to mind in that instant.

Erinalia looked over her shoulder at the Drow. "The more you lie, the closer I get to the truth." Turning back to the body, she looked some more. "Nobody would transport a plagued body; that would be ludicrous."

Shimeq'ena's dark lips curled upwards, ever so slightly, into a meager smile. She said a quick, silent thanks to her god, Plaguess, the evil god of Death, for her lord had looked down on her with favor, giving her an idea. "Back away, boys, she does not know what she is doing," Shimeq'ena said, waving her arms for Tenz and Kermair to back away, which they eagerly did. "You cannot see anything wrong with their bodies now, but the plague worsens as the body rots -- you really should not open the other caskets," Shimeq'ena warned.

Erinalia closed the lid on Tund's casket and banged home the nails before moving over and opening the other rag-tag coffin to find Termi's body in the same condition. After some time rummaging around the corpse, the officer closed the lid and sealed it by pounding the nails back into place. Kord's casket was under Termi's, so the captain pushed Termi's shabby box across the small cart, exposing the finely crafted casket underneath.

"Back up everyone!" said Shimeq'ena, "You too, Derg, or whoever you are. You do not want to be near that cart."

Derg snorted. "Keep your silence, Drow," the soldier said, emphasizing her race as if it was a vulgar, insulting word.

"After a few days the bodies turn into what you will find in that casket, if there is anything left," said Shimeq'ena, pointing to Kord's coffin.

Erinalia pried open the final casket and lifting the lid, gasped at what she saw. Kord, without moving his head, looked with his voided eyes and could see the horror on the human's face. His mind went to the dagger at his side as he felt the urge to slash her throat. Erinalia, dropping the metal crow, which clanged on Kord's breastplate, quickly backed away, covering her mouth with her hand. "Why would Marshal Krugar order this?" said Erinalia, still a little shaken.

"I told you not to open it," said Shimeq'ena. "But now that you have, you might as well know." Stepping closer to the commander, she motioned for Erinalia to lean down closer, and as she did, the Drow whispered to her, "Marshal Krugar is testing a new plague and wants to see if and how it will spread in Feldor."

Erinalia straightened up, regaining her composure and confidence. "Despite what you may think, or how clever you think you are, your story makes no sense; this is not an honorable order the marshal would give. However," she continued, "we do not want you or your cargo to remain in Castor, so we will obey the order, and, in fact, do you one better." Pointing at the soldier who had brought the crow, she ordered, "Derg, assign six soldiers to escort these three and their cargo out of this city, immediately."

"Yes, ma'am," said Derg, who began to round up six men.

"Go close that coffin," said Shimeq'ena, looking at Tenz and pointing to the cart.

Tenz looked at the Drow. "Are you crazy?" Shimeq'ena gave him an icy look and used her eyes and a nod of her head to reinforce the command. Tenz gulped hard but grudgingly went over to the coffin, the lid still ajar. Catching a glimpse of Kord lying inside, he was horrified at what he saw and stood transfixed by the gruesome visage.

Kord turned his head, ever so slightly, but could tell Tenz took notice by the young rogue's eyes widening. "Do as you are told," Kord hissed menacingly.

Tenz looked around, unsure if what he had just seen and heard was real, hoping someone else had heard it, too, but nobody seemed to take notice, since everyone's attention was on Shimeq'ena. Tenz nodded, almost imperceptibly and, in his haste, fumbled about the task, but eventually was able to replace the lid and, hammering the nails back in with the crow that the Erinalia had left, backed away, trembling.

Coming out of the thirty foot stone passage, they emerged into the enormous city of Castor. The city was well planned out, with six main thoroughfares running east and west, crossed by three roads running north and south, with the keep located in the middle of the city, towering and lording over everything. However, there were innumerable side streets and alleyways creating a maze-like situation of turns and dead ends, almost guaranteeing that someone not familiar with the city, leaving the main roads, would get lost -- their only point of reference being the keep. Despite the late hour, there was still a good amount of activity in the city streets, but it, at least, had the outward appearance of being orderly. The six guards formed a loose ring around the cart and the three 'guests.' The distance was just over two miles, from the smaller east gate to the huge northern gate know better as the Dragon Wall, which was the only passage into No Land. It took them almost an hour to navigate the streets, but finally they arrived at the massive gate. Derg, who had accompanied them, met with an officer, handing him the parchment with the order that Shimeq'ena had presented to Erinalia. Erinalia had, in turn, herself written onto the order, confirming that, despite the off hour, the Dragon Gate should be opened to allow the small unsavory group to exit the city. The commander of the northern gate was also dressed in fine plate mail, but was shorter than an average human. He had an unfriendly look about him but, after pondering the decision, allowed them to pass. The wall ran east to west and was forty feet deep, with towers and other fortifications bristling along the ramparts. The gate was comprised of three overlapping doors, each one hundred feet wide: the outermost section being a metal portcullis, with five inch diameter bars and six inches of space between them, the second wall was solid six-inch-thick Taper wood, metal reinforced gate, and the third and final component was another metal gate, similar to the first. Altogether, the gate was assumed by most people to be impregnable to ordinary means of force, although in its thirty years of existence, the wall remained untested by an enemy force. Given the weight of each section of gate, it was a tightly kept secret by which mechanism the gates are raised, but once the commander gave the order, the clanking of metal and the sound of it being pushed to its limits erupted from within the walls, and sure enough the gates, one by one, lifted just high enough for the small group, with their horse and cart, to exit the city.

They were barely clear of the deadly gate when the outer gate slammed down behind them, shaking the ground and startling the horse. Two more ground-pounding quakes followed, and the Dragon Gate closed once again. As usual, a small throng of people were camped out around the Dragon Gate, waiting for entry into Castor, but the crowd was small compared to the multitude of people that made up the shanty-like cities surrounding the east, west, and south walls of Castor. Still, the crowd of people were amazed to see the Dragon Gate raised in the night and unsure what to make of the three humans, or humanoids, that emerged with a horse drawn cart.

"Keep moving," said Shimeq'ena to Tenz and Kermair as some of the more curious bystanders moved in for a closer look. "We have a lot of ground to cover. Pergate is just a day away, Erdeep, another day, and then one more to the North Wall."

They traveled for a full mile, making sure the crowds were well behind them, before Tenz spoke up. "So, what the hell was that back there?" he asked, but Shimeq'ena remained silent. "Do you know what is inside that fucking box?" he asked, pointing at Kord's coffin.

"Of course, I do," said Shimeq'ena.

"That...that thing ain't plagued," said Tenz haltingly. "It is something undead."

"So what?" said Shimeq'ena, stopping and turning to face the human. "We have a task, and we do it. Period."

"And Pergate is almost fifty miles," he said, gesturing to the north with his hand. "There ain't no way we is getting there in a day, walking. So, we better find some other god-damned horses."

"I know that," said Shimeq'ena, once again hiding her rising temper, her voice level soft, almost sweet. "There are many travelers along this road, and we will simply acquire two more horses."

Tenz nodded. "Alright then, but if that dead son of a bitch comes out of that coffin, you will be on yer own." He looked over at Kermair for reassurance, and the shorter pale-skinned, rogue nodded.

The small group plodded on for two more hours. Shimeq'ena

could tell Tenz and Kermair were tired, worn out by the stress of the night, and with only an hour or two left until sunrise, the late hour was dogging the two humans. Sensing an opportunity, she gave the black band on her left ring finger a slight twist. Whispering a command, "dissipati peribunt," she vanished from sight. Tenz and Kermair were practically sleep walking, and it took them a second to realize that Shimeq'ena was no longer walking with them.

"Hey," said Kermair, snapping awake, his senses fully awakening. "Where is Shimeq'ena?"

Tenz, startled, quickly looked around. "Shimeq'ena!" he shouted into the night air, but he hardly had said her name when he felt a sharp pain. The shock was sudden and overwhelming, and while intense, he felt the pain only briefly. Shimeq'ena blinked back into sight behind Tenz, her dagger inserted up to its hilt into Tenz's neck. Given the angle of the attack, the blade no doubt extended into the back of the rogue's brain. Blood spurted from the wound, running down the dagger, onto the Drow's hand.

Kermair jumped backwards, drawing a short sword, a confused look on his face. "What the fuck?!" he shouted, half question and half astonishment. Shimeq'ena pulled the dagger from Tenz's neck and let the young rogue's body fall to the ground, leaving her face-to-face with Kermair. They were both about the same height, he being short for a human, but aside from that similarity, the two were almost physical polar opposites. Her skin was dark, and he was almost an albino. She was well groomed, and he was comparatively filthy and unkempt. Shimeq'ena pulled her hood back so she had better vision of what was around her. "How about we just part ways right here?" Kermair asked, looking for a way out. "I will give you an oath stone," he said frantically, his eyes darting every direction looking for an escape route. "I will do anything you say, just tell me what you need," he added, holding the sword in one hand and holding his other hand up, gesturing to keep her at bay.

Shimeq'ena twisted her ring again. "dissipati peribunt." In that instant, the ring's magic enchantment imperceptibly drew some energy from the negative plane and, unleashing it, made the Drow invisible once again.

"Oh shit!" exclaimed Kermair, who began running away from the cart and swinging his sword wildly about him. He kept it up for a couple minutes, then his swings became slower, his arm growing tired. Cutting the air in front of him, he was surprised to hear a clang as his sword was halted in mid-swing, as if it had just hit an invisible metal wall. That oddity was quickly followed by an agonizing pain as Shimeq'ena blinked back into sight, right in front of him, holding a long dagger with a curved hilt in her left hand, which she used to block his sword, and in her right hand, the other, already bloodied, dagger was plunged into his chest, piercing his heart. He could feel his strength dissipating and he could no longer hold onto his weapon, which fell out of his grasp to the ground. With all his remaining strength, he put both his hands onto the Drow's shoulders, leaning on her to stay standing, but his legs were rapidly going numb and he felt colder than he ever had. "Why?" he asked, his eyes searching hers in the moonlight.

Shimeq'ena relished the adrenaline rush of killing. 'Especially humans,' she thought to herself. Stepping backwards, she pulled the dagger out of Kermair, who fell over face first now that his support was gone. Bending down, she wiped the dagger on the back of his already filthy clothes, and spitting on his back, she hissed, "All I needed was your silence, and now I have it." Standing back up, she sheathed both the daggers behind her, in the small of her back, while walking back to the cart. Climbing up onto the small wooden bed of the cart, she pushed the two shoddy coffins off the back end. Hopping back down, she opened them up and dumped the bodies out. Stripping all four of the dead bodies naked, she looked through all their belongings, searching for any documents that might pertain to their identity or the task they had been assigned. She didn't expect to find anything but couldn't take the chance. Finding nothing, she piled their clothes onto the cart and dragged all four of their lifeless corpses thirty feet off the main road into a small natural ditch. In the same spot, she also broke the coffins up as best she could, so it just looked like a few scattered, worthless planks of wood. She knew the bodies would inevitably be found but moving them further off the path would allow her to put on a few more miles of distance from them and her when that finally did happen.

Dawn came too soon, and the late Octu sky was all too clear for her comfort as the sharp rays of sunshine beat down on her uncomfortably. Despite the hood of her cloak shielding her eyes, it still burned her retinas to look where she was going. She climbed up onto the horse's back and rode while it pulled the cart with the one remaining casket. Shimeq'ena was only four feet and eight inches tall, not unusual for a female Drow, as dark elves were typically a little smaller than other elves, which had some advantages, and, of course, some disadvantages. Today, it was a disadvantage, since Shimeq'ena was forced to travel in broad daylight, through the human-infested region of No Land, and to humans she looked like a ten-year-old traveling alone. She made good time until she veered off the main road leading to Pergate, deciding to not go through the town. It was a much less traveled path, but it cut directly north, skirting the town, and would take her directly to the road that led north to Erdeep, the last town between them and the North Wall — Thayol's own great defensive structure, built to hold back any potential Kardoon attack.

The side trail was rough and slowed her down as Shimeq'ena was extra careful, not wanting to risk the cart tipping its cargo out. Well into the afternoon, the sun was dipping lower into the sky to the west, but still was bright enough to hurt her eyes. Growing tired herself, she finally decided to pull off to the side of the trail and rest for a moment. Climbing down off the cart, she sat on the ground. Taking advantage of the long shadow that the cart cast, she rested her back against the large wheel of the cart. The shadow, giving her some relief from the sun, she closed her eyes.

She was able to get a little sleep, but not much, before she heard the noise of horses approaching. Her eyes shot open at the unwelcome sound and she looked around to get her bearings. The sun was much lower in the sky and getting ready to set. 'How long was I asleep?' she wondered to herself, bolting to her feet and searching for the source of the noise. A small group of four riders approached from the north, all human, heading south down the trail. They were all wearing chain mail armor, and carried shields with the symbol of a dove on them, marking them as No Land soldiers...more like peace keepers, sworn to neutrality and served as law keepers between the walls, sworn to neither Thayol nor Kardoon. They served the No Land Governor, a position that had a term of two years, and the two kingdoms, Thayol and Kardoon, took turns nominating the governor, ensuring that neither side could hold sway over the region, which meant nothing ever changed, or if it did, the change was undone shortly after it was affected -- just the way the two kings wanted it to be. The current governor was Wabaon Elkstaff, elected by Cayax Thayol in Janu of 1172.

The riders, not seeing Shimeq'ena behind the cart, dismounted, and looked around warily. "Odd," said the shortest of the three humans. "What crazy fool would haul a dead body around?" Without waiting for an answer, he waved his hand to the others behind him. "Go search the cart and the casket."

Shimeq'ena frowned and left the comfort of the shadow thrown by the cart, the sun now shining from directly behind the four humans. Despite the hood, she held her black gloved hand up to shield her eyes. "That will not be necessary, thank you," she said in her most polite and humble voice. "I was just resting but will be on my way now." Hopping up onto the wheel of the cart, then onto the back of the horse, she took the reins, but before she could do anything further, a heavyset human grabbed the harness and held on.

"Hold on there, little one," the heavyset man said.

Looking down at the husky man, she thought to herself, he had soft eyes and a kind face. "Please sir, let go, and I will be on my way," she said. The man tried to see past her hood, but she turned her head to prevent him from seeing.

The short soldier now walked closer to her cart. "No Land is a safe place for travelers, but even here a small girl should not be traveling at night alone." He, too, was trying to see into the darkness of her hood. "If we were traveling north, we would gladly escort you, even in the dark, but we are heading to the Dragon Wall on business."

"Oh, that is not necessary, really," said Shimeq'ena, continuing to use her pleasant and meek tone. "I do not want to bother great men on important business, as you surely are."

"We were going to travel a bit farther, until the sun set, but we will stay here with you tonight, and you can sleep well, knowing you are safe," said the short man with a black goatee and wavy black hair. "Well met, young lady, my name is Sergeant Kurseragim, but my friends just call me Gim," he said we a slight nod of his head. "This is Tyad," he said, indicating the tall thin warrior still standing next to his horse, "and this is Rayear." He motioned to the husky man holding onto her horse, "And this is Lepeth," he said, looking back at the last human, bald, smiling, and unlike the others, who had swords as their primary weapon, he was carrying a mace.

'Shit,' she thought to herself, 'a damned cleric.' The sun was hurting her eyes, but it wasn't hard to see the holy symbol hanging around the priest's neck of two crossed arrows, with both tips pointing upwards. The symbol of Tulas, the good god of comfort, was well known, and to her, it meant this group of good soldiers would see her race as a threat. "Really, I do not mind, and I do not want to be a burden on you, and I really must get my poor father to Erdeep to see him buried properly," she said.

"Nonsense! I will not have the death of a little girl on my conscience," said Gim. "Hop back down and we will eat together before getting some sleep tonight."

Shimeq'ena hesitated, long enough to plant a seed of suspicion that Lepeth, the cleric, couldn't ignore, and grabbing his holy symbol, he said a quick prayer. "Concedimi il potere di individuare le forze delle tenebre e del male." Focusing on the cloaked figure, Shimeq'ena's body resonated with a pinkish hue, only visible to him. "Hold on Gim," said Lepeth, holding his hand up in a halting manner, "this one is evil in nature." The warning was heeded by all three of his companions, as each of them moved their hands to their weapons.

Gim drew his sword. "Pull your hood back, little one," he commanded.

Drow were a feared race, but they were also despised, so revealing her identity would not be helpful. She regretted using her ring twice already today, it only had one more charge until it would have to recharge over a day's time, but her race was feared for a reason, and she had more tricks up her sleeve. Shimeq'ena reached out to the negative plane and drew in the dark energy, an ability that was a natural gift to her race.

"Invoco tenebre impenetrabili," she canted, the magical words dripping off her tongue as she released the spell. Immediately the area was enveloped by complete and utter darkness. Shimeq'ena couldn't see in the magical darkness, either, but it gave her a chance to gain an advantage over her opponents, since she knew it was coming.

"Darkness!" shouted Lepeth. "Watch out!" The sounds of three swords being drawn from their scabbards rang out like that of three hissing vipers.

"Nobody here wants to hurt you, whoever you are!" shouted Gim. "There is no reason to fight us!" There was no answer, so Gim added, "We will leave you be, to be on your way, just remove the spell," he said in a loud voice, not quite yelling. Hopping down as silently as she could, she crouched by the wheel of the cart. She could hear the heavy breathing of the horses, followed by nervous neighing until the animals finally bolted out of the darkness, drawing a grunt of pain from Tyad as he found himself sandwiched between two of the horses trying to get away. During the confusion, Shimeq'ena ran to where she knew the edge of the darkness spell was, and as if stepping out of a giant black glass cylinder, she emerged into the daylight, but she was prepared, having drawn her hood over her eyes, shielding them from the sudden explosion of light. She ran around the outside of the curving thirty foot diameter cylinder of darkness that she created. She could see the four horses still running away, but slowing a hundred feet away to the south.

"We need to move out of the darkness!" shouted Tyad, some fear in his voice.

"No, I can dispel it with light," said Lepeth, confidence in his voice.

"I am not waiting!" shouted Tyad, moving blindly through the darkness until, finally, his body emerged back into the sunlight.

Shimeq'ena was waiting, and as Tyad raised a hand to shield his eyes from the bright light, she struck with both daggers. Her first dagger, pierced deep into the dazed soldier, just below his kidney, sliding through the chainmail, breaking the interwoven links as the blade drove up and into the man's body. She immediately swiped with her second dagger, aiming for his throat, but just missed. Tyad screamed out in pain, dropping to his knees, barely enough time and energy to look at his assailant before falling forward, unconscious.

"Tyad!" shouted Gim, then waited a second, but with no response, shouted again, "Tyad! Are you okay?" he asked, true worry in his voice.

"Invoco la luce," canted Lepeth, and the darkness vanished. It only took a second for the three remaining soldiers to get their bearings and spot the Drow, her hood having fallen back during the attack, her white hair and dark skin, in stark contrast, still hovering over Tyad's fallen body, her dagger dripping with blood in the setting sun's light.

"By the gods, a Drow," said Gim. "Drop your weapon, mistress, and you will get a fair trial and an easy death."

Shimeq'ena snorted in derision. "Who is next?" She sneered, twisting her ring, and saying the command "Dissipati peribunt", she vanishing into thin air.

"Dammit," said Gim, "get in a circle, so our backs are not exposed." The other two did as asked, and the three men closed together, their backs against one another, their shields up and weapons covering the area just in front of them.

Lepeth, reaching out, tapped the positive plane and drew in the warm energy, canting the spell. "Confondi i miei nemici, rendendo la mia persona intoccabile."

Shimeq'ena, now invisible, stalked her prey, at first choosing the cleric, but then the priest cast a spell, and she could not seem to focus on him. She could see him but couldn't bring herself to attack him. Not giving it a second thought, she switched her target to the husky man named Rayear. Quietly sliding her daggers back into the scabbards in the small of her back, she pulled out two long bamboo tubes that she slid together to make one long blowgun. Reaching into her inner pockets, she pulled out a small leather pouch. Unfolding the flap, she revealed four darts with light feathery tails. Carefully pulling one out, she loaded it into the tube and, closing the flap, put the remaining darts back into her pocket. Moving silently, she got as close as she dared, it would be an easy shot, as she took aim at the husky man's exposed neck. As the air exploded from her lungs, the dart rushed out of the tube with a small but audible 'whump,' and Shimeq'ena became visible again, but in that small amount of time, she dropped the blowgun and was already moving away from the soldiers, drawing both her daggers.

Rayear felt the prick in his neck and, letting go of his shield, reached up pulling the dart out. "She shot me!" he said, looking at the small needle in his hand. The poison was expensive, and rightfully so, as it was very fast and effective. Rayear felt a jarring pain in his abdomen and his right hand went numb, causing him to drop his sword. "What, happ-app-ning." He stumbled, struggling to get the words out as the paralysis spread, until he finally fell over, squirming on the ground briefly before his heart stopped, and he died.

Gim looked at his fellow soldier, then back at Shimeq'ena, who was standing thirty feet away, daggers drawn. Her dark metallic skin, white hair, and red eyes a vision of pure viciousness. "You may frighten a lot of folks, but not me, you devil elf," said Gim, moving toward the Drow.

"Now you can go on your way, are you not glad you had to meddle?" Shimeq'ena asked with a sneer.

"Out of tricks, are you?" asked Gim, closing the distance.

"I do not need tricks now," replied Shimeq'ena, readying herself and her daggers. "I will take the odds of two to one."

Gim launched his attack, his longsword slashing through the air, Shimeq'ena ducking below it. Coming back up, she stabbed with both daggers, but neither penetrated the warrior's chainmail armor. Before Gim could adjust, the Drow spun around and jabbed her right-handed dagger into his side, the chain held, but the tip bit into his flesh. Her second dagger, late, was blocked by his shield, and Gim immediately swung his longsword in a hard downward strike. It would have been fatal, but the Drow moved quickly enough that the blade, although stinging the top of her shoulder, glanced off, doing only a little damage. As she leaned away and the longsword passed to her side, she moved in, closing the distance, stabbing with both daggers, and this time each blade bit, penetrating the chain mail.

Gim growled with pain, "You are going to die, elf!" and lashed out with his longsword, but missed by a wide margin.

Lepeth, seeing Gim bleeding, moved in, casting a healing spell. "Benedici il mio tocco con il potere di guarire le ferite lievi." He placed his hands on the back of Gim, releasing the energy into his body.

Gim, feeling the cleric's healing spell surge through him, smiled. "You cannot win this battle; lay down your daggers and submit."

"You may be right, but I will give you one last chance to leave alive," said Shimeq'ena, her voice serious and dark.

"You must know something I do not," said Gim. "I am offering you mercy," he said.

"I warned you," said Shimeq'ena, giving Gim a sinister look. "Kord!" she yelled as loud as her lungs could muster.

"What is that? Another trick?" asked Gim, "It will not work." He was about to attack when he heard a loud cracking noise from behind him, where the cart was. "What is that, Lepeth?"

Lepeth looked back and saw the top of the coffin knocked off, the lid lying on the ground near the cart. "Something disturbed the lid of the casket."

"What? What do you mean?" asked Gim.

"Better run, motherfuckers," said Shimeq'ena, her daggers dancing in front of her.

Lepeth continued watching when he saw a gauntleted hand reach up out of the casket, followed by the Death Knight pushing himself, unnaturally, to a standing position. He looked like a giant standing up on the cart, the large bastard sword in one hand, the full plate armor, dented and stained, the rays of the setting sun glinting off it, and the face...oh, the horror of the face, Lepeth thought to himself. Kord leapt down, landing powerfully on both feet, impossible for any man dressed in full battle armor. "Tulas protect us," murmured Lepeth. Turning back to the Drow, the cleric said, "We accept your terms, we will leave!"

Shimeq'ena shook her head, a sinister smile playing across her thin red lips. "It is not me you gotta convince now," she said, gesturing with one dagger at Kord as he approached, "and he is not nearly as accommodating as me."

Gim risked a look over his shoulder and had to do a double take, not believing his initial sighting of the Death Knight. "What in the eight hells are you transporting?" he asked, presumably to the Drow, but his attention was now focused on Kord, forgetting about the small elf to his rear.

Turning his back was a fatal mistake. Shimeq'ena closed the ground silently, her padded boots barely making a sound, as if she were walking on the very air above the hardened dirt. Leaping up, she grabbed Gim around the waist with both legs, slitting his throat with two blindingly fast slashes from each dagger. Gim staggered for a second, the Drow releasing her legs and using her hands to push him away as she gracefully landed back on her feet. The mortally wounded Gim took two steps toward Kord, his eyes searching the Death Knight for answers, but his strength seeped away too quickly. The daggers had done too much damage to his throat, not only robbing him of life, but also the time or ability to even ask one question. The good-natured soldier fell to his knees, grasping lamely at his neck, trying to stem the flow of blood, but it was too late. He fell onto his side, dead. Shimeq'ena turned to the cleric, but something was still holding her back, she couldn't bring herself to attack him. The Drow hissed in anger, her red eyes spewing hatred at the man. She waved her daggers menacingly but was unable to make an attack.

"Kill him," said Kord matter-of-factly, taking a step forward.

Shimeq'ena growled, "Dammit! He cast a spell on me or something...I cannot!" She spat at the ground near the priest.

"Please," said Lepeth, "let me go. I will tell no one anything, I swear!"

Kord moved closer to the cleric, within striking distance. Looking at the holy symbol hanging around the cleric's neck, the crossed arrows... Tulas, the information popping into his head, released from one of innumerable unmarked memories. "Curse Tulas's name one time," said Kord, "and you can go free."

Lepeth's face cringed, his eyes starting to well up with tears. "No, please do not make me do that."

"That is the price you must pay for your mortal life," said Kord.

"See," said Shimeq'ena calmly, "he ain't as easy to work with as me." She paused, then, with fury in her voice, she shouted, "All you had to do was fucking leave me alone!"

Lepeth looked back and forth between his two assailants, tears making trails down his dust-covered cheeks from the long day's ride, "I cannot renounce my god, I might save my mortal life, but I would damn my eternal spirit..." The priest sobbed lightly, falling to his knees. "Please, I will say nothing, I swear on Tulas, I will live my life quietly in the brotherhood."

Kord swung Slice, stopping just in time at the cleric's neck. "Last chance..." he said, his voice scratchy and unnatural.

"Tulas, I..." The cleric looked at Kord's face, the voids of his eyes haunting him. "I...I ask thee to receive my --" Kord didn't allow him to finish, Slice severing the man's head in one easy stroke.

"Yessssss! The taste of bloodssssssss!" hissed Slice. "Killssss the Drow, too! Kills her! Kills her now!!"

Kord looked at Shimeq'ena. He felt the urge, the desire, to kill her, and Slice was adding fuel to the fire. He started to raise the sword, but as he did, Shimeq'ena walked up to the headless body of the cleric and kicked it. Free from the sanctuary spell the cleric had cast, she bent down and drove a dagger into the dead man's chest. "Fuck you and your god-damned spell!" she said to the deceased cleric's body. Unknowingly, Shimeq'ena's actions had bought her a few precious seconds, enough for Kord to calm his impulses, and using his iron will, he hushed Slice and sheathed the blade on his back, watching as the Drow rifled through the priest's belongings. Finding nothing, she moved on to the others, searching them as well.

Kord remembered the voice, back in the Cruel Pass. 'Sacrifice a heart of a good cleric to me, and I shall provide what you seek.' Looking down at the corpse of the cleric, Kord drew out his jeweled dagger and crudely cut Lepeth's heart out of his chest.

Shimeq'ena heard the commotion and turned to watch the spectacle. "What in the eight hells? What are you going to do with that?" she asked, intrigued and curious.

Kord ignored the question and raised the heart up into the air. "Blick, I give you this heart to curse all his kind and his god!" There was a short delay, and then a thunderous crack shook the air, knocking both Kord and Shimeq'ena to the ground. The priest's heart, which was firmly in Kord's grasp, disappeared, his hand, now clutching nothing, collapsed into an empty fist. Kord looked around, not sure what to expect...but after waiting a few moments, nothing happened.

Shimeq'ena hopped up right away. "What was that?" she asked, but again Kord did not respond. She watched as Kord just sat there, looking around. "What are you looking for?" Again, there was no response. "Look, we need to get moving -- we cannot be found anywhere near these bodies or they will hang us for sure." Then chiding herself, she added, "Well -- maybe they will hang me; I have no idea what they will do with you." But Kord just sat there, unresponsive. "Hey! Kord! We gotta get moving... It is not safe here." But the Death Knight would not move. Shimeq'ena pulled on his armor, trying to get his attention. "Kord, get up, we need to get moving."

"Leave me be, Blick will provide," Kord said, although he did rise to his feet, always an eerie sight to behold, as the movement was not humanly possible.

"What can he provide to get us out of here?" asked the Drow.

"I do not know," said Kord, his voice distant and trailing as he continued looking around, assuming he'd know it when he saw it.

"Look, if you are not going to move from here, then we are going to part ways," said Shimeq'ena, "because I am not gonna sit here waiting for a miracle while the No Land soldiers close in on us."

Kord stopped his search and locked his gaze on the Drow. "Then be gone," he said with a wave of his hand.

Shimeq'ena felt the Death Knight's cold stare, the voids of pitch black, looking through her, but she did not feel fear. "Returning to Windred without you is going to be bad for me, so get your shit together and get moving!" she ordered, her voice confident and strong. There was a long pause as they stared each other down, his dark voids and her bright red irises both unblinking.

"The gods are mysterious in their ways, are they not?" said Kord, relaxing.

"Indeed, downright fucking random, if you ask me," she said, crossing her arms, her eyes still locked on Kord. "Now, can we get the fuck going?"

The last vestiges of light were peeking over the horizon. "I will ride, myself, until we get closer to the wall," said Kord, eyeing the horses now grazing off the road a hundred feet away. As he started to move toward the distant horses, a large swath of air in front of him wavered, as if it was made of water, or like that of an illusion. It lasted only for a second, and then a large jet black steed materialized. Its appearance was a strange mix: on one hand it was gaunt, its ribs showing, but on the other hand, it projected immense power. Its eyes were fiery red and its mane was a combination of black hair and flickering flames. Flames also danced around the beast's hooves and with each outward breath, soot and flames flared from its nostrils.

Shimeq'ena backed away. "What in the eight hells? Where did that come from? Did you summon that?" she asked, uncertainty creeping back into her voice.

Kord stopped in his tracks while the black horse, moving closer to the Death Knight, seemed to be inspecting him, sniffing at his body. Kord reached out to touch the horse, but the beast reared its head to avoid the contact, snorting as it did so, flames and soot shooting out. Kord put his hand back down, and the horse returned to nosing him, circling around him.

"That will not help us," said the Drow, motioning toward the black steed. "It will only draw more attention to us at the wall, and we do not want attention."

His fickle memory, so often a source of frustration, in this case, granted him access to its vault of information, allowing him to instantly recognize the legendary beast known as a nightmare. "You are wrong," said Kord. "You do not see the steed in front of you for what it is. It is magnificent," he added with true respect and admiration in his voice. As he spoke, he reached out to touch the nightmare's black muzzle, but once again the steed neighed, shooting out flames and black soot from its nostrils, and, rammed Kord in the chest with its head, knocking the Death Knight backwards several steps. Backing away, the fiery steed gave its head a visible, almost human-like, shake. Recovering his balance, Kord straightened himself up. "Yes, I see now. He does not think I am worthy," said Kord, reverence in his voice. "He believes I have not suffered enough for Blick."

"How would you know what a horse is thinking?" asked Shimeq'ena.

"Unclasp my breastplate," Kord said to the Drow.

"We do not have time for this!" protested Shimeq'ena.

Kord spun around to face the Drow. "Do it," he said, his voice low, resonating, demanding, and filled with pure evil.

Shimeq'ena hesitated but then relented. Running behind Kord, she unclasped the belts that held the breastplate of his armor together. As she undid the last belt, Kord pulled the armor off, revealing a tattered layer of chain mail, and a filthy undershirt, both of which the Death Knight removed, pulling them over his head and tossing them to the ground. Shimeq'ena put her hand to her mouth and backed away, aghast at the wounds and carnage that she saw, accompanied by a horrendous stench of sores, pus, decay, and death. Like his head, his body was covered in its entirety with open gashes and wounds, the skin was sickly and hanging, the scars were innumerable, and the open wounds were deep and festering, with yellow pus in an unending cycle of draining and drying. Kord sank to his knees, his arms upraised to the heavens. "I am the Prince of Suffering on Thran!" he shouted to the gods above, and despite the lack of proper geography, his voice echoed in the fading light. "To see me is to know true suffering! Tortured and slashed by a thousand knives, a thousand times over! Blick, I am here to do thy bidding!" As the echoes of his voice faded, he looked at the black steed, and rising, his arms still spread wide and uplifted, he approached the horse again. "Am I not worthy?!" he said with such force that it shook the air, and as he neared, he repeated himself, pausing ever so briefly between the words. "Am. I. Not. Worthy?!" Again, the air and ground trembled. The black steed hesitated, then bowing its head, it lowered itself on its front legs in obedience. "Yes! Now you see! Now you both see!" Kord spun around, facing the Drow again. "Tell me you see!" he commanded.

This time, Shimeq'ena did not hesitate. Dropping to one knee, she said, "I see, I see, you truly are the Prince of Suffering on Thran."

"Yes!" shouted Kord up to the heavens for all the gods to hear, his arms still upraised, his grievous wounds on full display. "All will tremble and then suffer before me!" His voice echoed again as the sun finally set, the darkness overtaking Shimeq'ena, Kord, and the black steed. Lowering his arms, he looked at Shimeq'ena, his dark vision showing her in full detail. "I will teach the entire world what I know about suffering." Walking over to the steed, he placed a hand on its mane, its flames more prevalent now, alighting and dancing in the new found darkness. "And nothing can stop me." His voice was cold, deathly, scratchy, ominous, and punctuated by the steed, who let out a snort of flames, which briefly lit up the night air. "I will call you Vativerrix," said Kord to the black steed. "Now rise, as we have much to do."

"Kord, I still do not see how this animal will help us get past the guards of the North Wall," Shimeq'ena said, also rising back to her feet.

"Help me with my armor," said Kord, "and you will see."

Shimeq'ena nodded. "Very well, but we must hurry, we must get far away from this place." Kord said nothing, but moved next to where the upper parts of his armor were lying on the ground. The Drow was surprised to find the plate armor to be much lighter than she expected, only possible through some magical enchantment. Still, the numerous buckles took time to fasten correctly, and her small stature made buckling the higher straps difficult. To the dark elf, it seemed like an eternity, made worse with the dead bodies of the No Land soldiers lying all around, and to add insult to injury, the black steed was taking bites out of the dead cleric and eating the flesh. Finishing the last buckle, she let out a long breath. "There, done. Now, can we get the hell out of here?" she asked. "I will go fetch one of those other horses."

"No need," said Kord, giving a short whistle that got the attention of Vativerrix and the beast obeyed, moving rapidly to Kord's side. The Death Knight, deftly grabbing the horse's mane, pulled himself up onto its back. Holding out his gauntleted left hand, he offered it to Shimeq'ena.

"I would prefer to have my own mount," said the dark elf.

"Nonsense," said Kord, "those horses cannot go where we are going." Opening and closing his hand, he motioned for her to take his hand.

"Where are we going," Shimeq'ena asked skeptically.

"Windred, of course, our objective has not changed," said Kord, an evil grin on his marred face.

"I hope you know what you are doing," the dark elf replied, grasping Kord's strong hand.

The Death Knight, easily pulling her up, swung her into a seated position behind him. "Hold on, you will not want to fall," said Kord. Without waiting, Kord gave the steed a sharp kick with his heels, causing the nightmare to leap into the air, easily carrying both riders as it flew up into the night sky. Turning northward, the air around the trio wavered as the steed, calling on its natural ability, slipped back into a shadowy parallel fourth dimension known as the ethereal plane. With the same abruptness of its appearance, the nightmare vanished with its passengers, leaving behind the quiet, dark, night sky...and the grisly scene below.

CHAPTER THIRTY-ONE
Gone, Gone, Gone

"KEEP MOVING! GET THROUGH THIS SHIT!" hollered Fellpon as he used his two-handed sword and longsword like machetes, cutting through the blades of grass that were coiling around his legs. But the Minotaurs were not faring as well and, despite their size and strength, all struggled to move forward except for Jumdug and Magzig, who were both making steady progress toward the group of humans. "Do something about this, you miserable dwarf!" Fellpon commanded without looking back toward the dwarf.

Back far enough, not to be caught in the flailing grass, Skik sneered at Fellpon's command, knowing he could do nothing for them. Instead he surveyed the scene unfolding in front of him. The humans were waiting for Fellpon and the others to come to them, some getting through the grass faster than others. 'Clever,' he thought to himself, 'but that only buys them a little time.'

"Nice work, York!" shouted Mikell, trying to make himself heard above the shouting and howling on both sides.

As Fellpon, Jumdug, and Magzig broke through the snaking grass, Isa, Brutal, and Tyberius all moved up to engage them. Fellpon, growling with rage, met Isa head on, but the gnoll was even quicker than the monk and his nine foot frame and large weapons gave him an extensive reach. The gnoll brought his massive two-handed sword, which he managed with one arm, down, slashing Isa on the left shoulder, which he quickly followed with his left arm, swinging the longsword across his body, trying to decapitate the monk, but Isa ducked, rolling forward, avoiding a more severe hit by the two-handed sword and dodging the longsword altogether. From his rolling position, he was able to stand back up inside Fellpon's defenses, and he punched the gnoll squarely in the gut, but the strong chain armor and last second turn of his body, made the blow a glancing strike that did no damage.

Ariana, moving about behind the front line, tried to find a view of the dwarf, but the bulky Minotaurs and the chaotic melee created veritable wall through which she could not see clearly. "Dammit!" she shouted in frustration, just as the first group of Minotaurs and the large gnoll broke free from the grass. Seeing Isa and the gnoll already entangled in their duel, she noticed a massive Minotaur charging Tyberius, sending a mixture of excitement, fear, and adrenaline flowing through her body. Foetore, sharing the rush Ariana was feeling, stuck his head out of the backpack, watching the battle unfold over her shoulder. Focusing on the charging Minotaur, Ariana opened a gateway to the positive material plane and began drawing in the familiar and tantalizing magical energy. Raising her finger, she uttered the command, "Invoco missili di forza, infallibili nella loro volo." Releasing the magical energy, she focused it out through her extended index finger. Three red bolts shot out, racing to their target, mystically dodging all other combatants and burying themselves into the chest and side of the large Minotaur, who howled in pain and rage.

Brutal, charging, raised the huge bastard sword and swung with all his might, but Magzig, the largest of all the Minotaurs, blocked the sword with his double-bladed ax and countered with a backhanded swing that deflected off Brutal's breastplate, doing no damage but emitting a small shower of sparks and a loud clang.

Mikell felt the urge to join in the combat, the Sundrudden mace feeling cool and deadly in his strong hand, but before the fight began, everyone pleaded with him to stay in the back so he could safely use his healing powers. He knew that was for the best, but the battle was just beginning, and he already could feel the urge to engage as he found himself selecting a Minotaur to attack. As he started to make his way to the front, he halted, chiding himself, "They need Zuel, not a rash idiot," he said, lowering his mace, and instead of charging into combat, he honored his companion's wishes. Moving up behind Brutal, he said a small prayer. "Zuel, Benedici il mio tocco con fortuna e salute." Touching Brutal's back, the priest cast a spell increasing Brutal's life force, protecting from damage and making his attacks more effective. As he released the magical energy, it briefly shimmered around Brutal's body like a globe, then snuffed out, but Brutal could feel the difference immediately.

Recoiling from the impact of the three painful bolts, Jumdug traced them back to their origin, Ariana, but with the sorceress safely in the rear, he could not charge past the tall human standing in front of him. Letting out a powerful roar, he raised his double-bladed ax, swinging downward at the smaller human who, moving to the side, dodged the main force of the blow, but Jumdug continued his swing and cut a gash in Tyberius's left leg.

The pain of the ax blade and the feeling of the blood now running down his leg sent a powerful wave of adrenaline through Tyberius's body, and he could feel his blood begin to boil with the high intensity he was beginning to covet. Reeling backwards from the initial blow, he immediately felt the heaviness of the flail diminish, almost as if it wasn't even there, and the armor he wore felt light as a feather. His outward appearance also began to change: his eyes began to redden, bloodshot, and his arms and legs began to mottle with blood as vessels popped underneath his skin. His muscles began to bulge from the massive increase in blood flow, his heart now racing to keep up with the demand. Regaining his balance, he let out a roar of his own and launched himself with reckless abandon at Jumdug. Swinging the flail in his left hand, he smashed the spiked ball into the right side of the burly Minotaur. A smaller or weaker opponent would have been knocked off his feet, but the Minotaur, stood his ground, surprised by the strength of the smaller human and hurt by the penetrating spikes of the ball.

Julius could see the dwarf standing far into the rear, behind the front line and, nocking an arrow, fired two in rapid succession. The first arrow flew true, but at the last second, just as it was about to penetrate Skik's chest, it deflected away, not seeming to do any damage. The next arrow, a second behind the first, passed narrowly over the dwarf's head. "What the hell?" Julius said in astonishment and frustration.

Skik cackled, his ashen face breaking into a grin. His main target, he knew, was to be the sorceress, but he could not get a clear line of sight to her, and although he could hit her with his missiles, he reached into his pouch and pulled out a tiny rod of glass and a pinch of fur. The ranger would pay for his feeble attempts to kill him. Then, almost as a gift from Vundune, the evil god of magic, the human priest of Zuel stepped backwards from the human with the serpent-etched armor, putting himself in a direct line of fire. 'Perfect,' he thought to himself. "Con la carica degli dei, scagliato dalle mie dita." As he spoke the magical incantation, he traced the ancient somatic command, and at the conclusion, the small glass rod and fur vanished, consumed and transformed into magical energy, which Skik released from his outstretched right hand. The bolt of lightning flashed forth, splitting the air right between Fellpon and Magzig, and arced and forked directly through Mikell and Julius before disappearing over the canyon behind them with an almost simultaneous thunderous clap. Mikell and Julius cried out as the charged bolt of electricity shot through them, causing their muscles to spasm violently, knocking them each to one knee, doubled over in pain.

Ariana, standing just a few feet away from Julius, could feel the hairs on her arm and the back of her neck rise in response to the nearness of the bolt passing by her. "Oh my god! Mikell, are you okay?" she asked as she ran up to the cleric. She was about to help lift him to his feet, but she could still see tendrils of electricity jumping here and there throughout his chain mail armor.

The cleric raised a hand. "Stay back, I am fine," he growled in a thick drawl, using his mace to push himself back to his feet.

Julius also managed to stand back up. His face was charred by the bolt and blood trickled out of his left ear, but despite the wounds, there was a deadly determination on his face as he reached back, pulling an arrow from his quiver as his elven eyesight began tracking down the dwarf. Seeing the ranger fall, York put his flute away, his mind going immediately to the coin that he always kept handy, and for a brief moment, he thought about letting fate make the decision, but the question was more out of habit, and he quickly dismissed it. "Not with this one," he said under his breath as he ran to the half-elf's side. Pulling out a small snip of mistletoe from a pouch on his belt, he said a quick prayer to Linkal, the neutral god of fate, "Benedici il mio tocco con il potere di guarire le ferite lievi," and touching the ranger on the arm, released the healing power of his spell.

Julius, interrupting his search for the dwarf, glanced at York. "Thank you," he said before resuming his search. York nodded, his eyes lingering for another long second on the ranger before turning his attention back to the front-line battle, as well.

Bealty moved carefully, walking in a slightly crouched position so that he could see just over the top of the grassy field. He heard the thunder of the lightning bolt, which startled him a little, but fortunately he was able to see where the bolt originated. 'Aha,' he thought to himself, 'there you are.' Eyeing the dwarf, careful to stay out of the druegar's peripheral vision, he decided to quicken his pace, more than he liked, because he knew time was important -- the dwarf had to be stopped.

Jumdug, using his right arm, knocked the ball of the flail away from his side where it had stuck while slashing with his double-bladed ax with his left hand. Tyberius, enraged by this point, was not being cautious and did not see the blade until is slammed into his right side, penetrating the chain mail and opening a deep cut. Jumdug snorted and roared in glee at the blow, but Tyberius paid the wound no attention, as if it were no more than a mosquito bite, and instead he spun around, using the momentum of the spin to speed up his swing. The heavy metal ball slamming again into Jumdug's right side, almost in the identical spot as last time, the spikes burying deep into the Minotaur's side. Jumdug would have roared in pain, but the force of the blow was so hard that it knocked the wind out of him as he stumbled, almost falling over, barely able to keep his feet.

Ariana, now standing right next to Mikell, could see the dwarf clearly through a small gap in the line of battle, between the large wolf-headed gnoll and Isa, and the Minotaur and Brutal. "Let us see if this hurts," Ariana said to herself, remembering the ashen dwarf's comment about her being burned. In her anger, she found herself reaching out to the negative material plane to draw her magical energy, something she hadn't done before, which filled her being. "Invoco missili di forza, infallibili nella loro volo," she canted, releasing the familiar red bolts, which streaked through the fighting line of humanoids, striking the dwarf in rapid succession.

"You bitch!" he howled, the pain breaking his concentration as he was beginning to think of his next spell. Tapping the blue lapis lazuli stone on the ring of his left hand, three images of himself materialized around him, mimicking his every move.

Magzig, still sparring with Brutal, thought he saw an opening and swung his ax downward, as if to split Brutal in half, like a log of wood, but Brutal stepped to the side, allowing the ax to pass by, narrowly missing his body, while he stabbed the large Minotaur. The long dark blade of his bastard sword sunk deep into the stomach of the beast, but he quickly pulled it back and, doing a quick pivot, swung the large bastard sword in an arc over his hand and slashed Magzag's exposed left thigh. The blade cut a deep gash, only stopped by the thick tough femur of the beast.

Isa leapt backwards, his large frame belying his agility caught Fellpon off guard. As the monk somersaulted away, the gnoll leapt after him, but that was what Isa was hoping for -- and without missing a beat, when the monk landed from his back flip, he immediately sprang forward with a flying forward kick, which struck Fellpon directly the chest, knocking the gnoll backwards and allowing Isa the opportunity to land a withering punch with his large fist, right into the gnoll's gut. Both blows were devastating attacks, but Fellpon kept his balance and composure, striking back with rapid swings from his two swords, trying to create some distance, which he did accomplish -- although none of the blows landed on the monk.

Julius, seeing the multiple forms of the dwarf appear, was confused as to what he was aiming at and decided to switch his target to the smaller Minotaur, Rusta, who was still struggling to make it through the entangling area of grass. He rapidly loosed two arrows; the first one glanced off the tough hide of the beast, and the second missed entirely, flying high and to the left. "Dammit! Sindu!" he cursed to himself, again recriminating himself with the slang term for a useless member of elven society.

Mikell knew he had been hurt badly by the lightning bolt, and although he felt a little guilty healing himself, he knew he needed Zuel's help. Without further thought, he chanted the prayer. "Benedici il mio tocco con il potere di guarire le ferite lievi." Laying a hand on his chest, where the bolt had gone through, he completed the spell. He felt the warm healing sensation flow through his body. "Thank Zuel," he said softly, with true appreciation.

Bealty, finally closing in on Skik, witnessed Ariana's magic missiles home in and slam into the dwarf, who immediately tapped his ring. "Aha, what do you have there?" he whispered with some intrigue to himself, followed by a silent curse, as the mirror images of the dwarf appeared. Carefully sliding a dart out from his belt, making sure he made no noise, he stood up and threw it at one of the images, hoping it was the real Skik, but the missile sailed right through it, causing the mirage to blur, then blink from sight, leaving only Skik and two images left. The dwarf spun around, but too late, as Bealty had already ducked back down into the grass, the halfling's camouflage combined with his innate ability to hide, made spotting the rogue nearly impossible.

"Come on out, you little bastard!" shouted Skik. Scanning the endless sea of grass, he felt, for the first time, a little fear creep into his consciousness. Looking up into the sky, he muttered to himself, "Where is that son of a bitch?"

Bealty, watching the dwarf, noticed the quick upwards glance. Looking up as well but seeing nothing, he whispered to himself, "Great, just what we need," he said, remembering the creature that had been spying on them from above. It was nowhere to be seen now, at least, he thought to himself.

Dartag, a husky looking Minotaur, finally burst out of the writhing grass, on the far right flank of the companions. Being nearest to Tyberius, Dartag let out a roar as he charged the warrior, lowering his enormous head and horns, ramming into the redheaded warrior, head-butting him in the head and upper body. Tyberius's helmet helped absorb a portion of the blow, but it still knocked him backwards a step, and the crushing blow smashed the helmet into his face, breaking his nose and sending a stream of blood down his face, mixing in with his red goatee.

Finally catching his breath, Jumdug was relieved to see another clan member rushing to his aid. "About time, you worm!" he cursed Dartag. Seeing the tall warrior being knocked backwards a step, he sensed an opportunity. His double-bladed ax had a spike on the end of it, and using his ax like a pole arm, he stabbed at Tyberius's chest to knock him down, but Tyberius moved just enough for the spike-tipped ax to miss. Still off balance, Tyberius tried swinging the flail down onto the back of the over-extended Jumdug, but the counter force of swinging his flail forward, and his own instability, was too much, and he stumbled, falling onto his back.

"Shit!" shouted Ariana as the mirror images of Skik blinked into view. But there were only two images left, and she could see the dwarf was beginning to cast another spell. She had to try and disrupt the spell, so she canted the missiles again. "Invoco missili di forza, infallibili nella loro volo." Again, the three red bolts streaked through the line of battle striking Skik -- but when they landed, the image blinked out of view. "Dammit!" she exclaimed, worried now about what was coming next.

Skik, reaching into a pouch, pulled out a small stinky ball of tallow with a mixture of sulfur and iron shavings in it as he began to incant the spell. "Invoco una sfera di calde fiamme bianche per ustionare i miei nemici." As he concluded, the ball of tallow vanished, consumed by the arcane spell, and a burning ball of flame, ten feet in diameter, burst into being right on top of Ariana. Mikell, who was standing next to her, tried moving out of the way and almost made it completely, but his arm was burned by the flames. Ariana was caught flat-footed as the ball completely engulfed her. Mikell looked in horror as he could see the shadow-like form of her body inside the ball.

"Ariana!" Mikell yelled, then realizing she wasn't moving out, he closed his eyes and ran into the ball of flames, grabbing her as best he could and diving out of the flames to the ground. Ignoring the blisters that the intense heat left on his exposed forearms, and the foul smell of his singed mustache, Mikell turned his attention to Ariana. He quickly examined her for injuries, but aside from a little scorching on her clothing, she looked fine. "Are you okay?" he asked with great concern in his voice.

Ariana coughed, sucking in the fresh air. "Yes! Yes, I am okay!"

Then a concerned look came over her face as she could feel Foetore's racing heartbeat. Quickly opening the flap on her backpack, she was relieved to see Foetore poke his head out, letting out a squeak of irritation, as some of the fur on the top of his head had been burnt away. "He is okay," she said, closing the flap and pushing herself back up to her feet.

"Thank the gods," said Mikell, "that you both are okay." But as he spoke, the ball of flame began moving toward them. "Shit, we gotta move!"

Bealty saw the large ball of flame rolling toward Mikell and Ariana, then realized what was happening: Skik was using it to drive them over the ledge! The halfling looked back at Skik, but there was still one mirror image left. 'Even odds,' he thought to himself, then wondered if Graff, the good god of luck and fate, could hear his thoughts, and if he did hear his thoughts, was that what praying was like? The ball of flame was pushing them closer to the edge, and Bealty, snapping out of his brief philosophical thought, moved quickly through the grass, drawing out his short sword and dagger. His nimble feet barely made any noise, but at the rate he was moving, and the direct line he was taking, he had to concede some rustling of the grass. He just hoped the dwarf would be too focused on killing Ariana and Mikell, as odd as that sounded. Closing in on the back of the dwarf, Bealty thought about his "Day One" training, and all the vulnerable sites on the body. He was confident in where to strike, but what really had him worried was which of the two images to strike: left...or right? Left...or right? He debated the whole way, finally deciding to attack the Skik on the right, because it had to be "right," he thought, a half grin on his lips. He was about to spring his attack when he caught a whiff of an awful stench...the southerly wind blowing from his left to right. In that split second, he realized his mistake. Changing targets, Bealty leapt at the left image. Hearing the grass rustle behind him, Skik drew his own dagger and spun around, swinging the dagger in a wide, extended arc. But Bealty was too quick, ramming his dagger deep into Skik's left kidney while his short sword pierced through the dwarven mage's right armpit with such force that the blade protruded through the top of Skik's shoulder. Simultaneously, the dwarf's arcing dagger sliced through the air directly at the right side of the halfling's face, but once again, Bealty's reflexes saved him. Letting go of his weapons, now solidly lodged in the dwarf, the rogue arched his back, leaning away from the oncoming blade, causing it to miss by no more than a hair's width. Skik's eyes were wide with shock as the momentum of his blow swung his body around. The dagger falling out of his hand, he staggered backwards one step, then another. The dwarf's eyes looked wildly around until they locked onto Bealty's, and a peacefulness settled across Skik's face, followed by a small grin on one side of his mouth, "You..." he gurgled as blood filled his lungs, his windpipe, and finally began running out of the corner of his mouth, choking his words. The dwarf stood there for what seemed like an eternity to Bealty before falling backwards, the last of his mirror images winking out of existence, along with the ball of flame, which had nearly driven Mikell and Ariana over the cliff.

"About fucking time!" yipped Fellpon as Dar joined him in his fight with Isa. "Flank him!" he commanded. The large gnoll was swinging his swords in a weaving pattern in front of him as a kind of shield from the monk, but as Dar began to move to Isa's left flank, the monk turned to face the new threat. At that moment, Fellpon moved forward, first stabbing with the two-handed sword, which Isa blocked with his forearm, but Fellpon struck quickly with the longsword in his left hand, slicing Isa on the right side, drawing blood, which began to blot the monk's robes. While Isa defended himself from Fellpon, Dar swung his large battle ax, but Isa deftly ducked out of the way. Being closer to the larger gnoll, Isa tried a backwards kick, striking Fellpon a glancing blow, not doing any damage, but it did force the gnoll backwards one step.

"Yes!" shouted Julius, watching Skik fall, but his excitement was short lived, seeing Tyberius falling to the ground in a prone state. Nocking his bow, he loosed two arrows at the Minotaur, who had just bowled Tyberius over. The first arrow hit Dartag in the right shoulder but bounced off the hide armor. The second arrow struck Dartag a little lower, grazing the Minotaur, but still succeeded in drawing blood.

Brutal was still locked one on one with Magzig, the largest of the Minotaurs, but he knew he had wounded the large beast, as blood was running out of both the stab wound and the slash he had just delivered. Eyeing the wounded side, which Magzig was favoring, Brutal feinted his thrust there, and when the Minotaur overreacted by trying to swing its ax to block, Brutal ducked and spun around, slashing Magzig badly on the right leg, Brutal's blade once again hitting bone. Magzig roared in pain. Snorting a mixture of phlegm out of his nose, Magzig swung his ax overhead, hitting Brutal in the shoulder. Luckily, the blade glanced off the metal armor, away from his neck, but the blow still hurt, severely bruising his shoulder.

York, seeing Tyberius fall, drew his longsword and engaged Jumdug. His attack was easily parried by the Minotaur leader, but it was successful in distracting the beast and preventing Jumdug or Dartag from taking further advantage of Tyberius's prone position.

"You mangy half-orc!" Fellpon shouted in his best common tongue, cursing the monk in front of him as he spun his two swords in his hands, looking for the right opening. Dar, hefting his large double-bladed battle ax, also looked for an opening in the monk's defenses, keeping a careful eye on the monk. Fellpon struck first, his large two-handed sword, which he easily wielded in his right hand, struck first, an overhand blow that Isa dodged by turning his body and allowing the blade to pass by, barely missing, but the monk wasn't ready for the quick slash the Fellpon followed up with, his longsword striking Isa solidly in the back, the blade cutting through the fabric and into flesh.

Letting out a vicious sounding "Kiiiiaaaa!" Isa let out a powerful front kick, which landed in Fellpon's crotch, causing the large gnoll to yelp in pain while doubling over, allowing Isa to land a smashing left-handed uppercut to the gnoll's jaw. Fellpon's jaw let out an audible crack as his lower jaw shattered, and he fell over backwards, motionless on the ground. But before Fellpon had even hit the ground, Dar let out a roar, striking a quick and heavy blow, his large ax sinking deeply into Isa's right side, gashing the monk terribly. Blood immediately began to seep out of the deep wound at a concerning rate.

As Skik fell, Bealty drew his second dagger and leapt onto the dwarf, but as he pinned the dwarf to the ground with his knee, he could tell Skik was already dead, his lifeless eyes looking skyward. Unable to resist his curiosity, the halfling quickly rifled through the dwarf's belongings, stuffing anything he thought might be useful into his backpack. Remembering the ring with the deep blue stone, he slipped it off the dwarf's finger, stuffing it into a deep pocket for safe keeping. Worried he was wasting precious time, he retrieved his short sword and dagger from Skik's body, stood back up, and began running back to rejoin his companions, but abruptly stopped, standing on the edge of the writhing grass, which was reaching out, trying to grab his legs and feet. "Damn," he whispered to himself, amazed at the magic but not allowing himself to dwell on it, he immediately began running northward, along the eastern edge, to make his way around it.

Magzig, seeing Brutal stunned momentarily from the shoulder blow, immediately struck again, but his blow was hasty and ill-timed as Brutal had already moved, the large ax blade swishing through the air where Brutal was standing a second ago. Brutal swung his bastard sword, its darkened blade severing both of the Minotaur's extended arms at the elbow. Reeling, Magzig raised his bloody stumps, his eyes wide in horror, but Brutal didn't wait, immediately plunging his sword through the chest of the almost eight-foot beast. Pulling his sword back, Magzig slumped to his knees and fell forward onto his face.

Mikell breathed a sigh of relief as the ball of flame winked out of existence, but didn't waste a second wondering why it had disappeared. Seeing Isa suffer some serious blows, he made his way to the monk. Canting the healing prayer, "Benedici il mio tocco con il potere di guarire le ferite lievi," he laid his hand on Isa's shoulder, releasing the pent-up energy and healing power. It didn't have the effect he was hoping for, but some of the grievous wounds mended partially. Seeing the fight raging, he couldn't help but utter, "Zuel, protect us."

Tyberius sprang back onto his feet, but as he did so, it opened an opportunity for Dartag to swing his ax downward, but Tyberius's chain mail deflected the blow. Dartag quickly followed it up with another swing, but Tyberius raised his shield and easily blocked the second attack as well.

Seeing Magzig fall, both Rusta and Gors, who had finally made their way through the entangling grass, charged Brutal, plugging the brief hole in the line. Gars lowered his head, trying to ram Brutal, but missed as Brutal side-stepped the charge. Rusta was smaller and thinner and wielded two scimitars instead of an ax. Although Brutal managed to avoid the charging Gors, he inadvertently exposed his flank to Rusta, who slashed twice, in rapid succession: the first blade cut the left side of Brutal's face, leaving a deep gash, which began to instantly bleed, while the second blade struck his right forearm, just below his elbow, cutting almost to the bone, and causing him to drop the heavy bastard sword as he recoiled away, cursing from the blows and the pain.

"Mikell!" Brutal shouted, knowing he had just been dealt two devastating blows.

Ariana, hearing the shout for help, spun around, looking for Brutal, just in time to see him drop his sword and fall back a step. "Brutal!" she screamed as she ran forward, feeling rage welling up inside of her as she once again reached out to the negative plane, drawing in the dark energy. As she neared Brutal, she placed her hands together, thumbs touching and fingers spread like a fan, pointing at the two Minotaurs, Gors and Rusta. Incarnating the spell -- "Invoco pareti di fiamme!" -- she released the energy through her extended hands, which resulted in a sheet of flame that roared angrily engulfing the two Minotaurs, who reeled backwards, giving Brutal a little space and allowing him to pick up his sword, but the flames only lasted for a few seconds. As the flames died out, Gors and Rusta both snorted, eyeing the sorceress with malice.

York looked warily at Jumdug. The towering Minotaur looked bloodied but still very fierce. Jumdug, literally drooling at the prospect of killing an elf, roared as he lurched forward, swinging a powerful blow with his large ax, the strike slashing through York's hardened leather and cutting into his rib cage. The elf's eyes narrowed, holding back his desire to scream out in pain, and with inherent grace, swung his longsword with deadly accuracy, slicing at Jumdug's exposed throat. The blade slipped over the outreached arms of the Minotaur, cutting a deep slit across the beast's throat. Jumdug dropped his battle ax, grabbing at his throat as he took two steps backwards. Blood continued to pour through Jumdug's fingers and finally, as his strength faltered, he sank to his knees while the world began to go dark around him. He was able to stay upright, on his knees, for a moment longer, before falling to his side, dead.

"Get back, Ariana!" Julius called out, worried that she had inserted herself too closely to the Minotaurs. Hoping he could drive them back a little further, Julius nocked an arrow. Taking aim, he unleashed two rapid shots at Gors, who was directly opposite Ariana. The two arrows flew straight and true this time. The first lodging into Gors's right shoulder, and the second punching through the tough hide armor on the Minotaur's stomach.

Ariana knew she was vulnerable and had to take a chance at disengaging. She tried to back away quickly, but as she began to pull away, Gors, ignoring the arrows that had just struck him, licking his chops, lashed out at the sorceress, his ax easily cutting through the thin leather on her shoulder, leaving a gruesome gash. Screaming in pain, she awkwardly fell backwards, breaking her fall with her hands and landing squarely on her butt, her legs splayed out in front of her. The only silver lining was that she was at least behind Brutal now, and, for the moment, out of imminent danger.

"Are you alright!?" asked Mikell, stopping to help her up and looking at the bleeding wound on her shoulder.

"I am fine," she gasped. "Brutal needs you more than I do!" Seeing Mikell hesitate, she reached out with both hands and pushed the cleric away. "Go!" Mikell frowned but turned and moved toward Brutal. Ariana took another step backwards, watching as Mikell left, noticing that she was getting awfully close to the edge of the canyon.

Bealty was running as fast as his short legs could carry him, finally making it around the corner, and was heading south, down the western edge of the spell area, back toward the group. That's when he saw it: a large creature that looked like half giant eagle and half... "What the hell is that?" he asked himself out loud, trying to make sense out of the large rack of antlers on top of its head as he ran. "An elk?" The creature was diving at a rapid pace, right toward... "By the gods..." Bealty said, huffing as he ran, "they do not see it." Everyone's focus was on the battle in front of them, with the minotaurs, and nobody was looking behind them, thinking the steep, deep canyon walls were protecting them. Bealty started running faster, even trying to jump to make himself more visible above the top of the grass, and with each jump, he shouted as loudly as he could, "Look behind you! Look behind you!"

With all that was going on, Ariana couldn't hear, or ignored the halfling's cry, but Julius's elven ears picked up the high-pitched shouting.

The half-elf looked at the running halfling, who seemed to be going berserk, running and jumping and what? Pointing? 'Is he pointing at me?' the ranger wondered. "What is it?!" shouted Julius, confused.

Bealty kept running with all his might, pointing up into the air. "Behind you! Behind you!" Julius frowned, still unable to make out what Bealty was saying; there was too much other commotion and noise going on.

Ariana, hearing Julius shout at the halfling, now noticed the rogue running and jumping and pointing. 'At me?' she thought. As her brain spun trying to figure out the halfling's meaning, she immediately began to worry that there was something wrong with her, or that something was on her, and she frantically looked, and felt, herself over. Not finding anything, she frowned, giving Bealty one last quick dirty look before turning her attention back to the fight raging just fifteen feet in front of her. "Idiot!" she said out loud, shaking her head in disgust despite the fact that no one could hear her.

While Bealty was making his way back, the fight continued. Isa was down to one opponent, Dar, an average sized Minotaur with no real outstanding feature other than a large golden ring that pierced the inside of his nose and hung down onto his snout. Despite Mikell's last spell, Isa felt severely weakened, having lost quite a bit of blood, but he still had some fight left. The two combatants sparred, keeping the other at bay with quick, harmless feints and strikes. Dar stabbed the point of his ax at the monk, who easily knocked it aside with his left arm, and quickly moved in with a right front kick, but it missed. Dar was able to pull the ax back up into an attack position and brought it down, slicing Isa's outstretched leg, leaving behind another serious cut.

Gors had missed his opportunity at the sorceress, and now the human in front of him had his weapon back, but just barely. Not waiting for Brutal to ready himself, Gors charged, swinging his ax wildly and successfully landing a blow to Brutal's back. The ax blade didn't penetrate far, but it was enough to draw blood and a loud curse from Brutal, who reflexively spun away from the blow.

Back on his feet, Tyberius ripped his bear helmet off, shouting and cursing like a madman. Eyeing York for the briefest of seconds, unsure who his next target was going to be, he quickly settled on Dartag, the Minotaur engaged with the bard. Hollering curses, the tall redheaded warrior charged the bullish opponent, swinging his flail with ease. The sudden on-rush took Dartag by surprise as the flail caught him on the side of his large head, cracking against his thick skull. The spike didn't penetrate his skull but did fracture it, stunning Dartag as he tried to refocus his senses. As he brushed the cobwebs away, York stabbed with his longsword, sinking the blade into Dartag's exposed belly, but the large beast simultaneously grabbed the blade and kicked the bard squarely in the chest, knocking him backwards five feet where he landed hard on his back. Pulling York's blade out, Dartag threw it to the ground with a loud bellow.

Having seen Brutal take the vicious-looking blow to the back, Mikell quickly said another prayer to Zuel, "Benedici il mio tocco con il potere di guarire le ferite lievi," and, laying his hands on the warrior, released the healing energy. Brutal didn't have the luxury to respond but gave the cleric a quick glance out of the corner of his eye, and that was thanks enough.

Rusta, the scimitar-armed minotaur, saw the cleric heal Brutal and leapt in to attack, his scimitars spinning rapidly in a confusing pattern, as the bullish beast prepared to attack. The Minotaur lunged in; his first blade cut Brutal's exposed right bicep, drawing more curses from the warrior, but the second blade deflected off Brutal's strong breastplate. Sensing an advantage, the Minotaur pressed his attack, his scimitars still flashing rapidly in an almost hypnotic pattern. The first blade struck Brutal in the right leg, drawing blood, and leaving a two-inch laceration, but the second blade swished through the air, above Brutal's head, as he ducked just in time. Ducking under the blade, Brutal jammed his sword upwards, using Rusta's own momentum, along with his own considerable strength, to drive the blade into and through the Minotaur's left side. Without hesitating, Brutal pulled the blade back and, spinning around, slashed Rusta's right thigh, striking the bone, but this time the bone broke and the leg nearly was severed. The gnoll let out the pain-racked yelps of a dying animal as he crumpled to the ground, dropping his scimitars, his leg no longer able to support him.

Gors, watching the horrific scene unfold as Brutal dismantled Rusta, rushed in to help his comrade, swinging the large ax, which missed but did succeed in driving Brutal backwards several steps in order to avoid the attacks.

Isa and Dar, on the northern left end of the line, continued sparring. Dar feinted with a quick jab, but Isa grabbed the ax just below the blade and pulled Dar in close as he wound up with his left fist, delivering a powerful strike to Dar's right side. The blow knocked the air out of the Minotaur, who quickly swung his ax in response. The swing was weak but did drive Isa backwards, perilously close to the edge of the cliff.

Julius was still trying to figure out what Bealty was shouting, looking back and forth from the Minotaurs to the halfling, concerned he was missing something critical. Bealty, finally breaking into the area where most of the grass had been trampled down, could be seen more clearly.

"Look BEHIND you!!" he continued to shout as he ran, his boyish voice started to wear out from all the yelling.

This time both Ariana and Julius heard him and each turned their heads to see the large creature barreling out of the sky, behind them, at a frightening speed. Julius reacted first. "Notria, protect us!" he shouted as he turned to face the new threat and, nocking an arrow, fired off two successive rounds, each arcing through the intervening space.

Harpajash saw the incoming missiles but paid them no heed, allowing them both to strike him in the chest, just below his head. The arrows bounced off harmlessly. The Peryton cackled, enjoying the surprised and horrified look on the ranger's face. "Stupid, pathetic weaklings," he said in his dark language, continuing his dive.

Ariana's eyes widened, worried at seeing the two well-placed arrows bounce, futilely, off the beast. "See if these bounce, you son of a bitch," Ariana snarled, tapping the positive material plane, drawing in the mysterious surge of energy. "Invoco missili di forza, infallibili nella loro volo." Pointing at the beast, she released her magic, the three red bolts silently, but rapidly, zeroing in on Harpajash. This time the flying beast flared his wings, trying to change directions and dodge the missiles, but to no avail, as they mercilessly homed in, one striking his left wing, and the other two slamming into his underbelly, drawing forth a splash of purplish blood.

"Fucking magic users!" Harpajash cursed in his dark language, as he recovered his downward momentum, his focus still locked on his original target. Streaking in low, Julius threw down his longbow, trying to draw his longsword, but the Peryton flew into, and through, the ranger, its huge fourteen foot wingspan knocking the ranger to the ground. At the last moment, extending his clawed feet, Harpajash grabbed Ariana by the shoulders, his sharp talons digging into her flesh, while allowing his momentum to carry them both toward the edge of the cliff leading down to the river below.

Ariana let out a blood-curdling scream. "Tyberius!" Even in his enraged state, the redheaded warrior looked to his fiancée, just in time to see the huge winged beast grabbing her by the shoulders.

"Nooooooo!" Tyberius shouted, as he mindlessly disengaged from Dartag, who took the opportunity to slash the warrior's back with a quick blow, drawing blood, but the warrior, if he had noticed the damage, gave no outward recognition, instead bolting, using his freakish speed to charge the Peryton. He was quick enough to land one powerful blow from his flail to Harpajash's extended right wing, but the impact seemed to have no effect, the spikes unable to penetrate. "You fucking bastard!" he screamed as the beast pulled Ariana away.

Mikell, shocked to see the appearance of the large creature in the back of their group, cried "Zuel, help her!" as he charged the beast, swinging his mace and landing a solid blow on Harpajash's side, but once again the weapon seemed to simply bounce off the creature. Dropping the mace, Mikell dove, successfully catching hold of Ariana's legs, hoping his added weight would slow the flying creature down. Holding on with all his great strength, he was roughly dragged along the ground, with rocks, dirt, and blades of grass cutting, tearing, and pounding his face, arms, hands, and body, while the edge of the cliff drew closer with each heartbeat. At the cliff's edge, Mikell, forced to make a split-second decision -- hold on and go over the edge or let go -- held on as long as he could, but at the last possible moment, he let Ariana's legs slip through his grasp. His body, bloodied and bruised, skidded to a halt, so close to the edge, that his head stuck out over the ledge. Watching in horror as the beast carried Ariana into the open air, he shouted with all his might, "Noooooo! Ariana!!!!"

Bealty saw it all unfolding and had an intuition of what was about to happen. There was too much space to cover running all the way around the edge of the cliff, and Isa and Dar were blocking the way onto the little peninsula of land. Bealty, seeing Julius getting knocked over, Tyberius attacking, and Mikell diving, but unable to hold on, knew he was the only one left who had a chance to do...something, and as Harpajash and Ariana went over the cliff, he saw the opportunity. Still running as fast as his legs could carry him, he changed the angle of his path, from trying to get around Isa and Dar to heading straight for the edge of the cliff directly in front of him. The timing wasn't perfect, but it was his only shot, he thought to himself. As Harpajash cleared the far edge of the cliff, the added weight of Ariana carried the Peryton downward.

Mikell, still lying on his stomach, his face bloody and scrapped from being dragged, noticed, for the first time, Bealty running directly toward him, Harpajash, and Ariana. The only problem was that there was a twenty-foot gap of space with nothing but a two hundred foot drop to the river below. "What is he doing?" he asked himself out loud. Looking at the angles involved -- where the beast was and the direction the halfling was running -- he could see the intersection in his mind. Mikell felt the cold pit of realization wrench his stomach. "Oh my god..." he gasped, holding up his hand for the halfling to stop. "Bealty!! No, no, no, noooo!!! Do not do it!!!"

Bealty heard his friend's plea, but only lowered his head, and sped up. "Got to, Mikell..." he said out loud to himself, knowing no one could hear, "got to." He neared the cliff's edge, going as fast as he could ever remember running, and doing one last quick calculation in his mind, leapt into the air. Time slowed. Looking down, the emptiness of the canyon below him seemed to stretch forever. At first, he was going upward, but soon he felt himself leveling out. Then, just for an instant, he seemed to defy gravity, but it was fleeting, and soon he could feel the air rushing by his face as he began to fall. His mind kept running calculations with each passing fraction of a second, watching Harpajash and Ariana slowly falling in front of him and below him, as he tried to figure out the angles and trajectories while flying through the open, intervening space.

Mikell watched, horror stricken, as the halfling leapt off the edge of the cliff and soon was falling through the air. "Noooo!" Mikell yelled, scrambling to stand up.

"Oh shit," Bealty breathed; he had misjudged it. Harpajash was diving more quickly than he anticipated, and now he felt himself overshooting his target. For a split second, he thought he was going to miss completely, but fortunately Harpajash did not see him, and with no time to spare, the Peryton unfurled his huge wings as the large beast began to fly once again. As Harpajash's left wing expanded outward, Bealty reached as far as his short arms could muster, barely grabbing hold of the feathery and sinewy wing with both hands, but as the forward momentum of his body continued on, it ripped his right hand, and a fistful of feathers, off the Peryton. He dangled there, holding on for dear life, nearly losing his grip with his left hand as well, but fortune, as it often was, was with Bealty. Just as his grip was slipping off the wing, Harpajash banked to the left to steer away from the cliff wall that the halfling had jumped from. This act gave Bealty some new momentum, swinging the rogue, barely hanging on by one hand, inward and upward, slamming him into Harpajash's side, but this time Bealty was able to grab with his right hand and swing a leg up and onto the wing. Carefully, he crawled, tightly gripping the feathery back of the Peryton, until he was straddling it, as if he was riding bareback on a horse. Looking over the side of the beast, he saw Ariana below, her arms up over her head, holding onto the taloned feet of the beast, although that seemed unnecessary to the halfling, since Harpajash appeared to be holding on quite tightly to Ariana. "Fuck me," he whispered to himself, glancing down at the river far below and looking backwards, the distance rapidly expanding between himself and his companions back on the ground. He could see Mikell and Tyberius standing right at the precipice, watching as they flew away. "The die is cast," he mumbled to himself, blocking out the events still unfolding behind and below him, allowing him to shift his focus back to his own predicament, which, at the moment, appeared to be complicated and dangerous to say the least. Flying high up in the sky, the wind blowing in his face, he looked around, finally knowing what it was like to be a bird. He muttered, "It ain't all it is cracked up to be." But the gravity of the situation, both literally and figuratively, was very high, and his mind turned back to the serious business at hand. "Now what the hell do I do?" he asked himself, and if he was honest, he half hoped Graff, the good god of luck and fate, might be listening.

* * * *

Back on the ground, Mikell watched helplessly as the large beast flew rapidly away with Ariana and Bealty. "Zuel help us," he whispered to his god, then added, "Protect them."

"Nooooo!" shouted Tyberius, standing at the cliff's edge. His face purple with rage, he bellowed unintelligible curses in his enraged state, his body quivering with an overdose of adrenaline, like he had never experienced before.

Dartag, taking advantage of the ensuing confusion caused by Harpajash crashing through the rear of the companions, charged York, who was still on the ground, weaponless. Raising his ax, he brought it down with great force, but York rolled out of the way, causing the ax to break as its blade slammed into the ground, the shaft shattering into two pieces. Dropping the broken handle, Dartag wasted no time, kicking the bard as hard as he could with his cloven foot. The elf's hardened leather helped absorb some of the blow, but it was well placed, landing across his rib cage and launching him five feet through the air, landing at the feet of Julius. Suddenly, the field parted, and Dartag could see a wide open path between him and the tall redheaded warrior, who was looking outward over the cliff, his back turned, unwisely, to the still raging battle. 'The fool wasn't even paying attention,' thought the Minotaur, and, despite being weaponless, Dartag lowered his bullish head, leveling his thick horns, and began charging with all his might, every footfall thumping the ground like a quickening heartbeat as he neared Tyberius.

Julius, barely jumping out the way of York's flying body, was not in a position to stop the charging Minotaur, but it was obvious what Dartag was doing. "Tyberius!! Tyberius!! Watch out!" he yelled with all his lungs could muster, but Tyberius paid no attention to his cries. Mikell, however, did hear and looked back over his shoulder but was too late to react.

Isa heard the ranger's warnings, and although he was engaged with Dar, he risked a quick look over his shoulder in time to see the minotaur rapidly closing in on Tyberius. He looked back at Dar one more time, then turned and sprang toward the charging Dartag. This gave Dar an opportunity, which he took, swinging his double-bladed ax, which sank deeply into Isa's back. The half-orc roared in pain, but kept his focus on Dartag. Just as Dartag was about to impact Tyberius, Isa landed, intercepting the Minotaur. The large half-orc and huge minotaur collided with a fearsome impact, sending both combatants in opposite directions. Dartag was knocked backwards, at an angle away from Tyberius, as he stumbled sideways toward Mikell. Isa was knocked directly backwards, his first balancing step back found firm footing, and he would have stayed on his feet, but his second step, being over the ledge, found nothing but air. The monk's momentum was too much, and Isa fell backwards, passing next to Tyberius, who was still watching the Peryton fly away with Ariana. Isa reached out, trying to grab Tyberius, touching the warrior's arm, but was unable to get a firm grasp on the warrior. Tyberius saw Isa falling backwards, face up, grasping up at him, but in his enraged state, he couldn't think clearly or quickly enough to even attempt reaching out to help, leaving the monk to fall more than seventy feet before slamming into the side of the cliff, causing his limp body to start cartwheeling, slamming into several more ledges and outcroppings, until his body finally splashed into the ice-cold, fast flowing river below.

Dar didn't wait to see what happened to the monk after his fall, and with Isa out of the way, he charged Tyberius as well, but this time Tyberius saw the attack, ducking under Dar's swing. Dropping the flail as he bent over, Tyberius grabbed the Minotaur by the left leg and, in an incredible display of strength, spun the three-hundred-pound Minotaur around like a rag doll and, after two quick revolutions, threw the beast over the cliff. Dar roared in disbelief as he was flung around, flailing helplessly during his long fall to the river below.

Mikell, now standing up, moved passed the stumbling Dartag to pick up his mace while York, also regaining his feet, ran forward to pick up his longsword that Dartag had thrown to the ground. Julius simply dropped his sword, not even bothering to sheath it, and picked up his longbow, still able to fire one point-blank shot at Dartag. The arrow flew straight and true, lodging into the Minotaur's neck. Dartag grabbed at the pesky arrow, but his carotid artery was nicked and blood was gushing out of both sides of the puncture. The large beast sank to his knees, still trying to stem the flow of blood, but his arms grew weak, and he fell to his side as he slumped over, landing face first.

Brutal knew Gors was badly wounded, the two arrows still protruding out of the bullish man before him. "Enough!" shouted Brutal, feinting with a low attack that Gors lowered his ax to block, only to realize too late, as Brutal spun back around, changing the direction of the blow and the angle, that the quick feint to Gors's right leg ended up being a real attack coming at him from the left and at his head. Brutal's blade sank deep, too deep not to be fatal, into the side of the Minotaur's head, cracking its skull and sinking into the beast's brain. The blow had an immediate effect, knocking Gors down into a crumpled heap at Brutal's feet, and in that instant, the battle was suddenly over, causing an uneasy quiet to settle over the four stunned remaining companions. The only noise, once again, was the sound of the wind blowing through the grass.

With his flail lying on the ground next to him, Tyberius stood silently, watching, a horrified and confused look on his face, the distant dot in the sky heading northward along the river, growing smaller with each passing second. As the rage receded and his body diluted his adrenaline, he sank to his knees, unable to stand any longer. Tears silently wove their way down his bloodied face, around his broken, bleeding, nose, until they mixed into the red whiskers of his goatee.

"What the fuck happened?" asked Brutal, turning around for the first time, surveying the scene, immediately noticing the absence of three of his companions. He had heard the yelling and commotion behind him but was not able to look backwards. "Where is Ariana?" he asked, still trying to wrap his mind around what he was seeing...or not seeing. "... And Bealty... And Isa?" He could see the distraught look on Mikell's dirty, cut, and bruised face, but the cleric said nothing. Brutal looked at the others: Tyberius was on his knees while York and Julius were simply standing next to each other, no one able to answer his simple questions. A pit formed in his stomach, his large bastard sword suddenly feeling heavy in his right arm as the point of the blade slowly sank to the ground. "No, Mikell, tell me..." he begged, feeling his throat clenching with sorrow, making it difficult to talk, "tell me it ain't true," he said, slowly walking toward the cliff's edge, dragging his sword tip along the ground.

Mikell, now beginning to tear up as well, tried to hold them back, trying to respond. "Isa..." he began but was interrupted.

Tyberius, still on his knees, hands on his thighs, his voice cracking a bit, completed Mikell's sentence. "Saved my worthless life. I..." he paused. "I did not ask him to do that!"

"What about Bealty and Ariana?" Brutal asked, urgency and despair in his voice.

Tyberius pointed off into the distance. "That...that thing took them." After a short pause, he added, "I ain't never seen such a god-damned, cowardly fucking beast."

Julius, making his way to the cliff's edge with his friends, said, "It was a twisted freak of nature. I have never seen anything like it, and our weapons were useless against it."

"A Peryton, no doubt," said York, sheathing his sword and walking closer to the edge near Mikell and Tyberius. "I have never seen one personally, but the description in the lore I have read makes them hard to mistake."

"Why did he take her?" asked Mikell. "Why her?"

York hesitated before answering. "No way to know for sure," he said, shrugging his shoulders. "Maybe just because he could."

Tyberius, grunting with the extra effort, stood up and turned around. "Sounds like you be lying, York," he said, taking a menacing step toward the bard. "If you know something, you better fucking speak up."

York looked at Mikell with a silent plea for help. Mikell put a hand on Tyberius's arm. "How could he know Tyberius? Our best course of action is to figure out what we do next."

"What we need to do next is find where that thing is taking them!" shouted Brutal, pointing with a bloodied hand to the north.

"How are we supposed to find that out?" asked Julius. "It could be taking them anywhere."

Mikell thought for a moment, his eyes narrowing as he looked back out over the cliff at the diminishing dot in the sky. He said, "That son of a bitch is on 'Straight Time.'" Just as Mikell finished, an audible groan pierced the air, causing everyone to turn and look. The large gnoll, with the white wolf-shaped head, moved slightly, groaning again.

"Screw the halfling bullshit," said Tyberius, picking up his flail and walking toward the fallen gnoll leader. "I am betting this son of a bitch can tell us where they are going."

CHAPTER THIRTY-TWO
A Little Cut

"FOETORE," SAID ARIANA, calling her familiar telepathically, "I need you to get me a feather from this beast." As she finished her mental command, she gritted her teeth, trying not to scream, as another wave of pain shot through her shoulders as Harpajash squeezed tighter, causing his long talons to dig deeper into the soft flesh under her shoulders, along her collarbone. Foetore could feel her pain, and it made him sad and angry at the same time. Popping his head out of the backpack, he immediately felt the rush of air buffeting his white and black fur. Looking down, he was amazed at what he saw -- in fact, he could hardly recognize what he was looking at. Shaking his head and refocusing his thoughts, he looked up the large, feathered underbelly of the beast was overhead, but with nothing to hold onto securely, it was too dangerous to try and get a feather from there. The best option, he thought to himself, was scampering up the creature's leg and onto its back. Taking a deep breath, he was about to leave the relatively secure backpack when the beast violently shook to the left, then to the right, causing the ferret to dig its sharp claws into the leather backpack, barely holding on. The bucking motion also sent another wracking wave of pain through Ariana as Harpajash tightened his grip.

Bealty, up on top of Harpajash, pulled out his dagger, stabbing the Peryton in the back multiple times, as hard as he could, but the blade couldn't penetrate the beast. He even tried stabbing the back of the Peryton's elk-like neck, but there, too, the blade simply bounced off its skin.

"Stop it, you fool!" shouted Harpajash in his draconian tongue, shaking his body, trying to dislodge the troublesome halfling, but the rogue was dug in like a tick. "Weaklings," he mumbled to himself. Confident the halfling couldn't do any damage, the Peryton stopped trying to buck the halfling, as he didn't want to risk somehow losing the sorceress -- he had waited a long time to find a such a fine specimen.

Bealty had no idea what Harpajash was saying, but after several attempts to stab the creature, he sheathed the dagger, thinking to himself, 'Damn, something is protecting this thing.' Looking around, trying to figure out what he could do to the creature, nothing jumped out at him as a weakness.

Ariana let out a half growl, half scream as the sudden and violent shaking caused her even more pain, but finally the beast stopped its gyrations. "Hurry, little one," said Ariana, again connecting with Foetore.

The little ferret didn't waste any time and scurried out of the backpack, clawing its way up Harpajash's leg, before carefully making his way from Harpajash's thigh to his back, where he was surprised to see Bealty clinging with both hands to the Peryton's back.

"Foetore!" yelled Bealty, "what are you doing?!" Foetore could understand the gist of what Bealty had asked, but unfortunately could not respond in common.

Down below, Ariana's eyes shot wide open in stunned surprise, hardly able to believe that Bealty was somehow on top of the beast. "Get me the feather," she reminded Foetore with her telepathy. "Bealty?!" she shouted, trying to make herself heard over the sound of the wind rushing by.

"Yeah?! I am here!" answered the halfling.

"Give Foetore a feather!" she shouted back.

"A feather?!" Bealty asked, unsure if he heard correctly.

Harpajash, hearing them communicate, squeezed his claws tighter, causing Ariana to let out a scream of pain. "You son of a bitch..." Ariana said, cursing the beast as the pain eased, before turning her attention back to Bealty, repeating her command, "Yes, yes, get a god-damned feather!"

"Okay, okay," Bealty whispered under his breath as he yanked on a feather. It wasn't easy, but a large eighteen inch feather popped out of Harpajash's back, and he handed it to Foetore, who clamped it tightly in his mouth before scurrying back down Harpajash's side. "An odd request…" said Bealty softly to himself.

"Can you force him down?!" shouted Ariana.

"I tried, but he is immune to my weapons!" responded Bealty, exasperated. "Plus, if he falls -- we fall!" he shouted back, emphasizing the 'we'.

Foetore returned with the feather, which Ariana took, quickly letting go of Harpajash's left ankle. As soon as she had the feather, she quickly grabbed his ankle again, feeling more secure to hold on herself, in case for some reason the beast decided to drop her. "Do you have any rope, or something to tie us together?" she shouted up to Bealty.

"Hell yeah!" shouted the halfling, reaching back and pulling out a coiled silk rope, fifty feet long. "Of course, I have rope, that is 'IR one,'" he said quietly to himself, referring to inventory rule number one for a halfling rogue: always carry rope. While mulling over his early training, he began tying one end around his right leg, and, once finished, he threw the remaining coil over Harpajash's side.

Ariana saw the rope and reached out to grab it, even though that meant letting go of Harpajash's foot again. She fumbled with the rope, losing it in the wind a couple times, but finally caught it on her third attempt. Trying not to look down, she, for the first time, let go of Harpajash, just long enough to tie the rope around her waist, completing the task with a strong knot. "Okay, it is done!" she shouted up. "I will get us down safely, but you have to find a way to get this thing to drop me!" she shouted back up. If it weren't for the pain, she might have almost smiled at the irony of the predicament, she could hardly believe her life was in the hands of the halfling, of all people.

Bealty nodded to himself. "Okay," he whispered to himself, "how do you make a flying creature, that you can't physically harm, fall out of the sky?" Then, as he watched Harpajash flap his powerful wings, it dawned on him, a devilish, boyish smile lighting up his face with the revelation. Reaching into his backpack, he pulled out the grapefruit-sized bag of what York had called tanglefoot, the gelatinous mixture still moving mysteriously inside, making it difficult to grasp, especially in his small hand. Leaning over a little, he yelled down, "Are you ready?!"

Ariana closed her eyes, focusing her mind on what she needed to do and soon she could feel the myriad of distractions around her melt away, turning into a light background noise. "Do it!" she yelled back up. Gritting her teeth, and finding the courage within herself, she let go of Harpajash's legs with both hands, saying a quick prayer to Axis as she waited for what seemed like an eternity for whatever Bealty had planned.

Bealty slid backwards down Harpajash's back as far as he could, then getting up onto his knees, holding a bundle of feathers with his left hand to keep from falling off, he hefted the grapefruit-like missile in his right hand. "Just like at home, knocking rocks off the split rail fence," he whispered to himself, silently hoping that Andor Harn, the owner of the general store back in Telfar, hadn't sold him an expensive sack of mud and rocks, but either way -- it would be interesting to see what happened next. Raising the little sack, he took aim at the middle of Harpajash's back, the space right between his powerful wings. Taking a deep breath, he held it for a second, before exhaling in a slow, controlled, practiced technique. For Bealty, this slowed time down and helped him focus during what were often stressful tasks, and this was certainly no exception. Taking comfort in the meditative-like state, he sprang into action. Almost simultaneously, he threw the jumbled grapefruit-like sack while he sprang backwards, doing a somersault off the Peryton's back. For Bealty, it all happened in slow motion. He lifted up and away from the flying Peryton, watching as the little bundle flew at Harpajash, hitting right where he was aiming. The bag indeed exploded, shooting black, sticky tendrils out in every direction, some even attaching to him as he flew backwards, but quickly he fell below and behind Harpajash, and the few tendrils snapped as he fell. The mess of sticky tendrils covered Harpajash's backside and wings, crippling his ability to flap and maintain his flight. The sudden loss of control confused and scared Harpajash, and the Peryton let out a long bleat of anger and fear as he strained to look back over his shoulder to see what had just happened, but as he did so, he began to fall out of the sky. He tried, in vain, to flap his wings and break the sticky stands, but the more he struggled, the more bound up he got, and in his ensuing panic, he let go of Ariana.

Finally released, panic and fear gripped Ariana, freezing her mind and thoughts as she began spinning in her free fall, the world twirling around her uncontrolled descent. Closing her eyes, she focused her mind again, as she always could, then she felt a jolt on her abdomen and she opened her eyes again to see Bealty below her, connected to her by the silk rope. The ground was rushing toward them at a frightening pace, and she was running out of time -- maybe she didn't even have enough time she thought. Closing her eyes again, she focused her mind. Holding the feather tightly, she reached out to the positive material plane and pulled in the energy she needed and canted the spell, "Fammi cadere come una piuma." The feather vanished, the energy of its destruction re-absorbed into the positive material plane, as a gift, and immediately Ariana felt the rush of air stop and then a vicious tug on her waist as Bealty's downward fall was halted. Opening her eyes, she watched as she and Bealty drifted toward the ground at an easy pace, floating like a feather. Looking around, she saw Harpajash twirling like a missile downward and away from them. They were falling into a mountainous region, and the Peryton disappeared out of sight behind larger hills, off in the distance.

"Holy crap!" shouted Bealty, hanging upside down by his leg, up to Ariana. "Nice work!!"

Ariana couldn't help but smile, even feeling a little regret at not having trusted the halfling, or seen him to be very useful. She still did not understand how the halfling ended up on top of the beast, but it was not too far-fetched to assume that she would not have survived without his help. Certainly not, she corrected herself. But looking at the rugged terrain below them, she wasn't so certain they were out of the woods. It took several more minutes for them to fully descend, with Bealty landing first, rolling to his feet gracefully as ever, followed by Ariana, landing lightly on her feet, as if she had just taken a flight of stairs down.

Bealty, his boyish face covered in grime, his hat still stuffed with a crown of grass to help his concealment back on the plain, looked up at her. "That was amazing."

Looking around at the rugged terrain, she began untying the silk rope from around her waist. Handing it back to Bealty, she said, "Yes, well, I am not sure where we are, or where to go now." Bealty was about to respond when he felt a gut-wrenching pain in his stomach, causing him to bend over, fall to one knee, and vomit. "Bealty! Are you okay?" asked Ariana, quickly moving to his side and putting an arm around his slender shoulders.

Bealty looked up, his eyes watering from the violent heave. "I...I suddenly do not feel well..." he said, his voice sounding weak and scared.

Ariana looked at his boyish face, his black hat still had grass tied to it, making him look ridiculous, and he had wiped mud on his cheeks to help camouflage him in the grassy plain. Ariana reached up and grabbed his chin with her right hand, turning his face so she could get a better look. Taking a brown rag from a pocket in her leather armor, she poured a little water onto it from a flask and she dabbed away the dirt, revealing a shallow cut that went almost ear to mouth along his right cheek. Although not deep, it was an odd red color, and tendrils of black lines, like tributaries of a river, were spreading up and down along the wound in a worrisome display. "Bealty, you are cut," she said, her voice quivering a bit, "how did this happen?" Bealty started to reach up and touch it, but she stopped his hand. "No, you must not touch it."

"Why?" he asked, but as soon as he spoke, the gut-wrenching pain returned, doubling him over as he vomited again, this time with some blood. He looked back up, concern in his watery eyes. "Skik..." he said, "I, I thought he missed me," then he remembered the evil smile the dwarf had given him, and it made sense now. "He poisoned me, like Hammer..." he said, feeling cold and weak.

"But you can fight it, Bealty -- you can survive! Hammer was weak and you are strong!" said Ariana, feeling herself wanting to cry, but she forced back the tears, remaining strong. Pouring out more water from the small flask onto the cloth, she rinsed the wound out as well as she could. It looked clean now, but the black tendrils continued to spread slowly. She looked around but saw nothing that would provide them some shelter from the coming night and cold. "Stay here and rest, I will find us some shelter and build us a fire." Bealty nodded, and sat down, leaning back against a rock.

Ariana got up and began searching for a suitable place to camp for the night. At least there were trees, and enough small sticks and branches on the ground, so that making a fire should not be a problem. She didn't want to go too far, and was about to lose hope, when she found a small cave, perhaps five feet wide at best, and ten feet deep, tucked into the side of the hill. 'This will have to do,' she thought to herself and hurried back. She found Bealty right where she had left him, sitting against the same rock and thankfully still alive. "Can you walk?" she asked.

Bealty nodded weakly, but as he tried to get up, he fell back down onto his rear. "Damn, I, I do not think..." he started to say, but another violent heave interrupted him, and he fell over onto his side, retching up more blood. Ariana bent down, holding his shoulders to help support the halfling.

As Bealty settled down once again, Ariana stood back up, putting her hands on her hips. "Well, then, I will carry you."

Bealty looked up at the sorceress, her upper body was badly cut, scraped, and still bleeding, especially under her shoulders where the Peryton's claws had dug in. Her left shoulder was the worst, as the Minotaur's ax had cut her badly, the Peryton's talons only making it worse. Shaking his head, holding up a hand, he said, "No, you cannot do that, and that is okay."

"Do not tell me what I can and cannot do," said Ariana in a sisterly tone. "C'mon, help me out here," and with Ariana's help Bealty was able to stand up and the sorceress hefted the small halfling up into her arms, carrying him in front of her. "See, no worse than a bale of hay," she said, with a comforting, if forced, smile. With Bealty, limp in her arms, she began to make her way down the side of the hill.

"Could you not jostle me so much," said Bealty weakly, his eyes closed.

Ariana smiled again. "Do not push your luck..." she answered, pleased to see her friend's lip curl ever so slightly into a short-lived smile. She had to stop and rest a couple times but managed to carry the thirty-two pound halfling and his gear to the small cave, where she made a simple bed from some Spruce tree branches and built a fire that quickly warmed the small area. Taking off his backpack, she helped him lie down and soon he was asleep, or unconscious, she could not tell which, but he was unresponsive either way. She could hear him lightly wheezing with each breath, which she was glad for since it was a sign that he was still alive, and she didn't have to check on him every few minutes. It was going to be a long night, she thought to herself, and said a prayer to Axis to help her friend through the night. Having nothing better to do, she decided to go through Bealty's backpack in case there was something in there that could be of use. It was mostly thieving stuff, the bag of holding, full of useless coins, she thought to herself. Digging a little more, she found the ring with the blue gemstone, but not recognizing Skik's ring, she put it back into the backpack and continued to rummage. "What is this?" she asked herself out loud, pulling out a small black book. Opening it, she recognized the old, weathered book, the cracks in its dark leather cover, and the clasp. "You surprising son of a bitch," she whispered, looking at Bealty. "You took the dwarf's spell book." Sitting back, she began looking through it, and although she still could not read all the pages, some of them were now clear and legible to her. Turning the pages, she couldn't help but smile. Flipping one more page, this time, her eyes widened in recognition. "Yes... Ohhhh, yes," she murmured as she read the complicated spell. Pouring over the words, the somatic requirements, and the components, she committed them all to memory. She spent hours on the one spell, losing track of time, but always remembering to check on Bealty, his soft wheezing a constant reminder that, at least for now, he was still alive.

It was a long night, and dawn was close at hand. Ariana was exhausted, wishing she had taken some time to sleep, but memorizing the spell was complicated work and she couldn't help herself -- she couldn't resist the pull of the magic and the power she could feel welling up within her. Axis had promised her great power, but at even greater cost. Perhaps this was it? Bealty's life? Hammer's life? Was that the cost? The questions ran through her mind as she picked up a small twig from the floor of the cave and, tapping the positive plane, she cast her simple cantrip. "Invoco la luce." Focusing the target of the spell on the tip of the twig, it began to glow, emitting a bright light. She smiled, remembering the last time, back home with Brutal and Tyberius, when she had cast the cantrip -- how they were amazed and dazzled by the light she created. Thinking of the two men, so close to her, brought her thoughts back to the present circumstance and along with it, feelings of doubt and sadness. Doubt, beginning to claw at her confidence, about the dangers and unknown that now lay before her and sadness, thinking about how distraught and helpless Tyberius must feel right now, not knowing where she was or even if she were still alive. She pushed those thoughts out of her mind, wiping away a tear before it had a chance to fall down her cheek and scolding herself for the weakness she momentarily felt. Focusing back on the task at hand, she shone the light along the cave walls and all along the rocky floor, searching for a component of her new spell. "Bat shit, huh?" she muttered to herself. "Of all things." As she was searching, she suddenly noticed that the sound of Bealty's wheezing was gone, replaced by a cold silence. Looking over at Bealty, who was still lying on his back, arms by his side, his face pale, she hurried over to him, lightly touching his shoulder. "Bealty?" she said, but there was no answer. "Bealty?!" she said, her voice louder, shaking his shoulder a little harder, causing his head to turn, silently, limply, away from her. "No...you promised to fight," she whispered, and, unexpectedly, she felt a tightness in her chest, a pang of loss and dread. Already on her knees, she bent down, placing her ear on his chest and, using her free hand, lightly covered his nose and mouth, listening, feeling, and hoping, for a breath, a movement, or some sign that Bealty might still be alive.

The End of Thran Book I: The Birth

ACKNOWLEDGMENT

To do anything well in life, it takes teamwork and support from others: whether it's playing a sport, running a department at work, raising a family . . . or even writing a book! Writing Thran Book I: The Birth has been an education and a journey all wrapped into one huge experience, and although I am sure I could have published a sub-par novel all on my own, I was lucky enough to have three exceptional people help me make this book a better, more enjoyable, experience.

Artwork

We live in a visual world. Unfortunately, my artistic skills are comparable to that of a four year old. Stick figures and simple shapes are about as far as my skills carry me in that arena. Fortunately, in the summer of 2017, fate smiled upon me when my path crossed that of Natalie Marten. The first project we worked on together was the picture of Ariana — and I can still remember opening the rough black and white rendering. Simply fantastic. Natalie always had a knack, and still does, for interpreting my rambling, convoluted, descriptions and turning them into exceptional, unique, and innovative art. The rest is history, and all the artwork you find in this book, including the chapter headings, and on the website has been digitally penned by Natalie. Thank you, Natalie, for sharing your incredible talents!

Proofreading

After months of editing the book myself, I realized that I was too close and too familiar to see the errors staring back at me, plus who really knows how to properly use "lying" or "laying" and "who" or "whom"? So, I started searching for someone else to help make sure the book was grammatically correct. In the book world, that kind of help is known as "proofreading" (part of my education). Once again, I had to find someone with specific skills, and once again, I lucked out in a big way when Parisa Zolfaghari responded to the project I posted. She is a true professional, not to mention a grammatical black belt. She tackled the 243,000 word behemoth of a book in about a month, correcting an embarrassing number (dare I say myriad?!) of imperfections. Taking pity on me, she even threw in a few copy edits here and there, for which I am grateful as well. My hope is that she saw the book had a seed of good writing, and taking a little extra time, she watered it with her deep knowledge of the English language to make it bloom.

More than eighteen months after my initial publication, I reached out to another professional to give Book I a full line edit. I want to thank Roxana Coumans from Roth Notions, Book Editing for taking on the monumental task and doing a great job!

Spell Language

Magic plays a pivotal and vital role in the world of Thran. But it takes training and either mystical or divine expertise to wield those powerful forces. Part of that training and expertise is mastering the verbal components of each spell. While I commend authors who create a new language from scratch, that path seemed like a major undertaking with little reward when there are so many existing languages to choose from. I settled on Italian as the language of magic in Thran because it has a mythical, poetic rhythm to it that seemed to lend itself to the purpose. To help make sure the simple English gist of the spells were translated into appropriate Italian, I was very fortunate to have the help of Lilia Pino Blouin. I first met Lilia back in my high school days when she spent a semester with my family as an AFS student. She went on to be a very successful, world traveling interpreter/translator for many important dignitaries and other high-profile personalities. I owe her a debt of gratitude for saving me from publishing broken, garbled, nonsensical gibberish and providing a perfected Italian translation for all the spells.

Natalie, Parisa, and Lilia – thank you for your significant contributions, I am forever grateful!

About The Author

It was in the summer of 2012 when Brian McLaughlin dusted off all his old Dungeons and Dragons® manuals and picked up the pen for the first time. After eighteen years in the paper industry, it felt good to get the creative juices flowing and watch as the characters took on their personalities and drove the storyline in directions that he could never have foreseen. He's currently in the midst of writing Thran Book II (no title reveal yet!), and looks forward to seeing the adventure continue to unfold - hopefully as much as you do! He lives in Wisconsin with his wonderful wife, Lynda.

Made in the USA
Columbia, SC
15 November 2020